BEDE WAS WALKING THE NIGHT

"Where is he?" I asked, looking around the Chapter room.

"In Jarrow, dead these fifty-seven years," the Prior said. "How did *you* come to see Bede's spirit?"

"My mother has the night sight," I told him. "Perhaps I've a bit of it myself."

He seized on the phrase with a smile. "A Celtic belief in the ability to see fairies and elves."

I thought he must have been a Celt: only a Celt making his bed in Eng land would've been so desperate to suck up to the Engs and discredit Celtic beliefs.

"I saw what I saw." I shrugged. "Make what you want of it."

"Perhaps," the Prior said, satisfied he'd scored a damaging point. "Do you seek sanctuary?"

"Sanctuary?" I asked, unfamiliar with the term.

"The Church has the power to protect those who come to Her," he said. "So protected, the civil authorities cannot harm you."

"Why would they want to?"

"You're a Dane," he pointed out, "Irish or not. And from a Danish fleet raiding up the coast. That makes you an outlaw."

𝔗𝔥𝔢 𝔇𝔢𝔢𝔭𝔢𝔰𝔱 𝔖𝔢𝔞

FLIGHTS OF FANTASY

☐ **THE BROKEN GODDESS by Hans Bemmann.** When a beautiful woman demands to know whether or not a complacent young teacher believes in fairy tales, his life is forever changed. He follows her out of the everyday world—and into a fairy tale. So begins a strange quest in pursuit of his elusive princess, through a realm of talking beasts and immeasurable distances, of deadly dragons and magical gifts. (454871—$4.99)

☐ **A SONG FOR ARBONNE by Guy Gavriel Kay.** "This panoramic, absorbing novel beautifully creates an alternate version of the medieval world. Kay creates a vivid world of love and music, magic, and death."—*Publishers Weekly* (453328—$5.99)

☐ **THE HOLLOWING by Robert Holdstock.** When the body of young Alex Bradley is found on the edge of the forest, Alex's father refuses to believe his son is dead. And so he begins a search into the forest that sends him journeying from the ancient North American plains to a castle in the Middle Ages to the age of Greek legends and beyond. (453565—$4.99)

☐ **ARCADY by Michael Williams.** With one brother locked in the Citizen's war against rebel forces and the girl's own father immersed in grief, Solomon Hawken must turn to a magic he can scarcely control in an attempt to save his family—and perhaps the entire world. (455002—$12.95)

*Prices slightly higher in Canada

The Deepest Sea

Charles Barnitz

A ROC BOOK

ROC
Published by the Penguin Group
Penguin Books USA Inc., 375 Hudson Street,
New York, New York 10014, U.S.A.
Penguin Books Ltd, 27 Wrights Lane, London W8 5TZ, England
Penguin Books Australia Ltd, Ringwood, Victoria, Australia
Penguin Books Canada Ltd, 10 Alcorn Avenue,
Toronto, Ontario, Canada M4V 3B2
Penguin Books (N.Z.) Ltd, 182–190 Wairau Road,
Auckland 10, New Zealand

Penguin Books Ltd, Registered Offices:
Harmondsworth, Middlesex, England

First published by Roc, an imprint of Dutton Signet,
a division of Penguin Books USA Inc.

First Printing, May, 1996
10 9 8 7 6 5 4 3 2 1

 REGISTERED TRADEMARK—MARCA REGISTRADA

Printed in the United States of America

This book is for my mother, who's curious to find out what happens to "Scallywag," and my father, who saw the manuscript completed a week before he died but who never got to read it.

ACKNOWLEDGMENTS

I would like to thank the early readers of this manuscript for their encouragement and enthusiasm: Kate Arrington, Jackie Benamati, Paul Fling, Terry Lohman, Tom Stone, Sheila Ton, and Bob Zasuli. In particular I would like to acknowledge Burton Raffel and Seymour Epstein, who taught at the University of Denver and who treated me like a colleague instead of a student; they saw the earliest manifestation of this story and were most receptive. I would be remiss if I omitted to thank Richard Deakin and Jane Ireland, who allowed my partner, Jaci, and me to descend on them in the spring of 1993 and disrupt their lives while I did research in the British Museum Library. Richard Kemp of the York Archaeological Trust, who took time from his busy schedule to answer my questions on Anglian York. Roland Warzecha, who provided valuable insight from the perspective of a Viking reenactor, and who I met, together with his brother Peter, on Lindisfarne on the 1,200[th] anniversary of the sacking of the monastery. Mark Christodolou, of Mark Christodolou Books in York, and Edmund Bennett, of Bennett and Kerr Books in Abingdon, and Susan Naughton, of Naughton Booksellers in Dun Laoghaire, Ireland, who supplied me with books on the period, in many cases long out of print, without which my research would have taken years longer. Finally, I would like to thank Steuart Smith, friend of twenty years and patron of the arts, and Jaci Hjelmgren, who put up with a writer at close quarters, not a pretty sight.

The Family of Snorri Horsekicked and Their Ages at the Time of the Story

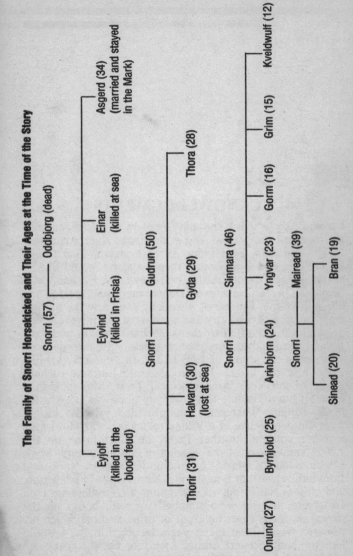

Orm Jarl's Family and Their Ages at the Time of the Story

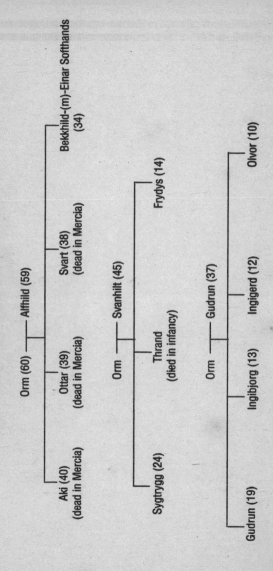

Irish Clan territories
780-800

Atlantic
Ocean

Ailech

Northern
Uí Naíll

Ernhaim Mhacha

Ulaid

Cruacha
Connachta

Southern
Uí Naíll

Tara

Drogheda
Clontarf

Ailenn

Eöganachta   Laigin

Cashel

Wicklow Mtns.

Irish Sea

N

The English Kindgoms
in the 8th century

Atlantic
Ocean

Orkney Islands

*Frisian
Sea*

N

Scotland

Antonine Wall

Lindisfarne

Ælfholm

Northumbria

Hadrian's Wall

Luel

Ireland

Man

Humber River

Clontarf

Lindsey

Yarrow Monastary in Newcastle

Offa's Dyke

Mercia

Severn River

Weogornaceaster

*Irish
Sea*

Wales

Tewkesbury

Gleawanceaster

East
Anglia

Essex

Cornwall

Wessex

Kent

Sussex

English Channel

Dounoc'h eo kaloun ar merc'hed 'vit ar mor douna euz ar bed
The heart of woman is deeper than the deepest sea in the world

Foreword

A snapping bow, a burning flame,
A grinning wolf, a grunting boar,
A raucous raven, a rootless tree,
A breaking wave, a boiling kettle,
A flying arrow, an ebbing tide,
A coiled adder, the ice of night,
A bride's bed-talk, a broad sword,
A bear's play, a Prince's children,
A witch's welcome, the wit of a slave,
A sick calf, a corpse still fresh,
A brother's killer encountered upon
The highway, a house half burned,
A racing stallion who has wrenched a leg,
Are never safe: let no man trust them.
　　　　　—The Sayings of the Wise One

On June 8, 793, the English discovered the Vikings. They discovered the Northumbrian coast was swarming with Vikings. It made all the documentation—Simeon of Durham's, the two Rogers', the *Mercian Register* the *Northumbrian Annals,* and all seven surviving versions of the *Anglo-Saxon Chronicle.* Here's a representative entry: "In this year, fierce, foreboding omens came over the land of Northumbria, and wretchedly terrified the people. There were excessive whirlwinds, lightning storms, and fiery dragons were seen flying in the sky. These signs were followed by great famine, and shortly after in the same year, on June 8th, the ravaging of heathen men destroyed God's Church at Lindisfarne through brutal robbery and slaughter."

All in all, for England the last decade of the eighth century was grim by so called "dark age" standards, or even by the standards of tonsured King Osred in York, exiled him to the Isle of Man, and accepted Æthelred back, apparently having forgotten why they'd driven him out twelve years before. South of the Humber, Beortric of Wessex married Ædburh, a daughter of Offa of Mercia.

In 791 Æthelred started to remind everyone why they'd driven him out in the first place. He dragged the two sons of Ælfwald, who'd been the beneficiary of his first exile, out of the sanctuary of the York Minster and hauled them in shackles up to Winandermere for execution.

In 792 Offa of Mercia, in his never-ending search for sons-in-law, invited Æthelberht, the East Anglian king, to Tamworth to marry his daughter Ælfthryth. The details are unclear, but Æthelberht's corpse left toes up and still a bachelor. Meanwhile, up north, Osred was set up with the usual whispered blandishments and lured back from exile on the Isle of Man. Right on cue his retainers deserted him and he was captured at Aynburg, killed on the fourteenth of September, and buried at Tynemouth before his corpse had cooled. Æthelred supervised the killing personally, during a small side trip on the way to Catterick to marry Ælflaed, who happened to be *another* of Offa's daughters. You'll hear more about that happy couple later.

I've already covered 793. That's enough to bring you up to speed. You get the point: life was cheap, business opportunities were where you found them, and Offa and Æthelred were fun guys.

Some people like to think of them as simpler times, except for the conveniently forgotten danger of parting with your head like old Æthelberht, or the chance that one of those dragons, the kind that flew or the kind that swam, might show up on your doorstep with an empty belly, or the absence of broad-spectrum antibiotics. Easy to smile now, at the end of a century in which the dragons have seemed less quaint. Dragons are where you find them and what you make of them: that's the lesson of the last twelve centuries.

What's all this got to do with you? Who are these people, and why should you give a shit? Stay with me, now; be patient, and you'll find out.

Even with everything else going on it was Lindisfarne that got their attention: the central event of three generations, an event of such magnitude that Offa's purges and Æthelred's liquidations were mere grace notes in comparison. It was the smoke over Lindisfarne that darkened their dreams, not the tangled dynastic struggles north of the Humber or the powerful forces of nationalism, capitalism, Christian supremacy, and the class system that were beginning to coalesce in the West. Lindisfarne was easier to perceive, an event not a process: you couldn't miss it.

The church was the major force of reason and order in the West, and Alcuin was the major voice of the church, but that didn't move him to be reasonable in the midst of the general panic that followed the burning of Lindisfarne. Instead, he wrote that famous torrent of correspondence, coming down hard on the generally iniquitous state of affairs in Northumbria and hinting at a specific laxness at Lindisfarne. According to him, the Danish *strandshug* was "God's punishment for the sins of His people."

It was easy for Alcuin to misconstrue a little casual pillage as divine pissoff and to blame the victims for getting what they deserved. That's a dynamic that's still with us today. Northumbria had enough trouble; you'd think a reasonable god would've given it a rest and not sent in Vikings on top of everything else, but no one ever mistook the Christian god for reasonable, and no one ever mistook Alcuin for an intellect, at least no one with perspective.

I was at Lindisfarne the day of the raid, and it wasn't much as military operations go and even less as divine retribution. It was four longships full of White Danes who'd accidentally stumbled on a monastery full of unarmed monks. A target of opportunity. The kind of target that tells you more about the White Danes than it does about the sins of the Northumbrians.

When I tell this story at Reenactment Events I usually skip the rat's nest of late eighth-century Anglo-Saxon plot twists; diverting as they may be, they're not for the average sunburned middle-class families that make up most of the crowd. But you're *my* family and I owe you the whole story. The truth's in there somewhere; I trust you to find it out.

It's New Year's Eve, and Anglo-Saxon plot twists are exactly what's wanted now that we're here, around the fire, wrapped in wool against a freezing fog outside with a pot of something hot simmering on the grate, and it getting close to the time when we see the Dead. It's time to remember, to resolve to do better, and resolution takes understanding. It's time you found out a little about your family; it's time you found out where you came from. It's time you found out who you are.

Stay with me, now. Don't get too comfortable and doze off. This isn't going to be your usual history lesson.

I was born in Clontarf, Ireland, ten years after Orm Jarl Skeggöx and seventy-five boatloads of kinsmen and followers dragged the keels onto the shingle where the rune posts had washed up and declared they weren't leaving. Orm had gotten himself into the usual trouble back in the Mark: a petty grievance, fueled by bored wives and dull-witted second cousins, had escalated into a blood feud of remarkable acrimony and violence, even for Danes.

Orm was a prosperous merchant who lived on a small fjord in Skäne. He'd begun as an amber trader, moved into horses and wool, built a forge and started making farming implements, expanded his fleet so he could trade east with the Balts in the Rus, down the rivers into the lands of the Slavs, Magyars, and the Volga Bulgars, and south across the Danewirke among the Old Saxons. Orm was in the right place at the right time with the right idea, always a recipe for success and the enmity of those who aren't as lucky. He rose steadily in social and military prominence until he became a jarl.

Here's how it was: one of Orm Jarl's neighbors, a man called Knute, and one of Orm Jarl's thralls, called Ulf, got into an argument over pasturage. Knute kicked one of Ulf's sheep; Ulf pushed Knute; and Knute knocked Ulf down. Then there was about fifteen minutes of chest thumping and in-your-face posturing before they parted on an ambiguous note. The next day one of Knute's thralls killed Ulf. He could have been under orders, or maybe he just wanted to avenge a perceived insult to his master, whatever. Orm Jarl asked for a shepherd's wergeld, and Knute refused on the grounds that slaves had none but market value.

That's how it stood until, in an effort to balance things and shut their wives up on the subject of how spineless they were, some of Orm Jarl's people helped themselves to some of Knute's cattle. Then some of Knute's people burned a couple of crofts and tore up some fence. Orm Jarl returned the cattle, beat the people who'd taken them, and served notice that he was going to bring suit against Knute at the Thing for Ulf's manslaughter and the vandalized real estate. Never considered a crack litigator, Knute tried to settle out of court by burning the house of Orm Jarl's brother in the middle of Beltane night when one more big fire on the horizon wouldn't attract any attention. A spy had assured him that Orm Jarl would be sleeping over without his berserks.

Knute and his men covered the door and hacked down everyone who ran out onto the bare, beaten earth at the threshold of the burning house. But no Orm Jarl emerged from the smoky interior, red-eyed, axe in hand, and when they lined up the corpses and sifted the hot embers and *still* couldn't find any trace of him, Knute realized he was in a world of shit.

With the slaughter of his brother's family the disagreement achieved its own momentum, and Orm Jarl gathered together his blood and foster relatives and declared a blood feud. Everyone put on their blue cloaks and started killing each other with the sort of uninhibited and purposeful abandon they usually reserved for drinking. Farms were burned, boats were scuttled, men were killed, women were raped, and favorite stag hounds were pickled in barrels of brine and sent back to their masters with runestaves shoved up their asses. It got so you couldn't go out to take a piss unless you were wearing ring mail and packing a sword. After a year of covert bladework, medium-sized skirmishes, and high-pitched wizardry, Knute realized he was getting the worst of it, so he appealed to Sigfred for protection.

Sigfred was kinging it in the Dane Mark, and in the south, Charles the Frank was doing a little ethnic cleansing among the Old Saxons with a zeal composed of equal parts religious fervor and the Frank's own special sense of manifest destiny. With all those Saxon refugees moving north, Sigfred didn't have any spare time for adjudicating blood feuds, so he delegated the job to his main enforcer, his brother Godfred.

Knute's relationship to the royal brothers, based on an attenuated web of marriages and fosterings, was never strong enough to satisfy Orm Jarl, but when Godfred finally comprehended the size of Orm Jarl's considerable holdings, fattened up over the years on the proceeds of trade to the east and south, it was strong enough to satisfy Godfred. The royal brothers were improving the Danevirke across the narrow neck of Jutland, and they were cash poor. Orm

Jarl was a rich man, and their share of the profits, once his estates were liquidated, would pay for a lot of moat and dyke. That was all it took to bring them down to Knute's side of the shieldwall.

With Godfred and Sigfred involved, Orm Jarl's wyrd was clear, so he spent the exceptionally bad winter of 763 putting his fleet in order and spreading the word to his relatives and dependents. When the ice broke on the fjord, he stripped his holdings of anything his enemies could possibly use, loaded his people and livestock into eighty-five ships, sowed his pastures with thistle, and burned every barn and building he owned. Then Orm Jarl turned his back on the Mark and his nose to the Out South to discover a more congenial place to live.

Wind and tide took him to the Orkneys, but contrary swells floated the rune posts back to the fleet and the rocks ate four boats, so they decided to move on. Scotland was inhabited by the Picts, who'd stripped naked, tattooed themselves with blue woad, and thrown themselves at Rome's legions for so long they thought that was how you were supposed to greet guests. After three landfalls, three skirmishes, and six lost ships, Orm Jarl coasted back to the Out South, keeping the inhospitable territory of the Picts off the port freeboard, and made landfall in northern Ireland. But the rune posts washed back again, and Orm Jarl coasted south into the Liffey Bay one April morning on a waxing tide that grounded the high seat pillars on a stony beach.

The local Irishmen weren't happy with the Danish presence, but Ireland was fragmented into kingdoms, petty kingdoms, and clan territories, and there wasn't much they could do about it after Orm Jarl's industrious followers had dug a ditch and thrown up an earthwork. The previous winter had left the Irish foraging for food themselves. One of the Irish leaders, a farsighted and ambitious clan chief named Oc Connol, regional leg-breaker for the Southern Uí Naíll, appreciated the appearance of Orm Jarl's seventy-five ships for what it was: a stroke of good luck.

Clan Connol, though small, had risen in power and prominence because of Oc Connol, who'd distinguished himself in the incessant warfare between the Uí Naíll and everyone else in Ireland. Clan Connol was distantly related to the Uí Naíll matrilineal, and their territory was in border country between the Uí Naíll and the Laigin, in the contested territory of the Liffey valley. But Oc Connol had a bigger problem than occasional cattle raids and local insurrections of the Laigin: the Wicklow Mountains hugged the coast from just below the mouth of the Liffey to the southern end of Connacht, straight to the kingdom of Munster, run by the Eóganachta, who'd no intention of bending a knee to the Uí Naíll.

There was a narrow corridor of unobservable coastline, like some kind of Dark Age off-ramp, that ran straight to the soft underbelly of Meath, only twenty-five miles from Tara, the main ceremonial site of the Uí Naíll since 467. This back door had been a major problem in the past, and Oc Connol quickly ceded to Orm Jarl all the land he required around the river mouth and headland, on the site of an abandoned missionary church called Clontarf, in exchange for a treaty of mutual support and nonaggression.

This accomplished three things: it blocked the back door to Meath from the Eóganachta, opened up a free trade zone and major port of entry for Orm Jarl's not inconsiderable merchandising empire, and it made Oc Connol the darling of the Uí Naíll. After Orm Jarl's retainers and their men mauled a few troops of Eóganachta cavalry in the Wicklow foothills south of Clontarf, the Irish kept busy fighting one another and left Orm Jarl alone. The Vikings in Ireland have a bad reputation, but they were pooftas compared to what the Irish routinely did to each other. As the clan wars dragged on, Oc Connol got comfortable with a Danish freehold at Clontarf. Orm Jarl's people were there to farm, to live as good a life as they could and not to bother anyone, at least, Orm Jarl being a neighborly type, not anyone in the area.

The Danes called the place "*Brunavanvik*" for the peat-browned waters of the Liffey and began to intermarry with the Irish, blood bonds were made, cattle got fat, and the hives burst with honey from the clover and wildflowers of Clontarf. My father Snorri was Orm Jarl's horsemaster. They'd been boyhood friends, shipmates as young men, and when Orm Jarl finally became a ring-giver, Snorri was one of his household thanes and oldest living friends. Their wyrds were woven together. Life was good.

Certainly better than it was in the Mark. No one in Ireland was trying to strip Orm Jarl of his wealth to finance defensive earthworks. And when it was all said and done, he craved the quiet life; he was ripe to become a ring-giver, a name-giver, and a settler of disputes. After the earthwork went up, Orm Jarl supervised traffic and trade into the Liffey, watched Oc Connol's back, and got even richer than he'd been before Knute started kicking his sheep.

Although moving his headquarters from the Baltic was a major inconvenience for a merchant prince like Orm Jarl, he was a Dane, after all, and he had a certain entrepreneurial flexibility. As far as he was concerned, the feud with Knute and the royal brothers was nowhere near conclusion. Every year a half dozen dragons swam out with Orm Jarl's knarr and made Knute miserable. The isolated farms of Knute's kinsmen mysteriously caught fire in the night. Knute's herds and flocks were rustled from under his nose. Knute's ships, sailing back across the Baltic, low in the water with trade goods, met Orm Jarl's dragons a day's sail from home. So the feud continued, and the yearly depredations of Orm Jarl's dragons bled Knute like a leech, and Orm Jarl ruled *Brunavanvik* in Ireland, far beyond the range of any retaliatory strikes.

And the years lengthened into one anther, and Orm Jarl himself voyaged less and less, neither trading nor raiding, content to let younger men take to the sea road.

1
Clontarf

It is always better to be alive,
The living can keep a cow:
Fire, I saw, warming a wealthy man,
With a cold corpse at his door.
— The Sayings of the Wise One

It was Orm Jarl's wyrd, as he drank in the hall one night, to let himself be badgered into a final vik by one of his younger and more restless thanes. As the years passed he'd been content to take his percentage from the high seat, hunting with Oc Connol and cementing the alliance that kept Clontarf safe, but called out in front of his people, what could he do?

Even now, the memory of that night's clear as spring water: all of us in the hall, Orm Jarl drinking from his gold-lipped horn, the shadows on the timbered roof, the dogs in the rushes, the smells of beef and mead and onions. Skallagrim the Skald had sung the story of Odhinn's blinding and the finding of the runes, and he was wetting his throat afterword. The smoke-thick air had the ozone tingle of an impending lightning strike; to breath it was to inhale recklessness.

At first it seemed the trouble would start with the argument between Skallagrim and Goltrade, the Irish priest. Those two were from opposite ends of reality. Skallagrim was an old man, even then; he'd learned much and traveled far. None of us knew for sure how much or how far, and he had wit to keep it that way, but he was no fraud. Skallagrim had grown up under the old gods; he was a rune-master, a linguist, a speaker, a wizard, and a healer. He observed the equinoxes and the solstices. He knew the secrets of the standing stones: he could read the stars, and he was a sometime-priest of Odhinn.

Skallagrim's white hair and leather face had been washed by time's water, but his fingers were sure on the harp strings, and his voice was clear and forceful. He had eyes like flint, and he was as prodigious a drinker as Orm Jarl. Exploded red and blue veins clung to his great hooked nose like autumn ivy. He was a tall man, straight and well fleshed, and he wore a thick cloak of northern wool against the wet evening chill with runes worked into the tablet weaving along the hem. The gold brooch that kept it about his shoulders was bright yellow in the firelight. He was an imposing figure in the hall.

Goltrade was not. A man of medium size with ink-stained fingers and an appetite for converts, which went mostly unfed during his time in Clontarf, Goltrade's Christian heterodoxy went unchallenged and unheeded by all but a few, and the majority of Orm Jarl's Danes were content to venerate the old gods or none at all. Goltrade was a fourth-generation Christian, fired and tempered in the Skellig Islands off the Kerry coast, and like all the Christians I've met, he was convinced that he had the answers. Those Christians made a strength out of everything that the old gods thought was weak: meekness, for example, and humility, charity, and chastity (which provoked the most laughter at their expense).

My father Snorri'd grabbed him up on a raid along the Frankish coast before I was born. Goltrade'd been on his way back from Rome, where he'd gotten the nod from the Pope and a commission to bring Christianity to the heathens in the western islands. He thought he was off for the Hebrides, but he had the usual weatherluck of priests, and the group he was traveling with—relic-laden pilgrims returning from a fleecing in Italy—was held up by a storm just long enough to run into Snorri and his crew, ranging a mile or two inland from the Loire, drunk and mellow on a wine the color of rose petals and the soft Aquitanian light.

Signing on as a slave in Snorri's household wasn't the vocation Goltrade had in mind, but with that irritating Christian resilience he decided it must have been the one his god had in mind, so he immediately set about trying to convert his captors. Snorri's crew balked at having a priest aboard because of their notoriously bad weatherluck, especially a priest who engaged in ceaseless philippic, so Snorri lashed him to an oar in the small boat and towed him behind the dragon's tail (with a man handy to cut him loose if the need arose).

It was just after Snorri'd assayed his only marriage with a Christian, my mother Mairead, and he had it in mind that Goltrade was a sort of present for her: a man who claimed to be learned, a man who could read the Roman runes. With a new groom's enthusiasm Snorri wanted to impress Mairead with his ability to make slaves out of educated men, apparently a desirable attribute in the Mark. That was why he didn't kill Goltrade when his psalm singing woke up the crew, asleep at their oars after a long day of pulling wood for home.

Mairead greeted this present with mixed emotions. She was a politic bride as much as a passionate one, and she recognized the affection the gesture represented in Snorri's pagan heart, but also the evil luck that enslaving a priest might bring. There were two faces to every coin, even then, but Mairead was a pragmatic Christian, and she interceded on Goltrade's behalf, saving him from the usual thrall work and setting him instead to teaching my sister Sinead and me our letters. He became her private chaplain and shepherd to the small flock of Christians (thirty-two) who lived in Clontarf.

He affected to be a culdee because of his "exile" among the Danes, but he had little in common with those ascetics except a fondness for hardboiled eggs and a certain downwind gaminess. Technically he was a thrall, but because Mairead's patronage made him bold, Goltrade preached as he willed within the earthwork, a concession that Snorri soon had to modify when Goltrade's continual importuning of pedestrians going about their daily routine grew to be a nuisance. Goltrade was allowed to preach whatever text moved him to whomever chanced by, but only from one strictly circumscribed spot of his own choosing, excepting the main gate, where traffic was heaviest.

After a little thought, Goltrade chose the vicinity of the common mead vats, well off the beaten track of daily commerce, but a main recreational goal. The people of Clontarf had to put up with diatribes about pagan excess when they went to fill their pitchers, but they seemed to adapt with good humor, and in the end Goltrade became the town mascot, their own tame priest.

After a few years Snorri tried to sell him, and when no one wanted to buy, tried giving him away. Finally only manumission seemed likely to rid him of the priest, but he wouldn't leave, and Snorri couldn't kill him because the Irish were too fond of their holy men, and no one wanted trouble. Goltrade expanded his ministry to the remote farmsteads, preaching, marrying, baptizing, and shriving the farm-bound Irish north of the earthwork, a day's ride or more away, in the heartland of the Southern Uí Naíll. He made many a baptism penny, and his quickness to advise his betters became a running joke on Snorri. But he bellied up to the boards from Clonmore in the south, to Clonfert and Clonmacnoise in the west, to Kells and Clonnard in the north, and everything he learned eventually came to Orm Jarl's attention.

As I grew, Skallagrim taught me Danish, Irish, and Anglo-Saxon verse and the cutting and sending of runes; Goltrade taught me to read, speak, and write the Roman language. If the priest wasn't after me with a slate and chalk, clicking out words and phrases for me to copy, the skald was after me with yew staves and a sharp knife, and one of the rune poems on his tongue. Those are my earliest memories of them, and my introduction to languages and learning.

That night in the hall, Skallagrim had been cutting runes at the table, and when he got up to sing he left the yew staves and his stag-handle rune knife among the shavings. Goltrade came in and swept Skallagrim's work aside with a flourish as he produced his slate and began to interrogate me about the grammatical relationships of the Latin words of some biblical admonition.

"What does this say?" Goltrade asked me as his chalk squeaked on the stone. The graying fringe of his tonsure shook with the righteous vehemence of some conviction regarding either grammar or scripture, you could never tell which, and his sun-browned head shone in the lamplight. His eyes were zealot red; your true zealot's eyes always burn like red coals.

"What have you done to my staves, priest?" Skallagrim demanded when he sat down after he finished singing.

"Swept your heathen beliefs aside, wizard," Goltrade snarled.

"Those runes have to be sent by midnight." Skallagrim peered into the shadows under the table, where the yew staves, about five or six inches long, were hard to distinguish among the rushes and dog turds. Skallagrim was a working magician, and he scheduled his magic when he could. Goltrade dragged his thumbnail across the slate to refocus my attention on sacred grammar.

"Your indulgence to this priest is foolish," Skallagrim complained to Snorri when he'd straightened up and rearranged the staves on the table. "Writing will ruin the boy's mind. How'll he remember anything if he writes it down?"

"He won't have to remember it," Goltrade snapped. "He'll be able to read it whenever he wants."

"I myself know thousands of lines in three languages," Skallagrim insisted, as he fingered the incised runes. "Learned one and all without reading. Harping learned without reading. Runes learned without reading—"

"Suppose he hears some lines you don't know," Goltrade interrupted. "Suppose he's far away and he hears some lines that he wants to tell you about, but you're not there. Now, if you could both read, he could write them down and send them to you, and you could commit them to memory if you wanted. The Church in the East is founded on writing, as the Roman Empire was founded on writing."

"Your indigestion is going to be founded on writing," Skallagrim promised him. "Either shut your face or you'll eat that slate."

"Runes are the closest you'll come to an education," Goltrade said pettishly. Part of his zealotry was that passion for new things some of them have, and in truth I had it too, for writing at least. True writing was just then making its acquaintance with the Danes, and most of the skalds who learned it were enthusiastic, but despite Skallagrim's vast runelore, he resisted it.

"Better a wizard than a thrall to writing," Skallagrim asserted, "or a priest whose wyrd was to be taken from fools in Frankland."

"My mission's here," Goltrade said tersely, pulling at my sleeve to force my attention back to the Latin he'd scratched on the slate.

"Your mission's wherever you're fed," Skallagrim snorted. "Your namesake killed those men with his harping all right, but not because of its sweetness."

Now, Goltrade's namesake was the mythic Irish harper who'd played so beautifully that once twelve men died of weeping when they heard him. That story was Goltrade's vanity, and he was a man of that robust and egomaniacal stock which set out to reclaim the vast pagan darkness for the light of Christianity, not a man particularly skilled at patient and reasoned argument. He was a Benedictine of the same cloth as Boniface, who, having exhausted logic against the Old Saxons, took up an axe, leveled a sacred oak, and dared Thorr to do something about it.

Of course at the time he'd been backed up by a troop of Franks with naked blades, but I've no doubt he was crazy enough to have done it without them. Goltrade's mood soured at that crack about the harper, and he broke the slate over Skallagrim's forehead. The skald came over the table with the rune knife, and they rolled together into the dogs, back against the wall.

Snorri picked up a bucket of water and emptied it over them, separating the only two scholars Clontarf could boast of just as they seemed about to resolve their debate. Someone kicked a barking dog, I righted the bench, and the excitement was over all too soon for the thanes, who were starting to wager on the outcome. In the lull that followed, talk was general and loud, and Kari Cut Nose picked his time. His nose was beyond picking, having been severed in a skirmish with an Orkneyman aboard one of Knute's ships, and he sported a leather patch over the hole in the front of his face where it used to be.

"Orm Jarl," Kari said, "in your day the raiding was easier and the sea calmer, but last season I took three boats into the Skagerrak and returned with four. How do you reckon it?"

Orm looked at him and wiped his lips with his beard before he spoke. "Perhaps you miscounted your boats?" he suggested.

There was laughter; Orm Jarl smiled. Kari smiled too, but it was a wolf's grin, and Orm Jarl knew it. Skallagrim moved back onto the bench beside my father and me. "*Ofermod*," Skallagrim said. A trickle of blood was meandering across his forehead, down the valley between his eyes, parting at the ridge line of his nose to course toward the wicks of his mustache. Goltrade picked himself up and sat down beside Skallagrim, holding the two halves of his slate together to reconstruct the Latin phrase, water dripping on it from his soaked head.

Snorri nodded, waiting for Kari's answer. Everyone knew Kari was ambitious. He'd commanded the last three fleets that sailed north to vex Knute, and he was thinking of expanding his compass; he was wondering how his ass would fit the high seat. He may have lost his nose raiding in the Baltic, but he'd come back with silver to show for it. What Skallagrim said was in the language of the West Saxons, which he'd picked up on his travels, and it described the only thing that really pissed off the Norns: "Overmuch mood."

"I counted right," Kari said. "And I reckon it cost me more than it cost you, sitting old and fat and taking your share in safety."

Well, that got everyone's attention. Orm Jarl was a graybeard, but not a man to treat with disdain: he was lord of Clontarf. He drained off his horn and handed it to Gudrud, his youngest wife. Everyone looked at him. "I can see that the Orkneyman taught you nothing about where to put your nose," he said. "He only made it so you couldn't smell death."

You could have cut the air with an Ulfberth blade, and it's a good thing all the swords were on the walls or no doubt someone would have. Only scramasaxes were handy, just the sort of weapon you ordinarily want for close-in work, but with Orm's housethanes moving around behind them, Kari's men were discovering discretion. Gudrud vanished into the shadows behind the high seat. I looked around and saw that *all* the women were gone. Even the wolfhounds were getting out of the way. The fire in the raised central hearth crackled as the logs relaxed into the coals.

"I see you've still got *your* nose," Kari said. "Come along and show us how it's done. Sniff out some plunder on the spring vik."

Orm Jarl, in his capacity as elder statesman, blinked a couple of times and then took the way that Kari held out. "After Beltane," he said. "We'll take out three boats each. The one comes back with less works for the other."

Skallagrim shook his head somberly. "Kari's right," he

said. "If Orm weren't too old, there'd be blood instead of boasts and betting."

"I'd expect you to prefer bloodshed to reason," Goltrade said.

"What reason was this?" Skallagrim asked, wiping at the tickles of blood beside his nose.

So that year Orm Jarl dragged himself away from his wolfhounds and sobered up long enough to outfit three ships for a vik to the land of the Engs. With at least one of his thanes growing restive, he wanted some relatively local action, and Baltic waters were too far away. It was a bad idea: it was 791, and that spring Offa, the Mercian Bretwalda, was marrying off one of his daughters to the king of Wessex as part of his master plan to ensure Mercian hegemony over the other six Eng kingdoms. It was into this context of power politics and sexual tension that Orm Jarl and Kari sailed, right up to the wedding feast where they demanded a danegeld, bold as you please. Offa and his new in-laws stropped steel on Orm Jarl and Kari and their six ships. In the end, they shared out equally. Whatever else you can say about the Anglo-Saxons, when you get a few thousand together for a wedding feast and pour fifty or a hundred hogsheads of ale into them, they're a match for any six ships loaded to the gunnels with *ofermod.*

The entry in the *Chronicle* for that year was a model of Eng understatement, and, characteristically, only half right: "Brihtric took Offa's daughter Eadburgh for his wife. In his days came the first six ships of the Northmen from Horthaland."

I was seventeen when Orm went to sample Offa's hospitality. Snorri would've been with him, but a horse kicked him at the Beltane feast. So Snorri was left to heal up and be in charge of Clontarf in Orm's absence, and when the news of Orm Jarl's end was finally verified by Welshmen trading with Einar Soft Hands, half a year later, Snorri oversaw the transition to Orm's only surviving son, Sygtrygg, who'd fostered with Snorri's family when I was a boy.

Everyone held his breath. Sygtrygg was a smoldering torch, and when he ignited, people were going to get burned. His fostering to Snorri had been as much to get him out of Orm Jarl's house and away from his four older brothers as a way of strengthening the ties of loyalty between Orm and his horsemaster. Sygtrygg had a reputation for dullness in all things but a fight, where his reflexes were quick and his sense unbeaten. These characteristics, while not considered undesirable in the eighth century, had to be tempered even in those more robust times. Snorri'd made a man of Sygtrygg, sharpened him as much as possible given the temper of the pupil, and sent him back to Orm less quick to cut when he suspected offense. Sygtrygg suspected offense whenever he didn't understand, which was often, so Orm Jarl was pleased with Snorri's work.

As the youngest son, Sygtrygg had been marked for mediocrity: a seat at the table, an oar in a boat, a small farmstead, and a wife to give him children and run things when he was on a vik. Orm Jarl had wasted no breath teaching him the skills of leadership or the wisdom of command. Instead, he'd fostered Sygtrygg out for whatever polishing he could get. Now Orm Jarl and his four oldest sons, Aki, Svart, Ottar, and Thrand, were dog food in Mercia. Snorri Horsekicked was a lucky man to have fostered the youngest son of his lord, Orm Skeggöx.

As I grew up, because of this fostering and Snorri's position as horsemaster and housethane, I was able to take advantage of the best training available in Clontarf: elementary and intermediate pillage, sword, axe, archery, basic and advanced principles of navigation, and boatbuilding. The usual curriculum. Like everyone, I spent my youth as a bloodthirsty punk leaning on anyone who wasn't leaning on me. Two things saved me from an early ride to Asgard: my mother and a vegetarian Geat.

Snorri had first seen Mairead when he was trading horses at the Lugnasad Fair at Tailltenn. Mairead was a woman of clan Ulaid, the clan that'd lost the most to the northern Uí Naíll, and, never one to haggle when he really wanted something, Snorri married her outright for the asked brideprice. She was eighteen years old. All Snorri's wives had been eighteen when he married them. He believed in the omen of that numerological equation: $1 + 8 = 9$. Nine was the most powerful of all numbers, and he believed it ensured domestic harmony.

Mairead was the last of his four wives, and she provided him with only myself and my sister Sinead. It didn't matter to Snorri, whose sexual rapacity was matched only by his ability to translate mead into urine, and who, not counting

Sygtrygg and two other fosterlings, had thirteen sons and four daughters, all of whom he treated with an egalitarian affection.

I caused Mairead some bad moments in my youth, but they were tempered by my apparent interest in the learning which she'd arranged for me. She always favored the finer ways of her Celtic heritage, loved the harping and the singing, and her aspirations for her only son lay in that direction. She'd persuaded Snorri to keep me back from the sea road, and in addition to having Goltrade teach me letters, she commissioned the lean Hebrew, Malachai, a merchant from the Moorish coast of Spain, whom Snorri'd taken, together with two of his ships (loaded to the freeboard with spices) during a leisurely cruise along the Cordoban Caliphate several years after my namegiving, to teach me the commercial aspects of the family business. He taught me only a little Hebrew, and without practice, it didn't stick. I'd never shown an exceptional interest in the horses, and my brothers had never shown *any* interest in letters, so Snorri agreed. I wasn't consulted.

I spent many reluctant mornings with Goltrade and Malachai, skipping the major mayhem that passed for play during my early adolescence, learning to read and write and to keep accounts. My real interest, though, during those years of my primary education, was theory and application of violence. In anticipation of my first vik, I spent my afternoons on the practice fields, hurling spears, swinging axes, wielding swords, shooting arrows, throwing knives, and my evenings in the hall listening to Skallagrim recite the "Sayings of the Wise" or "Baldur's Dream" or "Loki's Flyting," or, if there were Irish guests in attendance, the "Táin bó Froích" or "Togail bruidne Da Derga" or "Maccgnimrada Con Culaind": just the sort of heroic escapism and snide blasphemy that appealed to an adolescent in Clontarf, counting the months till his first vik.

I was fourteen and big for my age, swaggering around the vegetable market with my younger half-brothers Gorm and Grim. It was midsummer, sort of halftime in the trading season when the early fleet was stopping off for a rest in the friendly waters of the Irish Sea and the late fleet hadn't yet started to hopscotch the Frisian coast. The earthwork was busy with commerce: Baltic merchants, old colleagues and competitors of Orm Jarl's, had sailed down to see his new base of operations, and Irishmen from clan Connol were trading or buying at the stalls.

The Geat was crew on one of the dragons in the harbor; minding his own business and enjoying his shore leave, he was buying carrots, which struck me as one of the funniest things I'd seen in a long time. My brothers laughed when I did, and nothing's more dangerous than a fourteen-year-old wit with an appreciative audience. When the Geat slapped the *handsala* with the farmer to conclude the deal, I said loudly, "Maybe that carrot will stiffen his pecker," and grabbed up a carrot, planting it between my legs as I danced around. The three of us were laughing too hard to notice that everyone else at the farmer's stall was giving the Geat room. He'd been on the sea road for six months, but I didn't know what that meant, then. There was no room in his bag for insults from pups who'd never been Viking. He put the carrots down on the rough boards of the counter and turned around, smiling.

"I see the children of Clontarf play with swords," he said.

It was just the sort of bait I'd rise to at that age; he'd chosen his words well. I drew my blade, and Gorm and Grim had their scramasaxes out, following my lead. We thought we were formidable, arrayed there with our herringboned steel shining in the sun, but we'd no real skill fighting together, and I'd underestimated the Geat. He was only four years older than me, but he'd spent three of those four years harrying the Moorish coast of Spain, and before I could say "Baldur's balls," my blade was in pieces on the ground, and I was beside it with my face laid open from hair to jaw, wondering if a lightning bolt had hit me. Grim and Gorm dropped their scramasaxes and hauled ass, scattering a flock of geese that had been strutting through the market bullying the chickens.

"I'm Olaf," the Geat said, "a guest in Clontarf, and guest duty keeps me from killing you while you're down, but if you want to finish this, my friend will loan you his sword."

Another Geat separated himself from the crowd and put a hand on the hilt of his blade. I saw that the peace ribbons were in place, and I looked at Olaf's scabbard and saw that his ribbons were dangling, broken when I'd forced him to defend himself. I'd provoked this fight, and I couldn't win it. All I had to defend myself was the carrot in my fist.

"Forewarned is innocent," Olaf said.

"That's the law," his friend agreed. "Forewarned is innocent."

What they meant was that since I'd started the fight and survived the first exchange, the law said if I persisted after a warning he'd have my ass and be innocent of murder. No wergeld could be demanded, no sentence of outlawry delivered at the Thing, no blood feud declared: I'd die unavenged. I shook my head and stayed on the ground, my skull expanding and contracting with every heartbeat, and after a moment he sheathed his blade, picked up his carrots with a humiliating laugh, and walked away. How suddenly is the direction of a life changed. I'd started the fight pretending to be an adult, and they'd taken me at my word. The only thing that kept me from shitting myself was my preoccupation with the fact that my gaping face was covering me with blood.

There was laughter from the crowd and I saw a small group of Irish boys, a little older than me, talking in Irish, which they thought I couldn't understand.

"What a piss-poor showing," one of them said. "Do you suppose they all fight as badly?"

"If so, my father's men could wipe them all out in an afternoon," another one sneered. "Bleeding women and old crones would make a better fight of it than this coward."

I dropped the carrot and got up on my hands and knees, looking round for my sword. No use there, I realized when I focused on the broken blade. I crawled over to Gorm's scramasax.

"Pull out some steel," I said in Irish, "and we'll see who's a coward." I lurched to my feet, light-headed and clumsy. They gave a little ground and fanned out. I zeroed in on the one who'd called me a coward. He backed away and his hand went to the hilt of his weapon. Just then Sygtrygg stepped between us.

"My foster brother's wounded," he said. "And not up to another fight just now. Maybe I could take his place."

"Out of the way, Sygtrygg," I said as light-headedness covered me like a silk dust cover. Then I was sitting on the ground again, wondering how I'd gotten there.

I'd shown as much promise as any of my brothers in the martial arts, and gotten my share of cuts and bruises over the years, but that was the first time I'd crossed blades with a man who was prepared to kill me on the spot, and I was impressed. Although I didn't realize it at the moment, it was there, in front of the farmer's stall on market day in Clontarf, that I became a conscientious objector, and the appeal of the quiet life grew stronger with every one of the twenty-seven stitches Mairead used to close up the gash.

I was feverish for a week while Mairead persuaded Snorri that Malachai was getting neither thinner nor younger, and that someday he'd need another accountant. Snorri was agreeable and eager enough to have someone he trusted learn what Malachai had to teach, so from then on, after a few weeks of mostly token protest while I healed, I spent the bulk of my time going over the books and learning the less volatile end of the family business.

All that reluctant learning suddenly seemed like a found hoard. There were two warehouses full of booty: wool, linen, furs, amber, some silver chain and brooches, hack silver, gold coins, and rings, swords, spices, and incense. I spent my convalescence familiarizing myself with the value and contents of the inventory. My complaints about my new station were bitter enough to divert the taunts of friends who were coming home from second and, in some cases, third viks. They believed it was an imposed duty, and I was spared from accusations of cowardice and a flyting by my peer group.

It's funny how those things seemed important then. I winced all over at those stitches whenever Skallagrim spoke the verse from the Sayings of the Wise:

> A coward thinks he will live forever
> If only he can shun warfare,
> But in old age he shall have no peace
> Though spears spared his limbs.

That wasn't a tasty thought for a son of Snorri's to eat, one that wouldn't wash down no matter how many horns I drained, although I've learned a few things about cowardice since. And that Irish voice taunting me had rubbed the salt of that thought into the wound while it still bled. So I earned my new name, Bran Facecut, at small enough cost, though it seemed too dear at the time.

* * *

In the evenings I renewed my apprenticeship with Skalla-grim the Skald. He seemed more willing to teach me after I was marked by the Geat, as if he were confident now that I'd live to use it and his effort wouldn't be wasted. The eighth century actuarial landscape argued for a certain economy of interpersonal effort. We'd sit together in the mead hall while the women raked the ashes and rebuilt the fire for the night, and he taught me the rune poems, the art of kenning, and the composition of the alliterative long line. We practiced together, and I learned by rote the verses Orm Jarl and his thanes liked: "Lay of Erik," "Skirnir's Ride," and "Loki's Flyting." I wanted to write them down, to marry the two halves of my knowledge, but Skallagrim wouldn't permit it. "Quills are the leeches of poetry," he said. "And ink's the blood of verse. Carve stones if you have to scratch."

Skallagrim had as much of the old knowledge as anyone in the time when the Christians were first turning their attention to the Danes and the old gods were dying of disbelief. The food of the gods is man's belief in them, and when that belief goes, the gods starve, their power to make order deserts them, and men remember why they're afraid of the dark. Skallagrim taught me these things, and they've never proved false.

In those years of my first learning, my friends and brothers took to the sea road on their first viks. From the time the spring sun rose out of the standing stones until the balancing of night and day, when the dragons and knarr would come back laden with plunder and lies about why there was less or more, I learned whatever Skallagrim, Goltrade, and Malachai had to teach me. No matter that not everyone came back from those viks; as the years passed I squirmed more and more whenever the sails shrank away toward the Welsh coast, believing I would have been harrying Knute aboard one of Snorri's dragons but for the wyrm of fear that nested in my guts. I fingered the scar on my face unconsciously, but Skallagrim noticed and understood.

"You're no coward," he said. "You've battle luck, the best thing for a Clontarfman, and you've sense to the bargain, a thing that many lack. There's luck in your family: Snorri's was to be kicked at the horsefair, yours was to be facecut while

you could still learn from it. Orm's wyrd was to let himself
be baited by Kari, whose wyrd it was to want too much.
Would you trade with either of them, dead in Eng land? Your
wyrd wasn't to die for a poor joke about carrots, and Snorri's
wasn't to follow his lord to a bad place at a bad time."

He loved me in his way, and wanted me to find out what
my wyrd was without feeling bad about what it wasn't, but
I sensed a flaw in his reasoning. I thought about it a lot;
one of my earliest verses explained my new name:

A breaking of blades   and Bran went down.
  Gorm ran with Grim   scattering geese
The Geat was gracious,   a guest in Clontarf
  He let me live and   I learned my lesson.
   Face cut for carrots   Facecut I became.
  Where steel strayed   the serpent sleeps.

Six months after the news of Orm's death reached us, one
of Snorri's business initiatives failed to come home: two
knarr, built with borrowed money and crewed with a promised share of the profit, went down in a storm off Cornwall,
a day's sail from home. My brother Halvard commanded
the venture. He'd been Snorri's protégé as a horse seller
to the Irish, and he'd been eager to start amassing his own
fortune. He was looking to wive, and Snorri'd staked him
on the voyage so he could start building his own herd. Now
he was feeding the fish, and Snorri was out a son, his carefully trained successor as horsemaster, two ships, and the
cost of the entire enterprise. Snorri began to have an old
man's doubts, convinced the venture would've come home
if he'd been along, and went into a depression. He thought
he could see the better part of his life behind, lame and
old in Clontarf, unable to take the sea road and trade in
season, useless, telling stories in the hall at night about
things that were farther and farther behind time's keel.

Lost in this profound mope that not even his wives could
rouse him from, Snorri lost sight of the fact that he hadn't
repaid his investor, Sygtrygg. One night in the hall, as the
mead went round and the dogs fought for scraps in the
rushes, Sygtrygg advised Snorri that, as a housethane who
wanted to remain in good standing, he'd better give some
thought to repayment before the next Thing.

The idea of repayment hadn't been a part of Snorri's depressed and sodden musings, but one glance at Thord and Hjordis, the two berserks who always accompanied Sygtrygg like tamed trolls, and Snorri allowed as how he'd been giving it some heavy thought just that afternoon, and he presented Sygtrygg with three fine Frisian mares, as many swords as one of his trolls could carry, a hundred ells of spun wool, and me.

"My boy," Snorri told me that night, "the time's come to repay your old Da for all he's done for you."

Under the circumstances, what could I say? So I went to serve in the house of Sygtrygg Orm Jarlson, a late fostering in the house of my foster brother. In a settlement as small as Clontarf, relationships were bound to become tangled.

Because I'd held the office in my father's house, Sygtrygg handed over the part of his accounts that didn't touch on Snorri, for he was wise enough to know that allegiance shifted suddenly in face may take more time to shift in heart, and he didn't want me in charge of my father's account until then. Snorri'd taught him well.

As a physical move it wasn't much, a hundred yards up the timber street, and into the earthwork-within-the-earthwork where Orm Jarl's family lived, but it was farther away from home than I guessed at the time, and it was only the first step on the road to my wyrd. Outwardly, little changed. I still studied Latin with Goltrade in the afternoons and sang with Skallagrim in the hall at night. I still loafed around my mother's hearth while she separated the warp threads and tied them to the loom weights, or spun out wool with a spindle whorl, or gossiped with Gudrud and Sinmarra, Snorri's other wives. I still hunted with my friends and half-brothers, gamed in the mead hall, slipped the traces on the hawks, and the eel into any willing girl whenever the opportunity arose. I just spent my hours in Sygtrygg's counting house instead of Snorri's.

Now, Sygtrygg had a sister. What a flat and fatal statement that is: Sygtrygg had a sister. Actually, he had five sisters, but the one that mattered was Frydys. She was four years younger than me, but even at fourteen she was one of the greatest beauties Clontarf had ever seen. When she'd gone through her change, somewhere in her thirteenth year, she'd shifted shape from a dirt-faced child into one of those aching adolescent wish maidens that come along now and then to make men insane.

She was well favored in her features and her limbs, which is to say that her body was as wonderful as her face; her breasts looked like they carried the milk of the immortals, and her nipples, cold under her shift in the winter mornings, stood out like the taps on two kegs of mead. I once saw a man, watching her as he walked along, knock himself out against a post. She had hair like gold shot with copper threads, eyes as blue as a king's blood, and teeth like snow. But those breasts; Thorr's balls, it's true that straining impatiently against her apron were the most stunning knockers I'd ever seen.

She carried a pair of scissors on the silver chain between the turtle brooches on her dress, and they swung like a loomweight below those breasts. Men were always asking her to clip a stray thread, and, glad of the attention, she was always obliging. Too obliging for Sygtrygg, who inherited the duties of the ring-giver and the name-giver as well as the hall and the tribute. He had a mind to keep her for a while and make an advantageous marriage.

"Bran," he said one night when we were sitting on the earthwork looking at the early May sky. "That slut Frydys had better keep her knees together or there'll be trouble."

"What sort of trouble?" I asked him. "Girls do as they please."

He shook his head. "She's no girl of Clontarf, free to open her legs at will. She's Orm Jarl's daughter just come to her growth. She's my sister, and I'm lord of Clontarf now. She has duties."

"Are her duties the same as her sisters'?" I asked him. "I see Gudrun and Kalf Agirson inspecting the ships of an evening. Is Gudrun interested in boat wrighting?"

"Frydys has different duties, imposed by her beauty, as I've different duties imposed by the lordship, and you've different duties imposed by our foster brotherhood and Snorri's debt."

"We all have different duties," I admitted cautiously. Sygtrygg had obviously been giving this some thought, and I was worried about the result of this unaccustomed activity. "We're bound by the web of duty, each to everyone else, like fish caught in a net."

"Do you remember when we were young?" Sygtrygg

asked. "We used to roll down the earthwork to make ourselves dazed and then try to walk a straight line."

I smiled at the memory of those primitive sobriety tests. When Sygtrygg had fostered in Snorri's house, he'd been nine and I'd been five, and he was as near my age as my next oldest brother. I followed him everywhere, as Gorm and Grim followed me later on. We played in the home fields, slid on the winter ice, hunted, hawked, taunted girls, got into the usual trouble.

We'd sit on the earthwork and Skallagrim would tell us the stories in the sky, pointing out the stars against the Milky Way, which the Danes called the Path of Ghosts, and teaching us their names and uses to find your way. Now here we were, thirteen years later, looking at the sky and wondering where we were, and no stars could tell us the answer.

Weighted down by the burdens of the lordship, Sygtrygg didn't yet understand his mood. He was beginning to realize the days were gone when he could sail before the wind without his duties going further than to his shipmates, and I reckon he was trying to keep as much of his short youth as possible. He was just a twenty-two-year-old guy sitting in the dark, realizing that the easy life had been snatched away and replaced by responsibility to a settlement of twenty-two hundred people, looking to him for direction in a dark time.

We'd been friends and foster brothers, and Sygtrygg was nostalgic for a time he could trust. He'd learned about the friends the high seat attracts. Men who'd never given him a second glance before were toasting his health at the table and trying to wheedle larger fields or better ships or bigger legal settlements. Never the brightest bonfire to burn at Beltane, Sygtrygg was confused, and confusion drove him into himself, to come out in who knew what direction.

It seemed now the direction he'd take centered on his sister Frydys. Maybe he reckoned her beauty was the lodestone that would guide him out of the fog. Perhaps he had a profitable marriage in mind, or the continued promise of one dangled before many suitors. Now that he was lord, Sygtrygg was inventing subtlety. But his plan was jeopardized by his sister's own willfulness. If she opened her legs whenever she wanted, it was only a matter of time until she got a child and ruined her value. So his wyrd had brought us together on the earthwork once more to look at the stars and make the pronouncement: "That slut Frydys had better keep her knees together or there'll be trouble."

How prophetic. Scarcely any time had passed before he found her in the loft with her knees as wide apart as she could get them and someone unsuitable between. Sygtrygg split the unlucky man open as he rutted into Frydys and spent him before he could spend himself. There was screaming throughout the house, and I looked up from my slate to see Frydys running past, clutching her skirts to her bloody tits and cursing Sygtrygg in language scarcely fit for a dragon's deck. Then Sygtrygg burst in with wet steel in hand a moment after her bare ass, with a few straws still clinging to her beard, had disappeared round the corner.

"Where?" he demanded.

I knew what was coming, and I took him off in the wrong direction so he could cool down before he beat her.

"I told you this would happen," he said as he hacked a switch from the hedge and stripped off the leaves with a pull of his fist. "Now I'll have to pay a wergeld or risk a blood feud."

"Who was it?" I asked.

"I don't even know," he snarled. "I never looked at his face, just where his eel was swimming."

"We better see to him before someone finds the body and cries murder," I suggested. That brought him up. Lord of Clontarf though he was, it wouldn't do to be called out before the Thing as a murderer, which was possible if the killing went unannounced for more than a couple of days. He had to control the damage first and punish his sister after. We went back to the loft and found the corpse undisturbed, almost bled white into the hay. Sygtrygg cursed the corpse for draining into his loft.

"Now I'll have to burn this bloody hay and have someone rake in fresh," he muttered, pacing the perimeter of the stain while I rolled the corpse over. It was drawing flies already. I tried to put a name to the face, but I couldn't.

"A stranger," I said. "Well enough. We can set a wergeld and call it out for a week. Likely no one will claim it. He must be from a ship."

The setting of the price and the announcement were the short-term goals in a situation like that. Everyone had a death price, estimated by your position in society, your job, and your relationships. It avoided escalating death and feuds at every blood spilling. If a wergeld was accepted, vengeance wasn't required.

"Loki's bastard," Sygtrygg said, examining the dead man's shriveled dick with the point of his sword. "You don't think he's an Irishman, do you? That's just what we need: a blood feud with those turnip eaters."

I shook my head doubtfully. His clothes were in a heap a few feet away, straw kicked over them no doubt by Frydys's thrashing. I toed them out and saw I was right. "No Irishman wore these," I said. "This is northern wool, and man's hands have sewn the rips."

That was enough to put Sygtrygg at ease, and he hunted Frydys down, dragged her from her room, and striped her with the switch. Diverting as it may have been, I was not invited to witness this spectacle; no matter, everyone inside the earthwork could hear it going down. As it turned out, Frydys wasn't cowed, only silenced.

The next day Sygtrygg's Lawspeaker called out the wergeld in the market, and the captain of the corpse's ship came to collect some silver and half a beef for the voyage out, and, just to keep his shipmates cheerful, a cask of Frisian mead. We never knew his name.

Sygtrygg caught a break from the Norns that time, but what happened next had a greater civic impact. The fishing weir was in ill repair after the spring flooding, and the question was whether to fix it again or simply move it. Growing up, Sygtrygg and I'd spent a lot of time there spearing salmon and ling, and the day after the matter was brought to his attention, we went down to inspect the condition of the palisade weir. It wasn't the sort of thing the lord of Clontarf generally got involved in, but in view of time spent there as boys, we thought, what the hell?

It was the day before the cornplanting feast, and Clontarf had abandoned routine to prepare for the party. The oak pyre was built in the home field beyond the earthwork, the sacrificial animals had been selected and prepared, the banquet was in the making. There were eight of us, Sygtrygg, myself, the weirmaster, a few of the usual loafing housethanes, and Thord and Hjordis, Sygtrygg's two personal berserks. We crossed the west meadow in good spirits. The sun was warm, and the drone of bees, recently awakened from their winter's sleep and lazing knee-high over the clover, drifted like a current under the keel of our laughter. We reached the other side of the meadow and left the path to shortcut the weir. Sygtrygg pushed through the foliage at the edge of the trail and into the old Druid's oak grove, but before he'd gone three steps, he jolted to a stop and made a sound like he was vomiting up a futhark.

"Mnnahhrrggahh!"

"Sygtrygg," I yelled, drawing my scramasax, and Hjordis and Thord, whose job it was to go about armed and danger-ous, got in touch with their internal motivations and cut down a few saplings and slashed the weirmaster viciously on the arm as they drew their swords and hustled around to meet the imagined attack. The loafing housethanes flat-tened themselves on the ground and crawled for safety. Sygtrygg had wrenched the bearded axe from his belt by the time we caught sight of the problem, down on her back again, with her legs wrapped around someone's hairy ass.

The man, who we recognized as Bjorn the Weller, had barely rolled off Frydys before Sygtrygg's axe was whistling through the air in a stroke that made Bjorn's eel shrivel like a salted snail.

"Aaarrgghh," Bjorn screamed, taken with his pants down at the worst possible moment by the worst possible man. He reached over his head and grasped one of the rough-barked oak roots that writhed along the ground, pulling himself away from the falling blade and reflexively lifting and spreading his legs as much as the pants bunched about his calves would allow. The axe passed undeterred through the taut fabric with a twang of steel and sank a hand's length into a subterranean oak root, which held it fast.

As Sygtrygg tried to reverse the blow, Bjorn scrambled up and ran for his life, the severed halves of his breeches flapping about his ankles. That was when the berserks, transfixed by the sight of Frydys on the ground, remem-bered what they were supposed to be about and started after him.

"Don't kill him," Sygtrygg screamed when he discovered the blade was caught. "He's mine."

Bjorn was flapping through the oak trees like a monk on fire as the berserks closed on him, and Sygtrygg was strain-ing at the haft of the bearded axe, the muscles knotting in his shoulders and neck. That axe might have been held by the wyrm at the roots of the Yggdrasil for all the progress he was making, and then the haft snapped at the axehead, and he exploded backward into me and we both went down into the brush.

About that time Thord, the faster of the berserks, caught up with Bjorn and pinned him to a tree until Hjordis arrived. Bjorn was howling and frothing, but there was no escaping Thord's mastlike arms. Hjordis scooped up Bjorn's legs and they carried the thrashing well digger back to where Sygtrygg and I were heaped on the ground.

Frydys was on her feet now, screaming and kicking at Sygtrygg, and I was the beneficiary of the kicks that missed their mark, Sygtrygg's flailing elbows as he tried to lever himself up, and the oak roots grinding against my spine. The berserks planted Bjorn with a thud that I felt through the loam; Sygtrygg managed to push Frydys aside and got up, and I lay there trying to catch my breath.

Sygtrygg grunted and fumed like a boar in heat, waved the axe handle about, and, to gain a little time and punctuate his mood, cuffed Frydys upside the head with it, sending her sprawling against the tree trunk where she stopped momentarily, stunned, and then slid down into a sitting position, straddling a root with a look of dreamy contemplation. I shook my head and stumbled to my feet. Sygtrygg mastered himself and seemed about to make some pronouncement when he noticed a warm wetness down his flank and found my scramasax piercing the meat at his waist, where it'd buried itself when he'd fallen back against me.

If he'd been in a foul mood before, embarrassed in front of his berserks and housethanes by yet another display of Frydys' venereal disobedience, finding himself run through by a scramasax *really* curdled his mood. He pulled the blade out and looked at the bloody steel in disbelief. Bjorn, unmanned by the sight, relaxed in Thord's grasp with a moan, and an inside-out smell made our eyes water as Bjorn's well-digging bowels, unconstrained by the warrior ethos, opened and brought forth a turd two feet long and as big around as a spear shaft. It slithered out of him and coiled up on Thord's boots as prettily as a brown adder. Sygtrygg stepped forward and drove the scramasax into Bjorn with an upward thrust that lifted him out of Thord's arms and dropped him onto the ground between Frydys's spread legs, where he'd been surprised a few moments before.

"Who's going to keep the wells clear now?" Thord asked, shaking the shit off his boots.

Keeping the wells clear wasn't a consideration in the two months between Bjorn's last plumbing job and the Thing. In the week before Thingweek Snorri and I tried to cut a deal with Bjorn's family, but they were holding out for some fantastic compensation they refused to name. Bjorn's father made it clear that he intended to bring suit for manslaughter and put it to the Thingmen to decide.

The Thing was the annual folk gathering held during the week of the first full moon of July. It was the place where grievances were redressed, boundaries settled, laws modified, treaties compacted, marriages performed, divorces ratified, lawsuits pressed, and sentences passed. The deliberative body was composed of thirty-six Thingmen, generally upright or prosperous men from the surrounding hundreds, whose decisions were binding. That was the Thing in theory. It's been identified as an early manifestation of the democratic process, and consequently the invention of democracy has been attributed to the Danes by a certain type of nostalgic revisionist eager to rehabilitate the Viking image.

In fact, the Thing was as democratic as whoever ran it. Claimants had theoretical immunity once they got to the Thingplace, but many a lawsuit was preempted on the road by a few well-armed men. If you didn't show up, your case was forfeit. The wishes and attitudes of the local chieftain were no secret, either, and Thingmen occasionally molded their decisions to suit the prevailing mood. Gold and silver were also known to play their part in the decision-making process. Fair? No. Prudent? Well ... That point made, I have to say that the Things conducted by Orm Jarl, and Sygtrygg after him, were for the most part on the up and up. A few bribes were offered and taken, some minor coercion may have been brought to bear now and then, but in the main, the interests of justice were served.

The official in charge of the Thing was the Lawspeaker, and his first job was to recite the laws of the country. This took a full day and part of the next, and everyone listened closely to be sure that no unexpected nuances had crept in since the last Thing. People made a point of knowing the Law and took it upon themselves to be sure that all rights and technicalities were observed. It was a holdover from Druid times, when they believed that writing power words stole their power. The Druids never wrote, they memorized. They may have had a point: it's only after laws are written down and everyone forgets them but lawyers that things get out of control.

After the recitation of the Laws was over, the Thing recessed for the balance of the second day, and a great feast was laid on for the Lawspeaker and the Thingmen, and everyone got drunk. That was the traditional way of washing down the dry meat of so many words one after another. Because of the feast, no one wanted to have their suit heard the next day. The deliberations of Thingmen in the hot sun after a monumental drunk were notoriously unpredictable.

Scheduling Bjorn's family for the day after the feast was as far as Sygtrygg fiddled with the judicial process at the Thing, although Snorri seated the Thingmen on oak logs to urge them to swift and speedy justice.

As the day wore on, suits were presented, evidence heard, adjudications made, and verdicts announced by the Lawspeaker while the Thingmen rattled their swords on their shields to indicate agreement. That must have done wonders for their heads. The sun was hot, the day was long, and a procession of petty grievances was settled to the clatter of pattern-welded blades: Thorrkil the Proud's wife divorced him, a couple of neighboring farmers redefined their pasturage; an old women accused of casting a spell on a flock of sheep was acquitted when her sons offered evidence of bad husbandry on the part of the plaintiff. That's how it went.

The only remotely interesting thing was a manslaughter case between Bjarki Brynjolfsson and the family of Ketil Pike, whom he'd killed in a duel. Ketil had provoked Bjarki with insults and taunts after Bjarki had publicly warned him. His defense was the fundamental one: forewarned is innocent. But Ketil's family was demanding wergeld in compensation, and Bjarki was refusing to pay. On the surface it was open and shut, but Ketil Pike's family was famously litigious, and they'd bought a few of the Thingmen; also, the two witnesses had disappeared on Snorri's foundered ships, so no decision could be reached.

The only way to avoid a blood feud was to let them fight it out, so everyone retired to the riverbank for the duel. There was a small island in the river that was used for conflict resolution, and Bjarki waded out with his axe, sword, and shield, followed by Gunnbjorn Ulfsson, the champion Ketil's family had hired to fight on their behalf. Gunnbjorn was an able-looking man, but he was from one of the outlying farmsteads, and he didn't get to town much during the year, so he lacked a bit of essential knowledge about his opponent.

Bjarki was a berserk on Kalf Agirson's ship, which was the detail that Ketil's family neglected to bring to Gunnbjorn's attention, because he was surprised when Bjarki put on his bearskin headband and started frothing at the mouth and tearing off his clothes, screaming and pissing himself and swinging the axe in circles as he danced around the island with his eel writhing out in front of him.

Gunnbjorn looked across the water at Ketil Pike's family, and we could see the candle being lit as he realized why none of *them* had volunteered to defend the family honor, but it was too late to back out, and he had to make the best of it. Bjarki rushed him, naked, grunting rhythmically, eyes bulging, nostrils flared and spewing snot into his mustache, and Gunnbjorn took the force of the attack on his shield, trying to twist aside and get in a slash as Bjarki went by. A good plan but poorly executed under the circumstances: Gunnbjorn went down under his shield, and Bjarki stood on it, pinning him to the ground as he chopped through the oak with four or five well-timed blows between his feet, and then through Gunnbjorn with another two or three swings.

That suit settled, the Thing broke for lunch as Bjarki's friends threw a few buckets of water on him and gathered up his clothes while the thralls policed up both halves of Gunnbjorn. On our way back to the Thingplace, Snorri and I approached Bjorn the Weller's father with another settlement offer: a twenty-weight of copper, and two silver rings, the wergeld associated with a craftsman of Bjorn's well-digging skills. We all wanted the matter put as firmly to rest as Bjorn, who was sleeping under the binding runes that Skallagrim had cut. Nobody wanted to turn the corner some night on the way for a piss and run into the reanimated body of Bjorn the Weller, looking to finish that last job of plumbing he'd begun with Frydys.

With the recent example of what awaited an unreasonable plaintiff vividly in mind, Bjorn's father agreed to settle, and Snorri went off to inform the Lawspeaker the suit was withdrawn while I went to tell Sygtrygg. The news made him happy, and with the immediate crisis over, he decided to address the fundamental issue.

"I want you to talk some sense to Frydys," he said. "You've known her all her life; she's known you. Make her see reason."

"What's reason?" I asked, stunned by the request and eager to avoid the task. Several people had already sounded me out, in my capacity as Skallagrim's apprentice, on the ethics of cutting runes to make Frydys love them—hypothetically, of course, just out of curiosity. I told them Skallagrim handled all the spells himself and advised them to make an appointment. If anyone did, Skallagrim never mentioned it. Working magicians observe strict confidentiality, he often told me with obvious conviction.

"Make her keep her knees together," Sygtrygg said. "This suit was almost made, and I don't want another."

I frowned as we walked back to the Thingplace. "You could just not kill anybody else," I pointed out. "That's a fairly simple fix." My job description was evolving from skald and accountant to general fixer after Sygtrygg's fits of distemper. He'd hoped to have Frydys married off before the autumn equinox, but the word was out about her willfulness, Sygtrygg's temper was well documented, and suitors were scarcer than virgins in Trelleborg.

"I can't make her listen," he complained "You're a skald. You must have something in your wordhoard to cool her crotch."

"This is not a good idea," I told him firmly. Two serious beatings hadn't cooled her a single degree, and I doubted I had any arguments that would do the trick. "Have her mother talk to her."

"She won't listen to anyone," he said. "She's truly Freyja's daughter, not Svanhvit's, and maybe it's her wyrd to open her legs. So be it. Just make her wait."

"Marry her off and be done with it."

"As soon as one killing's forgotten, she opens her legs

and another killing's born. She's the mother of blood
feuds."

"So far they've not lived," I reminded him. "Foster her
out to some relative back in the Mark."

"She's sailed past the age of fostering to the age of
marriage."

There was no talking him out of it: I'd been so successful
fixing his killings he thought I could fix anything. "I'll see
what I can do," I promised him, stalling for time. "After
the Thing. But no magic, all right? Skallagrim takes care
of all the magic."

"No magic. You're my brother." Sygtrygg laid a hand on
my arm. "I need this favor."

Technically speaking I was only his foster brother, but
since all his real brothers were dead, he'd have to do with
me. Also, since my facecutting, he reckoned me too ugly
to be interesting to Frydys and so safe to trust with the job.

Snorri shook his gray head and laughed a laugh that made
the sparrows in the rafters fly away. "Trouble ahead," he
said. "Frydys in red. Until she's married, that girl's death
to anyone with a stiff cock. I've seen you look at her tits.
Odhinn's beard, *you've* seen *me* look at her tits. And
you've seen them in the flesh. What are they like in the
light of day?"

"They were covered with blood both times," I said. "Sygtrygg always strikes while the iron's in the fire."

"More than a clever kenning," Skallagrim said, joining
us. "A lesson for all men with a stiffness in their joints.
Your father's right. If you try to plumb Frydys it won't
be well."

"Plumb her? Bad enough he wants me to talk to her."

"Keep your mind on your task," Skallagrim said, and
Snorri nodded, *his* mind already on my task.

"I could always baptize her," Goltrade offered, eager, no
doubt, to save me from sins of concupiscence. We all
laughed at that idea.

No boats sailed from Clontarf in the autumn of 791. Yule
came and went without event, and heavy snows kept Clontarf quiet throughout the winter. But Sygtrygg sat uneasily
on the high seat, and no boats punished Knute in the spring
of 792, or in the early summer, but it was a busy year for

the Mark Danes. Things were changing in the north: there was too little land and too many men. Fortunately there were enough boats to accommodate them all.

Galt Thorrkil raised a staggering fleet of forty-three boats and sailed out of the Skagerrak as soon as the ice broke to harry far down the Andalusian coast, trading a little, raiding much. He battled a Moorish fleet near Gibraltar and lost twenty-seven ships and a third of his hoard; a storm blew in on the survivors and thirteen more ships went down before the remaining three limped into Clontarf on solstice day, having first missed the Liffey Bay in a fog and then suffered the amused pilotage of a couple of Irishmen in a hide curragh.

The boats that dropped their flukes off Clontarf made everyone knock wood, but Galt had managed to hang on to two thirds of his hoard, and he needed to refit his three ships with rigging and tackle. Losing forty boats on a forty-three-boat vik means everyone left gets a raise, so there was lots of discretionary cash on Galt's three boats, and the craftsmen of Clontarf were just the ones to sell him what he needed. Although everyone took it as a bad omen for viking that year, and went out to the grove to make sacrifices for weatherluck, it was an economic spike that diverted attention and bought Sygtrygg some time. His luck seemed to be changing, and if the price of hemp went up, if the cooper charged more for his barrels and the fletcher for his arrows and the carpenter for his oars, it only meant that Clontarf prospered from Galt Thorrkil's voyage in compensation for not outfitting ships of its own

Galt Thorrkil coasted in the nick of time. Before that, every wind wing that hovered the horizon or glided in on the liquid air to roost in Clontarf, bringing cargos of salt and silver, gossip and gold, reminded the thanes that they were stranded, and reminded Sygtrygg why. We thought Galt's meager trade would be Clontarfs' only commerce that year and that no knarr would come home with a cargo of trade, and that no dragons with bellies full of blood-feud plunder would swim home to shit out Knute's gold in Sygtrygg's hall.

Frydys was confined to the house and the doors watched after Sygtrygg spitted the weller, and when I looked for her I found her by the loom. She was sitting on a pillow to cushion the welts of the second striping she'd gotten, but the bruise from the slug she'd taken from the axe handle had faded. There was no shame in her eyes as she smiled at me and kept packing the warp.

"Good morrow, Bran," she said, in a tone of such sweetness that I could've doubted I'd heard her cursing her brother with her lover's blood on those perfect tits.

"Can you walk?" I asked, wondering who lived behind that face.

"I can walk where I may," she answered.

Her mother Svanhvit and her stepmother Alfhild and her sisters Bekkhild, Gudrun, Ingibjorg, and Ingigerd were busy at the two looms, pretending not to listen to us.

"You may walk with me outside," I told her, and she didn't waste any time following me to the door.

"Sygtrygg asked me to talk to you," I said. "He wants you to behave until he can arrange a marriage."

"Sygtrygg'll never arrange a marriage for me," she said. "I've a mind of my own and a will to match his."

"No doubt of it," I said. "But he's the lord here."

"Not *my* lord," she said. "I remember when he was puking up his first ale. He's not that much beyond me that I have to take his orders."

I could see it was impossible to get her to keep her knees together. She and Sygtrygg were struggling for power, and she might win if she could provoke a killing he couldn't buy his way out of. Someone might rid her of Sygtrygg. That's where this independence for women leads, Skallagrim often observed. When they aren't slapped around early and enough, they're nothing but trouble. Of course, that's an opinion that would've held up with Frydys as well as it would with any woman today, and I didn't offer it. In those days and these, women have a power of their own, and although marriages are often contracted, many of them marry for love, or spite, or whatever motivates them at the time. So it was and ever shall be, world without end, amen.

Frydys had her reasons, but I wasn't interested in them. The squabbles of the highborn are only trouble for those beneath, and Frydys and Sygtrygg were struggling for some power that I wanted no share of. She was just a temporary inconvenience to me. We continued to walk, but I was careful to stay in sight of the mead hall at the end of the street.

Snorri was right; there was no need putting myself too close
to the temptation of that body.

Meanwhile, Sygtrygg was shopping hard for Frydys's husband; he knew he needed to do something quick to make
his mark as lord of Clontarf. As a youngest son, he'd never
thought of himself as material for the lordship, and Orm
Jarl's death, scheduled for the worst possible moment by
the Norns, caught him as unaware as everyone else. He
had to learn quickly, a thing he'd never been good at when
he had all the time he wanted. Snorri was the oldest head
about and his foster father as well; there was no one else
to go to: all his other thanes were sons of their fathers,
dead in Mercia with Orm. Never a good situation, having
an untried lord with untried thanes; they all want to try,
and they usually try something they shouldn't.

"Send them off to raid Knute," Snorri advised when Sygtrygg came looking for answers, offering an old enemy for
new reasons. "We've half the summer left, let them plunder
the Skäne coast. They'll work off some of this restiveness,
and you can send Knute the message you haven't forgotten him."

"I have to go myself, if they're to respect me," he said.
"And I can't leave Frydys at my back, making what mischief she may."

He had that right, at least. Sygtrygg had been a crewman
on his brother Thrand's boat since the age of fifteen, and
commanded boats of his own the last several seasons, but
he'd never been leader of a fleet, and since Orm Jarl's
death, he'd not left Clontarf at all. Now that all his brothers
were raven's food in Mercia, Sygtrygg had to show his temper and prove the blade of his sense before someone
started thinking his own ass fit the high seat better. It
wasn't an original thought if it'd occurred to Kari. To have
followers who'll follow, you need a leader who'll lead. Sygtrygg needed a big win, and I was in his corner; I wanted
him to have it.

So I sent my sister Sinead to talk to Frydys. Sinead was
a tall girl, a year older than I, and handsome in the way
that Danish and Gaelic genetics can sometimes contrive.
She was a power among the younger women of Clontarf,
and I thought Frydys might listen to her.

"She'll never listen to me," Sinead predicted, "and why should she?"

"She's not listening to you, she's listening to Sygtrygg."

"Then let Sygtrygg speak. Is he mute of a sudden?"

Sinead and Sygtrygg had some history. She'd been in love with him when he'd fostered with us, and until she got wit to see he'd no future as a husband, she lived and died by his moods. The problem was his moods took him elsewhere. After he discovered the freedom of the sea, he'd decided Sinead's willfulness was a bigger geld than she was worth. It put a strain on things for a while, but we made it through without bloodshed.

"He's our foster brother and lord," I reminded her.

"You're like two dogs sniffing each other's assholes."

"No need to be insulting," I said. " 'Yes' or 'no' is enough."

"All right," she gave in. "I'll do it for *you*."

So she talked to Frydys, but what they said's a mystery, and Frydys remained unconvinced. When Sinead returned, all she did was shrug her shoulders and shake her head with a knowing smile.

2

The Unlocking of Frydys

Never reproach another for his love
It happens often enough
That beauty ensnares with desire the wise
While the foolish remain unmoved.
       —The Sayings of the Wise One

The local Irish chieftain was called Oc Connol. He was a man of canny political acuity who'd been quick to ally with Orm Jarl when the Danes had arrived in Clontarf. That alliance had paid off when the Eóganachta twice attempted to turn Oc Connol's eastern flank and strike at Tara. Once Orm Jarl had scattered a fleet that was coasting north to the Liffey, and once he'd surprised the Eóganachta on the low ground west of Clontarf. Both times there'd been monumental slaughter and taking of plunder. Oc Connol owed the Danes a great debt, and he'd been quick to pledge friendship to Sygtrygg and offer condolences at the news of Orm's death. Most importantly, Oc Connol was a man of great wealth in land and livestock who was looking to wive his only son.

In his efforts to find a husband for Frydys, Sygtrygg was looking closely at the boat captains who put into Clontarf to trade on their way back from a summer's viking. He reckoned that marrying his sister to a rich Viking from the Mark would profit him in two ways: first, aside from the immediate gain in bride-price, whenever his brother-in-law came back for a visit there would be presents and a share of the plunder, and second, Frydys would be safely tucked away in the north where she couldn't make trouble. There was a certain sense to his plan, but so far none of the boats that put in at Clontarf was captained by men of the proper mettle for Sygtrygg. Despite the undeniable benefits of relocating Frydys to Baltic waters, to marry her beneath her station would be a mistake.

So while Sygtrygg watched the horizon for sails, Snorri cast a wider net on his behalf. Why ship Frydys north for mere financial gain when he could get rid of her and ensure his power in Clontarf at the same time? A northern marriage would make Sygtrygg richer and get rid of Frydys in the short term, but what good was a powerful brother-in-law in the Baltic when Sygtrygg had restless thanes in Ireland? Snorri was looking beyond a Danish alliance, and he was beginning to look west.

Goltrade the priest ministered to the spiritual needs of Oc Connol's freehold, performing the marriages and baptizing the new babies. Oc Connol had his own priest, but Goltrade had a low opinion of him. Too long among his own kind, too complacent, too little resistance from the already converted. The Irish had been Christian for six generations thanks to the industry of the Benedictines, but Oc Connol was the kind of eighth-century liberal who didn't care who worshiped what gods as they were gods who didn't forbid a hard day's work. Even though a few of his retainers still walked the standing stones come Samuin and burned the Beltane fires, they all turned out when the Southern Uí Naíll needed an insurrection suppressed. Goltrade was welcome in Oc Connol's stronghold to minister and preach a Sunday mass and gossip with Oc Connol's resident priest, and try to convert who he may so long as he didn't interfere with production.

Although marriages between pagan Danes and Irish Christians were common, those were unions of individuals, not dynasties. Snorri, as a pagan who'd married a Christian, thought he had some insight into the problem. It didn't take him long to plant the seed of it in Goltrade, who saw an opportunity to make a high-profile convert and gain a foothold in the pagan aristocracy.

One night while we were drinking quietly in the hall over the *hneftafl* board, Snorri asked with drunken disingenuousness after Goltrade's latest visit to the Irish stronghold.

"Do their horses look in good shape?" he inquired. Snorri was finally recovering from Halvard's death and the loss of the two ships. He'd begun to train my brother Onund as Halvard's replacement, and it was a deft subterfuge.

"The herds seemed sleek enough," Goltrade said, moving one of the encircling pieces. "But Oc Connol did ask about having those two black Cobs to stud his Connemara mares."

"I haven't been to his stronghold since before Orm's vik," Snorri said. "And he's not been here since the last slave auction when he wanted to trade a half dozen of his fighting horses for the Cobs."

"He keeps his fighters close watched now his son's interested in them," Goltrade said.

"Fighters, is it? Last I knew the boy was riding after boar and looking for speed and endurance." Snorri studied the pieces on the *hneftafl* board and Skallagrim smiled.

"He ought to be old enough to wive by now. What're his prospects?"

"Oc Connol's at his wit's end," Goltrade snorted. "The boy's living a debauched life with his cronies—drinking, gambling, and getting peasant daughters fat with babies from here to there."

"Oc Connol should settle him down with a wife," Snorri observed as he watched Skallagrim move. "Has he been looking?"

"The boy's reputation's so bad no one wants to give their daughters over, even to ally with the warlord of the Southern Uí Naíll." Goltrade clicked his tongue to express distaste.

There was a pause while Snorri let us make our own connections. I couldn't believe my ears. Oc Connol's son was the boy I'd offered to skewer the day the Geat had sliced me up, the laughing boy who'd called me a coward and slurred the fighting skills of Danes. I'd run into him a time or two over the years, and he'd always gone out of his way to remind me how I'd offered to fight him with my blood running over my face, and how lucky I was that Sygtrygg had happened along before he'd had to kill me. He was a shithead, and if he hadn't been Oc Connol's only son, I'd have killed him a dozen times already.

"But," Goltrade said, taking up a *hneftafl* piece and rolling it between thumb and finger as he pondered his move, "if he found some in-laws as desperate to settle a daughter as he is to settle his son, maybe a wedding could be contracted."

"Maybe he should look to the Northern Uí Naíll," Skallagrim suggested with a snort, paying more attention to the *hneftafl* game than to the implications of Snorri's small talk.

"These Irishmen are fond of their daughters," Snorri empathized in the tone of one who understands indulgences to women. "But if there were a man of equal stature with, say, a sister, to marry off, maybe he'd be more successful."

Skallagrim looked up slowly as the true subject of the conversation dawned on him, then he laughed with an explosion of spittle that wet the gaming pieces. "You can't be serious."

"What's the boy like?" Snorri wanted to know, at least serious enough to sound the priest out. "As bad as his reputation?"

"He's a lout," Goltrade said honestly. "But a rich one. With all the cattle and horses Oc Connol owns, Sygtrygg could get quite a bride-price; and Oc Connol's debt to Orm Jarl would be balanced by a marriage alliance to anchor Sygtrygg here."

"What's your interest in this?" Skallagrim wanted to know, losing interest temporarily in the game.

"Once a man's dead, there's no converting him," Goltrade declared. "If Sygtrygg loses control of his thanes because he can't lead them out because he can't trust Frydys, there'll be dead Danes beyond the reach of the true faith," Goltrade said. "There are souls to save in Clontarf."

"Not to mention the lives of Frydys's future lovers," I interjected with a laugh.

Skallagrim hooted. "Have you learned nothing? Christianity has no matter for us. It's the religion of a warm place, and no good to people from a cold place. This Christ had no weatherluck, and his followers are geldings."

"It's true you heathens are an obdurate lot," Goltrade admitted. "It's hard to sow the seed of faith in your hearts."

"Obdurate?" Skallagrim said, raising up from the bench. "What's that mean? Why have learning if no one can understand plain talk?"

"Stubborn," I told him. "So what? How does this plan rid us of Frydys? She's no more Christian than Snorri, and no more interested in this son of Oc Connol."

"God's truth but Frydys is a beauty," Goltrade said warily as Skallagrim resumed his seat. "If she were baptized, Oc Connol would be glad of the match; he'll not want to marry his son to a pagan. If I can baptize Frydys, the match is good as done."

Skallagrim nearly fell off the bench laughing. The idea of Frydys, mother of blood feuds, up to her knees in the river with Goltrade pouring water over her head was too much. "Sound as a cracked pot," he sneered when he regained his breath. I withheld judgment. Snorri was first and foremost a horse trader, and I'd grown up in his house, where I'd learned a healthy respect for his skills. There was no counting the times I'd seen him come out ahead in a trade. Once he'd foisted off a couple of spavined fjord ponies to a man so impressed with their reputation for power that he *insisted* on overpaying. I'd hear him out before I dismissed him, especially since the object was the union of Sygtrygg's troublesome sister with Oc Connol's equally troublesome son. The more I considered it, the more it tasted like just desserts for all involved.

Snorri shook his head and scratched in his armpit. "This plan needs work," he admitted. "But it may lead somewhere after all. Once Frydys is married, he could command her to become a Christian. What's it to her, after all? And what choice would she have? It's not as if she were marrying a Dane."

Skallagrim wasn't swayed, and looked at Snorri in disbelief, but Goltrade's eyes betrayed some Benedictine machination I could only guess at. Snorri simply shrugged. I sat back against the wall and looked at him with respect. If he could pull off this deal, his reputation was secure and Sygtrygg was safe.

Some days later, Skallagrim and I were out on the barrow-down, a wide field where some great battle had been closed in the time before even the Irish had memory. There were fifteen mounds on the wide field, and a scattering of standing stones. The flocks of Clontarf kept it fertile and mown in summertime. Some boys were training a pair of kestrels with a bait and string, and I lay back on the grassy mound listening to Skallagrim practice the poem of the wife's lamentation.

> I drew these words from the well of my grief,
> From the depths of my own sorrowful life.
> I swear that in the years since I was born
> I have never suffered such sadness as now.
> I am tortured by the anguish of exile.

My husband forsook his family and lands
Went down to the play of the tossing waves; I fretted
At dawn as to where in the world my lord could have gone.
Then I left home, set out a solitary wanderer,
Hunting for the man whom to serve was all my happiness.
But kinsmen of my lord had laid careful plans
And schemed our separation, so that we should live
Most wretchedly, far from each other in this wide world;
I was seized with longings.

As he sang, I watched one of the hawks embrace the
wind, hang still in the cloudless sky, and then plunge like
a stone toward the field. The mound we sat on contained
a chamber where some hero of the battle had been interred
with his gear and maybe a slave or some of his animals to
help him when he woke in the next world. It'd been looted
by graverobbers sometime in the long past. The curse of
opening had been so swift and terrible that none of the
other mounds had been touched; the robbers had been
turned to standing stones. But now it was just a cave and
useful, after the spirit of its former occupant was properly
appeased with runes and sacrifices, as a place to wait out
bad weather if you were watching the flocks or to take a
girl on a summer evening.

I'd scratched one of my first couplets on the smoke-
blackened wall, celebrating the pleasures of a girl called
Thordis, dead of a fever these four years, and I found myself remembering her and wondering what she'd have been
like if she'd reached her growth.

Death was easy then; it was everywhere. All you had to
do was stand in place and within the hour death would be
sniffing like a dog at your ankles. The memory of Thordis
brought Frydys to mind. What did she want, after all? Just
to live her life and not be pawned so Sygtrygg could tighten
his fist on Clontarf. She wanted no more or less than I did,
or Sygtrygg: to take what pleasure she could. If she had
brideluck, she might hope for sons and a husband who
didn't beat her, but pawned off to the Irish in a political
alliance, she'd be expected to make the best of whatever
came to her, and if the son of Oc Connol was a loser, and
no doubt of that, then she was equally lost. Frydys just
wanted love, like the rest of us, and not to die of a fever

and be remembered in smokerunes on the wall of a trysting place that smelled of sheep.

As Skallagrim sang on about the lamenting wife, my mind was on Frydys, and the lament became her own. It was my fancy that I knew how she felt:

> My husband's kinsmen have forced me to live in a forest
> grove
> Under an oak tree in this earth cave.
> This cavern is age-old; I am choked with longings.
> There are so many lovers in this world,
> Loving and beloved both in bed together,
> When I in my loneliness dress before dawn
> And climb to the oak tree from this cave-dwelling.

I wondered if there wasn't some other approach to take that might leave everyone happy in the end. Finally Skallagrim noticed clouds scudding east from Connacht and covered his harp. We walked back to town, and I went to find Frydys.

Frydys was by the loom, weaving and laughing with her less well-favored sisters, Olvor and Gudrun, who were enjoying both her defiance and Sygtrygg's bruising retribution. Frydys was bringing some entertainment into their dull lives. Formerly, they'd been eclipsed by her beauty, but now it was one source of her unseating, and her will was the other: two things neither of them would ever have in equal measure. There was a jealous irony in it that appealed to them, and they were sure to urge her on to new acts of defiance. She didn't need overmuch urging by her sisters; so far her own urges had been more than sufficient.

Her sisters reasoned that when Frydys proved too much to handle, Sygtrygg would marry her off and they'd be rid of her. Then the men would have eyes for them when they poured the mead, and not be twisting round for a look at Frydys. This intelligence came from Mairead, who had a friendship with their mother Svanhvit, an understanding of the ways of plain sisters, and an occasional seat at the looms in Sygtrygg's house.

"Frydys," I called to her from the door. "Come out to see the hawking on the field."

She stood up in the laughter of her sisters like a swan

rising up in splashing water and smiled as she walked out with me. She'd become glad of my visits because she was only permitted out of the house with me. Frydys was losing her color for want of the sun, and her coppery hair flashed in the breeze as we tramped the road, skirting a work party that was replacing rotted logs, and passed through the gate in the earthwork.

The home fields that surrounded Clontarf were planted in wheat, rye, barley, and oats and surrounded by a stone and earth dyke that could serve as the outer defenses if need be. The pastures were beyond, no farther than the children could drive the cattle and sheep at beginning and end of day. The wheat was waist high; Frydys's hair shamed the blond tassels as we walked beside the field.

"Come again to persuade me to mind my betters?" she asked as we passed into the overhang of the oaks.

"Give it rest, Frydys," I said. "Name your better, and I'll marry her myself."

She didn't know how to answer me, so she walked awhile without speaking. It wasn't that she was a beggar for praise. She didn't need to be told she was pretty: the world had been telling her that for a year; men walking into posts had told her that; two killings had told her that; Sygtrygg's plans told her that. If compliments were gold, she'd have a wyrm's hoard. No, it wasn't that. On all my other visits I'd held to Sygtrygg's line like a drowning man, worrying her to lock her legs until a bride-price unlocked them; she took my new direction for a trick, and she was wary.

We pushed through the little woods that bordered the barrowdown. I heard the sharp cries of a hawk and saw it swoop low over the field, pass behind a mound, reappear, and flair to its master's fist with spread wings. The boy hooded the hawk and stroked its feathers as he set it on the hawktree stuck in the turf.

We climbed to the top of the closest barrow where some flat stones had collected the day's heat. Frydys sat on one of them. "It's cold in the house," she said. "I miss the warmth."

"What can I say?" I wondered aloud and shrugged. It was up to her whether she lived in sun or shadows of her own casting.

She spread her skirts and leaned back on her elbows, face up to the sun, shaking out her hair like a red-gold waterfall. The turtle brooches on her shoulders and the silver chain between sparkled. No wonder men were willing to risk Sygtrygg's temper for a go at her.

"Frydys," I said. "To say you're beautiful's to say night's dark or water's wet. What matter? Everyone knows it. We both know what a weapon it is, how cold it cuts, how deep it stabs. You know better than anyone the weight of beauty, like a hoard you can't carry and can't leave. It has a power. The thief who finally takes it can't be locked out. You know the curse of beauty, the thralldom of the looking glass, and the venom of the envious who reach for it without understanding it's a blade with two edges."

She was still as stone while I spoke. The breeze moved her hair a little, and that was all. Across the barrowdown, one boy unhooded the second hawk while the other swung the bait in circles. The bird rose on the stormsurge and disappeared against the darkening sky.

"Why are you making this speech?" she asked.

"It's what I do," I told her. "Sygtrygg wanted me to reach into my wordhoard and convince you, but his face was on all the coins, and they wouldn't buy a minute of your time. I'll mint my own coins, although I doubt he'd like the face that's stamped on them."

"Until now, your mouth moved; his voice spoke," she said.

"What do you want, Frydys? Why do you fight him?"

"Who wants to know?"

"I do," I told her, but there was no answer. She didn't know what to say. Maybe she didn't know what she wanted, just what she didn't want.

"Power is like beauty," I said. "It's a weapon too; it cuts; it's heavy to carry. Power has to be guarded because the thief who takes it has to kill you. You didn't ask for beauty, and Sygtrygg didn't ask for power. He was Orm Jarl's youngest son, and it was his wyrd to pull an oar, take a wife, raise cattle, get sons, and die. Orm never trained him to give rings and names and govern Clontarf. Can he learn power more quickly than you learn beauty? Does he have the wit for it if he had a lifetime to learn?"

"What matter?"

"Like power should like," I said. "You aren't enemies, you're Orm's children, and each of you powerful in your own way."

"Why doesn't he understand these things?"

"He understands other things," I said. "He was raised to understand pulling wood and burning towns, not beauty and power."

"How do you come to understand them?"

"I'm not sure I do," I told her. "I'm just talking. You tell me."

The boys were calling in the second hawk. She stood up and ran down the side of the mound and across the down as the hawk dropped over treetops and came to hand. I followed her, and by the time I got there they'd been dumbstruck by Frydys's smile. She stroked the hawks and asked the boys questions, but their answers were short and their eyes were on the ground, or on the silver scissors—I wasn't sure which.

"I saw a nest across the river," I told them. "Hatchlings should be ready for the taking soon."

"We have our hands full with these," the older boy mumbled, straining not to gape at Frydys. He was only three or four years younger than she was, still a year or so away from his legal age. Soon after that he'd be pulling wood on someone's ship.

"Well, no matter, then," I said.

The two boys pulled up the hawktree and took their birds to arm. We watched them walk across the field toward the woods. Frydys sat down in the grass and plucked at a clover blossom.

"You understand too much," she said. "No one's understood more."

"What is it you need, then, to leave it be?"

"I need to be asked," she said. "I'm not plunder to be shared out or a ring to be given. Can you make him understand that?"

"I can try," I told her. "He can't delay his first vik for another year. He has to make an autumn vik, but he won't go unless you're wived out or to be trusted at your word."

"He doesn't own all the honor in Clontarf," she snapped. "When I give my word it's kept."

"Well enough," I said. "I'll tell him."

There was a fork of lightning in the west, followed a second later by the thunder. The storm had come on apace while we talked. "Wayland's hammering a blade," I said.

She stood up as the first hail came out of the green sky, two hundred yards away, advancing like stones from slings.

We could see the leaves torn from the trees at the edge of the down and hear the clicking of the ice rocks as they bounced up from the beaten grass. The woods were too far away, so we bolted for the mouth of the grave mound and made it inside just as the hail overtook us, angling into the entrance and shattering into splinters. We were driven deeper into the barrow. I looked around in the sudden dimness and saw the pile of torches against the wall. I picked one up and shook flint and steel out of my pouch. In a while it was lit and I pushed it upright into a pile of stones. Frydys lit a second torch.

The ice on the ground made a cold wind come up, and we stood as close to the torches as we could without firing our clothes. The hail beating the mound reminded me of the custom of beating the grave of a debtor to deprive him of the rest of death. I lit another torch and walked back to the stone room.

If three men lay head to foot, they'd make the diameter of the chamber, and if a short man stood on a tall one's shoulders, they'd make the height. There was a pile of straw to one side and a thin wool blanket hanging on a peg driven between two stones on the wall above it. The walls were blackened from the occasional flashfire caused by the marriage of straw and torch. I looked for inscriptions.

"What are you looking for?" Frydys asked.

"Runes," I told her, looking round. She was shivering, and I fetched down the blanket for her.

"What do they say?" she asked.

"Who's been here," I told her. "And who with."

I could see that she was still shaking, despite the blanket. "Do you want a fire?"

"It's not the cold," she said. "Aren't you afraid of this place?"

"Why?"

"This is a hero's grave," she said. "It's cursed."

"That curse's long sped." I shook my head and smiled. "If it ever was. The story of the hero's ghost's supposed to work the other way round. We used to tell it so girls'd get closer under the blankets, not farther away. If they knew it kept the most beautiful woman in Clontarf away from the barrow, they'd never tell it again."

"Don't you believe in the spirits?"

"Not that one." I laughed. "Skallagrim's a wizard and

told me all about ghosts. And my mother's Irish, she sees them all the time, keeps a Fetch in the house to help her find whatever she loses."

"What did they tell you?" Frydys asked.

"Ghosts are real enough, but they only come back under certain conditions: if they have some duty to do, or an obligation that goes past death, or if the runes are cut badly. The ones that *have* to come back don't bother any-one, they just do what they need to do and go away, but the ones that aren't bound with true runes, they come back and scare the shit out of people, trying to do things they used to do when they were alive, moving things around in the house, milking your goats and cows, shearing your sheep.

"Whatever kind you run into, the important thing is the longer they stay, the more attached they get, and the harder it is for them to go back. You're not doing anyone any favors when you don't cut the runes properly."

"Jorunn Björnsdotter saw the warrior's ghost walking the barrowdown one night," she said.

"I don't think so. When the hero turned the robbers into standing stones, that was all he had to do. He wasn't let loose forever, he just dealt with the robbers and went back to death."

I held the torch up for better light to see if she was fooling me, but she wasn't; Frydys really was scared silly of the place.

"Haven't you ever been here before?"

"Never," she said in a tone that made me laugh again.

"Don't mock me," she snapped, but tears were close.

The drumming on the mound was the rapid pulse of the Connacht hailstorm. I took out my scramasax and scratched warding runes in the sooty walls, one in each direction, one in the ceiling, and one in the dirt floor.

"Nothing can get to us now," I reassured her.

She started to cry, and I put an arm around her. Better to let the spirits of everyone planted in that barrowdown come in and do their worst. She put her arms round me and turned against me, and I wiped away her tears with my thumb. Then she turned her face up and the next thing I knew we were in the straw. I had to scramble back to plant the torch I'd dropped, but she pulled me back with one hand. There was some grappling, and then we separated and started shedding clothes. Frydys was better practiced, and she was naked before I had my shirt over my head. She helped me lose the rest of my clothes as the torchlight splashed our shadows on the wall behind us.

That was how I came to know the pleasures the no-name Viking and Bjorn the Weller had died to know, but I never gave them a thought as I slipped inside Frydys and she pulled the blanket over my back. No ride on the night mare before or since has been like loving Frydys while the hail beat on the barrow.

After we finished, we lay in one another's arms and watched the shadows play over the soot on the ceiling and found dragon shapes in the smoke that climbed from the torch.

"I want you for husband," she said, moving against me. "Ask Sygtrygg for me in marriage."

"A poor joke."

"No one's understood me better," she said.

"Understanding counts for nothing. I've no property; I've never been viking; and I'd never make the bride-price singing in the hall."

"Understanding counts for much. Go on the autumn vik and make the bride-price out of your share," she said, opening her comb and running it through my hair to take out the tangles.

The woman had a mind of her own, all right, but Sygtrygg had other plans, and, while I didn't think for a minute he'd entertain my suit, I was *sure* of what he'd do if he found us together in the straw. The mound would be my grave; Frydys's too, maybe. I was glad I'd cut the runes of warding, even if they'd been just to placate Frydys.

"What about this?" I traced the scar down the side of my face. "I'm not considered fair-featured," I pointed out. "Some call me Bran Facecut."

"I've seen your face," she said. "It has no marks on it."

She kissed me, and we rode the night mare again, rolling about until we'd scattered clothes, straw, and blanket. By the time we finished, I was greedy for her; I never wanted her out of my sight. I had to remind myself of the weight of Frydys's beauty, understanding for the first time the urge to help her carry it.

"I love you," she said as she finished combing my hair and handed the comb to me.

Words cut on many a standing stone.

When the hailstorm passed, we walked out of the mound onto a field of ice glittering in the sunshine. The hailstones were the size of thrushes's eggs, cold as a witch's eyes. We scuffed across the down and into the trees. Limbs littered the ground, thrusting up through the white skin of the hail like broken ribs. I didn't know if Frydys loved me or only said she did, but by the time we reached the shattered cornfield I knew I loved her.

"Will you come tomorrow?" she asked.

"No." I shook my head. "Those runes only work in the mound. If Sygtrygg suspects, runes won't help. I'll come on Frydysday."

She smiled and took my hand as we jumped the little creek beside the barleycorn field, careful to release it when we were on the other side so no one would see. That gesture told me everything I needed to know. It'd occurred to me she might be setting up another killing, she might think it a great joke to open her legs for the man Sygtrygg had sent with arguments to keep them closed. A good way to strike back at him and rid herself of my visits. But I knew then I'd been wrong to suspect her. Understanding instead of commanding had been the key that unlocked Frydys.

We met a party of farmers going out to inspect the fields, fearing the worst.

"How are the crops?" one of them called.

"Beaten down," I told them. "But maybe not lost."

Inside the earthwork, the citizens of Clontarf had already turned to for repairs. The hail was thick in the cracks of the log street; everything was white with sudden winter. Women moved through their plots and cursed the storm that had beaten down their gardens. A strawman lay at the foot of his pole like a thane done down before his lord, and a figure stooped over him like a chooser of the dead. I could hear women wailing and men cursing as Clontarf mourned its stomping by the Frost Giants.

I took Frydys back to Sygtrygg's long house and left her at the timbered door. There were already ladders against the side of the building and men on the ridgepole with bundles of fresh thatch in their belts, trimming away the old where hail'd punched through. The ice melted into tongues of water that lapped at the sides of the house. I walked across the street and went into the mead hall.

Snorri and Skallagrim had met there to survey the damage. This inspection was thirsty work, and they'd already repaired to the ale vats in the side pantry. Skallagrim was abusing Goltrade in absentia about priests' weatherluck and suggesting that Freyr might spare us hail storms if they sacrificed him a Christian holy man. Snorri was looking up at the roof where sky was showing through in a few places.

"It won't do to have it rain on a feast," he said. "We've got to get the roof patched."

"Everyone's worried about the crops and their houses," I said. "The hall's the last place they'll fix."

"Sygtrygg must have a hall," Snorri said stubbornly. "He's small enough face as it stands; if he can't even offer his thanes a roof to drink under, someone else will want the high seat."

"The rafters are oak," Skallagrim mused. "But enough ice might bring them down." He walked down the length of the long hearth to check the mead vats.

"Untouched," he called back with relief.

"Where were you?" Snorri asked me.

"With Frydys on the barrowdown," I told him.

"Take a beating out there?" Skallagrim asked, returning with a full cup.

"We denned in the barrow," I said.

They looked at me without speaking. Then Skallagrim took a step and cuffed me on the ear, sending me back onto the bench. "Fool," he hissed, dropping the cup and looking round for a stave. I scrambled out of reach as he wrenched a stick from the woodpile. Snorri was hiding his face in his hands and shaking his head. They knew, somehow, what had happened; there was no use denying it.

"Are you mad?" Skallagrim demanded. "He trusts you with his treasure and you spend it under his nose. If you're discovered, you're dead."

"I want her to wife," I announced.

"You and half of Clontarf," Snorri pointed out. "You couldn't lift the bride-price, let alone pay it. What came over you?"

"I love her," I said.

"You slipped her the eel," Skallagrim corrected. "Your joint's wet with her still."

"There'll be a blood feud over this," Snorri pounded one fist into a pillar. "You've betrayed him as lord, as retainer, as trustee, as foster brother, and as friend."

"He'll never know," I said.

"Have you thought she'll tell him herself?" Skallagrim sat heavily on the bench and combed his fingers through his hair.

"She loves me," I told them. "She wouldn't do that."

"She loved that scudwalker from the spring fleet and Bjorn the Weller," Snorri reminded us. "Who hasn't she loved?"

"None of us but this deadman," Skallagrim said, pointing at me.

"You'll have to leave," Snorri said. "There's no other way. It's only a matter of time until he finds out, and then we're all lost. Not even Sygtrygg's thick enough to miss the smell of lust under his nose. If you're not here, it may blow over like the hailstorm. Take the next ship and don't come back until it's safe."

"How long would that be?" I wondered.

"After she'd had a couple of sons and you're forgotten."

"We leave together or not at all," I said.

"If it weren't for Mairead I'd kill you myself," Snorri said, a slight lividity creeping into his face. "I have an oath to Sygtrygg and it'd save more deaths later. Her marriage plans don't include you."

Skallagrim dropped the stick onto the woodpile and walked off without a word, and after another moment Snorri followed, shaking his head sadly. "A stiff dick knows no conscience," he said.

I sat down on the hearthstones and rubbed the side of my head. There was a movement in the shadows, a whisper like a guilty thought, and it seemed there was a swirl of black cloth, but when I looked closely there was nothing there, only the empty doorway that gave out onto the common mead vats behind the hall.

Clontarf was a week repairing the mischief of that hailstorm. The crops were damaged but not lost, and the ditch ran with icewater for the rest of the day, but soon the roofs were back in good order, and Sygtrygg sent a party aloft to patch the hall, so Snorri, Skallagrim, and Goltrade weren't inconvenienced at table and horn. Frydys kept to the long house, and we didn't see each other.

Sygtrygg asked me how my persuasion had fared, and I told him I'd penetrated her defenses, but, curious though he was, he didn't press me.

"If everything goes right, you'll be going autumn viking this year," I told him. It made his week. Things hadn't been going well for Sygtrygg: twenty-two years old, lord of Clontarf, dumb as a dead beaver, and a rutting sister like a quern stone round his neck.

I kept away from Snorri and Skallagrim in the hall, and hunted the far woods across the river as I tried to work out a plan for having Frydys and a long life both, but good plans were harder to find than the Brown Bull of Cuailnge.

After a long tramp one day, I came home for supper in Snorri's house. Mairead smiled to see me. Mairead was content, as a lesser wife, to spin and weave and share Snorri's bed when he willed, and since she was a handsome woman, even after two children and twenty years in Clontarf, he willed it often enough to keep a bloom in her cheeks. There was a squalling brat underfoot, one of my nephews or nieces, but a bowl of oatmeal and honey shut it up and left us in the quiet of the room with the whispering of the shuttle through the threads.

"I had a dream," she said. I nearly choked. Mairead's dreams often came true. She said all the women of her family had the nightsight, and she'd proven her own too many times to be ignored. I put down the bowl. "I dreamed you dead underwater," she said.

"Truly dead?" I asked after a moment.

"Thrashing naked in the water," she said. "Gasping for breath and going under. Snorri says there'll be an autumn vik this year."

"Yes," I said.

"I'm afraid if you go on it, you'll not return."

I tried to manage a laugh, but the croak that came out made her hesitate at the loom for a moment.

"Can you see me on a vik?" I asked her.

"And skalds never go viking?" she suggested.

"What else has Snorri said?" I wondered.

"Nothing more," she sighed. "The rest I dreamed."

"I've no plans to go viking," I assured her.

"Keep well," she said. "I fear it."

"Fear naught, Mairead," I said. I left her at her loom, pondering the significance of dreams and the safety of her only son, drowning alone.

Several weeks passed and Sygtrygg relaxed his grip on Frydys enough to let her serve in the hall, bearing round the horn after meat and bread. Every Frydysday we met in the woods and rode the night mare until we were saddle sore. The blue and yellow bruises that had mottled her naked skin were healed. We talked about life together and schemed to escape Sygtrygg's plan, but none of our schemes made sense.

The night after Mairead told me about her dream, Skallagrim was singing, and when Frydys started down the table he looked at me with a sharp cautionary eye. I was prudent, since all eyes followed Frydys as she served out the mead.

As she approached, Sygtrygg caught my eye and winked at me from the high seat. He didn't know what I was up to, but he'd noticed a change in Frydys and he assumed it was working. I nodded as reassuringly as I could with Frydys so close, offering the horn; Skallagrim across the hall, burning me down with a dire look; and my mother's dream spreading its wings like a raven in the rafters. I took the horn and stood, lifted it to Sygtrygg before I drained it off, little runnels of mead trickling down my neck.

Sygtrygg applauded and stood up, holding out his hands for silence. Skallagrim's fingers froze on the strings, and Snorri looked round for an exit. "Trading's been good this year," he began, "but we'll need to make up for the crop damage if we're to winter comfortably. I'll take out ten ships when the harvest's in the barns to raid or trade in Skäne. An autumn vik, back in harbor by the second week of winter."

Just the news everyone was waiting for. A cheer went up to the roof peak and startled the mice in the new thatch, and when I handed the horn back to Frydys she gave me a smoldering look that made my eel swim upstream, and her fingers brushed the back of my hand as she took the horn. She'd picked her time well: in the tumult, no one noticed. The only thing that would distract anyone from the lissome Frydys was news of an autumn vik. I looked round as she walked back to the mead vats and saw Gol-trade staring at me from the shadows.

The evening really took off after Sygtrygg's announcement. The horns went round and round, and by midnight the thanes and their men were drunker than moths on candlelight. Plans were made for the outfitting of ships and the equipping of men. It soon occurred to them that crewing ten ships would take every man and boy in Clontarf and leave the town undefended, so Snorri suggested a visit to Oc Connol to enlist any young Irishmen who wanted adventure on the high seas and a share of the plunder. The Skäne coast would be ripe after the harvest fairs. Knute's defenses, tuned to the breakpoint after a summer of expectation, would be relaxed; he'd not expect a late vik.

I had another horn and slipped outside into the cold night air to clear my head. Snorri was following the track of his plan, and I was tracking my own. The festivity was like heat from a fire: if you were cold for the sounds of a good time, you could've warmed yourself from Sygtrygg's hall that night.

"Bran."

I looked round and saw Frydys in the shadow of the hall. I was in her arms in a moment, and our tongues tangled in our mouths. Her breasts were warm against my chest. "Tomorrow," she said. "At the oak grove."

"I can come for you after noon," I promised.

"No need. Sygtrygg's given me run of the place again. What did you say to him?"

"As little as possible," I said. "We'll talk tomorrow."

"Talk isn't what I crave," she said, sliding her hand between my legs and rubbing what she found there. Then she broke away and slipped back into the hall.

"We'll have it settled this afternoon," I told Snorri over his bowl of breakfast oatmeal.

He gave me a bleary look and spooned a little more into his mouth. The ends of his mustache were collecting twin clumps of oatmeal as they scraped over the spoon, and they quivered tentatively as he chewed. His eyes were red from the lengthy discussions in the hall the night before, and the real estate itself showed a certain depreciation. Three of the benches were in splinters against the walls. One of the tables had been introduced to the fire sometime in the course of the evening, and the charred timbers of the legs angled stiffly out of the ashes like a lightning-blasted cow. There was an arrow driven into one of the rafters.

Here and there a few of the thanes were sleeping off the effects of the conference, and Snorri was answering in low, preverbal noises and a coded series of raised eyebrows and aborted gestures with the spoon. His method of communication had multiple purpose: he wouldn't wake anyone, no one would overhear us, and it was easier on his hangover. If I were him, I wouldn't have wanted to stuff that head into a helmet before nightfall.

Skallagrim was prone on the floor nearby, his forearm draped over his eyes. He'd finally volunteered, or been volunteered by Sygtrygg—it amounted to the same thing—to accompany the vik and compose poems to its success and the vision of its leadership. He was snoring thinly, his Adam's apple vibrating under his beard, and I assumed he was asleep, but the sound was merely the labor of drawing breath after the previous night's drinking.

"Dead before dark," he croaked to the rafters. His voice was thick and raspy with shouting and mead. I didn't like a raven voice telling me I'd be dead before dark.

"This vik is a way out for all of us," I told him. "Sygtrygg won't have to worry if Frydys behaves herself while he's gone, and now that she loves me she won't open her legs for anyone else. I'll go along and make the bride-price, and when we get back I'll marry Frydys."

"Where did we go wrong, Snorri?" Skallagrim wondered.

Snorri shrugged and blinked his red eyes. He was just playing with the oatmeal now, hunger momentarily superseded by a transitory queasiness. I could hear his stomach talking to him. Skallagrim was still motionless on the floor.

"This is brideluck and you can't see it," I insisted. "The alliance between our families will be caulked like neighboring strakes. No water will leak through."

" 'No one should trust the words of a girl or a married woman, for their hearts are shaped on a turning wheel, and they are inconstant by nature,' " Skallagrim recited with a fragrant belch, and concluded, "No such luck as brideluck."

"We make our own luck," I said. "It's time I made mine."

Skallagrim took his arm away from his eyes and regarded me with disbelief. His eyes were redder than Snorri's, and they'd sunk back into his head, glittering like two pools of blood in identical wounds. "The Norns weave our wyrd into their cloth," he said. "They make our luck and no one else. We can only make the best of our fate, not tempt it and not change it. I'd thought you learned Orm's lesson: nothing pisses off the Norns like *ofermod*."

I stood up from the bench and looked down at him from my full height. "You're wrong, Skallagrim. I'm following my wyrd. You just can't see it."

Skallagrim replaced his arm over his eyes and settled his head back down onto the floor. Snorri leaned over and vomited into the bowl. There was peripheral movement in the shadows at the back of the hall. I looked up, but there was no one there. As I left, Snorri was sniffing delicately at another spoonful of oatmeal.

It was one of those wonderful Irish days that send harpers out into the fields in search of inspiration and new melodies. It had already sent Sygtrygg and his housethanes out on horseback to visit Oc Connol. It was nearly half a day's ride, and they'd gone before sunrise; maybe they hadn't even gone to bed. It wasn't hard to imagine Sygtrygg driving them out to the stables with the flat of his sword while the mood was still on them and more sensible people were finding their blankets. He'd want to move before the euphoria cooled and hangovers settled in. Maybe he'd taken a cask along for the trip, just a roadie of mead to keep the right frame of mind.

Word of the autumn vik was all over Clontarf by the time I left the hall. The boatwrights were down at their sheds, working on the ships they'd begun during the winter. Those dragon skeletons had been neglected during the spring, first because of the planting and then because Sygtrygg'd showed no interest in outfitting a vik. Now they were busy fleshing out those ribs, shaving down oars, braiding tackle. The sound of axe on wood was like a hymn of praise to Sygtrygg's leadership.

I went over to the storehouse and supervised the dole in timber and iron, but my heart wasn't in it. I was counting the minutes till I saw Frydys. The morning was a slow procession of craftsmen, drawing out cordage and nails to use on Sygtrygg's ship. His boatwright had laid the keel of a long dragon the previous fall and worked on it as well as he might over the winter, given the indifferent patronage of his lord, and now he was putting all those modifications and plans he'd been keeping to himself into effect.

Finally, the sun was looking through the window high up in the wall, and I closed the storehouse and went to meet Frydys. The meadows were full of birdsong and warmth as I made for the oak grove. In Druid times Thorr's forest had stretched from the Sinnan to the sea, but now it was reduced by pasturage and cleared farms. The Druids had consecrated the oak grove to their gods and placed the stones there for their sacrifices, but the grove had older power than that. Skallagrim told me that the daughters of the White Goddess held it sacred long before the Druids had made their first blood sacrifices under its leaves.

The followers of the goddess didn't need to make stone altars because the goddess accepted the oak grove itself as her altar, and they worshiped there at night, dancing naked as the moon went through her phases from birth to death. At least that's what Skallagrim said. I'd always thought the oak grove was a power place, and Orm Jarl had felt it too, in his day, because no axe had ever bitten bark in its shadow. The trees were spaced apart like the columns in a Christian church, and when they were in leaf, only a green shadowed light reached the ground.

Frydys was waiting for me in the green air of the oak grove, at the base of one of the greatest and oldest trees. The grove seemed to be a favorite place of hers. I reckoned it was appropriate that Frydys, named for the goddess of fertility, had chosen a place sacred to the White Goddess for her venery, while I, a pupil of Odhinn and the warrior's way, had chosen a barrow for my sporting.

The tree was on the brink of a little bluff that overlooked the Poddle, and the various moods of the water had undercut the bank over the centuries, exposing its ancient roots. Frydys had already loosened her clothing, and she lay back in anticipation with her cloak beneath her. She'd scraped up the rooted loam to make a bed for us in the shelter of the roots. Her brooches and the silver chains were caught here and there in the rough bark and the scissors pointed the way to pleasure.

As I hurried to her, she threw aside her robe and opened herself to receive me, and I stumbled over a dead branch at the sight, launching headlong at her.

"We'll be married by Yule," she breathed into my ear as I hurried to free myself of clothes. "Our luck changed when we met."

"We make our own luck," I said for the second time that day, pulling my arm free of my shirt and throwing it aside.

She peeled my trousers down my legs with a quick motion and lay back as I entered her, and for a while I was only aware of the movement we made together, and the smell of her sweat and longing, and of my love for her. Then we spent ourselves together in a storm of biting and kissing and groping and moaning, and afterward lay as if we were dead, our sweat drying on our skin. Gradually the sounds of the grove returned: the birds, the whisper of the leaves, the scruffing and barking of two squirrels chasing round a tree.

"Sygtrygg's gone to Oc Connol's stronghold to enlist his men," Frydys said. "They rode off while the table was still burning in the hearth. How did you convince him he could leave Clontarf?"

"I told him if everything went well, he'd be autumn viking. Did he say anything to you?"

"Not to the point," she shook her head. "But he did ask if you'd talked to me, and I told him yes."

"I don't understand. Do you think he assumed I had a plan and acted on the promise of it?"

"He's acted on less," she pointed out with a smile, and kissed me again. "But what matter? It's just what we want."

It mattered to me. I like to understand why things happen.

"What shall we call our children?" she asked, running her hands over my chest.

"Ask me when they're on the way," I said.

"Best help them along," she said, crawling on top, her gold-copper hair falling over my face as she bent to kiss me.

So we made love again, and again Clontarf melted away as I lay back and watched Frydys sitting astride me, thrusting forward with a rhythm that made her breasts move across her ribs and her nipples thicken to the size of fingertips. The second time lasted longer than the first, and we traded places and positions, finishing with me astride her back, my hands cupping her breasts, her arms braced wide against the tree trunk, knees apart on the ground.

Again there were birds, the voice of the river below us, the sound of a party of men moving through the oaks in loud conversation. I lay with my arms around her, my face buried in the nest her hair made at the base of her neck. At the sound of the voices, I pulled out of her and looked back through the grove.

A dozen men were walking through the trees, as yet fifty yards away, but closing the distance. They'd not seen us, and I put a hand over Frydys' mouth as I looked for a hiding place. There was none. The interlocked branches of the green roof kept out the light, and the grove was free of underbrush.

"Sygtrygg," I whispered into Frydys's ear, and I felt her stiffen with sudden fear. "He hasn't seen us, but we have to get to the other side of the tree."

I gathered up her cloak and draped it over her. The motion must have attracted their attention. There was a shout, and I saw someone pointing. Others stepped around intervening trees for a look. There was laughter, and they changed their course to amble over and embarrass us.

We scrambled to the other side of the tree, out onto the lattice platform of exposed roots. There wasn't much room, especially with Goltrade already there.

"Goltrade," I hissed in confusion. "What?"

The three of us looked at each other, startled and blinking in surprise, and then our combined weight caused one of the roots to sag, throwing us off balance. Frydys slipped first, clutching at me, and as we went, Goltrade spread his arms and swept us off the root. We plunged down toward the water and met our growing reflections with a great splash and involuntary shout at the temperature.

The depth was overhead, and we came to the surface blowing and coughing. Frydys's cape came away and floated just under the surface. We swam for the opposite shore, but Goltrade was caught in his robe, and he went down again. I grabbed at his head under the surface, but my fingers squibbled off his tonsure, and I had to go after him. He wasn't too deep, and I pulled him along by the cowl until I felt gravel underfoot.

We broke the surface like whales breaching, Goltrade's black wool habit clinging to him as he coughed up water. I saw that Frydys was standing still, her arms crossed over her breasts. I snapped the wet hair out of my face with a toss of my head. Sygtrygg and Oc Connol were standing on the opposite bank, while Sygtrygg's housethanes and berserks were crowding for a look. Oc Connol's retainers were there too. Dane and Irishman pushing to witness my betrayal of Sygtrygg in front of the local warlord of the Southern Uí Naíll. This would set well.

Goltrade straightened up between Frydys and me and reached out, taking us by our necks and plunging us both under the surface. I breathed in water and struggled against his grip, but he had better leverage until I got my legs back under me. I thrust up from the river bottom and breached, but he didn't resist, pulling me up instead. I came out of the water sputtering and coughing and saw that he was withdrawing Frydys at the same time. Twin plumes of water streamed off her breasts; her hair, wet and darkened, looked like the trail of a water horse.

Goltrade was solemnly intoning Latin, but before I could catch the words, Frydys and I were on our way back under. I held my breath, coming to the surface at last, ready for anything.

"What are you doing, priest?" Sygtrygg was shouting. He had his hand on his sword hilt, but no steel was showing.

"Baptizing converts," Goltrade announced triumphantly. "Your sister and skaldling have embraced the faith."

Sygtrygg's mouth dropped open as he struggled to comprehend the situation: Frydys and I naked in the river being baptized by Snorri's slave priest. "But they're naked," he finally blurted out.

"I thought it best to have as little as possible between their souls and the waters of salvation," Goltrade said, casting a meaningful look at Frydys and then back at Sygtrygg. At that point the one monumental question was: would this insane lie work?

"Better baptized than dead," I whispered to Frydys.

She looked up at Sygtrygg, and he looked down at her. Oc Connol was looking too, and there was quite a bit to see above the water line.

"Their souls are clean now," Goltrade pronounced. "Would you do me the favor of throwing down their clothes?"

There was a general scurrying among the thanes and retainers to collect our clothes and in a moment they were floating through the air to our hands. We struggled into them under Sygtrygg's puzzled eye as Goltrade attempted to shield us from the stares of the flunkies with his wet robes winged out on his arms.

"This is a surprise," Sygtrygg said. "I want to talk to you."

I knew who he meant. We stepped out of the river and stood dripping onto the warm stones as Sygtrygg and his party moved back into the oak grove.

"What were you doing up there?" I demanded.

"Following you," Goltrade told me. "I didn't raise you up to see you spitted on Sygtrygg's blade."

"I thought Mairead had raised me up," I said.

"I was a better teacher than anyone," he said. "Most especially Skallagrim."

As we walked downstream I could see the shadows of Sygtrygg's party on the other bank inside the oak grove.

"There isn't much time," Goltrade said unnecessarily. "I'll tell him that I've been teaching you the ways of Christ ever since he killed that Viking, and that after he killed the weller, you repented and decided to seek forgiveness. You can tell him whatever you want, but if you tell him something different, we're worm's meat."

"It buys time," I said to Frydys. "There's no other chance."

"You'll have to act like Christians from now on," Goltrade said. "If he suspects we've gulled him, it's over as sure as if we confess."

"We're not Christians," Frydys said.

"You're baptized," Goltrade reminded us.

"Hardly that," I said. "Thanks for your help, but we're no more Christian than we were yesterday."

Goltrade was momentarily saddened. "Mairead and I baptized you when you were a day old," he said.

"You mean I'm a Christian?"

"I mean you're baptized. You're no one's idea of a Christian."

"Neither am I," Frydys said.

"Nor have I said you were," Goltrade said. "But if you want to live, you'll act like one."

"I'm in no danger." Frydys laughed, regaining her composure. After all, she was used to being discovered in these situations.

"Your brother and the man he needs just discovered you

trapping eel with one of his trusted retainers or in the middle of a religious experience. Which do you think will embarrass him less?"

"Let him be embarrassed, then," Frydys said. "I'll marry Bran Facecut after the autumn vik."

"You want to marry Bran?" Goltrade was stunned.

"If you like, you can perform the ceremony," I said.

Goltrade laughed. "Set your teeth for spinsterhood, then," he said to Frydys. "While Bran sets his for death."

We were at the shallow ford and Sygtrygg and his band were on the other side. There was nothing for it but to wade across and brazen it out. Sygtrygg splashed halfway out and probed into the water with his spear, fishing out Frydys's cloak and offering it to her on the butt end of the shaft.

She clutched it close as he stepped past her and took me by the elbow, guiding me back to the other bank.

"Was *this* your plan?" he asked. "To make a Christian of her?"

"Once bound by this ridiculous chastity, she'll keep her knees together until she's wived," I told him desperately.

"Who'll have her now?" he demanded, no doubt wondering what self-respecting Viking would want to go back to the Mark with a Christian wife in the hold.

"Oc Connol's son would make a good match," I said, blurting the only scenario that came to mind. "A kinsman like him to watch your back will help you sit easy in the high seat. He owes you that at least; Orm Jarl watched his back during the clan wars, and you'll do the same. It's time to settle accounts."

"Are you serious about this Christianity?"

"I had to submit so she'd go along. I persuaded her and the priest schooled us together."

"It's true Oc Connol got an eyeful. He'll take that story home with him. Macc Oç can't help but be interested."

"Don't press it," I told him. "Just say she's of an age to wive."

"Why not make the offer now?"

"Hold something back. Take Macc Oc on the vik and see what he's made of. Can Oc Connol object to that? At Yule, you can make what arrangements you think fair."

I had to go with Sygtrygg's gullibility. I didn't think he

had the imagination to guess the truth, and if I gave him a version he liked, he'd distrust any other versions he heard.

I'd stick closer to Sygtrygg than his smell when we went autumn viking. I'd defend him in danger. I'd compose lines about him. I knew I could get the bride-price, and make him indebted to me as well. So what if this son of Oc Connol came along? Arrows fly, blades cut, axes split: shit happens on a vik. I was optimistic. I was motivated.

"Good plan," Sygtrygg said, clapping me on the back.

3

The Vik

A man knows nothing if he knows not
That wealth oft begets an ape.
One is rich, one is poor,
There is no blame in that.
> —The Sayings of the Wise One

After Sygtrygg announced the vik, excitement visited every house like a guest before the Thing, traveled far and ready for a meal. Everyone understood that Snorri Horsekicked would stay behind to administer Clontarf's affairs, and that was a pleasing arrangement because civic administration wasn't the vocation Sygtrygg had been born to pursue. A good civic administrator in the late eighth-century had to settle disputes between neighbors about wandering cattle, plow rights, and rundown fence lines. He had to be sensitive to the familial duties aroused by casual manslaughter and adjudicate around a blood feud. He had to know when someone had really been cheated and not merely bested in a trade. He had to know the difference between a witch and an old woman who bathed only twice a year. He had to be able to spot a shapeshifter. And he had to be able to get along with the Uí Naíll.

Sygtrygg was glad to be getting back to what he understood best: the organization of a vik. The like of his mood hadn't been seen since before Orm's death. With the responsibilities of lord had come the grim business of settling trouble instead of starting it, and Sygtrygg had never been stellar in that role. Now that he was busy outfitting the ships, he made jokes, displayed unaccustomed largesse to his thanes and thralls, and once burst into song in the hall, startling everyone into a silence so awful you could hear the thatch mice moving in the roof.

When it came to helping Sygtrygg prepare for the vik, Snorri made sure he didn't neglect casks of fresh water for casks of ale and mead, or tradegoods for stones, arrows, and spears. Snorri's job was to concentrate on provisioning the two knarr, the deep-bellied cargo ships that would carry most of the provisions and whatever trinkets and goods were traded or extorted in Skäne. There was sure to be fighting with Knute's people; that was the purpose of the trip, to remind them blood feuds spanned generations, and that Sygtrygg's memory was keen to the injustice his family had suffered.

Something must be understood: the things you think of now when you think of viking didn't pertain in 792. Scandinavians were either Swedes, Norwegians, or Danes. A vik was a voyage for profit, generally mercantile, but occasionally piratical, since casual Baltic freebootery was considered nothing more than a small business initiative. It wasn't until the middle of the ninth century that "Viking" came to mean anyone with blond hair and a blade whose breath smelled of herring. That was after the inevitable population explosion caused by the pressures of Scandinavian polygamy and primogeniture: first sons inherited the farmstead; sons two through seventeen inherited what they were wearing when the old man died.

If they wanted their own land they had to clear it; if they wanted their own boats they had to build them. Both enterprises took money, and money lived mostly elsewhere. The purpose of the vik as an institution has been distorted through the centuries, largely because the people who wrote the histories felt the weight of an axe more often than a slap of the hands. The Danes were shrewd traders who knew that what couldn't be bought or bartered could often be extorted or taken. Only later were they privateers who sometimes gave the other side a chance to avoid blood by paying a danegeld.

I was born at the crossroads of those two ways of life.

So Snorri was busy going through the warehouses of Clontarf to isolate trade goods. There were bolts of spun wool and linen, bog iron, and buckles and brooches worked in the Irish fashion. He made lists and consignment sheets. Arguments about bills of lading replaced arguments about cheating at *hneftafl*. Snorri and Malachai were always moving through the warehouse with their lists, Malachai with his purposeful walk, and Snorri limping after with his weight on the shortened spear shaft he used for rapid locomotion.

Meanwhile, Sygtrygg and his stem-hugger, Rognvald, were busy outfitting and crewing the dragons, of which there were three times three, a lucky number that Sygtrygg was glad to command. Now, Rognvald was a strange man. A fierce fighter, as all fo'c'sleman were, he was a black Dane who'd come down from the Mark on a spring fleet and stayed when the fleet went on. A storm scuttled all the ships but one, which came limping back missing its mast and half the crew. Rognvald was considered to have weatherluck after that, and Orm Jarl wouldn't be parted from him aboard ship, though, in later years, when Orm went viking less and less, he gave Rognvald leave to go as he willed.

Rognvald married after coming to Clontarf, and his wife, Gunhild, gave him son after son as regular as the tide, all blond like their mother, each one a few inches shorter than the last. The year Orm Jarl had gone to Eng land, Gunhild delivered twins, and Orm Jarl let him stay behind. So the twins were also considered lucky, since they'd kept Rognvald alive, and they were named Wulf and Ulf. They made the number of Rognvald's sons three times three, another occurrence of those lucky numbers. All the omens were auspicious. While Sygtrygg supervised the martial aspects of the preparation, Rognvald supervised the nautical.

The boatyards smelled of fresh-shaved wood and pitch as the clinker-built dragons were repaired and recaulked for the voyage. Three new boats took shape in their clamps and braces: keels, stem posts, knees, strakes, decking, mast fish, and rudders. They solidified out of the morning mists over a few weeks. The boatwrights worked with their axes and draw-knives from dawn until dark, bent over the strakes, shaving the thinnest curls of oak, which collected around their ankles in the dragon's nest.

I was excited too, because all those preparations gave Frydys and me a chance to be together every day. We'd start out in the early afternoon, carrying a midday meal, a bottle of ale, and a few pages of laboriously copied scripture, which, we explained to anyone interested, we were off to study in the forest. Sygtrygg never reckoned our studies were exclusively biological.

"Bran," she said one day as we lay naked and exhausted after a couple of hours of unabashed fornication. "What will you bring me from the vik?"

"What would you like?" I asked, blowing softly on the hair under her arm as she held a leaf up before her eyes.

"A surprise," she said, squinting at the veins of the leaf between her face and the sun. "Bring me a surprise."

"Snorri brought Mairead a priest," I told her. "She was surprised."

"No priests," she said.

"If it weren't for the priest," I reminded her, "we'd be stone-cold dead."

"He was watching us," she said disgustedly. "That's where their chastity leads, peeping at lovers from behind trees."

"He assured me he was only listening," I said with a laugh, "and he was praying for our souls all the time."

"Do you believe him?"

"No matter." I shook my head. "He saved us, and we owe him."

"I don't owe him my soul," she pouted, spinning the leaf by its stem. I hoisted up on my elbow and watched the leaf shadow become a circular blur on her breasts, like some elf on speed that couldn't decide between them for a landing place.

"Frydys?" I asked her.

"What?"

"Have I told you I love you today?"

"Not in an hour," she said, reaching over and coaxing the eel to life. "Tell me again."

That's how my days went: sporting with the lovely Frydys in the forest far from the sound of axe on wood, gathering flowers, eating, drinking ale. For a long time I looked at that summer before the autumn vik as the best summer of my life.

One night I was sitting with Snorri, Goltrade, and Skallagrim, who were resting from their daily toil and refreshing themselves liberally with mead, when Sygtrygg approached us. The design of the hall was typical, the high seat was situated in the center of the north wall with a good view of the table and benches on the other side of the long hearth, where his thanes and housethanes arranged themselves according to their precedence in the retinue. We sat on the west end of the bench opposite the high seat, it being most approximate to the mead vats and the kitchens, and although Snorri had a place at Sygtrygg's right hand, he joined us after the first hour.

We saw Sygtrygg rise and guessed his intentions before he was close enough to surprise us. They were covering the usual topic: my colossal perfidy in bagging Frydys and betraying Sygtrygg. I was used to the nightly lecture, which was delivered by the three of them as a kind of roundsong, someone always available to take up the verse when a tired throat needed lubrication.

When Sygtrygg headed our way, Goltrade coughed and nudged Snorri, and the talk shifted smoothly to the provisioning of the fleet.

"We need more clench nails," Snorri asserted as Sygtrygg stopped in front of the table, "and more caulk day after tomorrow."

"Is it going well?" Sygtrygg asked.

"Well enough." Snorri shrugged. "Better if we had more time."

Sygtrygg grunted and dismissed the comment. "I've been thinking about what you said." He leaned on the table and regarded me as if I knew what he was talking about.

"When?"

"The day you and Frydys were baptized," he said.

The mood at the table congealed like a day-old porridge.

"What was that?" Skallagrim asked.

"About the son of Oc Connol coming on the vik."

"Didn't you ask Oc Connol when he was here?"

"I mentioned it, but only in passing, as you advised."

"And you think the time's right to press it?" Snorri asked.

"The fleet's almost ready, and the Irish will be gathering at Oc Connol's stronghold. It's another week before they're due, and the time's ripe."

"When are you going?" I asked.

"I'm not," Sygtrygg said. "I've things to do here. You and Snorri go tomorrow. Stay a couple of days, have a good time, but let Oc Connol know I want his son along. It won't hurt to talk up Frydys. I want Macc Oc to know what he's missing."

Snorri looked at Sygtrygg; Sygtrygg looked at me; I

looked at the tabletop; Skallagrim laughed. What had at first seemed ridiculous, and then only some kind of rare cosmic justice, now seemed like one of Loki's jokes, the kind only Loki appreciates.

"What's funny?" Sygtrygg asked him.

"Macc Oc and I aren't on the best of terms," I reminded him.

"That happened a long time ago," Sygtrygg said. "Get past it. I need your eyes there."

"Snorri's your man," I insisted, shaking my head. "He's the horse trader, and what's this if not a horse trade? Besides, it was his idea to begin with."

"I want you there," Sygtrygg said stubbornly.

I stood up and went round to Sygtrygg's side of the table. I put a hand on his shoulder in a gesture of fraternal confidentiality. "It's not a good idea," I said in a low voice. "Macc Oc's always been an asshole, and I've always let him know it. We don't like each other, and I'll just be a distraction."

"I know all that," Sygtrygg nodded. "That's what I'm counting on. He's too proud by half, and the idea that you'll be on the vik will squeeze his balls just when we want them squeezed . . ."

What's this we? I wondered.

". . . but most of all I want your opinion. Let Snorri negotiate, that's what he does best. You keep your eyes open and tell me what you see. Snorri sees with Orm's eyes; you see with mine."

He turned back to the table, where they were curious about our private sidebar.

"Goltrade," Sygtrygg said. "You go with them. It won't hurt to send a priest along to deal with Christians."

"I'll go too," Skalagrim offered. "Give them a taste of verse."

"Best not," Sygtrygg said, ending the discussion. "Be off at first light and back by week's end." He moved away, ambling along the table, working the room on his way back to the high seat.

"What's his reason?" Snorri asked.

"I'm supposed to shame Macc Oc into coming on the vik. Sygtrygg thinks just seeing me will do it."

"He's probably right," Snorri said, his expression changing as he looked after Sygtrygg, as if reestimating his foster son, and surprised to find it necessary.

"Time to tell all you know of Macc Oc," Snorri said to Goltrade.

"I baptized him myself," Goltrade began debriefing us after another drink. "A year before Bran was born. He's an only son, heir of the Connol and doomed to wealth and the high seat. His father fought the clan wars between the Laigin and the Southern Uí Naíll all the years of his childhood.

"Oc Connol fought to the end and harried the ancestral lands of clan Laigin, though it took him ten years. He burned their churches and monasteries, killed the men, and sold their women, cattle, and horses. Except for an occasional cattle raid or a fight over tribute, there's nine years of peace from Ailenn to Emain Macha. When he got back, he found his son had been raised by women.

"He quick set about undoing the harm, but his methods weren't to the boy's liking, or the mother's, for that matter. He's the hard hand of a man who's burned farmsteads, women, children, and all. The lad was put on a strict regime under Oc Connol's old teacher and expected to please."

"Did he?" Snorri prompted when Goltrade paused for a drink.

"Yes and no." The priest frowned. "His tone's rough enough to get results, but his manners were forgot in the process. He's got a way about him, but he's no leader."

"Sygtrygg wouldn't want a leader along," Snorri observed. "He's learning that trade himself."

"Well enough, then," Goltrade said.

"Which answers none of your problem." Skallagrim laughed at me. "Do you plan to sing that slut's praises to the son of Oc Connol?"

"That's Snorri's job," I said. "I'm just there to watch and keep my mouth shut."

"See you do." Snorri grinned wickedly at my dilemma.

"He may not want to come," I said hopefully. "He isn't the viking type."

"It's our job to persuade him," Snorri said, standing. "Sunup's early; I'm to bed."

"I'll preach to Oc Connol's people," Goltrade said, rising himself. "Good night."

"The hook's set." Skallagrim snorted. "I'm sorry I won't be there to see you landed."

The next morning our horses were booming across the ditch before the sun came up in the east. Oc Connol's stronghold was four hours away, and we digested our breakfast in silence as the August sun forced its way through the clouds. The road from Clontarf was a muddy cart track, crossing the road south to Aith Claithe at the Liffey ford a couple of miles out, and Snorri and I rode side by side while Goltrade followed after.

"Don't let your wanting Frydys interfere with your duty to Sygtrygg," he said.

"It's a little late for that song, isn't it?" I wondered.

"You'll never marry her," Snorri said, persistent if nothing else.

"Who knows what the Norns have woven?" I asked him. "We do as we will, and make the best of it."

"True enough," he agreed. "But sometimes wyrd is plain, and fighting it's what brings trouble."

"How do we know the fight's not part of our wyrd? We do what our hearts tell us. Did you hesitate to come to Clontarf twenty years ago with Orm Jarl? If you had, would you have met Mairead, would Sinead and I walk the home fields? What was your wyrd then? Did you guess it?"

"My wyrd was to do as I did," he said. "If I'd done otherwise, that would have been my wyrd instead."

"Your logic holds in this matter too," I said.

Snorri rode awhile in silence, digesting my point. He was a horsemaster, not a philosopher. Predestination didn't figure into horsemanship. Before he'd formulated a rebuttal, it was midmorning and Oc Connol's pastures broke out of the woods, the track widened, and we could see the stronghold in the distance.

Oc Conoll's ancestors had built well. The stronghold was on a hilltop, eight or ten hectares in area, walled and ditched, and the road coiled up the hillside so wagons had a comfortable climb but enemies were exposed to stones and darts from the wall. A couple of Oc Conoll's retainers were already on their way to meet us, capes flowing out behind them. Those Irish loved their horses, and more than that, Snorri liked to point out, they loved the way they looked when they rode them, a point of psychology that Snorri counted on.

They met us at the base of the hill and escorted us along the avenue between double rows of pikes. An assortment of fresh and less-fresh heads adorned the iron points, and the shafts were painted rust brown by the dried blood of hundreds of previous trophies. A raven was perched on one of the freshest, claws dug into the greasy hair of its scalp, craning over to peck at its eyes, a desirable morsel on the raven's menu. Flies buzzed lazily, landing on lips to explore the protruding tongues above us. I wondered if he took them down for Yule, or just put holly wreaths round their brows.

Oc Connol met us at the gate with the Irish bonhomie that had made him a favorite in those parts for twenty years and more, unless your name as Uí Fáeláin or Uí Laid.

"Well met, Snorri," he boomed. "My hall is yours."

"We accept your hospitality," Snorri said, grasping his forearm, concluding the formal contract between guest and host, and we followed him inside. The terms and conditions of the contract were well understood: he wouldn't try to kill us, and we wouldn't try to kill him, and neither would provoke the other. With that formality out of the way, we were free to devote the day to drinking while Goltrade attended to his ministerial duties. Macc Oc was nowhere to be seen, which was fine with me.

Oc Connol kept a good hall, the cups were full of brown mead when we reached the table, served up by a couple of bright-eyed women wearing torques of the Irish fashion: discrete gold wires bound by thicker silver cables. Their arms were adorned with rings, and the bracelets on their wrists and ankles sang when they walked.

It was a rich household; plenty of plunder from the clan wars kept the machinery well oiled and the mead flowing, which was all Snorri cared about for the first few hours, draining cup after cup of the stuff and pissing it into a cess bucket in the corner. Oc Connol had a harper in to play for us, and his tunes made old Snorri nostalgic for his wooing days, and he give him a ring for his troubles.

Well, that pleased Oc Connol, who called for food and feasted us into the night, trying to sound out Snorri on the stud services of his two black Cobs while he was mead-headed, but Snorri knew better than to trade horses then, adroitly deferring business for the next day as he steered Oc Connol in the direction of the impending vik. I was shitfaced and ready for the blankets by the time Snorri got round to our purpose, but Oc Connol kept returning to the

Cobs, so I left him to it and one of the servants showed me to bed.

In the morning, Snorri was already at the table when I limped in, my mouth tasting like swine shit, my head hammering, all light making me weep. Snorri and Oc Connol had talked long, and Snorri filled me in while we waited for cold meat to break our fast.

"The son's a loser," Snorri said. "Oc Connol wouldn't say as much, but that's how I reckon it. All his time for games and wenching and none of it for learning the ways of lordship. Thinks his shout's enough to make it work and doesn't see his father's shadow commands all the respect. Oc Connol'd like to see him go viking, thinks it'll make a man of him, but the son won't have it. He'd rather hump away the time between now and Yule, getting children on the peasant girls, making them moody and fat. He's pissing away everything the old man secured in the clan wars."

"That's done for it," I said. "After you've swindled him on the stud fee we can go."

"Not so fast, Bran," Snorri said. "The son's summoned to see us. Oc Connol will order him along, and we're to witness."

I frowned from inside my headache. "Let's get it over with."

They brought meat and ale, but I sent them back for milk and fruit. We were just finishing when Oc Connol came in with Macc Oc.

Macc Oc was a big lad, a year older than me and three this side of Sygtrygg's age, black in looks, wide of shoulder, carried himself like he owned the world. The sneering arrogance he'd displayed the day of my cutting had matured into a truculence that his father grudgingly endured. What choice? Macc Oc was his only son.

"You know Snorri, Sygtrygg's horsemaster and Orm Jarl's before him, and his son Bran Facecut." Oc Connol indicated us with a gesture.

Macc Oc barely spared Snorri a glance, but he smiled when he looked at me, that smile he'd favored me with over the years. "What of them?" he asked.

"They've come from Clontarf to invite you along on their autumn voyage. Their lord, Sygtrygg, son of Orm Jarl, wants you to lead the force of Irishmen."

"A true lord wouldn't need hired men," Macc Oc sniffed.

Snorri refused to be baited. "It's a custom of ours to accept men on a vik if they choose to come. It's well known there's glory and geld on the sea road for those with the balls to mount the windmare and ride after it."

"Don't worry," I said. "You have to work hard to fall off a windmare." I'd won a horse race a couple of years before when Macc Oc had fallen off his horse when it refused a jump. His ego was bruised worse than his ass, and it seemed like the time to remind him.

"Sygtrygg has a sister," Oc Connol said, ignoring my remark. "I spoke of her when I returned from Clontarf. Just found the true Faith. She and Bran were baptized the day I was there. Goltrade immersed them."

"The one with the tits?" he asked.

My jaw tightened, and I shot him a narrow look. I didn't want to hear anything about Frydys from this turnip sucker.

"Of course the Dane wants to marry her off to me," he continued. "Who else is there? I'll wager all the suitors in Clontarf are the like of this one [pointing at me], he never could hold a blade, and from the look of him he can't even hold down his drink, let alone a Danish bitch with the body you described." Macc Oc must have thought his insult was casual, just another way of reinforcing his superiority, but I was starting forward, hangover forgotten, as Snorri stepped in front of me with a smile.

"No doubt your worth as a husband's well known to the daughters of your clan," he said with a smooth ambiguity. "Marriage isn't the object of our visit. We're here to invite you along on the vik. If the prospect daunts, we'll certainly understand your reluctance to come for what it is."

Oc Connol motioned his son closer and when he was in range fetched him a sweeping backhand that split his lip and set him on his ass. "My son intended no insult," he said. "We're honored you want him to lead the Irishmen, and I promise you he'll be there."

"No insult taken," Snorri assured them.

"Perhaps you'd like a hunt while you're here," Oc Connol suggested. "My men are riding for boar today."

"We'd be honored to ride with your men," Snorri said. "Will you come?"

"I've business here," Oc Connol said, glancing at his son, still on the floor out of reach. "We'll talk when you return. My horsemaster will get you what you need."

Oc Connol's horsemaster, Mael, was an old acquaintance of Snorri's, and they had one another's measure. Mael took us outside and saw us outfitted with winged spears and uncontrollable mounts, one horsemaster's joke on another, and before I could think of a convincing objection, we were riding back down the hill between those rows of buzzing heads and into the forest for a hard day's tooth-rattling ride in search of two hundred pounds of ambulatory pork that, in a good mood, could disembowel a horse with a toss of its head. I lost my hangover with my breakfast, about five miles into the hunt, just as my horse leaped a ravine over my objections.

When we got back to the stronghold, Macc Oc was somewhere nursing a fat lip and his ego after a word from Oc Connol about insulting guests and emissaries from Clontarf. We ate boar that night, and before we got drunk Snorri made the arrangements for standing his Cobs to stud Oc Connol's Connemara mares. Onund would drive them over in a few days and come back with gold for their efforts, and Snorri would get the pick of the foals besides.

We were up early the next morning and Goltrade appeared magically when we were mounting up.

"Thanks for the help," I said as we rode out between the piked heads. "Who are these guys, anyway?"

"Uí Fáeláin wolfsheads," Goltrade said. "Died unshriven for stealing cattle."

"What a shame," I said.

"You did well without me," Goltrade said. "If you'd miscued, I'd have set you right again."

"Most appreciated," Snorri grunted as we entered the woods, turning our backs on Oc Conoll's home pastures. "Don't know what we'd have done without you."

The rest of the week passed slowly. I told Frydys about the trip and the husband they had in mind for her. She didn't take the news well. We were in the oak grove, and she sat looking out through the trees while I combed her hair and told her what an asshole Macc Oc was. A lesser man would have taken the opportunity to paint his rival in a bad light with exaggeration and lies, but Macc Oc was a self-made man: all I had to do was give her a truthful description.

"They've both got a lesson coming," she simmered. "This violates our understanding. I'll not be sold off."

"This plays to our advantage," I disagreed. "If he thinks he's keeping you for Macc Oc, there's no pressure to marry anyone else. Besides, a lot can happen on a vik," I said meaningfully.

Macc Oc showed up the next day at the head of a column of Irish, two hundred and twenty, boy and man, all decked out in their vacation clothes and ready for a cruise. Skallagrim and I were on the earthwork when they rode in. Macc Oc wore one of the few mail shirts in the area, and the slaves must have polished it for days because he glittered like a candidate for sainthood. He dismounted and looked round as if he thought Frydys should be on the ground with her legs apart already, but Sygtrygg met him instead, with the usual speech about host and guest, and led him off to the hall for a horn of something to cut the dust, leaving Snorri to billet the Irish and assign them to boats.

Skallagrim observed that Macc Oc had the dark Gaelic looks, the black hair, the square jaw, the broad shoulders, and the aristocratic bearing of a real asshole, and it wasn't necessary to throw the runes to verify it. I looked at Skallagrim and quoted him a couple of lines from the "Sayings of the Wise One":

> A man knows nothing if he knows not
> That wealth oft begets an ape.

By the time we got to the hall for a closer look at Macc Oc, he and Sygtrygg were beginning to cultivate the kind of slow, well-paced substance abuse that Orm Jarl had been so adept at. Their cloaks were in a pile on the table, and their shirts were open at the throat. Macc Oc's ring mail was a fifty-pound heap of links on the bench. Red-faced, they were trading toasts as fast as they could think of them. Frydys was standing by with a pitcher, and Macc Oc was taking every opportunity to drain the gold-rimmed guest horn so he could get his nose close to her tits when she refilled it.

Skallagrim put a hand on my shoulder to restrain me, and I realized that I was actually headed for Macc Oc with my hand on my scramasax. "Plenty of time for that later," he cautioned.

Then Sygtrygg waved us up to the high seat. "My skalds," he told Macc Oc, "Skallagrim and Bran Snorrison." Macc Oc looked us over slowly. "I know Bran." He smiled.

"How's the lip?" I asked him.

"They'll be coming on the vik to sing our victories," Sygtrygg continued, not acknowledging the exchange.

"I have my own bards for that," Macc Oc said. "No need to bring these two along and deprive Clontarf of such stories as they know until our return."

"No doubt your bards are up to the small task of singing your praises," Skallagrim shot back hotly, "but we're Sygtrygg's men and more than ornamental. We stand in the shieldwall when the arrowstorm falls and don't compose at second hand."

Skallagrim was as famous for his sensitivity about his skaldskill as Rognvald was for fathering sons, or Snorri for horse trading, and Sygtrygg moved quickly to head off trouble. His need of Macc Oc was making him more of a statesman than he was.

"We should have a contest," he proposed. "Your bards and my skalds will compose verse about the vik and sing them at Yule; the thanes will judge the winner."

"He better hope they sing better than he rides," I whispered to Skallagrim.

"Well spoken," Macc Oc agreed with a volcanic belch.

That suggested to Sygtrygg that he should fart, and soon the hall was thick with blue air as Macc Oc and Sygtrygg contested whose farts were louder, longer, of greater stench, and most satisfying. Frydys brought a bucket of ale to the table and left it between them, excusing herself. Skallagrim and I exchanged looks and departed.

By nightfall the Irish were comfortable in whatever houses, stables, and barns Snorri could find, and then there was a serious feast to celebrate the partnership between Sygtrygg and Macc Oc. It was the first cooperative occasion between the next generation of Dane and Irishman, and it was worth commemoration. The Danes and the Irish tried to outdo one another at table, and we had to broach two additional hogsheads of beer before first light. Three boars were reduced to skeletons, an acre of rye died to make the bread, a cellar was emptied of onions and turnips. All the hares the boys of Clontarf could hunt down went into the pot. No one went home hungry, which was a good thing from Sygtrygg's point of view. Now he was beginning to establish a reputation for himself, and one or two voices were heard to compare him favorably with his father.

The problem of what to actually *do* with Macc Oc and his men was a delicate one. On the vik, everyone had to pull his own weight and more, but the inland Irish were farmers and horsemen foremost, and not skilled on the sea road. True enough, the coastal Irish could handle a boat on the open ocean, and manage a coracle while they wrestled with a netful of salmon, and they'd been trading with the Welsh and their Celtic cousins in Brittany for hundreds of years, but they weren't born to the true sea road like we were. On a whim every boy and girl in Clontarf could sail a small boat round the Isle of Man, carrying nothing more than a lodestone and a light lunch. The inland Irish were better trusted on firm ground.

Snorri came up with a series of plans to account for them. At first he thought to distribute them across the fleet, so that on each chest a Dane would be the oarsman and an Irishman hold the shield, but Macc Oc vetoed that plan on first hearing. The idea of his Irish spread across the fleet made him uneasy, even though Snorri delicately pointed out there was no better way to teach men who had a lot to learn about the open ocean. Macc Oc wanted his men under his own command and not spread among the boats.

Snorri's second plan was to load four of the ships with Irish and leave the Danes at the oars and sail. Macc Oc balked at that when it came clear that the Danes would be in command. He was a chieftain's son, and he wasn't going to take orders from a Dane. By then Sygtrygg was beginning to appreciate the problem: if they couldn't agree on a plan to get the Irish aboard ship, how could they agree on anything? No agreement meant no vik, and no vik meant Sygtrygg had emptied his treasury for naught.

"Show him how well they'll do," Skallagrim suggested to Snorri one night. "The new dragons are ready for their first swim. Let the Macc Oc crew a ship with the best of his men and Sygtrygg do the same. Propose a race around Man; the winner will command the fleet and dispose the force. Let's see what Irish *ofermod* looks like."

"They'll never make open water." Snorri shook his head.

"That's the point," Skallagrim said. "Better put one ship on a bar and float it off than lose four ships for good in the North Sea."

Snorri knew the cost of making and provisioning ships, and though he wouldn't miss the Irish, the ships were worth a lot. "A cheap lesson's better than a costly one," Snorri agreed.

Skallagrim chuckled and ran his fingers over his mustache, looking around for Sygtrygg.

At the end of the week, Macc Oc had his men piling aboard the ship that Sygtrygg had given him. The ship was called the *Brown Serpent*, after the peat-stained waters of the Liffey, and it was a year old and already proven at sea. The dragon's head was stowed in the hold and they'd mounted a new weather vane on the mast.

Sygtrygg was aboard his new ship, a high-prowed dragon with twenty-two oars to a side, the same number of years Sygtrygg had lived and a good omen for his first voyage in the flagship, called the *Long Harrier*. I was aboard to get my sea legs back before the vik. I wanted to be near Sygtrygg to point out what a fool Macc Oc was and maybe compose some lines about the race for a good laugh later on.

The *Long Harrier* promised to be a fast ship, but it was her maiden voyage, and the fact was no one knew how she'd perform. It was a self-imposed handicap that Macc Oc didn't appreciate, but the Danes did and their measure of Sygtrygg increased. He continued to show promise now that something was expected.

There was general laughter and more or less good-natured rivalry between the Irish and the Danes. The Irish had behaved well, and they were widely liked, if regarded by everyone as poor sailors, so the mood that accompanied us all down to the water was one of a joke about to be sprung. The people cheered for both crews without discrimination, but they all knew the laugh was on the Irish, and there was heavy betting as to how far they'd get before they were in over their heads.

Snorri stood at the end of the dock and shouted the rules of the race as the two boat crews waited with shipped oars.

"We'll look for you in two days," he called. "Last back works for the other." He raised the horn to his lips and blew a great blast, and everyone cheered, and then the race was on.

Eager for a quick start and urged on by their leader, standing by the star board where he had a good view, the Irishmen unshipped the oars so fast they lost a half dozen over the side. In the scramble to replace them with spares from the oar rack, two of the Irish were knocked overboard by swinging wood, and the men on the anchor lines got out of time so that one set of flukes was still digging mud when the other came over the freeboard. With the oars in the water and everyone pulling hard, Macc Oc's dragon started making a circle round the anchor rope.

Sygtrygg's crew pulled away to give the Irish the room they needed to look foolish and then sat laughing at their oars. The people of Clontarf were hooting at the Irish, shouting advice and encouragement, throwing insults, gesturing, falling off the dock into the shallows in helpless mirth. The Irish who'd not been chosen to crew the ship formed a partisan rooting section on shore; they gradually switched from encouragement to laughter, but the Macc Oc and his crew were too busy to notice.

Macc Oc ran forward, shouting to his men to swim clear as he cut the anchor rope. The oarsmen sorted out their rhythm, and miraculously Macc Oc's boat began to make way toward open water. Sygtrygg shouted a few orders, his fo'c'sle man pointed out the course, and in a moment the *Long Harrier* was breasting the water and easily keeping pace with the *Brown Serpent*. We were a stone's throw apart, close enough to hear the grunts of the oarsmen and the groans of wood and hemp.

There was no wind, although we were confident of a breeze once we cleared the headland, so the crew that would soon be busy with the rigging were free to relieve their mates at the oars. This was an old trick, and easily accomplished without a loss of momentum, but when the Irish tried to copy it they lost their balanced pull. The distance between our two ships widened as Macc Oc's ship began to drift toward shore, where the Liffey and the Poddle had been emptying themselves of silt since the last Ice Age. The resulting bar ran straight out from the marshy river mouths, a mudflat at low tide and covered by a foot of water at the high. The children of Clontarf called it the crab flat because it was always good for a basketful if you don't mind the mud.

The tide was high but turning, and since those dragons drew two and a half or three feet, everyone with eyes aboard Sygtrygg's boat knew what the brown shadow just under the surface meant. Sygtrygg shouted a few words, and his crew eased closer to the *Brown Serpent*, cutting them off from rounding the point of the bar. Not that they noticed, pulling for all they were worth, thinking that if they beat Sygtrygg to open water they'd be first to feed wind into their sail's belly.

Those Irish pulled with a will, and they were strong men: they knew how to make an oar creak in the lock. Sygtrygg pressed them close. Then the Macc Oc decided to hoist the spar, and his men lay to on the sheets. The spar jerked up the mast tree a man's height on the first pull and another man's height on the second.

Rognvald shouted and his arm angled away to point out a new course. The oars on the left side of the *Long Harrier* came out of the water as the oars on the right side bit and jerked the dragon's nose to the right.

Then the first small gust blew Macc Oc's sail forward, blocking his view of his fo'c'sleman on the ship's prow. His men had another pull on the lines and the spar rose midway on the mast tree, the wool billowed, the oarsmen pulled, his ship leaped forward, and Macc Oc's fo'c'sleman, standing with his arm round the prow, saw the brown shoulder of the crab flat only twenty yards ahead. He turned to shout a warning, but all he could see was the sail blowing at him like a striped tidal wave. His shouts panicked the oarsmen forward the mast and their rhythm broke. There was no help for it with that bit of wind blowing them along, and when the keel chewed into the mud the ship went from ten knots to a dead stop.

The fo'c'sleman continued on course without benefit of deck beneath his feet, and we watched him tumble, arms flapping like a cormorant as he arced over the water and plowed into the mud. All the Irish were thrown to the deck; their heads hitting the planks sounded like an armload of dropped melons. The spar crashed down the mast tree, and the ropes sang in the blocks and flew loose like escaping sea snakes, one snapping around the star board man's ankles, swinging him forward, where he grabbed unsuccessfully at the stem before flailing back into the mast like a flounder being slapped against a post.

The ship bucked one last time as the wake swelled under the keel and then it settled down hard, throwing the Irish to the deck again. Macc Oc was shouting things, the text of which was lost on us, but the tone of which came through well enough. A rescue party was hoofing it through the cattails around the shore to the place where the crab ridge left the shingle. It would be an easy walk out to Macc Oc's ship, and an easy walk back.

"Macc Oc," I called across the intervening water. "I'm not too small a man to admit it. You ride better than you sail."

Macc Oc's head snapped round and he marked me as Sygtrygg's men lost their composure and let their oars go slack in the water. The grounding of Macc Oc's boat was a better joke than we'd expected, and they called to Macc Oc to collect a basket of crabs while we went back to get the water boiling. With everyone concentrating on Macc Oc's grounding, none of us noticed the sail coming in from the open ocean.

We heard a horn and lost interest in the Irish and their first lesson in seamanship. The incoming ship was high in the water, a big dragon tacking under a red sail with a great black raven stitched from seam to seam, wings spread and flying just behind the prow. The figurehead was shipped and there was a vane mounted in its place, but we knew the ship was a friend before we saw that because we knew who stood under the raven's red sail: it could only be Thorfinn Skullsplitter. The look on Sygtrygg's face when he saw that sail was an unexpected pleasure to top off the day. On the eve of his first vik as leader, Thorfinn was the last man he wanted to see.

Thorfinn, before he earned the name Skullsplitter, had been a kid on the fringes of Orm Jarl's group, big for his age, eager to prove himself, a nuisance underfoot. He was fully fifteen years younger than Orm and Snorri and that crowd of enterprising tourists who left the fjords every spring for the eastern Baltic, so he spent the first few voyages pulling wood with his mouth shut and his ears open.

No one killed him and he kept growing and learning, and he made his way up the career ladder until finally he was fo'c'sleman on Orm Jarl's own ship. Once every fifty years or so Danes like Thorfinn squirm into the daylight, find the quiet life boring, and go out and make a name for themselves in the sagas; Styrbjörn was like that, and Harald Hardrada, so after a while Thorfinn got to be too much for Orm to handle. There was friction with Orm's two oldest sons, Aki and Ottar, who were only a little younger than Thorfinn and jealous of their father's regard for him. So Thorfinn left Orm Jarl's company and set out in command of his own ship, crewed by fifty or sixty Vikings, all greedy for fame and fire.

Word of Thorfinn's career trickled into the fjords like fog, and stories about his courage and recklessness went round the fire in the winter hall. Thorfinn raided the Mediterranean coast as far as the Holy Land, and north into the Black Sea. He plundered Sicily and Malta. He burned Moorish towns on the edge of African deserts.

Then he *really* got serious. He took what was left of his original crew and sailed up to the gates of Jomsborg. Now, Jomsborg had a reputation for bull-goose craziness in a crazy age. It was a fortress town in the land of Wends, in the district of Jom. Enclosed within the fortress was a harbor big enough for three hundred ships. It was a warrior's wik exclusively, with the testosterone level to match, and dependents and slaves lived outside the walls. Jomsborg was situated so its ships could cover the belly of the Baltic and exact whatever tribute they wanted from the commercial lanes.

When they weren't levying a tax on passing merchants, they hired out to whatever king was fighting the biggest war. They were afraid of nothing, not gods, not men, not weather, not even each other. Only the bravest or the maddest went to Jomsborg, and having a cruise or two with the Jomsvikings on your résumé was enough to assure you a seat in any hall in the Norse world.

Their attrition rate was appallingly high, but they belonged only to themselves, so no one cared, unless you found yourself looking at them from the wrong side of the shieldwall. Thorfinn and his depleted crew sailed into the harbor and called them all pussies, offering them out for a fight to see who was tougher. That impressed even the Jomsvikings, who decided to give Thorfinn a seat by the fire instead of spending two or three ships to bring him to heel.

Stories about Thorfinn's exploits were nearly ready to pass from unofficial oral tradition into the formal repertoires of skalds. Now Thorfinn was dropping sail in Clontarf, come no doubt to visit and reprovision before he went out to lay waste the empire.

We forgot all about the Macc Oc, grounded and fuming on the crab flat, as Sygtrygg shouted to his oarsmen to put their backsides on the chests and pull away to meet the *Blood Raven.* Sygtrygg stared at the red sail trying to think what to say when he met Thorfinn.

Sygtrygg's brothers had a way of twisting every story Orm Jarl told to make Thorfinn out a fool. Of course, even though there was nothing to them but adolescent jealousy, Sygtrygg had no firsthand memories of Thorfinn, so he'd grown up hating the sound of his name, contending with the ghost of Thorfinn's reputation for Orm Jarl's praising. Orm Jarl held Thorfinn up to his sons as an ideal to be emulated but, of course, never equaled. And here he was, the living legend himself, blowing into Sygtrygg's life at the time of his proving as lord of Clontarf. He must have felt what little credibility he had slipping away as his oarsmen pulled toward the *Blood Raven.* None of us really knew what would happen, but we all had our expectations as the two ships glided to a stop beside one another and the crews shipped oars and caught thrown lines.

A group of the tallest, blondest, meanest-looking men ever to undertake a vik were clustered together around the mast, and when the oarsmen stood up at their benches, they were even meaner-looking than the mast-step berserks. Sygtrygg's crew, so cocky a few minutes earlier putting a boatload of Irishmen in their place, shrank into themselves at the sight of the Jomsvikings.

Then a man who'd been sitting on a chest near the helmsman stood up by the dragon's tail. He looked like a giant growing out of a melon patch. He must have been seven feet tall.

"Thorfinn Skullsplitter at your service," he shouted to Sygtrygg. "Come to see my old shipmate, Orm Jarl Skeggöx, lord over Clontarf these twenty years."

"Sygtrygg Orm Jarlsson," Sygtrygg called back. "And well come. But there's bad news waiting for you. Orm Jarl's dead last year in Eng land on a springtime vik."

Thorfinn shook his head and spat out the bad taste that

news left in his mouth. "Who's lord in Clontarf?" he asked. "Ottar Ormson?"

"Dead with Orm Jarl," Sygtrygg answered him.

"Aki Ormson, then," Thorfinn returned.

"Wolf's food in Mercia." Sygtrygg shook his head.

Thorfinn frowned, running out of sons of Orm. "Svart Ormson?"

"Svart drinks Agir's ale."

"This explains why no one's harried Knute this year. Who rules in Clontarf now Orm Jarl's dead?"

Sygtrygg looked at him in silence.

"What, you?" he asked. "You were shitting your pants when I saw you last."

This wasn't the most politic memory to dredge up, but Thorfinn was probably so taken aback at the death of most of Orm Jarl's line in Mercia that he wasn't thinking of his manners. I saw Sygtrygg wince, but he held his tongue.

"Orm Jarl dead with his oldest sons," Thorfinn mused aloud. "What's the world coming to?"

"Clontarf's hospitality's yours," Sygtrygg said.

"What's going on over there?" Thorfinn asked, pointing to Macc Oc's boat, where the Irish were beating the water with their oars.

"We're making ready for a vik," Sygtrygg told him. "The boat's full of land Irish trying their sea legs. They found the lesson hard. We'll spread them out in the fleet for their schooling. The boat captain's the son of the local Irish chieftain, a friend of Orm Jarl's these twenty years. He wants to marry one of my sisters, so we invited him along."

"I thought to winter in Orm Jarl's hall and renew our friendship," Thorfinn said. "But an autumn vik to avenge him would be a good tribute." Thorfinn smiled at the thought. It was a terrible sight. "Where are you harrying?"

"The Skäne coast," Sygtrygg said hesitantly. "We're off to teach Knute our grievance didn't die with Orm. It's been too long since we visited his home fields."

"Why not avenge Orm Jarl in Mercia?" Thorfinn shouted, and his crew cheered; it must have been a few days since they'd had any good revenge. Sygtrygg looked somber. The Severn had opened its jaws for six longships and swallowed them whole with never a belch after. They were all in the belly of Britain now. Sygtrygg wanted to cut his chieftain's teeth on more tender meat than Offa's army, but Thorfinn's arrival changed his wyrd entirely, and he knew it. Thorfinn would want to mourn Orm Jarl's death in some appropriate way. For a lesser man, that might mean raising up a stone, but one could only speculate to what lengths grief and rage might take Thorfinn Skullsplitter.

We turned tail and the *Blood Raven* followed us back to the dock, past the flailing oars of the *Brown Serpent* and Macc Oc's curses as he urged his crew to do the impossible. The crowd on the shore had doubled as word spread that Thorfinn Skullsplitter had come to visit. Snorri stood at the end of the dock, his arms folded, waiting for the ships. He was the only man in Clontarf who'd crewed with Thorfinn aboard Orm Jarl's longship. He knew what Thorfinn's arrival meant much better than Sygtrygg. When Thorfinn stepped ashore, Snorri embraced him like a prodigal son.

Forty-eight mud-footed Irish squished back into Clontarf on their own time, while a couple of small boats pulled the lightened dragon off the crab flat and towed it back to the dock so the boatwright's crew could inspect the keel. The Macc Oc was properly chastened, and Sygtrygg was ready with a plan: the Irish would be equally spread out in the fleet, but once ashore, they'd fight as a unit under Macc Oc's leadership. Curling his toes in the black mud in his boots, Macc Oc was forced to accept.

The Jomsvikings moved into Clontarf with the easy manner of men with nothing to prove. The peace bands were on their swords, their axes were out of sight, their spears were back on the *Blood Raven*. They were anticipating a more or less benign shore leave.

When they got to the hall, Sygtrygg put Thorfinn on the right-hand side of the high seat and sent Frydys to change into a more revealing dress so there'd be something worth looking at while Thorfinn got stupendously drunk. The thanes of Clontarf made room for Thorfinn's crew; weapons were hung on the wall; Skallagrim was sent for; casks were opened; and a yearling steer was killed.

"Where's Orm Jarl's mound?" Thorfinn asked. "I want to pay tribute to his memory."

There was an awkward silence. When Orm Jarl's death was verified, there'd been quite a debate about throwing up a mound. It wasn't only Orm Jarl, of course, but the crews of six ships, nearly two hundred men, which made quite an impact on the labor pool of Clontarf. It weakened us, and Sygtrygg had to think about how to make us strong again. The raising of mounds and the erection of cenotaphs hadn't seemed to be the first order of business. He'd never even had a stone cut.

I stood up at the table and said into the silence: "All of Clontarf is Orm Jarl's memorial. A mound would be insufficient to his memory; only a thriving town, rich in commerce, honored by the visit of Thorfinn Skullsplitter, Orm Jarl's old fo'c'sleman, does justice to the leader we remember with such affection: Orm the ring-giver, Orm the name-giver—Orm Jarl Skeggöx."

Everyone was looking at me as I finished, and I raised my horn and drank it back to Orm. They followed my example.

"Well spoken," Thorfinn said. "Come here."

He pushed back his sleeve and exposed an arm as thick as my leg. There were six or seven gold rings on it, and he slipped the smallest off and handed it to me. It was covered with the florid scrollwork of the Engs and must have weighed a full ten ounces.

"This is for your toast to Orm Jarl," he said. "I've always been proud of my friendship with him. He taught me much, and I always intended to visit him, but ..." He seemed to lose his thought. "Something always seemed to come up." He shrugged helplessly. He was a busy man. We all understood. "Clontarf is a most fitting memorial to a great man, but I'd like to do my own poor part and raise a stone. Have you a cutter hereabouts?"

"I'll cut the stone myself," Skallagrim said, stepping forward with his harp hanging at his side. "Skallagrim," he introduced himself. "A poor skald in Orm Jarl's service these twenty years, and now in the service of his son, Sygtrygg. This is my apprentice, Bran Snorrison, also called Bran Facecut."

"Son of Snorri?" Thorfinn's attention returned to me. "Your father was no less my teacher in the old days," he said. "Well met."

Snorri reddened slightly at such praise. To have Thorfinn Skullsplitter announce that he'd learned a thing or two from Snorri Horsekicked was a boost to the old man's ego. He'd been holding Clontarf together singlehandedly for over a year with no special recognition from Sygtrygg, who seemed to take it as his due.

Skallagrim and I returned to our seats. Sygtrygg gestured for Macc Oc to approach. There was some suppressed laughter as Macc Oc squished up to the table. First he was humiliated in the race and then supplanted by Thorfinn as the honored guest. It was a lot to ask of his Irish pride that he accept these reversals gracefully. I was enjoying the moment. I cleared my throat to get his attention, and when he looked I winked at him and tossed the ring Thorfinn had given me from hand to hand. There was silence in the hall as Sygtrygg presented Macc Oc to Thorfinn.

"Gulled by the Danes of Clontarf, eh?" Thorfinn asked. "Well, no matter. You didn't wager anything, did you?"

"Leadership of the vik," Macc Oc told him.

"You're better off the loser," Thorfinn said. "It's always something on a vik. I've been leading them for twenty years, and they're nothing but trouble. Someone always complains his share's too light; someone else doesn't like his mate at the oar bench; no one wants the night watches; and when it comes to negotiating a geld, *every*one could have done it better than you." He waved a dismissive hand. "Sygtrygg did you a favor," he concluded.

It was a gracious thing to say, especially since ridiculing Macc Oc would have been so easy. Macc Oc laughed. "I admit the Danes are the better seamen, but once ashore, we Irish can pillage and burn with the best of them. My men fought the clan wars for the Uí Naíll."

"It's true there's silver to be carried off on the Skäne coast," Thorfinn said, politely accepting the premise that the Uí Naíll were worth fighting for. "But there's revenge up the Severn. Offa sits fat in his stronghold while Orm Jarl's bones bleach. I say we balance accounts in Mercia before we harry Knute."

All of the Jomsvikings shouted his approval of this rash suggestion. That was enough for Macc Oc, who started calling for Offa's head and was backed by a chorus of mud-toed retainers. There was a general tumult under the rafters, and no one seemed to notice that most of the Clontarfmen were reticent to join in. We'd have liked to see Offa's head above the gate as much as anyone, but in less than a week Offa could raise an army that outnumbered the contents of our fleet by twelve to one. And given a month he could raise four more. Surprise was going to be the essence of this operation.

Then the first course was served, three hundred lobsters from the rocky shores south of the bay. They were red as Snorri's nose from their bath in the boiling sea water, and the three bushels of turnips and bowls of salt that followed took our minds off the destination of the vik as we tucked into the feast. The cracking of knife hilt on carapace filled the room, and voices got louder.

"That was well said about Orm Jarl," Skallagrim told me as he speared a turnip with his knife and dropped it on his trencher. "You saved Sygtrygg some embarrassment for not having raised a mound."

"Sygtrygg's a cheap bastard," I conceded, "but he'd better to do than raise a mound in Clontarf with Orm Jarl's bones in Mercia."

"Maybe." Skallagrim shrugged. "But with Thorfinn Skullsplitter getting thick-voiced at the thought of his old teacher dead, unavenged, and forgotten by his heir, you saved Sygtrygg's face."

"See you remind him when the time comes," I said.

In the week before we sailed, we worked hard to bring in the harvest while the weather was still cooperative. Even Thorfinn's crew turned to, harvesting grain shoulder to shoulder with Macc Oc's Irish and the people of Clontarf. With the big influx of manual labor, we were able to get the barley and rye in, the wheat cut, the corn up in the wicker cribs, the onions and turnips in the cellars, the orchards and vines picked clean, and the ships provisioned with a couple of days to spare. A sort of languid torpor settled over Clontarf at the end of Corncutting month. With salted fish smoking on the racks beside long strips of venison and pork, and the vats of mead ready to taste, there was nothing left but to have a harvest feast before we sailed.

I started dreaming about the Geat, reliving my facecutting every night from different angles, in slow motion, in color and black and white. Every night the Geat sliced me up, and every night I woke with a jump as I slapped my hand to the side of my face with the Geat's dream laughter ringing in my ears. Waking up every morning with Olaf the Geat's blade skittering off my cheekbone, the sensations of the hot stinging of severed nerves, the warm bath of blood on my cheek, and the cool breeze on the bone of my opened face, was starting to take its toll.

Skallagrim was the only one who wasn't too busy to notice my preoccupation. When we broke fast together, he'd eye me closely as he drank his breakfast ale. "You look like an anchor rope that's rubbing the freeboard," he told me one morning. "Every day a little more frayed."

"Bad dreams." I shrugged.

"Great dreams?" he asked. "Normal enough. Why not just stay here? Arinbjorn, Byrnjold, and Yngvar are going, Snorri's sons are well represented."

"You know why," I said irritably.

"Your plan falls apart if you turn tail." Skallagrim nodded. "Although that wouldn't be bad." He'd no confidence in my luck when it came to Frydys. "That bitch is death with tits," he often said.

Frydys and I were observing an unaccustomed celibacy. First the arrival of the Irishmen kept the women busy in the kitchens, and then Thorfinn had come and the focus shifted to the Jomsvikings. We were busy all day with the harvest, and at night, Sygtrygg had Frydys doing duty as Macc Oc's exclusive serving wench. I could see she'd no taste for subservience. She dropped the plate in front of him so hard the food jumped up as if it didn't like him either. She poured the ale so carelessly that more went down his arm than into his horn. Her manner, although outright rude by most measures, was a mere shadow of her capacity and a clear taste of what Macc Oc would drink from the bridal horn, but he licked it up like honey.

He was used to having his way, and he seemed to think his way was paved with rose petals as far as the foot of Frydys's bed. When he slapped her on the ass with a casual familiarity, I promised myself I'd cut that hand off and slap his face with it before I killed him. I started practicing with my weapons again. It had been four years since I'd given the martial arts any serious attention, but I went out to the practice fields daily and put in a couple of hours of blade-work with sword, spear, and axe. I was rusty, but I had muscle memory going for me and pretty soon my technique came back.

Finally there was only a single night left, and Frydys made sure that Macc Oc and Sygtrygg were well served with the oldest ale and the newest wine. We waited until the hilarity in the hall had reached new heights of farting, belching, and pissing into the firepit before we slipped off, leaving Skallagrim and Goltrade to cover for us if anyone noticed.

We met in Snorri's bathhouse. I'd started a low oak fire that afternoon, and the coals were red as a wyrm's eyes when I shoveled out a few of the hot stones and worked them into place with a stick. When Frydys poured cold water on them, they shattered with a loud crack and a great cloud of steam filled the bathhouse, as if wights had been released from a long imprisonment. I shoveled a few more rocks into the firepit, covered them with coals, and went to Frydys.

She stepped naked from the veil of steam, the love of my life, sweat beading on her breasts and her bush and the soft down on her thighs. She took me by the hand and led me to a low bench padded with fir boughs and covered with a linen cloth. The steam was like a hellish fog in the bathhouse. We could hear the faint roistering in the hall across town, rising and falling as toasts were proposed, agreed to, and drunk off with the kind of reckless goodwill that precedes a vik. I took her in my arms and held her close, inhaling her smell with the steam and incense of fresh pitch.

"I love thee, Bran Facecut," she said. "Come back rich and our children will eat well."

"I love thee, Frydys Ormsdottir," I answered her. "I'll come back charmed and we'll not need riches. But if I don't come back, will you marry Macc Oc?"

"Fear it not," she assured me with a catch in her voice. "I'll marry you or no one. I'll wait for you until I die, and keep my legs together until I open them again for you."

"I don't ask it. Only wait a year if I don't come back."

"Forever, I promised. I'll marry who I will or no one." She reached over to her dress, folded beside the doorway, and got her scissors. Before I knew what she was really about, she sliced my hand deftly on the ham, and then she served herself the same and clasped our bleeding hands together. "We've a blood oath now," she said. "What's past has no matter. I'll wait for you until you're back, and you spend time with no living woman until we meet again."

"Fear naught," I promised.

Everything's pretty much a steamy blur after that. I must

have heated more rocks, poured more water on them, released more wights, but I've done those things thousands of times and I've no memory of doing them that night. I remember Frydys's naked legs twined around my waist and the rhythm of her thrusting up from the fir boughs. The evergreen smell mixed with our sweat, our promises and moans, until finally there was only the weight of Frydys on my chest, the taste of her in my mouth, the thought of her in my mind. She took everything from me in the bathhouse and left herself instead. She was fourteen years old. I was eighteen and on the eve of my first vik. Nothing compares to it.

When I woke up, the steam had melted back into the air and the sun was lighting the bathhouse window. Frydys had gone, and I was sorry, because she was the first thing I wanted to see when I opened my eyes. Then I remembered what day it was, and I pulled on my clothes and stumbled into the house for a quick breakfast.

Mairead was waiting at the table with Gudrun and Sinmara, Snorri's other two living wives. They usually talked over their morning porridge, laughing about Snorri, although he could never prove it, and they would never admit it. Snorri's first wife was dead, and the three remaining always kept a place set for her ghost at the breakfast table because they'd loved her so much. Snorri had wived well. His women were all handsome and compatible, and there were no back-biters in Snorri's house. It was a good place to grow up, among twenty sisters, half-brothers, half-sisters, foster brothers, and stepmothers, with Snorri presiding at the table.

That morning they were hushed and their movements were slow and deliberate. Mortality was heavy on their minds. Gudrun's youngest son was dead on Snorri's foundered ship. Sinmara had just sent three of her seven sons with the fleet. I was Mairead's only son, and I was going too.

Gudrun and Sinmara left me alone with Mairead.

"Sleep well?" she asked, putting the inevitable bowl of oatmeal in front of me.

I smiled and nodded.

"I saw Frydys before dawn," she said. "Coming back from a pee while I was going. She acted like a daughter."

"A daughter by Yule," I said.

"A widow by equinox unless you're successful on the vik." She sat down and pushed a bowl of pears across the table. "Sygtrygg wants her to wed the Irishman, and you want her for yourself. You'd better take care not to stand too close to the gunnel in a storm."

"Your drowning dream's come and gone," I reminded her. "I was baptized instead."

"You were baptized the same day Orm Jarl sprinkled you with the holly leaf; my dream wasn't baptism. You follow Odhinn instead of Christ. It's your wyrd, doubly baptized, to follow the old gods instead of the new one."

"Orm Jarl sprinkled me before Goltrade had his chance," I said. "And what matter, anyway? Gods come and go."

"It's plain that Skallagrim's influence was greater," she said. "It's done. I hope whatever gods you follow watch over you."

Sinead came in with my pack and my weapons. It was strange to see her carrying a sword and axe and to know that they were mine. I hadn't carried anything but a scramasax or a hunting bow since the Geat carved me up. "I waxed the blades myself," she said, crying when she handed me the bundle. "They'll not rust in the salt air." She hugged me quickly and hurried out again.

"There haven't been any dreams you forgot to tell me about, have there?" I asked Mairead.

"No more dreams," she said. "The one I had's enough."

"Short leave-taking's best," I said, slipping my arm into the pack strap. I didn't want to go with red eyes. Mairead was standing by the table when I went into the morning light. Snorri met me in the dooryard, carrying a shield decorated with four black ravens.

"I had this made for you," he said. "Keep well."

I was touched by Snorri's concern, especially since I was only one of four sons he was sending off that morning, and I accepted the shield with mumbled thanks.

"What you learned before your wyrd took you to learn from Skallagrim isn't lost," he said. "When you need it, you'll have it. I hope this vik gets you what you want." Then he went into the house.

It seemed all of Clontarf was at the dock as every family offered up a son or husband or father to the autumn vik. Boasts were as loud as women crying, and men promised fantastic presents to loved ones and assured them there was absolutely no danger in avenging Orm at odds of twelve to one. There'd be some empty seats at the oars before the week was gone, and everyone knew it.

Goltrade met me as I walked through the gate and forced a leather-wrapped bundle into my hand.

"Parchment and quills," he said. "And pots of ink. You'll have plenty of time for writing. Practice your declensions and conjugations," he said. "Write what happens on the trip. You'll be glad of it later."

Someone called out my name, and Goltrade looked over his shoulder. "Here comes Skallagrim," he said. "Don't let him dissuade you from writing." Then the old priest slipped away, and I stowed the bundle in my pack.

Skallagrim caught up and grabbed at my arm. "I hope your last night with that slut was worth it," he whispered. "Sygtrygg started looking for you a couple of hours after you left, and I told him I'd sent you to make a sacrifice to Baldr for luck."

"My baptism must have slipped his mind," I commented.

"The Christ has poor battleluck," Skallagrim said. "There's nothing wrong with praying to a god who understands steel when you're going to vik."

"Did he look for Frydys?" I asked.

"I've enough to do saving your head without worrying after her," he snapped. "But if you weren't found, I reckon he didn't."

"I'm surprised he didn't want to dangle her in front of Macc Oc, just to remind him of the point," I said.

"Since Thorfinn got here, the point's been to keep your head on your shoulders," Skallagrim said. "This vik started out as a good idea at little cost. We could've spent a hundred Irish in Skäne and no one would've cared, but now that Thorfinn's declared a blood feud with Offa, we'll be lucky not to join Orm Jarl."

Skallagrim was particularly snappish because the sea road made him sick, and he knew he'd be heaving over the side by the time we were halfway to Skomer Island, about as far as you can get and still be in the land of Wales. He'd have plenty of company: the boat captains knew to give the Irishmen seats close to the freeboard. A confusion of personal belongings, families, barking dogs, and wheeling

gulls hoping for a handout cluttered the shore. Gunhild and
Rognvald's nine sons stood together like a patch of corn.

As I was about to step into the boat, I felt someone
beside me. Frydys pressed something into my hand and
slipped away in the crowd. I opened my fist and looked at
the rune *Othala* sparkling in my palm, a rune to keep me
focused while I was gone. Frydys wanted my eyes on the
prize. This is what the Rune poem says about Othala:

> Estate is very dear
> to every man
> if he can enjoy what is right
> and according to custom in his hall
> most often in prosperity.

Rognvald assigned me a place at the thwarts. There were
no oar benches on a dragon ship, you sat on wooden sea
chests that held your belongings and share of the loot, so
I opened my chest and dropped my pack inside. Most of
the crew was already aboard, and I could see Snorri at the
end of the dock. It didn't take me long to spot Mairead
and Sinead standing up the hill. Goltrade was near them.
Finally, I spotted Frydys, keeping a solitary well-faring in
the mild autumn morning.

After everyone was aboard, Thorfinn invoked Thorr and
Agir for weatherluck and battleluck. On shore, Thorr's
priest sacrificed a wolfhound and a hawk and lit a pyre for
them, so the smoke would carry the prayers to Asgard.
Then Rognvald blew his horn and everyone held their
weapons up to take an oath of brotherhood on the vik. It
was an oath I'd break in a heartbeat if Macc Oc wandered
by in the thick of battle, but I held my blade up with the
rest.

Then Sygtrygg, standing back at the star board, shouted
the order, and we took our seats on the sea chests. Rognvald blew another long note on the horn. The star board
man began to beat out a rhythm on the freeboard, and
Sygtrygg's dragon, the *Long Harrier*, moved ahead with a
smooth motion, pulling out in front where it belonged. The
Blood Raven glided to the star board and hung back a
little, and Macc Oc's boat, the *Brown Serpent*, commanded
by Kalf Agirson, maybe the best sailor in Clontarf, pulled
in to the left. Kalf was a devotee of Agir, and he'd made

his own sacrifices for the vik, offsetting, he hoped, the presence of Macc Oc on his boat. The rest of the fleet fell into
place like a wedge of sea geese as we moved out toward
the ocean. The knarr, slower and deeper in the belly, tailed
Sygtrygg's dragon inside the wedge.

When we cleared Liffey Bay, we raised the spars and the
wind filled the sails with a creak of wood and tackle. We
shipped oars and stretched after the first exertion of the
day, free from hard work until the wind died off, and I
crawled below to find a place to sleep. The close air below
still held the whole olfactory spectrum of a newly wrought
ship: the incense of fresh-trimmed oak, the astringency of
pine, the mephitic stink of tar caulk, and the musky smell
of oiled hemp. I sat alone against the mast step fish and
inhaled my first vik.

The wind held well into the night, and we made good
time toward Skomer Island. I stood an early watch,
wrapped in wool beside the dragon's neck, straining to see
the island bulking out of the darkness where the Land
South stars rose out of the horizon, but Skomer's shadow
didn't come up during my watch, and afterward I went
below and opened the bundle Goltrade'd given me. There
was a thick sheaf of parchment rolled around the stoppered
ink pots and the quills. I put my raven shield on my knees,
lit a candle, and arranged quills, parchment, and ink on it.

The red candlelight on the parchment was like a reflection of fire on a snowfield. I smiled and thought of one of
the first riddles I'd learned:

> I watched four fair creatures
> traveling together; they left black tracks
> behind them. The support of the bird
> moved swiftly; it flew in the sky,
> dived under the waves. The struggling warrior
> continuously toiled, pointing out the paths
> to all four over the fine gold.

I copied the riddle on the top of the first sheet, acting
out the answer as I formed the letters. It seemed a fitting
way to begin the journal of my first vik, and when I'd finished, I looked at the drying lines in the candlelight, like a
tracker reading the first sign of thought on the snow of that

parchment. When the ink dried, I rolled the bundle up again, stubbed out the candle, and went to sleep among the coiled ropes and the spare sail under the low deck of the ship.

When I woke, the sun was up and the boat was rocking in a bay on the Out South side of Skomer Island. The cries of seabirds echoed off the cliffs. The rocks above the tide line were crowded with harems of garrulous gray seals, displaying attitude problems. I picked my way carefully across a deck littered with green Irishmen to Skallagrim, who was huddled in his cloak, as sick as they were. Sygtrygg and Macc Oc were rowing to the *Blood Raven* for a little pep talk from Thorfinn, who, though technically not part of Sygtrygg's fleet, I suspected was preparing to take a more active hand in the administration of the vik now that Clontarf was well behind the dragon's tail.

I sat down beside Skallagrim. He'd settled in where the deck and the freeboards came together, and he'd made a little couch with his wadded cloak under the dragon's neck. Rognvald was standing beside him watching the progress of the little boat. Mairead had packed a few apples among my clothes, and I cut one and offered the halves to Rognvald and Skallagrim. Rognvald took his with a nod and ate it in three bites, but Skallagrim inspected his half with some reluctance, reckoned the odds he'd be able to keep it down, and then refused with a shake of his head. I cocked my thumb toward the *Blood Raven* and raised an eyebrow.

"What have I missed?"

"Nothing to make verse about," Skallagrim said, juking involuntarily as kittiwakes strafed the deck.

"We dropped the flukes at sunup," Rognvald elaborated. "Sygtrygg sent out a shore patrol top-heavy with seasick Irishmen that got lost for a couple of hours, discovered a creek when two of them fell in, and then came back with nothing special to report. Half an hour ago Thorfinn hailed Sygtrygg."

"How's Sygtrygg doing?"

Skallagrim laughed a weak laugh. "He paced around muttering to himself after Thorfinn's hail. Probably rehearsing his speech. Macc Oc took it on himself to go along, I suppose because he's ground commander of the Irish. He'll have a clearer understanding of his place before long."

"So will Sygtrygg," I said around a mouthful of apple.

"That's what I'm afraid of." Skallagrim stretched a little and shrugged out of his cloak. He spat over the side.

"Why didn't you go along?" I asked Rognvald.

"I wasn't invited," he said.

"Good reason," I said.

Skallagrim got to his feet, supporting himself against the prow. After a night of puking, he didn't trust his legs yet. I was glad to have slept through it. I'd seen Skallagrim puke plenty of times: the novelty was gone.

"Need a hand?" I offered.

"No, thanks," he said, assaying a few steps around the deck.

Then voices were raised aboard the *Blood Raven*. First Macc Oc's, then Sygtrygg's familiar bellow, and finally a sound that made the hair stand up on my neck, a sound like a bull having its scrotum bitten off by a dull-toothed wolf, a sound that could only have originated in Thorfinn's chest. The seals began barking in chorus, agitating the birds, and the din momentarily prevented speech, echoing round the little leeward cove where the thirteen ships were anchored together. Heads snapped round all through the fleet.

Skallagrim shot me a weak look and shook his head. "This vik isn't well begun," he said. "Sygtrygg and Macc Oc both could find themselves kissing Thorfinn's thin-lipped axe."

There was some activity on the *Blood Raven*, and then one of the mast step berserks pick up a man and threw him overboard. We strained to see who it was, and a moment later Macc Oc's head bobbed to the surface. One of the men in the little boat extended an oar to fetch him in. Skallagrim grimaced and eased back to the deck, gathering the cloak around his shoulders.

Macc Oc sat in the little boat with his back to the *Blood Raven* and didn't move again until Sygtrygg joined him. They rowed to Macc Oc's dragon, where they both climbed out and got lost in the crowd. When they came back into view sometime later, Macc Oc had changed clothes. A certain restlessness came over the fleet. Deck activity picked up a notch, and—on our ship, at least—I saw some of the men making their blades ready in case Sygtrygg decided to do something stupid. Not that they'd have hesitated, stupid or not, the warrior ethos being what it was; their choice would have been to follow a lawful order or be cut down in their tracks. This is what historians like to refer to as the grim fatalism of the Norseman.

The *Blood Raven* rocked in her anchor ropes. As I watched, one of her crew threw out a fishing line and sat near the prow with his feet dangling over the edge, spitting at his reflection. No danger of rash action from the *Blood Raven.* No one over there was worried about the other twelve ships blocking their escape. They knew the score.

Finally, Sygtrygg got back into the little boat and pushed off. In a minute he was aboard the *Long Harrier.* Everyone looked at him anxiously, but he came forward without speaking and blew the horn three times. That stirred up the seals and birds again. With all those shearwaters and kittiwakes wheeling overhead, the bird shit raining down on the decks was getting to be a problem, and one or two men raised their shields like umbrellas.

"I want to talk to you about Thorfinn's plan before the captains come," he said to Rognvald. "You too," he added, looking at me.

Rognvald and I stood by as Sygtrygg chased everyone aft, excepting Skallagrim, who was making himself comfortable.

"What happened?" Rognvald asked.

"Thorfinn's a madman," Sygtrygg announced unnecessarily. "He wants to hunt Offa down and take his head. He wants to rape his women, slave out his children, kill his retainers and thralls, burn his towns, and sow salt into the earth. And we don't have any salt."

"What did he say to that objection?" Skallagrim asked dryly.

"He said they'd enough salt in Droitwich to do the job." Sygtrygg threw his hands up in amazement.

"Maybe he was just exaggerating," I suggested. "The Romans salted Carthage so they wouldn't have any more trouble."

"Did it work?" Sygtrygg wanted to know.

"Whether it worked isn't the point," Skallagrim exploded. "The point is he isn't serious about the damned salt. He wants to have his revenge on Offa."

"What happened to Macc Oc?" Rognvald changed the subject.

"That idiot tried to tell Thorfinn how to deal with Offa.

I mean, this man's burned Byzantine cities; he's shown his bare ass to the Moorish fleet, and Macc Oc tried to give him orders." Sygtrygg shook his head at such a display of ego.

This was a fortunate turn of events. Macc Oc had demonstrated his ignorance of viking etiquette to the man who'd written at least a couple of chapters of the book. If Macc Oc's *ofermod* persisted, maybe Thorfinn would kill him. Maybe I could return without Macc Oc and a clean conscience to the bargain.

"This is the man you want for Frydys?" I asked innocently.

Sygtrygg looked at me with surprise. "Who cares about Frydys? Right now I'm worried about controlling the vik, not that rutting slut."

"What are you gong to tell the captains?" Rognvald asked as Skallagrim gave me a short jolt in the ribs with his elbow.

"I'll tell them we're going up the Severn," Sygtrygg said. "What else can I tell them? If I balk at the chance to fight beside Thorfinn Skullsplitter and avenge Orm at the same time, they'll desert the fleet. I may as well surrender Clontarf now."

"Will Macc Oc take the insult?" Skallagrim asked.

"It's that or walk home." Sygtrygg smiled briefly at the thought of it. "Although if it comes to a battle, I wouldn't put it past him to try to rid himself of Thorfinn."

"Been tried," I pointed out. "No one's had much luck so far. If Macc Oc tries, you'll have to look for another brother-in-law."

"Keep a tight rope on your hatred of Macc Oc," Sygtrygg demanded, "and your mind on the problem at hand."

Just then the first of the small boats scraped against the *Long Harrier*'s side and Sygtrygg and Rognvald went amidships to welcome the captains.

"Contain your excitement," Sygtrygg hissed. "It's not news Macc Oc's a fool; don't join him in his folly. If he goads Thorfinn and dies, what's Sygtrygg going to tell Oc Connol? What good will Frydys do you if Clontarf's burned to the ground?"

"If Thorfinn kills him, my problems are over," I hissed back.

"If he dies in battle or washes overboard, your problems

are over. If Thorfinn kills him, your problems are just begun. His father'll want to know why we didn't kill Thorfinn or die trying, which would be the result."

It was a ticklish business, all right. Getting rid of Macc Oc would be like getting thrushes' eggs out of a gorse bush without getting stuck. "I'll hold my tongue about Frydys," I promised.

" 'The gift of wisdom is beyond price,' " Skallagrim quoted.

Sygtrygg and Rognvald sorted out the captains in the brief meeting that followed, and they rowed back to their dragons with their sailing orders firmly in mind: first we'd stop at Rhymby, a trading camp at the mouth of the Rhymney River that Einar Soft Hands, one of Sygtrygg's captains, knew. We'd trade a bit and see what intelligence we could pick up about the Engs, then it was up the river as far as we could and hope to get back with our heads. We kept to the cove on Skomer another night. The Irish recovered enough to mount a hunting party that came back with a half dozen hogs they called "slow boar," and reports of an infestation of some species of vole that made the ground crawl with shadows in the moonlight. In a few days some anchorite, confused by an hallucinatory lifestyle of penance and self-mortification, would notice his hogs had vanished. By that time we'd be dead or alive in Mercia.

The hogs were butchered and divided among the ships, and we dined on pork and lentils. Thorfinn was so unconcerned about security that he raised the deck awnings on the *Blood Raven*, and, after a raucous supper during which a few disagreements about the size of the apportioned pork erupted, the Jomsvikings settled down. Finally, only bird cries and grumbling seals disturbed the darkness.

It took us a day, tacking against a contrary wind and rowing against the tidal race, to get from the leeward of Skomer to the mouth of the Rhymney. Rognvald used the time to start teaching the Irish the rudiments of blue water seamanship. He worked them in shifts, drilling them on the rigging of the sail, the fundamentals of tacking a dragon, and fleet operations. He had them shinnying up and down the mast tree and shipping and unshipping the oars. He made them stand to at the shieldwall while the oarsmen pulled. By the time the Welsh and Wessex shorelines began to converge on the Severn, the Irish were less apt to trip us up.

I sat at the dragon's neck making notes when we were under sail, and one by one the crewmen asked what I was doing. Writing was still magical then, and my ability to write Latin set me apart as a true runemaster. They asked me to send messages home, and to Agir for weatherluck. I cut them on yew staves and posted them on the ship's wake.

At the end of the second day we tacked landward of Flat Holm Island and held the fleet at the mouth of the Rhymney, a sheltered little bay that was deep enough for our shallow-draft boats. The Gwynllwg Welsh that lived upriver hated the Engs as much as any of their countrymen, and maybe more because they'd lost land when Offa built the south end of his dyke. They were as proficient at cattle raiding as any Irishman, and it wouldn't be hard to find someone familiar with the situation of the Engs on the other side of the dyke.

Einar Soft Hands, who was on the vik to get geld to build a new weaving shed, had traded wool with both the Gwynllwg Welsh and the Brycgstow Engs in Wessex, and Sygtrygg was counting on his connections. He went ashore at sundown with a few of his men, and we settled into our blankets to wait.

The next morning Sygtrygg had Ospak, the captain of the second knarr, set up a tent under some towering elm trees a few hundred yards from the shore. Pretty soon the Welsh began to trickle in, and we began to barter and collect intelligence. Einar had looked up old friends and spent the night drinking and gauging their mood. Once he explained we were there to kill Engs, the Welsh warmed up and offered to expedite our business.

Offa had built his dyke along the Welsh border from the Severn to the Irish Sea. It was quite a project, and he'd conscripted civilians to do their fortress work so it was finished in a year or two. The south end of the wall ran along the east bank of the Wye River, which emptied into the Severn mouth twenty miles upstream. The entire length was garrisoned at intervals, but troops from the fyrd patrolled irregularly, so you never knew where they might turn up.

This was good news as far as we were concerned. If the defenses were too formidable for ten dragon ships, why follow Orm Jarl to his wyrd with Skäne waiting like a drunken virgin in the hay mow? By midafternoon Einar and a couple of his Gwynllwg Welsh friends, dark-haired men with black eyes who crackled with hatred for the Engs, went into a huddle under the elms with Sygtrygg and the captains. This meeting lasted a couple of hours but no voices were raised, so I reckoned Macc Oc had learned not to give orders to men who knew what they were about. When the meeting broke up, Sygtrygg came back to the boat to tell us what would happen.

"In some places the Welsh lost land to Offa when he built his dyke, in some they gained land. In the south they lost it, and they're looking for an excuse to fight. There's a place not far up the Wye where the forest's so thick the Engs thought it was better than a dyke to keep them out, but the Welsh know a way through it. They'll raid east of the dyke to draw the Engs from the Severn, and we'll be able to get upriver."

"What happens if Einar's wrong?" I whispered to Skallagrim.

"Then you'll have something to make verse about," he told me with a smile. He as a skald of the "doomed but noble hero" school of verse, but I had no desire to compose in that genre.

"It will take the Welsh a few days to gather, so we've a little time yet before we pull wood upriver."

"Why are the Welsh so eager to help us?" Rognvald asked.

Sygtrygg smiled and ran a hand over his mustache. "They reckon the Engs will be more afraid of us and send their main force to the Severn; they'll have free rein among the Magonsætans."

Rognvald laughed. "Do you trust the Welshmen?"

"Einar trusts how much they hate the Engs," Sygtrygg said. "That's enough for me."

Sygtrygg gave the order to haul the boats out of the water and cover them with brush. We left a guard and the main force moved inland to Rhymby, which was a campsite, not a settlement. The Welsh delivered a herd of cattle, courtesy of the Engs, and we slaughtered a dozen and set them roasting over slow fires. The Welsh kept their distance. They were eager to speed us on our way, because the alternative was to continue to feed us.

The camp was organized by crews, and since the Irish were spread out across the fleet, Macc Oc had an excuse to inspect his men's accommodations. I was tenting with Skallagrim, and we were sitting on a log watching Thorleik Baster, Sygtrygg's cook, use a long grass brush to paint sauce on a side of beef. The smell of the barbecued beef ribs swirled round as Skallagrim strummed his harp strings and our stomachs sang.

As any master chef will, Thorleik had gathered his ingredients from what was locally available, and the sauce was pungent with garlic, leeks, rosemary, and dill. Few could resist Thorleik's barbecue, including Thorleik himself, which accounted for at least a hundred of the pounds he carried on his big frame. A crowd had begun to gather as Vikings finished making their hasty bivouac. Macc Oc made directly for us and stopped between me and the fire.

"This looks like a good spot," he said. "Get up so your betters can have a seat and something to eat."

Skallagrim stopped harping. I looked up at Macc Oc and smiled. "Think your teeth are tight enough to gnaw Thorleik's ribs without losing them?"

Macc Oc kicked me in the leg, and I was in his face before his foot was back on the ground. The Irishmen moved toward us, and the Danes moved toward them. One of the Irishmen kicked over Thorleik's bowl of sauce, and Thorleik grabbed him by the throat, lifted him off the ground, and painted his livid face with paste. Macc Oc reached out for me and I pushed him back into his friends to get some room. Hands grabbed me from behind, and Rognvald hissed into my ear.

"Settle down, Bran, or there'll be more trouble than you're worth, foster brother or not."

Kalf Agirson interposed himself, facing Macc Oc.

"Best save this energy for the Engs," he said, laughing indulgently like someone used to the tensions that built on a vik. "We'll need all we've got when the time comes."

By that time the commotion had attracted a wider attention, and Sygtrygg and Thorfinn pushed into the scrum. "What's going on here?" Sygtrygg demanded when he realized who the contestants were. Thorfinn stood behind him looking forbidding, and a crowd of his berserks stood behind *him*, looking even *more* forbidding. It was a tense moment, and Sygtrygg's first impulse was to blame me.

"Macc Oc started it," Skallagrim said on my behalf, but Sygtrygg didn't seem inclined to accept his word. "We were sitting here watching Thorleik when he ordered us off, and then kicked Bran when he wasn't fast enough."

"He was fast enough with his tongue," Macc Oc snarled, shrugging out of the restraining hands.

"Let's settle it with a horse race," I suggested.

Macc Oc started forward again, but Sygtrygg grabbed my shoulder. The look on his face brought me round more than his grip. I was going too far, and it was time to get control of my wit before I goaded Macc Oc into drawing steel.

"Skallagrim's telling the truth," Rognvald said. "But Bran didn't help matters."

"When has he?" Sygtrygg wondered.

"I don't know," Skallagrim said, sotto voce in his ear. "I thought he was a help when he toasted Orm."

Sygtrygg swallowed back whatever else he was going to say and turned to Macc Oc. "I'll talk to my foster brother about his tongue," he said. "But to save further trouble, since you're unfamiliar with viking customs, best take your cues from Kalf."

Thorfinn's berserks were dispersing the crowd like dogs working a flock of sheep, and soon it melted away. Thorleik set the basted Irishman on his feet and gave his nose a final daub. Kalf escorted Macc Oc to another ship's camp, and Sygtrygg turned to me when they were gone.

"Are you crazy?" he growled. "Where are your brains?"

"I don't need to take any shit from that turnip sucker," I said with comparable choler. "Besides, I thought I was supposed to keep him irritated."

"That's not the point and you know it. It's clear I'll have to separate you. Einar's sending some men with the Welsh, and I want you to go with them."

"What about my share of the plunder?" I demanded angrily.

"You should've thought of that before you baited Macc Oc. I need him with me more than I need you."

I spat into the fire and kept my mouth shut. What choice did I have? Maybe I could turn up some silver when the Welsh raided into Eng land. A bigger loss was the chance of killing Macc Oc when the arrow storm broke. I gathered up my cloak and went back to the ships to brood by myself, and no one offered to stop me.

4

Wales

With a good woman, if you wish to enjoy
Her words and her goodwill,
Pledge her fairly and be faithful to it
Enjoy the good you are given.
　　　　　—The Sayings of the Wise One

The next morning it was raining. I'd kept a dry but hungry night aboard ship, smelling the barbecue and thinking about wit and its rewards. My empty belly woke me up at dawn, and I stretched in my blanket as the gravel ballast crunched under my back. I could hear the patter of rain on the decking above my head, and I pulled the wool closer around my ears, but finally my bladder forced me to get up and piss over the freeboard.

Once upright, there was nothing for it but to go to the camp and see if Thorleik had breakfast going. The rain thinned until it was more of a mist, beading on the grass and the wool of my cloak. I passed the sentries and went back to my tent, which Skallagrim had enjoyed without my company to cramp his long legs in the night. He was already awake and about.

"Sleep well?" he asked.

"Dry but hungry," I said.

"Good. You're leaving in a couple of hours. There's just enough time to get some food and make your peace with Sygtrygg."

I knew he was right. My last breakfast course was going to be crow. Thorleik was stirring a cauldron under a hastily rigged cooking canopy, and I went over to see if food was ready.

"Hard luck, missing out on the vik," he commiserated. "I told Sygtrygg it was Macc Oc's trouble and not yours."

"Thanks, but he's right. We're better off separated now. I'll settle with him some other time."

I offered a bowl, and he ladled up a stew of the beef left over from the previous night's barbecue. There were loaves of bread on Thorleik's worktable, and I broke one apart and sat down to eat. I was blowing on my first spoonful when Sygtrygg walked up. We nodded at one another, he got a bowl of stew and sat down beside me. We ate without conversation, sharing bread, salt, and water from the bucket. When our bowls were empty, we wiped our mouths and settled back for the reconciliation.

"Well, foster brother," he began. "Maybe you were right after all. Everyone says Macc Oc started the trouble. It's the first time he's led a force and he thinks he's a warlord. Your quick wit didn't help matters, but Skallagrim reminded me of times it has, so I'm sorry I lost my temper."

An apology wasn't among any of the things I'd expected. I looked at him and shrugged. Now it was my turn.

"I should have taken the insult," I admitted. "I was too quick to react; with everything in the balance, I should have let him sit where he wanted."

He nodded. "It would have been better."

"What now?"

"Eyjolf and a few of his men are going north among the Welsh. They all speak the dialect, and you can speak the priest's language and a little Eng, so maybe you can help. I'd rather have you on the vik than Macc Oc, but this is the way it has to be."

"Where'll we meet you?"

"When we come downriver we'll wait for you here. Let the Welsh do the fighting, just make sure they don't change their minds. I'll keep out a share for you."

"Keep well, brother," I told him. "Trust Macc Oc to be what he is, not what you want him to be."

We stood up and embraced. A curious and unexpected thing was happening right before my eyes, something you don't see very often, even in a long life: someone was changing. I'd expected his famous temper, and I found an unexpected reasonableness instead.

I went back to the ship and got my gear, and when I returned to the camp, Einar was instructing his men. The Welsh had picketed horses in the trees at the edge of the forest. There were five Danes, all men in Einar's family or employ: his brother Eyjolf, Eyjolf's son Hrapp, and Odd-leif, Halldor, and Thjodolf. They were all trusted men in Einar's sheep farming empire who'd made many a past trip to Wales. Hrapp and Thjodolf had married Welshwomen and had kin in the area. I was totally unnecessary on this trip; they were as likely to need a Latin speaker as they were to need a midwife.

Einar spoke briefly with Eyjolf in private before he gave us a general exhortation to do well and bring no shame on the enterprise. Four Gwynllwg Welshmen sat their horses quietly just inside the trees, waiting for us to mount up, and Einar said a few words to them in their own language and waved as he left us. We mounted up and the Welshmen led the way into the forest. I fell in at the end of the column beside Halldor. A mist drifted through the colorful trees, and the sodden ground absorbed and muffled the sound of the horses.

"Halldor," I said. "Where we bound?"

"Thirty or forty miles north," he said. "The country here-abouts all drains into the Severn, so the quickest going's in the flatland along the water. When we get to the fourth big drainage there's a Roman road upcountry. We'll follow it over a pass into the Wye drainage. Hrapp's wife Angharad comes from there."

"So that's where we'll mount the raid?"

He nodded. "If we mount it at all. The Welsh are like the Irish: once you're over a ridge you've another clan to deal with. What's promised here may not be kept there. But they're like the Irish this way too: they all hate the Engs. Who knows what the Norns weave?"

We rode through the woods for another hour without speaking a word. We crossed at least twenty streams and a small river, but kept parallel the Severn. The ground to our left rose toward the red sandstone spine of the mountains. Splashes of red maple and yellow beeches mixed with the varied autumnal shades of elm, ash, lime, and whitebeam. We passed a few small villages where men watched cattle and sheep in their yellowed pastures.

About the middle of the day we stopped to rest and eat. The Welshmen, having put distance between themselves and so many Vikings, were finally talkative. When I tried out my Latin it provoked the misunderstanding that I was a priest. The one called Caradog in particular was curious about my status and questioned Eyjolf at length. Their language was familiar but incomprehensible, and when I tried out my Irish it had the same effect on them. Anglo-Saxon was another story, though. I wasn't fluent, but they understood my West Saxon dialect well enough. In an area of fluid borders, most everyone has to be able to get along in both tongues.

After our rest we rode along the foothills of the Black Mountains. Offa's Dyke was five or ten miles to the east. The forest was growing more dense, and the falling leaves made distance hard to measure and the confusion of bare branches and clusters of color made it difficult to detect movement. The infrequent forest habitations, small villages of no more than five or six huts around a clearing, were replaced by abandoned charcoal burners' huts. The path dwindled to a track, more a deer trail than a road, and all around us the forest pressed closer in the narrowing ravines that conducted the watercourses toward the sea.

We rode in single file, the column stretched out thirty or forty yards as the horses picked their way along the side of a ridge with the rock-choked stream to our left. I heard a shout at the front of the column, and then something buzzed under my chin like a hummingbird with pepper up its ass, and then an arrow flew out of the tangle of rocks and yellowing brackens ahead and hit Oddleif low in his right side. He shouted and twisted to the left as his horse lurched uphill, and he rolled out of the saddle into the brackens beside the trail. There were shouts in Welsh and Danish and Mercian. Apparently the Welsh weren't the only ones to make cross-border raids.

I snapped up the reins and turned the horse off the trail into the tall ferns with a kick in the ribs. A well-laid ambush would have a blocking force behind us, waiting for a headlong retreat. Snorri'd taught me to meet a surprise attack with a counterattack, where the line of attackers was thinnest.

I crouched low over the horse's neck and raked my heels across its ribs. An arrow glanced off my shield. The horse slowed as it reached the crest of the ridge, laboring to gain the last few steep yards and presenting an almost stationary target, and then it sprang forward with a scream, and we were on the flat ridge top. An archer stepped from behind a tree and drew his bow, and I galloped him down. He missed, and the horse shouldered him aside. I urged the horse forward for another twenty yards and then turned downslope.

The sounds of the ambush vanished on the other side of the ridge, as the horse plunged down the slope through the ferns. The drainage on this side wasn't as contorted and narrow, and when the ground leveled out I tried to whip the horse into a gallop, and knew immediately something was wrong. The horse tossed its head aside and a plume of blood feathered back from its nostrils, wetting its mane and my face.

I pulled up and the horse coughed. When I looked down, I saw that an arrow had missed my leg and gone into the horse's side, behind its left shoulder. The blood meant it had bounced off a rib and pierced its lung. Running had done the rest. The horse was dead; it just didn't know it yet. I looked back over my shoulder, but I couldn't see any pursuit. I jumped to the ground. The chest-high brackens quivered from the disturbance, and a quick look behind me showed a clear trail of broken and crushed fern. The horse staggered aside, gasping for air, drowning in its own blood. I grabbed the halter and pulled its throat to meet the blade of my scramasax. No use letting it suffer. It reared with a gargling sound, hit a tree, and caromed a few yards away before it fell. I didn't wait around to see what it did next. The noise it made dying, the spastic kicking and liquid neighing, would focus the pursuit. I shrugged the shield off my back to minimize the commotion and started through the ferns in a crouch, careful not to break the stems.

I ran as fast as I could, changing direction frequently and keeping the ridge line at my back. I was looking for thick cover and a place to den up. The bracken was still tall enough to hide me, but anyone on a horse could see every move I made. I needed something solid at my back, someplace with a restricted approach, preferably someplace back in Ireland, but, short of that, a hollow log or a cave would have to do.

Four or five voices shouted behind me, widely separate, as they searched through the brackens. Apart from Oddleif, I'd no idea what happened to the others, and I wasn't hanging round to find out. The ground started up again, and I climbed another ridge, but the way I chose was a dead end among the rocks. I looked back. The bracken was settling down behind me, so I slithered into the stone tumble and put my back to the hillside. I drew my sword and squatted behind my shield, facing the way I'd come. It started raining again and I drew the hood over my head. What a great vik I'd had so far.

I spent the rest of the day listening to them hunt for me. Only a few of them had horses, and the ones on foot were cautious as they poked among the ferns with their spears. They got within twenty or thirty yards a couple of times, and I got ready to fight, but they never picked up my trail: they were just blundering about, hoping to flush me from hiding. I tracked their progress by their shouts and the scurrying of hedgehogs and hares they disturbed. Leaves and bracken clung to the brown wool of the cloak. The leather that covered my shield was plastered with stray leaves and bits of fern, and that volunteer camouflage must have broken up my silhouette. I sat tight, and the rain fell harder. I was soaked and shivering, and my breath drifted slowly away low to the ground like a lost spirit. They broke off the search when it started to get dark, and I shifted my position and settled in for what little sleep I could get.

I dozed off for a few hours, and when I woke, I stood up and stretched. I took a piss against the side of the ridge to commemorate my tenure there. It's true that wet wool retains eighty percent of its insulating and warming ability, but the comfort must be in the other twenty percent. My situation wasn't all I could've hoped for, afoot in the dark in unknown territory, freezing.

I thought about retracing my steps, but dead reckoning and what I could remember of terrain covered on horseback could take me to Mercia as easily as Rhymby. I did know a couple of things, though. There were gaps in the dyke where the forest was thickest. The Severn River was east of me, and the fleet would be going up the Severn. I reckoned if I pushed for the deepest and most tangled part of the forest and headed east, with luck I'd pass through a gap in the earthwork and strike the river. Then all I had to do was wait. Not much of a plan, but the best I could do on the brink of hypothermia.

I scrambled to the top of the ridge. The movement warmed me up. I picked my way down the other side, up and down through the forest for more hours than I remember, crossing streams and following them for varying distances in case the ambushers tracked me with dogs. The rain stopped, and wisps of fog began to coalesce in the hollows, and tendrils drifted in the trees.

By the time it started to lighten, I had no idea how many miles I'd covered or even if I'd kept generally in the same direction. In the thin gray light I saw a dilapidated wattle hut. I stood cautiously twenty or thirty yards away, listening for sounds of habitation. The wet leaves swallowed my footfalls, and I circled the place slowly. There was no sign of life, but I found an old charcoal pit, which made it a burner's hut. The pit was cold to the touch.

The hut was constructed of woven saplings, and offered as much shelter as a fishing net now. There was a stone fire ring near the door, and I stepped over it and forced the door open. The hut was one small room, with a heap of dead brush against one wall that'd been the burner's bed. Water dripped from the roof, and there was a bird's nest in the loosely interwoven branches, and a few fragments of eggshell on the floor. The hut hadn't been used in a year or more. Colliers followed the raw material, and when they'd cut all the useful wood and burned it, they went where there was more.

I looked through the wall, but there was no indication of movement in the woods around the hut. Still, it made me nervous to stay there. Anyone hunting me was bound to check a collier's hut. I needed better cover. A post in the center of the floor supported the roof beams, and I eased my back against it. The structure creaked and a few twigs fell out of the roof, but it took my weight.

I slid my shield underneath me and drew up my knees. With something dry to sit on I felt better, and I closed my eyes for a little while, but like most little whiles, it turned out to be a long while, and when I opened them again, my body heat had dried out my clothes and the inside of my cloak. The forest was lighter than when I went to sleep, and a quick look up through the wattle roof showed me the clouds were thinning out. It was time to get moving, and I left the hut, stiff but refreshed from my sleep, and started north, looking for the thickest part of the forest.

The rest of that day I saw only the occasional bird, a few hares, and a polecat. That night I found a small cave in the hillside overlooking a river. I slept cold and hungry but dry, and in the morning the sun was out and a wind was stirring the branches and stripping off more leaves. The longer I waited, the less cover I'd have. I had a piss and a drink from the river as I crossed it, and started heading east again.

The woods continued to deepen and I reckoned I was heading in the right direction. I walked with sling in hand, relaxed by the familiar weight of a stone in the pouch and bouyed by the hope that a hare or squirrel would present itself in time for lunch. By midmorning I was still hungry, but I lost my appetite when I started to smell death. Death had a lot of different smells in those days: age, hot blood, cloven meat, sickness, the putrid stink of rot and decay. The death I smelled was definitely the rot and decay variety. You never smell that sort of death today. I'm not talking about the simmering summertime smell of death, but the smell of a corpse that'd been corrupt in life. What I smelled in the woods that September morning was the third world aroma of a dead leper. Nothing like that to bring you back into the conversation.

I stopped and looked around. The forest floor at that point was covered by waist-high ferns, and although I was never far from a thicket, the immediate area was relatively uncluttered by brush. The brackens were disturbed a few yards ahead, and I could see that some of them had been flattened by a weight. I slipped the axe out of my belt and stepped over to the spot.

I could see a swathed form, partially concealed among the brackens, quite still and just as dead as it was ever going to be. Flies were gathering on the fabric, exploring the surface in search of a way to get to the fertile breeding ground underneath. They moiled about in a glittering green cloud like a visible smell emanating from the corpse. I swallowed back the lump that climbed my windpipe and tasted vomit, like death's good-night kiss. A breeze through the trees brought the full smell to me, and I turned away and threw up what little was in my gut. The sound drew a small squadron of flies to investigate, and they liked what they found because they landed and began to explore it, with sharp, nervous movements of their forelegs.

I got down on one knee, supporting my weight on the haft of the axe, and heaved dryly in their direction, but they didn't seem to mind. Tears, squeezed out of the corners of my eyes by the spasms of nausea, trickled into my beard, and a little vomit thickened in my mustache as I snorted it out my nose. I sat down heavily, breathing through my open mouth. The forest was empty except for me and the flies, and I was getting sick of their company, so I hoisted myself up and started to put some distance between myself and the leper.

If it sounds strange that I'd get sick over one dead leper, you've never seen and smelled a dead leper, or a live one, either; there's a good reason for leper colonies. It's the idea that they rot while they're still alive that gets to me, the thought that they decompose before they die, lose fingers and toes, melt like wax. We're talking the living dead here, in a time when no one knew how leprosy was caught or transmitted, or that it was even a disease and not some supernatural pissoff. I was a child of my age when it came to lepers, a possessor of all the popular prejudices.

But my reluctance to turn my back on an unburied corpse was stronger even than my loathing. You have to observe the duties to the dead, no matter how compelling the reasons not to, and I hadn't gone thirty yards before I stopped and looked back at the spot where the corpse lay, and then I shook my head and started back. My steps were a lot heavier returning than they'd been going away, but finally I stood looking down at the bundled corpse, with my hand over my mouth in a futile effort to filter out the sweet and humid smell of disintegration.

In the woods, one spot's as good as another, so I walked round the corpse and moved a few paces away to dig a grave. The ground cut easily under the axe blade, like dirt happy to feel iron. I gauged the length of the corpse and cut the hole to size, laying aside the root-balled ferns and exposing the black earth underneath. I hoped the leper appreciated the trouble I was going to.

It was slow work because I didn't have the right tools, but after a couple of hours I had a hole that came to the middle of my ribs and a pile of black dirt to one side. The axe was chipped in a couple of places, but nothing that a little time on a grindstone wouldn't repair. I set it aside and climbed out of the hole.

"You'll be happy here," I said. "This is a good place to sleep forever, and the shade will keep you cool in the summer." I picked up a stone and brushed the dirt off its surface. The beard of my axe did an acceptable job of scratching binding runes with eleven clean strokes. Then I wet the stone with spit and cut them again, letting the grit work with the blade.

These were powerful runes, about which the rune poem says:

> Wealth is a comfort to one and all
> But he must share it who hopes to cast
> His lot for judgment before his lord.

And,

> The dust is dreadful to every noble
> When suddenly the flesh begins
> To cool, and the corpse must choose the earth
> As bleak bedfellow. Bright fruits fall,
> Joys pass away, covenants fail.

I set the stone aside and got up. All that was left now was to drag the corpse to its new home. I looked down at the leper, who was only getting riper while I put it off. Holding my breath while the flies buzzed around my face, I pulled the corpse's feet, half expecting them to come off in my hands. The earth held on for a second, and when it gave up its grip I lost my balance and went down on one knee.

"You could cooperate," I said. Dead men weren't so dead then as they are today. Now, no one expects to see a dead man again. Then, they had a tendency to give up life only with reluctance, and to come back if they got the chance or if they were obliged to. You always had the feeling they were never very far away, and that they could hear what you told them. Skallagrim always said that you should talk to the dead the way you wanted them to remember you.

The corpse began to slide through the brackens and weeds, moving quickly now that the earth had given up its hold. It seemed almost weightless, as if the disease had eaten it to a husk. I stopped when it was on the edge of the grave, unwilling to just drop it into the hole. I whipped my hair around to chase the flies. I squatted down and hopped into the hole. The corpse was right under my face as I lifted it off the edge; it was light as a corn-shuck doll. I lowered it into the grave and stood up. Flies were crawling over my beard, and when I shook my head they swarmed up in front of my eyes.

"Sorry it's not a softer bed," I apologized. "It's as good as I could manage and better than nothing."

I climbed out of the grave. Now that I'd removed the corpse, the flies lost interest and moved off in search of other dead meat. I dropped three silver pence into the hole beside the body. It was poor grave goods, but better than nothing.

I started scraping the dirt over the edge until the grave was full. When the dirt was mounded up, I set the ferns back in place and the binding rune over the middle of the grave.

I needed a bath and something to eat. I collected my gear and started east again. From twenty yards away, the grave was invisible, and in a week I probably wouldn't be able to find it myself.

My path continued through the forest for another hour until I came to a Roman road. There was no mistaking Roman engineering, and out there in the wilderness, no one had bothered the pavers. Thirty yards to my left, a bridge spanned a stream. I crossed the bridge and left the road, walking along the bank until I found a bend not far away where a meander had gouged out a pool that would serve, and I dropped my gear and stripped.

I dove into the stream. It was only five or ten yards wide, so I surfaced close to the other side. The water was warm, and I turned over and swam a little way with the current, spitting water into the air like a blowing whale. I swam back to the gravel beach and squatted in the shallow water to rub myself off with handfuls of wet grit. I got my comb out of the pack and combed my mustache to get any last bits of barf. The smell of the leper was gone, but I didn't start to feel clean until I'd scrubbed myself red with sand and rinsed off twice more.

I swam back upstream slowly, enjoying the freedom of moving easily in three dimensions, the liberation of skinny-dipping, and then back again and climbed out onto the path beside the river.

There are few feelings better than the self-righteous buzz you get from doing something unpleasant despite the fact there's no one around to appreciate it. Stepping up to your duty because it's your duty, not because you're playing to the crowd. That's how I felt when the smell of my good deed was washed away and I'd rinsed the taste of vomit out of my mouth. Self-righteousness is a drug that can get into your system harder and faster than opium.

But I didn't have time to enjoy the buzz. Before I'd finished drying off I heard the sound of someone coming through the brush. I dropped the cloak and grabbed the scramasax, spinning round to confront whoever was coming. I saw a figure struggling against the clutching vines beside the path, and I shifted my weight and brought up the point of the blade. Then the tendrils released the fabric and the figure turned, and I saw it was a woman. She stopped at the sight of me, and then she laughed suddenly and brought a hand to her mouth as if she wanted to grab her laughter back.

She took a long look to be sure of what she was laughing at. Her eyes traveled over me from head to foot and back again until her laughter overcame her and she had to turn away. I dropped the point of the scramasax and straightened up. She was alone on the trail. Then it occurred to me that she might be distracting me while someone came up from behind. I spun round and raised the blade again, but the trail was empty.

That made her laugh again, and when I looked back, she was sitting on the ground, holding her head in her hands, enjoying herself a whole lot more at my expense than I thought was polite.

"Glad to be able to cheer you up," I said, lowering the blade. "Anything else I can do for you?"

She shook her head and got control of herself. "I don't

think so," she gasped, wiping tears from the corners of her eyes. "I reckon I took you by surprise."

I glanced around one last time and then slipped the blade into its scabbard. As I stooped for my clothing, she got to her feet again, and I could feel her looking at me. She had a way of looking that made your back twitch, looking straight on, not in small glances the way some people do. She was a looking woman. My mother and sister were such women, and it was always getting them in trouble with people in Clontarf, mostly with men. Not everyone was as egalitarian as Snorri, or as immune to close scrutiny.

The kind of free enterprise practiced on the sea road, the opportunity to plunder and rape and burn professionally, made many a man difficult to live with, and divorces weren't uncommon at the Thing. Women were expected to keep the keys and manage the household, but that career path wasn't for everyone. Every year at least one formerly moonstruck daughter of some presently pissed-off father showed her bruises and announced her intention to quit living with her husband.

Sinead would never end up at the Thing showing her bruises. She was a woman who looked long into the faces of the men who came calling, and if the looking made them uncomfortable, they weren't welcome back. The ones that came back were generally men of Snorri's temper, but even so Sinead turned them all down. She was looking for someone else, looking far, looking for someone who didn't live in Clontarf yet, and maybe never would. Snorri more than once had to explain that his daughters made up their own minds about men who came sniffing round his house.

Mairead was a looking woman too. When Snorri met her at the Tailltenn Fair, she'd knocked him off his horse with one of those looks, and he'd never been the same after that. Looking women were rare enough, but I'd grown up in a houseful, and they'd prepared me for all the rest I'd ever meet. There's only one way to deal with a looking woman, and that's to look back, so when I was dressed again, I had a look at her.

She had sun-blond hair the color of August wheat, but if you took her out of the sun, who knew what color it would be? Some sort of brown possibly. Her face was honest without making you nervous, straight ahead, openly appraising you, thinking about you behind those blue eyes without bothering to hide it. Her cheekbones were wide, and her nose had been broken, but she had a face that could accommodate a broken nose, and you didn't notice it after a minute, and never did again.

I guessed her age at near my own, give or take a year. She stood with the ease of someone used to work, the lithe grace of a woman accustomed to using her muscles, and that muscle tone and hair and the hardness of her hands made her a peasant. She was wearing an unbleached linen shirt and her legs were wrapped up in heavy trousers, belted with brown leather outside a tunic that went to the middle of her thighs.

"What brings you out on such a day?" I asked her.

"What better a day to be out?" She looked at me with that level gaze, the yellow leaves behind her and the sunlight on that sun-blond hair like a halo. That image of her, framed in that pellucid light, is as sharp now as at that second.

"What's your name, and how do you come to be dressed like a man?" I decided to take a direct approach to save time.

"My mother called me Caitria," she said, "after the saint the Romans couldn't break on the wheel. My clothing's the best I've got, although I've owned better. What about you? How does a foreigner come to be here naked in the middle of the week?"

"I worked hard today, and I wanted a bath," I said, shouldering the pack. "And now I want something to eat. As for being a foreigner, I'm from Clontarf in Ireland, and I was on a trading party."

"You're a trader, then?"

"Not exactly," I told her. "I'm a poet."

"What's an Irish poet doing in the Welsh border country?"

"Taking a bath," I said.

"And where are your friends?"

"We were attacked two days ago by Engs. One went into the bracken with an arrow in his side, and I don't know what happened to the rest." I had no idea if I was in Wales or Mercia, or, for that matter, if this woman was an Eng or Welsh. She spoke her Anglo-Saxon with an indefinite accent.

"You know this country?" I asked.

"I grew up here," she said.

"Where I come from a woman alone on the road's uncommon."

"I'm going to make my way in Gleawanceaster on the Severn," Caitria said. "Now my family's gone, there's naught for me out here."

"Where are you from?" These seemed important questions to me at the time, still paranoid about the ambush, and I was resolved to find out the answers before I went any farther.

"My family's farmstead was north of Ewyas in the golden valley," she said, holding back the branches of a hazel tree that extended into the trail.

Since I'd no idea where that was, all I could do was shake my head and grunt, but it was an old story: the flight from the rural to the urban, the migration of the young from the primal rhythms of country life to the artifice and temptations of a swinging town like Gleawanceaster, another place I'd never heard of.

"Wales or Eng land?" I asked.

"Wales," she said, "at the moment. When I was born they paid tribute to Offa. When did you have those blade cuts?" she asked.

I looked over my shoulder. "Ask away," I said.

"Why should I wait?" she wondered. "It's not like your body has any secrets, now you've shown me both sides of it."

"If you weren't going around unwatched, you'd have missed it altogether. What're you doing off the road, anyway?"

"The Engs have raided into Wales, the Welsh are raiding back. It isn't safe to stay on the road."

"Unless you run into armed strangers," I said.

"One look at you told me I'd naught to fear."

That made me smile. All men, even if they're hauling ass across the border from Wales to Mercia as fast as they can, like to think they possess a dangerous cutting edge of madness; reminding them they don't always stings, but I assumed she meant it as a statement of trust, and I shrugged it off. She was right. Once I saw she wasn't dangerous to me, *she'd* naught to fear. She talked too much for a wight, and she'd faced down iron, not something a shapeshifter was generally up to. Still and all, in the early autumn of 792 it paid to be careful.

"How long ago did you drop off the turnip cart?" I asked her, feeling the urge to dispense advice, one of the four or five most dangerous urges known to man. "When you get to Gleawanceaster don't take appearance as a guarantee of anything."

"I can care for myself," she said. "I was running a farmstead when I was fourteen," she informed me in the tone of someone who'd been underestimated and wasn't taking it well.

"I don't doubt it," I conceded.

There was a standing stone beside the bridge abutment with runes worked into it in the Anglo-Saxon style and gripping beasts circling the stone as if they were holding it together.

" 'This bridge was made by Hywel. Branwyn, his wife, raised this stone in his memory. He was a good man.' " I read the inscription aloud, and Caitria looked at me with a little more respect. That was a good trick when almost no one knew how to read or write, but now it leaves women unimpressed. "Who do you suppose they were?" I asked, but she only shrugged.

Building bridges and maintaining roadways was as civic-minded as it got, even in a wasteland like the border country, and to be remembered as a maker of either one was a good legacy. In addition, Branwyn, which meant, in Anglo-Saxon, "white skinned" or "fair skinned," had found Hywel to be a good husband. That wasn't such a bad thing either, I reckoned. I imagined one of those milk-skinned women that abound in the land of the Engs, long-haired, full-breasted, outliving her Welsh husband and raising a stone so travelers would pause to remember their names and their marriage, which she'd found to be good.

Rune stones are lithic messages in the bottle of time, weathered and faded by the years, and they always make me feel sad when I read them. The Mark was littered with stones commemorating sons who'd gone to vik and never returned, wives and husbands ghosts before their mates, sons and daughters taken ahead their time, all dead and mourned, and remembered as long as those stones stand, cheating the void.

"She must have loved him," I observed.

"I suppose it's possible," she admitted. "But more likely he smelled of sweat and leeks, and never shaved, and thought he was a prize, and she thought so too, God knows why."

A little way beyond the bridge, she reached into the weeds at the side of the road to fetch out a scrip. "Since we're no danger to one another, and may even be a help, what if we keep company?"

I stopped and looked at her. The rules of companionship were complex and rigid, as were almost *all* the rules in 792, and I wasn't sure I wanted to be saddled with a woman while I walked across the land of the Engs. Most especially not one that looked at you as nakedly as this one: a looking woman, which variety, in my experience, attracted the most attention and caused the most trouble. I wanted invisibility, not attention. Oaths of partnership were oaths of equality in all things good and bad, with an equal share of everything. She seemed to read my mind as I hesitated.

"I said I can take care of myself." Her eyes narrowed. "Don't think you're necessary. But there are times when a companion's a help if you're not too proud to accept it."

"There's a pretty trap," I said. "If I accept, I'm unnecessary, and if I refuse, I'm too proud."

She laughed again and shrugged while I considered it. At least she had some wit, and she probably knew the land around here. I could use someone who knew how to get to the Severn without running into the Engs.

"All right," I agreed.

"What's your name, then?" She started off ahead of me without even a pretense of waiting.

"Bran," I said to her receding back. "Snorrison."

"Well, hurry up, then," she said. "Day's short this time of year."

We left the road again not far ahead, and Caitria led the way east. She walked with a sense of purpose, but she kept an eye on the available cover. "We're about five miles from the dyke," she said.

"I hear there's a gap where the woods are thick."

"Did you think I was going to walk up to the ditch and present myself?" she asked with an edge to her voice.

"I just want to know what your plan is."

"My plan's not to be seen if I can help it."

That was a plan I could endorse. With the border country

stirred up by raids and counterraids, not running into any-one was our best hope of staying alive. Still, I required a little more detail.

"We're headed for the gap in the dyke, then?"

"You're right," she said, stopping to look at me. "There's a gap in the thickest stretch of the forest, but that might not be the best place to go now. Everyone's probably headed there. There's a good chance that we can find a stretch of dyke that's not manned."

She gave me a quick smile and started walking again, leaving me to stay or follow as I wished. I'd known her for less than an hour, and she was already irritating. I hurried after her and fended aside rowan branches that snapped back as she moved on the edge of a thicket. "You're going to try to cross the dyke?"

She stopped again. "Do you know where you are?" she asked. "Do you know where the dyke is? Do you know where the gap is? Do you know *any*thing about this country?"

"No." I gave her the short answer. "I never said I did. I just want to know what you've got in mind. It's a reason-able request, since I don't know anything about you. You're Gwynllwg Welsh, you're Magonsætan Eng, you're whatever you say you are; how do I know I can trust you?"

"And you've told me all *your* story? Trading among the Welsh, are you? Trading what, swords and shields? And if you're attacked by Engs, why head east?"

It's true there were a few omissions, but what I'd *told* her was true. Why clutter up my story by mentioning the vik?

"Trading wool," I said. "Einar's traded wool in these parts for fifteen years."

"Einar? That doesn't sound Welsh to me. Come to that, neither does Snorrison."

"We're Danes," I told her. "We've lived in Ireland for twenty years."

She just looked at me and shook her head. "Irish Danes," she said with a small laugh. "Trading wool with swords and shields."

"Stranger than a Welsh Eng going to a Severn town alone to make her way?"

Before we could continue this stimulating debate, we heard the sound of horses in the woods and burrowed into the rowan thicket. The stalks were thick and it was tough going, but we managed to insinuate ourselves deep enough to get out of sight. I could see a mounted troop, about twenty men, heading west, carrying spears and definitely going somewhere, not looking for us. After they were gone, we waited a few minutes in case there were more. It gave me time to think, and I decided to tell her the whole story, or more of it.

"The lord of Clontarf was killed last year on a voyage up the Severn. We've come to avenge him, and I was part of a group that went to get the Welsh to help us. After the Mercians attacked us, I reckoned I had a better chance of cutting the Severn than finding my way to the Welsh."

"So there's Danes from Ireland, Welsh raiders and the Magonsætan Fyrd all roaming around the lower Severn?"

"Right," I said.

"This isn't going to be easy," she said. "Who was it killed the lord of Clontarf?"

"Offa and Beorhtric," I told her.

"They harried this land when I was ten years old," she said. "If you can avenge yourself on them, you have my blessing."

"Then help me get back to the Severn."

"That's what I'm doing," she said. "And you help me get to Gleawanceaster."

"Fair enough," I said.

5
Orm's Geld

I know a third: in the thick of battle
If my need be great enough
It will blunt the edges of enemy swords.
Their weapons will make no wounds.
      —The Sayings of the Wise One

We moved more cautiously for the rest of the day, and just before dark the bulk of Offa's Dyke loomed in the distance. In these days of smart bombs and television war, satellite reconaissance and infrared guidance systems, the most elaborate defensive earthwork you're likely to find is a two-man foxhole, but for most of recorded history, if you wanted to keep out an enemy you dug a ditch and threw up a wall behind it, and that's what Offa'd done to keep out the Welsh.

It ran from south to north, cutting off the entire Welsh peninsula, except for gaps in the southern quarter where the forest was impenetrable (or not, depending on who you talked to) and the northern third, where an older earthwork called Wat's Dyke, about which no one pretends to know much, took up the slack.

With the exception of the Chinese, whom we didn't know about at the time, Offa'd built the best of all the extant earthworks. It was longer than both Roman walls combined, and more formidable than the Danewerk. It was fronted by a ditch about six or eight feet deep and fifteen or twenty feet wide from edge to edge, and the timber-reinforced dyke topped out at twenty-four feet from the bottom of the ditch. This wasn't a casual accomplishment.

Taxation was less monetary in the eighth century. You were more likely to be assessed in barrels of wine, bushels of barleycorn, and cheeses than silver pence, but there were three duties that everyone owed the state: *feorm,* which was food rent sufficient to feed the king and his retinue for twenty-four hours; *brycg geweorc,* which was the building of bridges and defensive structures; and *fyrd geweorc,* which was military service for a specified term every year.

There were other duties, of course—the eighth century was a rat's nest of duties and concomitant penalties—but in Eng land these three were the ones from which there was no exemption. Well, crouching inside the treeline about fifty yards from the edge of the ditch, I could see that Offa'd gotten his due from his peasants. The dyke was quite the most formidable example of public works engineering I'd ever seen, and it stretched off in both directions across the rolling countryside without a break in the face that it showed to Wales.

"Where are we going to cross?" I asked Caitria.

"Where we can do it unseen," she said, studying the earthwork.

"That's what I reckoned," I told her. "Do you happen to know where that might be?"

She stood up and shook her head, looking round the woods for something. "Not yet. C'mon, let's walk a bit." She started moving north, keeping inside the trees. The Engs had leveled a killing ground about thirty yards wide in front of the ditch, taking care to leave the tree stumps about a foot or two in height, too small to hide behind but big enough to seriously hinder any cartage that might be wheeled up to the ditch. The chief engineer was obviously a man who understood the requirements of siege and attack.

The brush was clear-cut between the woods and the ditch, but the ground along the edge of the trees was jammed with shrubbery, in thick contest for the light, so we had a good screen from watchers on the top of the dyke. I hurried through the dusk after Caitria, but she came to a stop at the foot of a wych elm before I caught up. She was studying it critically.

"Drop your gear," she said, putting her back to the tree and cupping her hands at thigh level, "and I'll give you a leg up."

"Up where?"

"Up the tree. Ever climb a tree in Ireland?"

I looked at her and up the elm and across the open space at the dyke. There was still enough foliage on the tree to hide me if I kept the trunk between me and the dyke, and not enough to hinder my view along the earthwork.

"Well, shake a leg," she said, gesturing with her cupped hands.

I dropped the pack and shrugged out of the shield and harness. Stripped of my weapons I'd be lithe as a monkey, but it really made my ass pucker to leave them on the ground and climb a tree, possibly right under the noses of the Magonsætan fyrd. "Why don't you go up the tree?"

"Pretend it's a mast," she advised. "We're losing the light."

I tossed my cloak aside and put my foot in her hands. In a moment she'd launched me upward, and I was shinnying the elm. Elms don't branch near the ground, so I kissed bark for twenty feet, until I attained the first contorted limb; after that it was easy, and in no time I was fifty feet in the air with a good view of the dyke. There was nothing in sight, no smoke or fire glow behind, and no water in the ditch.

"It's clear," I said when I was beside her on the ground again.

"Let's leg it," she said, and she was dodging the stumps in the clearing before I could collect my gear. I slipped the harness over my head and clutched everything else to my chest as I followed, but she was off again, scampering along the lip of the ditch before I'd crossed half the distance. She squatted by a stump, sat down on the edge, and disappeared into the ditch. When I got to the spot I saw she'd let herself down using the exposed roots of the stump. I dropped my gear to her and followed.

In the ditch we were at least out of sight. "Let me know if I'm holding you back," I said. "I'll pick up the pace."

She graced me with a faint frown and shook her head. "Not enough to matter," she said. "Don't worry, I won't get too far ahead."

It crossed my mind to hit her, but she was already out of reach, moving along the palisaded inner side of the ditch, and when she found a loose timber she scurried up like a squirrel. In another moment we were at the top of the dyke, and then we scrambled down the inner face of the earthwork safe in the woods of Eng land.

There was no apparent difference between one side of the earthwork and the other. At least there were no troops about. Maybe not for miles. Or maybe a hundred yards away and coming fast, for all I knew. I didn't linger, and I didn't wait for Caitria; I started putting distance between me and the dyke as soon as I hit the woods.

That night we burrowed into dead leaves to keep warm. It was going on three days since I'd eaten, and food fantasies were starting to occupy a place of importance in my idle moments, so when I woke up to the smell of roasting meat I thought I was dreaming. I shook the leaves off and crawled out to find Caitria squatting over a low fire turning four hedgehogs on a spit of green wood.

"Not very careful," I said nervously.

"There's more danger someone'll hear your guts rumble than smell the smoke," she said, turning the spit over the flame.

I looked down at the hedgehogs and then around the forest. We'd put the dyke a couple of miles behind us before we stopped for the night, but that didn't mean we were safe. She stood up and kicked dirt into the fire, and then trod it into ash.

"Breakfast's done," she said. "Let's eat on the move."

There isn't much to eat under a hedgehog's bristles, and what's there isn't too tasty, but it tasted like roast beef and horseradish to me, and I took the stick and ate while we walked. I ate what I could from two of them and then offered her the other two.

"Are you serious? I don't eat hedgehog," she declined in a tone of mild disgust.

"I'm too empty to be particular," I grunted, starting on the third hedgehog. When I finished, I wiped my hands on the hem of my cloak and had a drink from a stream. The sun was up, but it was only middling warm by noon, and clouds scudded to the east. We passed a few deserted huts and a fenced paddock. The shit was fresh, and the huts had been vacated in a hurry.

"There's activity around here," Caitria said.

"Must be friendly or the place would be burned," I observed. Evidence of rapid evacuation told us little; the fact that the village was still intact was the salient clue. When armed men were about, a wise peasant beat feet without waiting to identify them. Friends were as liable to kill you as enemies; the difference was technical.

There was nothing to identify what had scared off the inhabitants, but there was a small ham suspended from a rafter in one of the huts that I confiscated for lunch. Caitria found some onions and tucked the greens through her belt. The whole search took under five minutes.

"Where are we?" I asked, munching ham and eating an onion as we walked.

"The Wye River's ahead, and then we'll cut a Roman road. We take it north until it forks. The right fork goes to Gleawanceaster and the Severn."

"How far?"

"Maybe twenty miles," she said.

We made better time east of the dyke. The peasants grazed their animals in the forest, and the absence of underbrush and shrubs made for easier walking. It also made for no cover and easy detection if we ran into anyone, but I had to make as much time as I could. This was my third day on foot, and I had no idea where the fleet was. I wanted an oak deck under my feet again and the company of hundreds of heavily armed friends. I'd had enough forest rambling.

The Wye River valley twisted through southwest Mercia, steep and wooded, and never very wide. The last twenty miles of it formed the border between Wales and Mercia, sometimes taking the place of the ditch in front of the dyke, sometimes backed up by dyke and ditch both, and sometimes, in those places where the terrain made it possible, unaccompanied by either one.

We waded a sheltered ford without incident. Caitria certainly had stamina. She stepped out at a forced march pace, leaving me to follow as I might. I was in good shape, if a little malnourished, but I had to work to keep up. She knew it too, and I think she wanted me to ask her to slow down, but I wasn't about to ask it, so we kept going without conversation for the rest of that day.

The forest pushed back to the south, so we cut the Severn close to the channel and turned upstream. We had to stay close enough to the river to see the ships, and at that point the river was still wide, but later that afternoon we came up to the first of the big meanders. The watercourse turned due west for almost a mile and then doubled back on itself.

There was a small village on the west bank, fisher folk,

judging from the flotsam of the sacking. I found a few Irish arrows and some blood trails leading into the forest, but I didn't follow them. There were a pile of heads near the water. Macc Oc and his men had reverted to one of their less civilized Celtic hobbies: headhunting. I wondered how Sygtrygg had liked that. Those heads could have been firmly attached to the shoulders of Eng slaves where they were worth money instead of drawing flies by the Severn. Someone would have to curb Macc Oc's boyish excesses or the vik would lose money.

Caitria looked at the heads and then at me. "You reckon these fishermen killed the lord of Clontarf last year?"

"This is the work of Irishmen," I said. "It's a waste. The leader of the Irish is an asshole who thinks this proves he's a warrior."

"Why have him along?"

"It's a longer story than we have time for," I assured her. The rain was sizzling on the hot timbers as Caitia poked through the ashes of the fishermen's houses.

"Will they stop at night?"

"They'll probably sleep on the boats," I told her. "We should go as far as we can before we lay up."

It was late in the afternoon when we got to Gleawanceaster. It was about the size of Clontarf. The smoke over the town indicated the fleet had been there ahead of us. All that remained of the structures nearest the water were their charred bones. The defense *burh* had been breached and pulled down. The civilians were returning. We sat on the riverbank and watched the activity on the other side.

"They had their revenge on Gleawanceaster too," Caitria said.

"Revenge is where you find it," I observed with a noncommittal shrug. I had nothing to be apologetic about; for all I knew, the Engs of Gleawanceaster had danced on Orm Jarl's bones. "Let's go find out what happened."

"What happened's plain enough," she said.

"Not to me," I said. It took me about twenty minutes to locate a boat, run up a small creek and hidden under some willow branches. I poled out of the creek mouth and down the riverbank to get Caitria. The Severn was about seventy-five yards wide, and it didn't take us long to cross. I tied the small boat off and we walked through the ruins. There were a few bodies, but most of the fighting had happened at the *burh*, not by the water. Caitria disappeared for a minute into a house.

"Best keep your mouth shut," Caitria said when she rejoined me. "It won't do to show off your accent."

"I've got to find out when this happened and which way the fleet went," I told her as I laid the palm of my hand on a charred beam. It was as warm as a rock that's been in the sun all day. I reckoned that the fire had died out that morning.

"Grandmother," Caitria called to an old woman passing nearby. "What happened here?"

"Foreigners in ships," she said. "They came yesterday morning and attacked the town. The levy was off fighting the Welsh, only a few stayed behind in the *burh*. They were no match for them."

"Where away after they attacked?"

"Upriver." The old woman laughed bitterly. "Their mistake. One troop of the fyrd's on their heels and another's coming from the west. They'll be cut off before they can get back to the Severn Sea." The old woman looked at me with a suspicious eye. "You best hurry if you want to catch them up."

"They've stirred up the Engs right enough," Caitria said as we walked away. "And the old woman's right, they could be trapped upstream."

"Well, I've got to follow them if I want to get back to Ireland. You're in Gleawanceaster. Thank's for the company."

"What's left of it, you mean. Your friends are pretty thorough."

"No good being half-assed about revenge," I said.

"Let's get going," she said. "Will we take the boat or walk?"

"We? Got a mouse in your pocket?"

"I can't stay here," she said, gesturing at the ruins of Gleawanceaster. "What's the point?"

"Opportunity." I smiled at her. I'd watched her back for three days; now I was going to show her mine.

"There's naught here but gravedigging." She put a hand on my arm. "We're still partners, since your friends razed Gleawanceaster."

"So I'm stuck with you? I don't think so."

"How far do you think you'll get with that accent? The

first time you open your mouth, they'll know what you are."

"A Danish poet/sheep trader from Ireland?"

"Laugh all you want. You'll be laughing out of the other side of your mouth when you're hanging from an oak tree."

The old woman was watching us talk, scratching her eczema thoughtfully. I took Caitria's elbow and led her back toward the river. "All right," I conceded. "Gleawanceaster's not what it was. I'll take you to the next big town upriver."

"That's generous." She laughed, shaking my hand off. "There's only one town between here and Weogornaceaster, and there's nothing much there."

"You kept your part of the bargain," I admitted. "And I will too. We'll find a place for you."

"Let's get to the other side of the river, then. This is Hwicca country; Magonsætan land's on the west bank."

We got back into the boat and I poled into the current. The Severn was still tidal that close to the channel, and the banks were reedy and overgrown with cattail. It was a pestilential place that smelled of ooze and rot, and only the lateness of the season kept us from being eaten to the bone by bloodsuckers. The boat had the handling characteristics of a log, and I could see it was going to be more work than it was worth. The dragons would make eight knots while I pushed the barge along at two.

"Walking will be faster," I said. "You know the river country?"

"Well enough," she said.

"Then you're back in the guide business." I nosed the boat into the reeds as far as it would go, and we got out and slogged through the muck to solid ground. We put up some ducks on the way, reminding me that my ham and onion lunch had been a long time ago.

"Shit," I said. "We should have gotten food back there."

"I found a few things," she said, slipping her hand into her pack and bringing out two eggs.

"It's a start," I said as she produced two more, and then a loaf, and without a pause three sausages. "You were busy." I grinned. "You didn't find a pot to cook them in, did you?"

She reached into the pack and came out with a small bronze cooking pot. The look on her face was characteristically wry. "I had to leave the tripod and cauldron," she said, putting everything back in the pack.

"Slacker," I complained. "Let's get some distance from the river and make a fire."

"All you do is eat," she said. "Maybe I can find some nice hedgehogs to go with."

We hiked into intermittent woodland and meadow. The sky was starting to cloud up again, so I stopped at the first suitable place and got a small fire going. Caitria cooked up the sausages and cracked the eggs into the bottom of the pot and scrambled them. I sliced the loaf. When we were done we had the famous English breakfast: greasy eggs, underdone sausages, and cold bread. It hasn't changed at all in twelve hundred years, but now they're so used to it they think it's good. Under the circumstances, it tasted pretty good to me. My half was gone before Caitria got started on hers.

We pushed on after dark, but we couldn't make headway in the tangled forest.

"How much farther is this town?" I asked.

"A few miles," she said. "If they haven't burned it and gone upriver, you'll be with your friends tomorrow morning."

"I'll be glad," I admitted. "I'll see you're dealt with fairly."

"So there's a reward for finding you lost in the woods?"

It's reward enough I didn't kill you, I thought, sneaking up on a man when he's just had a bath.

"Half of what I get from the vik," I said. "Sygtrygg told me he was keeping back a share."

"I haven't earned half a share," she said, "just for letting you come with me to Gleawanceaster."

"It may not be that big a share; don't get your hopes up."

When we were too tired to go any farther, we curled up under a deadfall and tried to get some sleep.

We woke up in the thin dawn light. There was fog among the trees like dry ice vapor in a low-budget movie. After another hour we struck the Roman roadbed and turned east. One more mile took us to the river, where the pylons of a ruined stone bridge were tumbled into the water. There were mast tops sticking out above the fog.

"Hello the ships," I called out.

"Who is it?" someone called back.

"Bran Snorrison."

I heard the thump of someone jumping into a small boat, and then the creak and splash of oars. In a moment one of the small boats slipped through the fog and grounded where the roadbed ran into the water. My brother Arinbjorn jumped out of the boat and ran up to me.

"We thought you were dead," he said, gripping my arms. "Thjodolf came back from the mountains wounded. He thought everyone else was killed."

"I saw Oddleif go down," I said. "I don't know about anyone else. Someone must have gotten through; the Welsh are moving."

"Where have you been?"

"Following you upriver. The Engs are calling up the fyrd. Are Byrnjold and Yngvar well?"

"Yes, but Yngvar got a cut when we burned the *burh* in the first town. He'll be showing it off when he gets home."

It was at that point that Arinbjorn looked over at Caitria. "Got yourself a captive too?"

I laughed and translated for her. "He thinks I captured you."

She stepped forward and delivered up a fast right to the middle of his face. He staggered back into the water and went down on his ass. "You better explain how things are," she shouted. "I don't plan to end up slaved out with the Engs."

I grabbed her arm and pulled her back. "This is my brother," I told her. "What are you doing?"

"I could have left you wandering around west of the dyke," she said. "Now you're planning to slave me out?"

"Take it easy, no one's slaving you out. It's a natural mistake."

I helped Arinbjorn out of the water. His nose was bleeding, and it looked like Caitria was in for a beating, or Arinbjorn in for a gutting, unless I intervened.

"This is Caitria," I told him. "She's half Welsh and half Magonsætan Eng. She helped me after the ambush, and we threw in together to get away."

"What'd she hit me for?"

"She's a little touchy," I said. "It's been a rough three days."

Arinbjorn rubbed his nose gingerly and looked at the blood on his fingertips. He was one of Sinmarra's sons, a few years older than me, and generally a fairly mellow sort, but there was assault and battery in his eyes when he looked at Caitria.

"Don't do it," I told him. "I owe her for getting me across the dyke and helping me avoid the Engs."

He straightened up slowly and nodded. "You better have a talk with her," he advised, more for my own good than hers. He got back into the boat and sat at the oars.

"Let's go." I gestured to Caitria. She sat in the stern keeping an eye on Arinbjorn, who watched her as he pulled the oars. I pushed the boat off the bank and went forward. The fleet was lashed together in the middle of the river, and everyone was up and getting ready to storm the town. There was a lot of purposeful movement on the decks. Arinbjorn called out as we approached the middle of the clutch and someone fended off the little boat with the butt of a spear. We bumped into the *Ice Skimmer,* Eirik Whale's boat. Eirik was stamping around by the tiller bar to get warm. He was wearing his mail shirt and swinging an axe in each hand to limber his shoulders.

"Eirik," I called out. "Where's Sygtrygg?"

He pointed down the line of ships with one of the axes and yawned prodigiously. Arinbjorn tied off the little boat, and I extended a hand over the gunnel to Caitria, which she ignored, putting a foot in an oar hole and vaulting over the shieldwall.

"She'd get along all right with Sinead," Arinbjorn said.

I nodded agreement. "Come on," I said to her. "Our ship's down this way."

We went over the gunnels from ship to ship until we got to the *Long Harrier,* at the end of the line. Rognvald saw me when I was two decks away and shouted out, "Sygtrygg, here's Bran back from the dead."

My shipmates greeted me when I stood on the *Long Harrier*'s deck again, and Sygtrygg pushed through them to give me a hug.

"So, brother, we thought you were dead in the woods."

"It was close," I admitted, "but my luck held and I got away."

"You always need luck," Skallagrim said, stepping up to greet me. "Sometimes luck's better than brains."

"This is Caitria," I said. "She helped me get out of Wales, and I told her we'd set her down where she wanted.

Arinbjorn took her for a captive and she bloodied his nose for him, so watch your step around her."

"She an Eng?" Sygtrygg asked, looking her over.

"Half and half," I said. "She was going to Gleawanceaster, but you burned it down first."

"They could've bought their town back," Sygtrygg said, "but they were too stiff-necked to pay."

"And too few to fight," said Rognvald, "but they fought anyway and paid in the end."

"Where do I stay?" Caitria asked, returning Sygtrygg's look with a challenging stare of her own.

"I'll find room for you on one of the knarr," I told her.

"The knarr are almost full," Skallagrim said.

"So you're not the only one can speak Eng," Caitria said, looking Skallagrim over.

"There aren't many," Skallagrim said, "but on Einar's boat they all speak Welsh."

"I'll stay with you," Caitria said to me. "You might get lost again without me."

Skallagrim looked at me with a smile. "You get lost back there?"

"I've been looking after him for three days," she said.

Skallagrim laughed and shook his head. "I've been looking after him for eighteen years."

"I don't have to stand for this abuse," I informed them, looking round for Thorleik Baster. "I want a bite before we take this town."

Thorleik made half a cold chicken appear, and I made it disappear while they untied the boats and drifted them apart. The thinning fog showed a town and *burh* through the trees on the east bank. A few solid strokes at the oars beached the boats and the Irish poured out. Sygtrygg made a gesture and the crews assembled by the prows.

"This is what it's all about," Skallagrim said as the pitch of energy and excitement aboard the boat reached a crescendo. "Now you're going to burn your first town. You stay here with me, girl," he said to Caitria.

It was a grim prospect. I could see the peaked roofs of the houses and the hall above the earthwork, and the thatch looked the same as Clontarf thatch. I thought about Snorri and Mairead and Frydys, as I hesitated at the gunnel, axe in hand. I had nothing against these people. I mean, Orm Jarl had been good to my family, but just because it was *his* wyrd to eat it big in Mercia didn't mean it had to be mine. I couldn't think of a single reason to burn that town: it wasn't going to bring Orm Jarl back, it wasn't going to bother Offa or Beorhtric, it wasn't going to give up even one man's weight in silver. There was no cost-effective business case for it, but there we were, shouting, screaming, slashing at the sky with our blades, getting ready to do what Vikings became famous for.

And there I was, not first in line, but not last either, running beside Rognvald over the well-trodden ground that led to the ditch and the earthwork as a fusillade of arrows and darts and stones began to full onto our assault. The jaws of the battlewyrm closed around the *burh* like it was a cake. Then Macc Oc's Irish breached the gate, and we pushed inside.

It was a typical Anglo-Saxon town. The common fields, stubbled after the harvest, were outside an earthwork topped by a log palisade equal to everything but catapult or flame, or mad Irishmen doing what they knew how to do. Once inside, you could tell civic planning was primitive. Two main streets divided the town into quadrants. There were seventy or eighty houses and a hall where the Ealdorman drank his beer, and the quadrants were subdivided by alleys. There was a spring inside to help them wait out a siege, but *siege* wasn't in Sygtrygg's wordhoard.

Soon there were six hundred Danes and Irish inside the walls, elbowing each other aside to get a piece of the two hundred Hwiccan Engs who'd formed up a shieldwall at the intersection of the main streets. It didn't last long, and in less than an hour the air was filled with the lamentations of women and the screaming of children and the whining of the gutted dogs as we moved among the bodies, finishing off the wounded and turning the place inside out in search of gold and silver.

The women were herded together and the quartermasters of the knarr appraised their worth on the open market. They were just cargo now, and if they wouldn't fetch back the cost of their keeping until the sale, there was no point in taking them aboard; they'd be driven off into the woods. Children were another thing. There was always a market for a child with thirty or forty good years of work ahead. Slaving was a profitable business.

But we were at the confluence of the Severn and the

Avon rivers, the juncture of two major Roman roads, and Sygtrygg expected the town to be at least as prosperous than the first one. True, they'd had time to escape, but they were affluent for Engs, and we knew middle-class pragmatism had convinced them to bury what they couldn't carry off. That's what people always did. It was easier to bury wealth and come back than to try to escape with it.

But at first we couldn't locate any hoards, and after putting the question to a few captives who died claiming ignorance, we resigned ourselves to whatever silver we could find on our own. All we really wanted to do was row back down the Severn and feel the salt wind again, but with Thorfinn along, Sygtrygg couldn't stop short of some significant event in this mad revenge saga.

Skäne was my idea of easy pickings; my ass puckered whenever I looked at the trees that crowded the Severn banks. Open-ocean raiding was what I'd signed on for, a quick assault on a beach out of the afternoon sun, maybe a *straandshug* up a shallow creek with one of Knute's farmsteads at the other end, but not worming my way up the ass end of Mercia like a Viking enema.

We spent the next couple of hours ferreting through the town looking in the same old hiding places. People are stunningly unoriginal when it comes to hiding their goods. The Hwiccans liked to plant their hoards in graveyards, on the mistaken theory we'd be afraid to dig up a fresh grave.

A fact about Vikings that's escaped general knowledge is that our town tossing expertise was specialized, generally because of our day jobs. A weller would plump the well, a thatcher would probe the roofs, a farmer would inspect recent cultivation. It was rare that we ran into something one of us didn't know well enough to tell if it hid loot. As it happened, there was a graveyard specialist among us.

There were four fresh graves in the boneyard: the first contained an old woman, dead of that disease; the second a man who looked like he'd fatally pissed off a boar sometime in the last week; and the remaining two were full of silver and plate. Sygtrygg let the men take their time, and Thorfinn, whose experience was wider than anyone's, directed the dismantling of walls and crofts, the uprooting of freshly paved surfaces, and the plumbing of wells with an expert's eye for each task. There was a goodly hoard to be squeezed from the town after all; enough to make us wonder what they'd carried off.

"Bran," Sygtrygg said when we ran into one another on the village common. "You know halls; have a poke through this one."

I looked round and spotted the hall, the largest building in the village, and nodded. "I doubt I'll find anything, but I'll have a look."

The doors had been torn out of the frame; one was on the ground in front of the threshold and the other hanging drunkenly on its top hinge. I stepped into the shadowed interior.

Eighth century halls had a common architecture no matter where you were. They were typically rectangular buildings, with the high seat opposite the door, in the middle of one of the long walls. There was a hearth down the center of the room. Benches were built into both long walls, and trestle tables, put by this time of day, stacked against one of the short walls. There were neither the clutter of a morning meal nor the remains of last night's supper, although a small neglected fire was burning itself out in one end of the hearth. They'd spent their night preparing to fight us. It must have been short rations at the ramparts.

I sat on the bench. Where would I hide something in a hall? Under the rushes? I swept the rushes up against the walls, but no one had been digging in the dirt floor underneath. In the walls? I had a look at the walls, but the timber slabs were intact, and only one plank thick. The roof beams? There was a ladder against the wall by the trestle tables, and I fetched it against one of the exposed beams and started up. My sword immediately got in the way, and I slipped the harness off my head and dropped it on the bench.

I was only on the third rung when someone came through the door. I looked down and saw Macc Oc.

"I thought you were dead," he said.

"Sorry to disappoint you," I said.

"Maybe you haven't." He was carrying one of the long-handled war axes the Engs liked, and he hefted it meaningfully. I had to laugh at the situation. I'd had something like this in mind for him. A sense of irony can save something from even the worst situations. I dropped off the ladder and looked over at my sword. It would be close, but I thought I could get to it before he could reach me with the axe. After that, we'd see what we'd see.

"So I reckon you're not here to help me look for loot."

He started to swing the axe as I dove for the sword. I got to it and rolled aside, expecting the axe to fall at the same time, but when I looked up I saw that someone had stepped into the hall behind Macc Oc and grabbed the axe just below the head, at the exact moment in his swing when the least force would have the most effect. He strained uselessly into the swing, an involuntary grunt erupting from his lips. I grabbed the sword hilt with both hands and tossed the scabbard aside.

"Chopping wood indoors?" I heard a familiar voice ask.

Macc Oc turned around, still a little off balance, and Caitria put her boot into his gut and shoved, letting go of the axe. He toppled into the hall and fell across the hearth, exposing his belly. I laid the point of the sword on his throat and leaned over him.

"I ought to open you up," I said. "Don't you think I ought to open him up, Caitria?"

"He was going to open you up," she acknowledged. "It only seems fair."

"See, it seems fair to her," I translated for Macc Oc.

He squirmed. The bed of coals was hot underneath his ass. That's when I realized where you hide something in a hall. "Get up, asshole," I said, lifting the point away from his throat.

"Who is this?" Caitria asked, stepping down into the hall.

"This is Macc Oc," I said as he got to his feet. "Warlord of the Irish Vikings."

"Why was he going to split you?"

"Long story," I said.

"Everything's a long story with you," she complained. "Isn't there a short version?"

"You're lucky," Macc Oc said, brushing the ashes off his ass.

"I'd say you were the lucky one." I shook my head. "You're lucky I remembered not to kill you; it almost slipped my mind." I picked up the axe and started probing the ash bed. "Go lead your men," I said. "They must be lost without you."

Macc Oc glared at me and started out of the hall, shouldering Caitria aside on his way out. She gave ground and slipped her foot between his ankles as he passed, so he stumbled headlong out the doorway into the common.

She came down beside me and watched me digging in the ash bed. "Lose something?"

"Looking for loot," I said. "What are you doing here?"

"Saving your worthless head again," she said. "No thanks necessary."

"Thanks anyway," I said. "It would have been close if you hadn't happened along."

"You can't count on me saving your ass all the time," she said.

"I'll remember that," I assured her, turning back to the hearth. The axe wasn't the tool I needed, though, and I discarded it in favor of an iron spit. I stirred the ashes with it for a minute or two before I snagged something. It didn't take long to improve the hole, and in short order I exposed a brass vessel. Its surface was hot from the fire, and as I toed it out of the hole, coins rattled inside it.

Caitria wrapped her hands in a sheepskin from the benches and picked it out of the hearth. It was stoppered with a fist-sized lump of baked clay that crumbled when I hit it with the spit, and she poured a double handful of silver coin onto the bench at the foot of the high seat. That was a worthwhile little haul, and I sat back with a satisfied smile.

Caitria swept the coins into the sheepskin with the side of her hand and weighed them roughly. "Worth the story of why that Irishman was trying to kill you?" she said.

"If you want the short version, this is it: he's an asshole and I let him know it whenever I have an opportunity, but Orm Jarl's son, Sygtrygg, who's ruling Clontarf now, wants him to marry his sister to secure us with the Irish. Sygtrygg's my foster brother, and he's asked me to leave Macc Oc alone."

Caitria nodded as if she comprehended the gist of the story. "Looks like it's too late now, if you've pissed him off to the point he'd come at you with an axe."

"He's a hot-tempered lad," I conceded. "I may have pushed him a little too far."

"What makes you think so?" she asked dryly.

"Find anything?" Sygtrygg came into the hall with Thorfinn and Skallagrim.

"A pot of coins in the hearth," I said.

"And an Irishman with an axe," Caitria added.

"What?" Skallagrim asked.

So I had to tell them what had happened. Sygtrygg wasn't happy about it.

"Did you provoke him?" he wanted to know.

"Only if you think defending yourself's provocative. He just came in with an axe and announced he was going to murder me."

"If I hadn't come in, Bran would have been split," Caitria finished the story for me.

"Maybe." I shrugged. "Maybe not. But there would have been a fight, no doubt of it."

"We have to do something about this," Thorfinn said, sitting down on the bench. "We can't have Macc Oc killing anyone, any more than we can have anyone killing Macc Oc."

"I could have taken his head, but I let him go," I said.

"Very sensible," Skallagrim said.

But before we could discuss it, Flosi Stemhugger, the fo'c'sleman on the *Arvak,* came into the hall looking for Sygtrygg.

"The fyrd's on the other side of the river," he said.

It's always something on a vik. The Magonsætan had levied three hundred men since the fleet had been on the Severn, a hundred men a day, not as many as they could raise in a month, but enough deal with the Welsh force that had come across the border. There was no use trying to sort out who was attacking and who was counterattacking, the causality of violence on the Welsh marches was long past reduction to first causes.

After they'd skirmished with the fyrd for the better part of a rainy afternoon, the Welsh had simply melted back into the forest and left the Magonsætans to police up their dead and wounded. The fyrd was about to disband when a messenger caught them up with news of boats on the Severn, and they'd force-marched east along the Roman road for Tewkesbury, which was the name of the town we'd just burned.

Their untimely arrival made us leave off looking for loot. They came to the smoke of the burned towns like bears to a cloud of bees, already tasting the honey, and while the Magonsætans who'd fought the Welsh were assembling on the west bank of the Severn, two columns of Hwiccans arrived on the Roman road that ran north from the ruins of Gleawanceaster.

Sygtrygg ordered everyone into the boats and we pulled out into the river to wait for them. By early afternoon they'd pushed out of the trees on the south side of Tewkesbury, crossed the Avon, and moved quickly to the riverbank. We were in a good position; they couldn't get to us and their force was split by the river.

There was a half hour of shouting and sporadic archery while they ranged their troops on the riverbanks and rattled their blades on their shields. Half the dragons faced the east bank and half the west. Caitria looked at me with apprehension.

"If they take the ship, I can always tell them I was captured downriver," she said, planning aloud for that contingency.

"No one's taking this ship," Skallagrim told her. "But you ought to stay below the freeboard in case their aim improves."

The tension was building on the Severn. Sygtrygg was wearing his mail shirt, a garment which he only put on for ceremonial or exceptionally paranoid occasions. Course encouragement passed from bench to bench, forward and aft between Rognvald at the prow and Sygtrygg at the star board as the crew psyched itself up for the afternoon's work.

Then we heard a voice rise from the *Blood Raven* in punch-line cadence, followed instantly by an answering chorus of laughter. One of the Jomsvikings was telling jokes. We looked at each other in disbelief, and then the tension melted like dew. Thorfinn's crew wasn't worried, and they knew better than anyone what to expect.

As if the laughter of Jomsvikings could cut fog, it began to thin out and finally the sun burned through to the deck. Cloaks came off, spirits warmed, and we took a good look at the Anglo-Saxon fyrd. They were a nackered-looking lot, showing the effects of the march, but they were drawn up in smart battle formation in case we came ashore.

When I looked down the line of dragons, I saw that the boys in the *Blood Raven* were all business now. No more jokes and pissing over the side. The shieldwall was up, their spears flashed in the sunlight, and the archers were standing to with nocked shafts. The berserks were gathered in a tight circle at the mast, impatiently testing the weight of their axes. I felt a peculiar itching between my exposed shoulder blades.

"What do you want?" shouted a voice from across the river in a kind of mangled, secondhand Danish that had us exchanging bewildered glances until we figured it out.

The Jomsvikings laughed, as if they'd been waiting for the cue. "We want revenge for Orm Jarl's death," Thorfinn shouted back, taking the initiative as spokesman.

"Who?" came the answer.

"Orm Jarl Skeggöx," Thorfinn shouted back louder, as if volume alone would jog the man's memory.

"Never heard of him."

"Killed a year ago by Beorhtric and Offa," Thorfinn attempted to clarify our mission.

We could hear Magonsætan and Hwiccan laughter from opposite riverbanks. "*That* fool?" came the answer. "The one sailed up to Beorhtric's wedding feast demanding money?"

"There's a blood debt," Thorfinn announced.

"Anyone who'd avenge a thief must be equally a thief," came the answer from the greenwood.

A dozen arrows whistled from either bank toward the *Blood Raven*; no one moved as the crossfire raked the deck. Two of the arrows hit Thorfinn square in the torso and the shafts buckled. He must have been wearing a mail shirt under his tunic, but the effect as the arrows shattered was electric. He opened his arms in a wide embrace and bellowed out a defiant laugh. His berserks all bowed to the mast, hoisting up their shirttails and dropping their pants to show the startled Magonsætans and Hwiccans their bare Jomsviking asses. "I hear you Engs practice shooting at butts on the common. We'll give you targets you're accustomed to," Thorfinn called out.

Another flight came out of the trees, but the sheer gall of the act unnerved the archers, because the closest they came was to hit the mast above the berserks' backs. Most of the arrows buzzed into the water with a liquid *thurp*.

"As much fun as this is, we're here for Offa," Thorfinn called to them.

"Offa's preparing for Yule," their leader called back, "and not to be bothered by thieves on the Severn."

"Who're you?" Thorfinn demanded.

"Wulfstan," the man told him. "Ealdorman of the Hwiccans."

Thorfinn turned to the west bank and called out: "Who's in charge of you rabble?"

"Oslac, Ealdorman among the Magonsætans."

"Offa's sent his dogs to deal with us," Thorfinn shouted to the fleet at large. "He's hiding in his stronghold while we punish his people. Engs can't amount to much if they stand for that."

"You've leave to come to ground and see how Beorhtric's dogs bite," Wulfstan shouted out, and the Engs on both riverbanks rattled their blades on their shields.

"Where's Offa keeping Yule?" Thorfinn demanded. "I've a mind to visit him."

"He badly wants to see you," Wulfstan answered. "He sent me to bring your head. The rest of you may follow or hang about waiting for your leader's return."

The Engs laughed; we all knew that Wulfstan's idea of hanging about involved hemp and oak limbs. Skallagrim stretched out his legs and yawned. These flytings could go on as long as men had the wit and breath for it, and he was making himself comfortable. Caitria sat beside him, listening with great interest. I joined them.

"Any verses coming to mind?" I asked him.

"I've twenty each devoted to the towns we've sacked."

"Forty verses is a start. What about Sygtrygg's bravery?"

"Oh, he's brave enough," Skallagrim admitted. "I watched him on the earthwork three days ago when he put his axe in his teeth and tore the burning palisade apart with his bare hands."

"You'd think that deed would be good for a couplet at least," I mused.

Skallagrim smiled. "I thought you were going to take care of praising your foster brother."

"I don't want to compete with you," I told him.

"Fair enough," he said. "I'll compose about Thorfinn, you compose about Sygtrygg, and we'll both compose about the vik."

"It's a deal," I agreed, and we slapped hands on it.

Meanwhile, Thorfinn and Wulfstan had progressed to the predictable insults about one another's parentage.

"Your mother sucks Walloon cocks for," Wulfstan

shouted in a sparkling syntactical blunder as he tried to put together a creditable flyting in an alien tongue. Forcing them to speak Danish even though we had linguists aboard was a brilliant ploy to keep them uneasy and slightly confused.

"Your mother *has* a cock," Thorfinn rejoined.

"If she has, your mother's sucked it," Wulfstan shot back.

It was clear that there was little literary gold to spin from the dross of this witty badinage, so I closed my eyes and tried to catch some sleep. It was a no-hoper, though, and as I tried unsuccessfully, the level of discussion sank even lower. I opened my eyes to see Wulfstan pointing his spear in Thorfinn's direction and making masturbatory gestures.

Just then, Macc Oc seized his opportunity to join the discussion, which had finally sunk to a level he could grasp. When Thorfinn stopped for breath, Macc Oc shouted out Wulfstan's name and bent over to show him his bare ass. Macc Oc had scarcely grabbed his knees when an arrow in a flat trajectory homed in on his exposed behind, penetrating both cheeks and pinning him to the mast.

The Hwiccans lost their composure and fell to the ground laughing, and the commotion as Kalf set about the task of unpinning Macc Oc kept them helpless. He'd been solidly hit, and Kalf first had to slit his pants down the back and then slip the open jaws of the rigging shears into the valley between his cheeks and cut the shaft before two men could pull him away from the mast. Then Kalf put a foot on Macc Oc's hip, grasped the feathered end of the shaft, and pulled it free.

The laughter and shouts drove a flock of ducks up from the wetland on the other side of the river, and their quacking as they wheeled over the fleet echoed the Engs' laughter. Several Hwiccan spearmen in the front rank fell into the Severn. Macc Oc shook his fists as he stood stiff-assed on the deck, but it only incited them to new heights of ridicule, shouting, and clutching their asses.

Then the *Blood Raven* glided past us, heading straight for Wulfstan. I got a good look at Thorfinn's face as they went by, and my knees went weak at the sight. He was red as the *Blood Raven*'s sail and veins stood out like cords against his skull. The berserks were moving to the foredeck, axes in hand, and the oarsmen were laboring to drive the boat right up on the beach among the Engs. Macc Oc had interrupted Thorfinn's flyting and made fools of us all, and now Wulfstan was going to suffer for it. None of the other boats had time to react as the *Blood Raven* closed the distance to the riverbank, and the Hwiccans, japing at Macc Oc, didn't seem to notice until the dragon's head loomed above them, but then it was too late.

The *Blood Raven*'s keel scraped on the muddy bottom and momentum carried the boat two spear lengths onto land before it stopped and the dragon's head listed a little to the left, as if listening for the rest of the fleet. Ten or fifteen of the Hwiccans were knocked aside as the bow pushed into them, and then the berserks were overboard, blades humming, axes biting, spears collecting Hwiccans like beads on needles.

Thorfinn moved his archers to the prow behind the berserks, and they poured a half dozen volleys into the Hwiccans, so the men retreating from the advancing axes began to stumble over the bodies of their fallen companions. Then the second wave tumbled off the *Blood Raven* and moved into the open space the berserks had created, finishing off the wounded with deft thrusts of sword and spear, and the archers rose up again and poured more arrows into the confused flanks.

The berserks formed a kind of flying wedge formation and pointed it right at Wulfstan. Then they settled down to the sluggish work of hacking their way through the wall of flesh that separated them. By the time our keels scraped bottom along the open bank of the Avon, Thorfinn, fighting at odds of ten to one, had already achieved ground superiority. All that was left was for us to kill the confused and leaderless militia. The Irish swarmed ashore to avenge the insult to their leader, but Macc Oc himself would be waiting this one out.

I dropped to the ground and took a step, immediately falling over something round and hard that turned out to be a severed leg. I lost my axe when I went down, and it was kicked away by those who followed me, tripping and getting back up to push on toward the Hwiccans. It was a completely different battle from the ground, and as I rolled aside to avoid being trampled, I gained a new appreciation for the melee. Thanks to Hollywood, when you think of swordfights you think of Basil Rathbone and Errol Flynn

parrying steel with ringing steel. Nothing could be further
from the truth. Your average eighth century fight involved
someone hacking at your shield while someone else tried
to spear your uncovered flank or chop off your feet with a
dull axe.

Most wounds by far—as many as seventy-five percent—
were leg wounds, which accounts for the number of swords
called "Legbiter," "Legbeater," "Legsmasher," "Leg-
mauler," etc. Legs were the most vulnerable part of a man
protected by a ten-pound shield and a three- or four-pound
sword and maybe a fifty-pound mail shirt, if he was rich
enough to afford one. All that ringing steel and flashing
swordplay and flowing lace was invented for a soundstage
about twelve hundred years after the battle at the confluence of the Severn and Avon rivers. The day Macc Oc had
his cheeks stapled to the dragon's mast it was hacked legs,
severed arms, and smashed skulls. Lots of blood and unattached limbs down there on the ground where I was scrambling out of the way.

Without an axe my offensive options were limited, so I
scurried back into the water and pulled myself along the
side of the *Long Harrier* until I could climb aboard. Skallagrim and Caitria were standing amidships watching the fight
develop, and they gave me a hand over the side.

"Back so soon?" Caitria asked.

"Madness," I told her, leaning against the spear rack aft
of the mast as I shook the water out of my hair.

"Not going out to play again?" Caitria inquired.

I ignored her as best I could and held up a shield against
stray arrows. Meanwhile, the battle was winding down
along that stretch of riverbank. Wulfstan had come out of
the town and taken up his position at the ferry landing that
connected Tewkesbury to the Roman road on the west
bank. The Hwiccans weren't able to array their lines to
best advantage because of the ruined town, and so they
couldn't reinforce their center, where the ferocity and sheer
insanity of the *Blood Raven*'s assault had carried the day.

It was the first time we'd seen Thorfinn's crew do their
stuff, and they were impressive: in the time it took me to
get back aboard, Thorfinn's lads had carved a swath halfway through the closely packed militia, caught between
Tewkesbury and the river, and killed nearly a hundred

Engs. When the Engs finally realized they ought to run for it, they didn't have the chance.

The other crews had sliced through the thinner ranks on either end of the battle line and flanked them through the town. I could see men running in the dirt streets and hear shouts as the Hwiccans were hunted down and killed. If any escaped the hour, they'd have to be swift and unencumbered by extra weight.

Half the fleet had beached on the other side of the river, but the Magonsætans, with a good view of what was happening to the Hwiccans and a pitch battle with the Welsh in their own recent past, didn't seem all that interested in fighting Danes. They fell back into the forest ahead of the attack, and Kalf Agirson realized the insanity of pursuing them into the wilderness before it was too late. He imposed order on the assault, called in the Irish, and left a force to secure the west. By the time the mast's shadow had moved closer to the dragon's neck, the Irish and Danes were coming back laden with the weapons and ornaments of dead Hwiccans and Magonsætans.

The berserks had taken Wulfstan, wounded but alive, with his standard, and they brought him to Thorfinn at the prow of the *Blood Raven*, where the captains gathered to see what he'd do to the man who said his mother sucked Walloon cocks for.

"Wulfstan," Thorfinn said amiably as the berserks threw the Eng to his knees. "Any last words?"

"Your mother doesn't suck Walloon cocks for," Wulfstan said.

"Well spoken." Thorfinn laughed, raising his axe.

"Now I think of it," Wulfstan mused, "it was a Geat that told me about her. He said most of the whores in the Dane mark had sucked him off, and your mother had the sweetest lips of all."

Thorfinn laughed in appreciation as Wulfstan refined his insult in the face of death. It was the sort of bravado he understood. "Greet the ravens for me," he said, taking Wulfstan's head off with a smooth sweep of arm and blade, like an effortless nine iron to the green. Thorfinn and the captains stepped aside as Wulfstan's headless body sat back gushing on its heels. Thorfinn picked up Wulfstan's severed head and regarded it thoughtfully.

"Not much of a fighter," he said. "But a ready wit in the face of doom."

"There's a few others," said Hoketil, one of the dragon captains.

"Bring them out," Sygtrygg commanded.

After the captains spent a minute admiring Wulfstan's severed head and Thorfinn's technique, they moved aside as four Hwiccans were pushed forward. One had lost his left leg below the knee, and another was dyeing his tunic red with the blood from a slash that should have severed his arm. We wouldn't be getting anything out of them. Thorfinn nodded to the men holding them up, and the prisoners were dropped to the ground and killed quickly. "I hate to see captives suffer," Thorfinn said, shaking his head in distaste.

The other two were less severely wounded. Sygtrygg looked at them for a minute while he decided what to do.

"Do you know where Offa keeps Yule?" he asked.

"Close enough he can be here in a week with a host," one of them promised. "Stay awhile, and Offa will come."

"Pity we can't wait," Sygtrygg said. "We've wasted too much time on this piss puddle of a river already." He nodded at the men who were holding the Hwiccan's arms, and they wrestled him to the ground, pried open his mouth, and had his tongue on the point of a knife in under half a minute.

"You," Sygtrygg said to the other one. "You'll have to tell Offa what happened here; your friend will guide you."

"I don't need a guide to Offa's court," the Hwiccan said.

"Even in the dark?" Sygtrygg asked him. In another moment the Hwiccan was blind.

"Bind them together," Sygtrygg ordered, and while the blind man was being tied to the mute, he gave them their marching orders.

"Tell Offa we came to avenge Orm Jarl Skeggöx of Clontarf, killed last year in the spring. Tell him we'll be back next year to collect a danegeld or plunder, whichever he pleases. Tell him that Sygtrygg Orm Jarlsson and Thorfinn Skullsplitter broke his fyrd."

Thorfinn took the arm of the blinded man and threaded his fingers into Wulfstan's hair. "Give him his dog's head," he said. "And tell him I'm sorry I couldn't bring it myself."

The captains shouted and drove the two of them away with the flats of their swords.

There was quite a haul in torques and arm rings and brooches, not to mention twenty-two pounds of silver and three of gold from the purses of the dead. The wapentake was impressive too: dozens of swords and axes; hundreds of spears, arrows, knives, five mail shirts, twelve iron helms, carved horns, clothing. Since Offa wasn't coming to hand, it would have to satisfy Thorfinn's thirst for revenge.

"Offa can send his dogs pack after pack," Thorfinn announced when the wapentake was finished. "We'll be worn down to nothing if we wait. I'll kill him some other time."

That cheered up the Clontarfmen considerably, Sygtrygg above all, and we loaded the plunder into the knarr and turned the dragons downstream to swim with the current for the open sea.

We weren't sorry to turn our backs on Eng land, and Eng land wasn't sorry to see them, but before we'd gone a mile downriver, the sniping started again. Caitria and Skallagrim went into the crawl space below the deck. Arrows felled on unprotected men in every boat. One of them whistled by my head as I bent forward over the oar on the return stroke and nailed the man across the deck. Whenever the river narrowed a little, the arrows flew, so Sygtrygg ordered the Irish ashore to sweep down the banks.

That put an end to the sniping, but it slowed our progress. The Irish couldn't move through the woods fast enough to keep up with the fleet riding the downstream current, and we had to hold the boats back so we didn't outrace them. It took us the rest of the day and all night to gain the mouth of the Severn, more Hwiccans and Magonsætan barking after us every mile. We lost thirty men going downriver, and all the Irish had to show for it when we collected them was a mere sixty heads, and twelve of them were women. Finally, the river widened, and the sea mares began to buck as the Severn poured itself into the ocean. We were all glad to have open water around us again.

"We never got to the next big town on the river," I told Caitria, "so I reckon we'll set you ashore here."

"What's here?" she demanded looking at the Welsh coast. "It's the same as what I left."

"You think you've bought a passage?"

"I think you owe me a town that's not on fire," she said. "That was the bargain we made."

Skallagrim shrugged his shoulders and smiled. "She can earn her keep helping Thorleik Baster," he said.

"The cook?" she yelped. "I'm not a scullery drudge."

"You're a Viking now," I pointed out. "And Vikings do what they have to do to make their share."

"Think it over," Skallagrim said. "We'll be back in Rhymby soon; tell us what then."

We spent the first day off the Severn beached at Rhymby, and Einar met his Welsh friends and we picked up Eyjolf and his son Hrapp. Oddleif and Halldor had died in the woods.

Caitria had a look round the land of her birth and decided to come along as Thorleik's assistant. We traded some of the Hwiccan slaves for a few beeves and slaughtered them for food.

The next morning we were well out in the channel before Sygtrygg blew the horn for us to come together. The sky was clear and the wind calm, and we tied the boats together head to tail, so we could walk the length of the clutch on dry feet. The Jomsvikings were in a mood to celebrate because Thorfinn had avenged Orm Jarl, and the rest of us because we'd survived. I was happy to be breathing salt air and pissing over the side; many weren't there to enjoy those sensations. The vik had cost us upward of ninety dead, but the cost to Offa was more: two towns and seven villages razed, and three hundred men at arms laid low. It was Orm Jarl's geld.

6

Coasting Eng Land

Bandy no speech with a bad man.
Often the better is beaten
In a word fight by the worse.
    —The Sayings of the Wise One

We were in a partying mood, so we hauled out one of those beeves and opened a few kegs of looted beer and got an early start. Cooking on the deck of a wooden ship's a ticklish skill, but Thorleik soon had everything in good order: the beef roasting on the spit, the onions and beans boiling in a saltwater soup. Lines went over the side and an assortment of fish were quickly swimming in the pots. Then we finished off the beer and broached the first cask of ale and started toasting ourselves.

The sunset was spectacular, crimsons and ochers, lingering pinks and madders; Thorfinn was moved to tears at the sight of it. It was good to be alive, and we knew what we were talking about: what we did to those towns up the Severn might happen to Clontarf someday. It was the eighth century. Things like that were common, and that knowledge led to the sort of shoot-first-and-ask-questions-later existentialism that all of us had been schooled in since birth.

After the first cask of ale was empty, we sampled some more Hwiccan beer. It was brown and heavy-tasting, the kind of brew that has weight: liquid bread—an unfastener of tongue and bowel. After a few horns of it, Skallagrim offered to recite his first verses about the vik. Thorfinn and Sygtrygg were not a little shit-faced and agreed to hear them, but before he could properly lubricate his throat,

word of the impending entertainment went round, and
Macc Oc limped over with his two bards.

Macc Oc hadn't been much in evidence since he'd shown
his ass to the Hwiccan fyrd. Thorfinn and Sygtrygg were
pissed at him for interrupting the flyting, especially since
Thorfinn had been getting the better of Wulfstan. Macc
Oc's foolishness had broken his rhythm and embarrassed
us all. The fact that the Hwiccans had paid Macc Oc for it
by pinning him to the mast was no matter to Thorfinn.

Macc Oc came slowly from one boat to the other, hobbling on his spear, his two bards in his wake carrying their
harps and cushions for Macc Oc's wounded ass. Conversation stopped as he stepped gingerly over the gunnel to the
deck of the *Long Harrier* and came aft, where Thorfinn
and Sygtrygg, the boat captains and fo'c'sleman, and Skallagrim and I were lounging around with horns of brown beer
and bowls of bouillabaisse.

"If the time's come for harping," Macc Oc announced,
pausing to look for a place to sit and finding that no one
was making room for him, "I've brought a fine pair to pluck
the strings."

"Have a seat, then." Sygtrygg offered malignly, gesturing
to the bare oak deck. "And tune them up while I slip the
traces on my word hawk and let him soar."

Skallagrim smiled and took a breath, when Macc Oc
interrupted.

"Let the old raven rest," Macc Oc suggested. "We'll
begin with the best and hear the croaking of the mediocre
when the ale's nearly gone, the better to appreciate it."

Skallagrim stood up slowly, and I saw Thorfinn smile; the
thought of an old skald slipping steel in this Gaelic peacock
amused him no end. However, while the traditional immunity for skalds in voice might be stretched to cover killing
Macc Oc if it came to a defense at the Thing, the Irish
weren't bound by our laws, Brehon law was a different
thing, and Macc Oc dead for impugning Skallagrim's skaldskill was as bad as Macc Oc dead for interrupting Thorfinn's flyting, or for coming between me and Frydys.

"I set the order of singing," Sygtrygg announced.
"You're on the *Long Harrier,* not in your hall, but there's
merit in getting these two hummingbirds out of the way.
Let them give us a tune."

Skallagrim stiffened and looked around at Sygtrygg, who

placidly returned his look and nodded for him to resume his seat. "More ale," he called, and Caitria brought more ale aft in a small cask and sat beside me to listen.

The harpers dropped their cushions on the deck, and Macc Oc lowered himself to such comfort as he could find there. While his bards tuned, we drained the cask and called out for another. Macc Oc had to ask for a horn, and one came with the next cask, accompanied grudgingly by a plate of cold fish and a spade-cut turnip. Then the bards sang *The Destruction of Da Derga's Hostel,* a story that begins with a dreaming druid and ends an interminable time later with bodies from horizon to horizon and someone pouring water into the mouth of a severed head. Under ordinary circumstances, it was an entertaining story, but that night the audience was disposed to be rude, and the captains talked loudly about the possibilities for plunder in Skåne, and the quality of low-country ale.

Macc Oc was too arrogant to let it affect him, and so the bard sang to an unappreciative audience. Skallagrim and I listened as a professional courtesy. When the first bard was finished, Sygtrygg belched and announced that Thord the Jolly would warm up the crowd before Skallagrim's turn.

Thord walked to the mast. He wore his usual smile, for Thord was a man who was amused by life's secret joke, and it was this characteristic which earned him his nickname, but while he may have attained a sage's detachment about his wyrd, one vanity he cultivated was vast pride in his hair. Now, almost all Danes had great hair; it was one of our less ferocious attributes that history omitted to record and which archaeologists had to reconstruct to explain all those combs they were digging up. But Thord took an inordinate pleasure in his wavy sun-blond hair, which he was always grooming with a comb fashioned out of whalebone and elk antler.

In his capacity as stand-up comic, Thord the Jolly, leader of the *Bloodraven*'s berserks, used this implement to direct audience response as he built the rhythm of his routine, and to comb his hair, which he wore thick and loose across his shoulders.

"Have you heard about the Irishman goes into a mead hall carrying a leather bag and walks up to the Jarl and demands a seat, big as you please. 'I'm a famous berserk and I've a thirst,' he says.

"The Jarl's insulted but in fact he recognizes the Irish-man as the famous berserk McOak of Uí Naught, so he invites him to the table despite his manners. The Jarl's woman serves up the guest horn to McOak and he drains it off in a long pull, ale dribbling out of the corners of his mouth and down his neck.

"He hands the horn back to the Jarl's woman and says, 'Another,' and then the leather bag starts squirming on the table and out pops a little gnome of a man dressed like McOak of Uí Naught, wearing the same shirt and pants and laced-up boots and carrying a little blade like the big one McOak was wearing when he came into the hall. The little gnome draws his blade and starts down the boards, kicking over cups and striding across plates loaded with food, leaving gravy tracks from plate to plate, booting on-ions into the chests of the startled warriors, and stabbing out with the miniature sword at anyone who makes a grab for him. All the time the gnome's cursing and screaming oaths in the vilest speech. When he gets to the end of the boards, he turns round and goes back, stepping onto the plates he'd missed on the way up and elbowing over the remaining cups of mead. When he gets back to McOak's leather sack he steps into it and pulls it up over his head.

"Everyone in the hall's stunned and they all look at McOak with their mouths open. 'More ale,' McOak shouts, and they all move again, and the Jarl's woman brings back the guest horn. The Jarl doesn't say anything to him be-cause he's a guest, and no one else can ask him about the little gnome in the sack.

"McOak tosses back another horn and belches out his appreciation for the brewing and the sack starts squirming again and the gnome sheds it like a snakeskin and starts up the other end of the board, kicking over cups, stomping carrots under his boot, splashing through venison and pud-dles of gravy. He stops and pisses on a loaf of rye bread, then he goes back to the leather sack and gets inside again.

"This time the Jarl has to say something, so he waits while the commotion settles down and his woman brings McOak of Uí Naught a third horn of ale.

" 'I have to ask about the gnome in the sack,' the Jarl says. 'He's wrecking my hall.'

" 'Oh, him,' McOak says. 'Once I found a hoard and there was a gnome guarding it, but I took him by surprise and captured him. He offered me wishes to free him, and I told him I'd take three.

" ' "Fine," says the gnome.

" 'Now in a situation like this, your first wish should always be for wealth,' McOak tells the Jarl. 'So that's what I wished for and the gnome trebled the size of the hoard with a snap of its fingers and gave it all to me. Ever since I've had gold and silver without end.'

" 'Next I tell the gnome I want victory in every contest, of whatever kind. Battle play, word play, woman play, weather play, whatever the contest, I'm to have victory.'

" ' "Granted," says the gnome. "But that's more than one wish."

"And McOak reminds the gnome that he was fair captured and that McOak could kill him if he wanted.

" 'Ever since then I've never lost,' McOak said. 'I've become a great berserk, cut off the heads of every enemy I met, spoken more pleasingly than any skald, won the girl of my desire without trouble from any rival.'

"Then McOak starts to drink off the horn again, but the Jarl puts a hand on his arm and stops him.

" 'What about the third wish?' the Jarl asks.

" 'I wished for a twelve-inch prick.' McOak gives the leather sack a nudge with his elbow. 'And that's him.' "

It was a variation of the joke that Snorri'd told me when I came of age legally on my twelfth birthday, and the audience, seeded as it was with Thord's own berserks, like comedy club regulars who'd never heard one of Thord's stories they didn't like, erupted with laughter and started slapping one another on the shoulders and wiping away their tears. Macc Oc looked like a man whose head was about to explode with a murderous distemper, but Thord was too formidable an opponent, so all he could do was seethe.

It was plain that Macc Oc didn't have the proper mindset for viking; detachment and the ability to enjoy a joke at his own expense were beyond his grasp. I fancied I could see Sygtrygg reassessing his plan. Marrying Frydys to Macc Oc meant kinship with Macc Oc, meant feasting with Macc Oc, meant the duties owed a brother-in-law. Maybe Sygtrygg was ready to consider an alternate.

Thord left the mast and Skallagrim took his place. I sat ready with ink and paper to record Skallagrim's verses, and after another splash of beer to wet his throat, Skallagrim

lost no time delivering this modest panegyric to the bravery
of Thorfinn Skullsplitter.

The ring-giver gave   a good account of
The killing of Orm Jarl   of Clontarf. How the keelroad
Took him off to feast   at the feast of Offa's
Daughter wed.   The whaleroad rang with the laughter
   of Orm.

As he offered a geld   to Offa of Mercia. Then
Thorfinn the strong   the splitter of skulls
Came to greet the goodly Orm.   But the gods had willed
That the ring-giver rotted,   ravens' food in the land of
   the Engs.

And Sygtrygg his son   sat in the high seat
Giver of rings, greeter of guests.   Goldfingered Sygtrygg
The lord of Clontarf, loudly   he laughed to meet
With Odhinn's foundling,   fearless Thorfinn, Orm's

Companion in younger years.   In the skullsplitter's youth,
He'd ridden the rough seas   to raid with Orm
To drink with Orm the draught   of death, blade-toasting
Foes, reddening swords, feeding   brightly the flames of
   doom.

He came to Clontarf not expecting   Orm to be dead
   in Mercia.
His raven flew upon the wind   to feed with his friend
A friendship feast but found   instead his friend the food
Of wolves in Mercia. Wyrd   is the woven fabric of our

Lives, and blind is the heart   that loses sight
Of duty to the dead.   And so delay was not a thing
That bladebreaker could abide   or calmly bear a blood
   debt.
Clattering blades called for killing   keen for blood in Mercia.

The Raven flew in Sygtrygg's flock   and few would feast
When wind-wings soared   and wounds were scored in
   Offa's
Land. But Offa's boasts were   given breath by Offa's dogs
Among the ranks, and blades were reddened.   Red the sky

Above the burning towns below baptized in blood in
  Hwiccan land.
The arrowstorm, the awesome sight of shattered shafts
  on Thorfinn's
Chest, the shining moons that smiled and shone
In sunlight on the Severn such sights the archers

Foiled, and flights of arrows found no marks.
We burned the towns, to tell the truth, we tortured Offa's
Wardog Wulfstan. Thorfinn wounded him with words.
His wyrd it was to wrestle twice, two wounds he felt

Before the sun had soared higher in the Severn sky.
The first was dealt with deftness and delivered to his pride.
The next was not so gentle: not another time would
Wulfstan see the starbeard spread across the chin of night.

"Come here, Skallagrim, you're embarrassing me," Thorfinn said, hoisting up that twenty-four carat sleeve. Gold
rings caught the red light of burning torches and made rich
lightnings on the hawktree he offered for Skallagrim to
perch on. "If I keep listening to this I'll start to believe it
myself. Take what you want."

Now, at any one time, Thorfinn wore enough gold on
that arm to drown a fat woman, so an offer like that was
a stunning gesture of appreciation: to refuse would be insulting. Skallagrim selected the third ring in line, and when
Thorfinn stripped the other two off to get to it, he threw
them in as well.

Even in Orm's day, verse wasn't so well fed. Although
Sygtrygg was beginning to show some promise, such gener-
osity would make him look like a market-day ceorl, stingy
with the pin money. But before Sygtrygg had to ante up,
Macc Oc stuck his nose in again. I was beginning to wonder
what passed for manners among the Irish aristocracy. His
father was always courteous, quick with condolence,
pleased to aid Sygtrygg with the vik. Maybe he too was
hoping that Macc Oc wouldn't come back from his little
vacation cruise.

"I never had an ear for the Danish verse," he said. "Too
many consonants clacking together like stones in a bag, but
well enough for those who grow up on it."

Thorfinn was slipping the rings onto Skallagrim's arm,

and he took the opportunity to hold it firmly, stopping Skallagrim's rotation toward Macc Oc. "I'll take a raven over
a hummingbird anytime," Thorfinn said. "A much sturdier
bird, and more pleasing in the long run, as Odhinn found
when he hung on the Yggdrasil."

"Let's have a song about a hero," Macc Oc suggested,
and his other harper launched into *The Boyhood Deeds of
Cu Chulain,* a vastly hyperbolic lie about a Gaelic ragamuf-
fin who ran round the island saving his betters and embarrassing his inferiors, although ferreting out the latter was
his greatest boyhood deed.

While the bard sang on, Skallagrim came over to Caitria
and me to display his new ornamentation to good advantage in the torchlight.

"Is Thorfinn elfshot, or what?" I asked him, examining
the rings in disbelief. "Have you cast runes at him?"

"He's a patron of the arts," Skallagrim said. "Are you
implying he'd have to be under a spell to want to pay so
much for it?"

"Well, you do handle all the magic," I reminded him.

"I've never had to resort to it when I composed," he
assured me. "And if you've been saving some lines about
the vik, now's a good time to spend them. Thorfinn's in a
giving mood, and Sygtrygg will have to match his gifting or
look a cheapskate."

"Sygtrygg *is* a cheapskate." I set the parchment aside.
"And you sucked up to Thorfinn without shame."

"But Sygtrygg can't appear to be cheap in front of Macc
Oc," Skallagrim pointed out. "And sucking up's just another skill."

"You can't believe Sygtrygg still cares about Macc Oc,"
I asked. "He's treated him like the turd he is all evening."

"We're not reading the same side of the rune stave, are
we, boy? What's passed has no matter," Skallagrim said.
"Macc Oc's manners aren't the point: it's all those horses
and cattle and his father's goodwill. A sister's a small price
to pay for security in Clontarf. That's what was learned on
all those viks you missed. Didn't you read it in the ashes
of those Hwiccan towns?"

Thorleik called for his assistant, and Caitria left us.

When the beef was done cooking, they brought us great
steaming slabs of it on a silver platter that Orm had
grabbed once in the land of the Picts. Knives were out and

the slapping of beef on plate drowned out the bard, who tried gamely to sing over the noise of Vikings at feeding time. Talk turned again to the Skänian coast, and the second bard finished his verses. He sat down and took a plate with his friend; they ate apart, as if they didn't want to be associated with Macc Oc.

The *Long Harrier* was in the midst of the other dragons, and when Skallagrim had begun to sing, the Clontarfmen had moved closer to hear. When the beef was served, they sat where they were and ate, and the noise of their audience was replaced by the sounds of their eating. It was a comforting and familiar sound as I sat there draining the last of the brown Hwiccan beer I'd been nursing for an hour. When the first mound of beef was eaten to the plate and another cask of ale was going round, Thorfinn caught my eye and waved me to my feet.

"You spoke well in the hall when I came to Clontarf," he said, "and Skallagrim named you his apprentice. Have you any lines to sing, Bran Snorrison?"

Not only did I have lines, I had just enough brown beer on board not to care who heard them. Snatches of advice and observations from the last couple of weeks came back to me out of the darkness like bats returning to their cave, and I looked at Macc Oc and smiled.

"My voice isn't so polished as the horn from which Skallagrim pours his word-brew," I said to Thorfinn, "but I hope it's pleasing enough. My brew's called the 'Edda of Macc Oc's First Vik.'"

I'll spare you. The alliterative long line's an intricate and acquired taste, and early verse is often an embarrassment. Suffice it to say I've made better verses since, but few more successful with an audience than those lines about Macc Oc's vik. I was on a roll and working in the skaldic tradition of the lampoon, a necessary literary form when you versified about some of the biggest egos in the eighth century.

Thorfinn nearly pissed himself with laughing and a surfeit of ale. Sygtrygg didn't like my sly references to his selling of Frydys, but at least he could take a joke. Macc Oc was another story. If he could have moved faster, he'd have probably slipped a blade into me before I was halfway finished, but the four wounds in his ass had stiffened, and he could only manage a slow climb up the spear shaft he was using for a crutch.

The fact the Irishmen were laughing as hard as the Danes only enraged him more, and by the time he'd pulled himself to his feet, his face was redder than the *Blood Raven*'s sail.

"Look," Thord the Jolly shouted. "Moonrise."

That set them all off again, and Macc Oc came toward me in a stiff-legged gait that made him look like his balls were glued to his knees. The lookout on the mast, laughing too hard for his own good, lost his grip and flailed half the distance to the deck before the safety line around his waist snapped tight and left him spinning like a loomweight above us.

"I'll avenge this insult," Macc Oc promised, his hand moving to his knife. Before it reached the hilt, there were four ship captains between us.

"There's no insult. Skalds have immunity when they sing," Sygtrygg said. "Sometimes they make verse we don't like, but if it's good verse you've got to have a sense of humor about it."

"We're far from Clontarf," Macc Oc said.

"This deck is Clontarf," Sygtrygg said, pushing through. "Where I sit is Clontarf, and the skalds of Clontarf compose what they want."

Macc Oc backed off a few steps. Uneasiness slithered underfoot like an adder, like a lie whispered in a shadow, passed quickly across the crowded decks as new friends realized they might soon be ordered at one another's throats. Macc Oc was capable of any rashness, even ordering his men to start a fight they couldn't hope to win with ten fathoms under the keels and no place to run.

But he mastered himself and gave one last angry look round before he left the *Long Harrier* for Kalf Agirson's dragon, two decks away. His bards began to follow him, but Skallagrim stopped them a moment. He slipped one of the rings off his arm and dropped it to the deck. Then he took an axe from the belt of a handy Dane and chopped it in two.

"Take half each," he said, handing the two arcs of gold to them. "Songs must be paid for, and not everyone here's ill-mannered."

They thanked him and left the ship, and when the crews were sorted out, Sygtrygg ordered the lines cast off. The clutch of dragons broke up, each boat pulling a little away from the others so that there was room for easy sleep.

"You're a bigger fool than I thought," Skallagrim said to me.

"You said, 'What's passed has no matter,' " I reminded him.

"Don't quote me to myself," Skallagrim said. "You only prove you misunderstood in the first place."

"You said treating Macc Oc like a turd had no matter."

"Treating him like a turd isn't rubbing one in his face," Skallagrim said. "How can he ignore those verses? His men will remember them and carry them home. Our men will remember them and want them again in the hall. What then? Will you insult him again at Yule when we compete with verses about the vik?"

"By Yule, Macc Oc will be an unpleasant memory."

"The wisdom of youth." Skallagrim shook his head. "I wish I had it still. You'll be lucky to outlive the vik."

"I'll outlive Macc Oc," I promised. "If he dies, there's no insult. I'm as ready to praise that oaf dead as I am to lampoon him alive."

"There are twelve boats in Sygtrygg's fleet," Skallagrim said. "And Irish on every one. What happens if Macc Oc gives an order? Can his men refuse any more than we could if Sygtrygg wanted something done? Decks are slippery; the sea road's full of ruts."

The next morning the wind came up, and the dragons coasted south and west along the Cornish coast without sighting sail, and Sygtrygg spread out the fleet so no one stole another's wind. The knarr had gained weight and settled into the water, slowing us down, but it was a good voyage: no time at the oars, the wind at our backs, and always a few lines out to troll for fresh fish. I filled two more pages with words, to Skallagrim's irritation: he was after me to fill my memory, not sheets of parchment.

Caitria, who spoke no Danish, helped Thorleik, who spoke no Welsh or Anglo-Saxon, and we all survived their cooking, so they must have found a common kitchen language. When they weren't preparing a meal on the deck, Caitria sat with Skallagrim and me in the shallow hold, questioning us on the ways of viking, which she found intensely amusing.

"So you invite this man along to appraise him for marriage to Sygtrygg's sister," she said, summarizing the events of the vik after we'd answered her questions. "And then you goad him into a fight."

"He started the fight," Skallagrim corrected.

"Technically, I suppose," she admitted. "But are you innocent?"

I shrugged.

"Then you raid upriver, and he's shot in the ass. And you make jokes and verse lampoons about him in front of his men, and when he objects, you tell him he's got no sense of humor. That about it?"

Skallagrim and I exchanged looks. That was about it.

"And what are the chances he'll marry this sister now?"

"You've never seen her," Skallagrim dismissed her skepticism. "She's a beauty. He'll want her regardless, unless Sygtrygg changes his mind, and I doubt there's much chance of that."

"And where are you in this story?" Caitria asked me.

"Right in the middle," Skallagrim hooted.

"Are all viks like this?"

"All the ones I've been on," I said.

We entered the treacherous water off the tip of Cornwall after a full day's sailing. Then we coasted from point to point along the bottom of Eng land, across the mouths of five or six large bays, until we made landfall at Wiht Island at the end of the second full day away from the Severn. It was late afternoon, and Sygtrygg brought the ships together for a talk. All the captains came to the *Long Harrier* in their little boats, and Macc Oc accompanied Kalf Agirson. He was moving around a little better, but his tight-assed walk provoked a few sniggers as he passed. Sygtrygg warned me to keep clear, and it was good advice, because as soon as Macc Oc came aboard, he called the Irish together. One or two looked my way as he spoke, and when he released them he came aft to Sygtrygg and the gathered ships' captains.

I'd listened with half an ear while I watched the Irish, but what Sygtrygg had intended as a routine meeting of the captains soon took another direction because of seasonal mathematics.

"We've another week at least to Skäne," Thorfinn was saying, "say a couple of weeks to make your point to Knute, and then another two back to Clontarf. We've been gone almost two weeks now, that makes eight weeks altogether, and that's if we don't run into any trouble on the way. What are the odds of that?"

"We're pushing the storm season." Kalf nodded in agreement.

"Storms have a mind of their own," Kalf's brother-in-law, Bui, said indifferently. He commanded the *Sea Snake*, a long dragon that had swum in Skänian waters before and come back with plunder, but if you asked me, Bui was letting past success and present association with Thorfinn get the better of his judgment.

"Why tempt the Norns?" Kalf wanted to know.

"I want Knute to spend the winter knowing the feud's still alive," Sygtrygg said forcefully. "He's had a year of rest; maybe he thinks we've forgotten him." Sygtrygg was fixed on harrying Knute as a point of family honor, and I had to admit that harrying Knute was a better idea than harrying Offa had been a couple of weeks ago.

"He's got to quit hiding behind Orm," Skallagrim said in my ear.

"Give him time," I said. "He's making it up as he goes along."

Soti, the captain of a sleek ship called *Tir's Blade*, shook his head. "If we die in a storm, what have we taught Knute?"

"Let him wait another year." Eirik Whale laughed. "Let him fill his storehouses so there's something worth taking."

"He's waited enough," Grundi shouted. "Let him feel our steel."

"It's a long cold sleep at the bottom of the sea," Einar Soft Hands said mournfully.

"Afraid of a little blow?" Bork wanted to know.

"Only a fool isn't afraid of the autumn storms," Toki said evenly.

"That's enough," Sygtrygg shouted before it got out of hand and someone said something we'd all have cause to regret.

I'd been counting as the captains argued, and they were lined up six to six for a Skänian raid. That's what comes of a fleet with an even number of ships. Sygtrygg would have to make up his mind now and take his chances the dissenting captains would stay with him. They had a point: the North Sea storms could take all thirteen ships without a blink. Sygtrygg took himself apart from the captains and went to the maststep fish to think it over. Rognvald, Skalla-grim, and I went with him in case he required our counsel, and after a minute, Thorfinn followed.

"What is it you want Knute to know?" Thorfinn asked. "And how can you best teach him?"

"That Orm's feud didn't die with Orm," Sygtrygg told him.

"Do you think it's likely he knows Orm's dead?"

"That's as may be," Sygtrygg said. "But last year was the first in twenty that Orm didn't send ships to bother him. What's he to make of that? You asked about it yourself."

Thorfinn shrugged. "If he thinks the feud's over, what matter? Let him think what he wants. Eirik Whale had a point: if he has a couple of years without worry, his store-houses will be full, and his guard will be down. All the easier to take him."

"What do you suggest?" Sygtrygg asked.

"If you were to stop in at the Orkneys with slaves and plunder to show, you might teach Knute a different lesson."

"What lesson?"

"That Orm's dead and you're avenging him against the Engs. He'll think you've too much on your trencher and rest easy. Then, next year, he's yours."

"What would be gained?"

"You need a good vik to ensure your place in Orm's stead," Thorfinn said. "You've already wet steel on the Engs and avenged him, you have silver and slaves and you'll come home covered in good words from your men; you should be secure. Next year you can punish Knute if you want."

Back by the star board there was a general discussion among the captains while Sygtrygg looked at the coast of Wiht and chewed the inside of his mouth, deep in thought. It struck me then that Thorfinn was intentionally bringing Sygtrygg along, teaching him the skills that Orm had ne-glected in favor of his older brothers. Maybe he reckoned that training Sygtrygg was a better tribute than raising a stone or killing Engs; whatever his reasons, Thorfinn was giving Sygtrygg time to invent his own plan.

Sygtrygg shrugged deeper into his cloak and walked for-ward to the dragon's neck. That was Orm's manner, and we all saw it, except Macc Oc, who was getting impatient while Vikings discussed the business of viking, and who couldn't keep his mouth shut.

"Just put us ashore anywhere, and you can lay off the coast where it's safe. We'll be back with silver in a few days and you won't have to expose yourselves to danger."

He smiled and puffed up his chest a little as he insulted us, and only his profound stupidity kept him alive. All the captains looked at him with flat eyes, as if they were wondering why his father hadn't exposed him at birth.

That was enough for Sygtrygg. He came back from the dragon's neck and stood face-to-face with Macc Oc, looking into his eyes for a long moment before he turned away. "We'll head for the Orkneys," he announced. Then Sygtrygg put it to the captains, and they voted for the plan: an easy pleasure cruise around Eng land, putting in to trade or raid as the spirit moved us. "After all," Thorfinn said with a shrug, "trading is just raiding with a *t*."

The captains went back to their dragons, but Thorfinn held off, speaking with Sygtrygg at the star board. After they'd talked awhile, Sygtrygg called me back.

"Thorfinn thinks Macc Oc wants you dead for your verses," he said.

"He wants me dead for more than verse," I said.

"Macc Oc's pride was wounded badly, and even with so much, such a wound must've come close to the heart of it. You're not safe on any ship with Irish aboard." Sygtrygg spat over the side. "Your tongue'll get you killed yet, foster brother."

"There're no Irish on the *Blood Raven*," Thorfinn said. "You'll be safe there for the length of the vik."

"Skallagrim can stay here," Sygtrygg said. "If he goes, Thorfinn will weight him down with so much gold he'll drown if he goes over the side. Your verses aren't worth so much." He laughed at the look on my face. "A joke," he assured me, and slipped a ring off his arm and gave it to me. "This is down payment for your verse."

"Here's my share," Thorfinn added, adding another ring.

"When are we going?" I asked.

"As soon as you get your gear," Thorfinn said.

Skallagrim and Caitria came over as I collected my equipment from the chest.

"Patrons are good," Skallagrim agreed. "They keep you warm in winter and alive while it suits them. Now you'll sail with Thorfinn Skullsplitter. Your future's assured if you keep your eyes open and make good lines about it."

Caitria disappeared and returned with her pack.

"Where're you off to?" I asked her. "Fancy the coast of Wiht?"

"We're together until you set me ashore in a town," she reminded me. "We agreed."

"I'm not arguing it." I shrugged. "But you'll have to keep here. The *Blood Raven*'s a Jomsviking ship, and they don't haul women."

"No women?"

"They're very strict about it," Skallagrim assured her. "You wouldn't like the accommodations. Stay with me while Bran hides out from the Irishman."

He insulted me, but he hugged me hard before I went over the freeboard into Thorfinn's small boat. "Keep well," he said. Caitria stood on the foredeck clutching her pack as if I'd deserted her.

As we pulled away, I realized I was leaving my home behind for the first time in my life. And not only that, I was leaving it for Jomsborg. I looked ahead at the *Blood Raven*, disappearing on the far side of a swell until only the upper half of the mast remained in view, and then rising up magically out of the green water as the small boat sank in a trough.

"Sygtrygg says it's your first vik," Thorfinn said. "Why?"

I traced out the scar on my face and shrugged, looking at the strakes of the little boat. "I was cut young," I told him, "and sent to work keeping accounts. Skallagrim thought I had promise in the hall."

He must have known, seasoned war leader that he was, that I had doubts about my nerve. "A pretty cut," he nodded, admiring it. "I myself have none that show. If you have to have cuts, they ought to be out where everyone can see them. I knew a woman in Hedeby, once, who was quite indifferent until I had my clothes off and she saw the Moorish slashes I got in Sicily. They have a strange, thin blade that cuts on the draw and leaves a thinner scar than ours." He pulled his tunic up and showed me four long scars in a crosshatched pattern across his chest. They'd healed white against his skin, scarcely the width of a leaf stem.

"You had these four at once?" I asked.

"That Moor moved like lightning," Thorfinn said, dropping his tunic. "I let him inside my shield for a second and he did that. It's a combination of the blade and the technique. Our blades are made for cutting leather and wool in layers. Maybe a ring mail shirt. We fight with the weight of our arms and backs and ward blows with a shield. The Moors live in a hot land and wear a thin cloth. Their armor's light and their shields are small. If you ever come up against a Moor, remember this: they can reverse a blow and draw it back on you quicker than you think possible."

That bit of wisdom dispensed, Thorfinn turned his attention to the *Blood Raven,* which was looming above us on the swell. He shouted a couple of orders and the oarsmen moved the little boat accordingly as someone from the dragon tossed us a line. When it was made fast, we were alongside and scrambled over the freeboard onto the deck.

Thorfinn motioned one of his men over. He was a pink-cheeked man with raggedly cut blond hair. His face was smooth, in contrast to prevailing fashion, but he had the ice eyes of the fjords. "This is Knute Stromborg," Thorfinn said. "It's his first vik too. He'll show you where to stow your gear."

"Everyone calls me Stromborg," Knute told me. "Stromborg from Jomsborg. They think it's quite a joke."

Stromborg had the face of some bloated cherub from an illuminated manuscript. He looked a little older than me, but he was really a few years younger. He stooped over a hatch and grabbed the iron ring to heave it open.

"How's it come to be your first vik?" I asked.

"My father needed help on the farm," he said, stepping into the open hatch and dropping into the hold with a thump, head and shoulders still sticking out. "My brothers had all gone off. I stayed until my sisters married and their husbands were there to help."

"Where are you from?" I asked, dropping my pack down to him.

"Oslofjord," he said. "My father sailed with Hardbein Hjrolfsson, when they raided with Halfden the Black. He used his share to buy the farm and settle, but he never begrudged his sons their will, and only asked me to stay until my sisters were married."

"How did you come here?" I asked him. I sat on the

edge of the hatch and slipped down into the shadows of the hold. Generally a gravel ballast covered the keel like a blanket, but the *Blood Raven* had another pine deck below, floating on the gravel bed.

"Ulf Thorhullasson, Thorfinn's fo'c'sleman, was a mate of my father's, and he asked them to take me as a favor."

I crouched down and stashed my pack in the angle of the strakes and a curving knee. There were runes carved into the beams overhead, and I reached up to let my fingertips read them. The *Blood Raven* was a true oceangoing dragon: deeper in the belly and wider abeam, she was wrighted larger in all proportions. There was more room below the deck. No ships of the *Blood Raven*'s class have survived, so the Oseborg and the Gakstadt and Skudelev ships are the representative hulls that scholarship has to work with. A clinker-built dragon like the *Blood Raven* had twice the size.

"Where's my oar?" I asked.

"You've no oar," Stromborg said. "You're the skald here. No skald pulls wood on the *Blood Raven*. Make verse," he said. "We've heard your work."

Back on deck, I went aft to Thorfinn. "Stromborg tells me I've no oar," I said.

"It's true," Thorfinn said.

"I have to pull my weight," I said.

"You'll pull your weight in verses," he said. "We talked it over."

"Who talked it over?"

"The crew and I," he said. "If they're to pull your weight, they have to agree to it. I don't keep slaves; we're all free men here."

"What'll I compose about?" I asked him.

"Don't worry," he said. "Something will turn up."

Stromborg introduced me round the ship, but it was only a formality; they knew who I was. They'd all heard me sing Macc Oc's praises four nights before.

As the wind was up and favorable, there was nothing much to do but try to be inconspicuous. All they required was that I didn't get underfoot. Stromborg left me alone and went to play a board game set up on a chest.

Stromborg's opponent was a man of Stromborg's size; in fact, they were all of a size. I was the smallest one aboard. He wore his hair in a thick braid, pulled away from a great burned patch on his skull where the skin had scarred and shriveled. At the ends of his mustache he'd tied small silver bells that sang when he talked.

"Greek fire," he said, when he noticed me look at the burn. When you've a scar a hand's length snaking along your face, you can study other men's scars without making enemies. "I was with Thorfinn fighting the Moors on the Bosporus. They threw Greek fire at the boat and a spit of it set my hair alight. There wasn't time to get my helm off, so I jumped overboard to kill the flames."

"Geat," I said, pointing to mine. "Vegetable market in Clontarf."

He pursed his lips and looked at the scar approvingly. "When we get back," he said, "remind me not to haggle with the asparagus seller. I'm Steinthor Bollison." He motioned me to sit beside him.

"Where's this game from?" I asked.

"It's a Moorish game Thorfinn taught us one winter in Corsica."

"Thorfinn taught you a game?"

"He said it would teach us to think like Moors."

"Did it?"

"We walked away with our heads," Steinthor said, turning his attention back to the board. "I liked it and since I can carve, I made a set for myself."

The pieces were carved from whale ivory, the pawns as tall as my fist, the other pieces larger still. The workmanship was remarkable: the faces were individually carved, and the opposing ranks of goggle-eyed warriors were light and dark, Dane and Moor, dressed and equipped correctly and posed in combative attitudes. Steinthor studied the board for a moment and then moved one of the pieces on his side. Stromborg pondered the new situation Steinthor's move created.

"I haven't played very long," Stromborg apologized. "I'm slow."

"Take your time," Steinthor said indulgently, taking his braid in his fist and giving it a tug, which rang the bells on his mustache. "Thorfinn's still thinking," he said.

Thorfinn had settled with his back to the tail of the dragon and his feet spread wide. His sword was across his thighs, bright in the sunlight like the silver tongue of a wyrm. It wasn't typical pattern-welded iron; it was all steel, a kind of blade that was beginning to make an appearance thanks to the advances of eighth century metallurgy and the addition of carbon to molten iron. He was honing the edge with a slow, rhythmic sweep of his hand, turning the blade over as he finished a stroke to expose the other edge to the whetstone. The steel made a noise like a wyrm purring, a clear low tone that we could hear amidships.

Thorfinn's eyes were half closed as he concentrated on some inner dialogue, and I found Thorfinn mediating on the voice of his sword an unexpected sight and chilling, although I understood from the general indifference that the crew took it for granted. No one approached him, and except for the movement of the stone on the edge of his sword, he seemed to be asleep in the sunlight against the dragon's tail.

"Thorfinn's a teacher and a thinker," Steinthor said. "He thinks every day while he sharpens Spineripper and prepares his lessons."

Stromborg moved another chessman, and Steinthor countered without hesitation, removing one of Stromborg's pieces from the board. "Never forget the bishop," Steinthor instructed with a smile. "If you turn your back on a churchman, it's always the worse."

I passed the afternoon watching Steinthor beat Stromborg at chess while the fleet crossed the Land South miles along the coasts of Sussex and Kent. Thorfinn sat in the stern of the boat for a couple of hours and then suddenly wiped the blade and slipped it back into the scabbard.

"Thorfinn's finished," Steinthor announced.

Thorfinn stood up and stretched, then passed a few sociable words with the star board man before he went forward to talk to Ulf Thorhullasson, his fo'c'sleman. I had a paramount fascination with Thorfinn and the crew of the *Blood Raven*; they all had the look, but none of them had it more than Thorfinn Skullsplitter. I'm talking about the *viking* look, the one that's associated with Scandinavians living between the ninth and eleventh centuries, particularly those who plied the tourist trade: big, blond, blue-eyed, ruddy-complected, bearded or at least elaborately mustached, handy with edged weapons, adept at navigation, keen to plunder any geography beyond the Scandinavian archipelago: *that* look.

Ulf took a bucket from the ropes coiled by the dragon's

neck and dipped it over the side, pulling it back and tasting its contents. He nodded, and Thorfinn took the horn from its peg and blew a couple of notes. Ulf pointed out a new course, the star board man responded, and the *Blood Raven* turned toward the shore.

"He's trying to taste a river," Steinthor said.

I went aft and loitered near Thorfinn.

"Wonderful afternoon, wasn't it?" he asked.

"Yes," I agreed, startled once more by an expression of sentiment from Thorfinn Skullsplitter.

"Looks like it will be a fine sunset." He gestured toward the west, where a band of clouds was motionless above the horizon line, and the sun was dropping toward the edge of the western sea.

We stood there on the afterdeck with the helmsman, who was braced comfortably on his seat with his booted foot on the tiller, gazing up at the weathervane on the top of the mast.

"Do you think we'll get back to Clontarf without fighting? No one's going to mistake us for traders."

"Raid or trade, it's much the same." Thorfinn pursed his lips and looked at me. "We've trade goods in the knarr, slaves from the Severn, bronzework from Ireland, linen, glass, jewelry, ivory, and whalebone, and the Orkneymen have amber, salt, wine, and silver."

"You plan viks," I reminded him. "I make verse, Skallagrim takes care of the magic. I've no ideas on viking, though most men think they can wright a line or cut a rune."

Thorfinn laughed shortly. "If we can find a river and the tide's right, we could *straandshug*. It wouldn't hurt to take another town or two. Speaking of Macc Oc," Thorfinn said, although we hadn't been, "why'd you gore him so deep the other night? It's true he's a fool, but you stuck him worse than that Hwiccan archer."

"I want to see him dead," I said.

"There must be a woman in this," Thorfinn mused. "Nothing else explains it. Is it that sister of Sygtrygg's with the great tits?"

"Frydys," I said, amazed by his intuition.

"Sygtrygg said you made her a Christian to keep her knees together. Is that true?"

"I made her a fake Christian to keep her for myself," I

admitted. "But neither of us is a Christian. Sygtrygg sent me to talk to her, and I grew to love her instead."

Thorfinn threw his head back and laughed to shake the sail. "I've known women like that," he said. "How old is the girl?"

"Fourteen," I told him.

"Barely a woman," he said. "And Sygtrygg wants to use her to keep the high seat?"

"Then he's told you his plans?"

"He told me nothing." Thorfinn shook his head. "But now it makes sense why he's put up with that Irish hummingbird so long. Odhinn's eye patch, you've gotten yourself into a mess, haven't you?"

"How do you mean?" I asked cautiously.

"How do you think I mean? Don't worry; I won't tell Sygtrygg anything he shouldn't know."

I looked at the deck and didn't say anything.

"I thought as much." Thorfinn laughed again. "Only fourteen and tits like that. She must be a valkyrie in the hay mow."

"I thought to make the bride-price on the vik and marry her," I confessed, hoping he'd be sympathetic.

"The bride-price isn't your problem here," Thorfinn said. "It's that Irishman with the sore ass."

"And I can't kill him first without bringing trouble."

"Unless he falls in battle, we're bound to avenge him." Thorfinn nodded agreement.

"Something may happen yet," I said.

Thorfinn said, "Does she love you?"

"She says so," I told him.

Thorfinn accepted this in silence, staring off into the sky as if remembering something; then he shook his head and quoted from the *Sayings of the Wise One*:

> The false love of woman, 'tis like to one
> Riding on ice with horse unroughshod—
> a brisk two-year-old, unbroken withal—
> or in a raging wind drifting rudderless,
> like the lame outrunning the reindeer on bare rock.
>
> Heed my words now, for I know them both:
>   mainsworn are men to women;
> we speak most fair when most false our thoughts,
>   for that wiles the wariest wits.

Fairly shall speak,　nor spare his gifts,
　　who shall win a woman's love,
Shall praise the looks　of the lovely maid:
　　he who flatters will win the fair.

At the loves of a man　to laugh is not meet
　　for anyone ever;
The wise oft fall,　when fools yield not,
　　to the lure of a lovely maid.

'Tis not meet for men　to mock at what
　　befalls full many:
A fair face oft　makes fools of the wise
　　by the mighty lure of love.

"That makes it unanimous," I told him. "Counting you, five people know, and all think she's false."

"Who else knows?"

"Snorri, Skallagrim, Goltrade the priest-slave, and my mother, Mairead."

"I'm the most ignorant of all," he said. "But I knew a woman once, in Trelleborg, who gave me her promise, her love, and her body within the space of a month. She was beautiful, and I was wearing a younger man's boots, so I believed her."

Thorfinn paused for a moment, and I looked at the other ships in the fleet, a little embarrassed by Thorfinn's romantic confidences.

"I think she believed it herself," he continued, "but we were both wrong. When I got back from the dolphin's playground, she was suckling another man's child."

"What did you do?" I asked.

"Went to Jomsborg." He shrugged. "It seemed like the thing to do at the time."

"And you think Frydys will play me false?"

"I don't think anything," he said, "but you should think everything."

I went back to see how Stromborg was doing at chess and meditate on Thorfinn's advice. Steinthor was teaching Stromborg the most valuable lesson of gamesmanship: never gamble. A crowd had collected to watch Steinthor clean out Stromborg's purse, which, like the purses of all

Jomsvikings, was made of the tanned scrotum of a former enemy.

"What happened?" I asked.

"Stromborg won a couple of games," Steinthor said innocently, "and then suggested we put a value on the pieces to help keep score."

"After that I won two more games," Stromborg said. "Then I started losing."

"How many've you lost?" I asked, trying to keep a straight face.

"Seven," he said. "But I almost won the last three. All I need is a little luck to make back what I've lost."

"He almost had checkmate twice last time," Steinthor said, managing to sound genuinely disappointed.

"How long have you been out of Oslofjord?" I asked Stromborg.

"Six months," he said, puzzled by the question.

I gave Steinthor a long look, and he gazed off toward the Kentish coast, biting his lip and making those little silver bells jingle. If he thought he could get away with hustling his shipmates at chess, who was I to say anything?

We settled down to watch the sunset make the striped sails glow with immanent light, turn the sky flame-red, and silhouette the gulls that flew above the masts. The wind held and we settled into our cloaks and blankets, except for Steinthor, who prowled the deck with his chessboard and a small oil lamp, looking for another sucker. After the sun slipped into the void, the light only lingered for a half hour, long autumn light that made everything gold and bronze, and then the moonless night.

We spent the night lashed together off the Kentish coast. We started out again at dawn, the crew pulling against the current from the Frisian Sea. All that pulling soon lost its charm, but the off-duty Jomsvikings seemed to be having some kind of angling competition, hauling in fish, which they measured against the length of a scramasax and then threw back, like the sportsmen they were.

At the appropriate times we ate, took a piss over the side, and pulled wood until we picked up a favorable wind. Steinthor never took a turn at the bench or pulled himself aloft or wrestled the rigging, and, as he had no apparent job, he was free to teach me the game. Soon I was belly up to a sea chest for instruction. Steinthor told me how he'd learned the game on Sicily, a place that had assumed magical proportions for him.

"They have orchards of trees," he said as he studied the board, "that gave a green fruit with a hard stone in it. They crush this fruit to make oil, but they also eat it whole. And they have whole hillsides given over to grapevines, from which they make a wine that will melt your brains. And they bake a kind of bread with slices of meat, and the cheese of cattle, and peppers, and onions, and the blackened fruit of that tree, and a kind of fungus that grows in pastures, and little salted fish all swimming in a red paste that eats well with the beer of that place. Freyja's tits," he concluded, "if you ever have a chance to plunder Sicily, don't pass it up." That was old advice, even then.

The October storms were coming, and none of us wanted to get caught in open water when they blew up with that sudden viciousness that October storms are known for, but the weather was still good, and if we could get round Britain and stop in at the Orkneys for a last bit of trading and self-promotion, we'd be back in Clontarf in a week. With the knarr along it was risky business. During the regular season a fat fleet would ordinarily sail home rather than risk running into a lean fleet, but it was late in the year and we were counting on having the Frisian Sea to ourselves.

But we were bored, and Sygtrygg's mood was to worry the Engs as a prank, so he had Rognvald course close in to the East Anglian coast to send them scurrying for the back country.

It was an easy cruise across the Wash and then we were passed from river mouth to river mouth, pulled or pushed by tidal races, helped and hindered by wind and current, and generally had a good time. But the Norns had a surprise for us at Tynemouth. We were passing a lazy day of slow sailing and drinking as the British coast passed the port freeboard. We'd been into that Hwiccan beer for a good two hours, and I, for one, was having trouble finding my dick to piss over the side, when the lookout saw the sails of a fleet coming toward us out of the river mouth.

"Twenty sails," he called down to us, pointing out the bearing.

I was writing some lines and nursing a cup of beer back at the star board when the lookout sang his song, and I wasn't prepared for general quarters. Thorfinn took the horn and blew out a long wail to announce company, and the crew of the *Blood Raven,* half drunk and listless, flowed to their feet now that something worth paying attention to had come up. Weapons flashed, and the shieldwall went over the side. The lookout's arm pointed the bearing to the English fleet and the star board man brought the *Blood Raven* around until the knife edge of his hand pointed between the dragon's ears.

The berserks shrugged out of their cloaks and limbered up in preparation for the wielding of bearded axe against English beard, talking to one another in rising tones of encouragement. Thord the Jolly moved among his men and slapped backs, tightened harnesses, commented on the smiles of their axes. The archers and slingers collected on the foredeck, untying bundles of arrows and spreading the mouths on sacks of stones. The crew's transformation was accomplished with a liquid ease equal to their previous indolence; except for that brief fit of pique when Thorfinn had attacked Wulfstan, the Jomsvikings had taken their time, as if there was nothing much to challenge them. Now they moved at full speed.

"Better get ready," Thorfinn said, smiling. "Verses come later; now's the time for deeds."

I went below and exchanged my pens for the raven shield and my weapons. My heart was pounding in my throat, and it tasted like it had been marinated in copper and brass. Our fleet was outnumbered, and the knarr were too heavy in the water to outrun the coast watch. There was nothing to do but fight. *Ofermod,* I thought. Orm's affliction ran in the family.

Steinthor came from the forward part of the ship, wrestling an object wrapped in canvas into the light under the open hatch.

"Some help here, skald," he said, and I sprang forward, glad to have a task to keep my mind off what was about to go down.

"What is this?" I groaned as I slipped my axe into my belt and took up some of the weight.

"It's time to work," he said with a malicious grin.

Together we got the object into position under the hatch and he whistled up for help. In a moment arms reached down and grabbed the canvas. As the bundle rose up to the deck, he hurried forward again, waving me to follow.

Under the prow of the dragon below the deck there was a space where the wrapped object had nestled in with the spare tackle. Two more bundles were laid by, wrapped also in waxed canvas and secured by hemp. A dozen spear shafts protruded from the bottom of the bundle. Steinthor scurried to the heavy end and stooped to lift it. I grabbed up the shafts.

"What is this?" I asked again.

"My speciality." He laughed. "Greek fire."

We made our way back to the hatchway, stumbling a few times over the strakes as the *Blood Raven* pitched into the troughs of the Frisian Sea, and when he fell, I noticed that Steinthor was careful to cushion his burden.

Back on deck, I saw that the distance between the fleets was rapidly closing. The berserks had begun to mill around, mumbling eagerly to themselves, taking their clothes off and laughing wildly at some private joke. The archers were slowly spinning arrows between their fingers and sighting along the shafts or waxing their bow strings. Slingers were whirling stones about their heads to loosen their arms. Someone was singing near the prow of the boat, a song in a Baltic dialect with a nice rhythm and a snappy chorus.

"Sygtrygg's sending the knarr ahead," Thorfinn shouted to anyone interested. "They'll wait for us in the Orkneys."

"Where do you want me?" I asked, joining Thorfinn by the star board as one of Thord's berserks easily lifted the bundle and carried it forward to a cluster of men busy on the foredeck.

"Stay back here with me," he said, "You'll have a better view. I told you something would come up, didn't I?"

What an obliging guy Thorfinn was: always eager to please. I reckoned that hanging round Thorfinn Skullsplitter, master of the *Blood Raven*, as he was about to battle a numerically superior Eng fleet would be good for a few lines if I survived to write them.

The lookout dropped down the mast tree and took his weapons from the rack. I could see Stromborg and Arnfinn working at their oar. Like all the other oarsmen, they wore shields slung over their backs for protection. The archers on the first of the English ships bent yew and let fly.

"Arrows," Ulf Thorhullasson called back and ducked behind the dragon's neck as the flight struck mast, deck, and oarsmen's shields. Steinthor's little crew formed up a small shieldwall to protect themselves and the two bundles, now partially unwrapped.

I raised the Ravens, but the closest of the arrows hit a few yards away, quivering in the planks. Thorfinn laughed. "Give them a lesson," he shouted, and the archers who'd been crouching below the freeboard stood up and returned the volley. In response, the Engs hurled stones, and we ducked as they smashed into the deck and bounced around the freeboard. There were scattered yelps as they ricocheted into the exposed legs and ankles of the oarsmen. I stooped and collected a few as they skittered up to my feet. They were as big as hen's eggs, river-smooth and deadly. I took my sling out of the shield boss and fitted a stone.

I gauged the rate of closure, focusing on the biggest cluster of men on the deck of the English ship as I brought the stone around my head in a fast windup. Three orbits to pick up lethal velocity, and then I released. The stone passed over the gunnel beside the dragon's head and kept climbing: for a second it seemed I'd misjudged the rate of closure. The stone passed over the figurehead of the English ship, and I thought it would be a clean miss, but the swell was lifting the ship and the rock caught their lookout full in the face and plucked him off the spar. He fell ass over elbows into the men below. The Jomsvikings let out a cheer.

"Steinthor," Thorfinn called forward. "Are you ready with the dragon's breath?"

Steinthor waved and his crew moved aside and I saw Steinthor's specialty. Fastened to the two bronze cleats on the foredeck was a small catapult. It was a kind of ballista, with two limbs fitted into the frame. Two of Steinthor's men strained to draw it, and a ratchet slipped into place and held the limbs. Steinthor fitted one of the shafts into the channel and stood clear.

The shaft was a curious thing, ending not in an iron head to pierce the gunnel of the approaching ship, but in an odd terra-cotta vessel, about two feet long. The shaft had been sealed into the base of the vessel with tar. Hard behind the terra-cotta they'd wrapped a torch head. One of them poured oil on the torch and another lit it.

Steinthor waved back at Thorfinn and Thorfinn brought up a scream from somewhere around his knees. It was like no sound I'd ever heard a human being make before that day, like no sound I would have reckoned a man *could* make. It made the hair on the back of my neck stand up and I swallowed that lump of brass and copper back into my chest.

Steinthor moved the frame a little against its restraining ties, eyed the drift of the smoke with a professional eye, and realigned the device with a couple of taps with his boot. With a deft flick of the wrist he released the trigger. The shaft leaped away from the humming cord, trailing a thick smoke from the torch, directly at the bellied sail of the closest of the Eng ships. I watched the projectile reach the top of its arc with a sort of paralyzed fascination, and so did the Engs as it began to fall down the back side of the parabola. It struck the sail, as hard as a stone wall with the force of the wind behind it, the terra-cotta shattered, and the sail wool erupted in flames.

Tendrils of liquid fire spilled down onto the deck and the closely packed Engs in their battle gear. The ship's momentum died as the sail vanished. The warriors on deck ran about, flame clinging to them like a bad odor, arms flailing, clothing, hair, and shields ablaze. Some of them jumped overboard. The rigging burned away, fanned by the wind, and the spar fell to the gunnel, breaching the shieldwall on either side. The fire spread across the deck as the blazing liquid ran along the planks with the motion of the ship.

The Jomsvikings shouted to the Engs to swim for it or burn. Steinthor's men loaded the ballista again, and as the *Blood Raven* closed with the helpless ship, another blossom of Greek fire opened its petals by the star board. When we glided past them, all thought of combat had gone as they tried to save themselves by throwing helmets of water at the fire, which only spread it more efficiently.

The star board man steered for the next ship, and before they could tack to safety Steinthor had dealt with them the same way. Two of the English ships were ablaze, and I had a little time to look round. Sygtrygg's fleet had turned in place to meet the Engs, presenting a ragged line, spreading out north and south from the *Blood Raven*. The Engs were bearing down from the east in the usual tactical array. Preferably sea battles were joined in calm waters; the fleets were moved into place and the ships lashed together so that combat could move from deck to deck, mimicking a land battle.

They had planned to overwhelm us, two or three ships to one, and then lash together and crush us with superior numbers. What they hadn't planned on was the *Blood Raven* and her resident specialist in Greek fire, Steinthor Bollison. As the *Blood Raven* disrupted their battle plan, the odds became more favorable.

Soon two more English ships were blazing to their waterlines, and one of them lost rudder and veered into the path of another, which rammed it and promptly ignited as well. Fifteen ships to go and confusion was spreading through the enemy fleet. We tacked into them, spreading flame and death, breaking their formation as they pulled wood to escape us, and then one of their ships was alongside, and the hooks were thrown and the shieldwalls scraped together by the star board.

"Odhinn. Put the battle-fetters on these Engs," Thorfinn shouted, swinging his sword overhead.

Stromborg shipped his oar and rose up with a shout to catch one of the Engs as he leaped the gunnel, passing clean over Arnfinn; Stromborg turned under the Eng's weight and threw him into the berserks, who reduced him to his constituent parts in seconds. It was slice and dice at the mast step, as Thord the Jolly ripped his own tunic in two. His hair was flying serpentine in the wind and he drew his fingernails across his chest and wiped the blood on his face.

He screamed incomprehensible words with a gargling voice, and then foam and spittle erupted from his open mouth. He was unarmed, but he was at least six feet four inches and twenty stone of seriously deranged Dane as he led the berserks in the rush on the English ship.

I moved aside to give Thorfinn room. An arrow bit into my shield, and I saw an English archer fitting another shaft when Thord got to him and tore the yew bow out of his hands, bit through the string, and snapped the bow over his forehead. Then he grabbed the archer by the balls and the head, inserting his thumb and forefinger into the man's eyes, and lifted him up off the deck. When he was at the proper height, Thord bit out his throat and spat it back in his face. The archer's blood gushed everywhere as his heart pumped its last, and Thord threw the body aside with a

wicked laugh, looking round for another career challenge
to sink his teeth into.

Another English ship was heading our way, and I slipped
my arm through the shield strap so my back would be covered. The axe in my hand seemed light, everything slowed
down, and I saw myself running toward the mast, where
some of the Engs were trying to chop through the base.
When I was within a few yards of them, I somersaulted
forward, offering them the shield on my back as I crashed
through. My momentum brought them all to the deck, but
one of them got his knee on my shield so I was pinned
there belly up like a thrashing turtle. As he was raising his
arms for the downward thrust I drove the butt of the axe
into his gut and his spear missed. He was about to try again
when Thorfinn killed him and then took care of the others
with an elegance of technique that even they must have
appreciated as they tried to scramble away.

He kicked the dead Eng off me and pulled me to my
feet. "No more craziness from you," he shouted. "I've berserks enough."

Then the second ship scraped against the port side of the
Blood Raven. The berserks were laughing and jabbering
and biting the top of the shieldwall, and Thorfinn stepped
over the bodies of the dead Engs, got a foot up on the
bench, and cleared the gunnel into the middle of the English deck. He started cutting them down from behind as
Jomsvikings followed him.

"These Engs are hungry for steel," I yelled to no one in
particular. "Let's see they're well fed."

I looked over at Thorfinn and saw that one of the Engs
had worked around behind him and was trying for position
to finish him with a spear. I chanced a throw with the axe,
and although the spin of the shaft was in the Eng's favor, the
weight of the axe head was in mine. The inertia spun the haft
into his face as he was drawing his arm back for the thrust
and dropped him to his knees. Thorfinn noticed and turned
to finish him with a slash of Spineripper. Then I got to the
other side of the spar and met the knot of Engs rushing
me from the stern.

I could feel the tapping of arrows in the shield on my
back, but until they bit, I had no time for them. The first
of the Engs took a cut at me, and I leaned back from it.
His blade caught the mast and held, and I took his arm off

with my scramasax as he tried to pull it free. Another jumped up on the spar and I hamstrung him as he came by. I deflected a spear, but it pulled me off balance, and the next Eng drew blood.

As we fought, no one was paying much attention to what was happening in the south. The Norns must have been really pissed off at Sygtrygg's *ofermod,* because in addition to the Engs they sent a storm down on us. The Land South sky was black, and the sea started to heave as the wind came up. The lines that held the ships together strained and snapped, and the storm broke. Who said those Norns don't have a sense of humor? The Eng that was trying to kill me stepped back and looked up at the sky. I looked up too, and then we looked back at each other and nodded our heads. He looked round for his mates. The one whose arm I'd amputated was already going over the shieldwall, so he helped the one I'd hamstrung to his feet and dragged him to their ship.

The storm couldn't have taken more than five minutes, after showing its black grin over the coast, to howl down on us, and Thorfinn barely had time to get his men back on the *Blood Raven* before the boats separated in the downpour and breaking sea. There was no transition from the battle frenzy to the gale. The fleets were scattered in the first minute, everyone running ahead of the wind as it drove north toward the Orkneys. Thorfinn got the wounded below; everyone else fell to tightening up the rigging.

Gathered below, we finally had time to assess the damage. Five of the crew were missing, dead or trapped aboard the English ships when we broke apart. Twenty were wounded, and we were stopping the blood with whatever was at hand, binding ourselves up with Frankish linen and cotton traded up from Africa, silk from the kingdoms of Persia. Something swam around in my stomach at the smell of all that living meat and blood.

I leaned over and threw up, and Arnfinn waited until I was done before he picked up the raven shield, which I'd shrugged off when I dropped through the hatch, and lurched over to show it to me. There were fifteen or twenty arrows in it.

"You looked like a rabid hedgehog," he said.

Some Northumbrian had my range, all right, and the leisure to try to bring me down. When I saw the arrows, my knees got weak. It was a good thing I was already sitting down and a good thing I'd already thrown up; Thorr's crutch, what was I doing there?

"Great shot with the sling," Ulf said. "Never seen better."

I smiled thinly and nodded, swallowing back the meager contents of my stomach. Me neither, Ulf. Arnfinn plucked out the arrows and presented them like a bouquet of long-stemmed flowers. "Keep these for the hall," he said. "It'll make a good story if you exaggerate a little."

Stromborg was across the hold, and I crawled over to him. He'd taken a cut on the leg, and he was binding it with a wad of cloth.

"Some fight, eh?" He laughed, slapping me on the back. "Nothing like that ever happened up in Oslofjord."

"Yeah," I said, "the quiet life, who needs it?"

Steinthor was asleep beside Stromborg, bored or exhausted. Thord was leaning back against the hull, muttering to himself and smearing drying blood over his face and neck like he was washing up after a hard day's work.

But Thorfinn stood in the hatch, where the water splashed in from the deck, and helped the men going up and down to their duties, taking the swamping that came, whenever a wave broke over the side, with a laugh that we could hear above the wind. Then, hair and mustache dripping salt water, he turned to those of us closest and gave us a fragment of riddle:

> Sometimes I swoop to whip up waves, rouse
> the water, drive the flint-gray rollers
> to the shore. Spuming crests crash
> against the cliff, dark precipice looming
> over deep water; a second tide,
> a somber flood, follows the first;
> together they fret against the sheer face,
> the rocky coast. Then the ship is filled
> with the yells of sailors; the cliffs quietly
> abide the ocean's froth and fury,
> lashing waves, racing rollers
> that smash against stone. The ship must face
> a savage battle, a bitter struggle,
> if the sea so buffets it and its cargo
> of souls that it is no longer under control
> but, fighting for life, rides foaming

on the spines of breakers. There men see
the terror I must obey when I bluster
on my way. Who shall restrain it?

The sight of Thorfinn standing there shouting the lines
of the riddle, as if he were daring the storm to come down
and name itself, is something I still see in my dreams after
all these years.

After three hours the shore started coming up to port, and
Thorfinn had to send more men to work the oars. If the storm
drove us into the rocks, we were done for. After surviving the
fight with the Engs, I wanted to live long enough to tell someone about it. Macc Oc might even be dead, for all I knew. I
thought it was time to do my share, so when Thorfinn called
for oarsmen, I pushed Stromborg back and went in his place.
I needed the air and the space. The hold was starting to smell
like the belly of some beast. I wasn't worried; I knew my way
around a deck, and I knew how to hold on in a blow. What
I didn't know was how bad the storm was or how much blood
I'd lost from the wound in my side. No sooner had I crawled
onto the deck than the *Blood Raven* slewed, and I skidded
hard into the freeboard under the thwarts.

The *Blood Raven* was weathering the storm as only a
dragon could: one minute the keel swam in air as the sea
fell away on all sides, and then the water swamped the
freeboard. The foam spewed across the deck and sloshed
down into the hold. The star board man was lashed to the
dragon's tail, listening to the creaking of the joints and
watching the caulk lines for ruptures as the strakes twisted
out of true and back again with the force of the waves.

I grabbed at a line and caught it, but I'd no sooner pulled
myself to the closest chest than the next wave broke over
the deck and flushed me back along the scuppers, past the
legs and feet of the men who were already at their oars. I
caught at another rope and slid along with the force of the
sea, and the bite of the rope and the sting of the salt in
my bleeding wound cleared my head enough for me to
realize coming on deck was a big mistake. I pulled myself
back along the rope, but the *Blood Raven* flew in a different direction and the last I saw of her, as I passed over the
gunnel, the dragon seemed to be turning like a spindle on
the hub of the mast. Then the black, bone-numbing water
of the Frisian Sea closed over me.

7

Lindisfarne

The man who stands at a strange threshold
Should be cautious before he crosses it,
Glance this way and that.
Who knows beforehand what foes may sit
Awaiting him in the hall?
            —The Sayings of the Wise One

I woke in sunlight. Truth to tell, I oozed back to consciousness. This is how it was: I was floating somewhere warm and damp, and then hardness came into the picture, and with it, a sense of gravity and the direction of the earth. Warm, damp, hard, up, and down. Rough was next. Followed by painful. Soon after painful, I remembered how to open my eyes, and almost immediately I remembered how to throw up. With throwing up came a wide range of involuntary movements: spasms, leverings, counterbalances. Then a brief return to oblivion. Sometime later I woke up in the more proper sense. Consciousness returned; I opened my eyes; I resisted the urge to throw up; and I moved voluntarily.

I was lying half in a tidal pond. I rolled over, gasped, and squinted up at the blue sky; the light was like a weight, and tears squeezed out of the corners of my eyes. Inhaling was like breathing fine wires into my lungs; sharp rocks cut into my back. The stale and brackish tastes of bile and the Frisian Sea competed for attention. The cries of birds filled the air, thousands of them, shrill and raucous, and every one was like a gimlet boring into my eardrums.

There was pain in my head, my midsection, and my left leg, and the general bruises and lacerations I'd sustained from the slapping of the waves and my reintroduction to land when I'd washed up. It's safe to say pain was as close-fitting as a hair shirt.

So how long had I been in the water? Good question. I turned to get a bearing on the angle between horizon and sun, and the resulting sensation of festive agony produced an involuntary yelp. I tried it more slowly until the horizon stabilized and the sun hovered in my peripheral vision. What I assumed was the shoreline of Britain was a dark blur, which put the sun in its ascension—I reckoned about midmorning.

I had to get oriented. The light was a flaming weight on my eyes, but my shadow and the low September sun gave me the general direction of north. I was on some offshore rock that might be dry come high tide and might not. I relaxed for a moment, preface to standing, and found myself nose-aloft a surprisingly large puddle of stench that I recognized as the former contents of my stomach. This motivated me, and I lurched up into a three-point stance that spared my left leg, swaying there for a moment as I gathered strength.

In the four or five seconds I was upright, before dizziness overcame me, I saw that I was on a small rocky island with visible marks of weathering above a discernible waterline. It was devoid of vegetation except for a few small shrubs, and whitewashed with bird shit. Terns hovered close above, feinting at my head, and about a million stupid-faced puffins stared solemnly from the rocks.

I quickly lowered myself to the ground and let the blackness pass before I tried again. A small roiling cloud of hallucinatory gnats collected before my eyes, and as I swatted at them they evaporated. I waited a few minutes, and then I stood again. I made the mistake of putting a little weight on my left leg, and the consequent scream from my nerves melted away all residual dizziness like pissed-on snow. My leg was bent in an unaccustomed angle below the knee. I'd seen that kind of thing before, generally associated with a fall from a moving horse. No bone was sticking through the fabric of my pants, so maybe I'd lucked out with a simple fracture.

Two men were sitting among the puffins, hugging their knees a safe distance away and not taking their eyes off me as the terns wheeled over their heads like feathered auras. Or were there three? It didn't matter, I reckoned them as ephemeral as the gnats until one of them stretched his legs. They wore black robes of a rough and apparently stifling cloth, and their brown heads, shaved clean on top in the sort of cut I'd watched Goltrade maintain every few days for as long as I could remember, were glistening with sweat.

That made them monks. I raised my hand in a greeting and smiled feebly, but the croak that emerged from my mouth was no word in any language. The salt water I'd swallowed, the hours I'd lain on the sun-bleached rocks, the blood I'd lost, all the delightful experiences of the last twelve hours, had robbed me of speech. My right leg quivered with the strain of supporting my weight, and I tried to take up the slack with my left. Even resting it on the ground was too much, and I blacked out again.

When I came to my senses the third time, I felt the rocking of water underneath me and the rough texture of uncured hide against my face, and I heard the slapping of paddles and grunts of exertion. I was curled into a fetal position with my left leg as extended as it could be in that cramped place. The two men were disposed on either side of me, and the jarring of their movements was transmitted onto my leg with great fidelity. I deduced from these clues that I was in the bottom of a coracle and assumed that the two monks were taking me ashore to turn me over to someone who would kill me.

I thought about escape. After all, these guys were only a couple of monks, handicapped by idiotic vows and whatever insufficient diet they managed to forage for themselves on the shit-dusted rocks of the Frisian Sea, and I was a Viking, lately in the company of Thorfinn Skullsplitter, recently engaged in harrying up the Severn River, with one short episode of berserk behavior in my immediate past. Could they possibly be a match for me? You bet: my life depended on whether I'd happened to fall among pacifists.

I lay motionless until I felt the hide bottom scrape the rock shore, and then I made the appropriate snarl of agony. The coracle bobbed as the monks hopped out and then the real pain came as they dragged it farther up on the strand. I whined and sobbed at the pain, sounds that came out of me without thought and seemed to come from someone else.

They still hadn't spoken, so I'd no idea of their provenance. Maybe they were under vows of silence, vows which Goltrade had spoken of at length. Then they grabbed me under the armpits and lifted me out of the coracle. I wept freely, teetering on the brink of unconsciousness as my leg slid over the rim of the craft. They stood me upright and supported me while I got my balance. Unless that smell was emanating from me, they might also be under vows not to bathe. One whiff of those two at close range cleared my head better than a night's sleep under a down quilt.

They'd beached on a stony shore rising almost a hundred feet out of the sea at its highest point and curving round to block my view. To the north the land flattened, and the smoke of a hearth fire drifted unmistakably behind the low hill. A flock of sheep gazed below the ridge, attended by a couple of bored dogs.

I shrugged out of their grasp and tried to hop a few feet away where the air was clear. My hair and beard were salt-caked, my mouth was dry, my head felt like horses were fighting between my ears, and I was ready to piss myself from pain. Aside from that, things were looking up. No one with weapons was in sight. Betting on the tonsures, I addressed them in Latin.

"Where am I?" I croaked out.

They exchanged startled looks, and then one of them said, "Lindisfarne, in the Farnes, Northumbria."

His accent was Irish, from north of Clontarf, but not unfamiliar to the ear. Sooner or later, everyone came through Clontarf on the Liffey Bay, Ireland's foreign merchandise mart, and anyone with an ear could speak Norse, Irish, the pidgin Hiberno-Norse dialect of people with no skill in languages, and maybe one other language: Welsh, or Frisian, or one of the Eng dialects.

"We found you on the rock where we were stranded last night in the storm. We thought you were dead."

"Were you waiting for me to rot?" I asked them.

"We thought you were a Viking from the battle," he said.

I looked down at my clothes. I was dressed in the Danish fashion of Clontarf, a cut of cloth I was sure he knew.

"What do you know about the battle?" I asked.

"One of the Northumbrian ships that chased the pirates came by this morning," he said. "The Danish ships broke up on Longstone, and the coast-watch was killing the survivors. Were you there?"

"Temporarily," I said, shaving the truth as closely as I could without drawing blood.

"Well, you're free now," he said.

"Not so free as the birds in the air," I said with a gesture to the wheeling terns close overhead. I saw no reason to help him refine his theories. "How did you two come to be there?"

"We provision the anchorites who live on the Farnes, and the storm caught us."

"Where are you from?"

"Iona. I'm Brian, and this is my brother Brendan. We've lived on Lindisfarne for almost a year."

"Well met," I said, switching to Irish as I began to sag. "I'm from Clontarf." They ran forward and grabbed me under the arms again. When it came to a choice between the smell and the pain, I was willing to accept the smell. Maybe it had anesthetic properties.

"We were born in Drogheda," Brian said, pinning down the accent. I'd stolen cattle near Drogheda with some of my Irish cousins in my more impetuous youth, before I'd gotten facecut.

"Wait. Clontarf's a Danish town," Brian remembered. They both looked more closely, or were there more than two? For a moment there seemed to be four or five of them.

"True enough," I said. "What of it?"

"You weren't a slave on that ship, were you?"

"I never said I was."

"You're a pirate," Brian concluded, giving me a shake.

"I was washed overboard in a storm," I yelped. "We were bound for the Orkneys and the Engs attacked us without provocation as we came by the Tynemouth."

"Were you harrying the coast?"

"We were drinking beer and eating bread," I snarled, "and I was writing down some verses I'd composed."

"You can write?"

"And read too," I added.

That warmed his mood. In those days, respect for intellect was something the Western church beat into you early because then, as now, knowledge was power, and the powerful were sure to demand respect. Even though they understood Latin I doubted they could read or write, and it would have been impolite to ask. They had peasant's looks and peasant's paws.

"The father Prior will want to meet you," Brian said.

"Bring him on if he can do something about this leg," I said.

"Let's go, then," Brian said, and they started up the path toward the crest of the hill.

When we began the climb, the pain wrapped its arms around me like a poor relative at Yule. I made a noise like a clubbed seal pup and tightened my grip on their necks. My toe caught in the tendrils of the dune grass, and I squirmed in their arms; they lost their balance, and we fell. Suddenly I was on my knees, and the ground tilted up and hit me in the face. I remember a mouthful of sand and the earthquake sensation as the two monks rolled down the hill beside me.

After that I was in and out for some time. Hours. Days. Memories have no sequence. Incidents have weight relative only to the pain which accompanied them. I remember a litter being lifted toward the sky, a protestation of pegged lumber, a long ringing of bells, and strange, monotonous singing. I remember vomiting into a wooden bucket and a face peering down at me and the slow descent of a thin sharp blade. I remember the sunlight like lime in my eyes and the fragrance of a new poultice and the stink of an old one. I remember the cool touch of a hand on my forehead.

When I was again aware of myself and my immediate surroundings, it was late evening. The light was dim and there was absolute silence; all reality was suspended in the alembic silence that filled the room. Then the faint whisper of a turned page, and I passed out again.

I coughed up some broth or medicine that someone fed me with a wooden spoon. Voices were speaking Latin, Irish, Danish. Faces: Mother, Snorri, Skallagrim, Goltrade, Frydys, Thorfinn, even Macc Oc, hovered over me. One face was distorted as if seen through water, a drowned face that looked a lot like mine smiling up from the bottom of a lake. There was an elixir of warm, liquid tranquillity that washed all pain from my mind, filling me with an almost postcoital placidity, like a bottled orgasm. Another face, light, dark, silence, pain evaporating and returning a little weaker each time.

When I woke again, it was daylight. I was lying in a

framed bed, mattressed by rushes sewn into a sack and supported by a woven grid of ropes. I was covered by a sheet and a wool blanket, but the bedclothes were tented up below my waist. The bed creaked like the tackle on the *Blood Raven* when I shifted my weight. I focused on the wooden table beside my bed. There was a pitcher and cup, a stoppered bottle, a spoon with teeth marks in the wood.

There was a smell of wind-dried cloth close by, and I realized that my head was pillowed on goose down cased in linen. I tried to move my hands, but my wrists were bound to the sides of the bed. I noticed that the cut on my hand was bandaged. I tested the strength of the straps and found that they were beyond me. The exertion left me weak and dizzy.

There was a row of beds against the wall, a center aisle, and another row of beds on the other side. The walls were stone, judging from the exposed casements. Each bed had a table, and there were a few stools scattered round. The last bed in the row across the aisle was occupied by a very old man. I could see his profile: a hooked nose thickened with the fat of age, toothless gums exposed by a sagging lower jaw, a spotted scalp with a fringe of thin white hair. A young man sat on a stool beside his bed turning the pages of a book.

The old man stirred distantly in his sleep, the rhythm of his breathing became erratic, and the young man looked at him solicitously. Then he noticed that I was awake, reached to the floor, and rang a small bell. Almost immediately I heard footfalls outside the room. I relaxed back into the pillow and closed my eyes.

Someone walked down the aisle and stopped beside my bed. I looked up and saw a round-faced man wearing the same cloth Goltrade wore: a black cowled robe belted with wide black leather. He was carrying a leather bag. His face had a dreamy familiarity, one of the faces from my delirium. He put the bag on the floor and rolled up his wide sleeves. Then he put a hand on my forehead and peeled back my right eyelid with his thumb.

"How's your leg feel?" he asked in Latin.

"Better than it ought," I said.

"Good." He smiled, pulling the stool to the side of the bed, and sat down. He opened the leather bag. "Awake long?"

"Not long," I said. "Minutes only."

"Did you want to vomit when you woke up?"

"No," I said. "How long have I been here?"

"This is your fourth day on Lindisfarne," he said.

That was a shock. Four days gone like water leaking out a hole. Memories had the quick elusiveness of fish when you try to catch them by hand, the slipperiness of an almost-remembered name. I gave it up as he moved the pitcher and cup aside to make room for a few things from his bag.

"Where're the two that brought me here?"

"They're about their duties," he said. "I'm Alban, the Master of the Infirm. You're in my care until you heal." He mixed the powdered contents of a couple of envelopes and a stoppered bottle in the cup. He consulted a complex triangular diagram on a sheet of vellum as he worked. Words were scratched in a quick and indecipherable Latin inside it. Alban seemed to be about Snorri's age and a little fatter than he needed to be, the result, I supposed, of working inside among the herbs and preparations of his profession. His fingers were stained yellow.

He sat quietly for a moment, and I had a good chance to observe him. He was a round-faced man, and his round face was red as he bent forward. The collar of his black wool scapular ridged the skin on his neck. His nose was generous in size and redder than his face. Then he straightened up and looked at me, and he looked like a middle-aged Eng who'd been out of the sun too long.

"Many fear the doctor," he said, examining closely the texture of the powders he was grinding. "Many have reason to, but it's generally the individual they ought to fear, not doctors in general."

I reckoned he was about to tell me that he knew his business.

"I learned my craft in Francia, where they had their learning from the Andalusians, who had it from the Arabs, who had it from the Egyptians. The medicine of the Greeks and Romans also traces to the Egyptians, but these days we work from a rational and empirical base, not out of superstition."

What a relief. I was in the hands of a practitioner of modern medicine. That made me feel better about the vile green paste he was concocting. When he'd achieved the correct proportions, he filled the cup with water and stirred it with the handle of the spoon. I knew what was coming next.

"Drink this," he said, supporting my back with his free hand.

"Why are my hands tied?" I asked, playing for time.

"You were restless," he said as he eased me back to the pillow. "I was afraid you'd harm yourself."

"Am I a prisoner?"

"Of course not." He undid the knots that held me to the bed.

That accomplished, he looked into the swirling contents of the cup and prepared to expatiate on its contents.

"There are three schools of medicine, two descended from the Greeks, the other modern. One holds that the body is subject to imbalances of the four fundamental elements: earth, air, fire, and water. These can be corrected by the application of herbs. The second teaches that disease is a disharmony of bodily humors, and the cure, according to Hippocrates, is to restore that balance. The third is the Science of Signatures, which holds that herbs and plants have a signature which tells the herbalist what maladies they're useful in treating."

Well, that made me feel better: a scientific approach.

"Which school do you follow?"

"I use the best from all schools," he said reassuringly.

So he was a freelance healer, a devotee of that most dangerous of schools: the school of common sense.

"Well, what are you doing for me?" I asked him. As a consumer, I thought it was a good idea to know what was happening, and he seemed pleased enough to talk, as though no one ever took an interest in his life's work. It's still a good way to curry favor if you're prepared to risk death by boredom.

"There are three types of herbal activity," he began, and already I found myself fighting to stay alert. "Building herbs, eliminating herbs, and neutralizing herbs." He drew back the blanket and sheet and examined the wound in my side. He'd no doubt recognized it already as the signature of iron and not the rocks of the Farne Islands, but he said nothing.

"To treat these injuries, we need herbs that knit bones and cuts, so I've prepared yarrow, comfrey, and ginseng.

Does this give you pain?" he probed the wound in my side with his finger.

"Nothing gives me pain," I answered him. I'd been around cuts and slashes all my life and endured my share. I thought I was probably a better physician of blade cuts than he was, but all my previous injuries had hurt like Loki's poison. I couldn't understand why I felt so damned good.

"It's redder than I like," he said, putting his hand beside it. "And warmer to the touch. It's not draining properly. I've opened it twice, and it still has an ugly look."

"It feels a little stiff," I managed. "No more than that."

He nodded, unconvinced. Then he offered me the drink again. I drained it off, finding that it tasted no worse than many other drinks I'd drunk in my time—green mead, for example, with badgers floating in the vat to give it body. Then Alban took a jar out of his bag and swirled it about to disturb its contents. When it was agitated to his satisfaction, he addressed the open mouth of the jar with a pair of wooden tweezers and extracted a leech. This was the cutting edge of medical practice in the waning years of the eighth century. Medicine men haven't changed much, and recently leeches have made a comeback, but when you get right to it, I just don't like the idea of intentionally applying blood-sucking annelids to my flesh. Call me a pussy if you want.

"Our little friend will eat the poisons from the wound," he said.

"Not my little friend." I pulled away from the tweezers, shuddering when I felt the leech's clammy kiss.

"Don't disturb it," he advised me. "When it's full it'll drop off. If you remove it before, the power goes out of the purpose."

"Right." I nodded. I didn't need the directions; I'd worn leeches on my face after the Geat cut me, felt them get fat and warm in the space of an hour as they filled up on my blood. The cut had finally healed, and my beard covered half the scar, but somehow I'd never learned to like our friend the leech.

"Why don't I feel my leg?" I asked.

"It's the elixir," he explained, tapping the stoppered bottle. "It banishes pain like the sun chases dark. A potion the infidels exact from a flower that grows in the land of the Turks."

He poured some of the green liquid on the wooden spoon and held it to my lips. It had that taste I remembered from my dreams, a warmth that spread out like honey on my tongue. I felt the flush of it redden my cheeks; my ears hummed. I blinked at the ceiling, surprised that Steinthor hadn't mentioned discovering it on Sicily.

"No trouble." Alban smiled. "We've a dying man who's earned the right to die in peace. He knew the Venerable Bede."

Good for him, I thought. I didn't know the Venerable Bede from a clam's asshole, but if the old boy across the aisle was ready to become a ghost, I'd let him do it in peace.

Alban collected his medicines and stood up. "Are you hungry?"

Until he asked I hadn't realized how empty I was.

"I'll send food round," he promised. "Nothing heavy at first. Fruit and soup, I think, until we see how it stays down. If you need me, have the novice ring the bell." He walked down the aisle to the old man's bed. The novice closed his book, and they whispered over the old man's still form. Then Alban walked into the hall, and I heard his steps creaking away on the timber floor.

Lindisfarne. I searched my memory for anything Goltrade had ever said about monasteries, but he'd said little. His ecclesiastical career had been passed inside the earthwork of Clontarf, preaching from his pulpit by the common mead vats, or hoofing the countryside to marry, baptize, and bury the Irish.

When he spoke about monasteries, he used the example of Clontarf and its organization, as if the warp and woof of obligations and duties were similar, but I couldn't remember any details. There was a high seat, and someone sat in it. What else was there to know? I closed my eyes and tried to sleep, but I was all slept out. I drifted, listening to the turning pages and the breathing of the old man.

True to Alban's promise, a bowl of thick soup and several apples arrived in a little while. A novice quartered the apples and propped me up while I spooned down the hot soup. The kitchen helper stayed until I was done, disappearing with the tray when I'd finished the soup, leaving me to eat the apples without his supervision.

My mood improved with a little food, but strength didn't flood into me. I was only borrowing strength for a little while, and the leeches were taking back what they could. It must have been a thin broth for them. When the leeches dropped off, Alban came back and returned them to their jar, changed the poultice, which he explained was composed of powdered comfrey, bread molds, the dregs scraped from beer kegs, and crushed mint. Better than leeches, I thought. A little while after that, another reader came to wait with the dying man, and sleep finally took me off to the sound of turning pages.

The autumn sun came up early, pouring through the deep casement in the Farmery, burning through my closed eyelids and into my brain. Unfortunately, the little bit of food I'd eaten the evening before forced me to call to the novice. He rang the small bell again, and after a minute the footsteps moved across the protesting boards. One sure thing was that no one could come up on you in that place without making noise.

"How are you?" Brian asked.

"Ready for a pot," I told him.

"I'll help you to the 'dorter,'" he said.

In a moment he had me upright, my right foot on the floor and my left leg straight as a stump, wrapped in burlap and braced by a couple of planks. Brian's smell hadn't noticeably improved in the days I'd been away from it, and the effect of the elixir amplified his odor. I nodded to indicate that defecation was imminent, and he hurried me down the aisle and through a doorway.

We were in a long room with stalls and a holed-out bench that had the look, if not the smell, of a place where men went to relieve themselves. With Brian's assistance, I lowered myself onto the cool, smooth wood, buffed by the behinds of the countless monks. Brian left me to my privacy, and I thought about my situation.

My geography wasn't precise, but I knew I was on the other side of Britain from where I wanted to be. Unless my luck had changed and Macc Oc had been killed in the sea battle with the Engs or gone over the side in the storm, by now he was in the Orkneys.

That might not be such a bad thing: much could still

happen in the Orkneys; after all, those people had been interbreeding with the northern Picts for almost a century, and the genetic fusion of Pict and Dane was nothing if not volatile. If he favored them with his insults, they might stake him out in a tidal pond with the slops and watch the crabs pick him apart.

But such thoughts were little more than happy fantasy. The Norns didn't consult me when they threaded their loom. As I sat with ass aquiver on the second hole from the left in the rere-dorter of the Farmery, I knew that Macc Oc was probably safe aboard the *Brown Serpent*, protected by Kalf Agirson's weatherluck, Thorr's patronage, and the survivors of the storm, all constrained from their better impulses by the obligations of a blade oath.

Once he was back, he'd be unopposed as a bridegroom, and his share of the profits as commander of the Irish would be more than enough for the bride-price. I had to beat them back to Clontarf, and that meant I had to cross the island, find or steal a ship, and cross the Irish sea ahead of Sygtrygg's fleet. Hey, no problem, right? Only the small detail of a broken leg kept me from starting after breakfast. That and the Northumbrian wilderness, infested by roaming bands of itinerant Picts marauding over the border, not to mention domestic outlaws, lepers, heretics, escaped thralls, and dead men looking for preternatural redress, together with the wolves and adders I reckoned were the usual population of any outback.

I unwrapped the bandage and examined the cut. I imagined the effect my reappearance would have, now it might enhance my reputation in Clontarf, how the details could be embellished to my credit. It was a well-known fact that the wilderness of the Engs was littered with hoards, carried off and buried ahead of one advancing enemy or another and subsequently forgotten. Even the Romans had buried treasure against their return. Orm had once assured us that you couldn't take a piss in Eng land without wetting something the Romans had left.

But first things first—what did they have to wipe with? I found a bundle of cattails and reduced it by a few, and then I called Brian to help me get back to the bed. As we came out of the latrine, Alban was making his rounds. He stopped at the old man's bed, had a whispered conference with the watcher, and then came over to me. Brian lowered me onto the mattress.

"Feeling better?" Alban asked as he set his bag on the table.

"Fair," I admitted. "The food helped."

"We'll try something heavier. How's the leg?"

"It started to ache last night."

"The elixir wears off after five or six hours," he said, opening the bottle again and pouring some on the spoon. "When you feel the pain, I want you to wait as long as you can. How long you wait tells me how the leg heals, and I need a true account."

"What's wrong with the old man?" I asked.

"God let Wilberht live a long life," he said as he replaced the discolored poultice, "and now He's calling him to his reward."

"How old is he?"

"Ninety-one," Alban said with some respect.

I was impressed. I wanted some of whatever they fed those Engs. In Clontarf seeing the far side of fifty was an accomplishment. Of course, that had a lot to do with edged weapons and violence, but in 792, disease wasn't exactly on the run. Whatever treatment was available and its efficacy had exclusively to do with the attending herbalist. If he was someone who knew some medicine, you had a slight chance of surviving, whereas, if he believed in magic or the primacy or prayer, you were done for. Fortunately for me, Alban had been trained by Franks, who had their knowledge from Arabs, who were the only ones who had their scientific shit together in those days. I didn't know if his treatment worked, but at least I didn't feel much pain, and I was willing to settle for that.

Alban examined the splint with professional efficiency. "How was it to move around?" he asked.

"There was some ache," I said, "but the sharpness is gone."

"That means the yarrow and camfrey are mending the bones," he said. "You're as good as healed."

"How long before I can walk?"

"Five or six weeks," he said. "But you can start moving around with a crutch in a few days. It'll hurt, but I've seen men turn themselves into cripples favoring a broken leg, so I suggest you put up with the pain."

By the time I'd be in shape to cross Northumbria, the winter storms would've brought everything to a standstill. The Norns wanted me at Lindisfarne, and it looked like I'd better get used to it. I reckoned they were teaching me a lesson about *ofermod*. But all I could think of was Frydys, how every hour put Macc Oc closer to Clontarf. It all came down to the weather. If the Orkney ice came even a week early, they might be caught in Scapa Flow until spring.

Alban finished his examination and creaked away down the aisle. I wondered at how deep a sleep Wilberht slept not to be awakened by the sound of the shortest stroll across that floor.

In a little while Brian returned with food, and I ate everything but the plates and wanted more.

"Any news of Drogheda?" he asked.

"Sorry," I said. "I've heard nothing in a year or more."

"It's been five years since we were home," he said.

"The news I had was of a cattle raid," I told him.

"That's not news." He smiled. "It's sport."

"True enough." I laughed. "Thanks for fetching me back from the rock. If you'd left me, I'd be dead now."

"We could do nothing else," he said, picking up the tray.

I spent the rest of that day watching the light move around outside the casement, the clouds scud across the little strip of blue sky, the seabirds drift in the air. The silence was measured out by the voices of bells, the turning of pages, Wilberht's breathing. How many breaths does a man have in his bag? I wondered. How many sunrises? How many trips to the shitter? How many women like Frydys? The answer to those questions was the same: not enough.

When the elixir wore off, Alban came round and changed the poultice. It wasn't draining as much, and he informed me that the comfrey was closing the cut. He had it in mind I was interested in medicine, so he told me every detail of the treatment.

When he'd finished his discourse on the relationship of comfrey to the prevalent seasonal humors, he came through with another spoonful of the elixir, and I was able to sleep. Darkness came, and the watcher lit a candle by Wilberht's bed for light and comfort.

In the days that followed, the blade cut healed and Alban discontinued the poultices. During that time he weaned me from the elixir until I was cut off completely. His judgment was accurate: I didn't need it, but I sure missed the way it made me feel, and a little of the feeling hung on, like a memory over a space of time. Another benefit of the elixir was that it prevented me from feeling any anxiety when I thought of Frydys. I knew that the fleet was in the Orkneys, or back in Clontarf, but that was a pain as distant as the pain of the broken leg; it was only after the elixir wore off that I became embittered at my wyrd.

Monks came to the Farmery to sit with Wilberht, who seemed to occupy a position of some importance in the affections of the place, but only Alban and Brian spoke to me. Wilberht lingered on in some private place, still breathing, still accepting nourishment and medicines. They cared for him as if he were the king of the isle. Brian said it was because Wilberht was at the end of his earthly journey and at the beginning of an eternity in heaven. Maybe, but they took care that no one died alone, and they performed the proper duties in the proper time. I respected them for it.

Wilberht finally died at the beginning of my third week in the Farmery. The novice had fallen asleep on his stool. Since I had nothing else to do *but* sleep, I did it often and not too deeply, but the deathwatch was additional duty for the novices, who caught what sleep they could in a full schedule; if *they* slept it was likely to be deep, and that's how it was the night Wilberht died.

I swam in and out of sleep like a dolphin, dreaming of fishes and birds, but the fishes were flying in the air and the birds were swimming in the sea. The floorboards woke me and the novice, but I was sooner alert, and I looked over at Wilberht's bed to judge the time by the length of the remaining candle. Novices who fell asleep on watch were in for a beating, and he snapped upright, wiping his eyes. The sound of the approaching watcher was loud in the darkness, and the novice went out to greet him.

I looked at the yellow pool of light swimming above the rafter shadows on the ceiling. Then I thought I heard a voice by Wilberht's bed and looked over. A cowled monk was standing beside Wilberht, partially obscuring the candle. With his arms folded in his sleeves, no part of him was visible, and I assumed he was the replacement novice. I was about to settle back into the pillow when he spoke:

"Thank you for reminding me to write that last line, Wilberht."

I got up on my elbow for a closer look, but he could have been anyone who'd stopped a few minutes beside the old man's bed in the last three weeks. I knew it wasn't the novice who'd stepped into the corridor. Then Wilberht stirred on his bed. The monk held out a dark stained hand to help the old man up.

"Father Bede," Wilberht said. "I thought not to see you so soon."

"Much time has passed in the world," Bede said. "Only an instant in paradise."

Bede pushed his cowl back, and I could see his profile in the candlelight. He seemed to shift shape as I watched him, appearing at first as old as Wilberht, and then as young as me. His eyes were ancient and knowing, his expression placid. He helped Wilberht to his feet, and then they both looked up at the sound of footsteps. Bede turned suddenly and set up a breeze that extinguished the candle, leaving only the ghost of the flame floating in my vision. Then the novice came in and relit the candle. Wilberht was back in his bed, and the novice bent over and examined him. Then he crossed himself and rang the small bell to summoned help. In a minute I heard Alban's familiar pattern of creaks and thumps.

"Wilberht's with God," the novice said.

Alban crossed himself. "Stay with him while I tell the Prior."

They gave old Wilberht quite a send-off. The bell started tolling soon after Alban left, and continued every minute without interruption for three days, which comes to 4,320 times. If you've ever been laid up sick, you understand why I know the exact number. They took him out of the Farmery to lie before the altar, where Brian said they still kept him company round the clock. I kept my peace about what I'd seen. I doubted they'd believe me. Lindisfarne didn't seem like a place where shapeshifters would hang out. I thought it was an extension of the dream about the birds and the fish. The elixir did some interesting things to my dreams; sometimes waking and dreaming were hard to differentiate.

When a man died in Clontarf, he was buried in the earth,

with a few of his best possessions in case he might need them on the other side. If he'd captained a vik, he'd be laid in a boat-shaped grave or a mound. If he was an ordinary man, his family might raise a stone. The funeral of a great chief, which I'd heard about but never seen, lasted for a couple of days, and a slave or wife might accompany him on the death ship, which would be burned or covered with a mound. In any case, it was done with the appropriate rites and binding runes to keep him in the ground.

I was familiar with the funeral customs of the Danes, but death in the monastery managed to be at once more austere and splendid. They chanted in a style called plainsong, a kind of endless monotony that discovered a strange beauty in the changing of a few tones. Brian told me that everyone associated with Lindisfarne who could was returning for the funeral. An official contingent from a place called Jarrow arrived last, the night before Wilberht's burial.

They sang without letup. The church was far enough away, and the walls thick enough, that the faint sound of their chanting, drifting through the corridors and across the courtyards of Lindisfarne, sounded elfish and weird. The wind carried it off and brought it back. I listened to it all morning, and when it stopped, I knew they had Wilberht in the ground. I hoped they had some way of keeping him there. I didn't want him returning to the Farmery and climbing into the wrong bed.

A few days after Wilberht's funeral, Alban came in with crutches and lay them down on the next bed. Now that I was alone in the Farmery, it was time for ambulatory convalescence.

"Let's get you up and take the measure of these crutches," he said, scooping an arm behind my back to support me as I swung my splinted leg over the edge of the bed.

He helped me stand on my good leg as he tried the crutches one after another until he had a fit. Then he helped me into the aisle, and I thumped down to the night stairs, reminded of Snorri Horsekicked hobbling around Clontarf while he organized the vik.

"Put weight on it," Alban said. "You've got to find the pain and work against it if you want to walk without a limp."

I gingerly put weight on the leg and felt the floor push back, forcing the ends of the bone into one another at the break. An unintended sound came out of my mouth, and Alban stepped over to support me. I walked up and down the floor and back a dozen times, letting a little more weight on the leg each time, and when I was done my face was slick with sweat.

"That's enough for now," he said. "I'll come back this afternoon and we'll walk to the courtyard for some air."

That afternoon he returned with my clothes, cleaned and mended, and a cloak of thick wool, and I went outside for the first time in almost a month. It was that time of year when the season can change overnight, and it seemed winter was only a few hours away. The salt air had the raw feeling that comes on a cold wind, and the color of the sky promised storms. We did a few turns round a small courtyard between the Farmery and the Herbarium, where Alban kept his fires and cultivated his art during the winter.

"Are all funerals like Wilberht's?" I asked him.

"All funerals here," he said.

"I was impressed by the way you took care of him," I said.

"Everyone here lives and dies under the Rule. He'd lived a long life, and we gave him the comfort of our company."

"He spoke to the last watcher," I said. "And when he stood up, I thought he'd somehow gotten better."

"Stood up?"

"Yes," I said. "Just before he died someone came to see him, and Wilberht took his hand and stood up."

"No one else came," Alban said. "You were dreaming."

"I was not," I insisted. I knew the man was there; it was only the shape shifting that was dreamed. "The novice and I both heard him in the corridor, and when he went out, the other man came in and talked to Wilberht. His name was Bede."

Alban stopped dead in his tracks and looked at me. "Bede?"

"That's what Wilberht called him."

"There's no Bede here," Alban said in a queer tone. "What did the novice tell you?"

"He said Wilberht died in his sleep," Alban said.

"We were all sleeping." I grinned. "But Bede's footsteps woke us: me, the novice, then Wilberht."

Alban didn't say anything for the rest of the walk, and after he saw me back to bed, he disappeared for the evening. A novice brought my supper and took the tray away. I walked around the Farmery to teach myself the crutches. I was asleep by vespers.

Alban came back in the morning, carrying clean clothing and news. "You're to meet the Prior today. He's anxious to talk to you about the night Wilberht died."

"I've already told you everything," I said.

"He wants to hear it from you," Alban said. "Are you well enough?"

"That depends on how far it is," I told him.

"Not so far as we walked yesterday," he said, helping me to my feet and offering the crutch.

I changed clothes and followed him out of the Farmery. The outer courtyard was wide and breezy, and the long grasses, browned by the autumn frosts, rippled under the sky. The layout was impressive: dressed stone walls, two-story buildings, a tower rising up from what seemed to be an inner court, and the church. It was the first one I'd ever seen, and I was amazed. Between twin turrets that seemed to scrape the sky was a great disk of colored glass. A long row of glazed windows pierced the west wall. There was a great double door of wood and wrought iron beneath the round window.

A cluster of wicker beehives sat like old women snoring together in the sunshine. The place looked like it went on forever, and I could easily imagine building after building, courtyard after courtyard, nested one within the next like some intricate mechanism of silence and tranquillity. A bell rang inside the buildings. A flight of pigeons rose beyond the roof and circled before dropping out of sight again. We approached a gate, and Alban held it open as I passed through. I was a step ahead of him, point man into the darkness of the gatehouse passage.

I had a premonition of the attack, a sensation from my crutch-supported left side, and then the shadow coalesced into a pissed-off, axe-wielding man. I pivoted on my good leg and dropped under his attack, bringing the crutch up to take his weight as I turned. I carried him through the sunlight that came in from the door and as he passed I recognized him as a Pict, as much by smell as anything. He went off his feet and rolled into a heap of black wool and grunts. He was the quietest Pict I'd ever seen. I hopped forward and brought the crutch down on him with the reassuring sound of cured hickory impacting solid flesh.

He rolled away and came to his feet in the shadows. I could see he was unsteady, but the loose fit of his black robe disguised the nature of his injury. In any case he wasn't sleeping off the effects of my hit. The blade of his axe was bright where it hung suspended in the light, and I could see the marks of a whetstone. Its edge curved up like Loki's smile.

I'd hoped to put him right out, but it was not to be. I hopped back into the shadow on the other side of the open door. The dust we'd stirred up roiled like fog in the sunlight between us and Alban's shadow preceded him into the passage.

"Are you mad?" he shouted at the Pict.

The Pict was noncommittal.

"What will the Prior do if you kill him?" Alban demanded. That made the Pict think a bit. As he stepped forward into the light and I got a look at him, I could see his eyes cloud over with the unfamiliar effort. He had a face ugly enough to turn gold into shit and eyes that tracked independently, so you couldn't be sure where he was looking. His breath carried a sweetness of decomposing wild onions and interested bacteria, and it was filling up the space in the enclosed passage a lot faster than I liked.

"It's been twenty years since Godric bought you from the Geats. You could've gone anytime. Think about leaving now."

He looked like he was beginning to appreciate the slimness of the job market for mute Pict axemen.

"We're going to see the Prior in the Chapter," Alban said. "Be about your duties." Alban put a hand on the man's forearm, but the Pict shrugged off his touch and looked at me with eyes like stones: dead eyes with an agenda.

"You want him gone, and he wants no less to go," Alban said, neatly summarizing the situation. "He'll go when his leg heals. Until then put up with him, or kill him and be off yourself with winter coming. Make up your mind."

A pretty gutsy offer with *my* life, I thought, but all my attention was on the Pict. The proof of that pudding would be in the tasting, and at that moment I wasn't sure how it was going to go down. The Pict absently rotated the axe while he figured it out.

But Alban had enough of waiting, and he stepped over to open the inner door. I stood there facing the Pict with my weight on my good leg and the hickory crutch in both hands. The truth was he had me, but he was still undecided, so I took a chance and followed Alban into the wide courtyard of the cloister garth.

"Who was *that*?" I gasped when the door closed behind us in the daylight garden, "and why does he want me dead?"

"Haki, the porter's assistant," Alban said. "When he was a child Danes killed his family, and he was slaved out among the Geats for years. He was traded around and finally came to a Christian who brought him here. One of his owners cut his tongue out. He's lived on Lindisfarne since he was fourteen. We're the only family he's got."

"All that must've happened before I was born," I said as we crossed a big rectangular garden, bordered by a gallery where stone tables and benches sat in the light of the lowering sun. At least that explained how this place of silence had its own silent Pict. Cutting out a Pict's tongue was the only known way to shut one up.

"Forgiveness is a hard virtue for some to master," he said.

"He's naught to forgive me for. I didn't kill his family."

"A Dane's a Dane to him," he said as we approached the door.

"I was born in Clontarf," I said. "Not the Mark. That makes me Irish."

"You've the look of a Dane," he said. "The sooner you lose it, the better you'll be."

Alban held open the door to the inner cloister, but I hesitated before I stepped through it, not eager to discover Haki the Pict knew a shortcut. The inner cloister was another court with a covered perimeter of benches and tables, and a pond and fountain in the middle. The splashing of the water filled the smaller courtyard with white noise, obscuring even the cries of the seabirds.

Alban indicated one of the benches that formed a pentagon around the fountain. "Wait here," he said, turning through an arch on the side of the courtyard.

I limped over to the pond. Fish swam lazily under the

surface, ducking under cold-curled lily pads as my shadow moved over them. I lowered myself to the stone border and splashed some water on my face. A bell rang inside the monastic complex, barely penetrating the water noise. In the Farmery there had been the creaking of the floor, Wilberht's labored breathing, and the turning of pages. Before that, on the ship, there was the wind in the rigging, the storm, the battles, the feastings and flytings, the shouting of Dane and Irishman: always sound. But in the inner courtyard garden of Lindisfarne sound was absent, noise was white, and the color of tranquillity was the blue of the sky: it was the epicenter of Silence.

I watched the fish. The sun was where I judged the gatehouse to be, where Haki the porter's assistant, pissed off by his past traffic with Danes, Geats, and Christian liberals, was no doubt whetting his knife and nursing his hatred. The Pict as the wetnurse of death has been a much-neglected image in literature, but at that moment it was an image of precise and unpleasant associations. After a while Alban opened the door and motioned to me.

"The Prior wants to see you in the Chapter House," he said. "What do you know about monastic life?"

"Not a lot." I shook my head.

"Higbald is the bishop of Lindisfarne, and the bishopric of Lindisfarne covers two thirds of the kingdom. Our land holdings are scattered all over Northumbria, and Higbald's absent much of the time attending to his duties. The Prior guides the monastic family in his absence," he said as we walked. "Apart from what's in the Rule, he makes all law in the monastery. He wants to see you before he decides what to do."

"What can he do?"

"Whatever he wants."

That sounded familiar. Higbald obviously sat in the high seat, but it sounded like this Prior warmed it when he was gone, and I expected that he'd be another variation on Sygtrygg, and Orm before him, in fact on every other ass that ever polished wood.

"We meet daily to read a chapter of the Rule," Alban explained as we walked down a long corridor. "After that we discuss business and matters of discipline. Whatever happens, remember this: don't talk to *anyone* but the Prior, and only if he asks you something. When he speaks, keep silent and listen."

It wasn't hard to see the lay of the land. Don't cross the Prior. "What is it you prize so much about silence?" I asked.

"St. Basil said, 'Quiet is the first step in our sanctification.' In general, voices are raised only in prayer and song," Alban continued, "and even outside the monastic precinct we only speak as necessary. We have a number of signals to make ourselves understood. You'd do well to learn them."

That explained the general dumbness I'd observed, but it didn't sound like a very stimulating way to spend your life, and learning hand signals was a low priority.

"Why are you talking to me?"

"The Rule allows the Farmerer to speak to his charges," Alban said. "Remember, no one interrupts the Prior."

I nodded. "Whatever you say."

The Chapter House was a large rectangular room, and the full population of Lindisfarne, over a hundred monks, was sitting around the walls. The high seat was opposite the door, and the man who sat there watched me walk in. I'd seen him come to sit with Wilberht a few times. The novices were always deferential, and he'd stayed a little while and gone without ceremony. He'd been accompanied by the two men who sat behind him now. One of them recorded what was said on parchment. The other's ferret eyes flickered from face to face, and when they passed over me it was like a cobweb brushing your face in the dark.

The Prior was a man approximately Goltrade's age; the fringe of short hair that circled his head was gray, and his shaved pate was brown. He had a whippetlike tension that made him seem ready to spring. I took him for a more sophisticated man than the rest of the monks; maybe it was something about his features, sharper and more alert than the broad Anglo-Saxon faces, or just that faint cologne of ambition that seemed to hang in the air.

I wondered what the proper mix of obeisance and spine would be. I didn't want to seem too arrogant, but, on the other hand, obviously sucking up wouldn't be good either. It was an old dilemma. I stopped behind Alban.

"This is Bran," he said by way of introduction. "Washed

up on Longstone in the storm, and a patient these weeks in the Farmery."

That was it. I gave him a little bow, as polite as I could manage with a crutch tucked under my arm, and we stood there appraising one another. The Prior was motionless, one elbow on the arm of the high seat, chin in palm, fingers covering his mouth as if keeping his words prisoner. It was an old trick I'd seen Orm play on traders to make them ill at ease before the talking began. But it continued longer than I expected, and just as I began to wonder if I was supposed to do something, the Prior removed his hand from his lips and spoke to me in Latin.

"We've been told of your discovery on the Inner Farne," he said. "You were lucky our novices came along before the militia."

"It was God's will," I said, dredging up one of Goltrade's clichés.

"You're Christian, then?"

"My father's Snorri Horsekicked, horsethane to Sygtrygg Ormson, lord of Clontarf. There's a priest there who baptized me at birth, and again a few months ago." I let it go at that. If he wanted more, he could ask, and maybe I'd already said too much.

"Clontarf's a Christian town?"

"There were Christians aplenty inside the earthwork when I left," I told him, thinking of the Irishmen. No one there was in a position to call me a liar if he inferred a Christian citizenry.

"I'm told you read and write, and I see you know the speech of educate men."

"Goltrade taught me," I said. "The only book he had was a Bible. I began to study when I was a child."

There was another long pause. I could feel the eyes of all the men in the room studying me, but I kept mine on the Prior, who was the only one that mattered. A breeze found its way through the open windows, carrying the salt smell of the sea, sharp as a cedar fire, and cutting the odor of closely packed men in ripe woolens.

"What made you want to study?" he asked, shifting his weight on the high seat.

I hesitated for a long moment, and then, considering how much silence was prized there, kept my own with a shrug.

"It's often so," he said, providing his own answer and

finding it agreeable. "God moves in us when He wills, not when we do."

He gestured to one of the men sitting nearest to him, who handed over a quill and scrap of parchment. The Prior passed them to me. "Write something, please," he said.

I took the quill and paper and searched my wordhoard for the correct currency, and I recalled a grammar lesson from Goltrade's Bible and wrote, in what I thought was a pretty acceptable hand:

> *In principio erat verbum,*
> *et verbum erat apud Deum,*
> *et Deus erat verbum. Hoc erat*
> *in principio apud Deum.*
> *Omnia per ipsum facta*
> *sunt et ipso factum*
> *est nihil quod factum.*
> *Est in ipso vita erat*
> *et vita erat lux hominus.*
> *Et lux in tenebres lucet*
> *et tenebrae eam non*
> *comprehenderunt.*

> In the beginning was the Word,
> and the Word was with God,
> and the Word was God.
> He was with God in the beginning.
> Through him all things were made;
> without him nothing has been made.
> In him was life,
> and that life was the light of men.
> The light shines in the darkness,
> and the darkness has not understood it.

Then I gave quill and paper to the Prior. He read the lines and folded the scrap. I was showing off, and I hoped it would work. I could have written a simple message to him to prove I could compose and not just memorize, but I thought the *In Principio* would get his attention.

"What do you know about Bede?"

The change of subject was accompanied by a change in the breathing patterns of the room. Now we'd gotten to the point of this audience; the story of my conversion and the business of writing had merely been ecclesiastical smoke and mirrors.

"Nothing," I could truthfully say, but now I was on guard. Bede was a sensitive issue, for some reason.

"You shared the Farmery with Wilberht," the Prior said. "Tell me what you saw when he died."

I repeated what I'd told Alban, lapsing into Irish and Anglo-Saxon when my Latin failed. When I finished, the Prior was silent for a long while.

"What do you know of Bede?" the Prior asked again.

"He the one who came to talk to Wilberht?" I asked.

"Some believe he was," the Prior acknowledged.

"Alban," he said suddenly to the Farmerer. "How much of the poppy was he taking?"

"Twenty drams a day, less as the leg healed. When he saw Bede he'd been without it for five days."

"We've yet to establish he saw Bede," the Prior said. "There must be an *advocatus diaboli*. How long does the poppy last?"

"It depends," Alban said. I settled back for a long disquisition on herbal science, but he cut straight to the chase. "In a man Bran's size, given the decreased dose, not longer than three days. After that, he'd be more alert, not less."

"Men dream strange dreams with the poppy," the Prior said.

"As did Bran," Alban conceded. "But dreams stop when the poppy's withheld. It was no dream of the poppy."

That conclusion seemed to disagree with the Prior, and he looked a long time at his steepled fingers, like the timber ribs of an unthatched hall. Nor was there a roof to his argument.

"The Celtic church is a church of mysticism and excess."

The silence in the Chapter deepened. When a group of quiet men gets more quiet, something's up. As far as the Prior's estimate of the Celtic Church was concerned, he seemed to know Goltrade.

"Christians of Celtic origin still hold superstitious beliefs side by side with revealed truth. They're prone error in their desire to believe the impossible. It was for this reason as much as the calendar that the synod of Whitby imposed the Roman rite."

Yeah. I knew what I'd seen, and I wondered why the

Prior wanted to blow it off. I didn't look at Alban. However it played out, I was on my own.

"Was this Goltrade a discoverer of saints?"

"Not to my knowledge," I said. Goltrade had discovered nothing but an attitude since discovering the mead vats.

"How did Bede look?"

"Old and young at the same time. Happy and sad at once."

I looked around the gathering, but I didn't see him in the Chapter room. "Where is he?" I asked.

"In Jarrow," the Prior said. "Dead these fifty-seven years."

Then I understood the look on Alban's face when I'd told him: someone had cut the runes badly and Bede was walking the night.

So many of the monks were crossing themselves that I reckoned this Bede must be bad business. I'd seen that look once before: when old Hoskuld had come back a month after his death to milk his goats because the runecutter made a mistake. Hoskuld's wife and one of his sons had gone to the goat pen at dawn and found Hoskuld, squatting on the low stool with his face against the flank of the goat. After a month in the ground, Hoskuld wasn't looking his best, and the sight propelled them screaming for Odhinn's priest and the runecutter. They had to act quickly because the longer a dead man hangs around, the harder he is to get rid of.

They woke up Orm, who was sleeping off the effects of the previous night's drinking, and then hid under the table until he sent for the runecutter. I was only ten at the time, just the right height to see them cowering under the boards while Orm tried to get the story out of them. The recut runes put Hoskuld to bed for good, but they sued the runecutter and won compensation.

Now a lot of it fell into place. Bede was a shapeshifter and a ghost, and he was prowling around the grounds, collecting people. So far only the old and infirm; who knew how long he'd be satisfied with them? Maybe the Prior himself summoned Bede. He had the look of a wizard.

"Why did he come for Wilberht?" I asked innocently.

The Prior looked angry, but it was a reasonable question, considering the fuss. "We believe the soul of a dead monk can return to guide the soul of the one who watched when he died," the Prior said. "Though I've never known anyone to witness it."

"Didn't the novice tell you?"

"He was ashamed he'd fallen asleep, and he merely said that Wilberht died peacefully. A caning made him remember, and a week's penance will absolve him of his lie."

That was one way to discourage spectral sightings, all right. A couple dozen strokes with a willow withe and a week on bread and water will make a rationalist of almost anyone. But the novice wasn't lying; Bede had left before he came back into the Farmery.

Christians believed that you were a ghost while you were alive too. That your ghost animated your body and that death released it into the next world to be about its ghost business, good or bad, depending on what kind of a life you'd lived. For some reason the Prior didn't believe that, or didn't want to, which came to the same thing in the end: a whipping and a fast.

There was a general stirring, and I saw that the monks were still crossing themselves. Apparently *they* believed in Bede.

"How did *you* come to see Bede's spirit?" the Prior wondered.

"My mother has the night sight," I told him, "as do all her sisters. Perhaps I've a bit of it myself."

"The night sight." He seized on the phrase with a smile. "A Celtic belief in the ability to see fairies and elves."

I thought he must have been a Celt: only a Celt would've been so desperate to suck up to the Engs and discredit Celtic beliefs. It was clear the Prior was making his bed in Eng land.

"Do you believe night sight enabled you to see Bede's soul?"

"I saw what I saw." I shrugged. "Make what you want of it."

"Perhaps," the Prior said, satisfied that he'd scored a damaging point. "Do you seek sanctuary?"

"Sanctuary?" I asked, unfamiliar with the term.

"The Church has the power to protect those who come to her," he said. "So protected, the civil authorities cannot harm you."

"Why would they want to?"

"You're a Dane," he pointed out, "Irish or not. And

from a Danish fleet raiding up the coast. That makes you outlaw."

"We weren't raiding," I protested. "We were going to trade in Orkney."

"Trade?"

I tried to look hurt by his implication. "Trade," I asserted. "The barter of goods, the exchange of items of equal value."

"I am familiar with the concept," he said with a little smile. "But Danes are not noted for it. Only a couple of weeks past a Danish fleet ravaged the country of the Mercians along the Severn River."

"There's a difference between Danes of the Mark and the men of Clontarf," I said with subdued vehemence, trying not to look guilty, though I was startled by the speed of that news.

"Perhaps." He shrugged. "I've never been to Clontarf. But if you don't ask for sanctuary, I must surrender you to the king's reeve in Bamburgh."

I didn't know what sanctuary was all about, but I knew I had a broken leg and that I was on a big island full of hostile Anglo-Saxons. I didn't have silver, weapons, or friends, and I needed time to heal.

"If I ask for sanctuary, what will happen?" There was always the fine print to consider.

"You'll stay in the community as long as you wish."

"Could I study?"

"Of course." He smiled.

"Then I want sanctuary."

"So be it," the Prior said in a tone of command. "Now Alban will take you to the Guest House."

"Thank you," I said, and followed Alban out.

"That went well," Alban said when we were outside.

"How could you tell?" I asked with sarcasm. "And what was the matter of Bede's ghost? I saw what I saw." I'd been ambushed, and I was angry that Alban hadn't warned me.

"I know," Alban said in a mollifying tone. "I never doubted you. But the Prior has a duty to prevent rumor from becoming belief, and he had to question you."

"He was doing more than his duty," I said. "And you know it."

"It would be sinful to attribute motives to the Prior," he

said, but I sensed that motives were plain enough to everyone but me. "He offered you sanctuary," Alban continued.

"What's sanctuary?"

"You'll be protected from the king's reeve," he said.

"What do I do in return?"

"What you're told." He shrugged. "Like the rest of us."

"I suppose that means keeping my mouth shut about
Bede?"

"If the Prior commands it." Alban nodded. "But he
didn't."

"Why not?"

"Because he felt your belief in the night sight made it
invalid."

We went back outside, across the little courtyard with
the fountain, and out another door into a third and broader
yard where the smooth facade of the perimeter wall was
broken up by small wooden buildings.

"Do you think it was Bede?" I asked.

"Night sight or not, I never doubted it," he said.

"Don't you have anyone to cut binding runes here?"
I asked.

"We're buried beneath the cross," he said. "Bede's soul
wasn't restless or distracted, as the ghosts who walk un-
bound. He came back with God's permission to pay the
debt he owned Wilberht."

"So I won't be running into him again?"

"Not Bede, but Wilberht may come back for you."

"With luck I won't see him for a long time," I said.

"With luck." Alban smiled.

The Guest House was on the other side of the monastery
from the Farmery, and getting there constituted a little tour
of the grounds. There was a forge, a tanner's shed, a small
mill, a granary, the unmistakable smell of a malt house, a
three-stall stable, and other small buildings I couldn't name.
They were self-contained on Lindisfarne. With serious fortifications and a few hundred men to defend the walls, it
would've been quite a stronghold.

"Are there many guests?" I asked.

"None at the moment," Alban said. "But the island
swarms with them at Cuthbert's feast."

"Who's Cuthbert?"

"Cuthbert was bishop in his time, but he's dead these
hundred years. He's buried behind the altar. Pilgrims come

from all over the island to pray at his tomb. Bede wrote his life."

"This Bede was a writer?"

"Yes," Alban explained. "He wrote the history of Britain and the Church." Alban showed me to the guest dorter on the second floor where there were rows of beds much the same as those in the Farmery.

"The laver is on the first floor," he said. "The guest master will come after Chapter."

I lowered myself onto one of the beds and nodded, and Alban left me alone. When I was rested, I made my way back down the stairs, where the water turned out to be cold. As I was drying off, Alban returned with Eadred, the guest master.

Eadred was a cheerful man who examined my bruises and cataloged my injuries as if accepting a cargo while babbling continuously about nothing I understood: random bits of monastic trivia, natural history, the weather, Christian prophesy, and personal hygiene. He suffered from a sort of natural geniality.

"Aren't you bound by rules of silence?" I asked him.

"For the guest master, as for the Farmerer, the Rule is relaxed," he explained. He looked closely at the rune that Frydys had given me, still around my neck. "The fish of Jesu," he said. "A handsome piece."

I was soon to learn that there were competing agendas at Lindisfarne in the late months of 792: some humble, some grandiose, some ecclesiastical, and some secular, but all of them carrying more *ofermod* than they could swim with. I thought mine was humble enough: keep a low profile until my leg healed. Not that I was in any hurry to actually *experience* the bipedal transition of Northumbria. It wasn't a popular jaunt in the late eighth century, unless you were a missionary, an anchorite, or a bunch of pissed-off Picts foraging for fun and profit.

While I'd been lying on my back in the Farmery, the routine of Lindisfarne had gone on without interruption. It was sheer coincidence that Wilberht shared it with me, bringing the frequent visitors coming one last time to see the oldest living monk who'd known the great Bede. And then there was the boffo eleventh-hour appearance of the great Bede himself. Whatever the Farmery was, it certainly wasn't the general routine of the monastery.

On Lindisfarne the routine began at midnight, a time when I was used to seeing the drunks in the hall finish puking and begin to get their second wind. The midnight bell at Lindisfarne signaled Matins. After that everyone went back to bed for a few hours until the bell summoned them to Lauds; after that they got something to eat and then fell in for Prime at about six A.M. Then they went to wherever they worked or read until midmorning, when it was time to sing Terce, which they rolled up into the Chapter mass, since they were in church anyway. Then they had the Chapter meeting.

After the Chapter meeting they had another mass and said the prayers for Sext. Then they ate again, had a siesta, tired out by all that prayer, and then in midafternoon it was back to church for Nones. Then they were free from *ora* for a little more *labora* until Vespers, followed by an hour and a half of work, then supper, and then Compline, the prayers for the last hour of the day. After that they hit the sack so they could start over at midnight.

My modified version of that grueling schedule began at sunrise with a tray of food. I was free to hobble around until the Chapter mass, which I attended, and then I was free again until the noon meal. I spent the afternoon reading, pillowed in a stone alcove with a southern exposure. Godwine, the librarian, guided my reading from a distance. One morning two books and a note accompanied breakfast. The note said: "These two books will explain many things."

And he was right. Basic to an understanding of what those Engs were about was Bede's history: *The English Church and People.* It began with the long procession of Old Eng clans and tribes, all but one of which claimed descent from Woden. Bede wove their subjugation by the Romans into the story of the emergence of the Christians, and the power struggles within the Church in the form of various heresies.

A heresy is a disagreement that appears to have merit, usually to disenfranchised peasants, and which is given voice by some up-and-comer too impatient to wait his turn. There were many in those years, chief among them Pelegius, a liberal who believed in free will and a general lightening up on the part of Rome. You can imagine how long it took them to come down on that; no less a personage than the great gardener Augustine took a keen interest in *that* hardy weed, and he did all he could to uproot it wherever it sprouted. In addition to the heretical rats gnawing at the Church from the inside, the Moslem expansion in the Mediterranean world made the Popes' asses pucker.

The second book Godwine sent me was the best one for understanding the monks and the life they'd chosen. Called, with utter lack of guile, *The Rule*, it covered every aspect of communal living. If your basic premise was the fundamentally communist proposition that everything belonged equally to everybody, you were on solid ground. However, this was a philosophy, and hence a volume, that would have been useless on a vik, another enterprise undertaken by men living communally but sharing out according to his geld and his deeds.

But I had to admit Benedict had really thought the whole thing out. Everything they did and why they did it was covered in that book, and to read it was to understand how to fit into that place.

As a historical document, *The Rule* said as much about the context the monks defined themselves in as it did about communal life. It was a context of emperors, overkings, petty kings, and warlords; thegns and wildmen from Scotland and Wales; and Frankish genocide: a context of Moslem expansionism from China to Portugal that threatened Christian control of the lucrative trade routes to the east. You had to understand all those things before you understood Western monasticism.

The Christians were like ants swarming over a roadkill: no question of the outcome, only how long it would take. The religions of the north weren't interested in making converts. They believed pretty much that what god or gods you worshiped was your business. It was Islam that scared the shit out of the Popes. The sons of the prophet made converts unhampered by a deity that insisted on love, mercy, and peace.

Moslems were expanding their belief system with fire, sword, and the Koran, and the Christians were inventing the just war rationalization and getting tooled up for the crusades in a few hundred years. So with the Old Testament ethos of Islam pretty much missionary-proof, and the Arabs as a whole completely immune to the particular blend of charisma, beard mange, and lice that ecstatic missionaries called their own, the Christians turned their attentions to the north. By that time, only the Danes, the Frisians, and the Old Saxons had resisted the blandishments of conversion, and Rome could afford the time to neutralize the northern gods. When push finally came to shove, they didn't want a two-front war.

Recent history, recorded by men who about half the time resisted the temptation to make their side sound like the good guys, was easy to find. There was a collection of letters exchanged by Pope Gregory and Augustine, a churchman with a lot of clout in the middle of the century. His book was there, too, *The City of God,* written while the embers of Rome still glowed in the evening sky in the wake of Aleric and the Vandals.

Very salutary, in terms of what I might expect once I was at large in the land of the Engs, were copies of the Laws of both Æthelred and Offa. The Engs were a well-regulated society, and I studied these codices thoroughly to avoid accidental fuckups when I finally hauled ass across Northumbria.

There were also volumes of Gregory's letters to just about everyone else who could read in the years between 590 and 604. There were treatises on obscure points of biblical interpretation, diatribes against rival schools of theological thought, breathless chronicles of fantastic miracles performed by itinerant holy men of suspicious means before witnesses of dubious credibility, all of which served to reinforce my idea of the Western Church of the late eighth century as a soap opera of conflicting religious and secular power.

Looking around Lindisfarne, I could see it played out on a smaller scale. The monks on Holy Isle were divided into many groups: craftsmen, middle managers, and the usual assortment of tradesmen, peasants all, and former members of the nobility, second and third sons of landed gentry, and in come cases members of various royal lines hiding out from death squads and purges. There was even one former Northumbrian king in residence, grown tired of royal responsibilities and the ingratitude of his thegns.

But the distinction that cut across all other categories was the distinction between Celtic and Roman observance. Outwardly they all observed the Roman rite, but there was a clean division between the careerist Romans and the spiritual Celts.

I never met Godwine in those weeks, but he sent books he thought I might find interesting, along with notes suggesting others. "Study the *Poetics* in particular," he wrote about Aristotle. "The third one," in Socrates' *Spartan Dialogues.* "The Campaign against the Helvetians, in Caesar's *War Commentaries.*" "All of Sappho and Tacitus."

After sampling the churchmen, I began Procopius's book on war, *De Bellis,* and his book of Imperial Roman gossip, *Anecdotes.* I chased Procopius with Virgil, Cicero, Xenophon, Sophocles, Aristotle, Plato, the complete works of Socrates in four volumes, and the *Encyclopedia of Arts and Sciences* compiled by Isidore of Saville.

For more insular reading there were the Welsh epics by Taliesin, Aneirin, and Llywarch Hen, and a wide selection of Old Saxon and Anglo-Saxon literature—the old stories were well represented, the great poems of Ireland, England, and Wales were there, and I had the pleasure of reading good versions of the *Tain,* the *Mabinogion,* and the *History of Arthur.*

The library had all two dozen of the great Arthurian epics, in both Latin and the Anglo-Saxon long line. They were a great read as I lay in bed knitting my bones: doomed love, dutyfetters, and a lot of axe killings and pitched battles. Conflicting wyrds all around: Celtic mysticism and necromancy mixed with a Romanesque urgency to unite England under one overlord; treachery and nobility, blood feuds, preternatural guests at the Yule table, internal and external threats, order and chaos, good and evil, being and nothingness. The great organic national myth of the Engs, invented and refined and spread by peripatetic gleemen with willow harps and a thirst for brown ale at the end of a long day, and finally recorded by monks on the royal commissions of petty tyrants who remembered them fondly from their youth. Confinement in the Guest House was not altogether unpleasant.

As the days grew shorter, day and night were only degrees of dimness and dark, and the weather turned to intermittent rain that never cleared off. My leg healed well, and by the end of November I discarded the crutch for a shortened staff. I walked twice a day round the great courtyard, and

Alban came daily to examine my leg, but for the time being my main contact with the rest of humanity was Eadred, who made the best of his dispensation from silence despite what the Rule had to say about idle conversation.

He respected my reading time, but it seemed that when I tired of reading he'd show up at the Guest House with some cloister gossip or news about the York Court or the royal palace at Bamburgh, as if I were a connoisseur of rumors about the Northumbrian nobility. But his prattling broke up the autumnal stillness of Lindisfarne. Days passed like coins dropping to the bottom of a honey jar, a languorous turning through a slow golden tranquillity contained by the clear vessel of the great silence.

One morning I came down for breakfast and found Eadred sitting on the stone sill of one of the window casements. "I've come to take you on a proper tour," he said. "We'll go the rounds when you finish eating."

I uncovered the Refectory tray, and Eadred talked as I wolfed down breakfast, a commentary of familiar rhythms requiring only a polite conversational grunt or nod.

"From now on you may join us in the Refectory and go unaccompanied wherever you wish, excepting the Chapter. You may leave the precinct of the monastery as you wish, because the island itself is sacred ground, but if you leave the enclosure, take care.

"The Prior hopes you'll find suitable work to give glory to God, and so we'll visit all the craftsme—"

I held up a hand, and Eadred stopped in midword, waiting for my response. "I want to see the library and the place where you copy books," I told him.

It was a cold, late autumn day. It had cleared off a little, which meant that the clouds were scudding overhead and the weakened sun was only half hidden. The wind ignored my wool clothes, and I began to understand what wintering on Lindisfarne would be like. The smell of a peat fire in the kitchen came and went on the breeze. High overhead a great flock of geese moved through the sky like a needle and thread sewing up the clouds. I watched them pass out of sight below the cloister wall. It was that moment when you first feel winter in your bones.

Eadred led me across the yard, working through his canned presentation of the highlights with the assurance of a man used to speaking, a man who liked to speak and had some pride in his ability; just another eighth century raconteur with a captive audience.

"Cuthbert used to go to the small island in the harbor to separate himself from the monastery, but in a few years so many people visited him he had no time to contemplate God's greatness. Then he went to Farne and drove out the evil spirits. He built a stone hut and an oratory, surrounded them with a ditch.

"Cuthbert lived there for many years encircled by an embankment so high he never saw anything but the sky where God dwells. Then Bishop Eata died, and the synod elected Cuthbert bishop. Trumwine went to the island and begged him to accept, which he did because Boisil had foretold it.

"After two years as bishop, Cuthbert returned to Farne Island to die. He wanted to be buried there, but the brethren begged him to let his body be placed in the church. After eleven years in the grave, while Eadfrid was abbot, they opened the tomb and found his body uncorrupted. They took word of the miracle to the archbishop, together with some of his vestments as proof.

"In after time, when Cynewulf was bishop, a guest master named Baduthegn was washing in the sea when he was struck by a seizure. He lay helpless before he could get up, paralyzed on one side of his body. He went back to the priory in great difficulty. His distress grew, and he determined to pray before Cuthbert's tomb. Crippled though he was, he went to the church and prayed, and finally fell asleep. He dreamed a great hand descend on him and touched the place in his head where the pain was, and when he woke he was healed of his disease. Thereafter, Cuthbert's clothing has had miraculous properties, and on his feast day, people come from all over to be healed of their maladies."

"Whoa," I interrupted. "You mean these clothes heal people's wounds and diseases?"

"Correct." Eadred beamed, pleased with my quick grasp of the thread of his story.

"When's Cuthbert's feast?"

"On March twentieth," he said. "The day before Saint Benedict's."

"I don't suppose Cuthbert could heal my leg any sooner?"

"He may if you pray to him," Eadred said optimistically.

As he related the medicinal properties of Cuthbert's bones and vestments, which I have to admit I found a little hard to believe, it became clear that these Eng holy men were at their most potent in the form of used clothing and hearsay, second- and third-class miracles as far as the Church was concerned.

One of the doors down the row of wooden buildings was open, and Eadred led me inside, where a number of men stirred a swirling yellow broth of hides in three great stone troughs. The odor of lime and green skins that rose to the ceiling as they wielded the heavy paddles, blackened from immersion in the hide soup, was the odor of all tanneries.

Other men pulled the wet hides out of the troughs, draped them over a board braced against their guts, and then drew a flat oak stave upward against the grain to remove the hair. They snapped the clots of hair aside for burning and stretched the clean hides on racks.

Drying them took days, and the drying room was heated with low fires to ward off the chill and moist ocean air. The hides had a pleasant smoky smell. After that the hides were scraped again in a room beside the drying room, where the men could carry the racks in and return them empty to be hung again with wet hides.

At a table on one side of the room, a monk trimmed dried sheets of parchment. There was a great stack, all of a size and weight, and he brushed the trimmed edges into a bin beside the table. Then he folded the sheets into folios and quartos. The finished pages were stacked in bins to be taken to the Scriptorium.

I'd never seen the making of parchment, and it was interesting to see them producing stacked pages of a pale and unblemished cream color that invited ink. The only noises were the sounds of the press, and the water that ran into the shop from one end became industrial effluent as it bathed the vellum in the lime-water trough and flowed out to drain into the sea.

The smell of the parchment paste was strong in the shop, but my head cleared in the fresh winter air. "I want to see the view from the tower," I said. I'd been in the church every day for the Chapter mass, but I'd never ventured beyond the first pillar.

Now I needed to orient myself, and the tower would

command a view of the entire area, so, as Eadred regaled me with tales of the restorative potency of Cuthbert's clothing, I made straight across the churchyard.

The cruciform church at Lindisfarne was a long nave flanked by two aisles, a transept where the high altar stood, and behind it the choir. No flying buttresses, but a sizable barn in its own right. Cuthbert's tomb was hidden from view by the high altar, but I wasn't interested in Cuthbert's grave, however much Eadred was. As I looked for the door to the tower, I was struck by the curious color of the ambient light. I stared up at the great circular window of colored glass, where a man made of light was standing with his hand upraised in greeting. With the late morning sun behind the glass it was a stunning sight, and I stood paralyzed like the old boy in Eadred's story. The light poured down like the slanting scintilla of a hard spectral rain.

All I could think of was that Heimdal, the good-looking god who guards the rainbow bridge, must look like that, but I knew Eadred wouldn't want me to compare his twenty-two-foot glass Jesus with Heimdal. However, an error in the direction of Cuthbert would be accepted with indulgence and a sense of warmth, so I asked him craftily if the image was Cuthbert's.

Eadred smiled. "It's the image of the risen Christ."

Let it not be said I have no eye for the main chance, but opportunism aside, I'd never seen anything like it, and standing there on the stone floor of the church at Lindisfarne, looking up at that window, I was as close to a religious experience as I've ever been. Finally Eadred tugged at my sleeve and nodded at the stairs.

They were made of stone as far as the loft in the rear of the church; after that they were wood, spiraling up the inside of the tower to a room where three great bells hung from oak rafters. It was hard work for someone on a staff, and Eadred followed as close as he could, complaining that Alban would forbid this and preparing to catch me if I toppled back. The bells were as tall as a man. A ladder stood against one of the walls, and I handed the staff to Eadred and mounted it carefully, leaving him to follow.

I raised the trap and climbed out onto the square, roofed top of the bell tower. There was a four-foot parapet of dressed stone and a slate roof to keep off the rain. The boards were white and dusty with bird shit, and the flutter of wings was loud when the trap creaked up, although the birds were gone when I finally gained the platform. Just as I'd hoped, I could see the entire island: the monastic buildings, the sheep grazing in three dog-tended flocks, the village on the north shore, the stony beaches, the dunes, and the rocky headland. Beyond the sheltered bay the marsh and the mudflats teemed with millions of feeding birds.

Even at low tide the harbor could hold five hundred longships. The island was watered by a spring-fed lake, which the industrious monks had channeled into a series of ponds and linking canals that carried fresh water to all the buildings and gardens. Situated on the Northumbrian coast, it commanded the Frisian Sea. I wondered what Thorfinn would have said.

But Thorfinn wasn't there. It was just Eadred and me, and, far below in the shadow of the wall inside the gate, Haki and Pict, his back against the stones as he watched. "Let's go," I said.

We went carefully down the stairs into the church. The floor was paved with great slates, quarried inland and carried to the island by pious men with strong backs, always a good combination. The vaulted lead roof was supported by stone pillars, darkened by the smoke of torches and candles. There were thin glazed windows in the walls.

A look at the sky outside told me that the storms weren't far away. I reckoned I was wintering at Lindisfarne. Sygtrygg and Thorfinn would be spending the time between landfall and Yule admiring their loot and sharing out rings and the proceeds from the slaves. Of course, because of this little detour into the Anglo-Saxon monastic experience, I wouldn't be there to collect any rings or take my share of the proceeds from the sale of the Hwiccan slaves. I remembered what I'd said all summer: "We make our own luck."

We went back through the cloister and across the courtyard. An enclosed stairway climbed straight from the yard into a large room occupied by about thirty monks who were bent over writing desks. The room was high-ceilinged and airy; lit from the south, it would have winter light as well as summer. The morning fires still glowed in the fireplaces on either end, banked against the November chill and ready to warm the clerics when the north winds came down again from the Mark.

The men who built Lindisfarne understood light in a way few men have before or since. They played with it, channeled it, colored it, sculpted it, made it sing. The round window in the church was the most spectacular example, but even the utilitarian light in the Scriptorium, by which men did, as they supposed, their duty to their god, was a light that had been played with by the architect of the room. The whitewashed walls reflected and suffused the light, and the opposition of windows and reflecting walls made it seem the whole room radiated a pellucid luminance.

The black wool of the monks' habits and the polished wood of the desks, shelves, tables, and lecterns stood out in that light so that no one could move without being noticed. Every gesture, turn of page, movement of quill was immediately visible. It was a room where no tongueless Picts could come up on you unaware.

A man I took to be the master, sitting on a raised dais, noticed us as we stood inside the door. The monks worked in silence, only the scratching of the pens, the protestation of parchment, and an occasional cough, climbing toward the smokeholes in the roof like a bird hoping for escape, broke the perfect tranquillity of that room and that light.

I turned to tell Eadred I wanted to work there, but he already knew. He gestured to the monk who sat on the dais, and the monk rose and came to us with a shuffling of sandaled feet, attracting no attention from the scribes, who were absorbed in their tasks.

We walked outside to avoid disturbing them. The man was older than Eadred, near Skallagrim's age or better, as I made it, and had clear piercing eyes like the blue ice that forms over deep water. He was tall, and his hair was gray around his ears. The prints stood out on his inked fingers like a contour map of everything he'd ever read or written.

"This is Godwine," Eadred said. "He's the librarian here."

So that was Godwine. I looked at him again, somehow surprised at the man he turned out to be. "Bran Snorrison," I said, "here to thank you for your guidance in my reading, and to say I'd like to work for you while I stay on the island."

"Would you?" he asked, without wanting to know, or

maybe already knowing—it was difficult to tell. "What can you do?"

"I can write," I told him.

"Everyone here can write," he said placidly.

I was stunned. In Clontarf, which was a fairly cosmopolitan place by the standards of the 790s, only two of us could actually *write*. But Godwine was unimpressed by such rustic credentials as the mere ability form letters in a row.

"Let's see a sample of your hand," he said.

We went back into the Scriptorium and collected a scrap of parchment and a fresh quill. On his desk was a small folio of a breviary. He'd been copying in a graceful script that ran away from an illuminated initial "A" like a stream from a spring. The phrase was *Abyssa abyssus invocat,* "the abyss calls forth the abyss." The folio sheet was faintly ruled, and he'd filled about half of the first column, working in red, blue, and black inks. The three inkpots, an ample supply of quills, a knife for touching up the points, the page, and a blotter were arranged on the desk.

Godwine stood by as I looked at his work, my mouth moving as I chewed the words on the page. He lifted the vellum from the desk, substituted the clean scrap, and gestured for me to sit. He offered the quill. I sat on the bench and hesitated, knowing I was about to make a fool of myself.

"Write the *In Principio,*" he said.

I dipped the quill in the black ink and began to form the letters. When the quill touched the parchment, ink ran in all directions, like a squashed leech bloated with Loki's blood. I swallowed hard and moved my hand farther down. The scrap was ruined now in any case, so why not scrawl out the words and then go find the sheep pens and pick up a shovel?

I wrote out the first four words in letters that looked primitive and diseased next to Godwine's disciplined text, then I put the quill down. Godwine studied the page, then placed the quill differently in my fingers and guided my hand on the page, copying the same words under the ones I'd written.

When we finished, he had me copy them alone. Holding the quill in the new way, and trying to force my hand to move as he'd guided it, I produced the four words again. They looked a little better, but no one was going to be fooled into thinking I was a cleric; finally, I wasn't fooled either.

"You need practice," Godwine observed. "I can give you a table and scrap. Come tomorrow morning after Prime."

That was that.

"You did well," Eadred said when we were outside.

"Right." I laughed. "I thought I could write until I came here."

"Learning one's ignorance is the beginning of knowledge."

"Uh-huh," I said. "At least I won't be shoveling sheep shit."

"Of course you will," Eadred said. "Everyone here writes, and everyone shovels shit. *'Ora et labora'* is the motto of the Order."

8

De Sanctis Insularis

The sitters in the hall seldom know
The kin of the newcomer:
The best man is marred by faults,
The worst is not without worth.
—The Sayings of the Wise One

As the weeks passed, my routine became established. Godwine gave me a desk and a supply of quills and set me to copying from an alphabet bestiary and an Anglo-Saxon grammar. At first I practiced on scraps of parchment and ruined pages, but after a while, when he was convinced they wouldn't be wasted, he provided full sheets of vellum. In a few weeks my letters and my understanding of Anglo-Saxon were improving.

I was free to write what I wanted, so I wrote the story of the vik. Maybe I exaggerated the virtues of the men who'd sailed out of the Liffey with Sygtrygg and Thorfinn, and if I did, so what? The way I remembered my first vik would be the way it was; what matter if I remembered it to everyone's credit?

When the copyists came to work, I abandoned writing and made myself useful around the Scriptorium, building up the fire, sharpening quills, refilling inkpots, and stocking the parchment bins. I warmed basins of water to ease their cramped hands, and brought fresh towels to dry them afterward. They were small enough services for the run of the library and the Scriptorium and the advice the copyists were glad to offer, whether or not I asked for it.

Scriptorium routine was more relaxed, and though the silence wasn't ignored, copyists and illuminators were free to confer on texts, glosses, points of technique, materials, or anything that touched on the matter of their craft. There was a whispered undertone that I never thought twice about until one morning when it suddenly stopped, like insect sound at night when a predator goes by, and I looked up to see that the Prior had made a surprise visit.

He stood inside the door, surveying the room with the subpriors at his elbows, their hands out of sight in their sleeves. I remembered Steinthor's comment about churchmen. The tension in the room made me nervous, and Godwine left the dais and walked to greet the Prior, since it was clear that's what the Prior required. The monks were concentrating on their work with maniacal focus.

After a moment Godwine motioned to me and stepped into the next room with the Prior and his entourage. I stood and walked across the Scriptorium, and the monks watched me from beneath their eyebrows.

"The Prior has a request," Godwine said, though I reckoned that a request from the Prior was as good as an order from the Pope.

"We would like you to read in the Refectory," the Prior said.

I looked at Godwine and shrugged. During meals it was the custom for a lector to read from the lives of saints, sermons, the bible, the Rule, whatever spiritual text the Prior desired. That was all right with me. Godwine's silence was icy.

"I recently received this from York," the Prior said. "You can begin to read it at the evening meal." He handed me a manuscript written in a competent insular script, and I opened it and read the title: *Beowulf.* A swift glance down the page was enough to reveal its secular nature.

"The script is unfamiliar to my eye," I told him. "I'd prefer to study it for a day or two so I can read pleasingly."

"As you wish," the Prior acceded with a patrician nod. "Day after tomorrow, then. I'll look forward to it."

He left the library with the subpriors behind him, and Godwine stood rigidly as the door closed after them.

"Did you know about this?" I asked.

"I did not," he said in a tone that communicated disapproval.

"What's this about?" I wanted to know, remembering the last time I'd been surprised by the Prior.

"Secular entertainment," Godwine said cryptically as he returned to the Scriptorium.

I spent the rest of the day reading the manuscript. It was a cracking good story, even if it was about a Geat, and I thought it would go over well in a hall. The next day, after a cup of diluted wine to lubricate my throat, I performed the first part while the monks ate their evening meal. It was a curious experience. The monks who'd come from the nobility listened with intelligent ears and seemed to enjoy it, but the monks who'd come from the peasantry ate their food without looking up and waited patiently until the Prior ended the meal. Afterward they sang the after-dinner prayer and left me to eat alone while the servers cleared the plates.

I read every day, and when I finished *Beowulf,* the Prior gave me a manuscript called *The Song of Roland.* After that, a selection of gnomic verse, and so it continued, and I had an opportunity to practice my technique every day.

One evening the Prior waited to talk to me after the meal.

"We have noticed," he began, "that not all of our flock seem to enjoy your reading."

I shrugged. "Maybe I'm not good enough to hold their interest." I had the feeling I was about to discover the strings attached to sanctuary, and from the center of whose web they radiated.

"False modesty is a sin equal to pride," he said.

I nodded and kept my mouth shut.

"There is discord in our community," he said, but I wasn't rising to that bait. "We would appreciate it if you would report anything you hear."

I looked at him noncommittally. I'd been waiting to see what my lectorship was really about, and now at least part of his motive was coming to light, like a corpse floating up out of a swamp, and it smelled just as good. "My door is always open," he said.

After I finished my meal and left the Refectory, I wandered back to the Scriptorium. Lindisfarne had begun to get comfortable, and the Prior was a good reminder that my stay was temporary. It was easy to lose sight of that. I was occupied in the library every day, and I read in their equivalent of a hall every evening. The strangeness about seeing Bede seemed to have blown over, and the Prior was treating me as well as he treated anyone.

Now he wanted me to spy among the monks for him.

Well, you may as well hate a dog for barking at the moon; after all, he was just being true to his nature, which I'd sussed out right enough that first day in the Chapter room.

There was a light under the door of Godwine's study, and I knocked. In a moment it opened, and Godwine invited me into a comfortable room with a fire and shelves of books. A bowl of spiced wine was mulling by the fire. Godwine sat in one of the chairs and motioned me into the other. Candles burned on a shelf. The stone walls were hung with wool that contained the heat of the fire and warmed the room. He put the bottoms of his sandaled feet close to the flames.

"My feet are always cold in the Scriptorium." He smiled.

I nodded. "Mine too."

"How have you fared here?"

"Well enough."

"The Prior seems to have taken an interest in you," he said, reaching for the bowl of wine and the cups.

"Why do you suppose that is?"

"One does not presume to guess."

"Why don't you tell me the matter of Bede?" I asked.

Godwine replaced the wine bowl by the fire and sat back to sip a little wisdom. He was smooth. He looked into the flames as he swirled the wine over his tongue and let it trickle down his throat. "The Prior isn't from Lindisfarne," he began. "Before he assumed these duties he was a student and then a teacher in the York school, and then he followed Alcuin to the imperial school at Aachen.

"He's from Ida's line, and he was taken into orders at the monastery of Iona. The Prior knows Celtic Christianity firsthand: it's the rite he grew up in.

"Two hundred years ago King Oswiu convened a synod at Whitby to decide on the preferred rite. Coleman of Lindisfarne held for the Celtic, and Wilfrid of Ripon spoke for the Roman. His arguments won the day, so Coleman returned to Iona with the monks who wanted to follow the Celtic fashion, and the rest stayed here. Wilfrid got his own bishopric at Hexham, carved out of the middle of Lindisfarne."

Godwine's face was a mask of concentration as he continued.

"But the faithful were divided, and when the people who'd converted saw the Church in disagreement, they doubted the wisdom of throwing down their stone gods. So the problem of the two rites threatened the integrity of the Church."

There was a noise in the library proper, and Godwine glanced out the open door. I heard the sound of wood scraping on the stone floor and then the door opened wide and Eadred came in, pushing a chair ahead of him.

"How are you this evening?" Eadred asked as he situated the chair close to the fire.

"Keeping well," I said. "Godwine's telling me the Prior's story."

Eadred filled his cup and then settled back. "Don't let me interrupt," he said, sipping a little wisdom himself.

"You were saying that the Prior saw where his meat came from and sold out to the Celtic rite for favor and advancement."

"I was not saying that," Godwine denied, "but some would say it has the same matter. The Prior went to Aachan, to help his master build Charlemagne's school. Because of the emperor's zeal to convert the Saxons, a difference of opinion developed as to how best to nurture the Roman rite. The orthodox approach discourages pagan ritual but uses their familiar feast days to ease the way into Christian light, which, as Socrates knew, can cause blindness and insanity if discovered too suddenly."

I wondered what the old Greek would have said if he heard Godwine's interpretation of the allegory of the Cave. Everyone was a theologian in those days. Theologies were common as assholes.

"The Prior insisted the surest method was to uproot the old customs and beliefs and force the people to learn the new ones. He argued that this would hurry them to the comfort of truth. He believes that the cults of the saints should be stamped out because they merely replaced the pagan gods.

"Fortunately, Alcuin knows that reverence for the saints is a way of strengthening the faith, but despite his admonishments, the Prior lectured on his belief in Charlemagne's school. Alcuin sent him back to York, and York sent him here to help Higbald administer the bishopric and to meditate on the sin of pride."

"Whether their choice of Lindisfarne was a joke or a penance we do not presume to understand," Eadred assured me wryly. "But he's been Higbald's Prior these four years and not discouraged belief in Cuthbert's holiness. He knows how to keep Cuthbert's Feast as well as anyone before him."

Godwine shot him an irritated glance at the interruption and continued. "Now, the story about the returning soul is a story you hear when you're a novice. Novices have told it for hundreds of years, because the deathwatch is the novice's duty; they're usually young and afraid to wait with a dying man."

He was right, some ghosts could be ghosts of convenience, like the one in the barrowdown, whose real purpose we knew without being told. But I'd seen someone who looked enough like Bede to fool people who ought to know, and I'd seen him shift shape. Shapeshifters have a way of sticking in your mind.

"I'd heard the story, but I'd never been convinced until now. Everything you said rings true. You never heard of Bede, and you saw him before you read his history. You didn't know he wrote, but you recognized inkstains on his fingers. The details are correct. What could you gain from a lie?"

"I'm a Dane washed over in a storm," I reminded him. "And before the storm I was in a fight with Engs; some might make a case for me lying to keep my head."

"Chapter fifty-three of the rule instructs us to welcome all guests as Christ Himself," Eadred said with a laugh. "There's no need to lie. And if you did, lying about Bede's ghost would be the worst lie to tell, given the Prior's dislike of cults."

"But what's it to the Prior, after all?" I asked, not bothering to mention that I'd not yet read Benedict's Rule when I'd stood before the Prior in the Chapter room.

"It's one thing to be Prior of Lindisfarne," Godwine said. "That's a penance he can endure. But it's something else again to have a miracle occur under his nose that might help Bede along the road to sainthood. The Prior thinks your belief in the night sight is enough to discredit your story, and he's using you to discredit yourself."

"How so?"

"By having you read these stories in the Refectory."

"By reading?"

"The lector should read matter of spiritual relevance,"

Godwine said. "Chapter thirty-eight of the Rule specifies the reading will begin with prayer. Also that the reading will be from the book."

"I don't understand."

"You may have noticed that while the community follows one rite, there are differences in its observation."

That was a delicately phrased observation that some of the monks were more worldly than others, and I smiled. "If you mean that monks from the nobility are more interested in a comfortable life, and monks from the peasantry are more interested in prayer and good works, then I've noticed."

Godwine looked at me over the rim of his cup, betraying nothing of his thoughts, and Eadred looked into the fire, betraying all of his. I was still confused.

"The Prior is interpreting the Rule in a most liberal way. It does not specify what the book should be, though it has always been holy writ. He has you entertaining, rather than enlightening. Telling stories in which ghosts and dragons and magic play a part. And though the high born monks are entertained, those of a more simple and spiritual nature are scandalized."

"What do I care?" I asked. "I just want to go home."

"The last thing he wants is you crossing Northumbria with the story of Bede's return. He plans to subvert your credibility by having the monks associate you with fabulous tales instead of spiritual truth. He hopes winter will keep you here until sermons on false prophesy can be preached throughout the See."

"What matter? Dead men come back. Everyone knows this. That's why we cut binding runes and you plant crosses."

"Why did you say 'we cut binding runes'?" Eadred asked me. There was a second's pause before I spoke, and the timing of that pause was enough to catch me out as a Christian of convenience.

"I'm not long practiced in the faith," I said, trying to recover.

"It could be reckoned in minutes," Godwine said. "No matter. We only care that you saw Bede. The people should know it."

Apparently they didn't care if my faith was convenient

or not; maybe a convenient faith only made seeing Bede more convincing.

"What do *you* want me to do?"

"Write down what you saw," Eadred said. "Tell the truth about it when you leave."

"I want to get home as quick as I can," I said, shaking my head. "I'm not preaching my way across Northumbria."

"Go as quickly as you can," Godwine said, "but don't suppress the news of this ..."

"Rather routine occurrence?" I finished for him.

"But special," Eadred pointed out.

"Oh, it's made a special impression on me," I agreed.

"Then there's nothing more for you to do," Godwine said.

There was a knock at the door, and we turned as Alban came in carrying a few more candles, which he lit and placed on the mantle.

"How's the leg?" he asked.

"Here's your cloak; what's your hurry?" I smiled.

"You mistake us," Eadred said. "We care about your welfare."

"And well faring," I added. "But there our interests overlap."

"Speaking of faring well, take care," Godwine said. "The Prior's got secular friends as well as ecclesiastical enemies."

"It's a long road from here to Ireland, and all of it's in Northumbria." Eadred nodded. "King Æthelred's his patron, and the subpriors are the king's cousins."

"Æthelred's never balked at removing an enemy, and he may grant a favor to the Prior if a favor's asked."

That was something to think about. Royal enemies had been Orm's downfall in the Mark, and I'd learned to avoid them. If the Prior wanted me to keep my mouth shut, it would be well if I did. But I drew the line at betraying my friends.

"There's something you ought to know," I said. "After the meal tonight the Prior told me to keep my eyes open and report to him."

"About what?"

"He mentioned discord in the community."

The three monks looked at each other, and I thought of Goltrade, Snorri, and Skallagrim, conspiring over their cups in the hall as Sygtrygg sat in the high seat, under the impression that *he* ran things in Clontarf.

The next day the first of the great storms of 792 descended on Northumbria. I had to fight through the wind to get to the church for the Chapter mass, and I hopped ahead of it on the way back. The wind screamed in off the water, driving spume, sand, seabirds, and sound before it. Not long after the mass, Eadred came to the Guest House with the Pict in tow. Haki was looking his best, as if he'd been found dead under a bridge just that morning.

"When the winter storms come, we draw into ourselves," Eadred said.

I stood there with two thick wool blankets pulled tight around me and looked at him. "What's that mean?" I asked.

"You'll live in the Cloister until spring."

"What're you doing here?" I asked, but Haki just returned my stare. That's what comes of questioning a Pict with no tongue.

"He'll shut up the building," Eadred said.

"Well enough," I said. They'd put the expert at being shut up in charge of just that function. The irony liked me well.

That first snow was like a shroud drawn over a dead face at night. The mourning sky was swollen and milky. The sea heaved below the monastery, and the ice-coated rocks invited anyone without wit or grace to fall. The months of Lindisfarne's isolation had begun, when all you could look forward to was a visit from the laymen who tended the closest grange on the mainland. There would be no pilgrims visiting Cuthbert's shrine, no travelers or itinerant monks looking for a night's lodging.

We crossed the courtyard and went into the Cloister. The fountains were still, and I saw fish trapped at the bottom until the cook came to chop them out. I wondered if they reckoned it in their little fish dreams. Inside, Eadred led the way down a long corridor I hadn't walked before. Windows looked into the inner courtyard and doors were spaced evenly along the other wall. Eadred stood beside an open door and I stepped across the threshold.

"This was Wilberht's cell," Eadred said, after I was inside.

It was a fell chill sensation, like climbing into a grave, dry and cold, a spartan shelter for the long years of death. I came to a quick halt. The monks didn't enjoy the same posh accommodations as their guests. *Cell* was an apt description for a stone room seven or eight feet deep and only five or six feet wide. There was a bed on a low platform, small table with a basin and ewer, and a few pegs hammered into the wall for hanging my clothes. A window overlooked the vegetable gardens, stubbled and lumpy under the sheared covering of blown snow, letting in enough light for reading.

"We've brought you a bed," Eadred said. Then, to let me know what a favor they'd done me, he added, "We sleep on stone." He smiled at the look on my face. "At least you're closer to the Scriptorium."

"Where's the Pict keep?" I sat on the bed.

"In the Gatehouse with the Porter. He'll abide by the terms of sanctuary," Eadred insisted, stepping into the hall. The small room was cloudy with the vapor of our breathing.

The sound of his going down the corridor eased my fears a little. No one could be sneaking into my room without making noise. Just to be on the safe side, I scratched runes above the door and the casement. Then I lay back on the bed and pulled the blankets closer.

The storms that winter were like falcons on a flock of grouse; the wind made the stones groan, and snow blew and drifted as high as the cloister wall, spewing over the crest in a plume of ice crystals. The water froze solid and clear as glass, and the monks in the Scriptorium shivered despite the fires burning on the grates. The cellerer distributed extra blankets, and everyone wore all the clothing he had. Respiratory infections spread through the community like a suspicion of guilt, and in a matter of days everyone was snorking back great echoing headfuls of snot as they sang the plainsong in the choir. Alban was busy making decoctions to combat the sickness, and I was charged with making sure the copyists and illuminators took their medicine.

It was an ugly business. After they swallowed the liquid, there was a ten- or fifteen-minute interval of lung-wracking coughs that produced a thick yellow phlegm of which the monks purged themselves freely, launching gobs of clinging mucus into the rushes.

The winter progressed as winters in that latitude will: the days were short and bleak, the nights were long and cold. Yule finally came at the end of Lent, which in those days was the last quarter of December. It was a time of fewer rations and extra prayer, flagellation and exposure to the elements, generally penitential behavior and depression, but it sure put them in the mood to celebrate the birth of Jesus Christ. Yule at Lindisfarne was quite a blowout: double helpings of meat and ale, some salt herring and wine, a worming and an extra bleeding, followed by a high mass in the church, sung in harmony with the wind.

It was the belief that bleeding a certain amount was good prophylaxis and maintained a balance of bodily humors, so every Thursday afternoon Alban put the leeches on ten or a dozen monks to cleanse their systems. Given the population of the monastery, this rotation meant they got a bleeding every six or seven weeks. There was more and better food, and silence was relaxed, making it a social and medical event combined. After food and a whispered discussion of Scripture, they were allowed to recuperate for an hour in the salt air of the cloister, which was quite bracing during the winter storms.

The Christmas bleeding was general, and there weren't enough leeches to go round, so they resorted to the blade. Alban's assistant, a novice called Eadfrid, who had a bad complexion and a raw nose from a constant cold, was busy running out to the stable to empty the basins of warm blood into the pigsty. His feet were collecting clods of ice, and he slipped and slid his way across the boards when he walked, balancing his steaming basin. It was the only time during my stay that all the monks talked in the Refectory, where they retired for refreshments after their treatment.

"I always feel better after a bleeding," Eadred said.

"Lighter of spirit," Godwine agreed.

I'd felt lighter of spirit the times I'd bled, like the top of my head was lifted off and my brain was floating away. I associated it with being on the ground with a Geat standing over me.

"Have you had your bleeding?" Godwine asked.

"I'll give it a miss," I said.

Just then the subpriors came into the Refectory and paused at the door like a brace of trained weasels entering a rabbit warren. They spent all of their time at the Prior's heels, like spin doctors poised to clarify whatever he said, and they seemed to have placed the fragile shells of all their career hopes in the Prior's basket. Good job they hadn't been with him when he was spouting heresy in front of the most prolific epistler in Christendom. They rolled up their sleeves and stood aside as the Prior made his entrance.

The Prior walked over to an empty table and the subpriors stood on either side of him as Alban administered a deft slice and tilted his arm aside to let it drain into a basin. He composed his face into a beatific mask and bled a bit for the crowd, and then Alban bound the wound and the Prior rose from the table, the happy beneficiary of modern preventive medicine. The hospice trestle across the room was piled with food and drink, but his glance passed over it. He surveyed the room, and I felt my insides turn over as his gaze swept my way.

When he spotted me, his slow pan of the room stopped and a hideous approximation of a smile came over him. Then he began to make his way over, and Eadred and Godwine felt the need to go load up on sweetmeats and brown ale. They floated up from their seats like ground fog and drifted away, leaving me to meet the Prior alone.

I prepared myself. Maybe he *was* a little bitter about his wyrd, but who wasn't in 792? Maybe he was just a guy who wanted to spend his time reading Augustine and extirpating the cults of lesser saints, misunderstood by the world at large. If he wanted to think that I'd hallucinated Bede, fine by me.

He glided through the room like an adder through a herd of sheep. The two subpriors stopped a respectful distance away; if you were talking to the Prior no one dreamed of intruding. He sat without invitation, his eyes never leaving me, but at least he relaxed his smile and assumed his normal face.

It takes all kinds to occupy the high seat: some lead by doing, some by ordering, and some by inspiring others with an incandescent and indescribable magic. Orm had been a doer, and men had followed. Macc Oc was a man who ordered. Thorfinn had mastered the magic of all three styles. The Prior of Lindisfarne was a leader by the whim of his superiors, and that was a creepy new kind of leadership for me: bureaucratic leadership, the first I'd ever seen.

"How are you keeping?" he inquired with a sinister silkiness.

"Well enough," I told him. "I'm busy in the Scriptorium."

"So I'm told." The Prior smiled. "Are you finding time to write?"

"More than enough."

"I'm interested in your work," he said. "I'd like to read it."

"Boring stuff, really, for a learned man like you. Just folk tales, old legends from the pagan times. Bedtime stories."

He smiled agreeably at this news, thinking no doubt he'd use it later on to his own purpose. "No invocations for the night sight?"

I ignored the remark. If he had something to ask me, he was free to do it plainly.

"Good. I want you to profit from your stay with us. I suspect you never thought to see the inside of a monastery, unless you burned one."

"I told you we weren't pirates in Clontarf. We're traders."

"There are many definitions of trade," the Prior pointed out as if he were examining a philosophical proposition. "The appropriate one depends largely on which side of the exchange you're on."

"This is true," I said. "My stay here, for example, could be viewed as a trade of services and labor in exchange for healing."

"And sanctuary," he reminded me.

"And sanctuary," I emended.

"As to that, you've nothing to report?"

"About what?"

"Voices of disobedience and discord," he said, tension creeping into his voice as he sensed my reluctance to play his game.

"I've heard nothing of disobedience," I assured him.

"You spend much time in the library and Scriptorium," he said.

"I've much work to do before I leave here," I said. "This is the opportunity of a lifetime for a skald."

"I'd like to read your verse," he said again. "Some evening perhaps you can bring it to me."

"I'd be honored," I assured him.

After all, he *was* a scholar. He might have valuable criticism. The Prior stood and looked down at me for a second. Then he was gone. That's how he operated, and no one questioned it.

Alban, Eadred, and Godwine were refilling their wine cups. I was rising to join them when one of the Scriptorium monks caught my eye and waved me over, sliding down to make a little room on his bench. He was called Cinewulf, and he was wearing the dreamy look of the recently bled. Cinewulf was an illuminator who drew the great initial letters and the marginal decorations on the pages of the Gospels, tracing them first in carbon and then embellishing them with colored inks and gold leaf. I didn't know it when I sat beside him, but he was about to bring a little illumination into my life.

"Bran," he said in the low voice the monks used when released from the silence, as if they were afraid the Prior might think they were enjoying themselves. "Have you had your bleeding?"

"I'll forgo that pleasure," I told him.

"I want to congratulate you," Cinewulf said. "You've good weatherluck after all."

I doubted it; my weatherluck was worthy of a priest. "How so?"

"I've had news of your fleet from a kinsman."

"What news?" I asked, somewhat too aggressively. "Sorry." I forced myself to be calm. "I don't know how they fared in the storm."

Cinewulf's face changed again; he'd been keen to share his news before I'd startled him; now he seemed reluctant to impart it. "Not well," he said, shifting uneasily and washing back the taste of his news with a mouthful of small ale. "My kinsman had it from one of the coast watchers after the storm. All the fleet was blown against the Farnes. Everyone drowned except part of a crew taken prisoner and a few captives. The Danes were killed and the rest slaved out."

There was bitter news: the whole fleet lost. I turned away and contemplated the grain in the table, thinking of the drowned faces I'd seen in the deliria of those first nights at Lindisfarne and understanding now what they'd been trying to tell me.

Skallagrim was dead and my brothers Brynjold, Arinbjorn, and Yngvar, and all the other Clontarfmen. The Jomsvikings were dead too: Sygtrygg, Kalf Agirson, Stromborg, Ulf Thorhullasson, Thord the Jolly, Steinthor Bollison, and, most difficult of all to imagine: Thorfinn Skullsplitter. Caitria had trusted me to set her ashore in an untouched town and she was drowned off the Northumbrian coast instead. Rognvald's weatherluck had failed him. And Macc Oc and all his Irish, led into a bad place at a bad time because Sygtrygg needed a vik and a brother-in-law. I alone escaped the Norns, and I'd been cursing them because of it.

"I didn't think," Cinewulf said with such contrition that *I* felt sorry for *him*. "Did you have family in the fleet?"

"Three brothers," I said, "and many friends." I stood up and looked round the Refectory as if I expected to see their ghosts, but I only saw the monks, arms bound and tongues loosened, having as good a time as they might while the wind screamed down from the Mark and my friends' bones were picked clean by fish in the Frisian Sea.

I went back to my room. At least now there was no more pressure to hurry home. Nineteen ships had sailed from Clontarf for the land of the Engs in the last two years, and not a dragon returned. Such was the wyrd of Orm's line.

February of 793 began with a few mild days to lull us into thinking spring was possible. Then in the middle of the first week, the final storm broke round us like Ragnarok. In the space of an hour the sky, blue and clear for three days, turned black as a frostbitten leg, and a wind so cutting it froze your tears slashed out of the north. The storm held Lindisfarne fast for five days of screaming blackness. Candles and torches burned during the hours when the sun should have lit the windows, and the Prior excused the monks from work, instead having day-long meetings in the Chapter room, at which I read an assortment of saints' lives and religious poetry to calm those who'd begun to see auguries of Apocalypse.

The day after the storm was over we went back to work in the laceratingly cold Scriptorium. I made a hundred trips up and down the stairs to the woodpile, to feed the hearth flames, hampered by the thickness of three blankets and a heavy cloak, as much wool as I could walk in. My hood was stuffed with fleece, and I was thinking of something warm as I stepped off the last tread and turned to find Haki the Pict. I looked for his axe, but his hands were thrust into his sleeves and he seemed to be unarmed.

The light was dropping off fast, and I was getting colder by the second, but we just stood watching one another. There could be a blade up that sleeve as easily as dirty fingernails. The muscles in his face contracted into a smile. Then he gestured for me to follow. I couldn't think of any reason to follow a Pict who'd once attacked me with an axe into the gloaming and a Force 7 wind; it sounded like a recipe for disaster, but he'd opened the way to the wood rick at least, and I stepped forward and pulled a sturdy length of oak out of the pile and weighed it in my hand while I decided.

Haki was impatient, and he waved me on, the wind blowing his hood off his face. I took a couple of steps in his direction, and he started across the courtyard to the cloister door. I kept ten or fifteen feet back. He opened the door and went inside, and I stopped cautiously at the threshold, but he'd gone off down the hall.

I pulled the door shut and went after him. The corridor was empty. Polished oak, stone walls glittering with frost, plumes of breath like the ghost tails of albino horses, the comforting sound of the Pict walking well ahead, these familiar images and reassurances combined to lull me into a kind of dangerous curiosity. Haki turned another corner, heading into a deeper precinct of Lindisfarne, and I stopped to reconsider.

After about fifteen seconds, he came back and waved impatiently. I started down the corridor and he went back into the side hallway. Before I got there I felt an arctic blast. The Pict stood in the middle of the archway connecting the monastery to the Priory. The door on the far side of the passage was open, and the Prior was outlined in the sunlight.

The Prior of a monastery that housed a shrine as important as Cuthbert's tomb needed a house big enough to accommodate the lesser nobility, who liked to be observed at piety, and those members of the emerging middle class that could afford the Prior's hospitality. Also, because Lindisfarne was a center of learning and a factory that cranked out the most beautiful illuminated manuscripts of the last millennium, the Prior needed a house comfortable enough to keep visiting scholars and clerics who came to work in the library. Finally, as a man who'd taken orders on Iona, studied at York, and taught at Aachan, the Prior's ego had certain spatial requirements.

The building had a silence all its own, showing its unbroken walls to the world. All the windows of the Prior's house looked inward to a small, galleried garden. A little fountain splashed there in the summer, and green plants must have grown in profusion, but now the fountain was a frozen mound of ice.

The Prior relieved me of the oak stave and slipped the blankets from my shoulders. "You won't need a crutch. I want you to have dinner with me," he said, closing the door on Haki, who was settling down in the archway like a guard dog. "I sent for your writing," he told me. "But I haven't had time to read it. I was surprised by the number of pages. I'm glad you augmented the Danish dialect you prefer with Latin."

We'd been walking along a corridor as he talked, and I stayed a pace behind to keep him where I could see him. We turned into a big room where a fire burned in the exact corner of the building, and there were fat candles in wall sconces backed by polished silver disks. There were wool rugs on the floor. It was the Prior's reception hall, made cozy by a roaring fire and interesting lighting choices.

The Prior opened a chest and took out a stiff leather folder. My verses were inside, tied up with a ribbon. Baldur's balls, he'd done that neatly: while I was out getting firewood, the subpriors were cleaning out my desk. He put the open folder on the table, and I saw a second sheaf under the first: the verse I kept in my room, twenty or thirty sheets only.

He'd sent his goons into my room, and the runes I'd cut hadn't kept them out. When I saw the second sheaf I knew how serious he was, and I hoped that what he was looking for was still locked in the writing desk in Godwine's study. I'd laughed when Godwine hid it there, but I'd humored him.

It was going to be hard to convince the Prior I didn't care about Bede's ghost if he had a manuscript about

Bede's ghost in his hands. I picked up the second sheaf, riffling quickly through the pages. I didn't find it, but that didn't mean it hadn't been found. There was no way to be certain until I saw it safe in the desk myself.

"Perhaps you'll read a bit," the Prior said. If he wanted me to read a bit, before the evening was over I'd be singing like a lark. The Prior, meanwhile, moved over to the fire and stood warming his hands and watching me. I didn't want to seem too anxious. Maps of the known world and chemical and astrological charts covered the walls. There were two shelves of books, and a chess set on a table between two opposing chairs. I closed the folder and stepped over to examine the pieces.

"Do you play?" he asked.

"I learned aboard the ship I was on," I told him. "The man who taught me learned it on Sicily."

"I played frequently with Alcuin, and several times with the emperor. Would you like a game?"

What a name-dropper.

He drew out the chair, acting like he owned time itself.

I sat down and moved a pawn, and five turns later I was checkmated by an offhand move which condensed on the board as he removed his fingers from his queen.

"That was stimulating," he said sardonically.

I looked at him as he began to rearrange the pieces and gestured for a more cautious opening move.

"How have you been keeping?"

"Well enough," I told him as I watched his fingertips brush the helmeted heads of his front-rank pawns.

"But you want to leave."

"My plans didn't include Lindisfarne, although I'm grateful for your hospitality. I've liked working in the Scriptorium, and I've written verse and learned from your library, but my family and friends think I'm dead."

The Prior took his eyes off the board for a second, glanced at me, and then returned his attention to the pieces. "The weather will break in a few weeks. This is the last winter storm. The spring ship from Jarrow stops here on the way to Iona."

"When's it due?"

"Two or three weeks after Cuthbert's Feast," he said as he took my queen with a bishop. "You'd have sanctuary on the ship to Iona," he said. "I wrote to Higbald in York to ask his guidance."

I looked back at the board and discovered that sometime during the Prior's little homily the chess game had ended with my king menaced from three directions. The Prior stood up, bored with the easiness of beating me, and led the way to the fire, where we warmed ourselves. There was a table laid with food to the left of the fire, and he walked over to it and prepared a plate.

The Prior lived well considering he'd been banished from Charlemagne's court. He filled his plate and went to one of the two chairs by the fire, where a trencher board leaned against the leg. The Prior sat down and pulled it onto his lap, arranging his plate and cup. I followed him to the other chair and, after a prayer of thanks for the food, we ate in silence, watching the fire.

The interior of his hall was appointed in oiled woods, polished and dark with years. Some of the walls were covered in tapestries with religious themes, made by the fingers of pious noblewomen whose needles must have flashed for lifetimes to complete them. Carpets of Oriental manufacture covered and warmed the stone floors, muffling the sound. There was nothing in the Priory to let you know when someone was coming for you.

The candlesticks were silver, and there was ample evidence of wealth in the furnishings of the room. The woodwork was covered with carved ivy and gripping beasts that clung among the leaves like household fetches. The chess table was the work of a master carver. The Prior had managed to land on his feet. I thought about Chapter sixty-five of the Rule, which discussed how some priors, puffed up by the sin of pride, got to thinking of themselves as second abbots. It didn't seem like the time to bring it up.

"How do you find the making of writing?"

Now, there was an interesting question. No one had asked me that before because copyists had a more graphic than literary interest in words, but the Prior was a man who'd confronted the unbroken ice of a blank page, and he knew the problems you found there. Looking at the Prior, easy in his robes and sitting by his own fire, I resisted the urge to show off a little, to let him know he wasn't dealing with just any wood puller from a passing vik.

"I like to tell stories. If you make up stories and tell

them it's called lying, but if you make them up and write them down, or sing them in hall, it's called composition."

"And how is the act of composition?"

"Like walking on ice in a blizzard. Everything's white, and there are white bears and holes in the ice and pressure ridges. Your footprints fill up as soon as you step out of them, and the wind changes direction. When you walk somewhere, the place you end up is hardly ever the one you started for."

The Prior looked at me without experience of sealing when a squall came up on the ice pack, but he seemed to know how a writer's block felt. He also seemed to have, if not a better, at least a different idea who he was dealing with, and I realized that, characteristically, I'd gone just a little too far. This wasn't a man you wanted knowing too much about you. Maybe he was a man with poor composition skills, a definite handicap when disagreeing with Alcuin of York, but he was connected and ambitious and I'd already pissed him off by not informing on my friends.

The Prior recomposed his expression and said: "Plato called that the realm of the ideal, and postulated that the purpose of art as *mimesis* is to approximate that ideal as closely as possible, knowing we'll never achieve it."

It took me a few seconds to puzzle out the meaning of that statement, hampered as I was by a wordhoard that didn't include *postulated* or *mimesis,* but I managed to get the thrust of his thought and nodded agreement as he stood to take away our empty plates in a sudden symbolic gesture of humility. He came back with the pitcher of ale, picking up the folder of verse on the way and handing it to me before he sat down. I opened the portfolio and shuffled the pages. Some lines from the *Sayings of the Wise One* caught my eye.

> The mind alone knows what is near the heart
> Each is his own judge:
> The worst sickness for a wise man
> Is to crave what he cannot enjoy.

> Never reproach the plight of another,
> For it happens to many men:
> Strong desire may stupefy heroes,
> Dull the wits of a wise man.

"There's merit there," he said.

"You sound surprised."

"The different things men believe are all the same."

I had a little trouble accepting this sagelike detachment from the Prior. "If that's true, why does the Church war with the Moslems? Why does the emperor convert the Old Saxons with fire and sword instead of arguments about error and mistaken belief?"

"It is possible," the Prior said after a moment's hesitation, "for the forms of a belief to be incorrect, the structure of a belief to be unsound, and the ceremony of a belief to be influenced by the Evil One, but for the essence of the belief to be true, notwithstanding. We are concerned with the distinction between essence and accident, and not essentially different things."

This is a good example of why the Prior had adopted a management style of ethereal disinterest, delegating the mundane administration of community life to the subpriors so he could slip into the ozone in the middle of a conversation, where few people without a doctorate in philosophy from the University of Utrecht could follow. This tended to exclude the average monk in his charge. I'd spent recent time reading through the library, sharpening my powers of reason, browsing the masters of antiquity, and I could only guess the direction his argument wanted to go in.

"Like what?" I asked, cleverly.

"The forms of a given heresy or pagan religion have been corrupted so as to lead the practitioner into the near occasion of sin, a direction away from the Divine truth."

"Well, who says?" I was certainly brimming with wit that evening as I debated the direction of the Western Church with someone who'd been schooled in Iona and York, and who'd twice beaten me at chess without my even beginning to suspect how.

"As the true Church of God on earth, it is our mandate to bring the light of Christianity into the pagan darkness. Without knowledge of Christ, you cannot enter the kingdom of heaven."

That pretty much summed up his position on spreading the light of Christianity throughout the dark expanses of paganism. The idea that a unified faith made it easier to unify a kingdom or an empire, and that the goals of the Church weren't that far out of alignment with the goals of the guy in the imperial high seat, didn't seem to cloud the Prior's logic.

"So much depends upon belief," I observed.

The Prior smiled in agreement. I smiled in understanding. We stood there smiling at one another across the manuscript of my verse, and I closed the portfolio, tied up the ribbon, and returned the folder to his open hands.

"I'll enjoy reading the stories you've written down," he said. "I'll send one of the subpriors to collect them every day."

So that's how it was going to be: I could write what I wanted, but he had to see it all. If there was anything he disapproved of, I didn't have to guess what would happen. I'd been with him for an hour and he hadn't asked me anything about Bede.

He put the folder inside the wooden box, locking it with a small key he had on his belt.

"We thank you for allowing us to see your work, and we will pray that your stay among us continues to be beneficial to your soul."

I knew an exit line combined with a thinly veiled threat when I heard one, and I followed him out into the covered gallery above the inner garden. The windows were a lattice of leaded glass that must have been beautiful in the sunlight. I recognized the pattern of colored glass as musical notation. Sunlight played that music as it moved from window to window, and only God could hear it, and maybe the Prior.

We went down the gallery and the Prior opened the door. The chill blew in and Haki turned to face the warmth of the Priory. The Prior draped the blankets over my shoulders, jerking his head at the Pict, who stood aside to let me pass.

"Thank's for dinner," I said. "And the chess lesson."

"You're well come," he said. "See you keep well."

I hurried down the archway, passed Haki, and heard the door close behind me as I opened the one into the monastery. When I turned, the Pict was squatting down with his back to the Priory door.

I was reassured by the sounds of my own passage through the hallways. Haki might be putting his rude head down in the Cloister, but he couldn't get to me on those floors; unless Heimdal struck me deaf, I'd hear a mouse coming a hundred meters off.

I popped into my cell and looked around. It took about a second to realize the place had been tossed by men who enjoyed their work. The verse had been out on the table, but they'd searched inside and under a straw mattress, through three folded blankets, under a cloak, behind a door, and under a table: not exactly a stretch of anyone's investigative powers, and they'd managed to leave the place in a shambles. There was straw everywhere, the mattress cover was a mass of shredded burlap, the blankets were tatters, the table was overturned, the cloak was in a heap behind the door. Orchids of ink blossomed against the wall and a few sheets of blank parchment were shredded.

No point hanging around there, so I went back to the library, moving quickly against the flow of post-Matins traffic. The reading room was dark. The door to Godwine's study was outlined by light. When I pushed it wide, the three monks looked up from their cups and smiled.

"How was the Priory table?" Eadred asked. "I only eat there at Cuthbert's Feast."

"He'll kick your ass at chess and criticize your verse," I told him. "And after that he'll show you the door, where, incidentally, the Pict now hunkers like a guard dog."

"He keeps a good table, then?" Alban asked insistently.

"Splendid," I snapped impatiently. "I assume he didn't get the lines about Bede."

"A correct assumption." Godwine laughed. "Is there anything you want to say?"

"You were right," I admitted. "Glad you're not rubbing my face in it."

"You needed a lesson in humility," he said.

"Well, now I'm humble. What next?"

"Next we find a way to get you out of Lindisfarne."

"The Prior just promised me passage on a ship from Jarrow."

"That ship will never sail." Alban shook his head. "The spring rains can keep us isolated for a month after the snow stops, but they're as reliable as any weather. They may come, and they may not. Cuthbert's Feast may be the best time to get you away. Lindisfarne will be full of pilgrims for a week. We'll find a party bound for Hexham. The Roman road runs straight as a string to Luel, and you can get a boat from there. You could be home a week after you leave."

"Sounds like a plan," I told them, pulling up a chair by the fire. "Who came for my verse?"

"The subpriors," Godwine said.

"And they never looked in here?"

"Of course. One of them cleaned out your desk and the other searched the study."

"Where was the verse?" I shouted.

"In the manuscript of Alcuin's letters." He smiled.

I shook my head. Clontarf and Lindisfarne had more in common than not; Goltrade's analogy had been right on the mark. "I need a place to sleep," I said. "They tore my bed and blankets apart."

"Stay here tonight." Godwine gestured around the study. "There's plenty of wood and good wool. We'll have the cellerer replace your bedding."

I was happy to take him up on the offer, and when the wine was gone and the three of them said good night, I locked the door. Sending off three old guys with wine on their breath was a familiar duty of mine, no matter where I was.

9

Cuthbert's Feast

It is best for a man to be middle wise
Not over cunning and clever.
No man is able to know his future
So let him sleep in peace.
                    —The Says of the Wise One

The weather changed in time for Lindisfarne's great feasting at the beginning of March: the snow turned to rain. Cuthbert's feast day was the twentieth and Benedict's was the twenty-first, and around the fifteenth the pilgrims started to show up, bringing their appetites and their ailments and hoping to be cured of both. It was serious tourism at its best, and Eadred finally got to earn his keep.

Higbald returned from York to preside, and the Prior disappeared into the woodwork without any indication of rancor. The Guest House filled up, and tents in the great courtyard accommodated the overflow. Eadred took on three or four assistants and needed more because every kind of brigand and con artist showed up for the trade. Christians in a festive mood are widely considered to be easy marks for such spurious relics as pieces of the true cross, rotting bits of fabric allegedly worn by unwashed holy men, stones from the manager Christ was born in, vials of water from the place where the Baptist had sprinkled him, dirt from his tomb ... you get the idea.

Then there were men and women who practiced street thaumaturgy by pretending some preternatural skill, generally the separation of pilgrims from their money in exchange for some sort of illusion. Changing water to wine was a favorite, as was multiplying loaves and fishes (although that one was generally restricted to cooler weather so the smell wouldn't give them away). They duplicated all

Christ's miracles, except the raising of dead men and the healing of lepers. Although the only miracles wanted at Lindisfarne during Cuthbert's Feast were Cuthbert's own, these sleight-of-hand artists were sure to do their share of business with people whom Cuthbert disappointed.

Entrepreneurs with legal businesses were also attracted to the feasting. Local fishermen sold herring and smelt. Bakers in Goswick, Beal, Fenham, and Fenham Hill sold round rye loaves by the hundreds. The village of Lindisfarne turned every available pasture into a paddock for the pilgrims' animals. The monastery kitchens worked night and day to take up the slack, giving away food to whoever wanted it, a practice that did nothing to undercut the fishermen or bakers, who paid tithes on their profits in any case. The Church got a cut of all the action on Lindisfarne, and in return they offered the lottery of Cuthbert's clothing.

The Insular saints weren't much on first-class miracles; mostly they lived lives of isolated poverty on small offshore islands or in caves in primeval oak forests. Some had been bishops, some had been martyrs, and some had written books, and some had been popular kings who'd died violently, but very few of them were associated with anything miraculous until they were ghosts, after which time their clothing and personal possessions achieved a kind of talismanic power.

Cults coalesced around the point of geography most closely associated with these late saints, frequently the sites of their death or entombment, which soon began to attract the crippled, the halt, the blind, the maimed, the diseased, the pockmarked, the afflicted, the smelly, and the unclean for purposes of getting right again. Not only was Lindisfarne unexceptional in this regard, it was prototypical.

Two days after the pilgrims started to arrive, the line to view Cuthbert's tomb stretched twice around the church from dawn to dusk, and as the feast day approached, it swelled with the aforementioned crippled, halt, lame, maimed, blind, and deaf, joined now by the stupid, the deformed, the gullible, and the devout. This assembly crawled, hobbled, clawed, and whimpered its way across the stones to get a glimpse of and say a prayer before the vestments Cuthbert had been buried in, and to kiss his grave and mumble their pitiful hopes into the worn stones.

Even the meanest and most desolate seemed to have a silver penny for the saint, which they dropped into a jar on the way out under the smiling visage of Ælfwine the Feretrar, who was in charge of Cuthbert's Shrine and whatever it raked in. They had an operation on Lindisfarne that Orm would've admired.

As the feast approached, I stepped up my preparations for departure. Eadred gave me a knapsack and travel clothes and a couple of elk hide scrips. Alban gave me herbs and medicines to take back to Mairead. Godwine selected a Book of Hours and a Psalter for Goltrade.

There was a lot of traffic between Lindisfarne and its granges. Flocks and herds were penned among the tall dunes north of the monastery until their wool, milk, and meat could be consumed by the rabble. Eadred prepared the guest chambers in the Priory and located the wooden box that contained my verse.

Eadred had written to his counterpart at Hexham, asking after the size and needs of the delegation, and we found out twenty-five monks and nuns were coming, escorted by twenty men at arms. Good news, I thought, an armed escort as far as the Roman wall, and then a straight shot to the Irish Sea, but the Prior anticipated me.

"We are concerned for your welfare," Higbald said when I stood before him at another Chapter meeting. "With so many people on Lindisfarne, we cannot guarantee sanctuary." Introductions had been brief and pro forma; with Cuthbert's Feast approaching, he had more important things to do than waste his time chatting up the resident Viking.

"No need," I said. "I can take care of myself."

"If we can't guarantee your safety," he said, "we fail our sanctuary duty. We'll take the necessary precautions."

I reckoned the necessary precautions would be a week in the Lindisfarne slammer, severe accommodations even by monastic standards. Chapter twenty-eight provided for a place of confinement for recalcitrant brothers until they saw the error of whatever way had put them there. But Higbald had my welfare at heart, after all. No incarceration for me.

"The pilgrims who come to Cuthbert's Feast are from all classes of mankind, and though the bishop concerns himself with everyone who comes, some require more attention.

We must be notified in enough time to greet these visitors as befits them, in the reception hall of the Priory."

"We have a system of signaling," the Prior continued with poorly concealed delight when Higbald paused for breath, "which requires a man by the causeway and a man in the church tower to drop a note below. From the ground it's quite impossible to hear a horn or see signal smoke.

"You have all the necessary requirements for this task," he said. "You can write, your powers of vision have already been demonstrated, and your experience as a lookout aboard a trading vessel will serve you well in the tower."

This was powerful reasoning and no denying it. No one would be able to say that Lindisfarne was reckless with its sanctuary duty, and neither would I be preaching the return of Bede's ghost to the unwashed multitudes. The Prior had maneuvered Higbald into running me up a stump for a week.

"Thanks," was all I could say.

That's how I found myself in the bell tower at the beginning of the week of Cuthbert's Feast. The subpriors and the Pict escorted me up the spiral stairs. Once again wings fluttered away when I opened the trapdoor, but there was only pigeon shit and loose down on the platform. A subprior handed me a bag of stones. My task was to watch for the smoke or fire, which signaled guests of sufficient rank to require a personal audience with Higbald, and drop a note to a waiting novice below.

The tower doors were locked to keep anyone from climbing up to take in the view. Ecstatic pilgrims had a known susceptibility to vertigo, which only made trouble for everyone. This year the security in the north tower was bolstered by Haki the Pict, who waited inside the locked door with his axe. At first it seemed there was no way out, but it was the Prior's conceit that showed me one. Always play chess with a man before you oppose him.

I was confident during the first two days in the tower, hunkered down on the pigeon shit as the monks laid out the temporary streets of the fairground in the vast outer garth, a faint grid of pegs and string to define the areas for gaming, fun, commerce, and flagellation.

A large tent in the garth housed Cuthbert's Court. In addition to the usual licensing fee for the privilege of having a fair, justice too was sublet for the duration. Attendees were subject to the judicial authority of Cuthbert's Court, presided over by the subpriors, acting as bailiffs, and enforced by the younger monks, acting as reeves. This court had jurisdiction over disagreements concerning trade and merchandise, set the tolls and fees for commerce and passport, collected fines for misdemeanor, and was empowered to arrest and detain criminals for the secular authorities.

I ran out of stones by midafternoon of the third day. By then the road from the west was like a tribal migration route, a great mass of movement and color. When the tide ebbed, as many as possible paid their pence and came across, and when the flood returned, they bivouacked along the shore from the causeway to Fenham while coracles ferried those who could afford it. The tide was the only thing regulating the onslaught, but even so the pilgrims soon filled the great courtyard, and the overflow pitched their tents in the pastures surrounding the monastery wall, coming and going unhindered through the open gates.

A dozen ships that had tempted the Norns with spring crossings from Frisia and Francia rocked in their ropes in the sheltered bay, eager for a share of the custom. These foreign merchants were housed in the monastery, where they rubbed elbows with middle-class merchants from Northumbria, East Anglia, Mercia, and Kent, and the Prior used the opportunity to milk them for news from the continent.

While their masters stopped in the Priory and the Guest House, the men at arms were in scattered billets, none too near another. They were a volatile bunch, always wound too tight and looking to perfect their technique, and it was bad enough they'd bump elbows as they shopped the vendors' stalls in search of just the right souvenir of Cuthbert's Feast.

The celebration of masses, the chanting of litanies, the praying of novenas, the hearing of confessions, and the dispensation of Eucharists reached a terrible pitch on the eve of Cuthbert's Feast. Cardinal acts of mercy were perpetrated upon crippled children, and silver pennies were lavished upon beggars with no pockets to hold them. Gangs of zealous laymen roamed the grounds in search of good works that needed doing; pardoners were engaged in a price war in a penitent's market.

Alban was busy treating the inevitable cuts, burns, hammered thumbs, sprained ankles, bad stomachs, and hysteria that were part and parcel of Cuthbert's Feast, and when he wasn't setting bones or applying the leeches, he was consulting with traveling healers about herbal lore and showing the stock of items he'd prepared during the winter or decoctioning compounds on the spot.

This gave him an alibi that an inquisitor from Saville and a crack team of Dominican interrogators would've had a hard time breaking, which was good because it was his chemistry that created the compound of poppy and alkaloids that Eadred slipped to Haki the Pict, baked into a dozen cinnamon buns and delivered by Brian and Brendan, still warm, with a small pot of honey on the side and a pint of the monastery's famous golden mead.

Brendan regaled Haki with stories of what a great time he was missing out on the grounds, in fact, maybe the only time when a gargoyle of Haki's lowness could aspire to be pitied enough by some servant girl that she'd open her legs for him. As Haki'd never taken vows and was a lay servant of the monastery he was under no duties of abstinence, and so was free to disport himself sexually as his opportunities and luck permitted.

This reminder of the cost of the Prior's favor agitated Haki so thoroughly that he didn't protest the presence of Brian and Brendan carrying more stones and the food. Haki's mood changed when he smelled the cinnamon and opium incense of a dozen warm buns. Here was what monastic communism was all about: a little something to balance out what he was missing.

He started wolfing buns as Brian started the long climb to the tower with the supplies and Brendan sat on the lowest stone step and talked about the wonderful things going on outside. The Pict ate another three buns, had a drink of mead, and sat down to ponder his situation about the time Brian got to the top of the ladder and tossed the trapdoor aside.

"How'd it go?"

"Just the way you said it would." Brian smiled.

"Learn chess," I told him as he closed the trap.

"There's a wonderful view from here," he said.

"I'm glad you like it." I walked over to the parapet.

"I had this duty two years ago," he said, setting a bundle

of shearling aside and taking out a book. No spartan watch for Brian, eyes peeled for smoke on the hill five kilometers from the tower. Whatever else you can say about a lad from Drogheda, you can't say that standing a twelve-hour watch in a bell tower teaches him nothing. Last out of the sack were a razor, a scissors, and a jar of water.

"Let's get this over with," he said, stropping the razor on his belt.

Some kind of reckless trust had rubbed off on me during the winter because I sat down and turned my back on a Drogheda boy with a razor in his hand. I was lucky to appreciate it before I went out into the crowd; no recklessness would serve down there among several thousand Anglo-Saxon pilgrims in search of a religious experience.

"Did you think you'd be getting a tonsure and taking the cloth that day you washed up on the Inner Farnes?" he asked as the scissors snicked the hair off the top of my head.

"Borrowing the cloth," I said, "and getting a haircut."

When my hair was short enough, he opened the water jar. He wet a cloth, lathered it on a cake of soap, and sponged it onto my scalp. The razor sang as he shaved through the jagged cropping on the top of my head, and little flecks of lather fell like sparks. It only took a minute to smooth the top of my head and throw a towel over it to sop up the blood from a few superficial nicks.

"You can tell it's the first tonsure you've had," he said, applying a critical eye to his work. "After a few years your head stays brown through the winter. Keep your cowl up and don't promise what you can't deliver."

I opened the trapdoor and started down the ladder. I wouldn't be sorry to get away from those bells.

At the bottom of the tower, the Pict was starting to feel the effects of a dozen mushroom-and-opium-loaded cinnamon buns washed down with a pint of mead. I pulled the cowl over my head and turned my face into the deep shadows of its folds. Brendan was watching Haki's dreamy smile with concern. Haki was on the brink of an experience most of the pilgrims outside would have sold their firstborn for, and he had no tongue to describe it. It was one of those ironies that made the late eighth century such a fun place.

"He'll be all right," I whispered. "Let's not waste time. I don't want to run into the subpriors."

"They're busy with Cuthbert's Court," he said.

Brendan gave me a look and adjusted the hood. I'd pass for a monk among many as we prowled about the grounds ferreting out games of chance, the vending of unauthorized relics, and the clandestine hocus-pocus of miracle workers, wherever they lurked. This was the reeves duty that Brendan and Brian performed for the court. They were the Feast Police, and now I was one of them.

It was good to be in a crowd again. I'd missed jostling the rabble, trading lice, smelling a few thousand unwashed bodies, having my toes trod on by thralls and corn merchants, and looking at the women. Since my thoughts had been occupied solely by Frydys, I'd forgotten about women in general. Suddenly the island was awash in them, and they all had those ecstatic glazed eyes which are the hallmark of a virgin longing to be possessed by a holy man.

I was only on the ground for a minute before I sensed the potential that lay in the unconfined adolescent breasts of the radiant virgin daughters of Northumbria. And there I was, charming and helpful in my habit and cowl, looking long into their eyes as I spoke to them, smiling suggestively as they pleaded for a look at Cuthbert's vestments or a private tour of the island.

If it weren't for my oath with Frydys, I could've had as many as I wanted. Not that I believed for a minute that the rapid porking of some Anglo-Saxon virgin would interfere with my loving Frydys—it was merely the biological scratch of a biological itch—but an oath's an oath, and even if there'd been no oath, there was no privacy. There were pilgrims everywhere, gawking at the church towers or the Farnes, six miles out on the ocean horizon.

They marveled at the sight with the credulity of tourists—bluff-faced and inhospitable Frisian Sea islands, they were invested with some geo-beatific importance because Cuthbert had manhandled a coracle around them. The rising ground from the point of Hole Mouth to the cliffs of Emmanuel Head was patrolled by couples and small groups discussing Things Spiritual and Cuthbert's intrinsic holiness.

Nowhere was there a little pile of hay where two people of average size and mutual carnal intent could shed their clothes and inhibitions for a few minutes of unobserved biological investigation. I had to pass up three or four clear

invitations in the first half hour, and it was all I could do
to keep my eyes open for the shadowy movements of a
cutpurse and his bumper working the congested areas of
the promenade where crowds gathered in front of acrobats
or jugglers or buskers miming the acts of charity that
Cuthbert reputedly inflicted on cripples and lepers. Dirty
work, I suppose, but someone had to wash their suppurat-
ing stumps.

As the sun rose it started getting hot in that black wool
cowl, and I was sweating freely and itchy as a dog in tall
grass. Two hours in one of those outfits made it clear why
the monks had their own peculiar odor, easily identified by
anyone downwind. That wasn't really saying a lot, though:
those years have never been celebrated as a triumph of
hygiene and personal grooming.

But now the pilgrims were pressing it on the church,
where Higbald, the Prior, and Bishops Eanbald of York
and Æthelberht of Hexham were about to concelebrate the
mass of St. Cuthbert's Feast, decked out in vestments elaborately embroidered with illuminated letters from the Gospels, threads of gold and silver shining in the candlelight
under the cool vault of the church. Cuthbert's vestments
were displayed in a gilded and elaborately carved frame
behind the altar while the heavyweights performed the ritual and the tightly packed congregation went quietly unconscious in the press.

Outside, there were less-conventional out-of-body experiences to be had. Sometimes, caught up in the moment,
men and women would begin to whirl about like spindles,
laughing ecstatically. Brendan was used to these moments
of gyrelike transport, but the ecstatics made me nervous,
spinning around like that, slapping pedestrians on the side
of the head or across the throat in good-natured Pentecos-
tal frenzy. The axiom "A crowd is an ugly thing" was first
spoken by someone who'd spent time in a mob of Anglo-
Saxons in hot pursuit of religious transport.

So I got worried when I saw someone spinning and
laughing as we pushed against the flow, and then I noticed
someone cutting purses at the fringe, deftly, almost invisi-
bly, with professional grace. I noticed the blade flash; I was
keeping an eye out for blades. The Prior's theory about the
dangerous nature of a Northumbrian crowd wasn't completely loopy.

I pointed the cutpurse out to Brendan, and we split to encircle him. We had a license for that guy, and we were getting ready to fill out the tag when the epileptic on the ground suddenly sprang upright and swung a fist the size of a roast partridge into Brendan's face, making his eyes turn outward for a hideous instant before they snapped back toward center.

As the cutpurse watched, frozen by the realization that such a simple thing as cutting a few purses could go so terribly awry in such a small moment, I hit him in the middle of his back with a shoulder that took the wind out of him and snapped his arms around, causing him to release both blade and purse into two unrelated but equally startled pilgrims. The one that took the blade merely glanced down at the handle, hanging loose in the left sleeve of his tunic, and the red welling soaked the cloth, but the one that got hit in the face with the purse and lost his front teeth in a shower of silver seemed to regard it as a reward for a good life.

I was on top of the cutpurse, pushing his face into the dirt as the crowd parted around us. The erstwhile ecstatic had evaporated, but Brendan sank to his knees and toppled over on us, rag-doll limp. There was a tangle of legs and arms and knees, and then the cutpurse was swimming through the crowd like a fish heading for deep water.

Brendan sat on the ground blinking himself back to the present tense as I slipped after the cutpurse, about as lithe in that black wool habit as a sheep in a hawthorn thicket. He seemed always on the verge of disappearing, and when he gained the edge of the crowd, he burst ahead toward the gate. He cut right to skirt the wall and get the curve of it between us. I angled to head him off, gained the highest rail of the fence, and scrambled to the top of the stone wall just as he panted into view around the clubhouse turn. I got my feet under me and dropped on his back with a scream.

My weight took us straight to the ground, and he was still as I got to my feet, but I didn't mistake him, as the Wise One advised: "A corpse still fresh is never to be trusted." I circled and gave him a solid kick from the rear quarter, but his body lurched gelatinously, the way only a deeply unconscious or dead man's body will, the way Brendan had just behaved, come to think of it, so I kicked the cutpurse again before I put my back to the wall to catch my breath. When he started to come round, I got up to search him.

Under his long cloak I found seven purses that had begun the day on other people's belts. He'd had nearly as good a feast as Cuthbert himself. I cairned them up in some loose rocks and rolled the cutpurse over to finish the search. I found no other blades, and I stepped back as his eyes fluttered open.

"You're going to Cuthbert's Court for a thrashing and a turning out," I told him. "Since your hoard can't be traced to its rightful owners, we'll give it to the almoner. I'm sure the poor would thank you if they could, but since they can't, I'll thank you on their behalf." Then I kicked him again, rolling him over on his side.

"What were you before you took the cloth?" he muttered.

"A berserk," I told him. "A skald aboard the *Blood Raven,* the memory of Sygtrygg's doomed vik—"

"Who cares?" he demanded. "I didn't really want to know; it was just a question, understand?" Then his demeanor changed as he remembered something. "Wait a minute," he said. "You *are* a Dane, aren't you?" He was talking as though he couldn't feel the bottom half of his mouth.

I shrugged and passed up the tempting offer of his unprotected flank. He was stunned enough, and I'd be able to control him now.

"I'm from Ireland," I said, exaggerating the accent. "A simple, pious son of the old sod saving your soul from a sin against the eighth commandment. But what sort of man would I be if I let you get away with hurting my friend?"

He shook his head and stumbled around for a second as a flush came and went, then he stood still and took a few deep breaths.

"It's true, then. I can't believe it."

"Can't believe what?"

"That monks took in a Dane from the fleet that harried past the Tynemouth last fall."

I shrugged. "Must have been some other Danes." Someone had spread the word about me. Maybe the Prior was advertising for that assassin he'd been so worried about in the Chapter meeting, or maybe some monk just mentioned it without thinking. Same result either way. "The Northumbrian coast watch attacked us. I'm the only one that survived."

"Bullshit," he said. "One thief to another, what was your haul?"

"Believe what you want." I shrugged. "What do I care? The fleet's bones are scattered all over the Farnes."

"Who told you that? From the Danish fleet, one ship only foundered. Called the *Sea Snake* or the *Sea Lizard,* or something like that. Half the crew lived, and half of them were slaved out, while the rest hung from the oaks while the ravens dined. It drew a great crowd and I took twenty purses over those two weeks."

That had the ring to it; a cutpurse would know what he was talking about when it came to public gatherings. And the *Sea Snake* was Bui's boat.

"What about the rest of the fleet?"

"All escaped," he said.

That meant that Skallagrim and Sygtrygg and Thorfinn and the crew of the *Blood Raven* were probably alive, had at least passed through the storm. They'd lost only one dragon and saved the knarr. Too bad for Bui, but Kalf had other brothers-in-law.

Then, like an anvil dropping on my feet, I appreciated who else had been spared—Macc Oc was alive, and in collusion with Sygtrygg to have Frydys at vik's end, and half a year had passed. I realized he might be having her at that moment, forcing her thighs apart and rutting into her. I walked over to the cutpurse and kicked him in the knee, folding him up on the turf again.

"What of the Irish?"

"What Irish?"

"The Irishmen aboard the Danish fleet."

"Nothing," he said. "They were all Danes at Tynemouth."

"I want the truth," I said redistributing my weight for another kick. "I'd friends in the fleet, and no word."

"You've word of them now, sweet Cuthbert's cock and balls. Don't kick me again."

For some reason, he'd parted company with the truth. There were as many Irish as Danes on that dragon, and I knew some of the survivors had to be Macc Oc's men. Since a man likes to talk before they hang him, it wouldn't have been a secret that some were Irish. The cutpurse was telling me what he thought I wanted to hear.

I kicked him once more, just a medium kick to let him know I was still waiting. "Still no Irishmen taken?"

"Some," he whimpered. He seemed to think I wanted to hear that no Irishmen had washed up, and he couldn't understand why I kicked him when he assured me it was so.

"How many?"

"There were a dozen slaved out and ten hung. Eight Danes survived, all but one hanged." His wrenched knee would make him a less deft crowd dancer. I hunkered down to face him, keeping out of reach.

"You're certain the rest of the fleet escaped?"

"Sure as sunshine."

I nodded and looked at my toes. Then he came out with the blade I'd missed in my search. What was I thinking about? A cutpurse with only one blade? Like a Viking with only one axe. I rolled back and he missed my throat by a half a foot. He was too hurt to follow me, though, and I picked up a big rock and threw it hard into his knee. He dropped the knife, and I put my foot on it as he rolled the other way. His knee was swelling like a sausage in hot water; he was sweating and his teeth were clenched.

"Hurts, doesn't it? So you slit purses while Danes fed the ravens?" I picked up the knife and laid my thumb along the blade. It was whetted feather-thin, and bone or leather would part under it like a virgin's lips. "Who knows I'm here?"

"It's a rumor I heard in the crowd. Who'd believe a rumor like that? Sooner a farmer'd raise a wolf. Rumors live in a crowd like hares in a cornfield."

"I live on Lindisfarne as a novice," I told him. "I've renounced my past and embraced the true faith."

"And I lost a manor in Andalusia when the Moors invaded."

"Pretty cheeky for a lame thief," I reminded him. His only geld was what he carried and he knew it. The man was worthless. It seemed like a good opportunity to point it out.

I thought once more about Macc Oc, trying to put an optimistic face on things. If they'd been too long refitting in the Orkneys, those first storms *might* have trapped them in Scapa Flow. It depended on how well the ships had fared, and what Orkney stores were available at the end of the season. Stranger things had happened. The Norns were famous for their sense of humor. Big kidders, the Norns. So if they'd been icebound in the Orkneys, they might be only a week or two in the Liffey; they'd barely be sobered up.

"The man who told me was certain as you the fleet was gone."

"Who was he?"

"A monk and kinsman of one of the coast watchers."

"As if the coast watch wouldn't have reason to lie. They lost half their ships with thirty-seven Danes to show for it. Maybe you'd double the number of ships went down, or multiply it like loaves and fishes if you could. What're you going to do to me?"

That was the next question, all right. I couldn't take him back to Cuthbert's Court with the subpriors presiding, but he didn't know that; he only knew what I told him. Maybe a little mercy was in order. But he had some serious groveling to do before he could appreciate it fully.

"You're in double jeopardy, my friend." I shook my head. "This crime is in the jurisdiction of civil and ecclesiastical courts, and both will punish you for desecrating Cuthbert's Feast day."

"It'll be a maiming, at least. Go through the rest of your life with your fingers tied in knots. Lose a hand or an eye, maybe. Finish up at the almsgate some winter night. They crushed a crowd dancer's foot in York last year and cut off his hands. He starved to death before he got the hang of begging with stumps."

"Please," he began, but without the proper hint of subservience.

"And when the reeve comes it's the king's own justice," I went on. "What would that be, do you think?" I didn't offer suggestions—it was up to him to imagine the punishment he dreaded most.

"If you turn me in, one or all of them," he wailed. "But if you let me go, none, and no trouble for you."

"Do you think the Prior set me loose to encourage cutpurses? Can I turn a blind eye to thievery?"

"Please, brother," he whined, clutching across the stones for the hem of my robe. "I repent. I've sinned, and I confess it freely."

I stood away from him and said, "Get up."

He crawled to his feet and swayed for a moment.

"Go away."

"My purses."

"Don't push your luck," I said in disbelief. "You've *lost* your purses. Say your prayers to Cuthbert tonight," I told him. "But say them on the mainland."

He started limping down the slope toward the penitents' way without looking back. He had the walk of a man with a sprung knee.

Brendan came round the curve of the wall and I waved to him. He was nursing a set of raccoon eyes, and his nose was swollen. His hair stood out in disarray from his tonsure. "Get your man?" he called as he approached.

"I gave him a good thrashing and let him go," I said. "How's your face?" Now that he was close, I saw that his eyes were black and blue and yellow and a deep sunset kind of red inside the lids, like a dog with alkaloid poisoning.

I looked back toward the causeway road, but the cutpurse had disappeared behind the first dune. Of course, now everything was changed. Frydys was no longer mourning my passing among all those other passings; now she was mourning my passing while Macc Oc comforted her, with Sygtrygg's encouragement. Considering the eyewitness accounts of my Frisian Sea swim, who'd expect her to wait a year for me?

I estimated my chances of slipping off the island then and there. With everyone focused on Cuthbert's Mass there wouldn't be a better time. The original plan had been to ingratiate myself with the party from Hexham, find out their schedule, establish my cover story as a wandering monk who was heading south after the feast, and con my way into their retinue when they departed. With Brian to vouch for me, it hadn't seemed like a stretch, but it had involved a return to the safety of the tower until they left. I couldn't count on remaining at large during the festival. Someone from the monastery was sure to recognize me if I stayed out there too long.

But after the news update from the cutpurse, I found myself fighting an overwhelming urge to split the island immediately. The party from Hexham could catch up. All

I knew was I had to get back to Clontarf as soon as I could. But the Norms had other plans, as usual.

Ten or twelve pilgrims who'd witnessed the original incident were waiting at the gate. One of them stepped forward and put a surprisingly light hand on my forearm. "I hope you weren't hurt in the struggle, brother," she said, and I looked down into those cornflower blue eyes they all seemed to have and almost melted at the sweetness of her face and the sincerity in her voice, instantly recognizing in her a vague willingness to give her virginity to a holy man. They're out there: priest groupies, safely tempted because the celibate object of their attention is comfortably off limits, enabling them to enjoy the sweet frustration of adolescent longing well into their adult years.

But, looking down into those concerned eyes, I resolved to give this one her wish. All that celibacy and fresh air were getting to me. What were the chances that Frydys was waiting for me? I knew the girl's history. I didn't blame her, I was just being realistic. "I'm as well as God wills me to be," I said to her.

Brendan looked at me with a kind of horrified understanding, probably because he'd had those thoughts himself a time or two, and because she was ignoring his obvious wounds to ask after my health. "We have to return to the crowd inside," he insisted.

"Aren't these pilgrims part of the crowd? Let's accompany them into St. Peter's Church for Cuthbert's Mass."

"Brother, we couldn't get through," one of the older men said.

"There's another door," I told him, putting hand on his back and gently shoving him toward the church. "By the side altar, not far from Cuthbert's grave."

"Could you do this, brother?" an old woman asked.

"Without trouble," I assured her, sweeping her up with my free hand. The rest of them fell in behind, and in a moment we were angling toward the low wall of the cemetery garth. Brendan followed in our wake, but I ignored him, and finally he forced his way to the front of the group to walk beside me.

We walked down the orchard path that ran behind the Chapter House and the Priory to the door in the south transept tower. At intervals there were statues representing the sufferings of Christ on his way to be crucified. This is a thing that Christians like to mediate on, and the figures of the Christ got increasingly bloody and tortured as we approached the crucifixion. Stone benches were placed for quiet contemplation of the scourging or crowning with thorns or nailing of hands and feet.

Odhinn spent some time hung up like that, bound to the Yggdrisil, but he made a better trade: an eye for the Runes and a drink from Mirmir spring, and when he came down again, he had something to show for it. The old gods had panache, and the farther back you went, the more they had. They were gods you could get pissed at, and who got pissed at you. They were gods you could have a relationship with based on getting drunk, reading poetry, fighting wars, planting and reaping, and riding the sea mare, not gods who demanded unconditional love and praise and in return insisted that you go meekly to your death on the promise of reward in the next life. This Christ provided churches where glass the color of wine translated light into discrete shafts of vaporous color, but then what?

"Eadred wouldn't approve," Brendan said, looking round in the crowd as if he expected to be apprehended by the old guest master.

"Eadred's concerned that the pilgrims have a good time here," I pointed out. "He wouldn't object to a little common courtesy."

"It's uncommon courtesy you've got in mind."

"What I've got in mind is between me and my confessor, should I ever go to one." As we spoke, we reached the gate into the inner cloister. The small oak door to the chapel in the south transept was hidden by the curve of the tower.

The eager pilgrims rushed past, jostling Brendan along, and as the girl came by I detained her with a subtle touch that she understood right enough. She lagged as they hurried toward the side door, and by the time we'd crossed the thirty feet, she was at the end of the group, walking just ahead of me.

They jammed forward, and when Brendan opened the door to avoid being pressed flat against the woods, they stumbled into the dark interior of the tower. The girl and I brought up the rear, bumping into each other in the crush, and conducting a mutual exploration of physiology from which I, at least, came away encouraged. I closed the door behind us, leaving everyone in a gloom as their sight adjusted.

A touch on her elbow indicated the direction, and we glided to the deep shadow by the tower steps. I turned toward her. She was breathing fast. We started up the stairs, climbing past the choir landing to the enclosed wooden stairs. All those really big churches had four towers, and St. Peter's church at Lindisfarne had bells in them all. The tower door was locked, but I knew where the key was.

The chanting acquired that strange sound human choral singing assumed in stone acoustics, like it was coming from the bottom of a well. Then we were in the bell loft. She looked at the bronze bells with awe. She'd grown to her present height listening to the voices of bells, but these were the first she'd ever seen. They were taller than me, and they must have weighed a couple of tons apiece. I have to admit I don't understand how they got them up there, but when she asked, I told her Cuthbert's spirit had levitated them into place under my direct observation.

"Really?" she asked, begging to be assured it was true.

"Of course." I smiled. "And I've seen the spirit of the venerable Bede, when I was ill in the Farmery for some weeks."

"I hope you're feeling better now," she said, moving closer, her hands partially extended as if she'd arrested an impulse to place them reassuringly on my arms.

"I'm feeling particularly well here," I said, stepping forward to show her whereof I spoke. She retreated a half step, a look of piquant alarm flickering in her eyes, and then moved off, her hand trailing around the rim of the bell. So that's how it was.

"Have you ever seen the view from a great tower?"

"Never," she said.

"Then climb this ladder, and I'll show you one."

She stepped aside and I went up the ladder ahead of her, slipping the bolt on the trapdoor and hearing the faint, familiar flapping of the Prior's pigeons as they took wing for a return to the dovecote and a date with a pie crust. I opened the hatch and pigeon down came swirling in like snowflakes.

I climbed out onto the platform with its fine view of the island, the only place that afforded the necessary privacy, and turned back to extend a helping hand. She opened her mouth and drew an involuntary breath, overcome by vertigo as she saw what only birds saw in those days, and monks who climbed towers, and girls who came with them. She sagged against me, and I put an arm round her for support, lowering her below the parapet to the rough boards and the fresh pigeon shit, and she spread her skirts out in a graceful gesture that told me she wasn't as vertiginous as she seemed.

I put out my hand as I sank to the boards with her, and I felt a sharp sting in my palm. I glanced down with irritation and saw a splinter had inserted itself across the white scar of Frydys's cut. I looked down at the expectant girl, sat back and slipped my knife point into the meat of my hand, pinched the end of the splinter between blade and thumbnail, and drew it out in one piece, leaving a blood trail under the skin, transforming the rune *Isa* into the rune *Nyth,* which makes the sound *n-n-n-n-n-n-n-no,* and is the rune of the great teacher disguised as the bringer of pain and limitation.

The girl moistened her lips with the tip of her tongue. I could see her nipples under her shift. I put my hands by her sides and lowered myself toward her. She closed her eyes and the ends of her mouth turned up in a little smile. Our lips were millimeters apart, and she shifted to receive the weight of my body.

The bells began to ring beneath us at that precise second, and the din and vibration levitated us both. I pressed my hands to my ears, a gesture she copied, although she remained prone on the rough boards as the three bells beneath us reached their full voice, and she writhed slightly, knees apart, as the whole top of the tower quivered sympathetically.

We were stuck there until the bells stopped after the distribution of communion bread and wine, a consummation somewhat different from the one I'd anticipated. It was no good going through the bell room now—the concentrated sound would burst our ears, and afterward we'd only hear what the Pict had to say. Besides, the girl was enjoying transports of pleasure, her lips parted and moving in ways that could only have produced moans of delight, if there'd been any way to hear them.

Finally the bells stopped, and I lowered my hands. She lay panting on the floor with her arms spread as if releasing someone from her embrace. I was glad she'd gotten what she came for, at least. I pulled myself up and looked over the edge of the parapet, where the congregation was streaming out of the church doors seventy-five feet below. I went over to the girl and helped her up. She had a glazed and dreamy look, and I hesitated to urge her down the ladder, but it was important to get back before they missed her. Her legs were elastic, and I supported her to the bell loft, where we rested as the bronze behemoths vibrated into silence.

She sagged against the wall at the head of the spiral stairs. Too bad she hadn't waited for me; I could only imagine what it might have been like. Too bad the splinter had formed the rune *Nyth*; too bad, too bad a lot of things. She put her arms round me and we kissed deeply, and then, as if actual human touch didn't measure up, she collected herself, slowly disengaged, and started down the stairs, one hand touching the exterior wall for balance.

I followed her, tasting in that kiss an echo of her experience in the bell tower. As we approached the ground, she went faster, and when we emerged from the stairwell, she was skipping, as if, having survived a brush with the transcendent, she'd returned to earth to remember it for the rest of her life. We found everyone milling around under the arbor, where Brendan was looking frantically for us.

"Did you enjoy the mass?" I asked them.

"Wonderful," one of the women said.

"Well, we've work now," Brendan said, guiding me away from the group, where the girl stood with a look of satisfaction that was easily mistaken for faith.

Brendan said nothing about the incident, and it was a loud silence. We found the party from Hexham hard by the forge, about fifteen of them, cooks, grooms, a few bladesmen and archers. The one in charge lounged against the side of a tent, observing the crowd with a practiced eye. We walked over and introduced ourselves.

"How's the feast?" Brendan asked amiably.

"How've we earned all this concern for our welfare?" he asked.

"What other concern have you had?"

"Four bladesmen came round before the mass and promised us a Dane was trying to sneak off the island. Had we seen a Dane, they wanted to know. Can you believe it? I said we'd seen a whole shipload last night but we ran out of mead about Prime and when we woke up, they'd gone."

"Just a joke," I assured him. "No Danes about."

"We thought so too, then a different pair came round with the same story. The second two said that all the men at arms have a contest to hunt him down. You tell me."

First someone had to tell *me*. How had this happened? Now I knew how the cutpurse felt; how immediate wyrd was then, or luck, or karma, or whatever you want to call it. A couple of hours ago I'd been on the top of the food chain, kicking a man's ribs to extort information, perfectly camouflaged as a churchman, and now I was a hunted dog on an island full of professional Dane killers.

I needed time to think this through. Maybe the Prior'd floated the rumor as a backup, an additional garnish to his security precautions, like crocodiles in a moat, or maybe it was the cutpurse's revenge. However it got started, serious interest in a rumor like that was the last thing I needed. Men at arms were thick as fleas in that crowd. Maybe if I spoke nothing but Latin my accent wouldn't give me away; mastery of the imperial tongue was a definite plus, and though my Northumbrian had much improved over the winter, it wasn't up to close inspection.

I was tempted again to make a break for it while everything was confusion and festivity, a chaos of quasi-mystical good humor, but for once I had the good sense to resist an impulse. Tomorrow all the movement across the causeway would be away from Lindisfarne. A solitary man, moving in a hurry while he tried to pretend he wasn't, would be pathetically easy to spot now. I doubted I could hide for another twelve hours.

As I made this debate with myself, a knot of soldiers pushed slowly through the crowd like stalking heron working a reed bed. Brendan and I stood there shoulder to shoulder as they came on, and I really started sweating under the wool cowl as I composed my face to look like a Benedictine. I've been in saunas cooler than that habit.

One of the soldiers looked at me for a long moment, and then he made straight at us, the flow of the crowd swirling like an eddy around a swimming wolf. Brendan got tense and said, in Irish, "I'll do the talking."

"Brothers," the soldier began. "Earlier I saw you fighting with a cutpurse, and three of us chased his helper through the gardens outside, but we lost him when he ducked back into the crowd. Did you find the other?"

"He escaped us," Brendan said.

The soldier looked at me, and I gave him a sardonic smile I hoped, for some reason, would throw him off the scent.

"There's a Dane in the crowd, brothers. We've been looking for him all morning."

"What does he look like?" I asked, accenting my words like an Irishman.

"He looks like a Dane," the soldier said.

"Then he'll be easy to spot."

"He may be in disguise," the soldier said.

"As what?"

"As not a Dane," the soldier explained.

"Oh," I said, understanding the search parameters. Anyone who didn't look like a Dane was suspected of being a Dane in disguise, and anyone who looked like someone trying not to look like a Dane was suspected of being a Dane who was a poor actor, and anyone who positively looked like a Dane was suspected of, what, being a really unlucky Dane? These guys had a license for whoever they wanted to harass.

"What about women?"

"A Dane might try to look like a Danish woman," the soldier realized, adding women who looked Danish to his working profile.

Just then a nun hurried over to us.

"Brother Bran," she said. "I've been looking all over for you. You're wanted at Cuthbert's Court."

Brendan and I were aghast. Now what? Who was this nun and how did she know my name? I looked at her as she pushed her veil aside. Her wimple was tight across her cheek, and she smiled as she took my arm to hurry me away. It was Caitria.

"If you see anyone suspicious, let us know," the soldier said, and started moving slowly to catch up his men, walking drag now, looking for anyone suspicious who might have slipped through the line of beaters.

I was stunned. I looked at her with my mouth gaping and she started to lose her composure. Brendan looked at her and then at me and then back at her.

"Wha— wh—" I was unable to formulate words.

"It's not often he's speechless," she said.

"Who is this?" Brendan asked me.

"Ca— he—"

"Caitria," she introduced herself. "I was in the fleet and stranded in the same storm as Bran."

"Whe—" I tried to ask.

"I've been in Bamburgh all winter. I washed up after the storm and an anchoress tended me until I was well."

"You're a Viking?" Brendan screeched, trying to puzzle out what was happening.

"We met in the south," she said ambiguously. "The fleet was going north to the Orkneys when the coast watch attacked. Then the storm blew us apart and I went into the water."

"Was the boat lost?" I managed to ask, finally coherent.

"No," she said. "I went into the water by myself."

"Me too," I said, looking at her outfit. "What're you doing here?"

"We heard there was a Dane at Lindisfarne, and the description sounded like you. I came to see. You're still obliged to set me down in a town. Is there a town hereabouts?"

"Fenham," Brendan offered.

"A town, not a sheep station with a well and bakery."

"Hexham's the closest town," he said.

"Maybe we should get started before those soldiers come back," she suggested, glancing after the Dane hunters.

"Too dangerous." I shook my head. "They're looking for me."

"They're looking for a Dane, not a monk and a nun."

"I'd never stand a questioning," I insisted. "I thought I'd join the party from Hexham, but not now. I'll wait until everyone's gone."

"*We'll* wait," she corrected me. "First you go to a ship where women aren't allowed. Then you hide in a monastery where women can't follow. You think I'll let you slip your duty that easily?"

"What's she talking about?" Brendan asked.

"He'll tell you later," Caitria snapped. "You better get under cover now. I'll send a message after the feast."

She melted back into the crowd, leaving us to our own resources. My customary optimism was beginning to fail.

Brendan and I went back to the church, but only Haki,

curled around some mute dream of a springtime meadow and naked women, lay in wait for us. Just another of the Prior's cruel jokes, to make sure the only safe place was in the tower. I climbed up to replace Brian while Brendan waited with the Pict.

10

The White Danes

A man should be loyal through life to friends,
To them and to friends of theirs,
But never shall a man make offer
Of friendship to their foes.
         —The Sayings of the Wise One

The next day was Benedict's Feast day, and while it may have been a double feast for the Benedictines, it was Cuthbert the crowds were interested in: a local boy made good, a dealer in healings, and past bishop of Lindisfarne. Benedict had no special favor among the rabble, so while the monks were celebrating the founder's feast, the rabble were striking the fairground, and I was treed in the bell tower until the tents and pavilions were packed up and hauled away.

The outlines of streets and booths were plainly visible in the trampled grass as laymen moved across the outer garth policing up the litter. The smoke of trash fires drifted away as the last of the pilgrims crossed the causeway and trudged into Northumbria. Higbald left for York with the bishop's party, leaving the Prior in command again.

I woke up to find the weather had turned foul in the night. The monastic rumor mill said it was a sign of Cuthbert's pleasure that he'd stayed the spring storms until after his festival. I'll bet that was a rumor that made the Prior's stomach burn. Apparently Northumbria's favorite saint was willing to let his devotees get swamped on the road home so their memories of his feast day would be of blue skies and miracles.

The swollen sky was a warning that the spring of 793 was going to be a meteorological freak show unrivaled since Noah's Flood. After a week of it I was convinced.

Fanciful stories of preternatural events filtered back to Lindisfarne in letters from Hexham (where they claimed to have seen a dragon in the sky) and York (where they claimed that drops of blood had fallen from the ceiling of the cathedral). That's the sort of fabulous tripe that doesn't go away even after you trace it to bad caulking in the lead roof.

The ground was sodden, and the creeks that drained into the harbor were yellow with mud. I bided my time, confusing the Prior and his boys with my tonsure. They didn't know what to make of me, and I clouded their minds with the same kind of disingenuous smoke the Prior was so adept at blowing in people's faces. I started keeping the canonical hours and going to mass; I worked and prayed with a novice's zeal; and I turned my lines over to the subpriors each day without complaint.

Storm after storm, the rains continued, and the villagers started to make their excuses for poor crops later on. Mainland rivers and streams overflowed their banks, sheep, their wool sodden and heavy, were falling over and dying because they couldn't get back on their feet.

There was no further word from Caitria. I had no idea where she'd gone. Brendan told Eadred about her, but what was there to say after I'd answered their questions? It seemed there was no getting rid of the woman, if I could be swept overboard into the Frisian Sea and find her waiting when I washed up.

Toward the end of April, a horseman showed up in a driving rain and stirred up Lindisfarne more than Cuthbert's Feast. Godwine, Eadred, and Alban were so incensed with his news that I had to piece it together from the fragments of their ranting.

The meat of it was that a noble named Sicga had killed himself a few months before, been buried, and now they were going to dig him up and rebury him on Lindisfarne. Bad enough a suicide was going to be planted in consecrated earth, but this suicide had also assassinated a previous Northumbrian king.

When the late and currently ripe Sicga was trundled up to the front door of St. Peter's Church, everyone turned to for the funeral mass. I kept out of sight, but the armed retinue was just security for Sicga's wife, three children, aged mother, and thralls. It was a mourning party of twenty-five, and seventeen of them were paid or owned outright by the mourners. Not many people were sad enough to slog through the storms to see Sicga into the ground a second time.

I gave them a head start so I wouldn't run into them down the road, but just when I was ready to leave, refugees started straggling down from the Forth estuary, forty or fifty miles north, on the Lothian borderland. They were carrying the odd belongings refugees seem to seize in moments of hysteria, like a cage of chickens, a patched copper pot, or a wooden milking stool and bucket, and they only stopped at Lindisfarne long enough to beg a meal and gibber about heathens coming in the night.

After that they were down the coast to Bamburgh and the protection of garrisoned stone walls. They were clearly terrified, and opinion was divided between Picts and divine retribution. I was betting on Picts. Circumstance pointed to another turf war brewing between the two kingdoms, and I knew there'd only be a narrow window of opportunity to escape. No one would be marching while the weather was bad, but when it cleared, if Æthelred took his army north, I'd be caught in the open ground.

When June came, the weather broke, and Odhinn's day of the first week found me on the high headland east of the monastery pretending to look for stray black-faced sheep at the tail end of lambing time, but a lot more interested in the sky over the mainland. All I needed was a dry stretch to firm up the roads, and the sun was warm and the sea was wearing a springtime face. The offshore breeze was carrying the smell of baking bread toward Frisia, and I began to hope for a pleasant walk across Northumbria.

Brian was with me, and two of the dogs that usually minded the mutton. We stopped to squint at the horizon while the long grass lashed our ankles, and I noticed the bump of a single sail emerging from the water, and then another sail joined it, followed by a third and a fourth. They were coasting south, beyond the Longstone.

I squinted between my fingers. They seemed to be tacking landward, and as I stared harder, the sails became striped, and the prows rose out of the water like the necks of sea swans. Brian called me, but I ignored him, watching the lines of the ships take sharper edge. Brian continued impatiently along the path down into a swale where a

marshy spring was sheltered from the wind. I kept an eye
on the ships.

Another few minutes passed, as they tacked seaward and
landward. I was sure they were four longships rigged and
cleared for action, and looking us over. The sails dropped,
and the oars frothed the water as they pulled wood against
the contrary tide. Four dragons down from the Mark—the
first vik of the season—had stumbled on Lindisfarne. They
were still tentative, not knowing for sure what waited
ashore, but I could see the ivory smiles of dragon's heads,
red-eyed, scaled, sniffing the wind and the smell of baking
bread from the kitchens of Lindisfarne.

They didn't know they'd discovered an unarmed group
of simple-minded copyists led by a Prior who'd been sent
down by Alcuin. They didn't know they were a short row
away from a hoard of silver pence from Cuthbert's Feast,
gold candlesticks on the altar, gold leaf in the Scriptorium,
silver censors and votive lamps at Cuthbert's tomb, jeweled
chalices and ceboria in the church, silk, leather, and vellum
in the bindery, and brass and copper in the craft shops. It
didn't matter what they knew or didn't know, what they
guessed, what they hoped, what they'd had for breakfast:
what mattered was that they'd just blundered into every
Viking's dream—an undefended pile of loot.

I sprinted down the slope. The outbound tide was a
break for us because it made rowing more difficult and
opened the causeway to the mainland. Brian was kneeling
in the grass with the dogs circling him, occupied with some
lambs, I reckoned. I waved to him to follow, but he was
slow to get the picture, standing indecisively and scratching
his tonsure. I concentrated on my footing as I crossed
stoney ground, slippery with sheep shit.

It was a mile along the curving shore to the monastery,
and I made it in about ten minutes. My legs were burning
as I ran across the great courtyard, through the outer and
inner cloister garths, and leaped the ornamental fish ponds
where Alban's herbs grew fragrant and lush beside the
water. I wrenched the door open and thundered down the
hallway. The urgency of my coming announced my state of
mind better than shouts when I slid up to the Chapter room
door, grabbed the molding, and careened in among the
monks.

I stood bent at the waist, gasping for air, and restricted

myself to the key concepts: "Danes . . . four ships . . . pillage and burn . . . kill you all."

There was instant furor. The Prior angrily hammered his fist on the arm of the high seat. As I gasped for breath, Eadred and Godwine guided me to the back of the room.

"Where did you see the boats?" Godwine demanded.

"Off the Longstone," I gasped out.

"How far away?"

"Wind and tide are against them. They'll be most of an hour."

"The causeway will be passable in an hour, and they'll still be on the east side of the island." Tide tables were the measure of when Eadred might expect guests, and I trusted his estimate, which meant I could collect my gear and verse and still be at the head of the line.

"I'll get my things," I said, starting out of the chapter room as the Prior's voice reimposed silence.

"Return to your places so we may resume the Chapter meeting."

"Resume the meeting?" I blurted to Godwine. "We've an hour to get to the mainland or we're dead."

"There's no proof they mean to harm us," the Prior said sharply in an attempt to quell the legitimate panic. "God and St. Cuthbert will not permit it."

The Prior was a name-dropper to the end, as if his unique relationship with God and Cuthbert precluded harm. Cynically invoking Cuthbert was a master touch.

"Who do you think those refugees were running from? These are the heathens that came in the night."

"This man is the voice of Chaos," the Prior shouted, pointing at me. "Don't listen to him."

"You're not getting the point here, are you? When those four longships leave, there won't be enough left to stuff up a duck's ass. We've got to get to the mainland." There was real danger at his door, and the Prior was acting like I was exaggerating the situation just to piss him off.

"We're in no danger," he insisted. "Lindisfarne's sacred ground."

"You'll end up with six feet of sacred ground next to Sicga if you waste any more time."

That wit was a mistake. He started to rise from his seat, longships forgotten because I'd mocked his self-importance. Then he remembered them and his eyes narrowed.

"We'll speak to them before we presume evil. We'll offer them provisions to assist them on their journey."

I was having trouble putting this together: the refugees had established the intentions of these Vikings pretty well, and here was a man who'd traveled, dabbled in Northumbrian court intrigue, broken bread with the head Frank, and pissed off Alcuin, and he wanted to *talk* to Vikings. Didn't he think anyone had tried that yet?

"This is a wind age and a wolf age," I told the Prior. "Wolves don't take one sheep and leave the rest, and four ships on a vik don't settle for sup and your good wishes and walk away from a hoard. It isn't natural. In a little while we're going to be all over Vikings."

But the Prior's expression was darkly intransigent, and I could see I wasn't getting through to him. I reckoned he'd show *me* who sat in the high seat. That was it for the Prior; he was out there on his own now. All that philosophy and court intrigue had finally gotten to him, all that *ofermod* had finally gotten too heavy to carry.

The two subpriors were rapidly losing their inscrutability, and the precentor, the feretrar, the burser, the cellarer, and the sacrist, all men with tangible physical inventories, seemed to understand the implications of a visit from Vikings quite a lot better than the Prior. Their eyes were wide, their breathing was shallow, and they were milling around on the verge of an entirely appropriate hysteria.

"Father percenter," the Prior said, "let us sing the psalm for the ending of the Chapter meeting. I must prepare to greet our guests."

"Greet the ravens for me," I said as the sacrist's cracked voice intoned plainsong. The monks were dumbstruck, and the precenter intoned again. Then someone began to sing, and others joined him, overcoming fear and confusion with structured Gregorian rhythms.

I slipped out of the Chapter room, and I could hear them singing as I made my way through the cloister. I wasn't going to waste any more time trying to persuade a man it was in his own best interest not to get killed. These Christians were an odd breed, and there were times when you couldn't imagine how they'd survive.

In a few minutes I had my bags from the undercroft in the Guest House. They weighed a couple of stone altogether, crammed with writing supplies, books, and assorted souvenirs. I'd just enough room for my verse and the purses I'd hidden outside the wall.

I slipped my arms through the straps and scooped up a travel cloak. I hurried back to the library, where I found Godwine directing the novices and selecting books from the shelves. I saw the great jeweled volume of the four Gospels pass under his worried eye.

"What do you want me to do?"

"Take the books across to the mainland," he said. "The Prior's forbidden us to doubt that God will deliver us. He says it's a test of faith and obedience."

"Why take a test you can't pass? If he's wrong, you die and your book hoard's carried off. If he's right, and he *can* talk them out of razing this place, then you get a penance, but you're alive to do it."

"The question of obedience is central," Godwine said. "You understand duty to your lord; this is duty to our Lord. We must obey even a mistaken command or risk sinning."

"Even Jomsvikings make up their own minds when the battle's lost. Duty's absolute while it makes sense; after that it's foolish."

"The bones of duty remain when the flesh is gone," he said.

"Oh, right. Does that make sense to you?"

"Articles of faith don't make sense," he said. "That's why they're articles of faith."

"So you're doing nothing? You're going to wait for the Vikings?"

"I have to wait, but the books don't. We'll load the carts and help you as far as the causeway."

I looked at him and shook my head. It was a wonderful moment, watching him step up to his wyrd. I had to respect his choice; even if I thought he was crazy, he thought he was doing his duty, and that's all that matters in the end. Two novices came out of the library carrying stacks of volumes, and I followed them down. One of the carts was a quarter full already, and the novices added their burdens to the load. Brendan was in the cart lashing the books down. I tossed my bags under the seat and went to help the carter hitch the horse to the second wagon.

The sacrist and the feretrar struggled out of the church supporting a huge reliquary chest inlaid with gold and silver and encrusted with gemstones. It took all they had to wrestle it up onto the bed of the cart, which sank under its weight with a creak of wood and protesting axles. "These are Cuthbert's vestments," the feretrar told me. "You must keep them safe.'

I shook my head. "They'll take too much room."

"They have to go," the feretrar protested.

"I can haul a hundred books if I leave the wardrobe," I insisted, prepared to take a hard line. I was happy to carry books, but not a set of talismanic and faded threads that once belonged to Cuthbert.

Then Godwine shouted down from a library window, gesturing for the reliquary to stay in the cart. I shook my head and walked away. They were his books, I suppose, but how do you reckon it? The cellarer came out with food and a skin of wine. Then Alban came up with his Leechbook of cures and techniques, the tome he'd composed over a life of practice as an herbalist and Farmerer. It was full of recipes, lab notes, musings, medicinal philosophy, and there were even a few cures between the covers.

"Thanks for taking care of me," I said.

"You're well come." Alban smiled. "I wish you were staying."

"Under the circumstances, I wish you were coming," I told him, grasping his arm. "There's no point in dying or getting slaved out."

"Obedience," he said, saying it all, and turned back into the monastery. He paused long enough to wave his farewell as he passed into the shadow of the cloister. This wasn't the well faring I'd planned. These men had been good to me; they'd healed me and taught me. They'd taken the place of my family and made me a better skald and a smarter man, and I owed them more than a slap on the back and hope for a quick death before I galloped across the causeway with my sacks of silver and vellum.

When the first cart was full, Brendan covered it with a canvas and jumped back to the cobbles, just another Drogheda boy headed for a bad end. "Brian and I will take the carts to the other side of the causeway," he said.

"You know what's going to happen here, don't you?" I asked.

"Everyone knows what's going to happen," he said, fighting his better instincts and staying calm.

"Wait with the carts until I get there," I said.

"We can't wait too long," he said.

I reckoned he wanted to get back in time for the slaughter. I nodded and stepped back as he climbed into the seat and snapped the reins. Brian was in the back of the second cart, which was as yet only half full. I wondered what was taking Godwine so long and hoped he hadn't been diverted by the rediscovery of some misshelved and long-lost volume come to light in the exodus.

I went to find Eadred. Reason had deserted the monastery at large, but I thought maybe all those years of exposure to the virulence of the outside world may have infected *him* with the sense God gave a fish. I went back to the Chapter room and found fifteen or twenty monks trying to carry on with that infuriating pluck that would make the Engs famous in stoic circles later on, while Eadred and the precentor argued as if there weren't four dragons swimming closer every minute.

The disputation centered on the interpretation of God's will in the matter of the four dragon ships. The dialogue consisted chiefly of Eadred recounting the tales of Viking depredations he'd picked up from the refugees and the precentor insisting that since the Prior had made it an act of faith and obedience there was nothing to discuss. At least Eadred was sensible enough to risk disobedience and doubt if it meant he'd see another sunrise, even though most of the monks were standing on the Prior's authority and riding on his luck.

"Eadred, I need help with the second cart," I called to him. I didn't have to tell him twice. He left the precentor standing there with his mouth open in midrefutation, and about a dozen monks followed us out of the Chapter room.

"Where are they?" he asked as we started down the corridor at the head of the group of monks.

"Brendan's taken the first one to the causeway: Brian's loading the second. I've got to collect my verse, but don't wait. I'll meet you across the water."

"Don't linger," he said as we parted company.

Lingering wasn't in the plan as I turned down the corridor to the Priory. I wondered how much the tide was holding up the longships; if we were lucky they were still a half hour out, which gave me enough time to collect my verse and the purses. Once the dragons were beached, all bets were off. There were no other footfalls on the oak floors. The Priory entrance was unguarded, and I went ahead cautiously.

Dead silence rang in my ears on the second floor of the Priory. I went down the quiet carpeting to the reception room, where I reckoned the Prior was getting ready to meet his wyrd, reviewing his career and getting right with God. I was wondering where the subpriors were, as one of them stepped out of an alcove ahead, his face a mask of anger and anguish.

"This is your doing," he shouted savagely.

"Pay attention," I snapped. "I'm getting out of here. If it was my doing, I'd stay to grab the loot."

"You led them to us with magic."

"Skallagrim takes care of the magic. I've come for my verse."

He had no answer to that enigma, but he gestured to his left and Haki the Pict stepped into the hallway, bent forward in a slightly tense posture, clutching his axe with the understanding that all constraints were gone.

I looked for a weapon and I grabbed a handy iron candlestick, knocking the fat beeswax candle off the spike. It weighed a ton, and I knew we wouldn't be fighting long before I was tired, but it was just the thing to deflect an axe. Haki advanced, and I gave ground. He flexed his shoulders and made several aborted chops in the air between us. The iron candlestick was rough under my fingers, and I had a secure grip. I probed back at his face with the short spike.

Then he rushed me, his mouth open in a silent bellow, specks of phlegm and spittle flying out and the stump of his tongue squirming like a red clam in a gaping yellow shell.

The blow made the candlestick ring in my hands, and the beard of the axe snapped off and flew into the wainscoting as the head came to a jolting stop six inches from my face, haft against the iron. I spun the candlestick and caught Haki on the ear with the base. He flopped against the wall at my feet. I didn't have time for this shit. I dropped the candlestick and headed for the reception hall.

The subprior retreated ahead of me, and the Prior came out of the door when I was still twenty feet away, looking beyond me down the hall. Before I could turn, someone hit me from behind, and I joined the Pict on the carpet.

I couldn't have been out long, because when I woke up I was still bleeding. They'd dragged me into a small room, wedged me into the corner behind the door, and left me for dead. The room was small and sparsely furnished, but there were a couple of those iron candlesticks on either side of a reliquary chest. I slumped into the chair and tried to get my bearings. A window looked into the interior garden, greening up nicely now that the fountain was running. I went over to the door and found it locked.

The wrought-iron hinges were bolted to a stone lintel, robust enough to resist the little knife I had in my belt, and the door itself was about three inches of oak. It was beginning to look like I'd have to make the twelve-foot drop to the garden, but I decided to have a try at the door first, so I picked up one of the candlesticks. It was no good just bashing away; it'd take a week to breach it that way. I pulled off the candle and examined the spike; fortunately, it was cast, not welded, so I jammed it into the keyhole and rolled my shoulders in the rowing movement I'd practiced on the vik.

Something inside the lock plate broke with a sound like walnut shells between teeth, and the door moved on the frame. I stepped back and gave it a push with my foot, and it swung wide on oiled hinges that made no sound.

I took a quick look into the hall before I stepped out, both directions this time, but no one was there. I hurried to the reception hall. Someone had been there ahead of me; all the furniture had been given attention with a war axe. The chess set had been scooped up, leaving only a forgotten pawn on the carpet. The high-backed chairs had been hacked apart, and one of them had been thrown through the panes of a leaded glass window.

I gave the place a quick search, but the box that held my verse was gone. If I wasn't out of there myself in three minutes, I might as well not bother. There was a bizarre sort of irony to the thought of being killed trying to get *out* of a Benedictine monastery. Bran Snorrison, memory of the *Blood Raven*, skald to Thorfinn Skullsplitter, foster brother of Sygtrygg Ormson: snuffed off by Vikings. The Norns were taking the lesson in wyrd a little too far.

When I think about it now, I can't imagine what I was doing, going back for parchments. Of course, the fact that they were the only extant copy of the complete works of

Bran Snorrison had some little weight at the time, together with the firm belief that lost work can never be re-created, but I wasn't crazy. I knew it was time to cut my losses and get out of there. I went back into the corridor.

Two White Danes who were walking casually down the carpeting leaped back with exclamations of surprise. White Danes, how do I describe White Danes? I reckon I could begin by saying that their clothing was in distinctively poor taste, and it was generally believed that they mixed their colors in ways meant to paralyze their enemies in disbelief. Although, from the safety of well-engineered fortifications, opponents had been known to shout such cutting taunts as, "How far did you chase the Walloon to get those britches?" or, "Was that cloak woven by a blind Geat?" or, "Did a goat vomit on your ring mail or is that your beard?" not, strictly speaking, a slander on their haberdashery, but a taunt which for some reason drove a White Dane into an unthinking rage.

I could also say that they ate garlic with every meal, and that they couldn't hold two ideas in their heads simultaneously, but the important thing about them was that they had incredible luck, and in the eighth century, good luck went a long way. It was time to see how far mine would take me.

They were carrying one of the tapestries hammocked between them, and it bulged with a hundred odd angles and scraped the floor. When they dropped it to go for their weapons, it gave up the muted ring of subtantially cast metal objects and a corner opened to reveal candlesticks, plate, chalices, incense burners, chains, silver inkwells, gold crucifixes, ceboria, and spare change.

Quite a haul for two sartorially splendid pilgrims such as these, and the capstone of a shore leave dedicated to the venting of all those nasty tensions and urges that build up on a vik, if the condition of the Prior's reception hall was any indication. My sudden appearance from a room they'd already cleared unhinged them enough to give me the upper hand; unfortunately, there was nothing in that hand that would intimidate them once they recovered.

"I wondered how long it would take someone to get wind of this place," I said, stepping toward them in good-natured greeting. Hearing a kind of Danish they understood in an accent they recognized confused them because the man who was speaking was a resident of the monastery they were currently pillaging. Fear and confusion will almost always induce cognitive dissonance in a White Dane, and that's the state of mind you want them in when they have weapons and you don't.

They drew their composure out of their scabbards. Muscle memory was asserting itself in the face of naked adrenaline, resolving their little fight-or-flight conflict for them: they'd given ground to an unarmed man, been surprised on that quiet carpeting just like I'd been, and they liked it about as much.

I spread my arms wide and walked slowly toward them. "I'm Bran Snorrison of Clontarf in Eire, a slave here since last autumn."

"How do you come to be here?" one of them asked.

"Sygtrygg Ormson's autumn vik was coasting up to the Orkneys when the Engs attacked and a storm blew up. I washed overboard. I was aboard the *Blood Raven*, skald to Thorfinn Skullsplitter."

"Thorfinn Skullsplitter? We heard the story in Orphir," one of them said, relaxing. Thorfinn's name opened doors, all right. They dropped their points to the carpet.

"When were they there?" I asked. At least they'd made it to the Orkneys.

"Last autumn," the other one said. "They left a week before we got there, just ahead of the ice."

"When was that?"

"A month before Yule."

"I've had seven months of preaching and thin broth from these monks," I said, tearing off the cowl. My accent and easy familiarity reassured them. "They worked me night and day, and look what they did to my hair, cut it like a mangy dog. Give me an axe."

The one in front handed me the axe in his belt. From its size I reckoned it'd done the work in the Prior's reception hall.

"We'll kill some black monks this afternoon," he assured me with a nudge and a smile, and then his eyes drifted to the tonsure and he looked away, as if embarrassed for me. Pity from a White Dane: it sealed his doom. Ever since I'd spotted the longships, a festering anger had been building up inside me, aggravated by the frustration of trying to argue against everyone's misplaced sense of duty, and now I'd an axe and a couple of White Danes in easy reach.

They turned to reassemble their loot, tossing candlesticks and chalices together with practiced hands. The edge of the wooden box that held my verse showed from under a corner of altar cloth. The one in front wrapped it closer to keep the surface unscratched and rolled up his end of the tapestry. They lifted the load between them, and we started down the corridor. I walked beside the hammock, getting the feel of the axe, swinging it around to find the balance point, limbering my shoulders for bladework.

The one in the rear lagged behind, gawking at the musical notation in the leaded glass windows. "Look at these designs," he said to his partner. Then shattered one of the windows with the scramasax in his free hand.

"Keep your mind on business," the one in front said over his shoulder, giving the load an impatient shake.

"How'd they treat you?" the music lover in the rear asked me.

"Bread, water, and beatings," I told him, glancing over my shoulder to verify his position. I spun on my heel and drove the butt of the axe into the bottom of his chin, lifting him an inch off the ground. The tip of his tongue squirted out between his lips, and he dropped his end of the weight, pulling his partner off balance. I turned the butt-stroke into a roundhouse blow and opened the top of the lead Dane's head. He went down on his face and kicked once, and I wiped the blade on his cloak while his partner gargled onto the carpet. Who were they to make fashion statements?

I walked a few feet down the carpet, breathing hard, and then walked back and kicked the lead Dane in the balls. "You pig-fuckers; these are my friends," I shouted. "I *live* here. What did we ever do to you? This was a good place until you smelled out the bakery, you cocksucking mutts." I kicked the musical one in the head about a dozen times, until his skull was a little pulpy and my leg was tired.

"That's the end of your life stories, isn't it?" I shouted at them as I paced around the hallway trying to get control of myself. Blood drifted like a crimson fog through the powder-blue patterns of Moroccan geometry as the Arab wool sponged up their lives.

I stood over the musical Dane and resisted the temptation to cut off his head. It would make too big a mess, and

I needed his clothes. His partner's were covered with blood, an improvement on the color scheme but a tip-off to even the most casual observer that something was amiss. A White Dane's threads would get me farther than Benedictine robes.

I slumped onto an alcove bench and shook with rage. Who did these guys think they were, coming to the place I lived and killing my friends? I loved those old monks. They'd taken as good care of me as Goltrade and Skallagrim, and I knew I couldn't run away from them now.

Mr. Music wore his sword in a harness across his shoulder, and I went over and drew the blade. It was pattern-welded, heavy, and long, with an Ulfberth Forge mark stamped under the cross guard. Its pommel was a heavy brass pyramid that would crack a skull on the downstroke, and it balanced well in my hand. I took a couple of practice swings while the first tenuous threads of a plan wove themselves together. I knew I could slip into the confusion masked by a White Dane's clothes. I was a lot more certain of my ability to pretend to be a Dane among Danes than my ability to pretend I wasn't a Dane among Christians.

Everything had changed again like an existential pinball game. If I could find Alban and Godwine, maybe I could get them out. I pulled the box out of the tangled tapestry and dragged Mr. Music down the corridor, discovering how uncooperative the gelatinous limbs of a dead man are when you're in a hurry to have his clothes. I pulled his britches and tunic off and gave them a quick shake to air them out. I already felt itchy and uncomfortable as I put his harness on and slipped the scabbard and axe through the belt. Then I picked up his leather helmet. Bloody or not, I'd need it to cover the smooth tonsure that marked me as a resident of Lindisfarne. Finally I threw the swag over one shoulder and headed back to the cloister.

The monks were about to find out the bells were a big mistake. The deep-voiced bells of the great churches of the eighth century were made to play accompaniment to a slaughter with fire and sword, as if it were a song imprisoned in them at the foundry, with the only release a resonance to the sound of blade on bone, and it wouldn't be long until they drove the White Danes into a berserk frenzy. They weren't much good for my headache either.

The Priory garth was too big to be able to call what was

going on out there confusion, but in a smaller enclosure there would've been no question. Some of the White Danes were running excitedly about, waving their weapons, while others gathered in a knot at the foot of the tower, awe-struck by the massive voices and the insane chromatic ravings of the bells. Smoke curled out of the craft shops where they'd found only tools and unfinished scraps. Now they were turning their attention to the church, where the bells and the chanted plainsong told them they ought to look.

I drifted unnoticed along the fringe of the crowd, just another psychopath in a bad suit clutching a sack of pathetic booty over one shoulder. They were trying to puzzle out the lock mechanism of the church doors before they surrendered to the urge to smash them. White Danes confronting an engineering problem are a volatile and quirky lot, and I left them to it, skirting the church and going up the night stairs to the dorter. I knew Alban would be waiting for his wyrd in the Farmery.

When I came through the door he closed his eyes and folded his hands, seeing only a White Dane until I spoke.

"Pull some rope off the beds."

"What?"

"It's me, Bran." I pushed the helmet back and grinned, then I dragged the mattress off the closest bed, exposing the rope. "I can get you out if you act like a captive," I said as I cut the rope and started stripping it out of the frame. "Wrap an end about your wrists and I'll pull you after me."

"I must wait here," he said.

I dropped the rope, grabbed his habit, and shook him until his teeth chattered. "The waiting's over; you're coming with me," I said. "We're going to the library to get Godwine."

He stood in confusion as I ran a few turns of the rope around his wrists. Then I cut the other end from the frame and pulled him into the corridor. The sound of running announced a group of White Danes, and we hurried down an angled passageway into the stairwell. On the floor below, they'd discovered the monks' cells, and they were complaining bitterly about the poverty of the place.

These bottom feeders were amateurs. The ones who'd tossed a monastery before weren't pissing away their time in the monk's quarters. They were heading for the library and the church, where valuable goods were sure to be found. I shouldered my way through them. No one gave me a second look when they saw I had Alban tethered and stumbling after me, but we had to defenestrate through a shattered casement to avoid a small but nasty fire that was licking along the dry oak floors of the lower corridor.

In the Cloister garth a naked Viking was spearfishing in the ponds and another was bashing the statuary with his axe and laughing as the heads of angels and saints spun into the flowers, yelling "Where is their god now?" with every stroke. The smells of trampled herbs were fragrant and sharp. I dragged Alban up the stairs to the library, where I kicked open the unlocked door for effect. The Scriptorium was empty, desks clear, copy stands arranged neatly and materials ready, as yet undiscovered by those Beau Brummels of the Baltic ravaging the garden outside. We hurried to the library. Godwine stood in the center of the great reading room, amid tables piled high with books and manuscripts, writing on a scrap of vellum. The emptied carrels looked like toothless sockets in a skull.

"I hope that's your will," I said as we ran in. He looked up at the disturbance: then he saw Alban and recognized me. "What are you doing?"

"Wrap up." I threw him the free end of the rope. "We'll get out of here alive if you keep your wits."

"We can't leave; the Prior forbade it."

"The Prior's dog food. They've overrun the cloister and they're breaking into the church, and this is just the first boatload. Your duty's sped, and you see how well the Prior analyzed the situation."

Godwine slipped the vellum into a book and tucked it under his cincture. He wrapped the end of the rope about his wrists, and I grabbed the middle of the length that separated him from Alban. Still they hesitated, and I had to pull them out of the library. Godwine stumbled through the door as the first of the White Danes loped up the stairs with their weapons put away and their eyes wide for a look at treasures monastic. Alban and Godwine jumped back as they came into the corridor, and I yanked on the rope to bring them to heel.

"These men are mine," I shouted.

"Where's the treasure?"

"In the church, you assholes," I told them. "There's naught here but parchment, and little enough of that."

Of course they weren't going to take my word for it, and they ran into the library to check for themselves. You could hear their hiss of disappointment when they saw I'd told them the truth. I knew what their first impulse was going to be, and I dragged Godwine and Alban down the stairs with a violence that made the rope bite their wrists. It was a good effect.

Outside, monks were scurrying about erratically, their heads inadequately protected by their tonsures. The White Dane ashmen let them get clear a bit and tried to bring them down with spears, the slingers got a chance at the rest, and the few who outranged the stones were archers' meat. I cursed at them to hurry as I thrust the swag into Godwine's hands and kicked Alban in the ass. No one gave us a glance. When we were outside the gate, the monks got their first look at the dragons, beached in the shallow water beyond Cuthbert's island.

The crews of two dragons were overboard in the knee-deep water, tying them off to exposed rocks. The only evidence of opposition was the Prior and the two subpriors, waiting at the edge of the water. We were only a few hundred yards away, higher by sixty feet, and our view was unobstructed. Alban and Godwine turned to look at me when they saw the Prior.

"Hey, I lied," I said.

The tide was running out across the sands, and mud was glistening on the sides of the current-scored runnels. Gray towers of worm castings rose from the exposed sand and rock. The water sparkled in the late morning sunlight. The Prior raised his hand in fraternal greeting, but no one from the dragons paid any attention to him. There was shouting from foredeck to mast step to tiller, and the two captains and their berserks gathered near the prows to talk things over.

I had a good idea what they were saying. Behind me, the bells pounded in the church, where the monks were waiting with Cuthbert, not that he was in a position to do them much good, his grave being so weighed down with crutches, entreaties, and guilt that runes of binding would have been superfluous. He wasn't climbing out from under that load of energy for a long time. But if it made them feel better about what was going to happen, who was I to mock it? We watched the ships' captains confer, and then the mob of White Danes separated into two groups. One headed for the sand beach where the coracles were overturned, just below the monastery wall, but the other bore down on the Prior.

He stood there holding his crosier, a polished yew stave that ended in a gold crucifix, a poor choice of accessories for the occasion, I thought, but an object with a certain utility if you swing it from behind in a quiet hallway. I rubbed the back of my neck and felt the brittle strands of blood-clotted hair. Clumps of greenish yellow seaweed were strewn on the rocky ground between the beach and Cuthbert's hermitage, where a low stone building still housed an anchorite. The prior's hand was raised in greeting and benediction; the subpriors flanked him, their silver censers seeping a blue haze in knee-level arcs. Silver censers were another negotiating gaffe. I wondered how the royal cousins felt, staring at the end of promising ecclesiastical careers. The leader of the vik was in front with his fo'c'sleman, and his men were just beyond. They stopped a few feet away from the clerics.

Words were exchanged, but not many, perhaps because the Dane only understood his own language, or maybe because the Prior began to follow the thread of some persuasive thought the Viking found boring, or maybe they were just on a tight schedule; whatever the reason, he brought the butt of his axe up into the point of the prior's jaw and lifted him off his feet. One of the Danes caught the crosier as it began to fall.

The Prior went back full length into the shallow water with a wide splash and the Danes laughed. Then one of the subpriors swung his censer at the head of the closest Dane, who dodged it easily and brought his sword down against the subprior's neck; there was a red fountain, and his ghost swam free of his body. The other subprior's nerve broke, and he started running, but a spear put him into the mud, and the White Danes acquired two smoldering silver censers. The gold crucifix on the Prior's crosier sparkled as the Danes walked over the bodies and onto the beach below us.

I'd seen enough, but there was one last gesture of futility to observe. Haki the Pict came out of the signal tower on the high ground facing Bamburgh. Smoke from the signal fire was starting to curl over the stone parapet. Haki made a stand facing the White Danes as they climbed up the hill. He waved his axe, the only one there who had any idea how to talk to them. The Prior could have learned a few things from him. It was a language without tongue.

One of the vanguards saw him and stopped. He threw out his arms and shouted to his companions. They hesitated, and Haki waved them on, capering about in excitement. Haki was a good thirty yards away and he had the high ground, but the White Dane laughed and made an assault up the slope, shouting and putting his shield up as he ran. There was a furious crash as they came together and Haki went clear off his feet, lifted up on the shield and thrown over the Dane's head. The Dane finished him before he could get up. The truth was the Pict had no technique with an axe unless he was confronting a cord of firewood.

I could see the causeway in the distance. The two carts were on the other side, and I started dragging the stunned monks after me down the road. The White Danes making their way up the slope waved to me and shouted questions. They took me for one of the advance party, already claiming a couple of likely slaves for later sale. They were beginning to feel that anxiety latecomers to a sacking always feel, a fear that all the good shit's already been looted. They surged forward, over the lip of the dirt road in front of the porter's house, across Haki's body, and through the open gates into the wider expanse of the Priory garth.

I cheered them on, shouting hyperbole about the vastness of the treasure that waited inside, and they threw themselves onto the running heels of the men in front of them. When the road was empty except for their dust, I led Alban and Godwine along the outside of the wall. The purses were under the pile of loose rock where I'd left them.

"What are these?"

"Tithes from Cuthbert's Feast. I took them from the cutpurse."

"This is Cuthbert's money," Godwine said.

"We'll just hold it for him," I said, starting for the causeway at as brisk a pace as they could manage. After fifteen yards, Godwine and Alban cast off the rope and hiked up their habits, and the three of us flew down the slope, out across the wet sand, crunching shells and crab carapaces underfoot and scattering the feeding birds. The silver in the purses jingled like bells on a bride's cloak. Speed was of the essence now. If anyone saw us they might assume I was chasing prisoners who'd made a break, but I couldn't count on it.

"Keep going," I shouted after them. "No one's following. Maybe we can cross before they see us."

Alban was already splashing along the line of posts and rock cairns that marked the pilgrim's way across the tidal flat, and Godwine was right behind him.

We crossed a few hundred yards of tidal ponds and rocks before we stopped to look back. Smoke rose behind the walls, and the disorganized bells were returning to silence, which meant the White Danes had finally broken down the church doors and the ropes were jerking above the bleeding corpses of the bell ringers.

"Let's go," I said, but Alban and Godwine were immobilized, and I had to drive them ahead of me with the flat of the sword.

"That's what happened to Lot's wife," I shouted. "Couldn't resist a look over her shoulder. The last thing my mother told me when I left home was, 'Never look over your shoulder when you're running from White Danes.' What did your mothers tell you?"

We made our way through two feet of water in the still-submerged middle of the pilgrim's way, forced into a choppy, hopping gait by the sucking mud underfoot. The monks who'd gone ahead of us were gathered near the carts, a little way up the side of the hill. Brian and Brendan, whose mother had raised no fools in Drogheda, were waiting with Eadred, watching the smoke climb over Lindisfarne, and when we splashed ashore, Godwine lost no time taking command. The horses grazed in their harness, and he snatched up the reins and got them pointed inland.

"Anselm, leg it down to Bamburgh and have them send for the fyrd. Godfred and Wilibald, take the carts to Goswick grange and then go on to Jarrow and tell them what's happened."

Godfred and Wilibald didn't need encouragement, and I hurried to retrieve my gear before they lashed the horses into a trot.

"We can't stay here. What's the plan?"

"We'll hide in Fenham until the fyrd comes. The Vikings won't come inland, will they?"

"Not with all the plunder on the island to keep them busy," I said. "They'll be the better part of the low tide getting it sorted out."

"How long will they stay?"

"As soon as their boats float, they'll be ready to go," I said without even bothering to think about it. "They may send scouts ashore, but they won't stay on a hostile coast."

Godwine was looking at me strangely, and I realized he was just beginning to understand the context I'd left when I washed over the freeboard of the *Blood Raven*. In a strange way, I was just beginning to understand it myself.

When I took a critical look at my life prior to washing up in the Outer Farnes, I had to admit I'd been a pretend Viking. I'd banged away at my friends with wooden swords until I'd been overmatched by a Geat in my first fight. I'd learned the craft of singing to make my sup, and hung out with three old troublemakers who'd lived long enough to learn how to make trouble interesting. Then I'd gone to vik so I could honorably boff Sygtrygg's sister. Up the Severn I'd hung in the rear of the action and avoided crossing blades with anyone until I insulted my way aboard the *Blood Raven*.

Then there was the craziness at the mast step, which I'd since been building up in my mind as an episode of berserk ecstasy, but it was really just temporary insanity, running at a half dozen Engs with a scramasax and slashing wildly in all directions when it looked like they were about to kill me. Picking that guy off the mast was luck.

The two White Danes were the first men I'd killed in cold blood. Oh, I was pissed about them burning the monastery, but they paid the price for a lot of things when I caught them feeling sorry for me about the tonsure. Those killings, which I'd have tried my best to accomplish with economy and dexterity last autumn and probably bungled, I'd carried off with a frightening elegance after wintering on Lindisfarne.

Relatively few people in these insulated days ever kill anything, but then killing was something you ran into a few times a week, on average, and you got used to it. But I wasn't used to it. The whole experience made me sick. A lot of fictions about myself were rewritten to accommodate this new talent. Was it guilt, I wondered, or just some fleeting hesitation and ambivalence? I wished Thorfinn were there to tell me. Something had happened to me over the winter; the place had its effect and no denying it.

Deciding to go to Fenham was one thing, but rallying the monks was another. The sight of the White Danes slaughtering their confreres had been too much for them. They'd backed the Prior as long as they could, and when his wyrd was clear, they'd saved themselves, and they felt terrible, as if survival were a sin against their duty. They were a pathetic lot.

Eadred and Alban were busy fighting the paralytic effects of panic. "Get a move on," I said. "Do you want to spend the night here where the Danes can find you?"

That argument had weight. The monks were terrified the Danes would follow them, although there was scant chance of it. The Danes were too amazed by their luck to care that a few monks had escaped. After sundown I reckoned they'd put to sea and decide whether to go home with their windfall plunder or throw dice with the Norns.

We cut inland to Fenham, through the low hills that fronted the shore, following a sheep track that skirted thickets and bogs, always keeping a significant terrain feature between us and Lindisfarne. We discovered Fenham had been prudently deserted by its residents, and we put up in a stable in the middle of the village. There were twenty-six survivors, not counting Anselm, who'd legged it down to Bamburgh and probably found the same desertion we'd found in Fenham, or Godfred and Wilibald, who were on their way to Jarrow with the bad news.

The citizens of Fenham had abandoned their livestock, and cows with distended udders wailed bitterly at the pasture gate, so Eadred detailed a few men to see to them, and soon we were passing round buckets of warm milk. I didn't see any reason why we should keep an eye on the Fenham livestock for free, so I ranged through the hen-houses, geese pens, and dovecotes in search of dinner.

I was coming out of a barnyard with a basketful of eggs and a sack of reluctant chickens when I saw Caitria walking toward me. She was still wearing a wimple and veil, but the hem of her robe was damp and muddy, and when she hiked it up I saw she was wearing her britches underneath. "Where have you been?" I asked her.

"Down Bamburgh way," she said. "When I saw the smoke I came running. What happened?"

"Vikings," I said. "They burned the monastery."

"You didn't stop them?"

"You think I know every Viking walks a deck? And even if I'd known them, I doubt I could have done much."

"Where'd you get the clothes?" She laughed.

"From a dead Dane," I said, struggling not to drop the basket as the chickens squabbled in the sack. "I'll shed them as soon as I can."

"I don't blame you," she said, standing back for the full effect. "Still wearing a tonsure, I see."

"Save your wit," I snapped, "and help me get this food back to the brothers."

"How many got away?" she asked, grabbing the basket handles.

"Not many," I told her. I twisted the neck of the sack tight and swung it hard against the ground. The chickens went limp. "Two dozen, a few more."

"Why didn't you go with the Vikings?"

"White Danes? Be serious. Those fools are an embarrassment to viking. Why lower myself by associating with them? Besides, they killed my friends and they tried to kill me."

When we got back to the stable, Eadred had everyone busy. He recognized Caitria from Brendan's description and bustled over. "God bless you, daughter," he said. "You're Bran's friend, Caitria?"

"Yes, Father," she said.

"I'm glad you're well," he told her.

"I'm better off than you," she said, setting the basket down on a table. "Are you safe here?"

"As safe as anywhere," Eadred said. "Where have you been?"

"With an anchoress called Iudelhild, who lives near Bamburgh."

"I know her," Eadred said. "Is she well?"

"Catch up later," I said. "There's other things to worry about."

He nodded and took the raw ingredients for the meal. While he was occupied with the cooking, I walked to the hilltop for a look across the tidal flats and marshes at Lindisfarne.

After dark, Eadred bedded everyone down in the loft, where there was hay to pad the boards, and then Caitria, Godwine, Eadred, Alban, and I sat below in the tack room and had a pull at the wine. It wasn't the most cheerful group I've ever drunk with, I can tell you that.

"What will you do now?" I asked them.

"We'll start again," Godwine said. "They didn't destroy everything. Lindisfarne's our home."

"What about you?" Alban asked.

"I'll help you," I told them.

Eadred shook his head. "If you're here when the fyrd comes, they'll kill you."

"I lived with you all winter," I said. "Why would they kill me?"

"I wouldn't count on sanctuary after this," he said.

"They're right." Caitria had taken off her nun's clothes and she was combing out her wimple hair. "The fyrd will hang you."

"I'm going back," I insisted. "You're going to need help."

Lindisfarne burned into the long June twilight, through the short night, and most of the next morning. I went down to the edge of the water to look for any others who'd gotten across the mudflats. A few were hiding inexpertly above the waterline, their trails of dried mud as easy to follow as the smears of garden slugs. After a night in the open, their lips were moving silently as they prayed for forgiveness.

I took them to the stable at Fenham common, and then went back and rowed a coracle across the channel to reconnoiter. The White Danes were gone, taking as many portable objects as they could carry and leaving ashes in their wake.

It wasn't pretty, but the only Danes left were the ones I'd killed, easily assumed to be casualties of a looting dispute, which was the truth, in a certain sense. They'd been overlooked in the rush to clear out, and their corpses were undisturbed. My discarded robe was still in a heap against the wall, and the loot was still there. I helped myself to Mr. Music's scramasax, the companion to the Ulfberth sword. A walk to the south end of the island satisfied me that the White Danes were history. Then I went back across the water and reported the situation to Godwine.

"We'll go back when the tide goes out. . . . Eadred?" he asked.

"Midmorning," he supplied. "Better get ready now. We'll borrow a couple of wagons from the village."

But the only wagons the Fenhamites hadn't taken with them were two dung carts behind the stable. There were no horses, so after they'd cleaned out the manure, the monks threw their shovels and picks into the wagon and harnessed themselves to the carts. It gave them something to do, mindless work to keep their thoughts off what they were going to find when they got home.

When we went through the monastery gate, the sight of all those gulls hopping among the hacked bodies drove the monks into the church to pray, where they discovered the corpses of their brothers who'd sought Cuthbert's help. Most of them were useless after they saw what the White Danes had done to Cuthbert's shrine, and they spent the rest of the day wailing their heads off or wandering the grounds like zombies.

The White Danes hadn't fired the library, preferring instead to hurl down the shelves and tear the leather covers from the books, leaving the room strewn with crumpled parchment. The library could be restored given time and patronage, so Godwine was the most fortunate of the surviving senior obedientiaries. Alban's Farmery had burned, and his herbarium had been wrecked: pots and jars smashed, cauldrons, scales, and crucibles stolen, pipettes shattered. Only his Leechbook had survived.

Eadred's loss was the largest. Even though the White Danes hadn't fired the Guest House, fifty or sixty percent of the physical plant was in ashes; empty walls stood in rising smoke, casements opened to depths of air. He was the only surviving senior whose duties involved the day-to-day details, the inventory and the routine logistics, and so the physical needs of the survivors devolved to him.

A hasty count and a little arithmetic disclosed sixty-four dead men that had to be put underground soon and fifty-three missing and presumed captured. Godwine detailed the three or four monks who'd kept their nerve to assemble the bodies and haul them to the south side of the church, where Brian and I were digging graves. It was hard work in the stony ground of Lindisfarne, and we had to stop frequently to sharpen the picks on a small grindstone the White Danes hadn't wanted.

The pile of bodies grew. And even though we had a monk detailed to keep the gulls off them, there was nothing we could do about the flies. Arms and legs and torsos went in one pile, unattached heads in another. When the parts were all assembled, Alban started trying to match them up. We buried them as fast as we might, and still worked two days in the graveyard. I made binding runes to hold them until there were crosses over the mounds. I dug a hole for the Prior beside Sicga, but we couldn't find his body.

I could tell Brian had something to say to me, and I knew right enough what was on his mind. A chilliness had descended on all the survivors. When they looked in my direction, they were looking at the guy who'd warmed water for their cramped fingers last winter in the Scriptorium, and who'd seen the great Bede do his ghostly stuff, and now they realized they were seeing a Dane. Evidence of what I'd been was stinking up the monastery, but evidence of what I'd become was in their memories.

There was only a token garrison at Bamburgh when the king wasn't resident, and the ton-reeve showed up after the heavy digging was over, looked around, and headed back right smartly when he had the story. The monks expected the Northumbrian militia any day, and no one wanted me around when they got there.

Caitria fretted anxiously while we worked, eager to be off the island. She was right. The climate wasn't healthy anymore. The monastery was burned, half the monks were dead, and, if the fyrd showed up, someone was bound to mention that I was a Dane.

The last grave wasn't filled in before guilty survivors started affiliating themselves with the Prior. We'd scoured the island shore and the mainland from Goswick to Beal, checking all the likely places the bodies would wash up, but the tides had taken the Prior and the subpriors out to sea, back to the land of the Franks, maybe. Wherever he was, not being *there* left it all open to speculation, and the monks were ready to speculate, already counting themselves fortunate to have been shepherded by the Martyr of Lindisfarne.

Rumors that he'd been translated into heaven began to noise about. The Prior achieved a more heroic stature in

death than he'd ever enjoyed in life, and there were rever-
ential conversations about how he'd walked out to meet
the Danes armed only with his crosier and his faith. They
began to insist to themselves that he was among the ranks
of the Northumbrian saints, breaking bread with Cuthbert
and the Venerable Bede.

After the bodies were in the ground, the survivors
elected Godwine Prior, pending the approval of Higbald,
who might have a candidate of his own in mind when the
news reached him in York. I talked him out of a horse to
speed our departure.

"How do you reckon it?" I asked Godwine when he
came down to the pilgrim's way to see us off. "Not dead a
week and already a saint."

"It would have horrified him," Godwine said.

"I don't know," I said. "He struck me as the kind of
man who would have preferred to be alive to enjoy his
sainthood."

"It's his late penance for disobeying Alcuin," Eadred
suggested.

"You presume too much," Godwine admonished.

"Maybe." Eadred shrugged.

"Any messages for Drogheda?" I asked the brothers.

"Tell them we're alive," Brendan said.

"You were first in my charge," Alban said, "and I cared
well for you. See you don't waste my work. Keep well."

"Fear naught," I said to them as we started across the
wet sand. "Look for me someday."

11

Ravenshill Moor

Better gear than good sense
A traveler cannot carry,
A more tedious burden than too much drink
A traveler cannot carry.
　　　　　—The Sayings of the Wise One

We stood on the hill above Beal grange and looked back at Lindisfarne. The roofless, fire-blackened walls of the cloister and the towers of St. Peter's Church seemed magnified in the clear salt air. It had been a long winter on Lindisfarne; I was surprised at how much I was going to miss that place.

Caitria stood aside and let me remember as much as I wanted. The grange was still deserted, the sheep were wandering the hills unattended. She sat on a rock and held the sides of her wimple away from her face to let in a little air. "Time to go?" she asked after a long while, and I nodded and turned the horse west.

"Eadred said we should make the other coast in four days if we don't have any trouble," she said as we walked.

"Eadred told me there's a town there called Luel." I nodded. "He said there's opportunities there, and I'd be able to get a passage to Ireland without any trouble."

"So long as your friends haven't been there first," she said.

"I reckon if they haven't, our partnership's over when we're in the gate. He told me to contact the priest with the news of the burning. It's a favor that will serve us well enough."

We were wearing our clerical disguises and carrying staves to pick our way along the route. In Chapter One of the Rule, Benedict dismissed wandering religious, which he called "gyrovagues," as the worst of the four kinds of monks and declined to speak of their disgraceful way of life, but they weren't an uncommon sight in the eighth century, and as long as no one examined the load and found the weapons, I was sure we'd pass a casual muster.

We had a general understanding that the northern landscape was hilly and wild. Eadred's directions were only marginally useful because he was familiar with well-traveled routes we wanted to avoid. We navigated the low ground between hills, and about five miles from the coast we crossed the raised Roman roadbed known as the Devil's Causeway. It was one of two main routes between the Lothian Picts and the Northumbrians. Those Roman pavers tempted us with convenience, but we were likely to run into other travelers on convenient routes, and I wanted to avoid people who trafficked convenient routes through the Northumbrian wilderness.

I reckoned we were quite a few leagues north of Hadrian's Wall, but there was no way to be sure how far. We were on the fringe of the Cheviot Hills, not the most congenial ground, even with a horse to bear the load. But the first day it was mostly low rolling hills and not too hard going. We came to the valley of the River Till a few hours after we left the coast.

The Till meandered through the center of the sheep country, and we saw the smoke of three or four villages in the southeast. It was the last reliable direction Eadred had given us. The Cheviot loomed to the south and west of the valley, and there was a royal ville at the foot of Yeavering Bell, a landmark hill that overlooked the approach of the River Glen. We crossed the Till a few miles upstream of its confluence with the Glen and pushed west into the Cheviot.

The Cheviot Hills weren't the best terrain feature to encounter after a forced march of twenty Roman miles, but they were the terrain feature of the moment, and there was nothing for it but to hump into them. We quickly discovered the ground might rise or fall seven hundred feet in any given mile, and the drainages were choked with brushwood and bogs. The hillsides were mottled by vast thickets of gorse, a nasty brush that's a cross between cactus, scrub oak, and barbed wire. Navigating round gorse thickets cost us hours and added miles, although at that time of year the gorse was blooming a beautiful golden color against the green grasses.

We made the best route we could. After a long first day, we camped in a disused hill fort. Every bit of high ground in that stretch of Northumbria had an earthwork to call its own. Unannounced Picts were known to come down from the north and ruin your day, and the hill forts were centrally placed so the people who clung to a truculent and bad-tempered existence in that latitude, herding the sheep on the moors, could get to them at the first sign of trouble.

"Not a bad first day," I said as we sat beside the fire that evening. I reckoned the anchoress she'd wintered with had observed the silence a lot more strictly than my friends at Lindisfarne, because Caitria hadn't said fifty words all day. That wasn't the Caitria I remembered from Wales.

"You'll soon be rid of me." She nodded. "And you can get back to your life."

"You'll find something in Luel," I told her. "Don't worry."

"I was heading for Gleawanceaster when we first met." She shrugged. "In Wales they held my Magonsætan father against me, and in Mercia they held my Gwentish mother against me. I wonder what they'll hold against me this far north."

"Probably being from the south," I guessed. "If not that, something else. People always hold something against strangers. But clerics, on the other hand, are welcome everywhere."

She was in a mood, though, and wouldn't be cheered up. She rolled over in her blanket and went to sleep, and I kicked out the fire and did the same.

We passed four days and four nights in the Cheviot without seeing anyone, and so we didn't have to run for our lives or try to brazen it out as a couple of gyrovagues. My travel luck was coming back. We weren't making the kind of optimistic time I'd hoped for, but we were moving almost every waking minute, and I was starting to relax as much as I expected to while I was treading Northumbrian dirt, and Caitria was rediscovering her original attitude and voice.

On the fifth morning we spotted a farmstead off across a field. The place was typical: a house, a few small buildings, a stable and a small shed for the grain and hay, all of it enclosed by a low wall. Defensible against homegrown outlaws—called wolfsheads because their bounty was the same as a wolf's—it wouldn't serve against a determined attack by men who knew what they were about. The hill forts were thinning out too.

The farmstead had been abandoned at least a year. The flat surfaces were covered with dust; cobwebs sagged across the corners like time's harp out of tune. There was crockery in the cupboard, and a copper cauldron hung from the iron rod that spanned the hearthstone. Four empty pothooks hung on the swing iron. Two clawed spits leaned against the wall, and the firedogs were soot-blackened above the ashes of the last fire to burn across their patient backs.

"See if the well's dry while I look through the house," I said.

"Who do you think you're ordering round?" Caitria swatted the dust off the bench and sat down, apparently disinclined to inspect the well then or ever.

"If you please," I asked her again. "I can only do one thing at a time, I'm tired, and dark's coming on."

"That's better." She smiled and got up again.

The house had three rooms and a loft. We were in the main room, one was a larder, and the other a place that served the sheep in winter, judging from the faint smell. The loft was infested with rodents, and as I gained the top rung of the ladder I could hear mice squeaking and scuffling underneath the straw.

Caitria came back with a bucket of cold well water as I was climbing down. She brushed aside the cobwebs over the hearth and poured the water into the cauldron while I knelt and raked the ashes away from the firedogs. Caitria went outside to get more water, and I looked for kindling. There wasn't any in the cottage, so I had to search out the woodpile, which turned out to be full of mice too. I wondered what the owls and cats did with themselves in the land of the Engs.

"What's keeping the fire?" she asked, returning with more water.

"Maybe you'd like to do it."

"Just don't take too long," she advised as she turned away.

"Where are you going?" I called after her.

"To see to the horse."

At least that got her out from underfoot; I reckoned when I was done with the fire I'd knock down some grouse along the wood line. I found some windfall branches in a little apple orchard behind the barn. It was going wild for lack of care, and last year's crop had rotted underfoot. I took them back into the cottage and shaved them for kindling. Caitria was gone.

I was kneeling over the hearthstone when Caitria came in and dropped two dead hares on the table with a clunk that made me gong my head into the cauldron. I rubbed the spot in the center of my tonsure and gave her a dark look. I was cut, and the blood was warm and thick under my fingertips.

"That fire didn't get any hotter while I was gone," she said, stepping over to the table to cut up the hares. She dropped the pink meat into the kettle, then, after few minutes' knife work, slices of onions and turnips.

She sat heavily on the bench and picked up an apple branch as I snapped a few sparks off my steel and ignited the kindling. "There's a grindstone in the barn," she said, examining the chop marks on the wood. "It'll be a while before that fire cooks anything. Maybe you should put an edge on your axe."

Not only was this woman amused by almost everything I did, but she had opinions about everything that didn't amuse her. It was already a long trip across a narrow island, and I was beginning to wonder at my luck in such a companion. If I'd wanted to be carped at, I'd have stayed home from the vik and taken in Goltrade's sermons.

"Why don't you do it? I'm sure you grind a good edge."

"You're right," she said, picking up the axe. I awaited her pronouncement of its design and balance, but she just smiled that serene and wistful smile as she walked out.

I fed the fire larger branches until it would burn without attention. The sweet smell of incinerated apple drifted around the room as I swept, redistributing more dust than I chased out. It swirled around in knee-deep clouds, and short of wetting the place down and mopping up, there was nothing to do but put the lid on the cauldron and go outside until it settled.

I heard the rasp of steel on a grindstone, and I strolled over to critique her work. The horse was tied to a rail eating some fodder, and Caitria was bent over the grindstone like a pro, taking care to keep the axe at the proper angle for a chopping instrument. An amateur always tries to put a razor edge on everything, but she knew the difference between a knife, an axe, and a sickle.

"Where'd you learn to sharpen blades?"

"My father taught me," she said without looking up.

"Was he a grinder too?" I inquired.

"Just a freeholder," she said. "Mother gave him only daughters, all dead now." She straightened up and scraped the blade lightly across her palm, satisfied with the edge. She offered the haft to me, and I checked her work. It would cleave kindling or ring mail, and everything in between. I slipped it into my belt and nodded.

"Good work." I expected her to make some sharp comment, but she only smiled.

"How's the stew coming?"

"I'm waiting for the dirt to settle." I grinned. "I'm not so good at sweeping as you are at grinding."

"Not a surprise," she said.

She had a tongue that would cut leather, and the will to employ it, and frequently my first impulse was to hit her, but something about her kept me from trying it. Caitria reminded me of Sinead and Mairead, but it wasn't that alone; despite her lip, she was good to be around. It wasn't her looks, which were plain enough but for those smiles. She didn't have the kind of easy beauty that makes men walk into posts. This woman was like gorse: a bramble that knew how to bloom. She'd get into trouble if she wasn't careful, and probably even if she was.

"Any good straw?" I jerked a thumb up toward the haymow. "The stuff in the house is crawling with rodents."

"Haven't looked." She reached up above the grindstone and took down a sickle from the wall. "I'll cut some fresh."

"Look in the apple orchard," I told her as we walked outside. "There ought to be plenty of good bedding there."

Caitria looked at me, her head tilted slightly to the right, her body a little to the left, a late breeze tugging the strands of hair that framed her face. The beginning of a smile was turning the corners of her mouth. The shadows defined those broad cheekbones, and her eyebrows were raised a few millimeters. The wood of the stable door, weathered into checks, covered with a faint verdigris of mold, was behind her. That's another of her looks that I remember with clarity: the look that preceded her sarcasm, the one that blossomed like an aura as she smiled and said, "Good bedding is the least of *your* worries."

I went back to the house to check the fire. The smoke coming out of the roof hole looked healthy enough, but it would want feeding. The dust had settled, and the stew was making the lid of the cauldron rattle. When I lifted it, the steam that rolled out made my stomach grumble. I put more wood across the firedogs and got the crockery.

Caitria wheeled a barrow heaped with fresh-cut grass up to the door. She knew her way around farm equipment, all right. While I worked, she piled the grass against the opposite walls and spread our cloaks. The room smelled of mown grass and stew, and I remembered how long since I'd put down in a house.

Such a domestic interlude made me think about Frydys, and I looked at the rune *Isa* on my hand. The circumstances of her waiting were a mystery, and so was what I'd do when I got back, but looking around the room I saw all I wanted out of life: a woman, a flat surface to compose on, and a meal cooking in the hearth. Someday children would make my wyrd complete. I'd had the Viking experience, the monastic experience, and more of life on the road than I'd ever craved; now I wanted to make verse and have a quiet life.

But first I wanted some stew, and the stuff on the fire smelled like it would do just fine. I swung out the pot and thrust my flared nostrils into the steam that drifted off the bubbling surface. A spoon dipped over my shoulder, and Caitria withdrew it under my nose.

"Not bad," she said, chewing with her lips open to cool it off. She stepped forward and spooned a generous helping on her plate and took it back to the table. It must have taken quite a reach to fill your belly on her farmstead. I filled my plate and sat across from her at the table. She was working that spoon like an oarsman. Life on the road gave you an appetite, no doubt, but she attacked every meal like it was her last.

"You eat like a starving woman," I said. "I reckon your meals with the anchoress weren't all that regular."

"Not so regular as I like," she admitted. "Iudelhild lived in a cave in Monk's House rocks, just upcoast from Bamburgh. She found me after the storm. We ate a lot of sea-weed and kittiwake eggs. How did you come to be at Lindisfarne, then?"

"I lost blood to the Northumbrians, and I was weaker than I thought. I went over the side, washed up on one of the Farnes, and Brian and Brendan found me with a broken leg. Winter trapped me while it was still healing."

"Why the haste to be in Ireland?" Caitria asked, scoop-ing more stew onto her plate. "Hurry attracts notice. It's been almost a year; a few weeks won't matter, or are you homesick for Vikings?"

I thought, why not? I'd kept quiet about my reasons for the vik and my urgency to get home for months, but there was a certain relief in being able to tell the whole story. Even though I'd been close to the monks at Lindisfarne, we weren't so close I'd come clean about the vik. It gave me a chance to hear some things spoken aloud and to think about them more objectively.

I told her the whole story while the fire burned down and the mice in the loft went about their mouse business. She was curious about foreign lands and customs, especially about the women of Clontarf, and I answered her questions for hours. Women had a different status among Danes than in Eng land, especially half-breed women from the Welsh border country, and I reckoned she'd had a life that made Sinead's independence seem fabulous. Finally I had to get some sleep. After wintering with 150 quiet men, I was eager enough to talk but out of practice.

The next morning Caitria was awake before I was. The fire had burned down, but the room still smelled like reaping time. It was the first chance I'd had to sleep past Prime in a long while, but she was taking no care to keep me in the land of dreams, clomping around on the board floor with surprising noise for a woman of her weight. She sloshed a bucket of water around in the cauldron. Then she splashed her face and put things away as if she were home instead of borrowing hospitality from ghosts.

"Time to rise," she said, nudging me with her foot. "There's plenty of road to travel while the morning's cool."

"I hope you're not always this cheerful." I rubbed the heels of my hands into my eyes, yawning. Not only was she a looking woman, she was a morning person too.

"I may as well be cheerful as the way you are." She laughed.

"That wit will keep you single," I observed, crawling to my feet and brushing the grass from my clothing.

"I'll never marry," she said matter-of-factly.

"Never's a long time," I said.

"I know that better than you." She pushed her hair off her forehead with the back of her hand and looked at me with old eyes that knew more about the passing of time than I did. That's what losing your family does to you, whether you watch them slip away one at a time or they all go at once. When your family's gone, time has different meaning and scope: soon becomes never, never becomes sooner than you want.

When she had everything put by to her satisfaction, we loaded up the horse and started out. The home field was littered with flowers: reds, yellows, and blues were scattered around like colors dropped from a hole in the rainbow's pocket. The sun was still low, and the soft light made everything more vivid and intense. Butterflies wobbled through the air like blossoms come to life and taken uncertain wing, and early blackbirds hunted the wet grass, moving line-abreast like beaters working a copse, stepping cautiously, listening with their heads cocked to one side, and then spearing down to pull out a worm or a snail. Their dark feathers shone purple in the morning sunlight.

We stopped awhile, resting on our staves as the blackbirds hunted across our line of travel. Meadowlarks clung to spikes of amaranth above the roadside ditch, calling out warnings to one another from the middle of their territories and singing for mates. We were passed along the road from lark to lark for half a mile until the woods closed in again and the forest sounds replaced the music of the open lea.

I took out my sling and collected a few stones in case we flushed something edible, but no hare or squirrel ran in front of us, no birds put up from roadside coverts to angle away across the open space. We passed more than one burned farmstead. At midday we came to a stream and rested in the shade of a bridge. I threw a line into the water without much hope, but it wasn't long before I had five perch. Whatever'd emptied the country had spared the fish. Caitria finished them off as fast as they were flapping on the ground, cleaned them, and wrapped them away in damp grass. With the business of finding food out of the way, we relaxed a bit, and I dozed off. She was gone when I woke up.

I called out, but there was no answer, so I went up on the bridge and scanned the area. The stone beside the bridge said: "Godric the Lean built me." I slipped the axe out of my belt and stepped back down on the creek bank. We'd been on the road six days without meeting anyone, and since we'd entered the burned country, that good luck was starting to make me more nervous every hour. Something had happened round there, and I wanted to know what it was.

The foliage was thick along the bank where it escaped the shadow of the trees to grow into the light. I moved along the path without making a sound, concealed by tall brush. I found Caitria bathing fifty yards upstream.

She was squatting in water to her ribs; she had her back to the stream bank. The muscles of her back rippled as she washed her arms and face, and I found myself looking at the first naked woman I'd seen since Frydys in the bathhouse on the eve of the vik. As I watched her, Caitria twisted around for a handful of the fine gravel from the bottom of the stream and saw me standing there in unfocused peripheral vision. She jumped to a crouch, dropping her center of gravity so her footing was solid on the streambed, and her hand came out of the water with a blade.

This woman had technique. An awkward moment passed, and then she smiled and stood up. She spread her arms and looked down at her body and let them swing to her sides, as if there were nothing much to do about what she saw, although it looked pretty fine to me.

"I'm not Frydys, am I?" she asked.

"Are you supposed to be?"

"I just want to be sure we both know it. Now, are you going to use that axe or not?"

I shoved the hickory axe handle into my belt. "One look at you told me I'd naught to fear."

She laughed and came out of the stream, drying off with her cloak while I waited for her, tossing pebbles into the water as she dressed. When she finished, she slipped the blade into her belt and we started back. Caitria stopped when we came to a side trail that led off through the trees.

"I found something you'll want to see. Come on." At the end of the trail through a small mixed wood we stepped onto the proverbial blighted heath where blackened and blasted grasses crumbled to ash underfoot.

There was a group of charred stumps in the middle of the heath, the remains of a grove felled for timber, I thought, but as I got closer I saw they were sheep. Their hoofless legs, heat-withered and burned to the bone, angled out from their roasted bodies. Their blown-out guts had drawn flies from miles around. There must have been fifty sheep and one small pile of cinders I reckoned was the dog that'd guarded them.

"What do you make of this?" I gestured around the heath.

"There's only one thing," she said. "It wasn't lightning."

"It must have been Thorr's fire to do this," I said. "Or a taste of what the Christian god did to Gomorrah."

"Only a wyrm could have done this," she said with an impatient shake of her head. "Let's go."

"A wyrm?"

"There was a wyrm scoured Gwent before I was born that did the same to the flocks there. Wales was wyrm country for hundreds of years. Why do you think we have them on our standards?"

Belief in wyrms was one of the things the average rustic held on to for a long time, together with belief in the power of Cuthbert's vestments and preventive bleeding. There was no more point arguing with someone who believed in wyrms than there was asking White Danes to pop in for tea and a color consult instead of burning your monastery. What can you say to someone like that? But she was quite willing, as true believers usually are, to explain her belief system to all and sundry, so as we walked back to the bridge, she shared her wyrm lore with a volubility that reminded me of Alban.

"They're from the old time, from before the goddess, from before the giants that stood up the stones down Sarum way."

"That long ago?" I asked, trying to sound less disinterested than I was for the sake of congenial travel.

"Longer," she assured me. "They're fallen angels who lost the battle with Michael and the archangels and escaped hell by hiding underground. They have the serpent's form

and they kept the ability to fly. They lurk for souls where
they may."

"What's their interest in gold and silver?" I asked her.

"It pleases them that gold and silver shine like the souls
of the saved and attract the souls of the damned," Caitria
said. "Everyone knows what happens when you touch a
single piece from a wyrm's hoard."

"It's terrible." I nodded as we regained the bridge and
untied the horse. Because of Skallagrim I'd believed in
trolls until I was thirteen, scared shitless to cross a bridge
in the woods because he'd said trolls lurked under them to
eat the flesh of unwary travelers. That Skallagrim—what a
baby-sitter he made. One of the male rites of passage in
Clontarf was to go on a troll hunt the first full moon after
Beltane of your thirteenth year, at which time you got the
shit scared out of you properly by men who knew how to
do it and in the process found out there were no trolls. If
I could get over trolls, Caitria could get over wyrms.

We stayed on the road for the rest of the afternoon. The
ground climbed out of the trees and into moorland. I didn't
know what had done that mutton to a terminal crisp, but
whatever it was, *I* didn't want to meet it. Maybe an elfish
party had gotten out of hand. Elves were notorious for
throwing a good party, and with most of the humans in the
area done for by a plague, there wouldn't be any interrup-
tions but the odd Pict, an easy enough contingency to deal
with. Elves disturbed at their midsummer revels had a nasty
reputation for spitefulness.

We crossed a high boggy moor with an unobstructed
view of miles of desolate land. There was no smoke, no
birds, no movement of any kind: an altogether lonely place
with a good view. I was glad when the ground dropped
again and we got back into the forest. When evening came
we were still in the trees, and it was clear that we'd have to
sleep out. We moved off the road a little way and scraped a
campsite out of the ground debris. I built a low fire while
Caitria wove a rack of green branches, so we could roast
the fish.

When we were done eating, we rolled up in our cloaks
with our feet toward the dying fire. It wasn't quite dark,
but then it never seemed to be *quite* dark in Northumbria,
and as twilight moved in among the trees and shapes began

to melt into one another, Caitria moved closer. Her gesture of trust made me feel a little necessary after all.

"Here," I said, handing her the sheathed scramasax. "Never know when you may need a blade."

She rolled over and took it from the sheath and stabbed it into the pine needles beside her. "Thanks," she said, "but we'll need more than this if we run into the wyrm."

In that case I doubted we'd need more, but I kept my opinions to myself. The sword was beside me on the ground in easy reach, and I was willing to put my trust in it.

Music woke us in the night. There was no way to judge how long we'd slept because trees blocked the stars, but it couldn't have been long because it was still dark. Music drifted through the air like mist; it was hard to get a fix on its source.

"Do you hear that?" Caitria whispered.

"I do if you're talking about the music," I said.

"What do you think it is?"

"Some late planting festival?" I guessed. "Beltane's come and gone, Lammas has yet to be. It isn't solstice time, is it?"

"A week away," she said.

"Suppose someone's getting an early start?"

"Who knows?"

Who knew, indeed? That far in the outback they still adhered to a lot of old customs and feasts, and although solstice day was near, there were always plenty of local cults conducting hybrid pago-Christian celebrations for fertility and good crops, observed by sweaty devotees who danced in the dark while the Christian priests slept. People still clung to what was familiar about the old gods while they got acquainted with the new one. If the Prior'd ever gotten out in the boondocks, he'd have understood that and not gotten himself into trouble with Alcuin.

"At least there's people," she said. "And a fair-sized village, from the sound of it."

"Shall we go look it over?"

"Better than spending the night here," she said. "At least there'll be a dry bed."

We stripped off our clerical robes and packed them on the horse before we set off in search of the music. It was a difficult task because of the shifting sound, but one that kept us moving. Caitria carried the scramasax in her belt, and I had the sword cinched up on my back; we swung our staves ahead to guide us. The horse got more reluctant as we went.

"Could be elves," I suggested after we'd groped through the dark awhile.

"I've never seen an elf," she told me.

"You don't want to surprise them."

"Don't you Irish believe you can extort treasure from an elf?" she asked in a tone that didn't bother to mask her amusement about my healthy concern for elves. Who was she to talk, the wyrm princess of Wales? When we neared the crest of the hill, the music took the shape of a wild and endless dance, full of reeds and strings and percussion. We could hear the bells on the dancers' feet jangling as they spun about. A bonfire lit the sky and sent sparks up to the stars, and figures danced round it in a circle.

Some wicker object had fallen in on itself in the flames, and when I saw that I put a hand on her arm and sank below the crest of the hill. The horse was skittish and about to give us trouble. Time to find another route.

"Wicker fires are sacrificial," I told her. "They're offering up something. Let's watch from here awhile. I don't want to burn in a wicker cage to some god who doesn't know he's dead."

"I've heard stories of the Wicker Man," she said.

Wicker Men weren't common, but some of the old Celts still wove them if the crops failed too many years in a row and famine smiled in the window. The Wicker Man was something Mairead had frightened us with when we were small. We'd scrape the bottom of the bowl for the last bean rather than face the threat of being tied into a thirty-foot effigy with sacrificial livestock and burned alive while the village danced round the pyre. That's a threat that has real weight when you're seven years old. Between her and Skallagrim, it's a wonder I didn't turn out a lot worse.

"I think we ought to give this hospitality a miss," I told her. "We can slip around the village before dawn."

"I'm for it," she agreed, and we backed down the hill again. "I've no interest in their troubles."

We put our backs to the glow of the bonfire and retraced our steps, but before we'd gone very far, Caitria veered off in the wrong direction. I caught her arm and stopped her.

"This way." I pointed to the left.

"No," she said. I could hear the frown in her voice. "This way."

"You're confused," I told her. "The road's over there."

"Confused?" There was more than a frown in her voice now. "I've never confused directions in my life. It's this way."

"You got turned round. I'm a hunter; I can't get lost if I try."

"Not too proud of yourself, are you?"

"Go ahead, then. Have a good time in the next Wicker Man. Oh, I forgot: virgins only."

Wrong wit is often the herald of doom. She tagged me with a fist that split my lip and made my ears ring. I stumbled back a step and squinted into the darkness for a glimpse of her, tasting blood. The horse shied away into the trees.

"You think you're thafe becauth you're a woman?" I yelped. "You're ath wrong about that ath you are about directhions. I'll give you the thrathing your father thould have."

"I'm safe because I'm a match for you," Caitria snapped back, giving me a direction to swing in. I caught her on the side of the head, and I was rewarded by the sound of her hitting the ground.

"A math are you?" I laughed, noticing my swelling lip altered the way I spoke. She scrambled up, and by instinct and sound I danced out of reach, caught her heel, and held it waist high.

"I tripped on a root," she hissed. "Let my foot go, and I'll show you the stars."

"I've theen the thtars," I told her. "But a look at them might get you turned in the right directhion."

Caitria hooked her heel into my back and leaped toward me. We went down, rolling across roots and through the leaves. She landed a couple of solid shots to my left ear before I finally controlled her wrists. I was taking the worst of this exchange. I was on my back, with her legs locked behind me, and I thrust up and turned under her. We rolled together, locked in a reflexive embrace, down a short steep hill and came to a tooth-jolting stop on the surface of the road.

We froze, looking up at two men standing above us with

upraised torches. Our entrance must have been pretty dramatic.

"He's come," one of them shouted, breaking the silence.

We jumped, holding one another's arms. The man who'd shouted turned and ran headlong up the road as if a dozen drunk elves were after him. The other man bent slightly and moved the torch over us for a better look. We must have met his criteria, because he straightened up and offered us a hand.

"We've been waiting for you," he said.

Caitria looked at me in the torchlight and grinned, immensely pleased with her handiwork. "Your lip looks like a sausage."

"Doth it?" I grinned back at her. "Your ear lookths like a dead mouth."

She put a hand to her ear and winced as her fingers brushed it. Then she looked at my lip again and laughed, taking the man's callused hand and hoisting herself upright. I stood up and faced her, just in case she tried to hit me again, but she seemed to think she'd punished me enough. The peasant with the torch looked at us both and shook his head.

"Walking in the dark often leads to stumbling," he said. "Oswald and I thought you were a boar."

"A couple of travelers temporarily lost," Caitria said, combing leaf fragments out of her hair with her fingers. "I followed him."

Before I could say anything, more torches were coming up the road, and we turned to face them, putting our backs to the woods. I saw her hand drop to the scramasax; my sword had come loose as we rolled down the hill and now hung under my right armpit. It would make for an awkward draw, but I figured Caitria was a match for any five peasants until I could clear steel.

"Othwald bringing frienths?" I asked.

"We've been waiting three days for you," he said. "We've burned the last wicker wyrm, and now we can start the feast."

Caitria and I exchanged looks as the villagers crowded up to us, holding their torches aloft and jabbering in Northumbrian, which, when shouted by two hundred throats at once, sounds like pack ice breaking up. They were un-

armed, but we put our backs together. The mob began to
move slowly back down the road, pulling us along toward
the village.

"Should we break for it?" she asked, her question nearly
drowned out by the crowd. Whoever they were waiting for,
they were going to be glad to see him; meanwhile, I wondered how glad they'd be when they figured out I was the
wrong guy. And then there was this business about the last
wicker wyrm. I didn't know what wyrm-exorcising customs
we'd wandered in on, or give a shit, but if they'd run out
of wicker and they needed something to burn, I didn't want
to be in the vicinity.

"If we're going to, noth the time," I said, my lip tingling
as sensation returned. "The clother we get to the village,
the farther we have to run."

We stopped and the crowd around us hesitated. She
turned to me and said: "What's passed has no matter." I
had a déjà vu: I saw her clearly, a split second out of
phrase, turning to face me. I saw her lips move and heard
the words like an echo of themselves in the firelit tunnel
of the forest road, and I saw myself put a hand on her
shoulder and then watched myself do it again. "We're true
partners now," I said. "We'll measure what comes on an
even scale: live or die, fail or prosper, stand or fall."

"So be it," she said, and turned round, starting to draw
the scramasax. This was it, then, time to cut our way clear
or go down. My fingers closed around the braided leather
of the sword hilt, and I started to ease it out of the scabbard. I could feel the adrenaline flooding into my head,
making distinct every shouted word, like the ring of coins
scattering on a stone surface from a dead man's hand. I
thought about going berserk again, but the thing about ber-
serking is you can't control it, and the requisite psychotic
state was unavailable when I needed it most.

A woman pushed through the front ranks of the crowd,
and I steadied the scabbard with my free hand as Caitria
lifted the scramasax free of her belt. The woman's face was
sweaty and dirt-streaked, and her hair, tangled from dancing, was confined by a wilted garland. Skewed ribbons fluttered down the side of her head.

She thrust a bundle into Caitria's arms and gave her a
pleading look. She'd been weeping, whether out of ecstasy
or grief I couldn't tell. Caitria grasped the bundle awk-

wardly with both hands, taking care to keep the edge of the blade away from it, and stepped back. The cloth squirmed in her arms, pushed out a tiny hand and a red shriveled face, and squalled louder than all the voices of the crowd.

"Please bless my child," the woman begged Caitria. "Please release us from the wyrm's curse." She snatched the garland off her head and offered it to Caitria like a crown.

Another woman came forward, pushing a child ahead, knee-high and frightened by the hysteria. "Bless my child," she pleaded with Caitria. "Help us," she begged, looking at me.

Then we were surrounded by women and their children, all wailing and lamenting.

"Any ideas?" she asked.

"Your blessings are worth as much as my help."

She turned and showed me the child, bending forward to whisper soothing noises to it. In the torchlight, looking at her hold the child, a great ache suffused me, a longing for the beauty of that image, a woman holding a child in dim light, her hair falling forward, backlit by flames, face in shadow, profile silhouetted against the light, and the child squirming, silenced momentarily by the tenderness of a whispered sound.

I let the blade slide back into the scabbard. We weren't going to be hacking our way anywhere now that Caitria was holding a baby in her arms and lamenting women were crowding around us on their knees. The night had just gotten worse and worse. I sighed and put a hand on Caitria's arm. "We may as well see what befalls," I said.

They led us into the village, past a great pile of embers that glowed like molten stones. Flames licked about the curves of osier ribs in the blackened skeletons of a series of wicker effigies. The air glowed red, and the coals looked hot enough to forge steel. That fire had been burning for days. Whatever they wanted, they wanted it bad.

"I don't have a good feeling about this," I told Caitria. The whole place looked new, as if it were freshly made for our arrival.

"These people are hungry," she said.

"They ought to spend their time hunting instead of dancing around fires," I said. "Burning wicker never filled a belly I know of."

"There's a wyrm," Caitria reminded me.

"Right."

We came to the center of the village, where two streets crossed and a post had been driven into the ground. Wilted garlands were lashed to the post; it was so thoroughly covered with blossoms that no wood showed. We could smell their faint perfume, even in the sweaty excitement of the crowd. An old man and woman stood on either side of the post, and the whole population circled, lighting with their torches the clearing they made. Caitria held the child, which seemed to be hers now, as far as the villagers were concerned, and I looked for the thinnest part of the encirclement.

I knew the custom of the Corn King; it was simple enough: when the crops failed, the Corn King got a chance to make them grow again, and if the gods gave them a good harvest, all was forgiven, but if the gods ignored his sacrifices and the crops failed again, the Corn King was next on the block, usually done for with a golden sickle and a lot of ceremony, but as dead as he was ever going to be, all the same. The twist was that the next man down the road became the new Corn King, and his first job was to sacrifice the old one.

That explained the burned sheep we'd seen in the meadow. These people went out and did the sacrificial flock the way a wyrm would: set it on fire while the sheep were alive. Apparently a whole flock hadn't been enough. That's the trap you're in once you start sacrificing: it's never enough to make the rains come or go, the crops grow, the insects bother someone else, or whatever it is you want. Now they'd taken to wicker effigies and marathon dancing while their children went hungry, and they waited for a new King, and Caitria and I wandered along, fat and dumb, into the middle of their hysteria.

They put garlands in Caitria's hair and led us to the old Corn King and his Queen, waiting for the end, placid as a couple of cattle. They must have reigned long and well to have reached such an age, but we were in the land of the Engs, I reminded myself, where people apparently possessed considerable geriatric resilience.

The old man stepped forward. Here it comes, I thought.

He's going to offer me the sickle and his throat, and if I refuse, we'll both end up in a wicker man.

"Well come to Ravenshill Moor," he said, offering his hand. We gripped each other's forearm and held for a moment. The old woman came forward and took Caitria by the arm, preparing to lead her away. I put a restraining hand on her shoulder.

"We stay together," I told her, shaking my head, "or not at all."

The crowd made way as the old couple led us to a raised platform laden with flowers where two pillowed seats faced the village. I held on to the sword with one hand, realizing irrelevantly that was as close to the high seat as I was ever going to get. Caitria took the scramasax out of her belt and lay it across her knees. Then the music began, wilder and louder and more feverish, now that they thought the Orkin man was there to handle their lizard infestation. A woman placed a stool beneath Caitria's feet and another did the same for me.

"What's the story here?" I asked Caitria.

"They've taken you for a wyrm slayer," she said.

I suppressed a smile, but it was certainly better than having to cut the old geezer's throat with a golden sickle.

Two of the women carried a trestle laden with food: fruits, roasted meats, potatoes, varieties of bread, honey, pitchers of mead, wine, ale. They bent under the weight of it, and Caitria and I looked at each other, and back at the scarecrows in the crowd, both coming to the same conclusion: it was time for a little largesse. I waved the trestle away and gestured to the villagers. "We'll eat what you leave for us," I said. "This is your food."

The two women hesitated and then turned back, carrying the trestle down and setting it at the foot of the platform. The villagers looked at us in disbelief, and then rushed it. Caitria watched them with contempt as they groped for scraps, surrendering to the feeding frenzy, forgetting their children as they pressed forward. Caitria leaped up and sent the stool rattling down the steps into the crowd. She held the scramasax with both hands and she was braced to do some work with it. The villagers fell over each other to get out of reach. Their instincts were correct: the only thing more disconcerting than a looking woman is a looking woman with a scramasax and technique.

"Feed your children, first," she screamed at them in a rage that surprised everyone. I'd wrestled with that woman, traded words and fists with her, and if she ever raised a scramasax to me I'd put a lot of space between us, but facing down a hungry mob in front of a table of food was a nervier thing than I expected. She penetrated the situation in an instant: understood that she was the Earth Mother now, not some farm girl from an abandoned freehold south of nowhere. She was the Word in Ravenshill Moor, and I realized, as she stood there communicating wrath to the burghers of Ravenshill, her hair bound by garlands, that I was the Law.

I got to my feet, pulling the Ulfberth sword from the scabbard as I rose. The scabbard turned on its chafe and fell in a slow arc onto the platform, rolled down one step, and came to rest, the belt buckle swinging to stillness with flashes of torchlight.

"What kind of shit-eating rats are you?" I demanded. "First you're on your knees for blessings and then you trample your children to get to food. You reckon you're worth saving?"

I swung the blade around so it made lightnings in the torch flames. It was pure street theater, and Caitria and I were making it up as we went, but we were doing pretty well, judging by the response: they'd all fallen on their faces.

"Not bad, huh?" I whispered to Caitria, lowering the sword.

"What kept you?" she asked.

I stood for a moment longer, letting them feel the guest of honor's anger, and then I sat down, but I kept the blade across my knees. Caitria stood beside me and put a hand on my shoulder in a gesture of solidarity. The women were the first to get up, leading their children to the trestle table and letting them have as much as they wanted. One of them retrieved Caitria's stool and offered it to her with no small hesitance, as if expecting a cuff for her trouble.

Caitria sat beside me, and we presided over the distribution of the food to the village children, frowning down from the high seats. The way they ravened into the food was an awful sight. There was hunger enough to go round in those days, but I never got used to it. Once you've seen real hunger, you know who the enemy is.

Then the adults took their share, moving with shamed restraint. The cost of killing wyrms had just gone up. When everyone was finished, two of the women heaped trenchers with food and brought them up to us.

There was still more on the trestle, and by the time we were halfway finished, the villagers were back for seconds, careful to see their children didn't cry out for more while they stuffed their faces. The Engs were a proud people, and I reckoned we were going to pay for this, but I couldn't imagine how much; I just knew it would be a lot. While they ate, I had to come up with some plan that would get us out of there.

"What do you make of this?" I asked her again.

"It's as plain as a plain sister," Caitria said. "They think you're a wyrm slayer come to help them out."

I shook my head and thought it over, coming back to the same thought; maybe there were worse things to be than a wyrm slayer. At least in those parts a wyrm slayer had status. A wyrm slayer was the man of the hour. The villagers were a little wound up, it's true, but all they wanted was someone to dispatch a mythical lizard and life would be sweet again. I didn't have to consider it long.

"We'll have to get out of here as quick as we can," she said. "Tomorrow they'll want you to kill the wyrm."

"Let's not be hasty," I said. "How hard can a wyrm be to kill?"

"Don't be mad. Nothing can pierce their scales, they fly and vomit flame, and they're as long as a cart and eight oxen."

"Still," I said reasonably, "there must be some way to kill them. When I was at Lindisfarne it seemed every Saxon monk that wasn't from someplace that ended in "-by" or "ho" was from someplace called Wyrmton or Wyrmhill or Wyrmsbane. You must have some opinions on it."

I figured Caitria was as much a subject-matter expert as I'd need to deal with the wyrm of Ravenshill Moor. All I needed was intelligence about what a wyrm didn't like; I could fake the rest.

"You can't kill them," she said. "Wyrms left those places or are still denned there. They're no trouble unless you disturb them, and then they lay waste. You can't stop one without magic."

"Skallagrim took care of all the magic," I said. "But maybe a little of it rubbed off, who knows?"

She wasn't convinced. She shook her head and leaned closer to me. "Don't try it," she said. "You'll be killed. When the feast's over, we'll slip out of here."

"Oh, I'm sure that won't piss them off after a welcome like this." I opened my arms to take in the entire village. The garlands were trampled in the dust and forgotten as the villagers squatted down in small groups eating their first meal in who knew how long. The bed of coals glowed red and black, emanating heat and a clue about their level of desperation.

"You'll be killed," she repeated. "Are you crazy?"

"You don't have much faith in me," I said.

"Of course not," she said. "You don't know what you're doing."

"Just tell me how to kill a wyrm and I'll take care of the rest."

"You *can't* kill one," she insisted with an angry look, and turned back to look over the crowd.

When the villagers finished their food, they took our trenchers away and the music started again, tentatively at first, as if they were afraid of our reaction, and then swelling finally into its former melody and rhythm. They danced in a long line that snaked through the village, around the post, around the fire pit and wicker ribs, around the platform where we sat on the high seats; the line was bowing and dipping, arms extended, holding their torches like flaming wings, undulating in concatenations of motion, as if they were swimming through the air in a sinuous flight, dipping and soaring without ever leaving the ground.

Then one of the musicians stepped forward and faced the line of dancers, holding them at bay with a reed flute in a gesture that I was certain mimed Caitria confronting them when they rushed the table for the food. She put the flute to her lips and trilled a scale that seemed hours or seconds long, and the line of dancers fell to the ground, collapsing from front to rear, torches rolling away in the dirt.

The old man and woman walked up the steps, offering basins of water and lowered themselves to the platform so they could wash the road dirt off our feet. I moved my feet away, but despite my resistance the old man pulled off my boots and set them aside. The old woman did the same for Caitria.

"I could get used to this," she said, wriggling her toes as the old woman laved them with water. Rose petals swirled in the basin and a few of them clung to her ankles.

"No doubt." I was preparing to stand when another woman offered me a clay cup. I took it cautiously and sniffed at the rim, then I wet my lips and drew a drop over my tongue. Not bad for a domestic. I sipped a little more and rinsed my mouth with it as if I knew something about wine. I made a face. I'd seen Einar Soft Hands do this little ritual a hundred times back in the hall at Clontarf, but it was the first time I'd ever performed it myself.

I indicated to the woman that I'd take a cupful, and she poured it out in a red stream, like the flexed translucent muscles on a demon's arm reaching into the cup with a handful of confusion. I drained it off in three pulls and held it out for another.

"That stuff cuts the dust," I announced, feeling a buzz.

"It can't feel better than this." Caitria sighed as the old woman kneaded the muscles of her calves with strong fingers.

The dancing began again, this time a more recognizable dance of weaving couples and swirling dresses as tambourines tapped and bells rang, strings hummed and flutes sang like nightingales. They wove themselves in and out, women and men going from partner to partner, laughing as they spun about, caught one another's hands, twirled, and danced away.

They brought Caitria a cup, and she sipped it as the old woman poured scented water over her feet. I'd been to worse parties in the mead hall. At least no one was throwing up into the fire, which makes a stench not to be believed as it bubbles away into the rafters. Open air was the place for a party, all right: build a bonfire, get the whole village dancing, break out the wine, and bring on the wyrms.

I looked at the starry sky and saw there were only a few more hours until dawn. Caitria stepped out of the basin onto a cloth the old woman had spread on the platform. Women gathered around her, screening her from view as they held out a dress and helped her slip into it.

I looked around quickly, but no one was heading my way

with new garments, and I was just as happy. I wasn't about
to drop my pants in Ravenshill Moor. I took my feet out
of the basin and dried them off. I had one boot on and the
other in my hands when they stepped away from Caitria
and I got a look at her in woman's array.

What I'd seen too much of by the stream to really see,
and not enough of when she was wearing men's clothes or
nun's weeds, came out like a sunrise in that dress, made of
a green silk that shimmered like light, flowed like the veil
of a waterfall to the flowers on the platform. It was cut low
in front, and her breasts, subdued into shapelessness by the
shirt and leather tunic she wore on the road, were partially
exposed, pushing against the silk, outlined in green light. It
covered her lithe waist like skin, clung to the width of her
hips, outlined one thigh. I wondered where these proles
had come up with green silk.

They replaced the wilted garland with three fresh ones,
and woven bands of flowers circled her head like a halo,
helixes of ribbon spiraled over her bare shoulders and
down her back. I'd seen her dressed and I'd seen her naked
and it continued to be the most curious thing about Caitria
that at any given moment there was nothing beautiful about
her, and yet she was a beauty. Not the same sort of beauty
as Frydys, or Sinead, or even Thordis, whose name I'd
scratched on the wall of the barrow all those years ago, but
a beauty without question. It's a quality that looking
women have, one of the things that makes them worth putting up with.

I couldn't believe she was the same person who'd fattened my lip in the woods a few hours before. She smiled
a shy and distant smile of profound sadness and looked at
me staring at her with my mouth drooping open like the
village idiot.

"It's me," she said. "Shut your mouth before a moth
flies in."

Whatever else you could say about Caitria, she had a
great sense of the moment. She picked up the scramasax
and sat down.

The Engs stood back looking at what they'd transmuted,
satisfied and a little stunned at the alchemy they'd wrought;
they smiled at the proof of their work, pleased with the
fairy before them, once imprisoned inside men's clothes,
now released by the mere understanding that she'd been

hiding there, only vaguely suspected by her somewhat dense traveling companion. They brought me more wine, but I could only watch Caitria as I drank it, feeling like a troll beside her in my dirty clothes and untrimmed beard.

I don't know what was in that wine, but more of it followed, and then I was dancing on the platform, still wearing only one boot, I noticed, and Caitria was whirling beside me, ribbons flying about her head, laughing as the green silk swirled about her legs, her breasts moving unconfined under the bodice, her hair streaming out as we linked arms and spun round and round. After that, everything was spinning round, and only more wine would slow it down. They removed the high seats, the sword, and the scramasax as we danced, and the flutes and tambourines played and the village clapped us on.

I woke up with a familiar feeling that it took me a few moments to place. At first I thought I was back on the Outer Farnes, facedown on the rocks, half in a tidal pool, waiting to feel the splintering pain of my broken leg. Then I began to remember the events of the past six months: the vik, meeting Caitria, the convalescence, the winter on Lindisfarne, the White Danes, the sacking of the monastery, the walk across Northumbria, Ravenshill Moor.

When I tried to get up, I discovered two things about my condition. First, that sensation I was having trouble recalling was an epic wine hangover. I felt like I had sand in all my joints, a wool sweater on my tongue, a kiln in my throat, and a weasel eating its way through my brain. Second, I was lying on my face with my hands bound tightly behind my back and my legs trussed to a noose around my neck. I sighed a desperate breath as I appreciated what an asshole I'd been, lulled into this fix by women with cups of wine.

And where was Caitria? What had these egg-sucking Engs done with her? I rolled over and my legs fell heavily onto the dirt floor, snapping my neck back. A massive burning cramp knotted up my right leg, like a piece of charcoal jammed into a slit in the muscle and sewn shut. I pointed my toe toward my knees and held it as long as I could, but it wasn't enough.

I shoved across the floor and got my toe against one of the roof posts, bending into the cramp and gritting my teeth as the hemp bit my throat. I held the position as long as I could after the cramp vanished, and when my temples were throbbing and I was light-headed, I relaxed and the cramp stayed away. It was a momentary victory, and I knew it. I looked around for some sharp object that would cut the ropes, some flame that would burn them, some animal that might be induced to gnaw them, but I was alone.

I tried to relax, to let the blood get to my brain so I could think clearly. My fingers were numb. There was no hope of picking the knots apart until some feeling returned, so I started pumping my fists to force blood back into my cold fingers. The door opened and several men came into the hut, the old man in the lead.

"A fine way you treat your wyrm slayers," I told them. "Where's Caitria?" My voice, deepened a couple of octaves by shouting and pouring wine down my throat, sounded like it belonged to someone else.

"She's with the women," the old man told me, squatting down so I didn't have to twist my head. "She's not harmed."

I said nothing. What was the point? I'd no threats that had weight, no wit that hadn't melted in the crucible of the hangover. The time had come to pay the supper check.

They cut the rope between my neck and feet, and the cramp returned with the sudden relaxation of my legs as they thumped on the dirt. They had to lift me to my feet. I had to be doing something wrong: all my arrivals on this trip had ended with men who smelled holding me by the arms while I endured pain.

They cut the ropes round my ankles and walked me around the hut while the needles of sleep melted in my legs, but they kept my hands tied behind me.

"Outside," the old man said.

I stumbled out into the daylight, still wearing only one boot, and tears came to my eyes. I was starting to remember my broken leg with a fond nostalgia for happier times. At least then I'd had the poppy. Now it looked like I was going to die with a hangover. Rather a more ultimate relief for headache, muscle fatigue, and queasy stomach than I desired.

In the daylight, I could see that the village *was* new. All the thatch was still green; all the posts still had bark on them. The grass wasn't yet worn off the paths between the huts. A low cloud of smoke curled into the blue sky from the fire pit. All the wicker was consumed now, and only embers were left, subsiding into gray ash, releasing their smoky ghosts.

They led me to the center of the village, where Caitria was bound like a heretic to the flower-covered post. Her garlands were gone; in the sunlight the silk dress was an intense competition among shades of viridian. The hemp that bound her to the post puckered the silk. Her head lolled forward, and her hair was moving slowly, whether in rhythm with her breathing or some vagrant draft I couldn't tell.

"Caitria," I said as they brought me up to her. "You all right?"

She lifted her head. There was a bruise on her cheek, and her nose was swollen a little, and I reckoned that somewhere in the village at least one man was on his back, nursing a crushed groin. She squinted through strands of hair that partially covered her eyes, trying to get a bearing on my voice.

"Bran?"

"Have they hurt you?" I struggled against the men who held my arms, but in my condition I was no danger to them.

"Bran," she said, perking up a little. "You look terrible."

I smiled. "They haven't cut out your tongue, at least." I was in front of her now, where I could get a better look at her. She'd been roughed up, all right; a looking woman who knows the business end of a scramasax and can kick must have been quite a handful.

"You look good in that dress," I said.

She made a face and snorted. "You look like a drowned man," she told me. "Your eyes are bloodshot, your face is puffy, and your breath stinks of wine and vomit. Lost your boot too?"

"Always count on you for a good word," I said. "What's passed?" They stood me up beside her and stepped away, leaving me to sag against the post. The old man and woman looked apologetic and sheepish in the daylight.

"Your woman tried to make you leave," the old man said.

"I'm no one's woman." Caitria was obviously clear on that point, and determined to hear it said out loud.

I pushed my weight off the post and stood on my feet. I

didn't know if Caitria was angrier because they thought she was my woman or because they'd caught us trying to skip out.

"What happened last night?"

"When you finished off the wine, I tried to get you to leave, but you were too drunk to do anything but puke."

"There's nothing to worry about," I told her, secure in the knowledge that the only dragons anyone need fear were made of oak and clench nails, flew on woolen wings, and swam on legs of yew. Not even my mother, with all her Celtic strangeness, believed in wyrms. The land about Clontarf was innocent of wyrms. Paidrig had driven them all out, to hear her tell it. Skallagrim had never told wyrm stories but one, the story of Sigurd the Volsung, a story about the mixed blessing of success. Heimdal's hard-on, my head was pounding.

"How long's this wyrm been plaguing you?" I asked.

"Since we reopened the old Roman works in the mine, and we went back to the old seam and started taking a good ore at once. Then the wyrm's curse started to work on us. Two went mad at the face one night and killed each other. Three more wasted away before our eyes."

"Wasted away?"

"They stopped eating, stopped speaking. There was no reaching them. They shriveled up like pears in sunlight. Died all three within a month after we found them huddled at the face of the seam. Then everyone who worked the mine started dreaming."

"The same dream?"

"Not the same dream, like, but dreams about the same thing. Men waking up in a sweat, screaming in their sleep and shouting out things as made no sense, but wanted to be speech."

"What were the dreams about?"

The men in the crowd all shifted nervously and looked away from one another. Whatever these people had dreamed about, it made them afraid even in the sunlight.

"Being alone," the old man finally answered. "Them was all about not having anyone around, like."

"What did you do?"

"We first had the priest from Bellingham, and he prayed and blessed everything, but it weren't no good, and the dreams kept on, and a man drowned himself in mine while his friends watched."

"Drowned?"

"Drowned himself. Walked right into the lake under the mountain, carrying his torch and all, until his head went under and the torch went out. He never struggled.

"The holy hermit from the Wark came and prayed, and he went mad too. After that we set the runecaster out to chase out the evil, but he said it was too strong and went away back into the wastes. Before they left they said a man would come down the road from the north country with his woman to deliver us, but they didn't know what from, and neither did we.

"Royal agents kept after us for ore, so we had to keep digging in the hill, though even the silver we got in payment had no good in it.

"Then Ælfnoth killed his wife and children, and we had to kill him. Three days later we broke into the wyrm's lair."

"You broke into its lair?"

"We broke open a sealed gallery and let out the wyrm. It killed all the miners at the face with a blast of flame. We were scattered in the woods for weeks, hiding while the wyrm hunted us down and vomited flame on us from the air. When it finally stopped harrying us, we came together and built this new village. We knew then what was causing the madness, and we knew we had to find someone to kill the wyrm. We can't do it ourselves. We know how to mine silver and grow a little food, we're not warriors."

"Only one wyrm?" I queried, adopting a professional tone. "Earth, air, water, or fire?"

"A fire wyrm," the old man said. "It flies high against the sun and spews liquid flames on us."

"Air and fire," I corrected him gently, in the voice of a craftsman talking to the uninitiated. "No problem here, just release me and I'll have a look at it."

A sigh of relief moved through the crowd like a wind through a rye field. As soon as they cut us free and pointed us in the direction of their wyrm, we could get out of there. I'd no idea what their problem was, but I'd volunteer to kill a hundred wyrms for them if they wanted, go up against them with my bare hands, blindfolded. Wyrms were the least of my worries.

"What matter?" Caitria whispered. "Nothing left to live for?"

"Don't worry," I assured her. "If there were wyrms, I'd have run into one before this."

"You're so far traveled you've seen everything?" she sneered. "Can't be surprised anymore? It's proven this place is a wyrm haunt, and where a wyrm's been, a wyrm can be again."

"There's no wyrm," I said confidently. "All we have to do is play along, and we'll be showing them our backs by noon."

"Noon's come and gone," she snapped. "Look at the sky."

I preferred to take her word. Looking at the sun would've blinded me for the rest of the day, and I didn't want to give the folk of Ravenshill Moor any reason to doubt my abilities. They needed a wyrm slayer, and I was going to give them what they wanted.

"This isn't wise," Caitria said, softening her tone.

"What choice have we? You faced down the lot when they rushed the food. How wise was that? Unless you've got a better plan, what matter? I'll be the one doing the slaying, not you. You're free to sit around and have your feet washed and wear green silk."

"You think you've such wit, don't you?" she asked. "What if there is a wyrm?"

"I'll be very surprised," I admitted, smiling the smile of a man who hasn't been surprised in a long time. "Where's the mine?" I demanded. "I want to get this out of the way before dark."

The old man cut Caitria's ropes. She sagged a bit, and I offered her what support I could, given my own condition and bound wrists, but she glared me off with those looking woman eyes. I was stung. After all, what did she have to be angry about? I was buying a little time, at the least. If she preferred to stay lashed to a post, maybe I should let her.

I turned to the old man. "Cut us loose," I said. "And let's go."

The old man shook his head. "She stays here until you're back."

"I'll need her help," I said.

"You'll do without it," the old man said.

There was a reversal, but I couldn't see any way around it. "While I'm gone, let Caitria free. If you hurt her, I'll the ride wyrm back and teach it to kill you all."

"She'll not be hurt," the old woman said. "We'll watch her. A wyrm slayer's woman isn't to be turned away from."

"I'm not his woman." Caitria bit off the words like jerked beef. "You ought to be sending *me* instead of him."

They looked as if they wanted to cut me loose just so they could watch me slap Caitria around. The men looked away, embarrassed for me, and I thought of the two White Danes, who'd pitied me as their last act on earth. These hicks were going to pay.

"What did you do to these people?" I asked her.

"What you'd have done if you'd any sense," she said plainly.

"I hope you weren't too hard on them. How they treat you while I'm gone depends on how many of them you mauled."

"Only three," she said. "They'll all live."

"Keep well," I told her. "I'll be back before dark."

All the men of Ravenshill Moor came out of the village carrying the tools of their trade: picks and shovels, tallow candles, ropes; one of them carried my weapons. They refused to unbind me, and we marched in silence. The village had been built on the edge of the moor, where the pine and oak forest ran out of a valley. The hills climbed upward behind it, through a tangle of bramble-choked ravines. The cataracts that washed across the path were cold, and I stopped and put my head under one of them for a moment of exquisite, head-clearing shock, like the shattering of a magic crystal, and exorcised the hangover.

The climb became difficult. The rocks were sharp underfoot, and the path wasn't well established. I couldn't imagine how they hauled ore out by this route.

"Isn't there a better way to the mine?" I asked.

"The wyrm watches it," the old man told me. "Our old village was on the other side of these hills, but it wasted our houses and fields. When we came together again, we built the new village on the far side of the hills to fool the wyrm into thinking it'd driven us off."

"How do you fool a flying wyrm?" I asked him. "From

up there, it can see everything. It can cross these hills like a raven."

"Have you flown a wyrm?" one of the others asked me.

"Only once," I told him. "A big wyrm, in the Mark, was harrying the land of the Wends. They asked Caitria and me to rid them of the pest. I fought that wyrm for two days, gripped its neck so tight that it took me up into the air to shake me to my death. We soared from Wendland to the south of Eire and back, but it couldn't shake me. When it landed again, I slipped my dagger into its heart through a loose scale and killed it."

They all looked at me with openmouthed awe, and I was afraid for a moment I'd overdone it, but if we learn anything from politics it's that you can't tell too big a lie; only the small ones trip you up. The trick about telling a lie is to believe it yourself, which breathes integrity into it. That's why simple lies are best, although adding detail, if you can keep track of the details you've added, makes it seem like remembering. Above all, never contradict yourself. If I spoke with conviction, these rubes would believe whatever I said.

"We're tonsured like priests," I said, "because a wyrm will hesitate to kill a holy man, and wyrmslaying's a holy calling."

I wondered what the real problem was. The rye fungus that makes you see monsters was a real possibility. Skallagrim once told me about a man who'd eaten a rye cake and thought trolls were chasing him. He'd slashed up four or five pedestrians and set a house ablaze before they subdued him. These Ravenshill people didn't look insane, but how can you tell?

Finally we topped the hill and rested. They all sat down among the rocks, took out food and water, and started to break their fast. No one offered to free my hands, but they did hold a bottle to my lips. The cold cataract had chased away the buzzing in my ears, and now the water from the bottle irrigated my parched throat.

"How much farther?"

"Now we have to go down the other side," the old man said. "But this part's faster."

"Untie me," I said. "If I fall going down this hill, I'll kill myself."

I could tell that it made them nervous, but they didn't

want to come that far only to lose their wyrm slayer to a loose foothold in the rocks. They discussed it and undid the rope. The man who carried my weapons kept far away—to prevent my jumping him and slaughtering the lot, I suppose—but they didn't have to worry about that. Even if I could've managed it, they were all armed with miner's tools, and a pick's as good as an axe for splitting a skull. Nor could I just leave Caitria to her wyrd. We'd made a partnership on the road, to take what came and split the results on an even scale: live or die, fail or prosper, stand or fall, doo da, doo da. I couldn't leave her any more than she could leave me, not until the journey was done.

After we'd rested half an hour, we started down the hill. The forest was a little thicker on that side, and the oak leaves were slippery underfoot. We were making too much noise, I thought, to be sneaking up on anyone, much less a flying lizard with preternatural hearing. It was plain they'd no woodcraft and less sense.

"Slow down," I called out to them. "It'll hear us coming, and you know what'll happen then."

After my warning they began to pick their way down the hillside, careful not to slip on the leaves, dislodge the windfallen branches, or kick stones that would plunge ahead to announce our coming. We cut our speed by ninety percent. I had to smile at the power a little conviction had. I decided to test how ridiculous they'd be.

"Everyone put a green acorn in your mouth," I said. "If your tongue's wrapped round a green acorn, no wyrm can understand your speech."

They all stripped small green acorns off the branches and popped them into their mouths. I was beginning to amaze myself, and I had to be careful not to gull them too far. Finally we struck a well-worn trail, and a little while later, the trail crossed the rutted cart track that led to the mine. They were hanging back now, afraid of what was at the end of the track, and I had to wait for them to catch up. Then the track turned sharply toward the hill, and we were standing at the mine entrance.

It was blocked. It looked like the roof had caved in, and they set about clearing a way through the rubble with their picks, opening a hole wide enough to crawl through. When they finished, the guy with the weapons climbed up the little bank and tossed them into the black mouth of the mountain. The old man gestured to the hole and offered me a sack of tallow candles and a holder.

"We'll wait here for a day," he said, his words bouncing around the acorn in his mouth. "If you haven't come out after that, we'll go back to the village and wait for the next wyrm slayer to come along."

"What about Caitria?"

"She'll be free to go or stay as she chooses," he said.

There didn't seem to be much point in drawing out the conversation. I knelt down in front of the hole. It was black as a Geat's heart in there. I lowered my head and shoulders into the opening and crawled forward on my belly. Barely enough light came in around me to let me see the tunnel ahead, but I felt the scabbards and the axe on the ground and pushed them ahead of me. In a little way the hole narrowed and I wriggled through the opening and was born into the mountain.

12

The Wyrm Gaefburnnah

Under Yggdrasil hide more serpents
Than dull apes dream of:
Goin and Moin, Grafvitnir's sons,
Sleepbringer, Unraveler, shall bite off
Twigs of that tree forever.
        —The Sayings of the Wise One

It smelled like the tomb of age in there: mildew, rotting bones, stagnant water, old death. I turned around to take a deep breath of the fresh air that was seeping in through the hole; they were already filling it again, and I watched it grow smaller and smaller until it was a slice of light, like the moon's frown, and then it was gone, leaving me in a darkness so complete not even hope could've escaped. I fit a candle into the holder and lit it after a couple minutes of effort.

Time was plastic: minutes or hours could have passed before the first yellow light from the candle flickered in the darkness. Of all the things that warp time—love, fear, boredom—darkness is the most sinister. I slid down the skree slope until I felt solid rock under my boots. The tunnel floor was uneven, and I had to stoop. I held up the candle to inspect the lintels and posts, a technique as old as the urge to dig in the earth.

The tunnel closest to the entrance held the oldest section of the workings, and as I went deeper into the mine, I moved forward in time, as the men of Ravenshill Moor moved forward in time, as we all move forward in chronological and linear time whenever we take a breath or a step. I wondered if the miners of Ravenshill Moor realized they were mining time; I doubted it. That kind of thought wasn't likely to cross the minds of men who stood around with green acorns in their mouths.

They'd replaced the older posts and lintels since they'd reopened the mine, and the new workmanship was tight and adequate. I was no miner, but I'd helped build enough longships to know good joinery when I saw it. The old timbers had probably been dragged off for burning, but a few had been thrown against the wall and left to rot. The ceiling was black from centuries of smoke. Water had collected in the ruts cut by the iron-rimmed cartwheel, and the sound of dripping water echoed in the blackness beyond the candlelight.

I found a rock, dripped a little wax on it, and stuck the candle upright; then I studied the flame. I reckoned that a mine that old had to have more than one entrance; all I had to do was locate the draft, follow it, and I'd be out the back door and halfway back for Caitria before the boys outside realized that green acorn mush wasn't going to do them any good. But I was disappointed: the flame steadied and burned true, and the smoke rose like a spear shaft until it surrendered to chaos just below the tunnel roof. I picked up the candle and went farther into the mine. When the tunnel forked a hundred yards in, I faced the ancient dilemma. The candle test was no help. The flame was straight as a Jomsviking's dick in a harem.

I examined the two passages for evidence of recent excavation, but they were identical. A pick handle, broken short and smoothed by the rubbing of callused hands, lay to the side of the tunnel, and I held it horizontally, spun it like a baton, and let it drop. The splintered end pointed to the left, so I decided on the right. It was a little test for the Norns. I recovered the pick handle to use as a tally stick; it would be easy to get disoriented in there. If I scored the wood every hundred paces I'd have a rough measure of distance. Now I had a plan, and I was a happier wyrm slayer than I'd been when the Engs shoveled the entrance shut after me.

I tried to keep to the high ground between the ruts, but so had every miner who'd preceded me, and the crown was as uneven and puddled as the cart tracks, forcing me all over the tunnel like a drunk in my quest for dry feet. The candlelight reflected on the water, and my shadow slewed around behind me. I stopped often to check for a draft. I heard a scurrying ahead, and I stopped in my tracks; after the sound of my heart left my ears, I realized that I was listening to rats going about the business of being rats, chittering and scrambling ahead of the advancing light.

I began to drink in the mood of the place, like the depression and dread I always felt after waking from a dream of the Geat standing over me. Shadows began to make me nervous; the echoes of my boots made me spin around to confront an emptiness. I remembered the old man's stories of madness and murder in the dark, and I tightened my grip on the sword. I breathed deeply to try to calm myself, but inhaling the cold humid air of the mine only made my attitude worse.

Graffiti started showing up on the walls, Ogham scratchings on the corners of the timbers, then the block lettering of some bored Roman overseer who wrote "Livia, your lips are moist for me in Aquila," with accompanying drawings that left no doubt about what lips he'd had in mind. I held the candle up and examined the words, aware that I was probably the first one in centuries who could read them, wondering who Livia was, what Roman mining engineer had scratched the words, and if he ever got back to Aquila. Maybe he'd gone under in Boudicca's revolt, or maybe he'd beat it out ahead of the pissed-off Celtic hoards.

Then I started to find runes in the language of the Engs: a note that the wyrm had killed the miners at the face. Who were all those people? There was no way of knowing. Their messages made me lonely, the way standing stones always do. Who had those people aspired to be? What had they become?

Just then a rat who aspired to be a fatter rat sauntered up the tunnel with a proprietary gait, quivering whiskers and eyes rubied by candlelight. He never hesitated; he came straight over and started to slip his incisors into the toe of my boot; I took a step and punted him against the opposite wall. Those rats were of a size to make a dog think twice, and I drew the sword as it got its little rat feet underneath it, a little dizzy from the unexpected impact, and fed it a few inches of Ulfberth iron. Its squeals exploded off the walls like shattering glass and set off other tunnel rats, who joined briefly in the chorus.

I knew a thing or two about rats, and one of the things I knew about them was their entirely unsentimental nature: that rat's immediate family would be stripping him to the bones five minutes after I left. I decided not to keep them from it, and I hurried down the passage.

After I killed the rat, I didn't stop to read any more inscriptions or admire the cave murals. I forced myself to keep going, thinking about Caitria waiting for me in Ravenshill Moor. If she could face the village down over a table of food, I couldn't let a little darkness get to me.

At last the flame of the candle began to flutter and tug ahead, but I couldn't feel a breeze in the close air. While I wasn't having trouble breathing, I was aware of the sound of my breath in my throat, a dry mouth, and a cold sweat trickling out of my scalp. I'd never been claustrophobic before, but the only cave I'd ever been in was the barrow on the down near Clontarf, where Frydys and I had first made the beast with two backs while hail pounded the mound.

This place was a different story, and the sight of the candle pointing the way to moving air cheered me up. I lit a longer candle and stubbed the short one out, but I walked another hundred yards before I began to notice that the floor was sloping down. I stopped and knelt to verified it: the water in the ruts was draining into the darkness ahead of me. I couldn't understand how the passage could *descend* to moving air, but my understanding of the phenomenon wasn't required.

Twenty yards ahead, the passage T-boned another tunnel. A noticeable breeze was moving through the second tunnel, and the flame jumped around, making me nervous; I didn't want to be down there in absolute dark. I squatted against the wall, retracing my steps mentally. There were eighty-four scratches on the wooden handle, which put me roughly a mile inside the mine.

I knew how long it took me to walk a mile, and, subtracting time spent punting rodents and admiring Roman pornography, I reckoned it at near half an hour back to the fork. I stood up and cut a notch into the post at eye level so I'd recognize it again, and then I cupped a hand round the flame and set off with the draft, hoping to find its source. What I found instead was a vast, still body of water, black as oil, which absorbed the meager light from my candle and the sound of my curses with equal ease. I reckoned it was the place where the miner had drowned himself. I threw a stone, but a splash came back instead of the sound of it striking the opposite wall. I pulled out my sling and fit a rock into the pouch, but greater range only produced a fainter splash.

There was nothing for it but to go back. Maybe the air was being blown into the cave instead of sucked out. It was the only theory I had at the moment. I passed the intersection of the first passage, and a second. Soon after that, the floor started to rise.

Another one, two, three tunnels intersected, and I marked the posts. Still the slope climbed. Evidence of recent working began to appear. Fresh scars on the rock, more recent timbering, thin, shallow ruts instead of deep ones. Then I found a charred overturned cart, the load spilled across the width of the tunnel. I stepped over the pile of ore and turned the corner into a stench that made the smell of all the lepers in the Eng land seem like clover in a springtime meadow. The hair stood away from my neck, the way it did the first time I saw Odhinn's fire, blue in the rigging during a storm on the open ocean. The draft had confined the stench to the end of the tunnel, and the smell was pooled in the terminus of the gallery. *Fetid* is a word that comes to mind, *putrid* is another, *moldy* is a third. Put them in a jigger and shake well and you have the smell that was in that tunnel.

I went back round the corner and sucked in a couple of lungsful of breathable air before I checked out the end of the tunnel, where the wall had crumbled completely. The air was moving with enough force to make the candle flame shiver. What I saw there made me take an involuntary breath.

Ten feet away a black-faced druid looked at me, his eyes glittering under his hood. He held a staff, carved round about with mistletoe and runes. When I moved the candle back and forth, his eyes sparkled inside the shadow of his face. The fact that human eyes don't reflect light loomed large in my mind. I was convinced some tunnel wight had materialized before me, but after a few seconds of deeply rooted immobility I realize the druid was dead.

I recognized the look once the initial fright wore off. Clontarf was surrounded by peat bogs, and once or twice a year the cutters unearthed people who'd drowned when the land had been swamp. The skin on their faces was tanned leather; even their fingerprints and the wrinkles round their eyes were preserved. That's what the druid was like, but someone had put gold coins over his eyes to reflect candlelight and make him seem feral and hungry. He stood in a niche, hunched forward as if the staff supported his weight.

That explained the taxidermied druid, but there was still the smell to account for. I stepped through the hole and held the candle up. The gallery had been sculpted out of living rock; the sides were cut to represent the thick trunks of oak trees, the texture of the bark exactly rendered, the floor was rough with above-ground roots, and the roof was a relief of interlocking branches. The shadows played among those stone trees like they would in a living forest. The place gave me a dreadful feeling; throats had been slit in that petrified forest, souls released, blood drunk.

The quiet hand of a nightmare familiarity lay softly on my shoulder, probably the same genetic knee-jerk that had scared the shit out of the Ravenshill Moor miners guild. I moistened my thumb and traced a binding rune on the druid's forehead before I turned my back on him. The smell was so thick I expected the candle either to go out or ignite it. Making my leaden legs advance was an effort. That should have been a clue. Ahead, gold coins were scattered on the threshold of the big blackness where the carved oaks stopped. I picked one up: it was stamped with Hadrian's triumphant profile.

There was a stirring in the darkness, and I prepared for more rats. The fairy chimes of hundreds of coins rang in the dark, retreating ahead of some heavy, slow movement connected to the smell, and which seemed deliberate, and reluctant, and bored. I stepped inside the door and the candle revealed the suggestion of a hoard. I looked on either side of the doorway, found torches, and touched one with the candle flame. It ignited with a flash that left me blinking scatterings of light, and I held it high, squinting into the room as confusing afterimages faded from my retinas.

There was a mound of coin and hack silver, plate, chalices, cups, torques, rings—all things worked in bright metal. I saw blades, mail shirts, jewels glittering red and green and white like the splintered light of dying stars. I held the torch higher and saw the scattered bones of men: femurs, pelvic girdles, gnawed collarbones, sterna, rib cages that had imprisoned twitching hearts, tibias shattered so the marrow could be sucked out, jawless skulls, scattered teeth, skeletal hands open in greeting and supplication. My eyes were watering with the stench of that place, and slowly I looked at the top of the hoard, where a great reptilian shape fully fifteen meters long coiled in bored repose like a green icon of evil and detachment.

Its eyes were vertical slits of yellow, and retina of red, brown, and black swirled and seethed like smoke as those yellow eyes opened. Its body was an unbroken cascade of tight jade scales. The wyrm's spine was ridged with spade-shaped plates that elongated as they drew closer to the tail. It seemed to *be* mostly tail, like a long armored muscle that burrowed in and out of the hoard, anchoring it to the treasure. I leaned against the wall. My heart felt like it was crawling out of my throat, and I actually swallowed to make it sink back to my chest. I put out a hand to steady myself. The wyrm's tongue flowed out of its mouth like a muscle of red quicksilver, sampling air that was laden with the smell of my terror.

"Why have you come here?" the wyrm asked.

"The villagers sealed me in," I told it after several attempts.

"The villagers." Coins repositioned under it. "The rats who dig in my mountain?"

I could only nod. Once I'd seen a viper fix a mouse with that stare. It was all I could do to move my hand toward the hilt of the Ulfberth blade. A laugh rumbled out of the wyrm at the movement, and its tongue flickered. There were hundreds of teeth in that mouth, all the thickness of a finger and the color of old ivory. Its leathery wings were folded against its sides, and it flexed them slightly to relieve a vague pressure.

"Go ahead," it said. "Let's see your sword."

I drew the blade and stumbled forward into a defensive stance, holding the point out before me; the wyrm's tongue snapped out in a blurred strike that sent the blade spinning against the stone wall, where it shattered like an icicle. My arm ached with the force of that blow; I could feel the muscles in my wrist stiffening. That left the scramasax, too light to stop a giant lizard, and the axe, which might do the job if anything could, but I'd have to drop the torch to use it. Fighting that thing in the dark wasn't something I was keen to undertake. So far the wyrm had only stirred, and my sword was scrap metal and my arm hummed with bone-bruised pain. A warm sensation moved down my leg, and I thought a splinter of broken steel had wounded me; I was relieved to see I'd only pissed myself.

"So you've come to join these others?" the wyrm asked, its eyes flickering about the bones at the base of the hoard. "They were all wyrm slayers in their time. All of them came for my head, and now their bones are dry and smooth."

"It's not what you think," I said. "I'm not a wyrm slayer."

"Then you're here to steal my hoard?" the wyrm's voice acquired an even more silky and minacious tone, but even more horrible than its tone was what it was doing as it spoke: becoming insubstantial, disintegrating in front of my eyes and replacing itself with Frydys, leaning back against the hoard mound as she'd leaned back against the burial mound before the storm.

Frydys smiled a familiar, seductive smile and parted her lips in a way I understood so well. Her voice was the low voice I remembered, the voice of the steam in Snorri's bathhouse, the barrowdown voice, the voice of the goddess' grove. "I wouldn't like it if you stole my hoard," it said.

"No matter," I assured it. "The thought never crossed my mind. I'm here because they *thought* I was a wyrm slayer and grabbed my friend and me on the road. They wouldn't let us leave until I'd killed you. Can you believe that? They sealed me in the silver mine. I'm looking for a way out so my friend and I can go."

"Good plan," the wyrm said, shifting shape again. "Too bad you found me instead." And there stood the Prior, his face bloated and picked over by crabs, his eye sockets empty and blue, tendrils of kelp clinging to his soaked habit, looking as serene and self-righteous as he possibly could under the circumstances.

I couldn't let the wyrm terrify me with apparitions. I mastered the impulse to fall down and cover my eyes. "Then there *is* another way out?"

"Of course," the wyrm said, becoming in a flicker the wyrm, and lowering its head gracefully onto its front feet, half closing its eyes. "How do you think *I* get out?"

"All I want is directions and I'll be out of here."

"Sorry," the wyrm said. "You can't go."

"Why not?"

"Part of the rules," it said, almost apologetically, as it became Thorfinn Skullsplitter, hair, beard, laugh, and all. "When the wyrm slayer finds me, we fight. Winner lives. That's how it works."

"But I told you, I'm not a wyrm slayer. I'm a poet."

Thorfinn became Skallagrim and looked me over carefully. "A poet? What sort of poet are you?"

Right then I was a poet with his own piss seeping into the top of his left boot. A poet who was beginning to reevaluate his ideas about the numinous universe. A poet who was sorry he'd ever left Clontarf. But of course I couldn't say any of that, so I said, "I'm the memory of the *Blood Raven.* Skald to Thorfinn Skullsplitter and Sygtrygg Ormson, pupil of Skallagrim, son of Snorri Horsekicked, enemy of—"

"What kind of *poet* are you?" Skallagrim asked again, cutting me off. "It's a long time since I've met a poet."

"I know the eddas and the sagas, and I compose on the occasion," I told the wyrm, adding a desperate and nearly fatal embellishment.

"Now's the occasion," the wyrm said, taking me at my literal word. "Compose."

"Now?"

"Of course, now," the wyrm insisted. "You haven't got long."

It was no time for writer's block, but that's what I had. I couldn't think of a kenning or a couplet. My mind was blank, and I was catatonic with stage fright. I knew lots of lines—all written down and rolled up in my pack. I began to fear the possibility that Skallagrim had been right all along: that what I'd always mistaken for a stubborn and paranoid distrust of writing *had* rubbed my memory clean of all the verses I'd known. I looked at the wyrm and tried to move my mouth, but no verses came.

The wyrm's tongue poured out as long as a long spear, and the tips quivered on either side of my face for a second before vanishing back into its spiked smile.

That was all I needed to prime the wordwell and bring some verses to mind:

I must fight with the waves whipped up by the wind
contending alone with their force combined,
when I dive to earth under the sea.
My own country is unknown to me.
If I can stay still, I'm strong in the fray.
If not, their might is greater than mine:
they'll break me in fragments and put me to flight,
intending to plunder what I must protect.
I can foil them if my fins are not frail
and the rocks hold firm against my force.
You know my nature, now guess my name.

"You embarrass yourself with riddles," the wyrm said.
"You're an anchor. Shall we play the riddle game?"

"No," I said nervously. "I just thought you might not
have heard that one. How about a few lines?"

"Sing on," the wyrm prompted.

I can sing a true song about myself,
Tell of my travels, of many hard times
Toiling day after day; I can describe
How I have harbored bitter sorrow in my heart
And often learned that ships are homes of sadness.
Wild were the waves when I took my turn,
The arduous night-watch, standing at the prow
While the boat tossed near the rocks. My feet
Were—

"That's enough," the wyrm said. "I've heard it."
Loki's lice, what if the thing had heard every line I knew?
Well, there were the lines I'd composed myself, so I recited
the saga of Macc Oc's vik, taking care not to speak too
quickly as I inched to the left, and tried to find some way
out of the wyrm's reach. There were torches set into the
wall, and I lit each one as I came to it, noticing the additional light pushed back the gloom, cast the wyrm into
higher relief, and made its slitted eyes narrow a little more.
When I finished, it opened its eyes and looked at me.

"Pedestrian," it said in a voice that was all too familiar.
Caitria stood there in her green dress, garlands askew and
fists planted carelessly on her hips as she critiqued my
verse.

"Everyone's a critic," I mustered enough courage to sneer.

Then the wyrm became Bran Snorrison standing calf-deep in the hoard, hands weaving patterns in the air, looking intensely into his own face and reciting in a paralytic rhythm:

> Arma virumque cano
> Trojae qui primus ab oris
> Italia fati profugis Laviniaque venit
> litora—multum ille et terris iactatus et alto
> vi superum, savae memorem Junonis ob irem.
> Multa quoque et bello passus, dum conderet urbem
> inferretque deos Latu; genus unde Latinum
> Albanique patres atque altaemoenia Romae.
> Musa, mihi causas memora, quo numini
> quidne dolens regina deum tot volvere casus
> insignem pietate virum, tot adire labores
> umpulerit.   Tantaene animus caelestibus irae?

"What's that?" I demanded.

"Virgil," I said pedantically to myself. "The *Aenid,* Book One, lines one through twelve."

"How do you come to know Latin?"

"Because I ate my share of Romans," the wyrm said, "and when I eat something, I know its language, what it knew, what it felt, what it wanted, what it had, what it was."

So the wyrm sucked the souls out of its victims when it took their lives. That must have made for some dull meals if it'd been dining on the people of Ravenshill Moor. A skald would be a spicier snack. My only chance was to convince the wyrm that verses heard were better than verses digested. It was a good thought, but I panicked in the execution.

"How about this; I learned it only recently":

> Hear me!   We've heard of Danish heroes,
> Ancient kings and the glory they cut
> For themselves. Swinging mighty swords!
> How Shild made slaves of soldiers from every
> Land, crowds of captives he'd beaten
> Into terror; he'd traveled to Denmark alone
> An abandoned child, he'd changed his own fate,

Lived to be rich and much honored.   He ruled
Lands on all sides: wherever the sea
Would take them his soldiers sailed, returned
With tribute and obedience.   There was a brave
King.   And he—

"I can't believe you're singing the song of that murderer
Beowulf," the wyrm said, as if it'd been considering letting
me off with a warning before I'd insulted it. It moved
around on the hoard to face me. Coins and plate rolled
and skidded down the mound like a golden avalanche, the
ringing of bells, the music of wealth. It was a social gaffe
I was unlikely to recover from.

"Yet the verse you sing is human verse; the thoughts you
have are human thoughts." I was saying anything that came
into my head. What did I have to lose at that point? "You
appear as people I know and speak with their voices."

"I speak in a way you can comprehend."

"You've shown me reflections of my own speech, or
ideas that I might have thought."

"Then hear you this," the wyrm said, and then ... then
what? How can I tell you what I don't understand myself?
What it did then had meaning, but not to me. The wyrm
began to sing its song, its eyes closing, and there was no
movement in the hoard room but the dancing shadows and
the invisible vibrations of the wyrm's song. There were no
words, only sounds, high and low, melodic and harmonic
sounds in ephemeral triads and octaves that came from
somewhere else, from another time, from a different reality.

I didn't understand its song, but I resonated to it like a
neighboring string; I quivered with the song of the wyrm,
wept with it, saw a flaming atmosphere and the ash of existence drift softly from the darkening sky of a nuclear winter
that would last for thousands of years, heard the death
songs of wyrms.

It sang its song for me in the hoard room, and the song
bridged my synapses like alien electricity; I thought its
thoughts, became the song of the wyrm, and it became me.
When it stopped singing, I was on the floor, weak and used
up, available to its lethal pleasure, but the wyrm was as
drained as I was, and it rested on the hoard and closed its
eyes. I willed my legs and arms to move, struggled to sit

upright against the inertia of that song, to crawl to my feet and stand bipedal once more.

The wyrm roused itself as I did, lifted its head, and laughed.

"So we spoke together. So we made our poetry, and you're still slime from a swamp."

"I'm a human," I said, pissed at being played with before I died. I wanted it over, and an animating anger burned off the lethargy of the wyrmsong. "A Dane from Clontarf, a skald on the *Blood Raven*. I can speak the Roman language, shape letters, wright words, and compose verse. I know the making of books, and the raven's banquet. If it's my wyrd to die here, let's get to it."

I slipped the axe out of my belt and dropped the torch onto the stone floor. I put my back to the wall and braced myself. The wyrm laughed like thunder in the cavern. I could feel the waves of its amusement surging against the rock behind me. The wyrm feinted with its tail, sending a shower of gold coins and jewels at me like battle hail, and I hid my face in the crook of my elbow. They spun past me, struck my arms and legs and chest, rang against the wall and bounced into my shoulders and back.

"You proud little rat." Its voice was genuinely amused. "You're so sure you're dead it makes you brave. You think you're everything, and when you come face-to-face with something *other,* something like me, what do you do? Draw a weapon. That's all you're good for, killing what you don't understand. If we'd been as good we'd have wiped you out when we had the chance."

"What are you talking about?"

"You don't even know—that's the pathetic part. How can you reckon time and space when your life's as short as lightning? We were here when you ran on four legs and gnawed roots. The full flower of creation evolved from our great saurian ancestors into beings of thought and sensibility, capable of living without bloodshed, capable of sharing sublime thoughts and emotions, innocent of fear or want, lacking only the inclination to hurt one another.

"Have you come near to achieving for more than a disparate handful of dynasties the paradise we enjoyed for millennia?"

"I was in a place where men live that life," I asserted. "A place of peace and quiet. An island of silence and thought."

"And what happened?" the wyrm sneered, as if it knew.

"Other men destroyed it," I had to admit. "But what matter? What happened once can happen again."

The wyrm spoke dreamily, remembering the time of its greatest pain. "Three hundred thousand of your generations ago we were extinguished by a stone from the sky. It turned the sea to steam, and the ripple of its striking washed continents clean. Clouds blocked the sun and everything withered. The air warmed, the great ices melted, oceans rose, rain and floods came, deserts became swamps, and mountains crumbled.

"Some of us went to the space between worlds. Most of us died. The last of us dream away the centuries in caves or at the bottom of deep lakes or the tops of mountains. Only because we live long are some of us living still."

The wyrm seemed a little bitter to me, but I didn't know about bitterness then, how in loneliness and isolation, bitterness is finally all there is to remind you you're alive. If you follow that road, after a while you're lost on it. It's all relative. For a man, a week of solitude can be more than enough; how much more abandoned to the madness of its own thoughts and speculations would a creature that lives for millennia be? And if I'd been *capable* of understanding such vast solitude, what matter? My immediate concern was that this lizard was planning to eat me, not that it was lonely. I wasn't its therapist.

"I'm sorry," I assured the wyrm, lowering the axe. "But you're not the last of your kind. What about the others?"

"We're aware of one another, of what passes in the world, of how you move into untainted places like a fungus that consumes everything. You bore into the earth to take out metals, and what does it get you? All these things I sleep on were taken from the ground, fired, worked, reduced to their bright essences. Someday you'll drink the world's blood, someday you'll burn the world up."

As the wyrm talked, a sword hilt angling out of the mound caught my eye. It was an ancient blade, forged and folded generations ago. I drew it out of the hoard and offered the carved ivory of its serpentine hilt to the wyrm. "Is this not a good thing?" I asked. "Aren't these objects beautiful? They were created by men, and the world is a better place because men find the beauty in it."

"You're so proud," the wyrm snapped. "Only a species

that can conquer self-awareness deserves to survive. When individuals become aware of themselves, they invent time. Past, present, and future begin to have meaning. There are memories and anticipation. Then they become aware of other individuals, of family, and then clans and tribes and nations.

"Then the notion of specialness appears, the delusion of the greater worth of an individual, a clan, a nation, or a race. Only the species that can overcome a belief in its own specialness will survive. That's the greatest and most subtle danger: the seduction of seeing specialness in itself alone."

While the wyrm talked, I idly scratched the sword point on the floor. Listening to its ideas made my head hurt; trying to follow what now seems the most rudimentary understanding of our place in a vast universe pushed me to the edge of the envelope. The simplest thoughts which any student today can invent over a bottle of beer seemed profound and beyond my power to articulate.

I looked down at the sword in my hand and saw it was a rune sword, a power object. "Who had this blade?"

The wyrm paused, glanced around the litter of bones, and indicated a skull with a nod. "That one," it said.

"Who was he?"

"It makes no matter. Better to ask who am *I*. You stand before a creature that was made as you were, by an incomprehensible power or a random event in infinity, and you wonder about an empty skull. The answer is he was another wyrm slayer with a weapon," the wyrm hissed. "As are you. Your poetry is sprung, your words have deserted you, and your time is over in the world."

In the yellow light, I saw the scratches the blade had made on the stones were runes. I squinted down at them and sounded the word on my lips. "Gaefburnnah."

The wyrm reared up suddenly, roaring out its panic and surprise, and a gout of flame rolled to the ceiling above its head. I got a flash-burn image of it, like one of William Blake's daydreams, its eyes blazing fearfully in the methane light, and the plates along its back rising up with a dry scraping. Its forelegs erupted out of the hoard as it fell toward me. I only had time to lift the point of the sword as it came, and the wyrm impaled itself on the blade, dragging itself forward along the steel to reach me.

"Gaefburnnah," I shouted into the wyrm's face, realizing

it was the wyrm's name. In those days names had power, they contained a thing's essence, and so to know something's name was to have power over it. For Gaefburnnah to hear its secret name spoken aloud was a terrible surprise. The blade, absorbing Gaefburnnah's energy all those years, had absorbed its name, and now it wanted out of there, and I'd happened along at a convenient moment and touched it. Once again I was delivered by the simple act of writing.

But not delivered unscathed. Gaefburnnah's claws raked my chest, opening me to the bone, one claw catching a rib and flicking me backward. I felt the rib resist and then crack as Gaefburnnah's heart's blood cascaded over me like a baptism of red brine. My back arched in my effort to get away from its face, its mouth agape and its teeth glistening with saliva, and I felt the wound in my chest open as the claw slipped out. I was instantly soaked as Gaefburnnah's heart pumped its life over me. I breathed its heart's blood and coughed it back into the wyrm's face, a foot from mine; as the smell of its death washed over me, I inhaled its last choking gasps.

I saw my face reflected in its eyes, then they dimmed as the wyrm's life ebbed away. I was pinned to the wall by its claws, which had gone clear round my chest and driven into the stones. A spasm racked the wyrm as it burped a gout of crimson blood into my face with its last breath. The light went out of its eyes, and it passed into whatever happens next.

I struggled to extricate myself from its grasp and got light-headed and slipped back against the wall. The wyrm's blood was still running down the deep fuller of the blade and flowing over me as its body became acquainted with death, muscles flexing and relaxing. I slipped into a daze, feeling the pumping of my own heart, the flutter of consciousness in my temples, tasting the wyrm's blood and my own. Awareness slipped away like a boring person's name, and my last thought was that I'd managed to bag a wyrm after all.

I woke in a stone room, naked and covered by the great weight of a sheepskin, which rendered me warm and immobile. The window was overgrown by vines that filtered the sunlight into a green haze except for two discrete beams, in which dust motes circled lazily, winking on and off in infinitesimal flashes.

I felt stiff and foggy-headed, and above all alone. I was wrapped in a solitude heavier than the sheepskin, an immediate awareness of individual isolation. I felt like the husk of fear. I couldn't remember what happened, but at last it started to come back, and I lay there piecing together the fragments: the memory of the wyrm, the hoard room, the rune sword, and the wyrm's death a foot from my face.

I moved my hands to my chest, but there weren't any scars. I didn't see how I could have been wrong about that claw pulling my rib away from my heart like a can opener exposing smoked oysters. When something pulls your ribs away from your heart, you know it. The wyrm must have laid me open from waist to neck, but I was unmarked. I heaved the sheepskin off and tried to sit up, but I could barely move. It was minutes before I could swing my legs off the couch and pull myself upright. I felt as if I hadn't moved in a month. I was too weak to stand.

I fell back across the sheepskin and gathered myself for another attempt. Then there was a sound behind me, and I saw Caitria standing in a door. She was dressed in her traveling clothes, the costume of the wyrm slayer's woman.

I put my hand out to her, and she came to the couch and took it. It was her touch that brought me back, like putting my head in the waterfall had brought me back on the way to the mine. The pressure of a human hand assuaged the loneliness I felt, and tears rolled down my face. Caitria supported me while I cried against her.

I tried to speak, but I was mute as Haki the Pict, and she brought me some watered wine to drink. When I swallowed, it was like swallowing a fear of losing myself into the unnameable void: I couldn't remember what I looked like. There was no image in my head when I thought of myself, no face, no picture of Bran to anchor me in existence. Instead, the faces of thousands of unknown men and women came when I closed my eyes. I could only suppose that my face was among them and wonder which one I was.

Caitria lowered me to the couch and hurried out, leaving me for a moment that was full of icy emptiness, a marooned and barren scattering of seconds. Then she was back with a basin and a cloth, washing my face and combing my hair, which was longer than hers, but not tangled or knotted.

She'd taken care of me for a long time, long enough for my hair to grow four times its length. How long had I been asleep? Then the real terror came: I tried to ask, but she couldn't understand the sounds I made.

I opened my mouth and spoke the language of the Celts. Then the languages of the Jutes, the Picts, the Bernicians, the East Saxons, the Anglians, and the Arabs. I searched for a language that Caitria would understand, but I couldn't find one. I spoke Frisian, Walloon, Geat, Southern Celt, Arabic, Roman, Greek, and languages I didn't even know the names of, languages of men whose civilizations had been in ruins for thousands of years, sunk beneath oceans, covered by mountains of ice.

The more languages came from my mouth, the more terrified I was. Caitria held me and rocked slowly, stroking my hair as I made sounds that were the languages of animals: whistles and grunts, growls, guttural pre-verbal sounds that must've been made by men before they knew they were men.

And in all those languages I screamed out the single question: "Who am I?" And when I finally managed to find Caitria's language, she whispered in my ear: "You're Bran Snorrison. You're a wordwright, a wyrm slayer, and my partner."

She lowered me to the couch and left for only another little while, seconds, but I was back in the void until she held a polished silver plate in front of my face. My reflection swam in it, a little distorted and warped, but a truer reflection than I realized. It was a stranger's face: long hair, full beard, eyes round with fear. There was no signature of daylight on my skin. I touched its outlines, felt my features, my beard and hair. The tonsure had grown out. I had a prisoner's face, out of sunlight for a long time. My eyes burned with a kind of feverish blue, like the hottest part of a flame.

I don't know what I would have done if it hadn't been for her. She took away the plate, whispered my name over and over again. We were there for hours. The light moved outside the window, the room dimmed, and I fell asleep hearing her speak my name.

When I woke, I was barely able to fight my way through the terror that waited for me. My wordhoard's too poor to explain how it felt, that isolation, that inconsolable and grievous abandonment. If that was how Gaefburnnah'd felt, I couldn't understand why it wanted to go on at all. It helped that I knew Caitria was somewhere nearby, and in a moment she came into the room as if conjured by my thoughts. I lay there breathing heavily and drew an arm across my forehead, which was slick again with sweat that burned the corners of my eyes. Caitria wiped my face with a damp cloth.

"Do you remember who you are today?" she asked.

"Don't mock," I told her.

"No." Caitria shook her head, and there was no trace of the mockery I remembered. "Yesterday you sounded like you were in wraithland."

"Wherever I was," I said, "I couldn't find myself or remember what I looked like, what I thought, anything. All I could do was talk in tongues and feel what the wyrm felt. Where are we?"

"In the mountain," she said.

"How long?"

Caitria hesitated before she spoke, her face dissolving into shadow as the last low light of day came through the foliage that covered the window. Then she smiled and brushed back a strand of hair. Her hand lingered on my forehead. "Two years."

"Two years. Right. Two years?"

"Wyrm lore says their blood keeps you from dying, keeps you asleep while you heal. They say surviving a wyrm's sleep makes you immortal."

Before I would've laughed at the idea that wyrm's blood made you immortal, but then I hadn't made the acquaintance of my late reptilian friend. Later on, someone said, "When you hunt the wyrm, you have to become like the wyrm, and when you look long into the abyss, remember that the abyss also looks long into you." He must have slain a wyrm to have made a thought like that.

"That's all I need," I sneered. "Immortality. The wyrm's twilight years were a bitter broth. Most of its kind were killed by some catastrophe from the sky, and the rest are pissed off."

"You know more about wyrms than you used to."

"Gaefburnnah was a real talker."

"You know its name?" she whispered.

"That's the only reason I'm alive."

"You have more luck than I thought," Caitria said.

What could I say? When she was right, she was right: I had more luck than *I* thought.

"Are we alone?"

"Yes. Now the wyrm's dead they work the mine, but they only came here to hang a door. They wouldn't look at you, and they wouldn't go near the wyrm."

"You mean they haven't cleaned out the hoard?"

"The hoard belongs to you. They won't touch it because the wyrm's still there."

"*That's* hard to believe." I shook my head at the thought of giving up a hoard already fired, minted, and cut, for raw ore.

"Were you surprised to see the wyrm?" she asked with that smile she smiled before she set a barb.

"I pissed my pants," I confessed without shame. I couldn't see depriving her of the right to gloat.

Caitria laughed aloud; it sounded like larksong. "Sorry I missed it," she said. "You were such a cocky wyrm slayer when you left."

"Don't worry, if we run into another, I'll show you my technique. How long was I gone before they found me?"

"They didn't." She shook her head. "They said if you'd killed the wyrm, you'd have come back. They said it was your wyrd to meet the wyrm without them. I made them miserable until they brought me out to the mine, gave me candles and a knife, and buried me under the mountain."

"How did you find me?"

"Not easily." Caitria closed her eyes for a moment at a remembered dread. I thought of Frydys's fear of the barrow and wondered if Caitria was afraid of ghosts, but she answered my question before I asked it.

"The rats," she said with a shudder, "came after me in the tunnel. I couldn't stop without rats at me. When I lived ..." she faltered for a few seconds and collected herself, "on the freehold, rats came at night and gnawed at my feet, and I couldn't feel them. They ate my fingertips, my nose and ears, my lips ..." she couldn't go on; she hugged herself and drew her knees up to her chest.

I put my arms around her and rocked her as she cried. "It was a bad dream," I told her. "You dreamed it in another life." That was something Mairead used to say when we woke after bad dreams, and it always made Sinead and me feel better, but it only made Caitria cry harder and clutch at my arms. I pulled the sheepskin round her, and we lay back until she cried herself out and fell asleep.

So it was rats. Who was I to mock anyone's fears? A pants-pisser and accidental dragon slayer, a bullshitter in the school of performance art. But I knew something about dreams from my talks with the dream Geat, conducted occasionally and always with reluctance, between the hours of darkness and light. If she'd lived with this dream of rats, going into the mine after me was an act of courage that made my conversation with the wyrm seem trivial. Those rats weren't interested in philosophy. One of them had tried to chew off *my* toes; the difference was I had thirty-four inches of Ulfberth blade to keep them honest.

I wrapped her in the sheepskin and went to look for my clothes, but first I had to remember how to walk again. I was the victim of a trampolinelike confusion of weightlessness and multiple Gs. I careened drunkenly off the walls until I got my land legs again.

Caitria's bed was in the other room, and a table and stool, and another wooden chest. I opened the chest and found my clothes, gear, and weapons. The runes on the sword were in no language I'd known, but since Gaefburnnah'd done for the former owner, I could read them without difficulty:

Confound my enemies with battle fetters, protect my friends with lightning, let evil not harm the bearer of this blade. I am called Garm. Wayland made me.

I swung the blade around my head, amazed by its lightness and balance. One of Wayland's true blades was a power object beyond price, and I had no doubt I was holding one in my hands.

Wayland hammered out a dozen blades for the gods, but his skill at smithy made the dwarfs covetous and they stole some of them; Loki, always on the snoop for an opportunity, took a couple more, so Wayland gave the rest to the Valkyries. He'd infused them all with a guardian spirit; that was a time when spirits lived in everything, in objects no less than in the men who made them. The *Lay of Wayland's Blades* was one of the first that Skallagrim had taught me, a perennial favorite in the mead hall.

In the lay, all but one of the blades returned to Valhalla,

and no one had a clue where the missing one was. When Wayland's blades are reassembled, Ragnarok's right behind. I looked at the blade I held in my hands. It made me nervous. A power object like that had a mind of its own, and it could turn on me if I crossed its yet to be determined purposes. In the meantime, I wrapped it in my wool cloak and laid it back on top of the chest.

After I got dressed, I found Caitria still asleep and decided to have a look round. I'd reckoned the place was one of those fabled temple complexes from when the druids ran things, but when I examined the runes cut into the trunks and stone limbs of the oaks, I saw it was even older: a shrine of the Goddess, cut and consecrated with the wyrm in residence. According to the runes, they'd made a pact with Gaefburnnah, whose name they'd never known: food, protection, and sacrifices for knowledge. In the beginning had been the wyrm, and the devotees of the Goddess came after.

The short passage went directly to the hoard room, where Gaefburnnah's reptilian corpse lay undisturbed, only a little shrunken now and desiccated. There were torches burning in all the wall sconces, and the true size of the wyrm was visible. I walked round it in amazement. Now that it was two years dead, the smell was gone, and it was just dried meat.

The brilliant jade of the scales on Gaefburnnah's back and sides had faded, and the scales on its belly and neck were now like verdigris on old bronze: mottled and dusty and shot through with blue striations. As I stood before the husk, I realized how beautiful a creature the wyrm had been, even in the shadows of the hoard room, even etched in the white light of its flaming methane breath, even dead. I was sorry I'd never seen it soaring like a jade butterfly in the sunlight. But the people who got to see *that* sight often didn't see much else.

I stood beside its head. The stones were black and encrusted for yards around with dried blood that was only now beginning to flake into a midnight-blue dust, a sand of immortality. I could see the skidmarks where I'd been dragged away, through blood that must have been teeming with some reptilian clotting factor but not yet completely dry. The imprints of Caitria's feet and the smears of my heels grew fainter like drying cart tracks beside a ford. I looked into the dead eye of the wyrm, its dull surface reflecting nothing. Its teeth were exposed in a rictus grin. A gossamer of cobwebs softened the longest of the fangs.

I walked up to the hoard. The mound of coins and gemstones was as high as the part in Thorfinn's hair, and as slippery as a winter deck. I scrambled to the top, where Gaefburnnah's tail was still anchored in the mound. The gold and silver coins were from everywhere: all the kingdoms of the Engs, Frisia, Frankland, Eire, the Mark, Rome, Iberia, Arabia, Byzantium, the Rus. There were gems both cut and raw, plate ornate and plain, cups simple and intricately wrought. Gaefburnnah'd gathered its bed well.

I picked up a goblet whose ivory stem was carved in the likenesses of three fairies, standing back to back, their hands linked and their wings supporting a cup made of hammered gold, deep enough to hold four gills of confusion. I started to fill the goblet with gems, but when it was brimming, more and rarer gems still sparkled in Gaefburnnah's nest. I slid to the bottom of the mound like a glissade on the song of opulence. At the bottom, I dropped the goblet and shook my head. It was impossible to choose anything that hadn't chosen me, and only Wayland's blade had come to hand on its own.

I went back to the stone chamber where Caitria was sleeping. Her breathing was soft and regular, a reassuring sound, a presence. I walked over to the window casement and tried to open a hole in the thick-stemmed vines, but they were too tangled. I reckoned the day was over, so I went back to the bed and crawled in beside Caitria.

The next morning we woke up together and stirred a moment against each other before we threw off the sheepskin. There was no fire, and the air was raw. I set about making flames while she went into the other room for bread, dried fruit, and meat. Breakfast was ready when I was finished making the fire.

"What do we do now?" I asked when we were done eating.

"Don't you want to go back to Clontarf?"

It dawned on me that almost three years had passed under the keel since I'd last seen Clontarf. I'd spent time so close to the edge of chaos that I'd forgotten about Frydys. I reviewed the facts: back in Clontarf they thought I was dead, which left Frydys fettered only by her belief in the rune *Isa* to wait for me in life and across death, or one year, whichever came first.

Even if Macc Oc was sporting with the dolphins, I doubted that Frydys had waited longer than promised on the unlikely chance I'd survived the battle, the storm, and the intervening time. I didn't doubt her love, but making herself a ghost's widow wasn't in her capacity; she was too young and beautiful for a widow's wyrd. Sygtrygg'd probably concocted another scheme to wive her out, or she'd opened her legs to some sympathetic Dane and gotten a child.

"Mairead and Snorri will be glad to see me," I told Caitria. "And Skallagrim and Goltrade, if they're still alive."

"They are." Caitria took a drink of spring water and wiped her lips with the back of her arm.

"Have you developed the second sight?"

"What I see with first sight's bad enough, but I feel it so."

"Sooner begun, sooner done."

"Luel must only be a few more days."

As the fire burned down, we organized for the trip. Caitria'd long ago traded off the horse for essentials and we weren't going to be able to carry much of the hoard on our backs. We needed some kind of transport.

"What's the chance of getting a horse in the village?"

Caitria smiled. "Since you killed their wyrm, life is good and they owe it to you."

"Then they can come up with three horses, and we'll ride out in style with more of the hoard."

"If we go now, we'll be back by midday."

We pulled cloaks around us and took up the staves that leaned beside the new door. Everything Caitria did had the familiar ease of a thing long done, and I knew she'd opened the door, stoked the fire, hauled wood and water enough to make those movements part of her dance. She'd kept up her side of the partnership even though her partner slept the wyrm's sleep. She'd kept faith with someone who might as well have been dead. Loyalty meant more then; partnership wasn't severed by life or death; duty and obligation remained as long as memory.

The path led down the side of the mountain, cut through a ravine, hopped a ridge, and dropped into another ravine.

The brush was thick, but the path was well defined. It joined the path we'd taken from Ravenshill Moor when I was bound and hungover, to meet the wyrm I hadn't believed in. I'd made them put acorns in their mouths and thought they were fools.

I tried to make peace with the idea of Frydys released from her oath and living a different life. If she'd decided that she wasn't duty-bound to wait for a corpse and married Macc Oc, or anyone, who was I to say no? That's what I told myself, anyway, or maybe that's just what surviving a wyrm does for you: one look into the void and you tend to take the long view, which looked pretty good compared to the languid latitudes of the wyrm's detachment that I struggled to keep at arm's length as we went to the village.

Ravenshill Moor had grown considerably, and this time there weren't any bonfires to greet us; instead, children were watching a flock of sheep. The squeal of swine came sharp and sudden from over the rooftops. There were three streets now, and corrals for cattle and horses. Ore carts were lined up outside the village where the path to the mine intersected the road to the south.

The shepherds saw us coming as soon as we left the cover of the trees and recognized Caitria immediately, but it took them a moment to figure out who I was. Then they hauled ass into the village, leaving the sheep under canine supervision. Before we were halfway to the first house they were pouring out to greet us.

"Careful. Last time this happened, we got drunk and danced all night," I reminded Caitria.

"But they did wash our feet," she said. "And massaged the cramps in our legs."

"Only your legs, as I recall, and they put you into a green dress that looked pretty good."

When they got closer I saw that the old man and woman were still alive, and they were even more deferential than before, but something had gone out of their mood. A new prosperity had seen that old enthusiasm fade like a flower. Now I was a reminder of how hard they'd groveled, and they were keen to see my back. None of them had spared a day to visit the guy who'd killed their wyrm, and now that I stood in front of them they must've felt the wyrm inside me.

"We'll have a feast for your return," the old man said.

"No, thanks," I said. "Let's have a look at your horses. We need three. Also a couple of good bows and a hundred arrows. Two spears would be handy. Water and food for a week's trip."

"Take what you want." He gestured to the horses in the corral and to the village in general.

Caitria went to inspect the horses.

"The last time I was here, I did a killing for you," I said.

"You did what you were sent to do."

"The Norns may have brought me here," I said, "and they may not, but all we need's the truth to make our own wyrd."

"We told you the wyrm was killing the village."

"You disturbed its sleep, and you tried to kill it."

"We have to live. You killed it or you wouldn't be alive now."

"You could've learned from it."

"What did you learn; how to turn a Christian cheek? You struck to save your life, like us. Like the wyrm. That's wyrd; that's what happens. That's the way things are."

Caitria came back with the three best horses, draft animals that could haul a cart of ore, and the horses she'd taken, shaggy-footed Dales ponies—a gray, a black, and a brown—were all broad in the chest and heavily muscled: cart pullers, open-road draft animals, the long haulers of their day with a good low range in the short run. They'd take us and whatever we wanted to carry and never notice they were saddled.

"The wyrm's bed belongs equally to Caitria and me. When we come for it, if one coin's missing, if you try to cheat us by a single plate, you'll wish you had the wyrm back."

We turned the horses away, and that was the last I saw of the good citizens of Ravenshill Moor. They called after us, but I didn't turn around. Going back to the mountain was like going back to the void, but it was a thing that had to be done. It was still a stone-chilling place, like being naked and alone in the centuries. I thought it was loneliness, but I didn't know what loneliness was; so far I'd only sniffed the cork of loneliness.

Where do you want to start?" Caitria asked.

"There's only two things to do," I said. "Get our gear and take what we want from the hoard."

"There's another thing," Caitria said, "maybe the most important. We've got to see to the wyrm."

"I've seen to the wyrm as much as I want," I said without guilt. "The wyrm and I have reached an understanding."

Caitria laughed. "Like most of your understandings, it's incomplete. You're not done yet."

"What else is there to do? Bury it?"

"There's the Taking," she said.

"What's that?" I asked, braced for more wyrm lore.

"The Taking of the wyrm's gifts."

"Which are?"

"Tooth and claw, blood and scale, and the craw stones."

"Mustn't forget the craw stones," I said with a laugh. "Fried up with garlic and butter, they're fit for a king."

"I thought recent experience might've chased your stupidity away; more fool me."

"What do you know about it? You think I'm having a good time getting used to Gaefburnnah's views on life?"

"That's another thing; even dead the wyrm's true name is a power word. Telling me was bad enough; don't tell anyone else."

I sat down on the wooden chest and bit the skin on the inside of my mouth while I looked at the mud on my boots. I could use a little understanding here. The wyrm's worldview, interesting as it was, existed in a vortex of nothingness, which I was unlucky enough to inspect from time to time, standing on the edge of ultimate chaos with my toes over the rim. I thought I deserved some room to brood if the mood overcame me.

"Stop feeling sorry for yourself," she said. "Opportunities like this don't come every day."

She acted like Being and Nothingness were things you got a handle on in an afternoon. What a resilient woman Caitria was proving to be; I was made of less elastic stuff.

"The wyrm still has powers in death, until its killer takes them. Parts of it are useful. The scales can keep you safe, and when its teeth are mounted on shafts, the arrows always return to the owner. The blood's a useful medicine. The claws cut anything."

"Let's get this over with. What do I do?"

"*You've* got to take them if their power's to work, and you have to do it with the blade that killed the wyrm."

"Let's get to it, then," I said, and she got the runesword

out of the chest and carried it ahead of me into the
hoard room.

Caitria stopped at the wyrm's head and told me to draw
as many teeth as I wanted. I cut them out with the point
of the sword. Finger-length, bone-smooth, and sharp
enough to do the job, I wondered about their utility as
arrowheads. I stopped at a hundred, and there were still
plenty left. Caitria carried them over to the silk dress she'd
spread out on the floor and lay them out.

"Which scales?"

"Bigger covers more," she said, so I climbed up the
hoard, scattering treasure as I lost ground to gravity and
the incline, pulling myself along by the drooped and stiffened plates that ran along the wyrm's spine. When the
scales were as big as they got, I slipped the blade between
them and sliced their roots, and they slipped off into my
arms. I handed them down to Caitria and she took them
over to the pile of teeth.

"Where's it keep its gullet?"

"Between its front legs," she told me, moving to the spot
while I slid down the side of the mound. "Put the blade
into the wound and pull down."

I slipped the first three inches of the runesword into
Gaefburnnah's death wound and slit downward, and the
wyrm unzipped, and with a dark clattering, like petrified
drops of heart's blood, nine stones the size of hen's eggs
fell out, smooth as ice, made of a mineral then called
wyrm's eye but called tiger's eye now. They were warm, as
if the wyrm were still generating heat.

I carried them over to the teeth and scales. I was
amassing quite a collection of body parts during my first
lizard autopsy, and I still had the claws to go. "How
many claws?"

"What you want," she said, so I went back and cut out
the three that'd hooked my heart.

"That's over with," I said when I came back. "Now let's
take what we want from the hoard and go."

"You're not done yet," Caitria said. "One more thing
to do."

She took my hand and held it over the carpet of dried
blood. "Wyrm's blood cures all wounds and diseases," she
said. "But you have to prime it with your own." She turned
my hand over and the rune *Isa* looked up at her. Caitria

frowned and opened my other hand and drew the blade across it with the same quick pull that made steers back on the freehold, and a warmth of my own blood welled up in it. I made a fist and squeezed it onto the dust. I don't know what went on chemically, but the dust turned to liquid under my boots, as if a spring had forced its way up from the ground.

Caitria went into the other room and came back with a handful of stoppered bottles and a measure and filled the bottles with blood. When they were full, she spilled some of the blood on my hand.

"The wyrm's blood will cure anything," she told me.

"What do I need cures for if I'm immortal?"

"You won't die, but you can be killed, just like you killed the wyrm. This will heal your wounds. If you lose your head, you're done for."

It didn't take us long to collect my fee: gold and hack silver for big-ticket purchasing power, gemstones for their portability and shock value, torques, objects d'art wrought in precious metals, rare gems, and rings. We carried three sacks to the packhorse, but we didn't put a dent in that mound, and the horse probably considered it a vacation from his work as the motive engine of an ore cart.

There was another trip to bring out the two wooden chests. We packed our gear and bedding around the bags of loot and wrestled them onto the packhorse. I made one last trip inside, to the druid I'd met on the way in. The staff in his hand moved easily, so I slipped it out of his grasp. I couldn't think of a better gift for Skallagrim, and the druid wouldn't miss it. Standing there empty-handed, he looked like he was waving good-bye.

Caitria was already in the saddle, impatient to be elsewhere. I couldn't blame her; I was hoping to leave behind the black rushes of depression that'd kept breaking over me at random moments. If I'd slept for two years, how long was this mood going to last? I meditated on its possible duration as the horses wound down the river valley to the southeast of Ravenshill Moor.

13

Ælfholm

Greetings to the host. The guest has arrived.
In which seat shall he sit?
Rash is he who at unknown doors
Relies on his good luck.
          —The Sayings of the Wise One

The road followed the river, and the river wound down through the hilly country southeast of Ravenshill Moor; it wasn't as direct, but it was an easier journey than trudging straight up the hills and across the high fells. You don't get much good trudging these days, but when I was young it was common as lice and just as welcome. But now that we had real horses, it would have been stupid to take a route that was too broken for comfortable riding.

Freshets and small cataracts fell out of the high ground and formed sikes, which became burns, which swelled into streams, which drained into the dale of the River Tyne. All that water was starting to get on my nerves. It rained just often enough that we were never really dry; every cloud heading east pissed on us in passing. We stayed on the road for the rest of the day, forded the Tyne upstream of Bellingham, and when the sunset began to blaze up red, we sheltered in a soggy hilltop earthwork. There was a ring of standing stones at the base of the hill. The land of the Engs was littered with dolmens, standing stones, and hill forts; that was pissing me off too.

We unloaded the horses, and Caitria hobbled them and let them out to graze inside the earthwork. I tried to dig a small pit in the turf for the cooking fire, but it filled with water as fast as I scooped. Even after I found a flat rock to build a fire on, it took me an hour to find dry fuel, and it wasn't really dry, only damp. Caitria hunted round the edge of a warren in the side of the earthwork and killed a couple of hares.

"When's the fire going to be ready?"

"When the wood dries out," I snapped.

"Don't bark at me," she warned.

"Then don't ask stupid questions," I told her.

She looked at me angrily and took herself a little way off. I felt bad, and that only made me angrier. I knew the last two years couldn't have been a good time for Caitria: alone while the months passed, tending to the no doubt revolting bodily needs of a living corpse, while she was holed up in the lair of the wyrm, listening for rats on the stone floor. Sounds like a great way to spend a couple of years, doesn't it? So what? Until you experience real loneliness, you can't appreciate how endless even a few minutes of it is. Thanks to Gaefburnnah, I'd broken the code on loneliness. Why couldn't she understand that?

Finally, after I'd blown myself dizzy coaxing the tinder, the fire was going in the underside of a log I'd had to drag up the hill. I fed it more dry fuel, and finally it was hot enough to dry out the log as it burned. I threaded the hares on a skewer and roasted them in the flames, and after a while the smell brought her over. We sat with the fire between us, eating and looking at the flames.

"What'll you do with your share of the hoard?" I asked finally, just to break the tension.

"Was you killed the wyrm," she said curtly.

"What matter? Partners share," I said testily. "You think I'm a cheat?"

"Wyrmlore says it's yours."

"That's what comes of killing wyrm," I pointed out vehemently. "You get to rewrite the wyrmlore. Half's yours, partner, you earned it. True, I killed the wyrm, but that was accidental. You came after me into the dark, through the rats; killing the wyrm was easy compared to that. I didn't even *believe* in wyrms."

"I owed you the looking," Caitria said.

"Right. And I owe you. What I can do's little enough: half a hoard. Be a power, control your life, make your wyrd."

"My wyrd's made," Caitria said.

She was a daughter of her time: a woman who'd gone into a dark place after someone who'd joked about her virginity and cuffed her upside the head; a woman who'd gone after someone who might have skipped, or, most likely was an hors d'ouevre for a giant winged lizard with an attitude; a woman who'd stood by a partnership made when we thought we were out of luck; but not a woman who could imagine making her own wyrd, even as she did it.

It seemed shortsighted to me.

After she was asleep, I looked at her profile against the fading firelight. It was a common enough face: a broken nose and wide cheekbones, lapis eyes, a small scar on her forehead. Who was the father of such a face, and who the mother? I saw something distinctly for the first time as I watched Caitria sleep: she had a real face that you could love, whereas Frydys had everyone's *idea* of a lovely face. So what? Despite any moody insights, I knew I still loved Frydys. It was too late to do anything about that. Three years had passed like smoke: as far as I was concerned, not even a winter had turned. I felt how I felt. Frydys might be waiting for me, but she probably wasn't, and either way I knew she'd be more trouble than treasure. She'd be *my* hoard to guard until someone wanted her badly enough to kill me.

It clouded up while we slept, and we woke in a heavy fog. Caitria had rediscovered her opinions on everything from my ability to start a fire (inadequate), to the distance the horses had wandered despite the hobbles (inconvenient), and the look of the weather (menacing). She predicted rain before midday and went grumbling after the horses, which had managed to get as far as twenty yards deeper into the lush pasturage of the earthwork. I reckoned when the size of her share dawned on her, she'd perk up; that much silver would put smiling lips on a leper. We broke fast on cold hare and apples.

We left the hill fort and not long after struck a Roman road from which no stones were missing, and the horses trotted along with the hoard bags jingling. It started to rain just before noon, as Caitria'd pronounced at breakfast, but the accuracy of her forecast didn't cheer either of us up. I drew my cloak around me and pulled on my hood, and the rain fell harder, but Caitria threw her face back and rode looking up into the sky as the falling rain splashed her face and wet her hair into dark ropes.

Whatever her mood, Caitria was in love with sensation; she had a child's enormous pleasure in immediate experience, and a child's ability to be surprised by the warmth of the day rising from a meadow, sunlight flooding through a rent in a cloud, a lark song, the coldness of water, or the texture of wool. She also had a child's displeasure at small frustrations, and I wondered how she'd like pneumonia. After another half hour we left the road to look for a dry spot in a nearby group of dolmens.

They stood together below some hills like loitering vagrants, at the edge of a little swale with a pond behind; lichen-mottled, gray, hulking, neolithic—just the setting to help us recover our good spirits. The low clouds held the sound close, and the ground rose up from the stones on three sides. We climbed down from the horses. The roof stones were wide enough to make a dry area in the center of the largest. Caitria hobbled the horses in the next biggest, which wasn't so dry but good enough for horses, and we got our blankets out of the trunk. The clouds were the color of watered milk. It rained steadily.

I was preparing to meditate on my mood until sleep overtook me, when I noticed a movement on the hilltop. The rainlight was dim and the colors washed together, but the contrast was good enough to see someone hopping the ridgeline. I watched for a few seconds and saw another silhouette following the first, and then two more. Just what I needed, external focus.

"Company," I snarled.

Caitria threw aside the blanket and got her legs under her. "Where?"

I jerked a thumb upslope. They were still fifty or sixty yards away, and we had a defensible position with the bog at our backs.

"It's always something, isn't it?" I bitched as I got to my feet. The bows and the rest of our gear were with the horses, and I crossed the space fast and got them out. As I was stringing yew, I heard a yelp from the other side of the clearing and saw Caitria scrambling across the turf with her knife out, slashing after a man that was crabbing away from her.

Then another man ran into the clearing, straight at Caitria. He had a bow over his shoulder, an axe in his hand, and the look of no friend I've ever had, so I put an arrow into him. He tumbled ass over elbows and skidded on his back a few feet across the wet grass before he stopped. He raised up on his elbows and looked at the shaft growing out of his side while I nocked another.

Caitria'd cornered her man against a stone; he was talking fast.

"Wolfsheads," he gasped.

I aimed the arrow just below his center of mass, and he turned his attention to me. "Æthelric," he panted, "son of Æthelwulf . . . march thegn . . . tracking wolfsheads . . . found too many."

I looked at the one I'd dropped. He wheezed and coughed a little blood. I'd clipped him in the bottom of a lung. He lay back on the turf and looked up into the milky sky, his breath rising like white ash on a thermal as he bled out in the rain.

Caitria squinted into the insubstantial daylight beyond the stones. She tensed as she looked up at the hilltop.

"Here they come," Æthelric said.

Caitria bolted across the clearing and slid into the cover of the dolmen. The horses stamped about at Caitria's sudden arrival, but they held their ground and calmed as she strung the other bow.

"How many?"

"I couldn't see."

Æthelric was looking for a hiding place, but there was nowhere to go: we were trapped with our backs to the little bog and the bad guys had all the high ground.

"Get his bow," I called over to him.

Æthelric stripped the wounded man's bow over his head, and the outlaw yelled out in pain. Then he came under the roof stone and pulled an arrow out of the ground. He was a lanky man in his late twenties, and he'd been hunted hard. His clothes were soaked and mud-spattered. His hands and elbows were bleeding, and his cheeks were lashed by branches.

Ten minutes passed. The only thing to look at was the dying wheezer. The arrow fletching moved in little circles as he breathed, like his ghost hovering above him. The iron arrowhead was cutting more pink lung with every movement. His wheezing began to sound wetter, and he turned his face to the side and coughed and blood ran out of his mouth. Then he rattled, and that was the end of him.

He became a feature in the landscape, a heap of guts in threadbare clothing with a hole in one boot. His beard was patchy; his thin hair hung down in lank cords, showing bare, fish-belly scalp. Just another dead wolfshead in a raw fog in the middle of Northumbria. Hey, I should let some asshole jump us in the rain and not get a little pissed?

"I found Hengest and his lot with a bunch of mongrel Picts," Æthelric said, his breath pluming out in front of his face. "A blueface sniffed me out and they've been after me since midmorning."

"How many?"

"Eight or ten, but the Picts are following after."

I stepped out of the dolmen and squinted around in the falling rain. I didn't see any movement, so I took another step. The body of the wolfshead was twenty feet away; the dolmen where we'd sheltered was ten feet beyond.

"Hullo the stones," a voice shouted out.

I jumped back as Æthelric slipped over to cover our blind side.

"What do you want?" I shouted out.

"Your silver and your horses," came back the shout.

"What do we get in return?"

"You get to live."

"Piss up a mast," I advised him diplomatically.

Caitria drew fletch to her cheek, held it, and released. There was a scream from the edge of the bog and the splash of a body hitting the water. She nocked another arrow as the splashing died.

"We've plenty of arrows," I called out.

"But not plenty of daylight," came the answer.

"True enough," I told Caitria. "The light's only going to get worse."

That was all I needed to say. She pulled the hobbles and got on her horse so fast I thought she'd levitated there. She tied the reins to her saddle and held her bow like she meant to use it.

"What are you waiting for?"

"Do they have horses?" I asked Æthelric as I tossed him the reins of the pack animal.

"No," he said, "they'd have had me in no time."

"Then we have to go before the rest get here." I

mounted up, Caitria looked at me with a look that said anything could happen, and then we were out of the dolmen, leaping the dead guts and pounding through the fog toward the Roman road. There were encircling shouts, proving there were a lot of them out there.

One jumped from the side, waving a cloak to startle the horses, but those draft animals were nervier than he expected, and mine shouldered him aside. I saw his ass and the bottoms of his feet as he arced into the fog, and then I was past him. Æthelric was behind me, holding on to the horse as best he might, and Caitria brought up the rear. I saw a shape to my left, drew back the arrow, and watched it fly toward the middle of a man's chest.

It only took us a few seconds to get through them and across the turf to the welcome sound of the paved road. We had to slow down after a quarter mile because of the fog, and when I reined in to listen for a chase, I heard only the breathing and stamping of the horses and the hiss of the rain.

After another couple of miles the pavement disappeared, which meant we were getting near some sort of habitation. The Engs tore up the Roman roads for building material when there was nothing else to hand, and even if there was, the convenience of paving stones already quarried and shaped being irresistible. So when we started splashing through great shallow marshes of rainwater and weeds where the road used to be, I knew that such civilization as there was north of the Humber was close by.

"Home's not far," Æthelric said, validating my logic. But the fog was getting thicker if it was changing at all, and the light was almost gone. A mud track crossed the roadbed, and Æthelric turned his horse into a moil of black muck that was full of rainwater and manure and the tracks of livestock.

"We're delivered," I said.

There was a ditch with a stationary timber bridge about ten yards long and wide enough for a cart, with space to walk beside. The horses' hooves boomed on the bridge, and fog swirled vaguely over the water. The gate was made from the heartwood of oak trees and wouldn't surrender to anything less than a siege engine.

"Look at this place," I said to Caitria as we crossed the bridge. "Those mutts aren't going to follow us in here."

"There's mutts enough to go round," she said.

A man sat in the guard mount above the gate, hooded and wrapped up in wool. He held his hand downward to absorb heat from a charcoal fire, glowing out of sight in a brazier. A couple of spears leaned against a roof support, and I could see one end of an unstrung bow above the parapet. He didn't move as we rode up, but I felt his eyes as soon as I could see him in the fog.

"Æthelhere, open up," Æthelric called up to him. "We've got Hengest and his lot after us."

"How many?" came the unhurried reply.

"Two of us," Caitria snapped. "Can't you count?"

The guard leaned over the rampart and looked down at her, holding the cloak tight around him.

"You must be from down in the Midlands where women talk out of turn. I meant how many after you?"

"About ten of them," Æthelric said.

"Out of turn?" Caitria began.

"Save it until we're inside the gate," I advised, afraid it would all unravel if Caitria started an argument with Æthelhere.

"Draw blood?" Æthelhere asked, in no hurry now, prepared to show us who had the keys to the gate.

"Subtract two for certain," Æthelric told him, "and maybe a third, and you still have too many, and there's worse news yet."

"What news?" Æthelhere stood back from the parapet and loosened his cloak.

"He's joined a couple hundred Picts."

Æthelhere stepped out of sight. Caitria seethed, but before she could say anything I put a hand on her arm. She gave me a look that would have glazed a pot, but she held her tongue.

In a moment the gate started to open, and Caitria leaned forward and swung it wider, urging her horse through. Æthelric and I followed her in. Æthelhere was standing beside a flight of stone steps; he closed the gate after us and threw the bar into place.

It was a wealthy place by the standards of eighth-century real estate, six or eight enclosed hectares, comparable to a small Danish settlement. It even had a hall. The Engs had acquired a taste for Roman rectangles, and they laid out their earthworks quartered by streets, with their halls in the center, running east to west.

The freehold was built on the site of a Roman camp, and the Engs had reengineered the wall and ditch. Wherever those Romans put down for the night, they threw up a wall and dug a ditch and set outposts along the main approaches. Paranoid camp discipline for paranoid times, but a lesson these Engs had learned.

In its day the fortification would have billeted a legion; now it was a village. Most of the buildings were timber and plaster instead of wattle and daub, and four long houses flanked the hall with a warren of smaller cottages behind, all built on stone foundations pried from the roadbed. I reckoned between three and four hundred people lived there, and nearly as many sheep and cattle.

We rode over to the stable and dismounted. There were eight stalls to a side and hay and equipment lofts looking down on a middle alley paved with Roman stone. A small fire threw shadows from the forge. The open back door gave out onto a paddock and fenced area. A livery man was waiting for us inside. He was wrapped up against the chill, but I could see he had Æthelric's wide shoulders, and he was short and heavy through the chest, clearly a brother.

He took the horses' reins. "Bad night on the road, eh, Æthelric?"

"Had better," Æthelric acknowledged. "I found Hengest up the Chevoit, meeting with Lothian Picts."

"Bluefaces?"

"Blue as Wodan's balls," he said. "I'd be dead if it weren't for these two. I met them at the circle bog. This is Bran and Caitria. My brother Æthelred."

"Well met," Æthelred said.

"Come on." Æthelric turned to us. "We'll find Æthelwulf in the hall warming his old bones."

Æthelric helped me wrestle the trunks off the packhorse, making a face when he pulled three arrows out of the wood. I opened a trunk and took out the edged weapons, hesitating to leave the hoard bags unguarded. There was a lot of silver in the trunk, and we needed it all, but those sacks came to about two stone apiece, and I couldn't carry them. I slipped a small bag into my belt and closed the lid.

The fog distorted the sound of our steps in the paved

courtyard. There was a single window above the doorway of the hall, and the sound of voices and clatter of jugs and plates floated out on the light from the hearth fire. The door was carved with zoomorphic figures, and the faces of gripping beasts looked out from the grain of the wood. I handed Caitria the scramasax as Æthelric lifted the door latch.

The hall was a single large room, about thirty yards wide and fifteen deep, with the benches running down each wall, facing a raised central hearth. The high seat was framed by timbers inscribed in the Anglo-Saxon futhark, the runetree of ten or fifteen generations of Æthelwulf's, together with footnotes about their potency, strength, wisdom, and good looks.

Shields, decorated in the geometric patterns and primary colors the Engs favored, hung from the rafters; stag antlers and the tusks of boars and the tanned hides of bears and wild oxen covered the walls behind the high seat and decorated the posts that supported the loft. Three hawks perched on the outspread arms of a hawktree and behind them a ring mail shirt hung in a frame. Tapestries depicting the deeds of all the clan leaders of Æthelwulf's line covered the wall. Racks of boar spears stood on either side of the door. Hunting and the martial arts would be hot topics of conversation in this joint.

The hall was half full of men and women, round the hearth or on the benches, hustling back and forth from the pantry, or grunting as they stacked firewood at each end of the hearth, where they were getting ready to lay a new log, a great trunk as big around as a fat man's middle and eight or ten feet long. A log like that would take days to burn, and while a couple of women scraped out the ashes of the last log, others laid kindling out on the bare stones between the firedogs to make a bed for the next. It'd be a warm night in the hall when that monster took off.

An old woman swept the floor with a rhythmic swish of broom on stones. She was so old I reckoned it was all she could contribute, and she swept with a rhythm perfected over better than half a century and a vacant look under white eyebrows. It was the first hall I'd seen since Clontarf, not counting the one I'd visited under less congenial circumstances during the Severn vik.

There was a quarter of a beef on a spit over a cooking

fire, and the smell of baked bread combined with the aroma
of beef and the sweet smell of unwashed humans to make
a broth as thick as the fog outside, nearly visible in the last
thin light of day filtering through the open windows high
up on either end of the building. If I'd closed my eyes, I'd
have sworn I was home. There was a pile of dogs in the
corner, and they were the first to notice us, poking heads
out of the heap of brown and black fur and sniffing the air
disinterestedly.

"You Engs live pretty well," I observed to Caitria into
the silence that fell over the hall just a second after they
noticed us.

One of the men sitting on the raised stones of the hearth
looked our way. "It's no secret it suits us better than living
poorly," he said.

When he stood up, I could see he was the father of Æthelric, Æthelhere, and Æthelred, and at least six more of
them, all with the same shoulders and chest, just different
editions of the same genetic pattern. His white hair was
gathered back into a braid, and his beard was winter fox
white. Intelligent eyes looked out of his red, seamed face.
His arms were heavily muscled, and his legs were a little
bowed; wrapped in wool pants and high boots, they disappeared under his knee-length tunic at a divergent angle.

"Where'd you pick up these two drowned kittens,
Æthelric?"

"They picked me up at the circle bog," he said. "I found
Hengest up the Chevoit, and they chased me until I ran
into these two. We rode through them and came home."

"I'm Æthelwulf. Well come to Ælfholm."

"This is Caitria, and I'm Bran; we're bound for Luel."

"Your woman?"

You'd have thought those Engs had gotten out of bed
that morning and agreed to piss her off; they couldn't have
done a better job if they'd planned it. That's how it was
for a looking woman in those days: even the way she stood
made people defensive, made them want to explain her in
some familiar way. I took a deep breath, and she didn't
keep me waiting.

"I'm nobody's woman," she instructed Æthelwulf in a
tone I was certain he wasn't used to hearing from the fe-
males of Ælfholm. "You must not think much of women if
you think we're property."

"More costly than property," Æthelwulf said ruefully.

I shook my head and turned to leave. If we hurried, the son in the stable wouldn't have the horses bedded down yet, and we could get back on the road ahead of the Picts. There was no point staying where Caitria was going to be insulted because it wouldn't be long before she told them what she thought, and who could predict where *that* would end?

I put my hand on her shoulder as she was about to respond and nodded toward the door. "There's no use hanging round here. You'll just kill one of them, and we'll have to run for it, so we may as well run for it now before we're trapped where we're not wanted."

Before she could answer there was a commotion, and we looked up to see the old woman beating Æthelwulf about the head and shoulders with the business end of her broom, which wasn't made of manicured straw but a bundle of willow shoots, and not a pleasant thing to be whipped with.

"I taught you better manners than to insult strangers asking for a night's hospitality." She connected at about every third word, speaking in a rhythm that matched her stroke, and Æthelwulf retreated round the fire pit with his arms up to protect his head. "You whelp," she scolded, pursuing him. "You clod-tongued, ignorant-of-courtesy, runt-pig, weasle-faced Walloon."

"Back off, Mother, I was only japing her a bit."

Caitria's anger turned to laughter as Æthelwulf's mother took him to task. "Have at him, Gamma," she cheered on the old woman. "They forget their manners when they grow beards."

Everyone was laughing now, and Æthelwulf, out of range on the other side of the hearth, dropped his hands, laughing too. His mother stopped chasing him, gave him a last blighting look, and then turned away, holding her broom like a spear. She walked over to us.

"Your pardon," she said. "He always was witless." Æthelwulf's mother was too old to reckon. Her hair was whiter than snow, and there was no telling what color it had been. Her tanned face, seamed as a riverbed, looked more like upholstery than skin.

"I see who runs the place," Caitria said. "No harm done."

"Æthelwulf runs the place," his mother said in a low

voice that only Caitria and I could hear, "but I run Æthelwulf."

"All is as it should be," Caitria said.

The old woman estimated me in a brief glance, as if she'd just noticed me standing there, but it was a strong enough look to make me blink.

"Who're you?" she asked Caitria.

"My partner," Caitria said.

"I'm Bran," I told her.

"Are you?"

"From Ireland," I added, although she didn't seem interested.

"I took you for a foreigner," she said. "What happened to you?"

"Nothing but Picts," I said.

"You're a poor liar," the old woman observed.

"Do you always call your guests liars?"

"Only when they lie." Æthelwulf's mother sounded pretty damned sure of herself, and while she was holding that broom I wasn't going to dispute her. Still, I wasn't *that* bad a liar.

Æthelwulf walked over as his mother finished putting me in my place, and she turned and pushed him aside.

"Sorry if I offended," he told Caitria. "We've an easy way about us here, and I forget strangers don't know what's meant."

"No harm."

"Come to the fire and talk about outlaws." Æthelwulf said, offering Caitria his hand. She took it and descended the two steps to the floor of the hall, and I followed them over to the warm stones beside the hearth.

"These are my sons: Æthelstein, Æthelstan, Æthelwold, Æthelbald, Æthelheard, and Æthelberht. Æthelred's in the stable, and Æthelhere's watching the gate. You've met Æthelric already." They nodded through their father's introduction, smiling his smile and laughing his laugh like a spectral chorus of Æthelwulf's youth.

"And my daughters: Branwyn, Blodwyn, Bronwyn, and Aud."

They gave us dry blankets, and three of the daughters began to dry Caitria's hair with soft wool towels. They were blond and clear-eyed, and their faces glowed with that limpid Eng paleness. I could see they were ordinary women, but Aud was near Caitria's age and a looking woman too.

Æthelwulf and his sons crowded round.

"What were the robbers like?" he asked, to start the debriefing.

"Threadbare," I began, and told him what we'd seen.

"Where'd you find them?" Æthelwulf turned to his son.

"Up the Stoat Crags," Æthelric said. "In that valley 'tother side."

Everyone nodded, familiar with the geography.

"Hengest, taken up with Picts," Æthelwulf said with disgust. His sons nodded agreement. "Pathetic," the old man shook his head.

"You know him?" I asked.

"Grew up with Hengest, fought the Straithclyde Welsh with him when Eadbert was king. Afterward we went our ways. He came back a few years ago and took up robbery as a trade. They steal a sheep now and then, but he mostly stays far enough away we don't run into him. Once or twice a year I help the king's reeve hunt him in the Chevoit. Good excuse for a ride, and we never get close."

"He's with the Picts," observed one of the older sons.

"Maybe he's devised a use for them," Æthelwulf speculated.

"Maybe Hengest's just stupid," Æthelstein said. "Since Æthelred married Offa's bitch, Northumbrian silver's minted into Mercian pennies. He ought to go south where the coins are minted."

"A smart dog knows his own territory best, Æthelstein. Even if the territory's poor, he's pissed on all the bushes." Æthelwulf scratched his beard. "His head'd be poled in a week if he went south, and he's wise enough to know *that*."

"Where's the fyrd when you need them?" I complained. "You'd think Æthelred would keep his marches clear of wolfsheads."

Caitria moved over beside me and listened to the end of the conversation. Her hair was beginning to shine in the warmth.

"Æthelred's interests only go so far as Offa's," Æthelwulf said dismissively.

I'd assumed from the way he'd summarily dealt with Orm's fleet that law and order was an item of particular

interest to Offa of Mercia, hence to Æthelred if I understood things correctly.

"Is business for a wolfshead so poor round here?"

"They have trouble stealing a nun's ransom. Hengest's
troop worked for Offa against the Welsh, and when the
dyke was finished the pay master shorted them in the last
payout. Hengest blamed Offa, and he's been raving about
foreign oppression since he came back. Bloody patriot all
of a sudden. Has no matter," Æthelwulf concluded with a
shrug. "He won't bother us in here, Picts or not. Æthelberht, take a couple of your brothers to Luel. Have Wulfgar bring the fyrd."

There was a scurrying as Æthelberht selected a couple
of siblings and the three of them went out the door. That
was good news as far as I was concerned. I wanted to get
back to Clontarf and see how it'd all turned out; I didn't
want to spend any more time in Northumbria.

"We'll be gone tomorrow," I told him.

"Not a bit of it." Æthelwulf shook his head. "I've got to
make up for the poor beginning: it's bed and board for you
two. I owe you for helping Æthelric. Otherwise he'd be
dead. We'll give you dry clothing and a meal and board
and bed as long as you want, at least until the rain stops."

Caitria stood up and followed Æthelwulf's daughters.

"Can you eat?" Æthelwulf asked.

"Hungry as fire," I said.

"Get a horn," Æthelwulf ordered. "Now the outer man's
warmed, we'll warm the inner. Æthelbald, fetch Bran some
dry clothes."

They brought me a frothing horn of brown beer, and I
put it away in one breath and belched a sweet-tasting belch
that I could roll around on my tongue and swallow again.

"Excellent," I said, wiping my mouth. Praising the beer's
always a good way to start out with an Eng.

"Then have another and tell us about yourself."

I peeled my wet clothes off and wrapped in the blanket
until Æthelbald came back with a dry outfit under his arm.

"It's a long story," I said, hoping I could elude a ritual
exchange of life histories. I wasn't in the mood for socializ-
ing with these farmers. I knew Æthelwulf's autobiography
would include rhapsodic celebrations of cattle and sheep
breeding, killing animals in the forest, and sowing barley
and rye: noble enough pastimes but not the kind of narra-

tive I wanted to endure. And *my* story was littered with unbelievable facts or those better left unsaid.

"Tell away," he said, settling back to listen.

So much for that ploy; there was nothing for it now but to tell Æthelwulf the abridged and sanitized G-rated version of my recent life and hard times. A simple tale of peaceful commerce interrupted by the Hwiccan fyrd, who'd misunderstood our intentions on the Severn, and the Northumbrian coast watch, who'd misunderstood them as we sailed to the Orkneys. And, of course, my stay on Lindisfarne.

Lindisfarne was a name that got their attention, and when I told them I'd been there the day of the raid, they all started asking questions, too fast to understand. The sacking of Lindisfarne was still big news two years after the ashes had cooled. Æthelwulf's clan was pretty knowledgeable about the place. They'd been there for Cuthbert's Feast the year before the burning, and they wanted to know were the old boy's bones really safe, were the buildings gutted, was all the gold from the church carried off?

So I had to detour into the monastic experience long enough to satisfy their curiosity about the condition of the physical plant and the body count, which gave me an opportunity to keep my word to Godwine and unload the story of Bede's return, which they listened to with respectful silence. But they had some interesting news to tell me in return.

"The Danes burned Jarrow last year," Æthelwulf said, "ravaged the east coast until the fyrd caught up to them at Wearmouth. A storm broke their fleet when they tried to escape."

"They're moving out of the north," one of the sons added, nodding his head. "What's the matter?"

I had no idea, but I knew better than to open my mouth on the subject. If there was *ever* a time to practice losing the look of a Dane, that was it. By that time Æthelbald was back with dry clothes that more or less fit—men's tailoring in Ælfholm ran to barrel chests and long arms.

After I was comfortable, I started to get interested in the telling, and picked again up with the burial of the bodies and our departure before the fyrd got there, but not why, and they were with me all the way, but when I told them the story of Gaefburnnah and the hoard, I could see they were skeptical.

Maybe it was a bad idea, but I had to tell someone: when you survive a fight with a wyrm, you want to let a few people know. There was no doubt I survived by accident, and I was pretty sure I'd used up all the wyrmluck I had any right to expect in one lifetime, however long it was going to be, but I still wanted to brag a little. Who wouldn't? I sure as shit wouldn't get much satisfaction bragging to Caitria.

And anyway, Æthelwulf and I had reciprocal duties now that hospitality had been offered and accepted: I was obliged that whatever I told him be the truth, and he was obliged to believe me, or act like he did, but it was obvious he thought I was bullshitting him about the wyrm. With Picts on the prowl I wanted active assistance out of Æthelwulf, not tight-jawed Northumbrian cordiality. I took out the small sack of gemstones.

"I had these from the wyrm's bed," I said, spilling out the stones onto the folded blanket with a chromatic detonation of gem-refracted firelight: reds, greens, blues, yellows, whites. Those Engs gaped. I picked up four of the stones and handed them to Æthelwulf. Now, Æthelwulf had no doubt heard a few stories in his time, but when he saw the gems, his expression changed to a look of respectful surprise.

"It's little enough for a night's shelter," I told him, hoping to put us on a fee-for-service basis and bribe our way out of his hospitality.

"I can't take those," he said. "We're not a hostelry."

"Take these for your daughters, then. A gift from a grateful man who'd be dead if you hadn't taken us in."

He pushed my hand aside a second time and smiled. "There's nothing here so worth a handful of gems," he insisted. "And stones from a wyrm's hoard, who knows what power they have?"

"It's in your power to give us another night's life," I pointed out. "It's payment in kind."

"He's right," Æthelwulf's mother said, leaning on her broom. "Take the stones. If that cow flop about the wyrm's true, he'll never miss them, and it would explain his surly mood. What's a hoard to one that hasn't 's alms to one that has."

I thought my mood had been fairly cordial under the circumstances, but she'd sensed the truth. Æthelwulf opened his hand and I dropped the jewels into his palm. He looked at them sparkling amid his calluses and then closed his fingers.

The sons of Æthelwulf gave a shout and welcomed me into the bosom of the family exchequer with claps on the back and bearish pushes and shoves meant to convey acceptance. I was surrounded by the flower of English yeomanry: the boys who'd come through later at Agincourt and Crecy, who'd shove off for the crusades following mad religious visionaries and cynical Knights Templar, who'd fight the Franks for a hundred years or thirty (what's your pleasure?)—profoundly stupid boys, in other words, who were willing to march off to whatever war the Bretwalda had going at the moment.

Then Caitria came back, and I got another look at what a shapeshifter she could be. She was wearing a tunic of white homespun and a russet mantle around her shoulders to keep off the chill, fastened with two brooches. She smiled shyly, as if embarrassed to be out of her travel clothes and dressed like a woman. I didn't know why; it was clear that she was meant to wear those clothes in a place like Æthelwulf's hall.

Æthelwulf took a long look. "You say she's not your woman?"

"We're partners, that's all."

"You're slow enough to watch sheep, aren't you?"

Æthelbald nodded agreement.

"Make her your woman," Æthelwulf said, slapping me on the shoulder in a gesture of roguish paternal admonition that jarred my teeth. "If she looks like that and can use a yew bow, what more do you want?"

What I wanted was to get home and find out what had happened, not cool my heels in an earthwork, waiting out the rain.

"We've each got our wyrds," I said, relying on a simple answer I reckoned he'd accept. "For the moment they're braided together."

"We make our own wyrd," Æthelwulf said.

That was a jolt, hearing my own words come from his

lips, and I looked over at Caitria, thought of Frydys, shook
my head, and raised the replenished horn to my lips.

"I might as well be drunk as this way," I said.

We pigged out on beef and bread, fowl and boiled greens,
fish, black rice, cheese, brown beer, mead, and cold rainwater; it was a time when cholesterol was the sound you made
when you cleared your throat. I was deluding myself about
paying for our keep; we were the guests of honor for rescu-
ing Æthelric. Caitria and I sat opposite the high seat, beside
which Æthelwulf kept an empty place and a full cup poured
for his dead wife's ghost. His sons and daughters and their
husbands and wives, and some of the older granddaughters
and grandsons and their wives and husbands, filled the
benches, singing and laughing into the night.

There were 489 Engs living inside Ælfholm: men and
women of all ages, children and babes at the breast. Of
that number, Æthelwulf's household contained 62 people,
not counting servants and slaves. There were 272 men at
arms, and 73 of them were blood relatives of Æthelwulf's
line. But food, beer, and the hearth fire did more to allay
my anxiety about Picts than the thought of so many blades.
When the trenchers were cleared, they brought out the
flutes and the harps and the tambourines.

After a few more beers, Æthelric stood up and gave us
the whole of his adventure, and one of Æthelwulf's grand-
daughters started to improvise accompaniment on the harp
as her uncle spoke. That girl had a gift: she could make
her harp sound like wind in the trees, a headlong run over
the moor, or a hard rain on stones.

The feasting broke up before midnight. Ælfholm was a
working farmstead, and everyone had day jobs. They'd be
rested and ready for labor come dawn. In Clontarf, the
thanes were prone to while away the hours getting drunk,
fighting, or hunting, three activities they regarded as an
essential part of their training regimen. Some of Sygtrygg's
men had farms round Clontarf, but they spent little time
there, unless some agrarian emergency demanded their
attention.

Æthelwulf's clan was composed of professional farmers,
men who could turn their hands to whatever came along:
hunters, coopers, fletchers, carpenters, smiths, weavers,
cooks, accountants, plowmen, reapers, and wrights. When

you're that diversified into areas of heavy physical labor, you need at least six hours of sleep a night, or five hours' sleep and an hour of great sex.

I knew it was going to be six hours of sleep for me as Æthelstein led us to a small loft in the building where Æthelwulf's two oldest sons kept with their families. There was room enough in the loft for our gear and blankets, but, shitfaced as I was, it took me a few minutes to scale the ladder. When Caitria'd handed everything up and followed after, Æthelstein reached the flame to her oil lamp and went back down the hallway to his bed, where his warm wife was waiting in the warm covers.

"Is Clontarf like this?" she asked, talkative with all the beer.

"Smaller," I said.

"So you're a wealthy lot in Ireland?"

"You're as wealthy as me. All you've got to do is shovel it out of the hoard room."

Now that I was out of society again, there was no need for pretense, but since she wanted the talk, I'd play along.

"Where's your homestead?"

"Northeast of Llangorse Lake," she said.

"You could improve it, expand the buildings, throw up a hall."

"It's nothing but cinders," she said.

"What happened?"

"It burned down. Do you feel anything strange about this place?" she asked changing the subject.

"Is this a riddle?"

"No, a question."

"I think you feel too much," I told her shortly, rolling over and making it plain I was ready for sleep.

"You think too much and feel too little," she replied. "That's what you learned at Lindisfarne."

"That's not where I learned it," I mumbled into my blanket, thinking how pointless the conversation was, how pointless everything was since I'd killed the wyrm.

Next morning, Caitria and I strolled into the hall about terce, looking for something to eat, and we found Æthelwulf and all his progeny in the middle of a free-form argument. Æthelstein, the oldest, was on his feet shouting when we came in the door, and judging from the body language, half the group was on his side. Æthelwulf was red-faced and nose to nose with his son across the trestle boards.

When Æthelwulf saw us, he cut off the argument with a gesture across his throat and said, "Hengest's followed you here with his Picts and camped out across the bridge. They're roasting the homefield boar."

"How many are there?"

"Two hundred plus, the cheeky bastards. I'll show Hengest who he's dealing with. I've only suffered him this long for old times' sake, and now he comes with Picts at his back, and he thinks he can stuff his face with my pork and give me orders in my homefields."

There it was, the reason Æthelwulf wanted to go forth and do battle before the fyrd arrived: Hengest had insulted him. It was personal. I reckoned that Æthelstein realized the craziness of leaving the earthwork before the fyrd reinforced them and was trying to talk the old man out of this scheme.

"If anyone kills this dog it ought to be me," Æthelstein shouted. "You stay back and watch from the wall. It's my right as oldest."

So much for that theory: they *all* wanted a piece of Hengest.

"You're only oldest because your mother wouldn't let me expose you, you looked so puny when you were born," Æthelwulf shouted into his son's face.

"Well, she didn't, and I'm claiming my rights."

"I'm not dead yet, and not likely to be anytime soon, so don't demand your heritage until I'm under a mound."

"Æthelwulf," I shouted. "What's the hurry? The fyrd will be here, won't they? Let's see these Picts and outlaws before you decide anything."

"We'll go to the wall, then," Æthelwulf said, and we all went out of the hall and across the enclosure. The fog had thinned enough so we could see groups of Picts huddled round fires out of bow and sling range across the ditch. Out by the Roman roadbed, a larger group was clustered round a cooking fire. They'd chopped up the mark post for fuel, and they were roasting the homefield boar on a hasty spit made from a wagon tongue.

Small watch fires surrounded the earthwork. The good guys wouldn't win this fight unless Æthelwulf waited for the fyrd.

"We'll over there, feed the ravens, and back by lunch," Æthelwulf promised with a two-fingered gesture of contempt for the armed force on the other side of the ditch.

I thought about those towns we'd tossed on the Severn and the White Danes at Lindisfarne, and I realized I was about to round out my education as a Viking by being *inside* an earthwork under assault. Then I thought, why not buy some time? The hack and the gold were only travel money, anyway; I just wanted to get back to Clontarf, find out my wyrd, and get on with it.

"I'll just give them the wyrm's hack," I said to Caitria after I'd drawn her aside. "What do we care? It's not worth losing blood over. They'll take it and think they've won, and while they're congratulating themselves, the fyrd will get here."

"You nearly died to get that silver," Caitria said, "and you want to give it up without a fight?"

"There's a couple of bags of loot here," I reminded her, "and a mound we'll need a wagon to carry back at Ravenshill Moor. What matter if we give up some hack? We'll likely get it back anyway."

"You killed a wyrm for it," Caitria said with a low vehemence that Æthelwulf couldn't hear. "And I walked through rats for it, not to mention listening to two years of your nose whistling, *that's* what matter. How'll Frydys take it if you come home without silver? Who'll believe your story if you've got nothing to show?"

It wasn't an idea whose time had come. Every Eng I knew had his or her back up, and they weren't in the mood for sober and reasoned bribery. I'd insult them if I made an issue of common sense at this volatile juncture. Now that it was a matter of honor and insult, there was nothing for it but to spill blood.

"Have things in the world come so low that guests throw hospitality in their host's teeth?" Æthelwulf asked through rhetorically clenched teeth of his own, as if he wanted to be sure I didn't try to jam any more hospitality down his throat. Apparently my discussion with Caitria hadn't been as discreet as I'd thought. His sons murmured assent. The moment was turning ugly.

"It's a guest's duty to keep his host well," I said. "And I'd be failing that if I let you fight without offering alternatives. A hoard's naught compared to a host's life, and it's a poor guest who'd say so."

Æthelwulf's sons looked at the ground and shifted on their feet, sensing I'd turned it round, somehow, but not quite getting it.

"I mistook you," Æthelwulf said after a moment, in a low menacing voice that indicated he was now even more eager to ventilate some renegade wolfsheads and Picts. "But don't worry. It won't take much to squash those ticks. They'll scatter when the gate opens; Hengest won't be able to keep 'em in line."

There it was. They were going to kick some ass before noon and then get back to farming and let the ravens police up the mess.

"Fetch my shirt," Æthelwulf said to his youngest, Æthelheard, who hotfooted it back to the hall for the ring mail. "Arm up and meet back here. Æthelstein, get your lot ready with their bows. Bran, you can fight where you choose."

What a break for me. I'd hoped to hear him say I could choose whether to fight; for a minute there, I was afraid I'd have to sit this one out where I wasn't in danger of getting killed.

"The things you saved out from the wyrm will come in handy now," Caitria said as we came down off the rampart.

She stopped someone and asked directions to the fletcher, and I hurried back to the stable and rooted through the chests. The scales and the teeth were on the bottom. I knew what Caitria had in mind. We were going to mount those homers on as many shafts as she could find and snipe from the battlements. Artillery's a good branch of the combat arms; less chance of a serious maiming back there if you stay alert. Caitria came in with an armload of shafts as I was closing up the chest, and she spread out a blanket and dropped them in the middle of the wool.

"Twine?" she asked.

I found a spool and sat across from her with the pile of shafts between us on the blanket. I put the bag of teeth beside them and took up my knife.

Caitria spread the mouth of the bag and shook the teeth onto the wool. She handed a shaft and a tooth across the blanket, and I fit them together. It was as if a socket had been machined into the base: it slipped just as tightly into place. I wrapped it with an inch of twine and tied it off. Once I got the rhythm, I was turning out four a minute. Outside we could hear everyone reporting back under arms. Dogs barked, and someone went by with the hawktree; the three hawks, balanced on spread wings, looked like they were just as anxious as everyone else to draw blood.

As I finished each arrow, Caitria picked it up and examined my work, sighting along the shaft and spinning it slowly in her fingers.

She nodded and set them aside "Passable."

"Sorry they don't measure up," I apologized.

"Time's short." Caitria grinned, letting me know her standards were relaxed.

I examined one of the scales. It was was nearly weightless and flexible in my hands, smooth on one side, about a quarter of a round shield in size, thick as a finger.

"They'll protect you from wounds," she said.

"They didn't do Gaefburnnah much good," I reminded her.

"The blade absorbed its power," she said, "and turned it against the wyrm."

The scale seemed to be made of tightly woven fibers, resilient strands that I could barely disturb with my thumbnail, and which stopped the point of my knife and came back like grass after a footstep. I slipped it into my tunic, rough side in so it would grip the cloth. Caitria positioned another against my back, and I cinched up my belt and walked around, moving my shoulders to shrug them more or less into place.

Then I strung my bow and drew empty a few times, but the scales conformed to my body and didn't interfere with the movement.

"Let's go," I said. "We should be able to point these arrows downrange and have a cuppa while they do their work."

"Not so easily," Caitria said as we went outside. The fog had thickened, and it was hard to see across the street. Shadows floated by carrying weapons and shields, and we had a hard time pushing our way through. Æthelwulf stood on the rampart above the gate as his troops formed up below.

"Why not?"

"They'll stay out of range once they see what's happening."

"Out of range? I thought these arrows always hit their targets and always came back to the owner."

"When you're in range," Caitria said as we found the bottom of the stairs.

"Then what's the point?" I demanded. "I live forever unless I get killed? I have a hundred magic arrows that only work if I'm in range? What else should I know?"

"There's no time to teach you," she said.

Far down toward the end of the street we could hear women chanting and singing. Below, the men of Æthelwulf's clan were practicing threatening gestures with the assortment of spears, bows, and blades they were carrying, and lifting their throwing axes into the air. They'd gotten their shields down from the rafters and they were ready to hack. Æthelwulf's youngest son, nearly buckled by the weight of his father's ring mail, struggled through the crowd. As soon as it came to hand, Æthelwulf shrugged it on.

"Æthelwulf," I said. "I have a plan."

Æthelwulf worked his shoulders around under the ring mail and turned to give me his attention. His look communicated a certain desire not to hear any more talk of bribery. I didn't disappoint him. I cut right to the chase. In the eighth century the famous Eng sense of what was sporting didn't extend much beyond killing your horse if it broke a leg, and then they'd eat it for dinner. When it came to combat, they preferred to enjoy overwhelming superiority in numbers and arms, favorable terrain, the approval of their gods, the sun at their backs, and an inferior enemy riddled with dysentery. And who can deny those are pretty good conditions for going into battle? Caitria shook back a corner of the blanket and a hundred wyrm's teeth bristled out of the crook of her arm.

"Magic arrows," I said.

It turns out no one can resist magic arrows: a superior weapon system will always find a home. Æthelwulf's yellow smile spread through his white beard, and he laid his hand lightly on the points. "Æthelstein, get your men over here."

Æthelstein's yewmen reported on command and drew five arrows each. "We've got to pull them up to the edge of the ditch," I said.

Æthelwulf mused on it as they slipped the arrows into their belt quivers and clustered round to hear the plan. I looked over the rampart. The other side of the ditch was ten yards away, but the fog made everything opaque another three feet beyond. There could be a thousand Picts out there, for all I knew. The bridge was a brown rectangle floating on cotton. I turned back to Æthelwulf.

"Can you get Hengest to fight a duel?"

Æthelwulf's face clouded with a frostiness that indicated he could, and before I could say anything else, he walked over to the edge of the rampart and cupped his hands to his mouth.

"Hengest," he shouted into the fog.

We all moved to face beyond the earthwork, pressing up against the timber. I drew Æthelstein aside as we waited for Hengest to answer. "If we can draw them up to the ditch while Hengest and Æthelwulf fight, we can cut them down where they stand. They'll have to get close to watch, and we can get a hundred before they reckon it."

He smiled and shook his head, directing nine of his men to the left side of the gate and the other nine to the right.

"Hengest," Æthelwulf shouted again.

"What is it, Æthelwulf?" Hengest was a resonant baritone, and his voice carried through the fog. It was the voice that had offered us our lives for silver in the standing stones.

"Only a scum-sucking pig fucker would work for Picts."

"It's time to be a power," Hengest called back. "When I break the fyrd, I can hold everything north of the wall. Then the thegns will rise up against Æthelred."

"Æthelred would break you in a day, but I'm going to do it first."

"I always knew you were Æthelred's dog."

"You and Æthelred are one to me," Æthelwulf shouted, and then he brought up a mouthful of phlegm and hawked it into the moat with a splat. "But you're on my threshold and he's not."

Hengest laughed, and we could hear laughter out in the fog, disembodied and strange, giving us a clue about the topography and the disposition of the enemy.

"I've more men than you," Hengest said. "And I intercepted your sons. No help's coming from Luel."

Æthelwulf had played that card once or twice himself. "Show me their heads," he shouted back.

There were two heavy plops and a couple of heads rolled out of the fog. One of them teetered on the edge and rolled into the ditch with a little splash. Ripples fled from it, and it floated facedown. We waited, but there weren't any more heads inbound.

"Can anyone tell?" Æthelwulf asked, and everyone leaned forward to see if they could recognize the head that had come to a stop on its left cheek a foot from the bridge.

"They could be anyone's heads, or they could be our lads and one got away." Æthelwulf gripped the edge of the rampart and shrugged, unable to decide.

"I'll have *your* head before midday," Æthelwulf shouted.

"Picts will be raping your women before that." Hengest laughed.

"Meet me on the bridge here," Æthelwulf demanded.

"What can I win?" Hengest wanted to know.

"If you kill me, my sons will join you," Æthelwulf said. "And you can have my daughters."

After a minute's quiet, a figure materialized on the other side of the bridge. Almost immediately the fog hid him again.

"You're lying," Hengest called out.

"Sniveling butt-fucker," Æthelwulf snorted. "Coward."

"All right, then. We'll fight."

Æthelwulf took Æthelstein by the shoulders. "Don't shoot your arrows until I've killed him," he instructed. I suppose it was something of a concession to fairness, but I could tell from the look on Æthelwulf's face he thought it was more than they deserved. Æthelbald was in front of the gate at the head of 250 Engs who were shouting like madmen and waving ash spears, axes, swords, and a scattering of farm implements which all seemed to be designed for disemboweling some large animal. There were twenty-four words in the language of the Engs for the act of disemboweling. It was a language of nuance.

Æthelwulf swung his blade a few times to limber up his arm. "Let's go, then," he said, taking up his shield.

They undid the bar and the gate swung wide. Æthelwulf stepped onto the bridge, carrying fifty-five pounds of ring mail, a fourteen-pound oak shield, four pounds of iron helmet, just over three pounds of pattern-welded steel, and a thousand pounds of righteous indignation, and his sons and armed retainers pressed up behind him, stopping at the threshold and clattering their blades on their shields. Æthelwulf walked to the middle of the span and kicked at the dirt underfoot to get a feel for the available traction. It was clear Hengest would pay.

We moved into place at the rampart, keeping our bows out of sight below the timber. Hengest stepped onto the bridge, and they moved toward each other, crouching a little behind their shields, their steel poised for the first blows. Hengest feinted and Æthelwulf closed with him, and before you could say "Let us reason together," their pattern-welded blades came together with a sound like hell's cloister bell: the din of steel edge against iron spine or boss or rim.

They made pass after pass, one time trying for a low-sweeping stroke that would hack a leg and the next slashing at exposed neck or uncovered chest. After ten minutes the shield bosses were dented and the rims hammered out of shape; splintered wood spun away with each blow. Across the ditch, shadowy figures pressed forward into the edge of visibility.

They fought without speaking, intent on the kill without sentimental conversation about the old days. Those two knew what they were there for, and it wasn't existential inquiry. They were men with a lifetime of muscle memory to draw on, but they were old men now, and they lacked the energy to use it for longer than ten minutes at full speed. Their endurance was shot; soon they were moving like drunks in knee-deep water; finally their blows took seconds to land, tracing slow arcs through the air, parabolas of iron and exhaustion which their battered shields came up to meet with a dreamlike slothfulness.

The Picts spread for ten yards on either side of the bridge, crowding closer in two tight ranks so they could all see.

Hengest and Æthelwulf panted circles around one another. Their faces were red under their beards, their eyes wide, and the corded tendons in their necks quivering with the effort of a full-bore duel. Hengest's footwork was suffering from oxygen depletion and hunger, and Æthelwulf, better fed but sporting the additional weight of a ring-mail shirt, was tripping over his own feet on the uneven surface.

Finally, when neither one could lift blade or shield, they faced off, trying to get enough breath for speech, now that fighting had failed. Communication: the last refuge of the nackered.

"Æthelwulf," Hengest began in peroration, "I never wanted ..."

But we never heard what Hengest never wanted, because a queer look came over him and he clutched at his chest. His eyes bugged out, and he gasped for breath. He rubbed his right hand down his left arm, as if it were suddenly cold, and then he grabbed his ribs, took a step forward, and splashed onto his face in the mud. Old Hengest certainly had panache. Surprise ran through Æthelwulf's people like a breeze through dead leaves, and I nudged Æthelstein.

Æthelwulf walked over to Hengest and pushed his body with the toe of his boot. Hengest wasn't so dead as yesterday's fish, but he was as dead as we needed him to be to declare act one of this preprandial pissoff a victory.

Æthelwulf turned to face his clan and paused, reaching deep into his wordhoard.

"They slaughtered the homefield boar! Let's gut the fucks!" he bellowed, and a shout went up as the clan spilled forward onto the bridge. Twenty baying hounds followed behind. Someone released the hawks, and they disappeared with sharp cries into the fog. Two or three of the assault force were jostled into the ditch, which proved to be about ten feet deep and stocked with an ugly species of carp, sporting disgustingly large gray and brown scales and bellies the color of sour cream.

I drew the fletching back and let go at a Pict, not bothering to take close aim. That arrow was on its own, and if it knew its business, that's all there was to it. The important thing was to lay down a base of fire that would break their ranks. Working quickly, twenty yewmen can lay down five volleys in twenty seconds, and we were working very quickly, letting those arrows go into the fog in five ordered flights, as the screams of bitten Picts were subsumed into the sounds of general rout on the other side of the ditch.

But even in the confusion a few Picts got their arrows off. One shaft flew out of the fog like a hummingbird, disappearing overhead into the freehold. Then one hit me square in the chest, knocking the wind out of me. I staggered back a few steps, and another one hit me two fingers away from the first. I gasped for breath. Caitria grabbed the two shafts and pulled, jerking me off balance as the scale held them fast.

I never saw the third arrow coming, but my luck was mixed because even though my turning made a smaller target, the arrow managed to hit me anyway, missing both of the wyrm's scales and making a nasty cut across my spine and ribs. I shouted when I felt the punch and prick of the impact and dropped below the rampart.

"You're not immortal," Caitria shouted. "That could've been it."

"I thought I'd heal."

"Not from a fatal wound, you idiot. You die from a fatal wound, just like the wyrm. You won't die in bed. You better get it straight while your luck holds."

"Right," I agreed.

"No one told you to make yourself a target."

"Am I ever going to see the end of this?" I snarled.

"If you stay careless, you'll see the end of everything."

"Give it a rest. Since we met I've been trussed like a homefield boar at Yule, sealed in a mine, nearly eaten by a wyrm, slept for two years, and been shot by Picts."

"And you thought it'd be boring," she said.

Æthelstein was looking at us with his mouth hanging open. I doubt anything like our road show had come through Ælfholm before. The third arrow hung loose in my clothes, and I reached around to pull it out, but the barb caught the fabric. I tried to ease it out, but I lost patience and just ripped it away.

"Tore your new clothes too," Caitria said.

I probed around under my tunic and felt the wound. I was cut to the bone and bleeding, but my ribs had absorbed the impact. I unbuckled my belt and sat down. The scale lifted away from my chest, but the arrows refused to come out of the scale. The points had penetrated, and I felt warm blood on my belly from the cuts. I recognized two of the shafts I'd fired into the fog a few minutes before. I worked one around in a fast tight circle and pulled it away.

The wyrm-toothed arrows had returned as advertised, though I'd have preferred to find them growing out of Picts when the fighting was over. I pulled the other one out of the scale and handed it back to Caitria. The forward edge of the battle area had passed into the fog, and I wasn't sorry. I preferred to be in the rear as long as there were ninety-eight more wyrm-toothed arrows unaccounted for. All I had to do now was find them before they found me.

On the other side of the ditch, it sounded like there weren't enough wolfsheads or Picts to go round. Before I could get across the bridge, the remaining few were throwing down their weapons and begging for their lives, after which it only took a minute or two to finish them off. I watched the Engs practice all twenty-four different methods of evisceration. When Æthelwulf's people realized there wasn't enough enemy ass to go round, they began to impose a little order on the dogs, who were gathering round the homefield boar with unmistakable interest.

While Æthelwulf's sons were collecting the heads and stripping and gutting bodies, Caitria and I moved through the carnage retrieving arrows. Some had penetrated shields, some had passed completely through bodies, some had struck from the front and some from the rear, but each of those shafts had killed its man. Caitria added the arrows to the bundle as I gave them to her. We could hear Æthelbald complaining bitterly about how desperate the Picts were as he supervised the stripping of the dead. They'd evidently been experiencing bad harvests, chronic business reversals, and extended revenue shortfalls, and this combination of vitamin deficiency and poor fiscal management had persuaded them that invading Northumbria was the answer to their problems.

"Those dogs don't have two coins to rub together," he shouted.

"Fifteen missing," Caitria said, walking her fingers through the shafts in the crook of her arm like a bundle of long-stemmed flowers.

"They've got to be here somewhere," I said, staring into the fog.

Two men pushed a cart out of the fog heaped with shields, blades, spears, and other abandoned battlefield litter, and a quick look at their loot recovered six more shafts. It made me nervous to leave the remaining nine, but they were going to have to wait until the fog lifted. We wrapped the bundle tightly with two belts and went back to the earthwork. Æthelstein and Æthelheard were ahead of us on the bridge, bending under the weight of the homefield boar as they carried it back to finish cooking over the hearth fire.

Inside the wall, everyone was returning to his or her routine except for the two dozen wounded, who filed over to the hall where Gamma waited with her needle and thread. None of their wounds were serious, which was lucky for them. I stood apart while Caitria went for some of the wyrm's blood.

Thorfinn would approve of the trellis of cuts on my chest, but it was the conventional arrow that had done the most damage. The clotted edges of the wound had glued themselves to my shirt, and I had to be careful not to open the wound again as I pulled it away. I was congratulating myself on escaping so lightly when Gamma spied me and came over with her assistant, the looking daughter, Aud.

I shifted away at the thought of the old woman focusing her rude medical skills and diagnostic abilities on my wound, but she was there before I could get away, spitting on her fingertips and probing the gash roughly as I winced.

"Men are children," she muttered to Aud.

"Ease up, Gamma," I said. "The wound's just closed."

Then she pinched the meat on either side of the gash in her callused fingertips and pulled it slowly apart, an experience I've had only the once and don't want to repeat. When the wound was open again, Aud irrigated it with cold water and Gamma forced the edges together and produced a needle and thread from the folds of her clothing. Before I could decline, she began a line of whip stitches through the meat over my ribs and across my backbone, giving the flax a tug between each one. She tied off the thread and bit the needle free. Alban's technique seemed centuries ahead of its time compared to Gamma's.

"Good as new," she pronounced, wiping the blood away with a corner of her apron. A look of malicious enjoyment crossed her face before she went on to her next patient. "Soon you'll be as sweet-tempered as always."

When Caitria returned, I was still gritting my teeth at the pain of Gamma's surgery.

"Gamma sews a straight seam," Caitria said, examining the work. She dusted it with powdered wyrm's blood, and the pain went away. I went into the hall for a drink.

Æthelwulf was sitting in the high seat with his legs splayed out before him and his chin on his chest, in the grip of some kind of Anglo-Saxon postcombat funk, or just coming to terms with another of life's landmarks gone forever. He ignored offers of footstools, blankets, mead, meat, apples, and a steam bath that were tendered in a babble of concerned voices. I sat down by the fire while Caitria fetched a pitcher of water and a couple of cups. It looked like Æthelwulf and I were finally of a mood.

"If I hadn't taken the scales, I'd be dead," I said gratefully when Caitria poured us a drink.

"Maybe. Maybe you wouldn't have been hit. That's what wyrd is. We can't prepare for it."

I shook my head. "I can trace being here back through all the choices I've ever made. We make our own wyrds; the Norns don't make them for us."

"What if you'd drowned in the sea?"

"What if I'd never learned to swim?"

"What if the storm hadn't come up? What if the White Danes hadn't come? Those were two things you didn't make happen."

"Danes come. It's how you meet them that counts."

"I suppose we make our wyrd after death too?"

"If we still exist, we must still have choices."

"The priests say the choices we make in this life decide what happens in the next."

"Priests say a lot of things, but I notice they only do about half of them. If what we do in this life decides the next one for us, it's like holding you accountable for what you did as a child. Death's a thing we don't understand. Who says it's the end?

"I knew a man once who was dead a month and came back to milk his goats in the morning, the way he'd always done, and scared the shit out of his family. He didn't *have* to come back to milk the goats because of something he did when he was alive, it was just his habit.

"Bede came back to pay off a debt and take his friend's soul wherever Christians go. They either come back because they have to, or because they're homesick, or just because they can. That's why it's good to cut the runes well; ghosts have other things to do. You're not doing them any favors by cutting the binding runes badly."

It was just coming on noon, and I'd already been shot, seen two hundred men killed, had twenty-five stitches and a philosophical argument. I was thinking about breakfast and another couple of hours in the hay. But before I could accomplish those two desires, the doors burst open with a shout, and the clatter and racket of a troop of armed men spilled into the high-timbered hall. Æthelwulf and his sons, still spring-loaded and cranked on adrenaline, scrambled for their weapons, knocking sections of the trestle table to the floor and upsetting benches. Dogs yelped underfoot and bared their teeth. Women screamed and headed for the back entrance as one of Æthelwulf's sons ran the length of the hearth, sparks and ash flowering in his footsteps.

A horse stomped on the threshold stone, and then a mounted man surged into the hall, his horse coming up hard on its haunches as he brandished his sword over his head. The horse righted itself and stamped in the rushes. A wolfhound lunged forward and barked at its hocks and the horse snapped back a kick that killed it before the mutt even noticed.

"Æthelwulf," the horseman shouted. "You're saved." He pushed his hood off his face and my spine did a little twist as I saw that it *was* Æthelwulf. Then I looked at the high seat and saw Æthelwulf standing *there,* dressed in the same mail shirt, same helmet, hair the same, beard the same, sword identical, looking at himself on the horse.

"Wulfgar," he shouted, "you're late. We've killed all the Picts."

"Timing is everything," Wulfgar said. "Look who I found on the road." He waved out the door and Æthelberht, Æthelstan, and Æthelwold came inside. Wulfgar's horse stamped nervously, and they gave it a wide berth.

"Wulfgar," came a shriek from the shadows. "Get that horse out of here."

Wulfgar's head snapped up like a hook had set in his jaw. He squinted the length of the hearth and sheepishly returned his blade to its bed. Gamma was advancing on him, grasping her broom like a bill hook and getting deep into his shit on the question of his manners. "We never have word of you," she scolded. "You could be dead, for all we know. And in you ride, after all the work's done, and your stupid horse shitting in the fresh rushes. Not coming to Yule again this year? Is that right?"

Wulfgar touched his spurs to his horse and urged it toward the door. "Sorry I broke your dog, Æthelwulf," he called over his shoulder.

"Sorry we killed all the Picts," Æthelwulf said.

"That's what they're for." Wulfgar shouted this last observation as the horse sprang up the three steps to the door of the hall and back outside.

The Engs greeted their errant brothers like they'd come back from the dead, and Caitria and I shook our heads.

"That crone calved twins," I said.

Wulfgar gone, Gamma redirected the last of her distemper toward Æthelwulf, who was still clutching the edge of a post, sword in hand, surfing the curl of a cresting wave of adrenaline.

"Put that away," she barked, and Æthelwulf gave her a bewildered look as he lowered his steel.

Then Gamma looked at me, and I felt my scrotum contract. "And you"—she grinned—"how's the back?" I winced involuntarily, anticipating pain, and I was left with a scrunched-up face and no discomfort. I relaxed as the old woman laughed.

"The wyrm's blood's healed it," Caitria said.

"So it's true, eh? Caitria insists she's not your woman," Gamma said with an incomprehensible look. "I'm not surprised, the foul temper you have."

"I'll bet she insists."

"And what do you say?"

"I just say no," I said.

"Then she keeps with me in the long house."

"And why's that?"

"It's our custom that single women stay under the family roof. Go fetch her gear."

Caitria nodded. "Gamma's asked me to keep with them."

"I reckon I'm just the muscle for this decision, that right?" I put the empty cup down on the hearthstones and started back to the loft. Outside, a hundred horses were boiling around. Now that the Picts were dead, the earthwork was awash in armed men. Wulfgar, still mounted and sitting fifteen hands above them, rose higher still in his stirrups and shouted. "Find beds for the night. We'll ride into the Chevoit tomorrow."

His men started to disperse as I hurried to the loft to get Caitria's bag and spread my gear out to reserve the straw. I didn't want to bunk in with a half dozen flea-ridden troopers from the northern fyrd. But they were going to the northeast quadrant of Ælfholm where the houses were thickest and the streets windy, not my loft. I got Caitria's pack and slipped a bag of hack into it so she'd have some cash on hand. Then I rolled up her blankets and went back to the hall. I felt the black mood coming back. I'd been with Caitria since I woke up, and separating from her frightened me.

I handed over her gear and turned to go, but before I could leave, Wulfgar was back with his blade in his belt and his mead-low light blinking intermittently. He was surrounded by men who could only be his sons: they all looked like him and Æthelwulf, and Æthelwulf's sons; now there were twenty of them, all counted, like one of Loki's cloning experiments gone awry.

"Thirsty work, galloping across the country?" Æthelwulf demanded.

"I could drink ox piss," Wulfgar announced. "Still serving it?"

"You city folk have lost your taste for real mead," Æthelwulf told him as they came together in a titanic hug that set their mail shirts ringing. They thumped each other on the back, and then Wulfgar lifted his brother off the floor in a sudden wrestling move which Æthelwulf countered, and they spun around looking for an advantage, becoming indistinguishable for a few vertiginous seconds before they broke apart. As their sons mingled, the twin brothers stood off by the door and spoke privately for a moment before they came over to the hearth. I had no idea who was who until Æthelwulf directed his brother toward us.

"Come meet the two saved Æthelric in the standing stones."

This ought to be interesting, I thought, as they loomed near.

"Bran," Æthelwulf said as we stood to meet them. "This is my brother Wulfgar, who went to town and got rich in the trades."

"Well met," Wulfgar said. "I'm the good-looking one." He appraised Caitria in a long glance and said, "Handsome woman. How long have you had her?"

The look on Caitria's face would have bubbled wax, but Wulfgar just smiled, anticipating her response. What he got instead was her fist in his ear, at the end of a trajectory that had begun at her belt and gathered speed all the way.

His head snapped to the side and his eyes wavered momentarily as he seemed to examine a spot up in the smoke-darkened thatch near the roof peak, then he took a step back and shook it off. "One of those kind," he said.

This is it, I thought, looking around for a weapon. It's all over now. Everyone descended from the fecund loins of Wulf looked as surprised as me, but one man: Æthelwulf surrendered to a prodigious laugh.

Wulfgar looked at him, comprehending the setup. "And you said she doted on him," he shouted as Æthelwulf sagged against the boards. "You said her greatest joy was to be this man's woman—and she hates him. Not only've you killed all the Picts, you got my ear boxed, you bastard."

But Æthelwulf had succumbed to a gargling kind of helpless laughter, and he couldn't respond. Then Gamma blew in like bad news and started working close with the broom before they knew she was there. The sons and grandsons of Wulf split like the Red Sea, a move they'd perfected over half a century of matriarchal pissoffs.

"I'd box your ears if it weren't well done already," she hissed. "You stay away for months and then come too late to fight and insult our guests. What would Wulf have done if he'd lived to see it?"

She stopped and they did too, equidistantly out of range. I could only imagine what it must have been like growing up with a mother so liberal in her application of the willow. A sense of humor must have helped, or else the old woman never managed to get in many solid shots. Whatever the reason, the reunion of the twins resulted in a sort of cubbish behavior that she wanted to see extinguished *instanter*.

"You're a guest yourself," she reminded Wulfgar.

"You're scolding the wrong man, Gamma," Caitria intervened. "His brother sent him thinking it was courtesy. I shouldn't have hit him."

Gamma turned her attention to her other son, indistinguishable from the one she'd just attacked; it must have been an easy transition for her, or an old trick on the part of her sons. "Always playing pranks," she said, feinting one way and lashing out professionally with the broom, tagging Æthelwulf alongside the head. He reeled aside and Wulfgar, anticipating the return stroke, jinked out of harm's way, slipped on some dog shit in the rushes, and skated toward the hearth, his arms flailing for balance.

Gamma looked round her for more trouble, and I raised my hands, palms open, to show I was a noncombatant. Caitria went over to Wulfgar, who assumed a defensive stance.

"I'm sorry," she said. "You owe it to your brother."

"Fear naught," he promised. "I'll see he gets it."

"Just a joke, Caitria," Æthelwulf said as Gamma retreated to wherever she'd been lurking. "From the moment you saved Æthelric you've been my daughter."

"These're my sons," Wulfgar said. "Wulfhere, Wulfric, Wulfrune, Wulfstan, Wulfnoth, Wulfwyn, Wulfbrand, Wulfhart, and just plain Wulf." I had that old familiar feeling as they jostled to greet us.

Since the formal introductions were over, and Caitria'd punched a son of Wulf and no one had died, I went outside. The gates stood open. I heard the dull rhythmic thud of pegs being hammered with a wooden mallet, and when I got close enough I saw someone was pounding the Picts' heads onto spikes on both sides of the gate. An older son of Æthelwulf was teaching the youngest the proper method of mounting a head on a sharp stick.

"Hold 'em by the nose, Æthelheard," the older one was saying. "That's what it's for, but if the nose is hacked off or too small, don't be afraid to stick your fingers in the eyes. Ravens won't mind, and the Picts won't either. Now, then, when you have it where you want it on the point of the stick, take your mallet and give it a couple sharp raps like this."

There were two brisk workmanlike thuds as the older brother seated the head on the stick. He set the mallet on the rampart and took it by the ears, centering it so it looked patiently into Æthelheard's face. "Then one good smack, sharp like tapping a keg, and you're on to the next one." There was a final thud from the wooden mallet and he stepped back to admire his work.

"You try one now," he said, offering the mallet to his little brother.

The impaled heads were arrayed on the earthwork like a troop of shiftless and unemployed laborers, the breeze tugging at their hair. It was such an Eng thing to do. A raven glided out of the sky and perched on one of them, holding out its wings for balance as the head turned slowly on the sharpened stake. I left Æthelwulf's two sons to their

Kodak moment, crossing the bridge under them and heading for the probable impact area to look for the rest of the arrows.

As I walked, dark gnomish figures hopped around in the fog, clucking and cackling among themselves, fluttering into the air and settling back again. Every habitation had its resident ravens, but a lot of other ravens had been invited over for the unexpected party. They were swarming over the killing ground like old women in the marketplace, complaining about unspecified illnesses, the freshness of the produce, and the closeness of the crowd as they did what ravens do: reduce corpses to bones so they're more easily disposed of. After the ravens took their fee, wolves would drag what was left back to their dens, and the new homefield boar would eat anything they overlooked.

I walked out across the homefield, toward a pasture where children were watching sheep. A couple of dogs were doing the actual work; the kids were just there for a little character-building discomfort and boredom. When I got to the far boundary I turned back and started a looping search pattern, alert for the fletching of wyrmtoothed arrows.

It was an odd errand, walking among ravens in the fog, and I could feel the wyrm's emptiness creeping over me, like the worst mood you can imagine, the worst depression and ennui, the most profound sense of lassitude, the silence of the entire human race: an incredible drag. That's the down side of killing wyrms you never hear about in the stories—you can look forward to being mugged by flashbacks of existential despair.

I wasn't keen to take another dip in my id without a spotter, and I reckoned I'd been depending too much on Caitria for that service. Better get used to it now, cut my losses. That's where partnership leads: to the necessity of having it and the pain of losing it. I searched for an hour, but I only found three more arrows. All this sorting through large numbers of corpses was getting to be distressingly routine, what with viking up the Severn, burying monks, and slaughtering Picts. No wonder I was depressed.

Caitria was sitting in the hall with Æthelwulf's mother. A couple of Æthelwulf's grandsons were scattering fresh rushes and mint sprigs on the floor. The hearth fire crackled under the carcass of the homefield boar.

The old woman looked at Caitria and stood up. "I told

you he'd be along soon." Gamma brushed her hand over Caitria's head as she crossed to the side door.

I pulled up a stool and sat down. "Three more shafts," I told her. "Six to go."

"If the wolves scatter them, they'll be out there still trying to come back," Caitria said. "Better you find them first."

"You're welcome to help," I told her. "That's what partners do."

"I've other things to do," Caitria informed me.

"Like what?"

"Like help you get better."

"There's nothing wrong with me that leaving here won't cure."

"You better discover a new mood," she advised.

"Discover the six arrows, partner," I said. "That'll help more."

"Don't wave this partnership in my face," she said firmly. "You've been asleep most of the time we've been partners."

14

Aud

Hew wood in wind-time, in fine weather sail,
Tell in the nighttime tales to house girls
For too many eyes are open by day
From a ship expect speed, from a shield cover
Keenness from a sword, but a kiss from a girl.
—Sayings of the Wise One

Æthelwulf was a host of the old school whose idea of hospitality included lots of drinking, eating, entertaining, and hunting. Now that he had something else to celebrate, he unleashed the hungry dogs of Northumbrian hospitality on his twin brother, Wulfgar. It started that night with the homefield boar, prematurely slaughtered by Hengest's roving pack of gourmets. Æthelwulf delivered a moving eulogy, praising its great girth and ferocity, its aggressiveness among the sows, the sweep of its magnificent tusks, the black bristles of its coat, the red venality of its eyes, the way its snout plowed the homefield earth in search of grubs, tubers, fungus, and field mice. When he was finished, women wept and men hung their heads.

The boar turned on its iron spit with no visible reaction to Æthelwulf's blandishments. Hengest's lot had done for him, the bastards, and every woman, child, and man among us was the poorer for it. We'd been cheated out of the party associated with the hanging and curing of the homefield boar, not to mention the party associated with the removal of the homefield boar from the smokehouse and the preparation of the Yule log, over which the lucky porker would be roasted. Æthelwulf made sure we understood the magnitude of the loss.

Wulfgar lifted his horn to the demised boar, whose head looked down at us from the iron spike reserved for whatever animal happened to be the main course at these little get-togethers, and we drank to it. Then there were tambourines and dancing. Aud played her flute, and the granddaughter with the harp made some music. When the meal was over, Æthelwulf called for silence.

"Æthelberht will take the troop round the marches to be sure there's no more Picts about," his father announced. "While they're gone, Wulfgar and I will hunt. In three days we'll exchange gifts."

Now there was no escaping the famous Eng hospitality, a slippery ride at top speed on the black ice of duty and obligation, and hunting, but at least the party was over for the night, and everyone collected their gear and walked out into the cool air to find their blankets. Æthelwulf's lot was well trained. I went back to the loft, threw my clothes in a heap at the top of the ladder, and crawled into the bolster and blankets, trying to be well-trained, too, trying hard not to think too much about the void.

I woke up late from a conversation with the Geat. After I was on the ground with my face hanging open, he was eloquent on the subject of what an asshole I was. I opened my eyes into the thin light that filled the loft, his laughter loud in my head, stirred and stretched under the blanket. My foot touched a leg, and I thought it was Caitria. My mistake: it was Aud.

It was the first opportunity I had to look her over, and she was a looker in her way. Her hair was a rich auburn, and her face was scattered with freckles. She had malachite eyes and teeth as white as cream. She would've been considered thin, but what they considered to be thin in the late eighth century was hardly anorexic. She'd turn heads anyplace I'd ever been.

"How do you come to be here when I wake up?"

"I came to get you up," she said with a laugh.

"I must have felt you come into the loft."

"That feeling's yet to be," she said.

I rubbed a hand through my hair. "What's the time?"

"Nearly midmorning. Time to be up and plowing."

"A hard thing while you're sitting on my clothes."

"Harder still if I weren't."

And before I could say anything, before I was even completely awake, she had the shift over her head and emerged in her innocence out of a shower of red hair. That was a sight: fair-skinned, heavy-breasted, near enough to smell, and naked as a promise. She smiled and fixed me with those green eyes. "Am I good to look at?"

"A bit on the thin side," I told her with a swallow, "but well formed in spite of it. What's this all about, before things move on?"

"Æthelwulf offered you board and bed. Now he knows you're not with Caitria, it's his duty to provide you a bed warmer."

Not for one minute did I believe that this green-eyed and utterly naked daughter (who was at that moment scratching the underside of her left knee with slow strokes of her fingernails) had been sent by Æthelwulf to warm my bed. Æthelwulf struck me as the kind of guy who'd have mentioned something like that. No, I suspected something else; I reckoned it was some kind of Eng test. The problem with tests like that are that you never know the penalties for failure until it's too late. I couldn't plumb this woman, despite an undeniable rigidity of interest.

"No, but if that's your story, practice it, get familiar with it, make it your own. Just don't tell me your father sent you. I've heard too many farmer's daughter jokes to believe it."

Aud looked straight at me and smiled. "Bed and board for guest's an old custom. It's seldom kept since the priests came, but time was women of this house were proud to comfort guests. Gamma remembers it."

"No doubt she remembers the Romans, but times change."

"She knows much. She knows about you."

"What does she think she knows about me?"

"She knows you're wyrmodd, and she wants to help."

"There's nothing you can do for me," I said.

"We make our own wyrd, but we don't have to do it alone." Aud was undeterred in her intention to offer herself. "Are you sure you won't take bed with your board?" She lifted her breasts in her hands. Her lips parted slightly, revealing those ivory teeth. Her breathing filled the silence that hung between us.

I shook my head and grinned and wet my lips. "No, thanks. I'm honored, but I've a blood oath with a woman in Clontarf."

"So you say." She shrugged. "What matter?" She wriggled back into the shift, and it slid over her breasts as she knelt and wriggled it. She shook her hair out and smiled as she started down the ladder.

I couldn't believe I was letting her go. I couldn't believe I wasn't inside her already, making a mess of the bolster and blankets. But I wasn't, and then she was gone. A pain collected in my groin. I got dressed and climbed down from the loft, found a barrel of rainwater outside and pushed my head into it. Contrary to popular belief, it did no good.

When I went to the hall, Aud was already there with Caitria and Gamma, sitting around a loom near the end of the hearth. Most of the loom work was done in the weaving shed, but the old woman had a loom in the hall so she could keep an eye on Æthelberht, the oldest of the middle sons, as he presided over the comings and goings of the working farm.

My interest in Northumbrian agronomy was minimal, so I drifted over to the pot to see what was simmering, ladled a bowl of it up, and retreated into the shadows at the back of the hall to be inconspicuous while I ate it.

The women at the loom spoke softly as they wove, and I couldn't make out what they were saying. The blocks clacked together as Caitria separated warp and woof so Aud could toss the shuttle and Gamma could pack the weave. They had the rhythm of all weavers, no matter where the skill's learned, the rhythm of all the weaving songs they'd sung and forgotten, and they worked together as if they'd been doing it for years. Seeing the three looking women of Ælfholm at the loom gave me a strange feeling.

I knew Gamma was teaching something that didn't have anything to do with weaving. She was passing on that looking woman attitude about living that would disturb men for centuries. They worked the loom at a reckless speed and didn't seem to give it the slightest attention. I watched them, safe enough in the shadows.

Æthelwulf and Wulfgar got back with an elk in the early evening. A commotion in front of the stable announced them, and I went out into a courtyard full of whooping and admiration for their skill. It made me wonder why Hengest's lot had been starving. They had to be able to poach an elk as well as anyone: unarguably the first hunting skill acquired by the yeomanry of the eighth century.

In fact, so many had the knack that Offa had commissioned roving bands of forest reeves sanctioned to deal harshly with anyone caught taking a deer, although poaching achieved its fully felonious flower only later, under Norman management. Offa and his son-in-law Æthelred had a sweetheart understanding about how to husband the natural resources north of the Humber that didn't include the likes of Hengest.

Fortunately, Æthelwulf's position as thegn carried hunting rights, and he was able to sidestep the royal game laws. The elk, a two-year-old bull, must have weighed six hundred pounds. They fell to, and soon the hide was sewn into a frame destined for the tanning shed, and the brain was pulled out of the skull and immersed in boiling water for fresh elk-brain broth as the women threaded the rear quarters onto spits over the hearth fire.

Æthelwulf and Wulfgar stayed out in the yard while the horses were wiped down and fed. The twins were having quite a time for themselves, striding around with their capes sweeping about their booted feet, waving their boar spears like they knew what to do with them. When Æthelwulf saw me, he gave me a great embrace of rib-cracking Northumbrian welcome

"Good day for yourself in the woods?" I asked as the hounds frolicked about, several of them bleeding from antler wounds.

"Excellent day. Saw four more elk and boar sign everywhere. No wolf spore at all. How're you finding board and bed?"

I looked at him blankly, feeling a stupor of comprehension slip over me like Aud's shift dropping over her nakedness.

"Aud's the apple of her Gamma's eye," he continued. "Keen to be off the farm, if you catch my drift. She's not like the other girls. Aud'd like to find a man who'd take her away from all this, and in you walked with Caitria, a girl as like her as another lark in the nest. Well, it make her feel like she'd never find someone, and then it turns out Caitria's not your woman, and you start to look like a possibility for a girl like our Aud. So I thought to bind her under the old customs, where she could share your bed and stay here."

"Why didn't you tell me before you left?"

"I knew it wouldn't matter to you, great git that you are, staying true to that bitch in Clontarf. That was the plan. Send her to you so she could see what assholes men can be. She's a bit young to be taking up with gleemen."

"It's a blood oath," I said. "Could you turn us over to Hengest?"

"Sometimes a host has to say a thing to a guest," he began. "The girl in Ireland, what chance is there she's waiting? You've been gone, what, almost three years?"

"That's as may be." I shrugged. "But those years haven't gone for me. And even so, wyrd happens. Jaws can snap, blades can bite, fevers can burn away. I have to find out before I do anything else. When I've seen for myself, the wind will still blow both ways."

"Do what you want," Æthelwulf said. "But answer me this: are you insane? You walk in here with a woman who's not interested, and I mean one in a thousand, and you find another ready to partner up, and you're worried about a bitch in Ireland who thinks you're dead? The Norns don't do things like this for fun, boy. They have something in mind. And while you're here, it's bed and board, no matter what you choose to make of it. A wise man knows the difference between honor and stupidity; what do you know the difference between?"

"Is this a riddle or a question?"

"It's a question, of course." Æthelwulf laughed, propelling me toward the open door to the hall. "Let me know what the answer is." His dogs swirled after him like a wake.

After the meal there was axe juggling, and Wulfstan and Æthelwulf told us the story of the hunt. As I'd reckoned, it was a long, discursive tale about riding fast after the dogs until they brought an elk to bay, followed by a detailed description of how the pack worried the beast until it lost a lot of blood and most of its patience, and then the details of how they killed the elk. The story included rococo sidebars about scats and fuments, tracks and blood spores, panting horses, shrieking hounds mortally done for by the flying hooves and slashing antlers of the elk, and, to demonstrate that it wasn't all work, there were interludes of drunken congregation for practical jokes involving defective equipment and high-spirited horses, resulting in a goodly number of laughs at each other's expense, casual humiliation delivered offhandedly and accepted good-naturedly, and the ritual exchange of lies about elusive and chimerical game. Hunting hasn't changed a bit since then.

The telling was begun by Æthelwulf and taken up at intervals by Wulfgar and the three sons who'd gone along, Æthelwold, the master of the hounds, Æthelhere, the best tracker, and Æthelstan, the nerviest with a boar spear. It drew to a close with a recitation of the return to the free-hold with the trophies, the skinning and cleaning of the meat, the grooming of the horses and the feeding of the somewhat reduced pack of dogs, ending finally at the point where the story had begun: Æthelwulf rising to begin telling it.

When they'd washed down the story with three or four horns of brown beer and gone out for a piss, Æthelwulf and Wulfgar turned their attention to us.

Caitria reported the progress of the tapestry she was weaving with Gamma and Aud, a record of Æthelwulf's career as a hard charger that went as far back as the days when he fought the border wars against the Lothian Picts and the Strathclyde Welsh. She talked about some of the adventures of Æthelwulf's life and described their representation in the tapestry. When she finished, the sons of Wulf drank a toast to her, and she gave them a heart-stopping smile and sat back down.

"And now, how'd you keep the day?" Æthelwulf asked me.

"Making verse," I told them. "The story of my trip. When gifts are exchanged, I'll sing them."

"Well enough," Æthelwulf agreed, as a quartet of grand-daughters started playing and the thralls cleared the tables and banked the fire. They played for the half hour it took the family, in twos and threes, to drift away to their beds, carried off by the sound of the music.

That night I dreamed of a dark place and rats, and Gaef-burnnah's voice, and Frydys's laughter, and the Geat, not so talkative this time, dead and blue-faced, stalking me through the dark tunnels of the mine. When I woke from those dreams, I found Aud sitting in the dim red glow of a trimmed lamp, which turned her hair the color of Gaef-burnnah's blood. She was wearing a shawl about her naked shoulders. It took me a few seconds to acknowledge her, and I braced up on one elbow, breathing hard from the dream. After my Geat dreams, I always wondered if there was something there to be learned, if dreams were some message in the broken language of sleep, a language close to the wyrm's, and so a language I thought I should have understood.

"You dream badly," Aud said.

"I dream too well," I disagreed. "How long've you been here?"

"Half the night's sped; I came to keep watch."

"Was watch needed?"

"Tell you me."

"I doubted you yesterday," I said. "I'm sorry, I'd ride the mare if I were free to do it."

"This woman must be lovely," she said.

"She was a nuisance, but we came to love each other."

"So it happens," she said. "And now she's the woman of a wyrm slayer," Aud said, the shawl slipping from one shoulder.

"That's as may be." I shrugged.

"She's a long way off," Aud said. "In another land, and another mood. You're three years gone, and she's three years older."

Aud dropped the shawl from her shoulders and knelt beside me. "I'm willing to warm your bed while this other woman's warming someone else's. Maybe you should take your warmth on the road in case the comfort's colder at home."

I held up my hand for her to see the scar of the oath-cut, white against the red of my lamplit palm. "This cut makes the rune *Isa*, the rune of ice and standstill. I swore to spend time with no living woman until I'd come back to Frydys."

"It's right to keep an oath," she said. "But half an oath kept amounts to naught. What about Caitria?"

"You know the intent."

"If the intent's to keep from fucking, no one's any worries about you. Let me under the blankets, at least; it's cold in here."

"If you want," I said.

"Fair enough." She slipped under the bolster and turned to blow out the candle. I lay on my back and watched the ghosts of the flame circle in the middle distance, listened to Aud's breathing until I fell asleep. She was gone when I woke up.

Wulfgar and Æthelwulf were hunting before dawn in weather even more miserable than the day before. The fog had become a raw mist that swirled over the homefield, despite which the two hundred spiked heads on the earth-work were beginning to give off a smell. The clouds seemed lower, and everything growing was that vivid green the land of the Engs acquires when it rains.

I crossed the paved street and went into the hall to break my fast. Gamma, Caitria, and Aud were near the loom, laughing and drinking mulled cider. They had a tapestry spread along the length of the table, coiled upon itself and spilling over the edge, collecting on the bench, and then falling to the floor like time's waterfall. Gamma was bent over it telling the girls some story, pointing at a section of the weaving and jabbing her finger into the cloth for emphasis; the three of them laughed and leaned back, like a flower of sound opening its petals.

I got a bowl of the hot substance du jour from the pot and retreated to my spot in the shadows. I was curious about the tapestry and the story, but I wasn't going over there for a look.

Gamma hurried forward through the woven time line, bunching up the past in one gnarled but nimble hand and then tossing it aside. Her finger followed the life of some ancestor, and she told another story, and they laughed again. Then they went back to the loom and took up their places, Gamma at the shuttle today, Caitria packing the weave, and Aud separating woof and warp; the tone of their conversation came to me across the hall, and I could see that Caitria was having a good time with two other looking women. She could go all her life and not meet another, unless she came home with me.

The second day Gamma's boys got home a little earlier, in high spirits, with a big boar strung up on a pole, its tongue lolling out of its great, tusked head. The dogs weren't so frisky as they'd been that morning. The pack was down by a few more, and the ones left were too tired to folic after the scraps when the butchers skinned out the beast; they just lay there watching. The boar had made them pay for his life, and they were showing the effects.

Wulfgar supervised the livery while Æthelwulf displayed the trophy head for everyone to admire. It was big for a feral boar, and the shadows of the moving torchlight made it seem even larger. It'd make a meal, and maybe something left over for the stew pot. Four sons carried the carcass inside for final preparation, seasoning, and introduction to the iron spit, and Wulfgar, the epicenter of a smell that had to do with galloping around on horseback for eight hours, came over and gave me a hug.

"How'd you fare today?"

"Well," I said. No use keeping Wulfgar from a wash-up.

"How was board and bed?"

"I kept my oath."

Wulfgar shook his head and grabbed his braid. If he had any avuncular advice, I wanted to hear it, but all he said was, "What *do* you know the difference between?" Then he went off to pour water over himself and take a piss. That was all the advice I was likely to get. Inside they were rubbing the carcass with herbs and salting the cavity, and the drudges were building up an oak fire that would burn down into coals so hot they'd turn from red to blue and back again, radiating intense dry heat to cook that boar to a turn.

Eight hours later, about compline time, the clan began to wander in and the noise level increased as they shouted to one another and laughed. Æthelwulf and Wulfgar took their places at the high seat, and Caitria came to sit beside me. When everyone was in place, the jugs of mead started round, and the appetizers: round rye loaves, glazed apricots, apples and cinnamon, cheeses, salt fish, and fruit.

Then there was more axe juggling. They never seemed to get enough of it. Æthelred began with three axes, laughing and talking to his audience, and then Æthelwold and Æthelbald joined him in the wide aisle between the high seat and the hearth, hurling axes and moving toward one another until they stood back to back, shoulder to shoulder, looking at the rafters, eyes focused on the middle distance, heads nodding faintly with the rhythm. There were nine axes in the air, spinning up toward the thatch, and applause began to ripple around the hall.

Then one of the axes veered off course and struck another one that spun into three more, and it rained axes. Two of them hit oak beams and angled toward the tabletops on either side of the hearth; one of them spun on its haft in front of a startled grandson-in-law, who toppled backward off the bench to get out of the way. Two ricocheted off the hearthstones with a blast of sparks, and one plunged into the fire and sent blue-white coals into the rushes, which had to be doused with water. A spinning handle struck one of the dogs, who'd just wandered by to drool under the roasting boar, and it levitated off the floor, emitting a turd from one end and a howl from the other. When the iron rain stopped, Æthelred, Æthelwold, and Æthelbald were crouched under the trestle table with their arms wrapped round their heads. There was a moment's silence while everyone accounted for their limbs and appendages, and then Æthelwulf threw his head back and laughed.

"No one hurt," Wulfgar pointed out. "No one hurt. You boys need more practice. When we were your age we never missed."

Æthelred, Æthelwold, and Æthelbald spread out to retrieve their axes. Their uncle was right: more practice was definitely needed. I realized that my ass was gripping the bench and relaxed my sphincters and lower back. One of the axes had bitten into the tabletop where the bread basket usually sat, an ugly, bearded profile of iron with a shining grin along its thin lip, just a short reach away. Æthelwold levered it out of the wood and slipped it back into his belt. It was a skill of limited entertainment value, but it pleased the Engs. Æthelbald pulled his last axe out of the hearth log and wiped the soot on his pants leg as he went back to his place. I had to admit the place was growing on me. It had its moments of lightheartedness.

"Some fun, huh?" I asked Caitria. "How are you keeping?"

"Well," she said. "I needed a rest."

"I'm glad to hear it," I said.

Then Wulfgar stood and began the story of the day's hunting, seeming to take for granted that we were interested. In the clan-based society of 795, with grocery stores still over a thousand years in the future, they had a relationship with their food that most people today would find alien. Æthelwulf's clan knew what a boar *was,* how it ran tossing its head from side to side to bring its tusks into play, how it could put its boar ass to a rock or a tree and tear up a pack of dogs before you could kill it. They knew how its blood smelled, how its meat tasted, what you could do with the pelt and tusks, and the medicinal properties of the hooves and gallbladder. Its hide would keep their feet dry and warm in the winter.

So when Wulfgar talked, they listened to a familiar story told new each time because it always rewrote itself. There were too many characters working at cross-purposes to arrive at the same ending twice: the boar, the hounds, the horses, the men, the equipment, and the gods of whatever place they all came together.

Wulfgar told us about the color of the leaves in the glade where they finally brought the boar up, the sound of the little stream that rimmed it, the only moment all day when the clouds parted for a second and a shaft of sunlight missed the boar by a foot, throwing the moment into a silhouette of frozen action: dogs stopped, boar stopped, horses and men stopped, only the sunlight on the green floor of the glade and then the disappearance of the sunlight, bringing them all back into motion again.

Æthelwulf took up the story at the point where the boar broke through the dogs and his horse bolted and put him on the ground in the way of a pissed off two-hundred-pound porker with sharp tusks and a bad attitude. He described the feeling as the boar charged, the vibration of its weight through the wet earth, and the blur as Wulfgar put his horse between and leaned into the boar spear as the swing came on, impaling itself on the iron. The boar's assault hurled the horse off balance and it fell toward Æthelwulf, who rolled out of the way as his brother came out of the saddle and landed on his feet with his weight against the weight at the other end of the spear shaft, still trying to reach him with those ivories even as it died.

And then the boar collapsed suddenly in its struggle, and they squatted round and watched it for a while to be sure it was dead, listening to the thin whining of one of the wounded dogs, the nervous stamping of the horses, and to their own hearts hammering in their ears, their noses full of the smell of death.

When they were sure it was dead, they pulled the spear, gutted the pig, and cut down a small oak to string it up for the ride back. Flies were gathering, laying their eggs in the puddle of blood and on the eyes and in the exposed guts

of the three dead dogs that the boar had killed in the first
minute after standing its ground. A few ravens fluttered in
as they rode away.

By the time the hunters were finished telling their story,
the silence in the hall was so loud it nearly swallowed the
fire. Æthelwulf stood up and walked around the table to
the hearth, where the boar was turning on the spit, and
carved out a strip of it with his knife, tasted it, and pronounced it done. People were on a first-name basis with
their food in those days.

Æthelwulf's clan tucked into the boar. It may have died
ferociously, but it had died well-fed, augmented by whatever it could root out or run down: acorns, truffles and
other edible fungi, the guts of carrion deer and elk, everything that found its way into that maw had been translated
to sweet wild pork. It took us two hours to finish the meal,
toast the high points of the day's hunt, and then settle back
to hear the daily report on the progress of the tapestry.

Caitria stood up and told him the weaving of the battle
with Hengest was almost complete. The section began with
our coming to Ælfholm, and had progressed as far as the
occult archery. There was another day's weaving at least
before they were done.

To listen to her, you'd think she'd grown up as one of
Æthelwulf's daughters, and the old boy beamed while she
talked, never talking his eyes off her, nodding to indicate
his encouragement and understanding. This was where she
belonged. Half a hoard could do some good in that place,
and they seemed sensible enough, for Northumbrians.
When she finished, the sons of Wulf praised her lavishly
and drank to her health.

"And how're you keeping, Bran?" Wulfgar asked.

"Making verse," I told him. "Full-time."

"Keeping your oaths?" Æthelwulf inquired.

"All of them," I assured the brothers.

I wasn't sure but another visit from Aud wouldn't make
a liar out of me. The myth was blown; I'd met too many
of the myth makers by then to believe that shit about how
much water duty and honor would hold when they were
coming over the shieldwall or crawling under the quilt with
goose bumps as big as their nipples, begging to be warmed
up. But maybe these Engs still believed in that. Maybe old
Æthelwulf had been more pricked by duty and honor than

by the premature slaughter of the homefield boar when he led his clan out of Ælfholm with the battle ice in his fist.

Despite the multiplicity of rules, there was as much gray in the eighth century as in this one. The difference was that then duties often conflicted, and now it's desires—although the results aren't easy to tell apart; all you had to do was go up on the wall and ask the Picts. Looking around the hall, I knew they'd like my verse when they finally heard it, shaped as it was to appeal to the famous Eng upper lip, built for carrying the yokelike mustache that conveyed mead onto their chins.

"Tomorrow we'll hunt fox," Æthelwulf declared. "Something this rag-eared and mangy pack of puppies can handle. Two days after that I have to be at the witan gemot in Hexham. Then I'll travel to Mercia while Æthelred pays tribute. Bran and Caitria, keep here another day, and Wulfgar'll take you to Luel."

That was the end of the party. The tables were cleared, the cups and horns collected, and Caitria joined Gamma and Aud, waiting by the door to Æthelwulf's house.

I went outside for a stroll on the rampart. The night was as miserable as the day'd been; the unseasonably chill mist was already making me shiver. There were faint rainbow coronas around the two oiled torches burning at the gate. The ditch was dark below the wall.

I passed under the spiked heads. They were pretty ripe, and I could only imagine what they'd be like if the weather weren't wet and cold. I said good evening to Æthelric, whose night it was for the watch, and we passed a few words about what moved in the dark: a few owls hunting, an otter in the bank of the ditch, a flock of slumbering geese under the bridge, the eyes of a fox or barrow wight shining in the dark.

Aud was already under the bolster, her clothing folded by and the lamp gleaming to light my way up the ladder. Her hair was spread out behind her, cascading over a silk pillow. It seemed like I was getting in bed with *her,* now, or else deciding to sleep in the hall by the banked fire. I was beginning to wonder if sex was all those Engs ever thought of, but intervening years have proven me wrong. My cloak was wet from the mist on the ramparts, and I hung it up on a peg. The lamp guttered and did things to the light, but then it recovered to reveal Aud's shadowy smile.

"What're we going to do about this?"

"Do what you want," she said. "But you'll be more comfortable doing it over here. There's a lot of ways to warm a bed."

Now that I was in the loft, I didn't want to go back outside and across a muddy courtyard to the hall. It was more effort than it was worth. She'd kept here half the night before and nothing had come of it. I suppressed a yawn, and Aud threw aside a corner of the bolster and patted the hay.

What the hell? I thought. I pulled my shirt and tunic over my head and took off my boots and pants. The straw was warmer under the bolster, and she leaned over to blow out the candle as I joined her, displaying the undercurve of an extremely desirable breast before the light went out. We lay in the swift profoundness of dark that followed.

"I want to give you something," Aud said. "You've kept faith with Frydys and Caitria and should have more than taunts for it."

"I've had more already. Your father's given a ring of water to protect us, some great meals, axe-juggling lessons, and an opportunity to be killed by Picts. And you're warming my bed. There's nothing more to be given or got."

"Then take a kiss of sisterhood," she said.

Hey, a kiss of sisterhood. What could be wrong with that? After all, Aud was there for the custom and to save face: a kiss would give them a little victory, and it wouldn't cost a thing. The terms of the oath were not to spend time, but that was time inside a woman, not time outside her. I considered it for a second, and followed her voice to her mouth; she slipped her hand round my head and our lips came together.

Aud had a different idea of a sisterly kiss than Sinead ever had. She turned into the kiss like she was delivering a blow with an axe, and my eel jumped up and bounced off her thigh. I took a sudden breath, and she breathed herself into me. Her hair trailed over my face, and I felt her breasts against my chest, and then, just as I reached the point where I had to decide whether to push her away or plumb her, she broke off the kiss and lay back.

"Good night, Bran Snorrison," she said, showing me her back.

I sucked back the gasp I'd surrendered and lay back under the bolster, my eel in the mast step tenting the bed-clothes amidships.

I didn't go to sleep; I finally passed out because of all the blood diverted from my brain. When I woke up Aud was still there, her warm ass curled into my lap, her spine against my chest. My arm was around her waist, and I don't reckon you need to be told what was imprisoned between her thighs. I came to consciousness in a fairly languid pace.

Where do you go when you fall asleep, anyway? Not even Gaefburnnah'd mentioned that, as familiar with the sleeping state as it was. Maybe you're translated into some other reality where fragmented and nonsequential dreams are your ordinary life, and maybe you're just asleep; in any case, that morning I woke up about to plumb Aud's well, and it was no dream. I was pillowed on her thick hair; my fingers bowed on her ribs like harp strings.

I rolled away from her, sat up, and got out from under the bolster. She stirred in her sleep, and I clenched my fists to the side of my head. It was chill, and I put on my clothes and went down the ladder, noticing halfway to the bottom that my eel was hitting the rungs and my balls felt like lemons hanging between my legs.

The sun was just beginning to throw a little sallow light through the low clouds. I could see the torches at the gate ringed in the spectral halos of another day mist. I let myself in the side door of the empty hall. No bubbling pot above the banked ashes of the hearth fire. The benches were put by and the tables up on their pegs. I went over to the hearth and raked back the ashes, threw some kindling on the exposed coals, blew on them, and stood back as the fire came to life for another day. I built a small structure of kindling and threw a few logs across the firedogs above it.

The hall held the heat; that's what a thatched roof's good for, and I took my cloak off and rolled it up for a pillow. I stretched out on the hearthstones with my feet close to the fire and looked at the ceiling. The light was beginning to seep in from the eastern window of the hall.

I hadn't seen the tapestry they were working on, but I'd looked at the sections that preceded it, hanging on the wall behind the high seat. The loomwork changed, depending on who was doing the weaving, but in general the style was common enough, graphic depictions with runic bordering top and bottom that explained the action. I'd seen that kind of tapestry before: Orm had one that Mairead contributed stitches to, and I reckoned shuttles in Clontarf had been tossed into the story of the last three years on a loom much the same as this one, there for me to read when I got back.

I got up and went over to the covered loom to have a look at the weaving, unable to guess what a triad of looking women would produce, but as I touched it the door to Æthelwulf's house opened and the sound of voices poured into the hall. I went back to the hearth and sat down. The kitchen drudges came in and started setting up for the day. One of them lugged the pot out and put it on the iron over the fire. I got up to give them room and they soon had my table ready in the shadows where I could curl up comfortably until breakfast was hot.

Then Æthelwulf and Wulfgar and a couple of sons came in for cold boar and a cup of mulled grog before the day's hunt, and Æthelwulf spotted me on the bench.

"Bran, Woden's woolly ass, I thought you *never* got up this early. You want to come along?"

"No, thanks," I said, pulling myself upright.

"Shame to miss a day as good as this," he said.

"What are you talking about? It's foggy and cold as a witch's kiss. Horses will fall and the spore will be hard to follow."

"Love a challenge," Wulfgar assured me. "That's the point of it. No fun when it's too easy."

"Why not ride sidesaddle, then?"

He laughed and slapped me on the shoulder. "We'll saddle a horse for you," he insisted. "Any side you want. Just the first chase. Makes a change. Æthelstein, get a horse ready for Bran."

Before I could decline again, Æthelstein was out the door, and Æthelberht and Æthelric were winking encouragingly from their bite and cup of grog. Æthelwulf started eating breakfast as if he understood it was the most important meal of the day, consisting of fried eggs, bacon, sausages, and stale pieces of bread toasted in a rack by the fire. The dogs reported in while they ate, a dozen still untouched and a half dozen limping wounded. They frisked around, whining for scraps that they weren't going to get.

"How do you reckon it?" Æthelwulf demanded of the dogs. "You pups weaned yet? Ready to put in a decent day's work? Today we're going after something that's going to run away—promise. No nasty tusks or antlers, no hooves to crush your soft heads, just a run in the country to earn your supper. You up to it?"

The dogs melted back at the tone of his voice, as if ashamed of their performance the last couple of days, sensing they'd let him down in front of his brother.

At least there wasn't a lot of heavy equipment to carry, just a boar spear in case we ran into some unexpected feral pork, and Æthelred and Æthelberht would deal with that. The rest of us would carry as little or as much as we wanted. If I was going, I was going warm, so I went back to the loft for a thicker tunic. Aud was gone, but the bolster was still warm and the pillow held her smell.

The horses were ready when I got to the stable, and the dogs were fighting over a fox skin to bring them up to speed on what was expected. My horse was a three-year-old with crazy eyes; we looked one another over, and I attempted to communicate the chain of command telepathically. The party mounted and crossed the bridge, skirting the homefield wall while the second-string boar, attracted by the activity, paced us inside, just another pig without a clue about what was in store for him come Yule.

The morning looked the same from the back of a horse as it had from the ground; the sky was just as sullen, and the fog as low over the fields. Visibility was about a hundred yards; after that it was a broth of shadow and suggestion. The dogs loped ahead, noses to the ground, tails in the air, casting for scent along the stone walls and into copses and thickets, pausing here and there to lift a leg. After ten minutes the dogs got excited, whining and quivering as they nosed the shrubbery along a stone wall. Æthelwulf rose up in his stirrups and strained to see the quarry, exhorting the dogs to be dogs for a change and earn their sup. And then the mutts got a positive lock on the scent and things started happening.

The dogs foamed along the wall and flowed over it in a smooth wave, baying and snarling and yapping happily. Æthelwulf and his sons became part of their horses and hauled ass after the sound of the pack, taking stone walls, streams, any obstructions that came out of the fog without hesitation. It always puzzled me that the Engs, who were great horsemen, only used their horses to commute to battle and never fought from them. They didn't get around to inventing mounted cavalry for a few more centuries; for the time being they just liked to ride fast and reckless after small mammals.

The horse was a jumper, unafraid of half the things it should have been, and it had a hell of a good time taking me over stone walls, hedges, streams, deadfalls, and ditches. I hung on hard enough to choke it to death, but once the others started off at a dead run, there was no holding that nag back.

Wulfgar put the horn to his lips and gargled out a few notes. We began to spread out at the jumps, and the others disappeared into the fog. I could hear them calling to each other, the horn, the dogs barking, but those sounds soon faded.

I finally managed to rein the horse in. It wasn't pleased to be brought under control and stood stamping the turf while I listened for Wulfgar's horn. I could hear them tear-assing around in the distance, the horses' tack and harness jingling, and the dogs wailing after the quarry resisting precise location in the fog. Visibility was now about fifty yards in all directions, and what lay in all directions was a green and brown expanse of rolling moor, which, under current lighting conditions, seemed flat and two-dimensional, like a poorly executed backdrop for trouble. Since the horse knew the way home, there was nothing for it but to stay aboard and keep alert.

Hunters are tightly strung animals, and mine was impatient to be doing something at high speed, now he'd had a ten-minute gallop to get his circulation going, and there I was making him stand still while I tried to decide between identically dim vistas. I could feel him building up to something I wasn't going to like, so I turned him generally in the direction I thought Ælfholm lay, gave him a nudge, and let him have his head. I reckoned he'd be willing to go home in the absence of direction from me, and if he didn't, I'd be no worse off than sitting there waiting for the hunt to circle back.

The horse wanted to go faster than I did, and the best

compromise I could negotiate was a bone-jarring gait that made my teeth rattle and my head snap out to the end of my spine if my attention wandered for an instant. The horse demonstrated mastery of three speeds—full stop, spine-rattling, and flat-out—and I was welcome to any of them.

You can say it's an equine joke, or merely the kind of cunning often confused with intelligence by people who anthropomorphise animals, but in my experience if you show a horse anything it can interpret as weakness it'll take advantage of you like any other opportunist. That was one of the reasons I'd never shown any interest in the family business; I understood horses well enough, I just didn't like them.

But the opportunist *I* was riding was heading somewhere with a confidence that he transmitted to me, and I changed my seat and started examining the countryside while I kept him under the speed limit. It was bleak and wet, end of report. Occasionally a hedgerow or a stone wall would drift into focus and then fade out again, but the horse continued, undisturbed, to follow a secret azimuth of its own understanding, and I was along for the ride.

When the ground began to rise, the horse discovered a new gear and slowed to a walk. I didn't remember any hills, but I thought maybe it was a shortcut; that dog food had all my confidence. Then the horse stopped and stood alert, his ears pointed forward, his muzzle lifted as it looked upslope. After a few seconds I flexed my legs and snapped the reins, but the horse ignored me. I brushed his shoulder with the leather quirt. His skin quivered locally as if dislodging flies.

Then the fog thinned out a little and I saw a huge chalk horse cut into the hillside above me. Before I could digest the image, the fog closed again and the horse started upslope on his own.

As the horse crested the hill, I saw standing stones. It was a true circle, ancient but still intact, granite post and lintel for 360 degrees, covered with mottled mosses and lichens. The horse made right for it, suggesting perhaps that the true purpose of those ancient stones was to radiate a bizarre equestrian magnetism.

But the horse stopped at the edge of the circle, and I almost went over the horn. The animal reverted to a stupid placidity and tried to sneak a few mouthfuls of grass to see if I was paying attention. I jerked his head up. He shook his ears back and looked into the circle. I shifted my weight in a way that communicated a desire for forward momentum, but the plug just lifted his tail and dropped a few road apples. I nudged him into a clockwise walk about the stones, which he began with little enthusiasm and completed with less, about five minutes later.

When we'd finished circumambulating the structure, the horse stopped beside the pile of road apples and waited for me to get off. I thought there was a better than even chance the nag would leave me there if I give him the opportunity, and I looked round for something to tie up to, a vain hope in the middle of that existential metaphor of a place. There was nothing in the ecology to loop a rein around but the lithosculpture we'd just circled, and the horse was clear on the point of not allowing himself to be ridden into it.

I could have just headed out in some other direction, hoping the horse wasn't being passed from circle to circle by barrow wights, creatures with some crawful of ancient pissoff at humans that I didn't want to involve myself with, but I needed five minutes off that horse; between the lingering effects of my nightly abstinence with Aud and the cross-country steeplechase, I badly required a piss and a walk on terra firma.

I swung my leg over the saddle and jumped. The horse twitched his ears at me and shook his head, surreptitiously testing my grip on the reins. I stretched and took a few tentative steps along the path, and the horse matched them without resistance. So far, so good. I walked out the kinks and eased the pain in my bladder against the horse's leg to show him what I thought of his navigational skills. The herbivore just browsed the low grass and swished his tail. Then I turned back, guiding his head around slowly, and as I transferred the reins from hand to hand, that dog-meat piece of shit snapped his head up and sent them whizzing through my gloved fingers like a match head across a stone, then he cantered away, trailing road apples like parting tokens of esteem.

I pinched the bridge of my nose and wrinkled my forehead. The morning was slipping away, and maybe more than that. I didn't have any idea where I was, and the fog was in its third day. I might be looking at a night on the moor, never a wise thing, and to make it worse there was nothing to make fire with in the hundred square miles of tarns and heaths and generally empty stretches of moor that made up that part of Northumbria. North of the Humber, where it wasn't forest it was moor, and where it wasn't moor or forest it wasn't, and at the moment everything was wet. I pulled the cloak round my shoulders and went over to the stones. They were runecut:

Prophecy of destruction! A row of bright runes I hid here. Through perversity and without rest, there is dreadful death to one who breaks this circle.

No problem. The stones had been cut and transported to this hill by people who believed something strongly enough to go to a lot of trouble about it, runes had been cut, blood no doubt spilled, solstices and equinoxes observed, computations made on the quarter days, elegant mathematical systems described—all forgotten now—and I wasn't about to deface it with graffiti or chip off any souvenirs. It was the only thing beside me and the horse that stood taller than eighteen inches off the ground, and I thought I'd have a look at it while I was there.

"Hey, wight," I called out. "Anyone home?"

"No wights here," Gamma said, straightening up from the base of a stone. She had a knife in her hand and a basket brimming with plant cuttings.

The look on my face must have betrayed my surprise. "Cutting woad for the dye pot," she explained.

We were alone in the circle. She hobbled toward me, and I backed off a step.

"Don't worry," she cackled, "I won't hurt you."

I kept an eye on the hand with the knife anyway. So far I hadn't sensed the same level of goodwill from the old woman that her sons lavished on me.

"It must have been a climb up the hill," I said.

"I'm not as decrepit as I look." She shook her head and dropped the knife into the basket. "I spend half my time in the fields collecting herbs and plants."

I'd already been the beneficiary of Gamma's surgical skill, and I hoped I never had to consult her as an internist. She was no doubt as familiar with wolfsbane and hellibore as comfrey and mint.

"The hunt got too far ahead," I told her. "I gave the horse his head to find the stable."

"It's not far." She gestured vaguely out of the circle.

I smiled crookedly into the fog and took her word for it.

"A long climb up the hill," I ventured again.

"You get used to it. I've cut plants here for sixty years."

I wondered how old she was; seventy at least, maybe older. In a time when the life expectancy was forty for men and thirty-five for women, she was at *least* twice as old as she ought to be.

"How old are *you*?" she asked, reading my mind.

"Nineteen," I said.

"A baby." She laughed. "I was nineteen when I jumped the broom with Wulf. He was killed when the gesithmen deposed Oswulf. We'd already buried six children by then, but the other nine survived."

I shifted my position and looked beyond the stones in the direction the horse had gone.

"In a hurry to be away?"

"Just wondering about the horse."

"The horse knows its way in these hills; it's you that's lost."

"Not now, unless you plan to leave me here."

"There's lost"—she shrugged—"and there's lost."

I walked over to the low heel stone sunk into the turf and sat down. She followed, put the basket between us, and sat down.

"We got off to a bad start," she said. "Let's start over."

"You called me a liar," I reminded her.

"You lied," she said matter-of-factly.

"It's the same start," I said. "Everything I told you's true."

"Then you're lying to yourself."

"About what?"

"About what happened."

"I see things more clearly than you think."

"What do you see?"

That was the question, all right. What did I see? I'd seen quite a bit. I'd seen how things could be and how things were. Now I was looking at how things were going to be, and the view wasn't pleasant. I sensed the ephemeral nature of life now that I was ambered in it. I was falling through life, accelerating with the passing seconds, and there was no influencing its endless trajectory. That was the essence of the wyrm's mood.

"I want to make my own wyrd," I said inadequately. What else could I say? How could I explain what I only felt? How could I describe that incapacitating dread?

"Make it, then. You know how."

"The wyrm's made it for me," I said, admitting what I'd denied since I woke up in the mountain.

"You're feeling sorry for yourself, probably because of this woman who's supposed to be waiting for you; the wyrm's another matter, that's all. How different was it from the Danes who burned Lindisfarne or the Picts who followed you to the gate? All different, but all things that happened, and you came through. Someday it ends for everyone and everything. In a long while or a little, who can say? Making your wyrd's what you do until then. Wyrd's just another word for living your life. Don't be in a hurry to do it."

"But to be the last one …" I stopped, unable to say more. That was the essence of it, that isolation. That's what the wyrm had felt and infected me with, that was the melody of the wyrm's song.

She shrugged and shook her head. "Someone has to be last. Some go too soon and some not soon enough. People come and go: that's the way things are. It's the lesson you learn if you pay attention. You already know that. Maybe you've just forgotten, or maybe you need to hear someone else say it."

What was learned? What did I know, and how long could I hold on to it? These are questions you ask again and again as you try to get the knowledge that keeps you from making the same old mistakes. If you're going to make it, the wyrms you have to confront are the real ones that live inside you, the ones you're so familiar with you ignore them while you waste your energy on the made-up ones out there.

It's an insight you rediscover time and again, and time and again you forget. If you're lucky, every time a little more stays with you.

The horse was browsing just outside the circle, the trailing reins caught in the stems of some tough upland shrub.

"I'm done here," the old woman said. "Let's go back."

"I'll get the horse," I said. "You can ride."

"I don't get on with horses." She shook her head and picked up the basket. "I'll walk." She turned away and started out of the stones, and I walked over to the horse and picked up the reins.

Visibility was improving; the mist had rolled back a little more. The horse's ears twitched when I untangled the reins. "I ought to leave you here," I said. "Wolves would find you before nightfall."

I straightened the stirrup and pulled into the saddle. From up there I could see a little farther. The circle was on top of a hill that rose like a shield boss out of the moor. Gamma's head was just disappearing below the horizon. By the time I rode around the stones, keeping my attention on the horse in case it had any more ideas about who was in charge, Gamma was at the base of the hill.

When I caught up to her, I dismounted and walked beside her. She surrendered the basket, and I fastened it to the saddle. We headed straight across a field that had been grazed and manured by sheep, and after a while I could see the earthwork, the rampart, and the ditch of the freehold. The gate was open, and Æthelhere was in the guard mount, warming himself with a handful of roasted chestnuts. He called a greeting down to Gamma, but she didn't acknowledge it. Once inside, Gamma retrieved the basket and made straight for the dye shed.

"How's the hunting?" Æthelred asked as he stepped out of the stable to take the horse.

"A bit raw," I said, handing over the reins. "The dogs put something up, and Æthelwulf and Wulfgar and the boys chased it."

I crossed the paved courtyard. I wanted warming by the fire, the warmth of hearthstones to sit on, and maybe a bowl of whatever warm was simmering in the pot to wrap myself around. Warmth was the operative concept. Not much time seemed to have passed in the hall. Caitria was at the shuttle today, and Aud separated woof and warp. I went over to the pot and ladled out a bowl of a brown stew, which revealed itself to be leftover elk, cooked with barley and vegetables and salted to the cook's taste. There was a bucket of well water, and I dipped a leather cup into it and poured a little into the bowl to cool off the stew. Then I went back to the table and ate. When I had warm stew in my belly, I lay back on the bench and closed my eyes.

It was full dark when Æthelwulf returned to Aelfholm. The leftover boar was warming over the hearth fire in iron cauldrons of brown gravy and onions, smelling up the hall; the loaves were cooling in wicker baskets, and everyone was sitting around listening to their bellies. The horn sounded from across the homefield, and the cheer that went up from the hungry clan woke me. I was laying back on the bench covered with my cloak. About half the usual complement was waiting at table; the rest were going about whatever late business they had until Æthelwulf and Wulfgar returned.

The early diners had apparently been making do with carrots and turnips and liberal doses of mead, unable to begin officially reducing the leftover boar to the bottom of the pot until their patriarch bellied up to the trencher, so they were ready to start the serious eating and drinking then and there, but it was another fifteen minutes before Æthelwulf and Wulfgar stomped into the hall shouting for liquids and warmth, preferably combined in the form of mulled mead. Early in that fifteen minutes I realized that I hadn't written down any verse, that I couldn't account for the day, and that I was in the same position I'd assumed when I lay down for my five-minute nap, for that matter the same one I'd been in that morning when Æthelwulf came in for his grog. It had been a fetal kind of day, and I wasn't sure what had happened and what hadn't, how much or how little of it'd been real, or whether I'd have anything to say when I opened my mouth.

Æthelwulf strode over to the fire, keeping his cloak around his shoulders, and offered his hands to the warmth. His braids were dripping onto the floor, and his cloak began to steam, faint mists becoming visible and swirling off into the air as if he were beginning to dematerialize.

Then Wulfgar made much the same entrance, reaching under his cloak and drawing out a badger pelt.

"We spent the whole day hunting," he said, throwing it on the table before the high seat. "And this is all we have to show for it. The dogs took us over the moor, and all they could run down was one old badger, and it was *lame*."

"Great pack of worthless mongrels," Æthelwulf shouted,

in a rage at his canines. "I'm sinking a bear-baiting post at the end of the hall. You'll find out how good you've had it up to now.

"Let's eat," he said, rolling his shoulders out of the cloak as he went to the high seat.

That met with general approval and the food started round before Æthelwulf had lowered his damp ass onto the cushions. I drained a cup of mead while the platter came round, and Caitria came from the shadows at the back of the hall. I moved down the bench to make room for her.

"We're out of here tomorrow," I said.

"I'll be sad to go," she said.

I looked round the room and nodded. I'd needed the rest, but now I was as rested as I was going to get, and it was time to go.

That's when the pork and wild rice arrived, and all conversation was forgotten as we tucked in. All around me was a frenzy of late dining, and when people finally came up for air, there was a chorus of belching, the sounds of weighted benches shoved away from the trestle, and then a general caesura of quiet satiation while we got our second wind. Then the food came round again, and we stepped up to the task and finished it. When everyone ran out of steam the boar was a memory, about to begin a new career as indigestion.

The time had come for the exchange of gifts. Wulfgar gestured to one of his sons, who came forward with an object that must have weighed a couple of stone at least, judging from the thunk it made when he sat it in front of Æthelwulf. It was wrapped in silk that shone in the light, and blue twine collected the edges into a bouquet of shapes. Æthelwulf pulled the knot out of the twine and the silk fell away to reveal a blue glass vessel, about the length of a forearm. It was stoppered with wax, and Æthelwulf slipped the point of his blade around the seam to unseal it.

He staggered back and suppressed an explosive retch. People all along the bench swayed away from the smell emanating from the glass jar.

"Newt's eyes," Gamma squealed with enthusiasm.

"Woden's woolly ass," Æthelwulf gasped, his nose wrinkling as he held the vessel at arm's length. His mother came up and slapped the lid back into place. Then she wrestled the vessel off the table and went out, bound for her apothecary, where she was doubtless low on newt's eyes.

Wulfgar was laughing helplessly after his brother opened the gift, and he wiped his eyes with his sleeve and sniveled for a few seconds on the edge of a relapse. When they'd fanned the smell away from the high seat, Æthelwulf gestured to his oldest son, Æthelstein, who brought out a wooden chest about as long as his shoulders were wide and about a hand's width tall.

"Once Æthelwulf sent me two barrels of cider that'd gone off," Wulfgar said as he held the chest in his hands. "So I sent him a box of fish caught the week before. Then he sent me a wagonload of manure. The next year I sent him a wagonload of pine cones, and that Yule he sent me a sixty-foot pine log. I had the log cut into a set of oars and sent back."

Wulfgar set the chest on the table and hesitated, nerving himself before he opened it with a quick movement. He stared into the chest, a puzzled look on his face, and reached into the box and took out something wrapped in silk. He unwrapped a beautifully buffed horn, rimmed in gold and bound tight by a silver web, and held it at arm's length. The cord was braided from the tails of black and white horses, and was thick as a thumb and just the right length so you could bring the horn to your mouth while you rode.

Wulfgar held it up to be admired. The hammer dimples in the silver webbing splashed the firelight into the hall. Wulfgar cautiously sniffed the mouthpiece; he shook it and held it up to the light. He smiled. "This is too good a gift," he said. "I don't trust it."

Æthelwulf shrugged and looked hurt.

Wulfgar raised the horn to his lips, sucked back a barrel chest full of the smoky hall air, and kissed the mouthpiece. The note that came from the horn sounded, in the high-timbered hall, like a thousand cattle farting simultaneously. Wulfgar dropped the horn and stepped back with his eyes bulging, and then he started to laugh at how neatly he'd been trapped.

Gamma returned and motioned for me to approach.

"I've made these for you," she said, offering me a leather bag, "from the wyrm's hack, so they have the wyrm's power in them. You're a runemaster, and you know how they work: these are for casting as you need to cast them; when you need direction, the runes will guide you."

I spread the mouth of the bag, peering into its shadows. It was full of coins, a bag full of futharks, I couldn't tell how many. I spilled them onto the trestle boards and grabbed a handful. Runes trickled through my fingers onto the pile.

"Power runes are always handy," I acknowledged in surprise.

She waved me away with a look of near warmth, which would've still bubbled varnish. "That's as may be," she said. "You'll know when the time comes. Runes may be the thing you'll need."

Caitria stood up and walked over to the loom. The tapestry was off the frame, folded on the small table against the wall. She carried it to the high seat where Æthelwulf and Wulfgar could see clearly as she unfolded the narrative.

The women had woven the death of Hengest, leaning on his blade in the center of the bridge one minute and facedown in the mud the next, as Æthelwulf's lot gaped in surprise. Caitria identified individuals in the weaving, pointed out the Picts who'd returned my two arrows, what'd happened when the Engs discovered how the pockets of the dead outlaws were, and how they spiked the heads when they finished dismembering them, how Æthelwulf's depression at Hengest's death had been restored by the arrival of his brother and missing sons, followed by three days of hunting and feasting.

Æthelwulf leaned forward on his elbows, following the narrative with interest, nodding at the appropriate places, grunting his praise at details in the weaving, smiling broadly at what a hero they made him out to be, defending the odal estate against starving bandits and their Pict allies.

When she was finished, Caitria regathered the length of the weaving and folded it back into a bundle. Then it was my turn, and I stood up at the table and walked down into the space in front of the hearth. I looked at Æthelwulf and Wulfgar, and old Gamma, sitting between them with a look on her face that would have stopped a wolf's heart. I waved to the granddaughter harp virtuoso, and she came forward to accompany. I let the tension build the way Skallagrim had taught me, and when they were ready, I sang.

By the time I finished, blood sugar levels had adjusted, and the clan had settled into a penumbral after-dinner glow, stimulated by the mead and the warmth of the open fire. Such postprandial ambience makes for kind critics, and the verse was well received, but I wasn't about to make the same mistake Gawaine had made.

I walked over to Aud and took her hand. She stood, and I led her before the high seat, where Gamma and the brothers waited.

"One last gift," I said. "Your daughter Aud, who offered herself to me in custom. My oath prevented me from accepting, and so I return her, untouched, and hopefully taught the lesson you wanted her to learn."

Æthelwulf smiled and stood at his place. "Gifts are exchanged," he said. "Dawn comes early."

There was no fluting or dancing to tambourines; everyone headed to bed while the tapestry was rehung.

Caitria came over to me as everyone left. "In your verse you made me out to be something I'm not," she said.

"Don't get confused. Skalds make things out of what they find around them. When people see something they recognize in a skald's words, sometimes they get the wrong idea."

"I know better than you who I am," she said.

"Skalds are allowed to fake it," I told her.

"Don't believe what you make up about me," she said.

"I never believe the things I make up," I said.

Caitria gave me a long look and followed Aud to the longhouse, and I went outside to check the horses. They'd been groomed, fed, and rested, and their hair shone in the light. These nags had made out, all right; reprieved from pulling carts, introduced to an improved diet, and not asked for anything they couldn't deliver. They were restless and ready for the road again. Securing our gear would be twenty minutes' work in the morning.

I went up for a last stroll round the rampart. Hengest and his lads were showing the kind of wear two hundred severed heads usually show after three days on the spikes. Eye sockets were empty, patches of smooth skull were showing through, a few strips of peeled flesh hung from their cheeks, and what was crawling around under that matted hair where the flies had laid their eggs didn't bear close inspection. The moon was showing through the clouds, winking in and out, painting the rampart with intermittent shadows.

After a single lap I went back into the empty hall for a last warming by the banked fire. The tapestry was back in place behind the high seat, and I stood for a minute with my spread cloak trapping and reflecting the heat, idly trying to discern the movement of the woven figures as they progressed from left to right across the fabric. When I was warmed again, I lit a taper from the night candle and went over for a closer look.

The weaving was remarkable. I wouldn't have believed it could be done in three days if I hadn't seen it. I studied the narrative and admired the detail. Too bad none of those Anglo-Saxon tapestries survived; they'd have shed a lot of light on the bullshit and conjecture that fills out the scholarship on the period.

When the weaving got to the hunting scenes, the power of the boar and nimbleness of the elk were rendered with an energy that came off the fabric at you. The horses galloping through the forest, the dogs bringing the quarry to bay, and the final confrontation were all images that've been made by hunters since someone discovered how to draw on cave walls with pigment and charcoal. When I got to the fox hunt, I saw that six hunters galloped after the hounds instead of the usual five. The sixth one was a small detail, woven close to the bottom hem under the larger figures of Wulfgar and Æthelwulf and sons. The figure riding along the hem soon got separated from the others in the fog, rode around for a while, and lost his horse by a circle of standing stones. While the others followed the hounds all over the map, the small one went inside the stone circle and talked to an old woman.

Then there was a scene in the hall where I recited verses and the tapestry was displayed to Æthelwulf. It was the story of how I'd spent the day, even though I'd told it to no one. When I got to the end of the visible tapestry I had that feeling of the hair on my neck standing up, that feeling of vague confusion that accompanied most of the things that had happened since I'd turned my back on the smoking buildings of Lindisfarne. There was one more section, obscured by a drape that hadn't been tied back. It was just long enough to contain the story of what happened after Caitria and I left. I fought the urge to look. The only way to know if wyrd was woven or made on the spot was to finish my trip and look afterward. I didn't want Gamma to weave my future any more than I wanted the wyrm to decide it. I wanted to make it up myself.

I knew one thing for sure: it was definitely time to leave. Things in the land of the Engs were getting too weird for me.

15

Last Tango in Luel

He who has seen and suffered much
And knows the ways of the world,
He who has traveled, can tell what spirit
Governs the men he meets.
                    —The Sayings of the Wise One

The loft was mercifully empty; I'd finally passed their test. It's another proof that timing is everything: I couldn't have held out another night. I stripped off my clothes and crawled under the bolster.

I woke up to the sound of someone making the kind of racket you make when you try to walk by quietly with a load of war gear. I got dressed, closed up my bag, and dropped it to the bottom of the ladder. Outside, the sky was still dark, but I saw the first stars I'd seen since Caitria and I had counted them inside the hill fort. Our saddled horses were waiting in the courtyard. Shadowy figures, burdened by an assortment of gear and weapons, were converging on the hall where the fire was going full blast, bowls of porridge were steaming on the trestle boards, and Engs were stumbling round in an early morning mental fog. Caitria was dressed for the road, now looking as out of place in those clothes as she had in skirts and broaches only five days before.

"Luel before noon," she said.

"I'm ready; this place's getting too strange for me."

"It must be getting pretty strange," she acknowledged. "But sometimes you have to open yourself up to the strange; sometimes you just have to say things are strange, but what matter?"

"What I'm saying is the time has come to open ourselves

to the strange in some other location, to move downriver to some as yet unspecified strangeness."

After the brothers Wulf broke their fast, they started haranguing the occupants of the hall at large about the valuable time they were wasting, prodigality of time on the road being an undesirable trait in eighth century Northumbria, even for groups of disembowelment experts like Wulf's clan.

There was little or no tourism to speak of in the north country, except for the annual pilgrimage to Lindisfarne, which was always undertaken en masse, with little time to gawk at the roadside attractions. A more casual tourism might have been something the rising Mercian middle class had the leisure for, but north of the Humber most of your day was spent ensuring you'd be around tomorrow.

Their progeny ignored the brother's sense of urgency, as if they'd decided that finishing off Hengest's lot had made Northumbria safe for their palely beautiful sisters and their sheepherder brothers-in-law, from Dumbarton to Durham. My nostrils quivered with the delicate piquancy of *ofermod* as they said good-bye to loved ones and relatives, their best arms and harness glittering on the table in front of them. If there were a couple hundred Picts grinning down from the spikes, who was to say there weren't a few hundred more out on the moors?

One by one they collected their personal gear and went outside where people lower on the food chain were saddling horses and packing supplies for the trip. The activity out there was more to the twin brothers' liking. Excitement spread to the horses; they stamped and blew, shook under their harness, tossed their heads, and twisted their ears out of alignment. The troop came to 223. Things were crowded in the courtyard, spilling out across the bridge and along the homefield wall. The moon had set, and the stellar conjunctions told us when the sun would rise. We worked quietly, doing familiar things in substandard lighting, trying to move efficiently and get on the road.

According to people who claimed to know, if we were expeditious, we could be halfway to the Roman wall when the sun came up. I checked the rigging on our gear and noticed our draft animals to be reassuringly bored compared to the hunters that Æthelwulf's men were riding. If the Engs relaxed for a moment, those mounts would treat them to the kind of full-bore horsemanship everyone seemed to take as a matter of course in Northumbria.

Caitria rechecked the harness. There's no such thing as too many eyes checking the harness; even though you've done it a million times, there's always the chance you missed something. But she didn't find anything wrong and we led the horses out of the barn. About half the troop was in the saddle, and the rest were milling nearby. Gamma and Aud stood near the weaving shed. I walked over to say my fare wells.

"Thanks for the stitches," I told Gamma, "and for minding Caitria, and for the talk in the stones."

"Caitria minds herself," Gamma said, "and the stitches were easy enough once the wound was clamped together."

"Not those stitches," I said. "The ones in the tapestry."

"There's naught of you in the weaving." The old woman never dropped a beat. "Weave your own tapestry, if you can. Though your hands're too clumsy for the loom, if you want my opinion."

"You're a charmer to the end, aren't you, Gamma?"

"Go look for yourself," she said. "There's naught of you in it."

"I haven't a doubt," I said, turning to Aud, whose wine-red hair spilled out of the folds of her hood, framing her face.

"I'll see you when I may," I promised. "Thanks for bed and board."

"I hope you liked what you had of it," she said from the shadows of the hood.

"I liked it very well. I'm sorry—"

"I've heard all I need to hear about your oath," she interrupted.

"Then take gift for gift," I said. "There's one more left to give. A kiss of brotherhood." I slipped my hands into the warmth of the hood where her red hair was thick against my palms and guided her lips where they needed to be, paused for a second, looked into her eyes, and kissed her at least three orders of magnitude more than she'd kissed me. She stiffened in surprise, and then her lips parted and the tip of her tongue slipped out to wriggle with the old wordwyrm. I inhaled her and breathed her back into herself. We started to become indistinct as we merged in the kiss, and some time passed, but all I can say for sure is the sun wasn't up yet when I stepped back and smiled.

"I miss you already," I said, turning away and walking across the street to Caitria, who was holding the horses. I took the reins from her.

"Go say your last fare wells," I told her.

She went across to them, and they talked as the last of the stragglers came out of the hall, and then Caitria hugged them and hurried back. I never saw them all together but from a distance, and I've often wondered what they said to each other.

Caitria was in her saddle when the last man still had a foot in the stirrup, and as soon as he was up, there was a blast on a horn, followed by a tremendous fart from the horn Æthelwulf had given his brother, and a general laugh, just an ice-breaking joke on the verge of a long ride, and Æthelwulf and Wulfgar led us across the bridge under what was left of the noses of Hengest and his associates. Then we rode down to the Roman road, making the comfortable sounds of a mounted column on the move: coughing men, blowing horses, creaking leather, and the low thud of hooves on the roadbed, sharply-etched, familiar sounds in the startling clarity of the bracing predawn air.

I patted my horse's neck a few times, which was as familiar as I ever got with horses and about all they seemed to expect of me, and the column spread out as the pace increased when we gained the Roman road, but the draft horses from Ravenshill Moor kept the speed sensible, and I didn't have to worry about holding my seat in the jumps.

Occupied by thoughts of reluctant horsemanship, I paid no attention as we climbed the rising ground to the top of the hill. The place was heavily wooded, and a tunnel of trees blocked out the stars. We topped out the ridge and went down the other side toward the King Water, forded the stream, and paced the marsh on the west riverbank, the residence of thousands of marshwiggles, frogs, and insects that croaked, slithered, and buzzed in the dark. Then road and river separated, and we crossed a pasturage and passed the lit window of a small freehold closer to the river.

The terrain seems tame on Ordnance Survey maps of Northumbria: the blue lines of all those burns drain out of the high ground toward the Irthing like purse strings pulling tight, the old forests have been reduced to tracts, new forests planted, the course of the Roman wall become a dotted line, traceable more by the ruins of mile castles and forts than ditch and dyke, and there's a pale blue grid of kilometers over everything, but there was no pale blue kilometric grid over Northumbria the morning we started for Luel.

After a couple of miles the sky began to lighten up. What that means in Northumbria in July is that we'd started down the road at three a.m., after going to bed around eleven p.m. and sleeping for a full two hours. Days are long and nights are short north of the Humber, and Æthelwulf and Wulfgar must have been happy thegns up there at the head of the column with a couple miles of imperial pavement under the horses' guts and full daylight still ahead. Caitria was beginning to materialize beside me.

"Another hour to sunup," she called over to me.

"How far to the Roman wall?"

"Gamma said an hour if we followed the river."

Then, just above the oxbow in the river where the ford was, a strap on one of the packhorses worked loose and began dropping provisions onto the pavement. A copper cauldron signaled the beginning of the inconvenience by gonging on the road, spooking one or two nervous horses in the column. Times of transitional light make horses nuts because that's when the predators are out. It was shadow time, the hour of the wolf, or the wolfshead, or a thousand Picts, and the horses were wired too tight to handle the sudden tolling of a copper kettle on Roman stone. Æthelwulf called a halt while the teamsters checked the lashings.

Æthelwulf and Wulfgar walked their horses down either side of the line to check on everyone. "How's the ride?"

"Always this early on the road, Æthelwulf?"

"Never too early on the road in this kingdom," Wulfgar answered.

"I noticed you have a little problem with Picts," I said.

"Picts are easy," Æthelwulf said. "It's us we have to worry about."

If I'd learned nothing else at Lindisfarne, I would have left with the understanding that Northumbrian politics defied description as merely Byzantine, and that the surest way to make a blood friend or start a blood feud was to discuss them casually. Wulf's clan already liked me well enough because I'd had a hundred magic arrows when they needed them, and they thought I'd saved a son's life. Why ruin a good thing with opinions on politics?

"How much farther to the wall?"

"Not far. We'll make good time when we get across the river. We'll cut the wall Gilsland. Wulfgar will take you to Luel, and we ride to Hexham," Æthelwulf said.

The sons had the gear picked up by then, and Wulfgar and Æthelwulf rode back to inspect the job. The dogs stayed near Æthelwulf's horse, ready to cast for scent on command. That's the thing about dogs, they're just about the worst suck-ups ever created, and their master's anger was forgotten on the chance he'd sail a scrap their way. Then the twins galloped back toward the head of the column, dogs boiling after, and we started moving down the hill to the oxbow and across the shallow ford, where Æthelbald detached himself to pay our way at the tollhouse. We went through a wood for ten minutes and then out onto another moor and found the sun had risen while we were in the trees.

It was a clear day, and from the high ground we could see how green the fells and forests were, stretching off to the south in the soft dawn light. Three miles to the south I saw the straight line of Hadrian's wall.

It was a landmark you couldn't miss. There were Roman workings all over the island, but Hadrian had only built one wall: seventy-six miles of fortified ditches, walls, and ramparts, sixteen feet high and twenty feet wide, backed by a paved road, garrisoned by a hundred men every mile, and supported by great legionary fortifications. And it *was* the line, or the end of the line, depending how you viewed it: the farthest reach of the Imperium; and just so no one got confused, the actual physical limit of the empire, a line in the ground called the *vallum*, was cut inside the wall, in some places through solid basalt. The Romans were nothing if not serious about marking their turf.

Six and a half centuries hadn't been kind to the wall, but Hadrian's engineers built to last, so there was still plenty to see when we crossed the ditch and went through the gate onto the road itself, which bisected Northumbria like a limited-access highway. Only a few hundred yards away, across the ditch and earthwork that protected the *vallum*, the impressive workings of a garrison fort sat on the plain with stolid Euclidian arrogance. We reined in and dismounted, and while Wulfgar sent someone ahead to see if there were any transients there who might want an escort to Hexham or Luel, Æthelwulf walked over to us.

"Short leave-taking's best," he said, hugging Caitria. "I've a daughter like you," he said, "and she'll be trouble all her life if she's not careful. You're as like her as makes no matter. Take care, and when your business in Luel's over, come home to us."

"I'll come back if I can."

"I'll look for you, then."

"I hope you see me."

Æthelwulf hugged her again and turned to me.

"You'd do well to forget that bitch in Ireland," he said. "She sounds like the marrow of trouble."

"And what am I?"

"You're trouble's meat." He laughed. "There's a big difference."

I escaped from his good-bye hug, and he made one of those grand turns, sweeping his cape out and obscuring himself as he walked away to share some fraternal joke with Wulfgar. Æthelwulf's sons came over to say good-bye.

"I'd be dead if it weren't for you," Æthelric assured us effusively.

"And we'd be dead if it weren't for you," I said. "Balance is restored."

"Take care," Caitria told him with a laugh. "I think you'll keep well enough in this family."

They went back to their horses, where the sons of Wulf talked and waited for the scouts to return from the fortification.

"What strangeness did *you* see at the freehold?" Caitria asked as she watched half of Wulf's clan prepare to ride out of her life.

"Nothing stranger than three women weaving in four days what should have taken them a hundred."

Wulfgar was slapping Æthelwulf on the shoulder, but he failed to knock him from the horse, and the brothers parted, Æthelwulf east on the stone road, Wulfgar west, between wall and *vallum,* where the way lay open as far as Luel. Wulf's clan let out a shout, and rattled their blades on their shields when we split up. We turned in our saddles and waved as our horses carried us into unknown territory across the fold of Gamma's tapestry.

We were twenty miles from Luel, and Wulfgar didn't let the horses stop to browse. The earthworks of Roman camps were regular and familiar features of the terrain, marking the miles as surely as stones.

"You have to wonder what stopped them," Caitria said, looking at the shoulder-high walls of a fort as we trotted past it.

"Mad emperors and lots of Visigoths," I simplified.

"Can you imagine what it was like?"

"For them? Pretty much a shit posting, I reckon. What did they have to look forward to but a trip to York once a quarter to have some fun? The rest of the time, they sat here knowing hoards of crazed Picts might be stripping off their clothes and covering themselves with woad on the other side of the wall. Not an easy life."

"Who's had one of those?"

"My life's been easy enough," I admitted. "Clontarf's a good place." That was putting a simple face on it. I'd had luck, there was no denying it. Oh, there'd been some inconveniences, like having a daughter of Freyja set me on the road to Lindisfarne and Ravenshill Moor. And then there was the wyrm. But on the plus side, Northumbrian thegns liked me, and my verse was well-received in the hall. All in all, things were looking better now that we were back on the road. My mood was easier to bear.

"You've good wyrd," she said.

"I can't complain," I said. "From now on life'll be as easy as you make it."

The Irthing flowed on our left in our direction. Waterfowl circled over the wetlands that flanked the river, and as we climbed the bluffs on the north bank, they glided in pairs to the feeding grounds. The river stayed below us for six or eight miles, and then the ground dropped us into the floodplain by Howgill. A couple of miles farther south we could see the smoke of the hearth fires of Brampton, far back out of the Irthing's springtime reach. The land rolled beside the river, and then the Irthing turned south to join the Eden, but we stayed north until finally, late in the morning, water and road converged at Luel.

It's bigger now, but Luel was still a fair-sized town, built up in one of the Eden's loops. It must have given Hadrian's engineers a lot of problems, but they'd shored it up well enough to last seven hundred years, and since it was the western gateway to the southern kingdoms, it'd been reen-gineered hundreds of times since then to strengthen it against a siege. The Picts had controlled it as many times as the Northumbrians. There were a lot of rivers at Luel, the Petteril joined the Eden on the west and the Caldew joined the Eden right below the walls. Luel was sited to command the water trade.

The Eden was tidal, and downstream it meandered through marshland to the Solway Firth. Like all ports on the western side of Eng land, I reckoned there would be Irishmen there, maybe even a boat heading back that we could catch a ride on. The road led straight to the town gates, where the gatekeeper somehow spied Caitria and me in that troop of hometown boys and held out his hand for the stranger's tax.

"Wulfgar," the gatekeeper asked as I dipped into my pouch for one of Offa's pence, "how many Picts did you get?"

"Æthelwulf bagged 'em all before we got there," he snorted. I was glad Wulfgar was keeping him busy with small talk. I tossed the gatekeeper the pence and looked hopefully through the portal, eager to get moving. Caitria hadn't displayed any rapport with gatekeepers so far, and I wasn't keen for her to involve herself in the discussion.

"This your woman?" the gatekeeper asked, right on schedule.

"She won't have me," I told him. "Says I sleep too much."

Wulfgar smoothly urged his horse between Caitria and the gatekeeper, and we thanked the old boy and rode into Luel before Caitria could clarify things for him. The main street was dirt, and we moved slowly through a crowd that was going about its business in the late-morning rush hour. We passed Cuthbert's church, dedicated by the old Episco-pal peregrinator himself during one of his interminable walkabouts through the Northumbrian outback, and across the street from the church a tithe barn, where the church collected its ten percent of the gross. After the fresh air of the open country, being inside an Anglo-Saxon town with three or four thousand Engs and their pet lice was a stifling experience. Cats strolled the sidewalks searching out rodent dinners; dogs roamed the streets looking for edible garbage or dead beggars. There was straw and mashed road apples in the gutters where the Engs emptied their slops. Wet clothing dripped on our heads from the windows that overlooked the street.

The troop began to disperse as soon as we passed the gate. Wulfgar and his sons clattered uphill, their horses scrambling for traction and gouging up wet dirt. People asked after the body count as we passed. Then we wheeled down a narrow street, the walls on either side unblemished by windows and topped with red-tiled roofs. There was a gate at the end of the street, and Wulfnoth leaped down to shoulder it open and wave us into the courtyard, where a fountain splashed into a pool and an orchard stood in ordered rows.

"The last Roman to govern Luel lived here," Wulfgar told us, obviously proud of his urban digs. "He had inside plumbing."

Caitria and I were impressed. Indoor plumbing had gone on hiatus with the dissolution of the Roman empire, except in Arab lands, and it wouldn't reappear for a thousand years. Wulfgar's place was a walled urban residence of late imperial design, with formal gardens that converged on the fountain and the symmetrical reflecting pools. Women, children, and the unattached female dependants of the family Wulf scurried out to meet their loved ones, and thralls peered from around corners and out of doorways.

Wulfgar led us across the courtyard and through a row of fluted columns to a gallery, set with small mosaic tiles, that ran the length of the house. We dismounted, and thralls took the horses to the stable. Double doors let us into the room where Wulfgar's wife was waiting. She seemed a woman like most other women, and therefore a woman who could be relied on not to weave like a runaway jacard loom or make anyone uncomfortable with her looks.

"This is Ælflaed," Wulfgar introduced us.

"Well come," she said, taking Caitria's hands. Ælflaed was middle-aged, in her third decade and starting to show it, but not as middle-aged as she'd have looked if she lived on the ancestral country estate, or anywhere else but the house of the last Roman to rule Luel.

"Listen to this," Wulfgar said, showing her the horn, and then blew another acoustically gut-wrenching note that echoed inside the house. "Sounds like King Æthelred getting an idea," he said.

Ælflaed made a face and took her hands away from her ears. "You'll have to send him something proper in return," she told him, leading the way to another room, where the fire was burning and the table was laid out with the kind of spread you like to see after a long day of horsebacking.

There were grandchildren at the benches, and servants carrying trenchers from the kitchen. How did the poor Engs live? I wondered. But I knew the answer to that one. There was no ambiguity between the rich and the poor, but it was clear the line of Wulf was doing *pretty* well for itself even though the middle class was only beginning to coalesce around places like Luel, where everyone's hand was out and the air smelled bad.

While we ate, Wulfgar told Ælflaed how the battle he'd missed had necessitated a few days of decompression for one and all, unless you were a Pict, in which case your head was a raven roost.

"He must've had a fit when they killed the swine," she said. "He treats his homefield boars like princes."

"They paid out," I assured her. "The Picts didn't last five minutes."

"Did he make a speech before you ate it?"

"People wept," Caitria said.

"They live for the Yule feast out there," Wulfgar said. "Losing the homefield boar after seven months of fattening must have made him berserk. Æthelwulf was the oldest and inherited the freehold. I came to Luel and made my own way, dealing with the Strathclyde Welsh. They're a strange lot, but their furs make a warm cape."

"How's your mother?" Ælflaed asked. "Foul-tempered as ever?"

"Sweet as the day is long," he said.

After we finished eating, about an hour into the afternoon, they took us on the A tour.

The house was built around three sides of the courtyard. If you faced it across the gardens and orchards, at the end of the ponds, the slaves' quarters were on the left, the common rooms were dead ahead, and the family rooms on the right. There were nine common rooms, including the summer and winter dining rooms, the guest rooms, and the kitchens.

Wulfgar's sons kept their apartments under the red tile

roofs that flanked the street to the gate, and the domestic sounds of squalling children and scolding mothers floated out of the second-floor windows. There was a bathhouse in a free-standing room that the Romans had contrived a way to heat in the winter. The pool was about twelve feet by eighteen, chest deep. It was tiled with cerulean stone, mosaics of underwater scenes set into the border; fish swam; monsters lurked. Columns at the four corners of the pool supported a galleried second floor.

"You can come back for a wash," Wulfgar said. Then they took us up to the second floor, where our trunks and packs were sitting in the middle of one of the big rooms. Caitria and I were bone-tired after almost no sleep and a long ride, but a pool of water was an idea whose time had come.

I went outside onto the gallery. Everything was quiet. I was two days from home and about to take advantage of indoor plumbing. After a minute, Caitria came out beside me.

The river was behind us, and we were facing the northeast, toward Ravenshill and Lindisfarne. The air was better out there where the wyrms and the Picts lived, and no one had their hand out unless there was iron in it. I realized I was waxing nostalgic for the Northumbrian outback, and I tried to get a grip.

"You have to wonder what stopped the Romans," Caitria said for the second time that day.

"Mad emperors and a lot of Visigoths, like I said before. Six hundred years ago it wasn't as congenial as these days. Not all of them lived like this. The troops out there just slurped back their gruel and counted the days till they could go home." Under ordinary circumstances I'd have been happy to discuss the Roman empire, but I wanted to wash off the smell of horses as soon as I could.

I went down to the bathhouse and pulled off my clothes. The water was warm and fresh, and I swam around the pool for a few minutes to ease out the kinks. It was going to be good to have a deck under my feet again instead of a saddle under my ass. While I was anticipating that, Wulfgar came in and stepped out of his cloak.

"Nothing like a soak after a ride," he said, stepping off the edge of the pool and disappearing under the water with a minimal splash. He surfaced a few seconds later, blowing out an oxygen-depleted breath and rolling back to lie on the surface of the water with his fingers interlaced behind his head.

"No rules here about where you sleep," he pointed out.

"Makes no matter," I said.

"Nor should it," Wulfgar agreed, doing an inefficient backstroke that wet the tiles on both sides of the pool. "We're more liberal in the city. Who sleeps where's no one's business but the people doing the sleeping. Too many rules out in the country."

I wondered where this was heading. An avuncular sagacity that had nowhere been in evidence at the freehold had suddenly joined us in the bathhouse. Wulfgar was preparing to deliver some opinion on my status; he had a theory.

"What're the rules here?" I asked.

"Here the rule's simple: don't kill anyone."

"Fear naught."

"And the girl," he began again, after he'd made the turn at the end of the pool and started back. "What about the girl?"

"Which one?"

"The one you're with, you know which one. There's naught to say about the others."

"What about her? She's a free woman; if you have something to say to Caitria, you ought to say it."

"When the time comes, I will; now's *your* time. Duty's a good thing and honor can never be stolen, but stupidity's it's own reward."

As a philosophy of life it had the merit of brevity, but I was no stranger to strangeness these days, and this conversation had taken a surreal turn that was all too familiar. I was prepared for just about any metamorphosis on the part of Wulfgar, but what he turned into, without any pyrotechnics, was a guy in his late middle age who'd taken a strange liking to Caitria because she was old enough to be a daughter and she'd boxed his ears. It may be argued that this event, in a context of facing down hysterical mobs with a scramasax or walking into rat-infested caverns with resident wyrms, was of minimal weight and significance on Caitria's résumé, but the requisite technique and a willingness to box Wulfgar's ears had gotten the old boy's attention.

"If things go bad in Ireland, look to Caitria or look at the reason why."

"I won't look any farther than I have to," I promised ambiguously.

"See you don't."

Then he finished his wash-up, climbed out of the pool, and wrapped his wet frame in a cloak spun from the wool of the Strathclyde Welshmen. I swam for a while longer, thinking how suddenly imminent the end of the trip was, like a rock coming out of the fog at twelve knots.

I spent the rest of the day recovering from the ride, lolling round the pool, conserving my energy, eating oat cakes with honey, and leafing through my verse. Caitria slept in the afternoon, and in the evening we ate with Wulfgar's family and exchanged small talk about the chances of finding a boat for Ireland.

We got up early the next morning, and while Caitria had a wash-up, I went to the dining room and found food on the table. The line of Wulf were all early risers, and Wulfgar'd been there ahead of me and gone. Ælflaed was in the weaving room, a large space with a window that looked over the town and the river beyond. She told me to enjoy their hospitality and make myself at home. Wulfgar was out in the town sniffing up some useless joke gift for his brother.

"Full day ahead," I told her. "Have to find a boat and gear."

"There are boatwrights along the river," she said, "and you can find whatever you need in the market."

Caitria joined us, eating an apple and looking refreshed. She was wearing clothes she'd gotten from Aud, a dress made of a pale blue linen embroidered with serpentine figures in the Anglo-Saxon style. She looked good, and I thought she meant to stay at the house while I went out, but she quickly put my mind to rest about that.

"We have to provision for the trip. Where's the market?"

"Town center," Ælflaed said, watching the loom. "Can't miss it."

We thanked her and started out. After a brief stop for more explicit directions, we made the correct combination of turns and downhill traverses and were soon on a main street, dodging chamber pots and slop buckets like all the other pedestrians.

"I thought you were staying here," I told Caitria as we

walked. "You're finally in a town that Vikings haven't burned."

"Partnership changed all that," she said. "It lasts till journey's end, and the end of this trip's in Ireland. An oath's an oath, as you've been telling all and sundry since we met."

"You'll like Clontarf," I said, pleased to hear this spoken aloud. "And if you don't, you can always come back, though I'd wait for the cold weather to dampen the smell, if I were you."

"When the trip's over, we'll see what befalls."

"Stablemen know everything," I told her, and it didn't take us long to find a stable exactly where a cripple, who'd been happy to direct us for half a pence, promised it would be. The stableman was lounging on a stump beside the open doors, talking to someone who looked like he had a successful career as a stall and compost engineer. They looked up as we approached, and the sweeper went inside. There was a dirty kid sitting laconically on the top rail of the corral, leaning against the side of the stable and dangling one foot into space, the first Anglo-Saxon punk I ever met. He was about ten or twelve years old, and the fact that he was destined for a bad end involving an edged weapon or a blunt instrument was written all over him, plain as insolence.

I could see empty stalls through the doors, and hay in the loft. Just outside there was a medium-sized heap of horseshit with a pitchfork angling out of it. The stableman walked over with a yellowed smile and breath like twenty-five years of garlic consumption, just another small businessman who was looking to turn a few honest pence in exchange for services rendered.

"Can you direct us to the riverfront?"

"Half a penny each, fee included," he said. "In advance."

Caitria and I looked at one another and laughed, and I pulled out the pouch and gave him a pence.

"River's that way," he said, gesturing generally to the south.

"Know of any boats for Ireland?" I was determined to get more for a pence than a vague hand gesture.

"No boats for Ireland now," he said.

"In that case, do you know a good boatwright?"

"We've marketing to do in that case," Caitria interrupted, "and we'll need a barrow to carry what we buy."

"Boy can pull a cart," the stableman offered, opening his hand again. "Two pence, no charge the cart."

I counted out two more pence, while he gestured the punk off the fence and into the harness of a small cart. Once he was in the traces, he looked anemic and hardly up to the task.

Meanwhile, the stableman was composing obscure directions to the boatwright, an honest tradesman much as he was, no doubt, and I found my mind glazing over. I could see this was going to be thirsty work, so I interrupted him.

"Where can we get a drink?"

"There's an inn round the corner and two streets up," he said. I thanked the stableman and we left him to find the inn.

"Maybe an innkeeper will be easier to deal with," I told Caitria as we walked up the street. "When there's money in it, these city Engs know everything but what you want."

Although I was bitching about urban avarice, I wasn't exactly taking a soaking. There were two kinds of money then; counted coin and weighed coin. Counted coins were the ones that hadn't been reduced to make change in business transactions. Since no one thought much of slicing off a quarter or half a coin to rectify a sum, there were a lot of defaced coins around; they were called weighed coin because you had to weigh the silver to get a real idea how much you had. I was unloading all my shaved coinage in exchange for tourist information.

The kid trudged after us, the wooden wheels bumping through water-soaked ruts.

"We'll have to be sure the load's not too heavy," I told Caitria.

"You can always haul it," she said.

"My cart-hauling days are over," I said. "I've come into cash."

"This is how it starts," she warned.

"The stableman'll get a pence for sending us," I said to Caitria as we tried to avoid the street traffic and stay wide of the drop zone under the windows.

"I think we ought to give the horses to Wulfgar," Caitria said. "What do you think?"

"We sure won't be riding them to Clontarf," I said. "Why not?"

We found the inn and went inside for a drink and a

conference. It felt good to walk again, and there was no use walking over on the strength of the vague directions we'd solicited.

The innkeeper brought us a couple of cups of brown beer (half a pence each) and suggested the mutton if we were hungry. We were, but we weren't brave enough to try the mutton, so we asked him about a boatwright. It developed that the innkeeper was full of advice and bursting to share it out, and he rubbed gingerly at a sty on his left eyelid as he shared his vast knowledge of men in the business of wrighting boats.

He directed us to a place on the river where he thought we might be able to find the best boatwright in town. I was pretty sure he had the same arrangement with the boat-wright that the stableman had with him, but maybe the intimate connection between information and money in Luel was making me a little paranoid.

"What about Wulfgar?" Caitria asked me. "Maybe he can help."

"Wulfgar?" the innkeeper asked.

"Do you know him?" I asked hopefully.

"For friends of Wulfgar I'd recommend a Strathclyde Welshman," the innkeeper said, "who has a small wharf at the foot of a crooked street by the market square, and then upstream along Fisher Street."

But that was as far as we got in terms of clarity. His instructions were equally long and obscure, and after a few minutes, during which he rephrased and backtracked, drew ghost diagrams on the wood of the table, and made sure we knew the difference between the most *direct* route and the most *scenic* route (which no doubt passed the busi-nesses of several friends), I found myself nodding and mak-ing encouraging conversational noises. Caitria seemed to be listening intently, so I concentrated on my beer; she could be in charge of land navigation as far as I was concerned. But when we walked outside, she turned and asked, "Which way now?"

"I thought you were paying attention," I told her.

"It didn't make any sense."

We went into a tanner's and asked after a Strathclyde Welshman with a boatyard somewhere on Fisher Street, but the tanner professed ignorance of any boatwright except a friend of his at a different location, which he would be happy to disclose for a small monetary consideration.

"Why isn't anything easy?" I asked her after I'd declined to pay up.

"We can find the river, at least," she said. "All we have to do is go down to the low ground."

It made sense that even the Engs would keep their river on the low end of town, but when we went to the lowest street we could find we discovered it was called Wall Street, because a branch of Hadrian's wall ran along one side of it, separating us from the river. We wandered about looking for luck or a way to the other side of the wall, whichever came first.

"We're always lost when you're in charge of the directions," I said.

"I think you're wrong," she said in a tone that indicated she thought I was horribly wrong in every instance.

"It was your directions in the woods that brought us to Ravenshill."

"You were turned round before I boxed your ears," she said. "You were taking us to the road, sure as flies. Good thing you weren't in charge of finding the Severn; you'd still be rowing up and down the coast."

"I'm all the navigator we're likely to need between here and Clontarf," I said somewhat hotly.

"I hope so," she said.

Then we came to a busy street and turned right, into a broad flat square where the marketing was done, in the old Roman forum, just south of the ox-baiting arena. The gate that led to the waterfront was on the other side of the market.

Most of the riverbank in Luel consisted of a wide board-walk along the docks with shops and houses backed up against the wall of the town. Outside the wall, the smell of humans was replaced by the smells of water and fish. There were boats tied up to the docks, but none to meet our needs. They were all fishing boats rigged to work the Firth or river craft to take goods up and down the Eden; none of them had enough keel, or any, and only a few had masts. We needed something that could walk the true whaleroad, and after I looked the first couple of docks over, I began to doubt we'd find it. I was surprised when I finally found a suitable craft.

We walked out to inspect it, our footsteps creaking on the planks. The boy waited for us in the shade of the cart. The boat wasn't new, but it still had a lot of miles left on it. I hopped in to look over the construction, and it moved under my weight as if I'd startled it awake. I stood braced as the boat quivered under me along the axis of the keel. Some might say a boat like this was touchy, and some might say it was unstable, but I'd say it was a craft a used boat salesman would want to unload.

That boat wasn't made for the river traffic; it had been a small boat on an oceangoing vessel and crafted the same. When I had my legs I stooped down and gave it a close look. It was clinker-built, and the nails were clenched through washers inside the hull, but they were lashed to the ribs with spruce roots and caulked with tar and wool. The mast and loose decking were pine, and everything else was oak. It only drew a little more than a foot and it would be flexible in a blow. Running ahead of a squall in a fifteen-footer wasn't any way to introduce Caitria to small-craft seamanship, nor was it the way I wanted to end my trip home.

While I was examining the joinery I heard footsteps on the dock, and I looked up to see the promised Strathclyde Welshman, who we'd managed to find after all, walking toward the boat. He was wearing a blue tunic and a hat rimmed with shearling. Black hair shot with gray fell into and tangled with a beard of medium length. He had a shaving axe over one shoulder as if he'd just come from crafting a hull, but it could have been a prop. We took one another's measure as he approached, a used boat salesman and a prospect. Same as it ever was.

"You could sail to Rome in that craft," he said, leading with hyperbole.

"Don't want to sail to Rome," I told him, bending down again to duck the hyperbole and have a closer look at the knees.

"Where do you want to sail?"

"A coaster's all I require," I told him. "How's the hull?"

"Tight as a drum," he promised.

I stood up and started to strip off my clothes. There wasn't any hope that he'd haul it out for a look, so that meant I had to take a swim to see how much this particular drum had been played.

"A serious buyer," he said to Caitria approvingly. "I get so many lookers I expect nothing else."

"Looking first, buying after," I told him, stepping over the gunnel and into the river. The water was cold enough to make me alert, and I took a breath and slipped under. As I pulled myself along the keel, I could see that the rivets were well set and the hull was free of worms and barnacles. There was wear from being hauled up on rocky shorelines, but within normal limits. I came to the surface on the other side of the boat and pulled myself onto the dock. The Welshman held out a blanket for me.

"Satisfied?"

"Who made it?"

"A wright in Annan. He owed me, and I took it in kind."

"How long ago?"

"Two years," he lied.

"More like three or four," I said, not bothering to point out that this hull had obviously been wrighted in the Baltic.

"Maybe," he admitted with apparent reluctance. "He said two."

"I don't make boats for a living, but I know four-year-old timber from two-year-old."

He let that remark go unchallenged, understanding now I wasn't going to fall for routine salesmanship.

"Fishing or trading?" he wanted to know.

"Yes," I said.

"You've a crew?"

"Just the two of us to get where we need to be," I said. "Plenty of hands there to help out. Haul up the sail."

He hopped into the boat and grabbed the lines, familiar with the craft's lightness and landing with his weight over the keel and his legs spread fore and aft. "Tackle's good," he said. "Hemp's new. The sail's been patched, but it holds the wind."

I watched him haul up the spar. When the sail was flapping loose, I could see the patches, but the stitching looked sound. When he lowered the spar I went aft and hauled it up again, paying attention to the block. I'd seen boatwrights get round problems with the rigging by knowing how to avoid them.

"I'll want some extra rope and a second tiller bar," I said. "Where do you keep your oars?"

"Up in the shop," he said, leading the way.

"Is it a good boat?" Caitria asked as we walked after the Welshman. The ferret-faced stableboy started to get ready, but I motioned for him to relax awhile.

"Good enough to get us to Clontarf," I said. "But I'd want something else for that trip to Rome."

Inside there were racks of oars, all different lengths so they'd bite water at the same time around the curve of a hull. I went to the racks that held the lengths we'd need and pulled them out. There were three benches in the boat, which meant six oars. Since there were only two of us, we already had spares. I set the oars aside and examined the rope. It was all in good shape, and I selected a couple of coils. The Welshman was totaling up the costs for my benefit, although he already knew what he was going to ask without resorting to whatever rude arithmetic he possessed.

"Can you make a cooking frame?"

"When do you want it?"

"Before we eat again."

"I can have it by midafternoon."

"Good." I nodded. "What will it all cost?"

"A hundred pence," he said with a straight face, which I immediately laughed in.

"A hundred pence. For that tub and some rope? Are you a Walloon?" Now phase one of the serious negotiating was at hand. I was willing to pay twenty weighed coins, or the equivalent in hack, even though it was price-gouging, but a hundred counted coins was naked theft.

"I reckon you've mistaken us for royalty," I said.

He laughed with me to indicate he was just testing. "Have to have a joke," he said. "Of course it's worth only seventy-five."

"Let's go, Caitria. We can ride up to Annan in two or three hours and have a new one for forty. Thanks for the use of the blanket," I said as I took Caitria's arm and started outside.

"Wait a minute," the Welshman said. "I'll let it go for fifty."

"I hope you don't have to wait long for a buyer," I told him as we walked out onto the wharf. The boy stood up again and put the brace over his shoulders.

"You're willing to pay forty in Annan," the Welshman said, following us out and putting his hand on my arm to detain me.

"For a new craft, not a ticklish coaster with a gouged keel."

"That's reasonable usage," he said defensively.

"That's as may be, but my top price for everything is twenty counted pence, take it or leave it and wait for someone who wants a quicksilver keel on their new fishing hull."

He pretended to hesitate, and then nodded his head. "The cooking's frame's extra," he said.

I shook my head. "Frame included. We both know this craft's worth thirty weighed pence at most, and that's if it's charmed. Take the frame out of your profits."

"Cash," he said, holding out his hand.

Now we'd arrived at phase two of the serious negotiating. I waved the stableboy back onto the ground and reached into my pouch as we went back into the shop. At Wulfgar's house I had two or three hundred pence liberated from the cutpurse on Cuthbert's Feast day and forty or fifty pieces of Roman gold, along with torques, rings, and stones, but I wanted to keep all that back for Snorri and Mairead. I opened a bag of hack and shook a pile onto the boards.

"I've only got hack," I said.

The Welshman frowned and looked at me. Not only was he being done out of counted coin, but it was for hack. He pushed the hack round the board with deft flicks of his right index finger, and then he scooped it up with both hands, weighing it. He frowned and put it back on the boards. I scooped it up and weighed it myself, and then I added a few more strands. Then with a flourish he produced a scale from under the counter and scooped the hack into the balance. He offered me his weights and I looked them over before I started adding them to the scale. When everything balanced to our mutual satisfaction, he made it all disappear under the boards.

"I need some other things," I said, almost as an afterthought.

"What other things?"

"A bearing dial, a lodestone, Weather Floke's ascension tables, a tilt spar, and some canvas."

"You can't trust that Dane's scribbling."

"A man I knew swore by him," I said.

"His name should have been Weather Lucky," the Welshman said. "I have a set of tables made by a country-man of mine, superior in every way."

"Just the lodestone and the bearing dial." I stepped over to a shelf that had a few of them gathering dust. "And the tilt spar and the canvas."

The bearing dial was a pretty ingenious instrument: a wooden disk with a spindle in the center, divided into quarters, eighths, and thirty seconds. You shot a bearing at midday by putting the spindle on the sun and rotating it until south was directly underneath. At night you could shoot the dog star the same way.

The tide race down the Solway Firth would just carry us to Man, and I knew the way home from there. When you grew up in Clontarf, taking a boat to Man and back was something you did from time to time to get away from things. It was a fat island, and fleets were always putting in there, as in Clontarf. For centuries it had been a favorite refuge for royal bastards from Eng land, merchants with crooked scales, free thinkers, and people who didn't do well under the constraints of the king's laws. When I turned, the Welshman pulled out some bound sheets, which he offered with a look of relief. I recognized Floke's work at a glance.

"Take them off my hands," he said, scratching in his beard. "No one trusts them. Though if they've such magic, why the lodestone?"

"There's still fog on the ocean," I reminded him, slipping Floke's tables into my bag. "Three pence for both."

"A deal."

The Welshman and I slapped the *handsala,* and Caitria and I went back out into the sun. The boy looked over at us but stayed sitting, and when I motioned him up, he twisted his face and spat, as if he'd had just about enough of being my yo-yo. But I was in a good mood; things were looking up: in town one night and already had a boat. All that was left to do was buy provisions and get something to eat, an easy afternoon's work. I went into the first inn we saw and got a cup of beer. The boy waited outside with the cart.

We sat at the window table and watched the pedestrian traffic in the market: a parade of thralls, villains, and peasants first class, on their way to or from their daily business, carrying sacks that squirmed and sacks that didn't, baskets of fish and poultry. Indifferent oxen pulled carts of hay, barrels, lumber, stone jars, grain sacks, tools. Herds of swine, sheep, goats, and cattle were barked at and harried through the street.

It was a pleasant afternoon, sunny and clear, and it seemed like the whole population of the town was out and about, including men who didn't wear the cloth of the Engs. Tidewater towns always have transients from aboard looking for work or passage or trouble. There were Frisians, Walloons, Strathclyde Welsh, Irish, Pictish, even Frankish faces, but no Danes, although there were churchmen to make up for the lack. A churchman's blade's no duller. I spotted Benedictine cloth, but they were walking with their cowls up, and I couldn't make out their faces. Maybe I'd run into someone I knew. The mendicants, the cripples, the beggars, the maimed, the pilgrims in search of expiation, the masterless road men, all of them began to have an accustomed look, as if I'd finally made it back to a familiar reality.

I opened Floke's book and showed the tables to Caitria. Old Floke was a strange one—spent his life living out on a headland, watching the sky, and writing down what he saw. The result was a record of the sun's position at midday for the whole year, a handy thing to have if you're planning a long ocean trip, or a short ocean trip that could turn into a long one without asking leave.

"Ever been to a town this size?"

"I've been to Weogornaceaster," she said.

"Where's that?"

"Up the Severn from Tewkesbury. Their minster was taller than St. Peter's at Lindisfarne."

"I give up. You've been inside a bigger town than I have."

"Weogornaceaster was full of stone buildings."

I was suitably impressed; stone buildings have that effect when you're used to two timbered stories and a thatched roof, or sunken cottages of wattle and daub.

"Let's walk around," I suggested when our cups were empty. "We still have things to get."

We went outside, and the boy stood up. The crowd, thickening as we walked into the market, was full of the smells and sounds that eighth century Anglo-Saxon crowds were known for. Caitria led the way, and I followed, one hand on the bag over my shoulder in case I ran into anyone from the cutpurse union.

"How much food do we need?" Caitria asked me.

"It'll be a day to the Liffey. This time of year, figure on an east contrary wind, maybe a storm; considering our weatherluck, we should provision for a week in case we have to put in somewhere. If the whaleroad's smooth, it'll be a fine trip," I assured her. "But if Aegir's pissed, we may have to put in for a few days."

We looked at the goods in the market stalls. I bought a couple of small hickory casks for water. I traded some hack for a bolt of linen and some leatherwork to give to Snorri. The boy arranged the goods in the cart and followed us. While I was buying souvenirs, Caitria was provisioning for the trip and leaving me to pay. Almost before I noticed it, the cart was piled with goods.

There were bags of turnips and leeks, a small cooking pot, a larger cooking pot, a ladle, skewers, charcoal, bread, salt, cheese, apples, milk, salt pork, an iron tripod, an assortment of grains for the breakfast gruel, and at the moment she was inspecting a cage of live chickens. The boy waited in the traces while she waved me over and gave the willow cage a shake to stir up the fowl.

"If we get four chickens," she said, "we'll have fresh eggs."

I was wondering if she thought we were homesteading when I spotted a couple of men diffidently browsing from stall to stall on the other side of the market walk. Just two men killing time in the market at Luel. Their cloth was English, but they had a Baltic familiarity. They noticed me and returned the look, and then went about their business as I knelt in front of the caged chickens, still watching them.

There was something *really* familiar about the second one, and then it all fell into place. It'd been seven years since I'd seen him standing over me in the vegetable market at Clontarf, a Geat who'd already spent four years harrying the Moorish coast. The last time I'd seen him, my blood was on his sword and my face was flapping open. He hadn't changed at all when viewed from the same height and angle.

It was one of those frozen moments when everything's quiet: stillness in the midst of motion, silence in the midst of sound, and the Geat, feeling my eyes on him, turning to look my way again, trying to place me, trying to reckon why I was so interested in him. All I had to do was turn away, drop my eyes, get interested in the chickens, and he would have gone on without stopping, but I couldn't do it. Our threads had come together again in the pattern, and I couldn't pretend they hadn't.

"Geat," I shouted, standing up.

He mistook my shout for a warning and jumped aside, jostling his friend, but when he saw there was nothing to be alarmed about, he shot me an angry look. He still didn't have a clue. I stood facing him across a moving crowd of marketing Engs.

Caitria must have reckoned what was happening, but she didn't say anything, and when my hand moved to the blade, she moved aside so I had room to work. The crowd thinned out of the middle ground. I traced the scar down the side of my face.

"Still eating carrots for your limp dick?"

I saw it come to him then, and he marked me, older now, grown and bearded, soon to learn I was on speaking terms with wyrms and Jomsvikings. He flung out his cloak, drew under the cover of the swirling wool, and came at me as I slipped aside, drawing my sword to deflect the blow. The song of steel: there's nothing like it to get your attention, especially if you're singing a duet. The Geat and I circled as the crowd closed in to watch the fight and make a killing ground.

We tried to get the measure of one another as we played for time, feinting and probing. What you learn about a man's bladework in one pass isn't enough to build an offense or defense around, and we studied one another's movements, looking for the same things: a limp, a favored side, anything that would suggest a way to get a quick kill. While we were dancing, Caitria faded back into the crowd.

"Olaf, isn't it?" I asked, trying to get him talking so maybe I could get a hint about how to take him.

"Who're you?"

"Bran Snorrison," I told him. "It's your wyrd to meet me here."

"So it must be," he agreed. "I hope you've got more skill than before to make a good death."

"You be the judge," I said. "Still follow the sea road?"

"Sometimes," he said. "I just did a job of work for Offa in the south. Campaigned across the dyke against the Powys Welsh. After I kill you, I'll get a ship back to the Skagerrak."

"Don't be so sure of yourself," I cautioned, and then I went for him with three quick movements, two feints and the real blow, and he fell for the second feint and only partially recovered, getting a long slash on the thigh for his sloth. "Poor technique." I laughed.

I came out of the exchange between him and his friend, and my back was exposed. I felt that feeling you get between the shoulders when someone's looking at the spot where they plan to stab you. While I was focused on Olaf, his friend was getting ready to do me from behind. Then Olaf made his big mistake.

"After you're dead, we'll ride your woman till she drops and then shit in your face."

This brilliant taunt was meant to distract me as his friend went for my backbone. They hadn't counted on the fact that Caitria'd worked round the spectators and was closing in from his right, or anticipated the effect that kind of wit had on her. She hiked up her skirts and kicked the legs out from under his backstabbing friend, who dropped like a sack of grain. Caitria's foot was on the backstabber's throat when he hit the ground. He grabbed her ankle and twisted, and she gave him a knee drop to the groin, which would take him out of the action for twenty minutes, if I was any judge of groin injuries.

"His woman?" she demanded of Olaf as his partner writhed and puked in the dirt. "What makes you think I'd have a layabout like him? You think fighting Geats in the poultry market is some kind of compliment?"

Olaf saw his friend done to the dirt by Caitria and came at me. He had to do something. He'd just lost his hole card, and he was bleeding into his boot from the cut I'd given him. I moved into his wounded leg and he was sluggish to follow me, exposing a rack of ribs which I carved as he went by. After two exchanges the score was two to naught, and the Geat's friend was on the ground. Not bad.

"Where'd you learn the battle ice?" Olaf asked as he limped away to reassemble his defense.

"From Thorfinn Skullsplitter, on the *Blood Raven*," I said.

The look on his face was worth the wait. He'd seemed so invincible standing over me that day, not big enough to ignore an asshole with a poor sense of humor but big enough to cut him down. All my memories of Olaf were a giant Geat deciding whether to kill me or not. And now all my dreams of him, shifting shape, mocking me, were smoke up the ass of the night. I was facing him again, I'd cut him twice, and I'd just conjured Thorfinn Skullsplitter out of the fetid air between the fish and the vegetables.

I pressed him hard, and forced him back against a market stall before he brought together a defense that stopped me. Then we settled down to business. We danced round the market, and the circled crowd danced with us, filling in behind when we advanced, falling back when we pressed each other, the last tango in Luel. Steel sang in the market-place, battle ice flashed, the crowd got bigger.

After five minutes, Olaf was getting weak, and his clothing was dark with his own blood; I was winded and sweating, but the blade seemed lighter with every passing second, as if the longer it stayed in the sun, the more it became like sunlight. A flock of geese waddled into the clearing and started hissing at us and flapping their wings, jeopardizing our timing and balance. I punted one over the heads of the crowd, and Olaf put together a flurry of slashes. I caught the first two, but the third slipped by and cut the laces on my tunic. Olaf laughed and backed off.

"Your face just looked like it did the day I cut you," he taunted. "Pissing your pants?"

"Who's bleeding and who isn't?" I asked menacingly. "Who's getting light-headed? Who's friend will piss blood for a month? Who sailed with Thorfinn Skullsplitter?"

"Anyone can say they sailed with Thorfinn Skullsplitter."

"But I said it," I pointed out. "And you'll soon believe me."

I circled. The blade was moving so fast that I was having trouble keeping up. It went where I thought, pulling my hands after, teaching me how to use it. I pressed Olaf with a blur of feints and cuts, making the iron in his hands hum. Then he slipped in some wet straw and went down into a pile of horseshit. On his way back up I met him with thirty-four inches of Weyland's steel. He stopped with his chin resting on the point of the blade, and we looked at each other for four or five seconds, breathing hard and blinking sweat out of our eyes while the crowd got quiet, waiting to see what I'd do. I stepped on his blade and he let it go.

I reckoned Lindisfarne hadn't managed to erase everything I'd learned all those evenings in the mead hall, not to mention the things I'd seen and done on the *Blood Raven*. It's true you can take the boy out of the Viking, but you can't take the Viking out of the boy. But for some reason I hesitated; after all those years and all those night sweats, something prevented me from letting his ghost out of a hole in his throat. I dropped the point of the blade and stepped back. It was vibrating in my hands, as if it smelled how close Olaf's blood was. Pissing off a runesword hammered by Wayland and fully charged by a wyrm's magnetic field wasn't anything I wanted to do. Maybe I'd been at Lindisfarne too long, hanging out with Christians.

Look where it was getting me. Olaf had changed my life, and now I was in the position to change his. I stood there with a certain knowledge that if I killed Olaf, he'd only be the first in a long line of souls that blade would suck dry with my help. That was Thorfinn's job description, not mine; the blade was for him. I was only the delivery boy, but it seemed unfair to let it taste Geat since we'd come this far to make the meeting.

I brought the blade up along the side of Olaf's face, or it brought me up, slashing long, deep, wide, and continuous from jaw to hairline, and the Geat's blood ran down the fuller toward my hands. He fell away from me, propped up on one elbow, trying to stanch the blood with his free hand.

"Get up," I told him.

"Losing your nerve?" he wanted to know, clenching his numbed face together as blood reddened his knuckles. "Become a Christian?"

"Your luck," I said. "Forewarned's innocent. Now you're marked in turn, and if I ever see you again, awake or dreaming, you're dog meat. Get your friend and get out of here."

Olaf picked up his blade and helped his white-faced friend stumble to his feet. Then they pushed their way through the crowd, which, now that the entertainment was over, was remembering its business and going back to it. Good thing; their smell was getting to me. Caitria was waiting by the caged chickens. The ferret-faced stableboy stood beside the cart with his mouth open. I slipped the runesword back into the scabbard. I had the shakes, and I put my hands into my sleeves to hide them. The goose I'd kicked flapped drunkenly around by a stall, trailing a broken wing.

"Go kill that bird and find out how much the owner wants," I told the boy, and as he picked up one of the iron legs of the tripod to dispatch the goose, I turned to Caitria.

"Never a dull time when we're on the town, eh?"

"I thought you'd kill him."

"So did I." I shrugged, holding out my hands for her to see the tremors. "But when I came to it, marking him was enough. I'm as scared as I was seven years ago."

"You didn't look scared," she said, taking my hands.

"Thorfinn once told me image is all. The blade did the work," I told her. "I just held on to it. I'll be glad to give it up. Whoever holds that blade's doomed to use it."

"You're more Christian than you reckon," Caitria said, releasing my hands.

"That's as may be." I shook my head. "Don't spread it round. I've got a reputation to live up to."

The boy came back with the limp-necked goose and threw it on top of the supplies in the cart. "No charge," he said.

I sat back on the cart and looked at my feet while my breathing returned to normal. I reckoned that you had to slice up someone in the marketplace to get a bargain in Eng land. The tiredness was on me, and I needed a few minutes to get myself together, but I saw Wulfgar coming toward us in a hurry, and I stood up to meet him. He had a cage under his arm, and when he got closer I saw there were a couple of ravens inside it, trying to make the best of the shaking up they were getting as he jogged along.

"The Wic-reeve's on his way to see about the fight," he said. "It's just like Æthelwulf to take in someone who brawls with Geats in the market and then shove him off on me. Do you think you're still in the outback? This is a civilized town."

I looked around at the flower of the Northumbrian middle and lower classes and wondered how he'd come to that conclusion; they'd gathered round quick enough when the bladework started, looking to see severed limbs twitching in the street; maybe the hallmark of civilization was sending for the Wic-reeve when they realized no one was going to die. Whatever the reason, he was on the way, and Wulfgar was concerned.

"We've got to get out of here," he said, putting the bird cage into the cart. "The reeve will arrest you for fighting, and I'll have to go surety for you as a guest. I told you the rule was no killing anyone. You're not in the Chevoits now."

"I didn't kill him," I pointed out, "but let's go to the wharf." I motioned the boy back in the traces. "The boat-wright may have the frame done, and if not it's no loss."

Wulfgar looked over his shoulder and hurried us along. The rest of our gear was at his house, but the first order of business was to get out of the marketplace. Wulfgar and I walked on either side of the cart, pulling it along by the shafts so the boy was trotting between us to keep up. We turned through the alley and onto the wharf with a rumble of wheels.

"How's the frame?" I called out to the Welshman, who was on his knees in the boat.

"All done but the dirt."

The boat bobbed under my weight as I stepped aboard. We unloaded the supplies as we talked, Caitria taking them from the cart and handing them on to Wulfgar, who tossed them down to me. The Welshman stood on the dock and took a-measure of the hurry we were in. The boy was catching his breath, but he didn't have long to do it.

"You know where I live, boy?" Wulfgar asked the stable snipe.

He nodded.

"Run up to the house and get their gear," Wulfgar told him. "Bring it down in the cart, and tell a couple of the boys I want them. Any couple'll do. Don't waste time."

The snipe disappeared round the corner in a moment.

"He'll be fifteen minutes gone and back," Wulfgar said, tossing the last of the packages to me. I stowed the gear forward the mast and covered it up with the canvas. Caitria was watching the opening between the buildings. If anyone came for us, they'd come from there.

"Let's settle up," I said to the Welshman, getting out of the boat.

"We're quit," he said. "Except for the dirt: two pence a pound."

I put my hand on the sword and looked at him meaningfully. "Dirt's free," I said, "and in the frame in ten minutes."

The Welshman slipped by us on the edge of the dock, started round the cart, and then stopped to push it ahead of him.

"Be sure it's dirt and not barn scrapings," I called after him. I didn't want to build a fire on dirt mixed with the shit of some herbivore. I was on to that trick: we'd played it on each other growing up.

"Why were you fighting?"

"Old blood debt," I told him, pulling my thumb along the scar the Geat'd left seven years before.

"Is that all? I thought he said something about Caitria." He must have thought it was all some elaborate joke by Æthelwulf. First the silver filigreed horn with a voice like the wet farts of Odhinn, and then the job of escorting me and Caitria to Luel, where we brawled in the market. Wulfgar just wanted to trade furs with the Strathclyde Welsh, not have visitations from troublemakers because of Æthelwulf's rustic sense of humor.

"He did, but she made his friend pay for it," I said. I went aft for a look at the spare tiller handle as the Welshman came back with the cart.

"Gravel," the Welshman said. "Good ballast."

I grabbed the edges of the canvas and lifted it over the gunwale as the Welshman stepped down. The boat moved around as we carried the canvas forward and emptied it into the cooking frame. Dust swirled around our knees, and the Welshman stowed the canvas under the gunwale before he went back on the dock.

There was a clatter at the mouth of the alley, and the boy came trotting beside a horse hitched to a cart with our gear in it. Wulfric and Wulfhart jumped out and positioned themselves to cover the street.

The gear was stowed in a churchman's minute, but when Caitria stepped onto the boat, it bucked under her foot like she'd put a spur into it. Caitria knew as much about walking a deck as I knew about flying. She grabbed the mast and steadied herself as the boat settled down. I turned away to hide my smile. There was no use provoking her with the boat already this nervous.

"Does this thing have a name?" Caitria asked.

"It's called the *Ged*," the Strathclyde Welshman said,

looking relieved now that he was about to see the last of us and the boat. Telling us the boat's name was like handing over the keys.

There were three benches, two aft the mast step and one forward, and Caitria eased along until she was sitting on the bench closest to the mast, her legs spread, tense for movement, but as Caitria relaxed a little, the boat calmed itself. A low center of gravity was definitely a good thing until Caitria got her legs.

"Relax," I told her. "The boat's picking up your fear and trying to throw you out. A seamare's no different than any other mare. You need the seat for one and the legs for the other."

She didn't look convinced.

"Have a good trip," Wulfgar called as he untied the painter. I sat at the star board and slipped the line that held the boat's tail. The tug of the surrendering knots made the vane turn in its greased socket, as if it were sniffing for wind.

I pivoted the star board out of the water and changed my seat to the last oar bench, sitting with my back to Caitria and unshipping the two pine oars through the wool padded oarlocks. "Do what I'm doing," I said over my shoulder. Wulfgar pushed off the bow with his foot and the *Ged* turned its face toward the middle of the Eden. "Stop back anytime," Wulfgar called after us, waving. I nodded as I leaned forward and let the oars bite water. The *Ged* jolted up like I'd goosed it and then glided out toward the current. I heard the scrape of pine on oak, and then a thrashing off the star board as the *Ged* jerked to the right and a splash of the Eden hit me on the neck.

"Keep the oars out of the water," I told her. "Make the motion but don't get them wet till you get the rhythm."

She kept pine out of the water, and I heard the rowlock creaking as she matched my strokes. "Brace your feet on the deck strip and use your legs more than your back. You'll feel better tomorrow."

"How long are we going to row?"

I looked over my shoulder at the end of a back stroke and saw that the vane was only moving with the motion of the boat. So far there was no wind, and even if there were, the Eden was as windy a watercourse as the Severn, and I didn't want to tack a square-rigged craft between its banks.

"Until we're out of the river," I said.

The first bend of the Eden was just west of Luel, and the Roman wall crossed the water and continued on the west bank. There were more Roman workings at the next bend, and they ran on both sides for a mile before they opened out, and then we were on the north side of the wall again, the first time since we'd left Æthelwulf.

The wall stayed on the north bank for another mile and then the river flowed into the first of the marshes that bordered the Firth. I rowed and Caitria tried periodically to learn the stroke, always a bit out of time and pulling the *Ged*'s vane toward one or the other bank.

"You're trying too hard," I said. "Give it rest. This boat will go well enough for me."

River traffic was changing. We passed boats coming back with fish in their bellies, men wrestling with nets on their decks. We saw fowlers with their hulls run into the reeds, lurking for the marsh fowl that came in low on their way to feed.

I shipped the oars and reached into the bag for the bearing dial and Floke's tables. It was about an hour after the middle of the day, but I could shoot a rough bearing and get an idea where Man was. We were in the middle of the channel, and the ground was low on both sides of us, though it rose up in the distance. Ahead was a sea of marsh grass, and beyond, the great mud estuary of the Firth. It'd be buggy as hell this time of year, full of geese and ducks and stinking in the heat, but it was the way to open water. The tide was running with us, and Man lay to the Out South.

"Maybe we'll find wind in the Firth," I told Caitria.

"There can't be more wind than we're leaving behind," she said, insisting on the last word.

The *Ged* settled down as the Eden widened and got saltier, and then we were on the Firth. The tide rush carried us out toward the Irish sea. Caitria practiced with the oars until I made her stop. The day progressed, the sun moved down in the sky, and I sculled to keep us in the channel. I didn't want to get caught on a mudflat for the next twelve hours and then have to move against a waxing tide. The channel hugged the south shore of the Firth, moving in the same drunken meanders that the Eden had adopted inland.

All the Eng rivers were treacherous where they met the sea, and I was hopeful we'd be well out by dark.

"Let's put this gear in order," I said, going forward.

Caitria kept to her seat above the keel, and I stepped around her and started sorting out the pile of equipment and provisions. The cage with the two ravens had been loaded in the confusion of our departure. They cackled and hopped about, and I thought about releasing them but decided they might come in handy if I needed a guide to shore. I looked back at Caitria, and it was plain she wasn't going to be moving around with confidence in time to help me with the gear.

"Can you swim?" I asked her.

"Yes, but I'm not eager to," she said without turning round.

"Don't worry," I told her. "This is a safe enough boat if you don't piss it off. Tie a line to your middle if it'll make you feel better. If you go over, I can always pull you back in."

"I'm not going over," she said. "I'm not moving."

"We'll be a day on this boat at least," I reminded her. "You can't sit there for a day."

"Watch me," she said.

"Well, how are you going to piss?"

"I won't."

She'd change her mind soon enough. I'd sat an oar bench, and I knew how she'd feel in a few hours. I turned back to my sorting, and she unbent enough to take a couple of things and pass them aft. I opened out the canvas and put the bag of writing materials on it, and then packed our clothes around them. I took out Caitria's travel clothes and handed them back to her, balancing the *Ged* as she stripped out of the skirts that Aud had given her with slow and deliberate movements.

"You've got to get your legs," I told her as she pulled on her road duds. "If you're going to Ireland, water's the only way to come back."

"I'll worry about the going, first," she said.

"Boats are like horses. If you can ride, there's no reason why you can't sail a boat. I'll teach you all you need to know in a few hours after you get your legs."

"And how do I get my legs?"

"By using them."

She stood up slowly and waited to see what would happen. Her legs were so tense I could see them quivering under her pants and soon the *Ged* was rocking on its keel. I was relieved when she sat back down.

"It's a start," I said, looking for something encouraging to say. I finished restowing the gear, sat on the bench beside her, and put an arm round her shoulders. I told her about the race to Man between Macc Oc's Irish and Sygtrygg's Danes, and how it had ended quickly on the crab flat, but it didn't seem to cheer her up.

The vane was still listless on the prow, so there was no use hauling up the spar. I squinted toward the shore. There were a scattering of rocks as far down the coast as I could see, but I unshipped the oars and turned the boat toward land. I turned the *Ged*'s nose into a large bay and ran up a creek mouth.

Once we were tethered, Caitria started to relax. The creek was about waist deep, and I got out and had a look round. There was a fisherman's cottage a mile down the shore where a coaster was pulled up above the waterline and settled on its side in the gravel. I found a spring that would fill the water casks. The tide was starting to turn, but the stream would take us to open water quickly enough. The rocks on the shoreline were exposed like Eng land's teeth, and I'd be glad to get into the deep water. There was a creak, and the vane turned its head with a shore breeze. Not enough to fill a sail, but a start.

Caitria was dog tired when I got back; all those muscles used in unaccustomed ways were making their objections felt. The oars took us out of the creek and through the channel to open water, and before Caitria could pull herself above the gunnel we were out in the Firth again. There was a wind, and I dropped the star board and slipped the tiller bar into place. Then I hauled up the spar. The sail bellied out, and the *Ged* jumped, putting Caitria on her ass again. She'd be good for some laughs till she got her legs.

The east wind steadied, and we started making five or six knots, good time for a craft like the *Ged*. I sat back against the star board and rode the tiller while the wind dried my hair. Running ahead of an easterly was a good omen for the start of the trip, and I was feeling better. The ravens were settling down to some raven discussion, preening as the breeze fluffed out their indigo feathers. I gave them a handful of corn and some water and thought about what it would be like to walk in with a woman, two ravens, and a boat that had a mind of its own after three years and no postcards.

It was just another voyage in a small open boat, with Caitria hugging the mast, two ravens talking things over in a cage, the Norns, like common household Fetches, sitting on the spar with their hair blowing in the wind, and a school of dolphins escorting us from the mouth of the Solway Firth to Man. All through the dark night on the Irish Sea, under a summer sky scattered with open ocean stars. I taught Caitria how to sail. We'd spent time together on the land road, looking at the night sky and counting stars, gaming, talking about wyrd and duty and the price of sheep, but the sea road wasn't the Northumbrian outback, and I was finally back under a sky I understood.

Dolphins showed up when we hit open water, matching our six knots without any trouble. We watched them, slipping through water and air with equal familiarity, shifting shape between fish and whistles and clicks and wetly suggestive noises, and after dark we could still hear them splashing and talking, and occasionally feel them rubbing their backs against the *Ged*'s keel as they passed underneath us.

"Caitria," I said when the stars were full out. "Come back here so I can teach you about the sky." She made her way aft with considerably more skill than she'd had that morning, when the *Ged* had only tolerated her; a couple of times I'd had to save her from being thrown out, but she finally had legs enough to walk around without pissing off the boat.

I taught Caitria how to shoot the dog star with the bearing dial and where to find it on Floke's chart. Then I showed her how to check it with the lodestone. Even though she couldn't read, she was a quick study, and soon she knew how to use the navigational instruments of the day. I answered her questions about how to chart courses and find your way across the sea. When she tired of celestial navigation we put out a baited line and pretty soon we had a good-sized fish flapping on the deck. Caitria made a charcoal fire while I watched the sail and rode the star board, and we ate fish and chased it with an apple and cold spring water. When we were full, and the fire was out, we wrapped in our cloaks against the sea chill and listened to the dolphins that swam around the *Ged*.

I showed Caitria how to ride the star board, and made sure she knew which stars to guide on, and when she'd passed a quiz I tied her to the bench with a short length of rope, told her to wake me if any weather came in, and rolled up in my blanket for a few hours' sleep.

I thought about the case Æthelwulf made for jumping the broom with her. Caitria was game for just about anything. She was smart enough to give good advice and sometimes smart enough not to. She knew about wyrms, admittedly an arcane subject, but one which I'd managed to find myself enmeshed in and might again, for all I knew. She was a looking woman, so things wouldn't be boring, and she got on with witches like old Gamma. I knew that Mairead and Sinead would take to her better than they'd taken to Frydys. So would Snorri and Goltrade. Even Skallagrim would come round.

I fell asleep thinking about how easily Caitria would fit into life in Clontarf, and in my dreams I saw her in the farmhouse, in the crowd of villagers on the road to Ravenshill Moor, in the wyrm's lair, in the dolmens, in Æthelwulf's hall, in the market in Luel, and on the deck of the *Ged*, wrapped in her cloak as she steered west.

She woke me in a few hours and we traded places, I corrected the course to account for the changes in the sky and shot the dog Star again. It was the time of year when the planet passes near the Oort cloud and stars were falling, and we lay beside the tiller and watched for the streaks of light against the path of ghosts.

Caitria saw twenty for every one I saw, laughing with contagious happiness every time and keeping score to show her superior vision. It pleased her so much I kept quiet about some of the stars I saw first so I could enjoy her mood. I'd nursed a mood of a different sort for days, cultivating emptiness like a newly discovered vice, and we needed a rest from snarling at each other; falling stars were just the ticket.

"Another one," she cried, pointing up at the sky. "Another one. You asleep? How're you missing them?"

"I don't believe it," I told her. "You're lying."

"You hope," she said indignantly, and rapped me on top of the head with her knuckles. "You're just blind."

"Not too blind to see that one," I said.

"Where? Now *you're* lying."

We laughed and argued like that for a couple of hours, wrapped in our blankets in the *Ged*.

Caitria finally went to sleep, and the dolphins played in their playground. A couple of hours before sunup, Man came up where it should have, growing out of the horizon, blocking out the low western stars. I woke Caitria to show her the proof of Weather Floke's genius and the stupidity of the Engs and the Strathclyde Welsh. I tacked south, keeping Man on our right. We spotted lights on the high ground, but they were only points—no buildings stood out. Then the dolphins left us; chirping and clicking their fare-wells, they dove under the boat and fell behind, into time's wake. Man stayed to our star board for the next two hours, through breakfast and a stretch and a piss over the side, through another short shift at the oars when the island stole our wind, and through another shot of the sun with the bearing dial.

I let Caitria do the navigation and checked her work. She'd learned it well enough the night before, and when Man started to fall behind us, we were on the right bearing. Gulls came out to look us over, and we saw the sails of a few small fishing boats closer to the island. My biggest worry was that we might run into a fleet from the Mark, passing through the Irish Sea. They should have been through already, but who could tell? A late start out of the Skagerrak was all it took to throw you off schedule. There was a chance that they might give us a lift, but there was an equal chance they might kill us and take what we had. A dragon, with more sheet to the wind, would make half again the speed of the *Ged*.

We passed the day without speaking much or needing to. Caitria was discovering the rhythms of the water, and I was getting used to them again. We fished, cooked the fish, ate the fish, and watched the gulls. I taught her a little more of sailing, how to handle the rigging, how to coax momentum out of a wind that wanted to work against you. She sat at the bow under the vane with the wind whipping her hair around, but no more dolphins were conjured from the sea. The sun dropped into the west, and Caitria took her turn at the star board. I went through my gear, sorting out the gifts and checking the condition of the vellum and the writing materials. Ireland was low off the star board; I was beginning to smell home.

Home has a scent laced with pheromones and memories, tempered by years and miles, filtered by experience, but a unique scent you always know when you smell it. Ireland's scent, carried out across the water south of Man, triggered memories, and the wyrm's mood came over me, and the boat seemed to be floating above the sea, and the sail seemed to become the spread wings of a white owl, clutching the mast as if it still grew in the forest, and Caitria, kneeling in the prow, became a living figurehead with her hair blowing forward across her face, and I felt ready to take off the masks of what I'd been and done and become and show my true face to my home.

When darkness came I could feel myself being drawn to it like a lodestone's drawn to north. And about two hours after sundown, I steered toward the shore, and the smell of that green place was like fresh-mown hay after the astringent sea air. I reckoned we'd make landfall a little below Drogheda, just south of where Paidrig had landed a few hundred years before, prepared to throw down the old gods and throw out the snakes.

Two hours later, just after I shot the dog star for the last time, a fog came up, obscuring the stars. The treacherous acoustics of the fog made Caitria nervous, and I assured her I could see through it with the lodestone. It turned out I was right, and the stone was enough; the *Ged* came out of the fog and into the bay of the Liffey just a little before the middle of the night. The sky was clear, and the lights of Clontarf showed across the water.

A small fleet dozed in the anchor ropes, more than a dozen dragons, their details indistinct in the darkness, their sails furled on the spars. I recognized boats from the vik: *Ran's Delight*, Grundi's boat with the net pattern on the sail; Eirik Whale's boat, the *Ice Skimmer*, the two knarr, *Skaldi* and *Gefion*; and the other ships, shadowed and quiet. The *Ged* slipped among them like a thought, glided up to the dock, and nudged it softly. An oil torch burned in a socket on the last pier. Caitria tied off the bowline, and I shipped the star board and tied off the stern. There was no movement from the town; no one had noticed our arrival.

Caitria and I looked at each other for a long minute, prolonging the journey now that only a few more steps remained.

This was not the homecoming I required: slipping in like an outlaw wasn't what I'd had in mind. I'd left in the midst of a greater enthusiasm, and I expected a greater enthusiasm for my return. The wyrm's mood made it worse, and I felt a flash of insignificance, realizing I'd been forgotten by my own people.

Caitria looked up at the sky while I sat on the gunnel of the *Ged*, one hand on the planks of the dock, looking at the lights on the earthwork and in the houses and cottages that had grown up on the outside of the ditch since I'd been gone. Finally she stood up, and I did too, and we took one another's hand and stepped out of the *Ged*.

16

Clontarf

It is safe to tell a secret to one,
Risky to tell it to two,
To tell it to three is thoughtless folly:
Everyone else will know.
—The Sayings of the Wise One

"Impressive coastal defenses," Caitria said.

I looked at her and smiled. "When did you become an expert?"

"All I've ever heard about Danes is how fierce they are, and the first Danish town I see's as well defended as a henhouse."

"You must mean those other Danes," I said. "The ones who rape and pillage and extort money from innocent civilians."

"Right," she affirmed. "Danes, like you."

I stepped back into the *Ged* and lifted our gear onto the dock. Caitria walked across the planks to work out the kinks. She stopped at the end of the dock and bent forward to touch her palms to the wood beside her feet. I was stiff too, but I wasn't about to attempt *that*. Behind her was the familiar outline of Clontarf's earthwork enfolded in the oak silences of Thorr's forest. I was back in god's country after a long trip in a time when gods had turf, and their turf was intimately connected to the people who lived on it. Returning to the place I was born made me realize where the center of the universe was.

Clontarf had drawn me back as straight as a salmon heading to its upstream doom, and I reckoned I knew what my doom was as I watched Caitria straighten up against the backdrop of my past. I had unfinished business, and I'd only really be home when it was finished, but that didn't mean I was going to walk on Clontarf dirt after three years with a bad attitude about wyrd, at least not right away: first I was going to celebrate.

I shrugged off the wyrm's mood as I put the last bags on the dock and stepped out of the *Ged*. The fog, lying a couple of hundred yards out, dampened and imprisoned sound, giving it an artificial hollowness. I didn't hear Caitria's step as she walked up on the planks, but suddenly she was there beside me.

"What's it like?"

"Hard to put into words. Three years under the keel . . ." I made a gesture of incapacity. The fog had wet us, and the water drops fractured and scintillated the torchlight in her hair and on the shoulders of her cloak. "Want to change clothes?"

"Still going for a big entrance?"

"Sure as salt. A big entrance can't hurt."

"Make your wyrd," she said. "But whatever you do, do it soon. I've been in that boat for a long time, and I want to eat."

I opened the big chest and took out Caitria's green gown. The silk shimmered in the torchlight as Caitria changed. I reached two of the bags out. The dock was littered with our gear.

"How are we going to get all this junk up the hill?" she asked as she took off her tunic.

"We'll send back for it later," I said, setting aside the scrips that I'd gotten at Lindisfarne.

"Don't you want to show off all the loot?" She slipped the dress down over her head and laced up the bodice.

"There's time enough. If it weren't for you I'd be back in the cave, so why not show *you* off?"

She gave me a look that would have blunted an axe. "Take a joke," I said.

"I ought to throw you in the water," she said threateningly, stripping the pants off and kicking them free. "It's your business if you make your homecoming wet." She gathered up her travel clothes.

"I intend to get as wet as I can get and stay that way for, I should think, about four days if I don't piss myself to death first. And when someone asks if you're my woman, you're on your own. Just don't hurt them." I closed the lid of the chest and picked up my baggage. Then I slipped the scabbard of the runesword through my belt, put the hood of my cloak up, and looked around. Skallagrim's staff was leaning against the side of the pile; I picked it up too.

Caitria laughed as she surveyed the effect. The two ravens shrugged off the fog, and I lifted the cage into the torchlight.

"What do you have to say for yourselves?" I asked them. They shook out their feathers without comment.

"Let's go," Caitria said.

"Don't whine," I said. "We're going." I started down the dock, but I was still dragging my feet, and when I hesitated, Caitria shoved me off the planks. I stumbled ashore in a song of silver and a complaint of ravens, burdened by the props for my entrance.

"I told her I'd come home charmed."

"More lucky than charmed, I reckon," Caitria said.

"Luck's not bad as long as it holds, but knowing what you're about and acting smart's even better."

Caitria looked at me and shook her head. "Your wyrd awaits."

"So be it." I nodded, looking at her with the eyes of a man for whom all things are again possible.

"You're home now," she said. "What's passed has no matter."

We started up the hill. I remembered the procession out the morning we left to teach Offa a lesson in revenge. I'd gotten two runes that morning and worn them since. They were the only things I still had from the vik. Everything else was gone.

"Doesn't seem that long ago I left," I told her.

"When you sleep for a couple of years at a time, I reckon it's like that," she said, holding up the hem of her dress.

The path took us through a cluster of fishing shacks that I didn't remember. On down the shingle, several hulls were growing up around their ribs in the shipyard, but no one was working the night shift. We passed through the sand that marked the high-water line and stepped into the lushness of Eire. The earthwork was a hundred yards away. There were more houses built outside it. Part of the homefield had been ceded to real estate. I wondered what other changes had occurred, whose ass buffed wood in the high seat, whose lives were about to be upset by my return.

We walked up the street without being challenged, or

even seen. A dog whined away from us in the darkness, and that was the only greeting I got, walking down the main street of my hometown, just another native son trying to do what he can't. Noise came through the window of the hall.

When we reached the door, Caitria hugged me. "Well, come," she said, and kissed me on the cheek. "Bran Snorrison's home, and nothing will ever be the same again."

I smiled at her and put a hand on the door latch. "Brace yourself," I warned her. "You've never seen Danes at home. Axe juggling's tame compared to it."

I lifted the latch and put my weight against the oak. When I cracked the door, the noise of the hall broke around us like water through a failing dam, and we walked inside. I was stunned. They'd built the hall out in a fashion I'd never seen before: cut out the wall on one end and joined it up to an intersecting hall in a nearly cruciform floor plan. It was more like the church at Lindisfarne than the place where I'd puked up my first mead eight years before.

The hearth was a T-shaped trough of stone and fire, and full benches ranged along the walls of both wings. Oil lamps were suspended from the oak beams, and now that the eating was over and the cooking fire had burned down, it was like the night sky outside: pinpoints of light hanging in the middle distance.

The high seat was opposite the door, the full length of Orm's old hall away, a good seventy feet. There must have been a hundred trenchermen on the benches, elbows and in some cases torsos on the boards, their backs to the door and their attention on a man standing where the two halls intersected, just below the high seat. I didn't recognize him, but I knew it wasn't Skallagrim. If he was singing verse, Clontarf had a new skald. Caitria and I stepped inside and closed the door, putting our backs against the oak to listen.

"A wizard was walking through the country of the Brondings," the man said, "and he came on a farm just at nightfall. The farmer was out in the stable with the animals, forking in some fresh straw, and the wizard asked him if he could put up there for the night.

"So the Bronding says, 'You can stay in the barn where the fresh hay will keep you warm.' The wizard sleeps there and has a dry night and warm. The next morning he gets up and goes into the house to thank the farmer. Now, the Bronding's making breakfast, and he has a place set for the wizard, makes him sit down and eat, cooks him up some nice sausages and eggs, and a cup of ale on the side. The wizard tucks in and soon he's got an empty plate and a full belly, and then he and the Bronding have another cup.

"So the wizard says, 'You've been very kind, and I'd like to pay you back. I'll talk to your animals and find out if anything's wrong with them so you can attend to it.'

"So the Bronding says, 'Thanks a lot.' And the wizard goes down to the barn, and he's gone for about half an hour. The Bronding goes about his business, and when the wizard's done he finds the Bronding out back.

"The wizard says, 'Your horse says you changed bits about three weeks ago to a different kind that hurts his mouth, and he'd like you to go back to the old kind.'

"And the Bronding says, 'Wodin's whiskers, I did change the bit three weeks ago. I'll go back to the old one today.'

"And the wizard says, 'I talked to your cows too, and they said now the weather's cold you're wearing gloves when you milk them and the woold scratches their teats. They want you to stop wearing gloves at milking time.'

"And the Bronding says. 'They're right, I've been wearing my mittens in the morning. I'll take them off when I milk the cows.'

"And the wizard says, 'And I talked to the sheep—'

"And the Bronding says, 'Those sheep are fucking liars.' "

A good Bronding joke always brought down the house, and that one was no exception. Halfway through the story I recognized Thord the Jolly, the leader of the *Blood Raven* berserks and general quarterdeck cut up. I nudged Caitria and caught her eye as I opened the ravens' cage and shook them out.

They shrieked and pulled their way into the air, eager to stretch their wings in the warm hall, flapping through the heated air above the dying fire in the hearth pit, jinking through the suspended oil lamps, wings wooshing and small fluffs of black down riding the turbulence behind them. Shouts of laughter became shouts of alarm and surprise, and men reeled back and slipped off the benches or stepped on one another as they stood. Horns and cups clattered on the table, and mead splashed to the floor.

The two ravens went straight for the man in the high seat, obscuring my line of sight and hiding his face. Thord the Jolly fell backward over the pile of firewood as they came at him, and the ravens flared for a landing in front of the startled and speechless face of Sygtrygg Ormson.

"What an asshole," one of the ravens said, looking at Sygtrygg.

"You said it," the second raven agreed in a clear voice.

Sygtrygg scrambled on his seat when the ravens spoke, and he was no less startled than I was. Thord threw wood on the coals at the intersection of the two hearth pits, and it sent a shower of sparks out of the coal bed, hesitated a moment, and blazed up as the ravens preened and strutted about, shitting on the boards and cackling raucously.

Sygtrygg's hawks spread their wings on the tree behind the high seat and screamed, but the ravens ignored them. More wood went on the blue-hot coals, and when the fire was blazing I stepped forward out of the shadows by the door, holding my arms out to show them empty hands. The hood shadowed my features. Caitria moved beside me into the light, and we stepped into the hall.

As we walked along the pit, I scanned the faces and only recognized a few men I'd known before and not well. They looked like they'd prospered since I'd seen them last. The rushes scraped under my boots, and the ravens hopped down the table with the arrogance of prince-bishops to tear an abandoned loaf of bread apart with decisive thrusts of those pointed beaks. I reckoned they'd rather be stripping a carcass, but they seemed willing to settle for bread. They slurped up some mead from a spill on the table and threw their heads back and gargled.

"This tastes like horse piss," one of them said.

Caitria and I stopped opposite the high seat, and I waited to see who'd do what. The people at the table in the new wing of Orm's hall were familiar: Sygtrygg's thanes, their wives and women standing behind them with pitchers of mead; Orm's widows, Alfhild, Svanhvit and Gudrud, sitting in a place of honor at the head table. Sygtrygg slowly overcame his surprise.

"Odhinn's eye patch," he said as he stared at us.

It was one of those times you wish you had a voice you could project from someplace deep in your middle to blow unsecured objects off tables, but I didn't have that kind of voice, then or now, and so I kept my silence. And what did I have to say that would top the ravens, anyway?

In the stories, Odhinn always wore a hooded cloak and was preceded by his two ravens. Huggin (thought) and Munnin (memory), and maybe had a wishmaiden at his elbow, one of the looking women of Asgaard. If there'd been a chance to convince Sygtrygg I was Odhinn, even for a second, I'd have tried it, but the theatricality of the entrance was all the magic I had.

"What's the difference between a Frisian woman and a catfish?" I asked.

His brows knit together, mistaking it for a cunning riddle and trying to unravel it. The ravens finished off the bread and came back down the table, subvocalizing a conversation in their own language that sounded like stones grinding together inside a leather bag. Sygtrygg's eyes wandered down the ruin of his table and then back to me, no nearer an answer.

"One has whiskers and smells," I told him. "And the other lives at the bottom of a river." The look on his face when I delivered the punch line was so exquisitely ridiculous that I reached up and pulled the hood off my head and smiled at him across the flames that were crackling in the hearth. "Haven't you learned *any*thing while I've been gone?"

If the ravens had made an impression, Bran Snorrison's face on Odhinn's body detonated with an altogether greater magnitude. Women and men screamed, hands flew up in the sign to avert, and I heard Snorri's voice behind me shouting, "Thorr's foreskin!"

I turned around. Everyone I knew was sitting in the main gallery opposite the high seat. Snorri, Skallagrim, and Goltrade were staring at me; Mairead and Sinead had their hands up in warding gestures, startled out of their wits. On the other side of the hearth, even Thorfinn, sitting on the bench with his arms crossed, looked surprised. Sometime, if you want to make a really good entrance, come back from the dead.

"Mother," I said. "Your night sight's failed you. I never swam in the deepest sea, for all Thorfinn's poor seamanship."

She dropped her hands as I spoke. I shrugged out of the cloak and let it drop into the rushes. Caitria slipped her hood off her face.

"This is my partner on the road, called Caitria, who isn't my woman and will make things unpleasant for anyone who assumes she is."

Mother and Sinead were weeping, and even Goltrade was speechless, but Skallagrim looked like he'd lost some lines, and Snorri was looking around for a horn and the wherewithal to fill it. Old Snorri knew the first item on the agenda. He wrenched a pitcher of mead from a woman who'd pressed herself against the wall, whom I recognized as Ingibjorg, one of Frydys's loom-sitting sisters who'd been entertained by the birching Frydys got from Sygtrygg.

Snorri vaulted over the trestle boards, landing off balance and teetering dangerously close to the hearth fire. I put out a hand to steady him, and when he felt my grip he leaped at me, spilling mead over both of our heads as his arms went round my shoulders. He picked me up and spun my feet through the hearth flames.

I saw the faces of my growing up whirling past, my half-brothers and -sisters, my aunt-mothers, childhood friends, the crewmen of the *Blood Raven*, Thord the Jolly, Thorfinn, all released from the petrification of their surprise by Snorri's greeting. Caitria stepped out of the way as they leaped over the tables and crowded round, and I saw her step up onto the platform and greet Mairead and Sinead. My ribs were cracking when Snorri released me. Sygtrygg pounded me on the back, and then the crowd parted like the Red Sea and Thorfinn grabbed me by the shoulders and shook me until my eyes bounced round in my head.

"I've owed this fat limping horse trader for three years because you washed from my deck," he shouted, "and now you walk in here with a woman and two ravens pretending to be Odhinn. Where've you been?" he demanded, holding me at arms' length.

Goltrade began singing the opening lines of the *Magnificat* in a voice that made the two ravens look at him with disbelief, and to my utter amazement, the scattered crew of the *Blood Raven* joined in like some a cappella street gang killing time by a steam grate. Thorfinn dropped me and stepped back as my crewmates, boyhood friends, and former fellow berserks crowded in to take his place. Things had begun to take a surreal twist with the intonation of Christian hymns from the throats of the *Blood Raven*'s crew, and I stepped up on the hearthstones so I was a torso above the room, eye level with my stunned mother and sister as Snorri leaped round, pummeling those nearest like an ecstatic at Cuthbert's Feast.

I put my hands out, gesturing for quiet, and after a little while they calmed down. The ravens perched in the rafters, looking cautiously over the edge at a room full of Danes in a partying mood. When even Snorri was still, I lowered my hands, conscious that I had nothing to say to match their excitement.

I remembered Aethelwulf's succinct exhortation before he led his clan out to confront the Picts, a major menace to the commonweal, but "They killed the homefield boar. Let's gut the fucks" didn't fit the occasion. I thought of a better exhortation, and seizing a horn from the startled clutch of a familiar-looking Jomsviking, I raised it to the rafters and shouted: "Let's get shitfaced!" It was an idea whose time had come.

Things after that are, as they say, a blur. When I was next aware, what I was aware *of* was a boot resting on my face, or rather, my face resting on a boot, and the fact that the mint in the rushes needed changing. After that, things went out of focus again for an unknown period, and then the clear memory of watching Thorfinn split a log over his helmeted head stands out like a rock in a fog bank. Then we ate. I looked around and several basic things came home to me: it was daylight, they were bringing a cooked meal out to the trestles, and the ravens apparently intended to take up a permanent residence in the rafters. They flew in and out the open window with nesting materials and a sense of purpose, and when they perched with their tail feathers flared over the rafter edge, they shat down on the Danes underneath, laughing quite humanly at the effect.

Then there was an axe in a beam, punctuation to some tale of lust and abandon in the Mark, and all new stories by Thord the Jolly about the strange sexual proclivities of the Brondings, followed by Skallagrim working the crowd with a strange malevolence of alliteration and rhythm that rooted them to their seats, hanging on every line he sang. Then more food and another sleep, although the sun was out when I closed my eyes and also when I opened them, so there was no way to know if it lasted an hour or a day.

This was a decadent, excessive, and egalitarian drunkenness, the kind of good time civilization managed to grind out by the middle of the eighteenth century and which was only briefly rediscovered in the sixties, an artifact of the cultural archaeology, fabled, rumored: the fact that pagan excess was a lot of fun. It compensated a little for the unceremonious docking of the *Ged*.

Snorri appeared several times in that gray period of whimsy and alcohol, but each time he tried to speak he choked up and had to go away again. Goltrade was characteristically loquacious, and I remember several arguments with him on arcane points of theology, the validity of threats by liberal heresies to the tranquility of the church, and the difference between the Roman and the Celtic tonsure. He looked younger and more engaged than I remembered him, and when I commented on it he looked pleased.

"I'm finally doing God's work among the heathens," he said.

"What work's that?"

"I've converted the crew of the *Blood Raven*," he said.

"That explains the *Magnificat*," I said snidely.

"I baptized them at the same spot I baptized you and ... what was her name? That sister of Sygtrygg's? The one, you know ..." The old boy'd put his foot in it, and his game efforts to recover were only taking him in deeper, like a fell pony in a bog.

"Her name was Frydys," I reminded him. "Big tits, even you noticed at the time."

Goltrade seemed as embarrassed by that remark as anything, and he slunk away to field questions on the Trinity for Jomsvikings. Then Skallagrim's gnarled fingers dug into my shoulders and he looked me in the eye and pronounced me a shithead whose return had ruined six hundred of the best lines he'd ever composed about my heroic defense of the *Blood Raven*'s mast and the picking off of the Eng lookout with a stone the size of a hen's egg at a distance of a quarter mile. He'd made me a hero, and, as far as he'd known, I was the safest kind of hero to invent: a dead one. Then I'd rematerialized, and his hyperbole was exposed.

"Look there," Skallagrim said, pointing up to the center of the rafter opposite the high seat. The raven shield that Snorri'd given me before the vik was hanging there with all those Eng arrows sticking out of it, gathering dust and cobwebs.

"Where'd that come from?"

"Sygtrygg brought it back from the vik like it was Thorr's own oakenshield and hung it first thing when he built this place," Skallagrim told me. "He commissioned the lines about the vik, and I had to pump the Jomsvikings for information about your time on the *Blood Raven*. How'd you stand them? Except for Thorfinn and a few others, they're the dullest lot I've ever known."

"It's your job to make them more than they are," I said. "That's what skalds are supposed to do. Didn't you teach me that?"

"Still quoting your betters to their faces, eh?" he asked. "Mark you this: when they all sober up there'll be trouble. You were safer dead." Leaving on that note was the sort of exit Skallagrim liked. The truth was I'd made an entrance that he'd never top if he lived another lifetime, and I'd raided his verse hoard too, and he was pissed. He went off to take it out on Goltrade, a chancier task now that the old priest was the spiritual adviser to the Jomsvikings.

"You're behind this, aren't you?" I demanded of Thorfinn sometime later, or perhaps earlier, but at any rate with conviction, despite the mead that was dribbling out of my mouth.

"What?" he asked with an innocent and wide-eyed look.

"This outbreak of Christianity," I said. "When we left there were fewer Christians than you have worms, and now it's a hotbed of religious zeal."

"It's the thing of the future," he told me. "The old gods are going down. There's no Ragnarok to mark it, just some barefoot peasant preaching peace and love. *That's* power. No steel, no Fenris wolf, no Frost Giants. The rainbow bridge just melted away."

"They may be selling peace and love out here in the provinces," I told him, "but at the top they're just like Offa or Charles the Frank, or any other ass that buffs wood. Peace and love mean what they want them to mean. Ask the Arabs."

"All the Arabs I've met wanted to kill me as much as the Christians," Thorfinn said. "There's just too many of them. They convert, they breed, their numbers grow. The old gods are too old now; they knew it would happen someday, and this is it."

I shrugged. When he was right, he was right, but I knew

that whether they prayed to Odhinn or Jesus, things were going to be about the same; belief renews itself in different disguises, changes location, and shifts shape, but it's still belief, with all the paranoia and desperation that belief packs along. Poles had shifted while I was asleep, monasteries had burned, and Thorfinn and the boys had stripped off their mail shirts and let Goltrade dunk them in a stream. Wheels within wheels were turning.

"Right after we came here," Steinthor Bollison was saying, "and saw how it was, we decided to stay." At some point, Thorfinn had changed into Steinthor, the old Greek fire specialist and chess hustler. I looked around for Thorfinn, but now he wasn't visible. The hall was dark again, and smoke was finding its place in the roofpeak, roiling above the ravens' nest.

"The vik was wonderful," Steinthor said. "Best I've ever made, except for Sicily. That storm blew us close in among the Farnes," he said. "Stone islands all around and running before a black gale, everyone in the hands of the Norns and the men at the star boards. We lost three ships: the *Sea Snake* ripped its belly out on a rock that was twenty feet under the keel a second before, right beside us, and we never saw *Tir's Blade* or *Arvak* again after the fight, so unless you know better, they're at the bottom of the deepest sea."

I told him what I'd heard from the cutpurse, extracted under duress, admittedly, but the truth if I'd ever heard it: Bui's dragon gutted on the stones and the crew hung up beside the road.

"The ravens got their fee from Clontarf," Steinthor said. "When we cleared the Farnes we headed for land's end, north of Dunedin, and then straight for the Orkneys, collecting the fleet on the way. The knarr bellied their way through the storm, but the slaves were all dying from the ride. We anchored in the Scapa Flow and when Sygtrygg and Thorfinn went ashore nothing more had to be said."

"Well, a few things have to be said to me," I told Snorri when he finally showed up, several days or hours into the feasting. "How've you kept?"

"Well enough," he said. "Your mother wept and thought her dreams were evil until I made Goltrade talk her out of that. Sinead's become a woman in her own right, and now keeps house with Thorfinn Skullsplitter."

"You can't be serious," I said.

"Serious as a burial debt," he told me. "They jumped the broom two Things ago."

"I can't believe it."

"The *Blood Raven* came to stay in Clontarf," Snorri said. "They sail out of here now. We hardly have to raid anymore, except for sport or to keep Knute nervous. Oc Connol holds down all the land between here and Temair, and we hold the river mouth and the coast.

"They've married Irishwomen and Clontarf Danes, listened to the laws three Things in a row, planted wheat and barley, and turned out homefield boars for fattening. There's naught amiss that Thorfinn should be my son-in-law and your brother."

My sister had apparently met the Viking of her dreams. I wondered how Thorfinn was thriving after jumping the broom with a looking woman, but before I could ask him, more food was served and Sygtrygg produced a fresh hogshead of ale.

Sygtrygg had been in and out of focus until then, but now he became substantial on the bench beside me. We were sitting with our backs to the wall and our feet up on the table, and women were serving out a liquid better off avoided but, of course, drunk down as if our intestines were on fire. Our horns were heavy with honeyed mead and confusion.

"You've done well in the high seat," I told him, thinking of our talks on the earthwork after Orm sailed off and never came back.

"That first vik secured it," he said. "And you made the first vik happen by unlocking Frydys."

"My pleasure," I assured him.

"I owe you for it," he said.

It wasn't a bad thing to have the guy in the high seat indebted to you, but there was something more on his mind than simple gratitude for my small part in making the good life possible. Sure, I'd freed him up from worrying about his sister, but Thorfinn and the *Blood Raven* had lined Sygtrygg's pockets with gold, not me. I hate it when someone thinks they owe you and you don't know why. How can you know how much or how little's owed, and what strings are attached? I'd made him laugh at the feasting after we escaped the Severn, but the upshot of that wit was protective custody on the *Blood Raven*. My grandiose plan to save his life had never happened.

"Where's Frydys?" I asked him. "So far no one's said."

"She wed Macc Oc," he told me. "I know why she gave her word, and how my wyrd went on the sea road because of it."

"How much do you know?"

"When you're dead, there's no confidence to break. Frydys never said a word, but Thorfinn told me about your oath." He took my wrist and held up my hand between us, the rune *Isa* white on the exposed palm.

"What's passed has no matter," I said.

"You better hear it now: she never waited," Sygtrygg said. "Macc Oc was barely off the boat when she had her legs round him, humping his brains out."

I was relieved to have it confirmed. "I reckoned she'd married him, but I thought she'd wait."

"She waited long enough for his eel to get hard," Sygtrygg told me. "After a vik it didn't take long."

I looked at the ruins of some meal or other, a pile of pork bones on a trencher, and shook my head. Could I really blame her? Of course I could. I expected at least a few months of grief, but here was Sygtrygg telling me she humped Macc Oc before he'd washed the salt out of his hair.

"Where is she?"

"At Oc Connol's. She must know you're back by now."

"How long have I been back, by the way?"

"Only three days," he said. "Time enough for her to find out."

"How's her marriage?"

"She's not divorced him," Sygtrygg said.

"That could mean anything," I observed.

"She's a power, now," Sygtrygg said. "Oc Connol has the heir he wants and a woman who keeps his son in line. The borders are quiet because the Southern Uí Naíll broke everyone else in the clan wars, and the fleets bring things they never had a hope of seeing without Danes as agents."

I understood now what the matter was: blood feuds had been waged for generations because of things like this. It was a gray area, and it all depended on how I chose to interpret the terms of the binding. Frydys had taken the chance that a man who'd been seen going over the side in a Frisian Sea gale wouldn't be coming back to cause any unpleasantness about the letter of the law.

Suddenly I was in a position to make a lot of wyrds. If I pressed it, conflicting wyrds could rip the belly out of Clontarf like the Farnes had gutted Bui's boat. Thorfinn and the Jomsvikings had duty to Sygtrygg, since they'd come to live in Clontarf, and duty to me as the man who'd hewed Engs at the mast step. My family and relatives had blood duty if I decided I'd been wronged, but they also had duty to Sygtrygg. And if Sygtrygg really thought he owed me for the high seat, that put him between Macc Oc and a hard place.

"How did Macc Oc turn out?" I asked Goltrade when he came round again. "Still the same?"

"Worse, now he doesn't have to worry about making a son to please Oc Connol. Wenches all over Leinster when he's out hawking with his mates. He'll learn what's happening when he gets too tired or too old for venery and finds out Frydys is in the high seat."

"Have you been there lately?"

"It's not that far," he reminded me. "Frydys became a true Christian in spite of you, and I go there often. I married them in Oc Connol's chapel and baptized their son half a year later."

"Half a year?"

"Do your sums," Goltrade said. "Plenty have, especially when Thorfinn told us about your oath. Snorri and I and the old druid expected as much. In a way, drowning was the best thing you could have done, saved everyone a lot of embarrassment."

"Does Macc Oc know I'm back?"

"I doubt it. He went south a week ago. He'll probably be gone another week at least, unless someone went after him."

"It'll take us a week to sober up," I told him, swilling down some more mead.

We went out for a sweat bath and a change of clothes before the telling, which everyone would assemble in the hall to hear. There were some iron-bound tubs sunk in the ground with fires between them to heat the water. We boiled some of the alcohol out of our systems and staggered around in the grip of electrolytic imbalance for twenty minutes, and that's the shape I was in when Caitria found me on my way back to the hall, still nursing a roaring buzz but temporarily coherent.

"How long will this go on?"

"After the formal telling of the story it'll be over."

"Mairead and Sinead fear a blood feud now you're back."

"I've got grounds," I said.

"Don't be stupid. So she didn't wait, so what? What were the chances you'd come back?"

"I waited," I said.

"You're just talking to hear your own voice," she said. "You've been playing with your friends too long and drinking too much."

"They don't want trouble," I assured her. "A blood feud would gut Clontarf."

"That's as may be, but a blood feud's yours for the asking."

"True. I wonder what I'll do."

"Don't wonder to me, just do it. This is the wyrd you always wanted to make. Make it or shut up."

"Things have changed. Sygtrygg's jarl now, Thorfinn's a Christian and Sinead jumped the broom with him, Goltrade has a congregation of Jomsvikings. How are you faring here?"

"Well. Clontarf's much like Ælfholm. It feels good to be here. I told them as much as I know of the trip, and with a truer keel than any version they'll get out of you."

"A truer keel? You're talking like a Dane, Caitria. Better be careful, who knows where it'll lead?"

"It rubs off. But I've no fear where it'll lead."

"I'll make you look good when I tell the story," I promised her. "Despite how shabbily you treat me."

"I ought to box your ears," she said, pushing me away and taking the path for Snorri's house, "but it will be more fun to see you hungover."

Skallagrim and Goltrade were looking at the bags of gifts and goods, having trouble containing themselves until the sharing-out. I took out the vellum folio, opened the folds, and weighted down the edges. Skallagrim produced a leather of his own and took out the verse I'd made on the vik. I smiled and read over it quickly.

"I had to get this priest to read it for me," Skallagrim said. "I've always wondered if he read it truly."

Goltrade, caught out now, looked a little uncomfortable. I reckoned he's assumed the role of redactor as readily and with the same understanding of my status as Frydys had married and Skallagrim had made verse: the understanding that I'd never come back to embarrass him about it.

"You were there when I sang these lines," I told Skallagrim. "Is your memory failing that you don't remember them?"

"Who thought these scribblings would amount to anything? You were just a lovesick and jealous pup sucking up a bowl of *ofermod* when you made these lines. I hadn't yet made you a hero."

"Well, that'll teach you to watch who you make a hero of. Next time be sure he stays dead."

"Be careful. Some'd be glad if you returned to that land."

"I've had trouble enough the last three years," I promised him. "Whatever I do, I'll make it easy on everyone."

So that night, or perhaps that afternoon, everyone who was anyone in Clontarf assembled in the hall, and while Huggin and Munnin cackled like a chorus in the rafters, I told them the story of what had happened after I'd gone over the side of the *Blood Raven*, adding verse as verse was needed, prowling the space between the tables and the hearth as Skallagrim had taught me, stopping for drink and food and questions, but keeping control of the rhythm and the room.

I told them about Lindisfarne, and the way it was in the church, and the Prior's *ofermod*, and the way the tongueless Pict had met the Danes with his axe and the monks had stood by the Prior until he was down in the mud with White Danes walking over him. That got a cheer from the benches, and they started beating the trestle boards while we wet our throats and Goltrade tried to explain to a hall of Vikings why they ought to be upset that Lindisfarne was burned.

The Jomschristians declared a blood feud with the White Danes and vowed to take the *Blood Raven* through the Skagerrak next spring to burn their towns and rape their women. It wasn't what Goltrade had in mind, since he thought he'd Christianized the lot, but maybe he'd done better than he reckoned. At any rate, he'd set something in motion that might just rid the Baltic of bad taste in clothes for a few hundred years.

I opened the gift bags and started the sharing-out. The psalter and a breviary for Goltrade, bags of herbs and a gold cup for Mairead, leatherwork and a jeweled torque for Snorri, the staff and a silver futhark for Skallagrim, cups and plate and hack for my family and friends. While I distributed the loot, they discussed what I'd told them and refilled their cups. When the hall calmed down, I resumed the story with the walk through the Chevoit, dodging Picts and outlaws.

Now, while I'd been pursuing a course of slow, well-paced drunkenness for the past three or four days, Caitria had been exploring Clontarf with Sinead, meeting people, doing a lot of swimming down by the fishing weir, and making a name for herself besides "the woman who came home with Bran," and there was whistling and applause when she volunteered to correct my version of the story. She stood and they all cheered.

Caitria'd been wearing the cloth of Clontarf as comfortably as if she'd grown up in it, but the night of the formal telling she wore the green silk from Ravenshill Moor, and the light and shadow in its folds danced and made her a changeling again, and there were a lot of eyes on her when she stood up.

She told her version of the walk through the dark woods and the sighting of the wicker fires, and the retreat through the forest during which, according to her, I lost my way and had to be taken to heel. I interrupted with the true version of the story, and let them choose which they liked better since they ended the same.

Then she told how she'd gotten the green gown, and the dancing, and the obviously drugged wine they'd given us, and the miming of the slaying of the wyrm, and the dancing that went on until neither of us could remember stopping. I told them about waking up the next morning and finding out they really wanted me to kill their wyrm, and agreeing to do it because I didn't think there were any wyrms to kill.

They were leaning forward in their seats as I told them about the mine, the scratchings on the walls, the rats, the subterranean lake, and finally the end of the tunnel where the druid, taxidermied by centuries of peat, stood guard with gold eyes. Then the story of the wyrm, what it said

and did, what I said and did, and what happened when I
scratched on the floor with the blade.

That's when I presented the sword to Thorfinn, and I
was glad to unload it, especially now that opinion was divided about my grounds for a blood feud. I didn't want
one of Wayland's blades in my hand if anything happened.
I'd only used it twice, and both times I had the feeling it
used me. That blade had a mind of its own, and I told
Thorfinn that it was only my wyrd to carry it to his hand,
not to keep it. Thorfinn held the blade out for everyone to
see, and I read the runes aloud for them.

Then we had food, and I told them how the hoard room
smelled, how big a heap it was, how the wyrm's long tail
had rooted it to the mound of gold and silver, and how it
sang its death song for me in the torchlight. I took out
the scales, the arrows, and the claws, and told them how
Gaefburnnah'd ripped my chest and bled its heart's blood
into me as we died.

Then Caitria told them about coming after me and finding me in a drying lake of dragon's blood, my breath bubbling around my mouth as I lay nearly submerged in it, and
how she'd dragged me out and taken care of me until I
woke up, two years later. In general they had the same
reaction as Æthelwulf's people, though they were less polite
in expressing it.

"A wyrm, eh?" Goltrade called out.

"A wyrm the size of a long ship," I said, producing what
I'd taken from the hoard, the bag of gold and silver, the
plate and chalices, the gems, shining red and green and
blue and white on the cloth in front of Sygtrygg's trencher.
My stock went up when I spilled the gems, like the wyrm's
tears, on the trestle table. The women serving meat and
mead looked at me favorably, and I knew I could have any
or all of them, but there was one last thing to do before I
wet my eel anywhere, and we all knew what it was.

Then, after we threw the bones to the dogs, Caitria and
I both told about Ælfholm. They liked Æthelwulf's sense
of humor, and I was glad to use the pause while they
laughed to have a drink and clear my throat for the rest of
the story.

It didn't take long to tell them about buying the boat
and shopping in the market. And the Geat. They all knew
about the Geat. In a town the size of Clontarf, how you

came by a scar a hand's length on the side of your face is never a secret. And when I told them our wyrds had come together, they were more interested in how it happened than in all the rest of the story up to then.

And so I made a good story of it, and when it was over they cheered that I'd marked him in kind. I skipped over the wyrm's mood, which I didn't want talked about. When I finished there was a long period of cheering and shouting and Thorfinn stood up and the runesword waved him round in the lamplight, while everyone admired the loot. More mead was served, and we settled down to the serious partying.

When I woke up again, under the immense weight of a standing stone that had fallen over on my head, everything hurt: my joints were packed with hot sand, someone had stuffed nettles under my eyelids, my fingernails ached, and my hair hurt with the effort of growing. The hangover at Ravenshill Moor was a joke compared to the one that waited for me after my homecoming party, and everyone else was in the same shape. They were lying around the hall, on tables, benches, and floor, as the hearth fire smoked fitfully.

I knew I couldn't stand many more wakings like the ones that'd become routine since I'd gone viking three years before. I struggled up to my elbows, squinting round the hall for evidence of life. Caitria was asleep on the bench, and I thought about waking her, but the effort of the thought was nearly too much for me; doing it would've been my end. I lowered myself to the floor, hoping sleep would return, but it was a false hope, and soon the rushes were as comfortable as a bed of stones.

When I was upright, I saw that there were other movements in the hall; here and there moans and small twitches, like the voices of the wounded and dying after a battle, revealed the presence of life and pain. I wondered what day it was, in fact, what was the week and month? I located Snorri, asleep in the arms of his wives, and Sinead, asleep against Thorfinn's chest. Sygtrygg's snores could be heard rising from beneath the high seat table.

I staggered down the length of the hearth and looked at the ash bed. The fire would have to be relit from scratch. I felt guilty that my return had been the occasion of the hearth fire going out, and I set about relighting it with the kindling and wood that was left. The effort was immense given my palsied hands, and it took me a long time to tease flames out of the pile of shavings, but when it was accomplished I felt better. Now maybe someone would make some herbal tea to ease the pounding in my head, but I was the only one with healing herbs, and so it was on me. When the fire was licking over the top of the hearthstones I added more wood and went to find a cauldron.

The new hall had a large cooking area and pantries behind the high seat, and I found all I needed there, including thralls who weren't hungover and were capable of understanding that I wanted water boiled as soon as they could do it. I went back and sat beside Caitria, and my weight on the bench woke her up. She was in disgustingly good health, and the first thing she did was look at me and start laughing.

"Five days and four nights," she said, "and you look better than you should, which is only awful."

The sound of her laughter was like a thorn branch being dragged through my head from ear to ear, and apparently the face I made was even funnier, because she whooped and put her hand to her mouth to trap her laughter before it could wake anyone.

Other people were stirring, and I was sure her laughter would have the same abrasive effect on them. Wounded boars, harried clerics, and hungover Danes all inhabit the same latitudes of touchiness and bad humor.

"Why don't you go swimming?" I suggested. "I understand you've been doing that quite a bit."

"Goltrade showed me the spot where he baptized you and Frydys," she said, "and all the Vikings in Thorfinn's boat. There's a hole there deep enough to dive into."

"I remember it," I whispered, supporting my head in my hands. "Go swim. Have a good time. Come back later and see who's alive."

"Nothing interesting's happening here." She stood up and made her way through the hall, stepping over and around the prone forms of played-out partiers, and the white light, when she opened the door, was like a nuclear detonation on my frazzled retinas.

The people of Clontarf woke up slowly as I limped around the hall looking for some kind of comfort, although

if I'd found any I wouldn't have recognized it among the
rushes, spilled mead, snoring corpses, discarded horns, and
broken crockery.

Stereotypes are invented for a reason, and since we'd
arrived home, I'd been looking at the reason for the myth
of the Danes as great drinkers, but they were fading in the
home stretch. Those pussies had only been at it for five
days and four nights and they were in terrible condition,
gargling back their own secretions and farting in their sleep.
It was embarrassing. The thralls came out of the kitchens
with a cauldron on a pole between them, and they transferred it to the iron over the hearth fire with a practiced
indifference, not spilling a drop.

"When's food?" I inquired of the most friendly-looking.

"When we bring it," she said.

Sygtrygg's egalitarianism was having a liberating effect
on the attitudes of the scullery drudges, that much was
clear. I looked into the cauldron and breathed in steam
from the simmering water.

"I want all the mint you have, and raw honey, chamo-
mile, and fennel." They looked at me with comfortable
hostility and went back to search their shelves. I found my
bags under the bench a few feet away. I opened the one
with the jars: powdered wyrm's blood was supposed to have
poly-restorative effects, according to my partner, who was
in charge of all wyrmlore.

The cast-iron cauldron held five or six gallons, and I
dumped the Benedictine herbs into it to steep. The kitchen
drudges returned with a pot of honey, more fennel than
camomile, and an equal amount of mint. I crushed the
herbs between my palms and dropped them in the pot,
stirring the honey into the mixture with the wooden paddle.
Then I opened the jar of wyrm blood. All the jostling it
had taken since Ravenshill Moor had reduced it to an even
finer powder, a brown rust so fine that it left a rouge stain
on my fingertips when I pinched a little of it out and
touched my tongue to the familiar taste. I remembered the
wyrm's voice and the smell of its breath, and songs sung in
dead languages.

This stuff had worked for me three times, topically applied, and I didn't see any reason why it wouldn't cure a
hangover taken internally. I tapped the side of the jar on
the lip of the iron cauldron, and a fine mist of red powder

dusted the surface of the brew. The character of the steam changed subtly, and I stirred it in until the jar was empty. Snorri made his way over, and I dipped the jar into the cauldron and swirled the tea round to wash it out.

"Take a swig of this," I told him. "You'll feel better in no time."

I handed him the jar and watched carefully as he sipped, inhaling the steam as he tilted it upward. Several seconds passed, and he remained in good health; in fact, he held out the jar for seconds. Sygtrygg wandered over, and I dipped the cup for him and then tasted the brew myself. It was sweetened by the mint, but the camomile and the fennel were detectable, and the wyrm's blood gave it an alien body and depth. I had another taste, and the hangover melted away like a sunburn's heat when you step into the shade.

Thorfinn and Sinead had their own cups and stood patiently as I stirred the tea, the way Alban had always insisted that stirring had to be done. My appetite was coming back, and I looked hopefully for the kitchen drudges, but they weren't in sight. The smell of bread was beginning to fill the hall, and I knew that was a good omen. I took a cup of tea to Mairead, the first of Snorri's wives to wake up, and she sipped it gratefully and made room for me on the bench among my sleeping stepmothers.

"You've been long gone," she said. "Are you any better for it?"

"Some ways, yes,"—I shook my head—"and some ways no. What can I say? I've gone on my last vik."

"Snorri said that when you were ten years old," she said, remembering a no doubt more dashing Snorri than the one who was hunched over his cup of tea a few yards away bringing up phlegm.

"How many more did he go on?"

"Eight more," she said, "but he stopped short of Orm's doom."

"If I ever go to another I'll need so good a reason I can't reckon it now."

"It's good to leave yourself a loophole," Mairead said. "On the matter of loopholes there's been talk lately about what makes a loophole in a blood oath, and how apparent death ought to be sufficient. Opinion's equally divided. Even the Lawspeakers can't agree."

"When have they ever? Fear naught," I promised her. "If I was angry, it's gone now. But I won't be home until I talk to her."

"That's what everyone's afraid of," Mairead said, drinking the last of her tea. "Talk often leads where it shouldn't. She's not the girl you knew that summer before the vik, if she ever was."

"Well, whoever she was or is, not to see her soon's just asking for trouble."

"I know," she said, handing back the cup. "But if you see her husband there's bound to be bladework."

"Not if I don't take a blade. I gave mine to Thorfinn, and I don't own another."

"Get me some more tea and don't be stupid."

She was right. No amount of goodwill would be enough to keep Macc Oc from killing me if he thought I was a threat. Who drew first blood wouldn't be the issue; after first blood was drawn, everything would unravel. I had to attend to it soon, but first I had to eat and have a look at Clontarf again; I hadn't seen it coherently since I'd been back.

The early risers were all gathered around the cauldron, Snorri and Mairead, Goltrade and Skallagrim, Thorfinn and Sinead and Sygtrygg, all scraping the bottom of the pot for the last of the tea. That brew had a remarkably analeptic power; they looked far better than they had even before the party started. For my part, there was no trace of hangover, only a nagging belly as the smell of the bread got stronger. I looked up at a clamor from the kitchens and saw that breakfast was served. The two ravens swooped off their nest and out the open window to find their own.

Having proved the efficacy of my herbal lore, I took a warm loaf and went outside to look at Clontarf. It was midmorning, and the town was going about its business in the usual way while men of military age, members of the comitatus, their families, and dependents tried to reassemble their wits after the night's revels. I climbed the grassy slope of the earthwork, chewing warm bread, amazed that I was finally home. Clontarf spread out below the parapet, and outside the homefields spread as far as the woods.

In the distance, across the bay where the Liffey met the Irish Sea, the mountains rose into the blue sky. Thorr's forest stretched out to the north and west. I'd forgotten how beautiful the land round Clontarf was. I walked along the earthwork, meeting people from my past, looking down into the streets and seeing things had prospered under Sygtrygg, a wild card who'd proved to be a good learner with Snorri and Thorfinn for teachers.

I went down to the dock to check on the *Ged*. It wasn't tied up to the dock pilings now, and I had to walk a way until I saw it beside Kalf Agirson's wharf. I got into the boat and sat there, thinking about the trip. Kalf was in the hall, but his wrights were busy over a new keel, and the sound of their work drew me over to watch. They barely acknowledged me, except for one who put his drawknife down and walked over, measuring me as he came.

"Just watching," I said. "Been gone awhile."

"I know it," he said. "I'm Eyjolf. I was on Sygtrygg's first vik. Didn't you used to be taller?"

"Not that I know of," I said, straightening up a little.

"You seemed taller on the vik." Eyjolf put his hand on my shoulder and gave it a squeeze. "Well come home," he said, and went back to his work.

I reckoned I was in for a lot of that. Thanks to Skallagrim, I'd grown taller in the hall than I proved to be in the daylight. Wyrm slayer or not, skald or not, I was always going to be shorter than people expected. It was then I began to think about going away. I'd half a hoard in Northumbria, friends on the fyrd, and a partner to travel with, and my presence in Clontarf, for all the gladness it brought my family, made everyone nervous.

I left the boatyard and went across the homefields, cutting through the oak grove where Sygtrygg'd killed Bjorn the Weller. The air was green under the oaks, and the noise I made in the dead leaves kept me from hearing the river until I was beside it. I found Caitria sitting among the roots of the tree where Frydys and I'd been discovered and baptized. She was drying out her hair, and she waved when she saw me.

"Feeling better?"

"I brewed some tea that took away everyone's hangover," I told her. "Alban's herbs, some odds and ends from the pantry, and a jar of the wyrm's blood perked them all up."

"The wyrm's blood? A whole jar?" Caitria stopped rubbing her hair. "I'm not surprised. How are they now?"

"They were well when I left them. Why? It didn't hurt me."

"It's in your veins, stupid," she said. "It wouldn't hurt you, but it'll be a strong tea for them to drink."

"They drank it like milk," I told her. "It cured them."

"We'll see. How's sobriety?"

"It's fine," I said, "but I have to settle with Frydys soon."

"When do we go?"

"We?"

"I'm seeing this through to the end. I've come too far not to."

"Then there's no reason to wait. We're half a day away." She stood up and threw the blanket in my face. "Let's go."

We went back to Clontarf and found Snorri and Mairead at home. As soon as we walked in, they knew what was afoot.

"You'll want horses," Snorri said. "Or do you want to walk?"

"Horses will do," Caitria said. "No use dragging this out. I'll be ready soon." She went back into the house to get into her travel outfit one last time.

"You ought to stay with that woman," Mairead advised me. "You'll look far and not find better."

"Whenever that suggestion's made, trouble follows."

"She's more willing than she lets on," my mother said. "Sort it out between you after you talk to Frydys."

"Would you like company?" Snorri asked.

"Thanks. I've got all the company I need. More would make it harder. It's better to ride up a visitor than a delegation."

"You're judgment's best," Snorri said, having made the offer.

I went to collect my gear. I reckoned the wyrm's scales might come in handy, and I took the bows and arrows. I found Caitria in the stable supervising the livery. It felt like I was doing everything for the last time, and a strange anxiety came over me as I thought of seeing Frydys again, a fluttering in my chest and a hollowness in my guts that was different than the sensation I used to feel, hurrying to see her deep in the oak forest of Thorr. It was more like waking from dreams of the Geat, wet with nightdew, my heart in my throat.

Only a week had passed since I'd marked the Geat, and I knew he was still out there somewhere, with his face stitched up and swollen, maybe infected, and certainly hating me. That's how it was in the eighth century: if you marked a man and the infection didn't kill him, you never knew when he'd step out of the shadows for a little quick bladework, and if you killed a man, you never knew when some relative would step out of the shadows for a little quick bladework, but if you got interested in inspecting the chickens when the Geat of your dreams showed up, you'd always be inspecting the chickens. We mounted up and rode out of the earthwork and onto the road to Oc Connol's stronghold.

The road was full of old friends taking shape in the shade or behind columns of sunlight. I recognized stream crossings, bends in the road, bridges, lightning-scarred trees. We passed the low stone wall, by the barrowdown, covered with grass and sheep; a dog was barking on the other side of a scattered, grazing flock. The outliers of Clontarf had expanded. There were a couple of new assarts before we got to the fork in the road, places that had been cut out of the oaks and built with the timber that industry provided. Smoke was coming out the roof holes, goats and pigs were impounded by stone walls, and there were sheep everywhere.

An hour from Clontarf, I began to feel the old paranoia. We were riding into the territory of clan Connol, and I was glad we were wearing our body armor. My experience when the Picts returned two arrows into my protected chest had made me a believer in the wyrm scales; they were the Kevlar of the eighth century.

"What's the plan?" Caitria asked. "You've kept it to yourself."

"When I have a plan, you'll be the first to know."

"Good. No plan, no magic sword, how do you expect to get out if they aren't won by boyishness and bad verse?"

"You're a full partner," I reminded her. "I don't hear any plans from you."

"It's your wyrd you're making. I can't make plans for you."

That was my turn of luck, suddenly, to find myself working in the dark with poor advisers and no net, though I did have arrows that always hit their mark and returned to hand, an attribute not without its downside. Our weather-luck was no better than usual either. A storm came up from Munster like some Eóganachta joke, first a wind, then black clouds and rain and a barrage of lightning that made the horses nervous, but not nearly as nervous as it made me. We got down and walked, our cloaks soaked and our boots sucking in the road mud. I passed the third hour of the trip wiping rain out of my eyes and listening to Caitria complain.

"I think it's your optimism that makes this partnership work," I told her. "Your ability to see the positive aspects of every situation."

"You like the way I am in the morning too," she said. "My cheerfulness makes you want to get out of bed."

"Only to strangle you," I assured her.

We were still discussing her irritating early morning pleasantness as we approached the Irishman's homefields. The rain had lightened, but a fog was coming out of the ground and everything had a strange look. It's always been my experience that when a fog comes out of the ground, bad things happen, and so I was a little dry-mouthed as the hill that Clan Connol had fortified began to take shape in the distance.

The spikes that lined the bridge were empty now; apparently peace ruled the land. The road looped up the face of the hill, slick under the horses' hooves and exposed to the whim of any wag with a weapon behind the palisade. It took us five minutes to climb the hill, laboring like salmon upstream because the road doubled as the main drainage sluice. Finally we clanged on the strip of iron that hung in front of the gate. It opened enough for one horse at a time, and I urged mine through, and Caitria followed.

Oc Connol's slaves took our horses and showed us into a warming room, where there was a fire blazing in a stone hearth. The wind sucked a fierce draft through the smoke-hole with a high banshee wail. We opened our cloaks to trap the heat, and steam coiled out of the wool as the fire did its work.

"So far, so good," I said.

"No plan yet?"

"How about you?"

"Still thinking." She shrugged and smiled. "After you forgive her, all will be well. They'll throw a big feast to celebrate; and you'll be a hero: the man who did the right thing even when it wasn't easy, and you can get on with your life."

"Hold that thought," I advised. "We'll see what happens."

One of Oc Connol's functionaries fetched us. Oc Connol's slaves wore brass torques, a clear identification tag if they decided to run, but this one didn't have a torque, which made him a hired employee or a family member. He took us through a maze of corridors and rooms, up a level, and into a big reception area.

"Wait here," he said, and left us looking at sparse but imposing furnishings, mainly from the clan wars: racks of blades, spears, axes, ring mail shirts, bleached skulls, the loot of the strongholds he'd burned—all trophies of the losers he'd killed or slaved out. A captured chariot stood in a corner of the room, the yoke supported on a stump.

"You think this is meant to worry you?"

"What, all these souvenirs of former enemies?"

"Is it working?"

"Sure it's working. As long as the old man's in the high seat we'll be all right, but when Macc Oc inherits he'll be in a position to use all this gear to make trouble."

"Well come, Bran Snorrison," a man's voice spoke behind us, and we turned around to see the Connol himself coming into the room, dressed to receive a dignitary who, I realized after a few seconds, was *me*. The last time I'd been there I was a second-level negotiator under Snorri's supervision, but now I was the man of the hour. "We were glad to hear of your return. Your loss was felt."

"So I understand," I said.

"My daughter was fond of you before you left," he continued, getting right to the marrow of the visit, "and there was an oath. We have to understand one another on this point. You were seen to wash over the side of a boat in a storm, on the other side of Northumbria. No one rightly expected you to live. It's my view that no one can be held to such an oath."

"Mine too," I said. "If I'd come back within the year the matter would be different, but three years late's two years past the agreement."

He relaxed then, and smiled.

"This is Caitria," I said. "My partner on the road."

"Well met," Caitria said, remembering her manners and not drilling him with one of her stares.

"And well come," Oc Connol said.

I sensed a peripheral movement and turned to see Frydys standing just inside the room. The weaving that covered the doorway behind her was still moving. She must have been hidden there, listening to Oc Connol's opening remarks and deciding when to make her entrance. She'd grown into her beauty in the last three years, and I saw the girl she'd been and the woman she'd become both standing there together.

Her clothes were in the Irish fashion, with gold running through the decorated hem of her dress and a gold torque round her white neck. Her hair was longer and blonder than I remembered. Clearly, she'd no one to tiptoe round these days, as she'd gone carefully around Sygtrygg that summer before the vik. Frydys ran the show here, or as close as made no matter, and she knew it.

We looked at each other, gauging the time passed, and then she walked over and kissed me on the cheek, the sort of sisterly kiss I'd expected from Aud. "I'm glad to see you alive," she said.

"Not as glad as I am to be alive," I said.

She smiled courteously. "I want to hear all about it."

"Someday. We've got other things to talk about first." I held up my palm and showed her the scar *Isa,* white against my flesh. "You cut me here, three years ago, and we made an oath."

She lifted her hand and opened her fingers. Her palm was unblemished; whatever scratch had been there was long healed. It was the kind of detail life hands you that sounds false when you tell it, but there it was: Frydys's unscarred right hand.

"I see you didn't cut yourself so deep as you cut me."

"When I cut your hand I was sincere."

"I've no doubt of it," I assured her.

"Let's go into the small hall and have something to eat," Oc Connol said, leading the way.

Frydys walked with her father-in-law, but Caitria put a hand on my arm and slowed me a bit as we followed.

"Learned her bladework better since?"

"I reckon she knew it well enough," I said.

The hall was a larger version of the warming room but

not so vast a place as the used chariot display area we'd just left. Food was already on the sideboard, and we ate without talking, a meal with indigestion written all over it. The fire crackled and the wood settled as it turned to cinders, but aside from a few comments about the weather, no one had much to say. When the trenchers were empty, we sat for a while at the table, drinking brown beer and watching the fire, feeling the tension screw tighter, and the combustion point in the room get lower, until I started to get worried that a stray spark would ignite the air.

"If you and Caitria keep here awhile, Frydys and I have things to say to each other." The tension leaked out of the room like hope out of a hulled boat, and Frydys stood and walked in the direction of the corridor. Oc Connol smiled and watched the fire.

Frydys was waiting in a window casement. There was a cushioned seat round the sides of it, and she was sitting with her back against the dark curtain that covered the opening, with her hand holding aside the folds so the waning, watery light of the afternoon softened her profile. She smiled, gesturing to the cushion on the opposite side of the window.

"How have you been?" I asked her. "I got to know him better on the vik, and I hope I'm wrong."

"I'm sure you're not," she said. "He's detestable in every way but one: he's not Sygtrygg. No one beats me here. I held a blade to Macc Oc's balls the first night and told him if he ever raised his hand to me I'd geld him in his sleep. A man would have killed me for that, but Macc Oc's solution's to stay away as much as he can, hawking and gambling with the Conmaicne.

"He's got women out there, and well come. But I marked him, too, and he always comes back. He's here just enough to please everyone. Oc Connol's got his heir and feels well rid of his son, backing me in all things. Doesn't even care who the boy's father is."

"Who is it?" I asked, surprised she was even bringing this up.

"You, of course, who'd you think?"

"Macc Oc?"

She looked at me with that old look. "I was sincere," she said, for the second time.

I said nothing.

"We rode the night mare well, you and I." She smiled.

"It's true," I agreed.

"There's no reason we can't ride that mare again," she said. "Macc Oc comes back once a month for silver. The rest of the time I'm alone with Oc Connol and his household for family."

"And our son," I reminded her. "What's his name?"

"Halfdan."

"Two years old."

"And a half."

If you held my hand in a fire, I'd have said a son didn't figure into my life until some years after I got back, say until I was in my middle twenties at least, and here was seventeen-year-old Frydys, who'd made herself a queen among the Irish because her brother beat her when she opened her legs for a weller and a deck hand from the Mark, offering me the position of official plumber to her majesty while Macc Oc was in absentia. In that moment I felt a kind of forlorn rapport with that Irish asshole, and I knew his decision to take up the venereal sports in other places was the right one. He'd had his ass nailed to the mast once, and I doubted even he was stupid enough to tempt the Norns again.

"I'll have to sleep on it," I said.

"You mean on your farm girl," she sneered.

I smiled at what would happen if she said that to Caitria, but she misunderstood my thoughts and smiled in return.

"Get rid of her," Frydys said. "We could have power together."

"I may go back to Northumbria." I shrugged.

"For her?"

"For a hoard," I said, giving her an answer she'd understand.

"You won't be going until spring," she said after a moment.

"I'll think it over."

"Do you still have the rune *Othala*?"

"No," I told her. "I lost it."

"You're lying," she said without hesitation. "*Isa* was the first rune I learned to cut and control. When I cut *Isa*, it stays cut, and when it's done its work, it comes back to its maker. And here's *Isa*." She grabbed my wrist and held it up, as Sygtrygg had done, so I could see the scar on my palm. "Where *Isa* goes, *Othala* goes too."

"I know what this one did"—I shook my hand in her grip—"but what was *Othala*'s work?"

"Its work was to keep you safe for me."

"Then you must have known I wasn't dead."

I could tell it wasn't the answer she wanted. Her face composed itself around a stare that would have knocked me off the bench if I hadn't grown up with Mairead and Sinead and been partners with Caitria. I only smiled back at her, and when she saw I wasn't intimidated, a bilious kind of anger spread through her.

"What did you think? That I was serious about making a marriage with Sygtrygg's dog? A boy with no geld? Why waste my time with you except to do Sygtrygg harm and advance myself?"

"That explains why you didn't wait out the year for me."

"Wait out the year? I couldn't wait till Yule, pregnant with your brat. I'd planned your wanting me would build the bride-price and the dowry and give me a bigger hoard to start, but getting melon-bellied before Macc Oc married me would have destroyed it all. When I heard you died, I cut a rune on Macc Oc. It's a rune that always returns, like yours."

"You'll know it's back when you have it in your hand," I said.

Frydys stood up and dropped the curtain. The runes had been unpredictable since I'd left Clontarf, either not working or working in ways I never expected, and maybe now I was looking at the reason. She was a runemistress, and she had witchcraft, all right, but not the kind you'd expect. It's funny how witchcraft makes itself known, strange how people employ it.

Frydys walked away without looking back, pushed the weaving aside, and went into the room where Caitria was waiting with Oc Connol. I was only a few steps behind her, but they looked round when I came in, as if they hadn't heard Frydys enter. Frydys knew how to move around without making any noise. Caitria tried to measure what happened, but she couldn't read my expression. I was glad, because if she couldn't read it, I knew Frydys couldn't. No runes were coming back to her this time.

Frydys got cups and a pitcher from the sideboard and

poured Oc Connol a cup of wine, and then for Caitria and me, and herself at last. Frydys raised her glass.

"To those who've crossed the deepest sea unharmed."

We all raised our cups and drank.

"There's no point in riding back tonight," Oc Connol said. "I haven't warmed and fed you to turn you out in the rain. You'll keep here and go back in the morning."

I looked at Caitria and smiled. Once invited, we were safe, unless someone asked Caitria if she was my woman, which was bound to get us uninvited just as quick and put us back in harm's way, but naught was said as Frydys took away the wine. "I'll show you where to sleep," she said.

Frydys took us to a room where a fire was burning and a great framed bed was covered with bolsters and furs. There was an oil lamp on the table, and she lit it and turned to go.

"Thank you," Caitria said.

Frydys turned and looked at her, but she didn't say anything. After a long moment she went out and closed the door after.

"She's a job of work," Caitria said, sitting down on the bed.

"More than ever I thought," I agreed, sitting down beside her.

"Some women never get over a beating," she said.

We looked at the fire for a while, and I felt myself getting drowsy. I stood up and walked to the hearth and stirred the coals a bit, sending sparks up toward the roof hole.

"We have a son."

"Sinead said as much."

"My sister learned her sums," I said. I opened my shirt, feeling unaccountably warm. Sweat was running down my chest behind the wyrm's scale. I hoped I wasn't getting sick from that ride in the cold Leinster rain. I sat down on the bed, and when I bent forward to take my boots off, my head got light and my ears buzzed. I felt a warmth at the base of my neck. I wondered if maybe I shouldn't just wear my boots to bed after all. I lay back and started to pull up the bolster, but I was asleep before I accomplished it.

I dreamed in that sleep: that Frydys came into the room in the middle of the night, and I opened my eyes and saw her standing at the foot of the bed, with the fire behind her, throwing her face into shadow and backlighting her hair like a kirilin aura. She stood there some span of dream time, and then walked over to the side of the bed where I lay propped up by the pillows.

She looked down at me and reached for my throat, her long fingers spreading as they got closer, her hand slipping under the cover, and I felt the cold tips of her fingers on my neck, soft as grass growing, brushing lower until she touched the silver chain where the rune *Othala* lived. She wrapped her fingers into the chain and slowly pulled it away from my neck, lifting my head away from the pillow until the chain broke and I fell back. It danced in her hand and the rune slipped off, and I saw it spinning toward my face, flashing in the firelight, and then she caught it, and I looked at the back of her hand as she opened her fingers to look at the rune. She smiled at me and closed her fingers again and turned to leave.

Caitria was standing between her and the door.

"What've you got there?"

"Something of mine that's come back to me, mistake it not."

"That's as may be," Caitria said with a shrug.

"Looking to partner with your betters?" Frydys asked her. "Being his woman on the road has no matter here. Go back to your cow shit."

"*His* woman? Are you serious?" Caitria asked, stepping forward as she brought something up from the vicinity of her knees and applied it glancingly to the side of Frydys's head. It sang like imprisoned birds, and I recognized the bag of futharks Gamma'd made from the wyrm's hack.

Frydys reeled back and clutched at the bolster, dragging it off the corner of the bed. Caitria followed her with a purposeful stride that brought her back in striking range. She dropped the bag onto the bed as she passed, and as Frydys regained her balance, Caitria's right fist knocked her to her knees. I sensed, as from a distance, that the situation had deteriorated. Caitria grabbed a handful of Frydys's hair and pulled her up. Frydys looked a bit disoriented; her eyes were tracking slowly around the room as Caitria lifted her to her feet and helped her find the door.

"That felt good," Caitria said, coming back to the fire after she'd tossed Frydys out into the hallway.

That was the only dream I had that night, a chilling enough dream, though not without its lighter moments.

After I woke up it took me a few minutes of lying there in the thick-brained warmth of the bolster to remember it and discover the rune *was* gone from my neck. Which meant Frydys had put something in that wine to freeze me while she took it back, just so I'd know she could, and on her way out she'd run into Caitria and made the mistake of pissing her off. Caitria was, of course, already awake, but her mood was less chipper than usual.

"Did you punch Frydys out last night?" I asked.

"Back from another of your convenient naps, I see," she said. "The love of your life drugged the wine."

"Tell me I dreamed you boxed her ears."

"No dream. I watched her take the rune and said naught. No matter, I reckoned, it's not a rune you need, anyway, and she didn't try to hurt you. But she said what they all say, and I lost my temper and stunned your runemistress with a bag of her own weapons."

"You just put us in good with the warrior queen of the local Irish." I nodded. "Don't help anymore."

"It's a poor partner doesn't help. What did you want with that rune, anyway? The one on your hand's trouble enough."

I looked at *Isa* on my hand, and then through my spread fingers at the last of the fire, burned low in the hearth. I got up from the bed and walked over to it. She had a point. The logs and branches had burned down into ash-whitened bones, and I reached into the hearth and picked one of them up. The nerves in my hand burned away in a second, so I couldn't feel it as the flesh wrinkled on my palm and fingers, incinerating the rune with a noxious smell.

"I'll be better off without," I said, trying to open my fingers to drop the branch and finding I couldn't. I hit the back of my hand against the stones, and the branch disintegrated, leaving my blackened and blistering fingers clutching emptiness. I plunged my hand into the water bucket beside the fire.

Caitria watched me without moving, and then went to her bag and took out a jar I well recognized, one that was full of the dry dust of the wyrm's blood. She opened it and pulled my hand out of the water. "You'll thank me for this later," she said.

She dusted the charred flesh, and the powder turned to a red mud in my wet palm. She continued to shake the powder onto the burn until a red paste formed, and then she rubbed it into the blisters. When she was finished she bandaged it with a strip of linen.

"Time for breakfast," Caitria said. "Think she holds a grudge?"

I started laughing a sort of insane laugh that set my own hair on end, and Caitria gave me a shake. "Get a grip on yourself and wait here, and no more grabbing what's left of the fire."

I sat there on the floor and watched the fire settle into ashes. The stones radiated enough heat to keep me warm. I wondered where young Halfdan was; somewhere in the stronghold I reckoned, doing whatever you do when you're two and a half years old. I thought about taking him away to Northumbria, where I was well connected with shape-shifters and professional disembowelment experts, but I knew if I did she'd make war on Clontarf instead; Oc Connol would have to burn it to avenge the loss of his heir. I expected Frydys with a blade any time now, or Frydys and six or eight Irishmen with blades.

But Caitria came back instead, carrying a bowl of sliced apples and some water, and we had a hasty breakfast before we made our way outside to the stable. Caitria saddled the horses while I got the bows and arrows from the warming room.

"I won't be sorry to turn my back on this place," she said. "We're quit of it now."

We rode slowly out to the gate, where the guard opened up without having to be asked. The rain had stopped in the night, but the road was a mud chute; if the horses slipped at all it was straight to the bottom. It seemed to take hours to get down to the ditches and out under the empty spikes. To tell the truth, before the day was over I expected to be looking down from one of those spikes with the same intense interest old Hengest had been showing when I saw him last.

The standing water was deep in the wheel ruts, and only a thin strip of ground in the middle of the road showed above the surface, but Caitria and I were used to wet horsebacking.

"Did you expect to live this long when we got there?" she asked when farm buildings began to thin out and the forest quickened close to the road.

"The day's not over yet."

"Her teeth are pulled for now," Frydys said.

"Let me explain this," I began. "The woman you punched out and dragged round her own guest room by the hair was the woman who made herself a power so she could throw her own brother down from the high seat for doing the same thing."

"Not for that," Caitria said. "Because she wouldn't be owned."

"You know, I started out thinking that was the true story. When I told her that on the barrowdown, she melted like honey on your tongue. Said all she wanted was to be asked, not ordered, and she had as much honor as anyone. *I* believed it. I wouldn't want to be treated like that either. Said she loved me, said she'd wait, made runes. Who was that? Who's she now?"

"Her wyrd took her that way," Caitria said. "But she'll not bother with me. I don't want to own her, and I won't be owned myself; I'm just someone who isn't afraid to say no to her. I'm not going to be her neighbor, and she won't go where I'm going for a while."

Maybe she was right, maybe not. The woods were dripping and noisy after the rain, and more green than anything could possibly be. I thought about Frydys.

Despite my itchy back, we took the whole day to go back to Clontarf, stretching the four-hour ride into eight, stopping frequently to walk beside the horses or sit a little while by a stream. If I was going to make my own wyrd, options were closing out fast. If I tried to preempt Frydys, it was war with clan Connol, which was really war with the Southern Uí Naíll, which was war with way too many Irishmen. A blood feud would waste Clontarf, if Clontarf didn't waste itself first.

Caitria truly believed her theory, but I couldn't rede it, and even if she was quits with *me,* Sygtrygg hadn't heard the last of Frydys. I'd have a poor story for him when we got back, though not the same poor story he expected. Northumbria was looking better every minute. I wondered if we ought to spend the winter or go back right away. It looked like we'd be partners for a while longer.

"How do you like the country here?" I asked her.

"There's peat all round and lots of pasture and woods. I'd hate to see it burned."

"If it burns it won't be on your account."

"Still, Northumbria has some things to recommend it."

"You hated everything north of the Humber. Too many Picts, you said. And thegns daughters trying to trip you up."

"Funny how you can change your mind about a place," I said. "I can't wait here for Frydys to burn down my house."

"You can do what you want," she said. "You've convinced me."

"You think I ought to stay?"

"I think you ought to make your own wyrd," she said. "It's your choice. After a while, the Norns will start to look good."

"What happened to all those opinions you were carrying when we met? You'd so many opinions I thought you'd never carry them."

"That's why I took on a partner," she said. "I needed help with my opinions, and who'd I meet but someone dumb enough to carry half of them."

"Well, you're stuck with me yet awhile," I said.

"No, I'm not," Caitria assured me. "I only joined until the end of the trip, and in case you haven't noticed, this is it. You've met her again and had your talk."

We got to the barrowdown in the long afternoon light at the end of the day, the best of all possible meteorological moments. The sheep had been driven back to Clontarf, so the grass was empty round the mounds. We left the horses grazing at the bottom of the biggest and walked up, where we had a good view of the sunset on the Wicklow mountains.

"So we're not partners anymore?" I asked her.

"What's passed has no matter." She took my hand and untied the bandage. There was still no sensation, and I expected quite a mess when she exposed it. She wound the linen round her own hand as she unwound it from mine, and I leaned forward to get a look.

The palm was seared into a calluslike hardness, my fingerprints were smoothed and melted nearly away and it would be a long time until they came back, but the rune *Isa* was gone. I tried to make a fist, but my palm was too stiff, and I could barely touch my fingertips to the heel of my hand.

"What's ahead?" I asked her.

"Let's walk down and see," she said, and she headed down through the long grass of the mound to the level down. The horses were eating their way toward Drogheda, their reins trailing behind, but she didn't stop to hobble them as she walked by. I followed Caitria over to one of the standing stones in the field.

"There's nothing on it," she said, a little surprised.

"They're supposed to be what's left of thieves who opened the barrow," I told her. "The curse of the hero buried there got them all."

"You believe that?"

"No, I think they didn't cut runes, or didn't know how. But the ghost of the warrior's supposed to walk. People have seen it."

"There's a ghost here," she said, shaking her head. "But not his. Where's the famous barrow?"

I nodded to a mound thirty meters away. She went over to it and around to the entrance, and I followed her. Why not? No use leaving any shrines to Frydys unvisited. I reckoned I needed to face down all those ghosts as soon as I could. The sun was on the west side of the mound, and it was already dark inside the entrance. I looked for torches and found an oil lamp instead. Progress. I got it going after some work, and Caitria sat on the side of the mound and watched the gathering blue line on the horizon. When I had it lit, she followed me inside the barrow. The floor was bare, and the dirt was packed down.

The roof, blackened by smoke, seemed lower than it was, so we had the feeling of straightening up when we walked into the burial chamber. I held the lamp up to look at the roof of the grave, but the runes were covered by layers of soot. Those were onetime runes, easy come, easy go, at least the ones I'd had anything to do with.

"So this is where you made the beast?"

"This is the place. She was afraid of the ghost."

"You've naught to fear from most ghosts," she said. "But I know how you like to tell stories, so why don't you tell me a road story I've never heard before?"

"You've heard them all," I said.

"Not all of them," she said. "You always have a story; you've more stories than ticks in a wolf pack."

"I can't think of any," I told her. "I'm told out for a while."

"Just a short story," she said. "You can do it. Short. Something you've forgotten because it's so short. A *little* story, understand?"

"No stories left," I said, putting the lamp on the floor and sitting down with my back to the wall.

"No one's lazier than you," she said, sitting beside me. "Won't even tell your partner a story."

"Partners again?"

"Until the story's over," she said.

I thought about something I'd never told her, and there was only one thing. "After the Magonsætans ambushed us in Wales, I hid in the bracken that first night," I began. "I knew I had to go east to the Severn. I slept in a collier's hut the next day, and then in a cave. The morning before we met, I found a dead leper. Smelly business, flies all round, but even though I tried to walk away, I couldn't do it.

"I cut out a grave with my axe. It wasn't as deep as it should have been, but it was up to my chest, and I put the leper into it and left what I could: a few pence.

"So that's the story you never heard. People don't like to be around you if they know you handle lepers, and you can hardly blame them, so you know why I don't lead off with it. Now we're no longer partners, what matter?"

Caitria listened to the story without saying anything, and when I was done we sat for a moment watching the lamp, in a round stone chamber, like the moon's kitchen, cool and quiet.

"That story couldn't be about anyone but you," she said, touching my arm. I turned toward her and she put her arms round me and kissed me. It was more surprising than an attack, but I liked it a lot more when I realized what was happening. All that time together, and I never knew she could kiss as well as she could kick.

We slid down to the floor, and then I hopped up and looked around for the blanket. It was still in its place, and I spread it out for a more comfortable couch. Her shirt was open by then, and I looked at her partially exposed breasts and felt an excitement that hadn't been my friend for quite a while. I hopped around pulling off my boots and tossed them aside, and then I unbuckled my belt so she could help me pull my pants off. She shrugged out of her shirt and rolled back, offering me her legs so I could strip her pants off.

Then we hesitated, as if we'd never seen each other naked. I lay down beside her and she moved against me. There's only one way to exorcise some ghosts, and I didn't want to remember riding the mare with Frydys every time I rode it with someone else.

We lay together for a long time, looking at the shadows on the sooty roof, and then we made love again. Three years had gone by, but I hadn't forgotten what to do, and she knew at least as much as me. After the second time, we nearly fell asleep in each other's arms with the blanket over us, aware of our mutual breathing and smell, and lulled by those primal sensoria into a postcoital drift, but then one thing led to another, and before I knew it we were making love again, tying our legs together in the tangle of blanket.

We did get to sleep then, or I did for a while, and I woke with a jump when I dreamed of Caitria laughing at me for falling asleep, and found her laughing at me for falling asleep, so we made love again, aware of a certain genital discomfort after that first abandonment to lust, and so more carefully and slowly. After that we both slept for a while, curled into each other as we'd slept clothed once or twice before, and when I woke up my eel was as stiff as if it were varnished. There was only one thing to do under the circumstances, so we did it again, enjoying the nuances of the act itself, aware of slow kindnesses within the motions, of soft sensitivity within the rhythms, the small gifts of our noises and sighs.

I understood at last that riding the mare with Frydys had every time been like some kind of religious experience, the religion of the stiffened eel, of which I was the high priest. Getting what you never hoped for is a mixed blessing, and losing it's worse.

Riding the mare with Caitria was getting to know her in another way, a way I incidentally enjoyed more than I'd enjoyed finding out about her hand-to-hand technique. She was never more carnally real than she was then, and I realized that Frydys, the most beautiful woman in Clontarf, had been real only in the carnal dimension all along. I'd begun the vik with every expectation of concluding it in just this way with Frydys, and at Lindisfarne I'd imagined the long years of living with her, riding the night mare when the sun went down until it came back up again—the yearnings of an eighteen-year-old pretty much anywhere, anytime.

When I met Caitria on the way to Offa's Dyke a partner was a convenience I hadn't expected, someone to guide me away from the Magonsætan fyrd, someone to delegate unwanted camp chores to, but it hadn't turned out the way I expected. Not much had, come down to it.

And now Caitria, sweating on me as we rolled over, mist-eyed, clinging together, a strand on her damp hair flickering on her eyelash, laughing and having as good a time as I was. We lay together when we were finished, and she looked like she was wringing every possible sensation from every moment of the time we lay together, absorbing the energy of an unbelievable act. I looked at the horizon of the blanket against the line of her shoulder and the curve of her back, like the lambent light of sunset on a vast moor.

I was ready to get into the *Ged* and start for Northumbria that night, looking in at Clontarf only long enough to tell them to watch out for Frydys. Then Caitria rolled away from me and sighed and blinked back a wetness in her eyes and started to get into her clothes.

"We'll go back to where your farmstead was," I told her, sitting up. "Or would you rather go back to Æelfholm first? We could use a half dozen of Æthelwulf's sons to help us collect the hoard. What do you reckon? Wulfgar will be real glad to see us again."

"I reckon you're going to be making your wyrd without me."

I shook my head and looked at her, blinking away her answer. "What're you talking about?"

"My work's finished," she said. "Our partnership's over."

"We'll make a new one," I said. "We've already made it five times just now, why not forever? We're young, rich, and you're good-looking, and I can make verse and sail from here to there, and read and write, and you're—"

"A ghost," she said.

"A ghost?" I got up on one knee and put my hand against the wall of the barrow for support. Caitria was pulling her pants on. "The ghost of what?"

"The ghost of whom," she corrected me. "The ghost of

the dead body in your story. The ghost of a dead leper, turned out of her farm when the neighbors burned it down. The ghost of a leper who watched them kill her family when they resisted, and then crawled five days into the woods until she died in the bracken, wrapped tight about with linen to hide her from sight.

"And along comes a Dane following his eel east who stops long enough to bury me. Where I grew up, that means a burial debt. No one else was paying three pence to put me in the ground; the good people of my parish had already seen to that, left me to wander Gwent while I rotted, left me to die alone so a Dane could bury me with grave gifts and runes.

"The next thing I knew I was on the bridge over that little steam, in a body that was clean, on a clear fall afternoon, knowing I had to go down the path because the man who buried me was there, and I had to help him.

"And you turned out to be such a fool about taunting Macc Oc and keeping your feet in a storm that we ended up wintering in Northumbria, so you could be an even bigger fool about things like wyrms and wyrd and which direction to go in the dark. When someone comes back from the dead, even if they want to, the longer they stay, the harder it is to return, and you nearly got yourself killed and ended up sleeping two years, while I got attached to life.

"When I was alive, I was a leper, and now I'm dead it's my wyrd to help someone who doesn't believe in wyrms and maroons me in the land of the living while he sleeps the sleep." She shook her head, mightily put upon by the turn of the wheel that had gotten her that prize.

This meant two things: that I was losing my partner just as I began to understand how much she meant to me, and that the best sex I'd had in my life was with the ghost of a leper. I sat back heavily on the blanket and looked down at my eel.

"Don't worry," she said. "It won't fall off."

"Can't you stay? You've been here two years already; I didn't know ghosts could stay that long. I didn't know ghosts could do what we just spent five hours doing." I gestured at the tangled blanket in the middle of the barrow.

"How do you think it feels to me? When I was alive I couldn't have hoped for someone even like you."

"Don't flatter me, please," I said.

"I had a chance to live a little life," she said. "And I lived it with you, longer than I expected, but what turns out like you expect? Now I have to go. You're as properly thanked for burying me in the woods as I can thank you; and for the little life, there aren't any thanks I can make."

"Why not stay until you can?"

"This is hard enough," she said. "The truth is you're not that bad: with a little work something could be made of you."

This woman had no future as an icon of finesse, nor as anything else if this ghost business were really true. Those Engs had a strange sense of humor. "Are you sincere?"

"No. I'm telling the truth," she said. She held out her hand, and a silver chain spilled out between her fingers like a quicksilver waterfall. "I saved this out, when Gamma made the runes for you. You lost a rune last night; you'd better have something to replace it."

"I've carried runes enough," I said, shaking my head in refusal.

"It's your rune, not mine," she insisted.

I held out my hand and she dropped the rune into it, *Gyfu* to the Anglo-Saxons, *Gebo* to a Clontarf Dane. It was a rune about which the Eng's own rune poem said:

> Giving, to men, is an ornament
> Displaying worth—and to every outcast
> Without any other is substance and honor.

But which the *Havamal* dealt with at greater length:

> No man is so generous that he will jibe at accepting
> A gift in return for a gift.
> No man is so rich that it really gives him
> Pain to be repaid

> With presents.   Friends should please each other
> With a shield or a costly coat.
> Mutual giving makes for friendship.
> So long as life goes well

> A man should be loyal to his friends
> And return gift for gift,

Laugh when they laugh, but with lies repay
A false foe who lies.

If you find a friend you fully trust
And wish for his goodwill
Exchange thoughts, exchange gifts,
Go often to his house.

It didn't look like Caitria would be coming over a lot,
but the rest of the poem was true: she'd been a friend to
me and seen it through to the end. Except that now I didn't
want her to go back to wherever you go when you're dead.

"Don't misunderstand what's happened," she said. "No
religious experiences have occurred. Gift for gift is all, and
well come. I don't want you mooning around being tragic
and stricken. Use this rune to remember me by, but make
your wyrd without me. Frydys's runes are trivial compared
to it."

I looked at the rune of gifts and partnerships and back
at Caitria.

"I'm not the love of your life," she said.

"Why not?"

"Because you can make your wyrd and I can't. You'd
better go back to Clontarf. You'll find people eager to talk
about your hangover remedy."

"What about you? Let's take the *Ged,* and sail together
out into the deepest sea."

"I'll not leave here," she said. "My bones are under the
bracken in the woods west of Offa's Dyke. When you're
gone, I'll be gone too."

I didn't want to leave her. I looked long into her eyes,
my hands on her shoulders, crying and not realizing it until
I tasted my tears. Caitria was crying too.

"I love you," I said. "I never thought to have a partner."

"Some things come unlooked for," she said. "I never
thought to have any life at all."

She put her arms round me, and we held one another
for a time, and I tried to memorize her smell, the feel of
her, all I'd have to remember her by except the rune *Gebo,*
and somehow I found myself walking down the passageway
with Caitria beside me growing more insubstantial as we
got closer to the night, becoming ephemeral, a mist, and
then she wasn't there, and I was standing out on the down

looking up at the Path of the Ghosts in the clear night sky over the barrow.

The horses had grazed their way back to Clontarf long before I came out of the grave. It was a nice night, I'd just said good-bye to someone I didn't even appreciate yet how much I loved, although I soon would, and I had a new power rune around my neck, so it seemed like I could afford to take my time. The gate was open, and I crossed over the ditch and scuffed onto the packed dirt and log area inside.

They grabbed me from behind, swarmed out of the shadows with ropes and that unmistakable sense of purpose that never turns out well for its object; they had me before I knew I was had. They made noise *then*, shouting for something to hang me from, describing what it was going to feel like when they reached up my asshole with hot tongs and pulled my guts out and tied them round my ankles and hung me head down by them. I was beginning to notice a pattern of extremes in the people of my hometown: six days ago they were so glad to see me they'd stayed drunk for four nights to celebrate, and now they were so pissed off they were getting out the billhooks.

They didn't seem to need a leader, pinning me securely, controlling my arms and legs and carrying me ass up into the hall. Maybe they assumed I was leaning in the direction of a blood feud or some other stupidity that would make their lives miserable, and they were preempting the problem. It was all I could think of.

They set me down in front of the hearth and turned me around, and I saw what else it could be: the bodies of Snorri and Mairead, Goltrade and Skallagrim, Thorfinn, Sinead, and Sygtrygg, arranged like a precision sleep team, hands folded across their chests, shallow breathing, deep in the land of REM.

"What happened to *them*?" I asked.

Ulf Thorhullasson and Thord the Jolly were standing nearby like interested spectators at a matinee lynching. It was their detachment that gave me a little hope. I looked around and saw that the *Blood Raven*'s crew was scattered about on the upper level where the trestle tables were, well in the back of the crowd. And Thorfinn was lying as catatonic as the rest of the people I'd hurried home to see, arranged like fresh mackerel on a bed of shaved ice.

"You tell us. A couple of hours after they drank your tea, they started folding up. If you've done witchcraft, now's the time to undo it," their spokesman was Kalf Agirson, and he was in a fair mood or I'd have been dead already. If all they wanted was a credible explanation, I was sure I could come up with something satisfactory.

"Skallagrim's in charge of magic," I said as I shrugged out of their restraint and walked over to inspect the bodies. They were warm to the touch, but they breathed so infrequently I had to rely on the faint pulse in their necks to be sure they were alive. I wondered if now was the right time to bring them up to speed on Frydys and, of course, my ghost partner and spectral lover, Caitria, who'd dematerialized in the barrowdown. I decided it was not.

"When we woke up yesterday they had a case of Odhinn's head, and I made up a tea for them," I said. "Some of the ingredients may have been stronger than they should."

"What's this mean?"

"That they may sleep a long time or a short, I don't know. But it looks like what happened to me after I killed the wyrm."

"And you slept for how long?" Ulf Thorhullasson asked.

"Two years," I said.

Thord started laughing at the idea of Thorfinn sleeping for the next twenty-four months. "He'll be pissed when he wakes up," Thord said, "and stiff."

But the Clontarfmen didn't see the grins in having their lord in a coma, and they only got uglier as Thord laughed.

"I was ripped open and drenched in the stuff," I told them. "I don't think it'll be that long."

"See it isn't," Kalf told me, and the crowd began to disperse, mumbling to itself in the time-honored manner of crowds everywhere, but none of the Jomschristians moved. I reckoned I was in for a grilling from these boys now, and likely it would be more direct than Kalf's interrogation had been, but, as I was about so much else in the last three years, I was wrong in my apprehensions. When the last of the Clontarf civic improvement committee had gone, Thord relaxed and came over and put his arm round me.

"Things are never dull around you, I'll say that. Anyone

who's able to make verse and charge a dozen of Engs is all right with us."

"What happened to Thorfinn?" Steinthor Bollison asked.

"He drank a tea of the wyrm's blood and the elixir of some poppy, and I reckon he's dreaming his way up the Severn right now, where he once said he liked the land."

We took over the hall while we waited for them to wake up. I told the Jomschristians how it was with the former pinup princess of Clontarf, how she was holding a grudge deep in her heart because Sygtrygg'd whipped her ass blue and yellow for fucking a plumber and a seaman first class from the autumn fleet. The Jomsvikings liked nothing more than a good soap opera, and Danish soap operas are among the best, especially when you know the players. They even claimed not to be surprised by Caitria, who'd always looked a little too hard at the majority of them, men who were brought up along the Baltic coasts by strict disciplinarians who would in later centuries embrace Lutheranism and even grimmer sects.

"She had a sort of distance to her," Steinthor said sympathetically. I'd risen in his esteem since he'd tried to hustle me at chess on the *Blood Raven*. I shrugged in a noncommittal way.

When Thorfinn finally stirred, along about midafternoon two weeks later, I'd just about played all the chess I wanted for the rest of the century. Soon the rest of them started coming round, blinking awake with a look of bemused disorientation, and then croaking out words that didn't make any sense, and wouldn't until they forced fluids and walked around for a while. They'd all accomplished that much by dark, and so we sat them down to a good meal and told them what they'd missed and why.

Opinion among them was divided about the goodness of this luck. Goltrade decided it was the return of Original Sin, a brush with the influence of the archserpent himself. Skallagrim was unamused and attacked Goltrade. Snorri fetched me a clap on the side of the head that put me on the floor, and he was looking for a stave to finish me off when Thorfinn got between us. It must have been a happy few moments for Snorri; I knew it was something he'd been wanting to do since he found out I'd given Frydys the eel. Thorfinn just laughed and waited for his in-laws to stop attacking each other. After everyone calmed down, we began a serious discussion.

"What will happen now we've drunk your tea?" Sygtrygg asked.

"I don't know," I said. "My wyrm expert went back to the land of the spirits after she beat Frydys cross-eyed with a sack of runes."

"I'd like to have seen it," Sygtrygg said.

"It's that impulse got you in this fix," Goltrade told him. I was surprised at how much having a congregation of Jomsvikings had liberated the old priest's inhibitions.

Snorri shook his head in agreement. "He's right," Snorri said. "Beating her was a bad thing."

"You never said so at the time," Sygtrygg said defensively.

"You had so much to learn that your old foster father had to neglect some areas."

"You neglected an area or two with Bran," Sygtrygg said.

"Let's not get into this now," Thorfinn suggested. "We can deal with the girl later, and who bent what oaths to who is too tangled a knot to unravel. What we need is someone to tell us what this tea will do."

Thorfinn looked at me as if I might have some ideas.

"We can try Æthelwulf's lot; they were strange enough to know about this. Or someone in Ravenshill might have an idea; after all, it was their wyrm, and we have to go there to get the hoard. And if that comes to naught, we could go back to Lindisfarne to see if Alban has a chemical or Godwine has a book in the library."

"I won't go back to the land of the Engs," Skallagrim said forcefully. "I was almost killed on that wretched cowpie of an island, and I don't want to go back. None of us would have to if it weren't for your ignorance."

"I was trying to cure your headaches," I said.

"We know how to weather headaches," Snorri said. "You didn't have to dose us with wyrm's blood."

"It seemed like the thing to do at the time," I said. It never fails: you try to do people a good turn and it never suits them.

I put up a stone in the barrow, cut with runes to give Caitria directions on where I planned to be, just in case she came back. I spent my nights on the down, wrapped in a blanket outside the barrow looking up at the Path of Ghosts until I fell asleep, and I worked on the *Ged* during the day. Kalf, once more my friend now that Sygtrygg was awake, hauled the *Ged* out of the water and gave it a close inspection, as much to understand the manufacture of the touchy craft as to verify the wrighting. We recaulked the hull and hung a new sail, but the wood was fine. He approved the bladelike design of the keel and studied the cunning way the wright had scarfed the strakes, nuances which were lost on me. When the boat wrighting was finished for the day, I went back to the barrowdown, where the wyrm's mood, combined with the loss of Caitria, rendered me morose and silent for hours. One by one my family tried to snap me out of it.

"This isn't good," Sygtrygg said, sitting beside me one afternoon. "She was a ghost, and a leper to the bargain."

"She was my partner," I told him, "and she helped me learn what I really wanted when all along I thought it was your sister."

"Your luck with women stinks"—Sygtrygg nodded in an attempt at sympathy—"but you killed a wyrm. How many men can say that?"

Even though he was trying to help, Sygtrygg didn't get it, and I didn't reckon he would; he wasn't exactly Mr. Sensitivity. Goltrade tried a characteristic churchman's approach.

"It's God's will," he said.

This was less comforting than Goltrade intended it to be, and after a few attempts to prove to me that God had plans for me and that this was a test of my mettle, he went away.

"There're other women, son," Snorri told me. "She helped in a bad time, but she couldn't stay. Now, Finnbogi has a daughter you'd do well to consider, and she's had her eye on you since you got back."

Snorri was more pragmatic, and I knew he was right, but I had no feeling for anyone else, certainly not Finnbogi's daughter, who served up the mead in the hall and herself to anyone who was interested.

"I'm sorry you lost her," Mairead said. "But a ghost's a ghost, and she couldn't stay in the land of the living. She wouldn't want you to stay in the land of the dead."

This was true, but no one was counting on the way the

wyrm's mood amplified my depression and loss. Apparently it was one of the benefits of the wyrm they didn't drink with their tea, and they were better off for it.

"You'll feel it until you don't feel it anymore," Thorfinn advised me, "and the change will be so slow you won't notice. It'll feel like it's taking forever. When I got back from that vik and found Bekkhild with her tit in a baby's mouth, I thought I'd never get over it, and I went to Jomsborg to die a good death. But look what happened instead."

"He met me, instead," Sinead told me, "and that made up for everything. Caitria's gone, but there're other looking women. When you stop looking for Caitria, you'll see them for yourself, and they'll see you."

"You're better off without women," Skallagrim said adamantly, and I began to understand his sour outlook on life.

They all made sense, more or less, except Goltrade and Skallagrim, but I had to ride it out in my own time and my own way, and make my wyrd as I found it.

While I was mooning around, they were all working out the itinerary and the plan. Goltrade wanted to take the *Blood Raven* as far as Luel, and held out doggedly, until we explained the effect that sailing the *Blood Raven* up the Eden would produce on the Engs, in the wake of the recent Viking depredations among their monasteries, and its undesirable consequences for our purpose. Skallagrim insisted he wasn't going back, and Goltrade insisted he was.

Finally a plan took shape they could agree on, the sort of compromise plan that emerges from committees all the time: the Jomsvikings would take us as far as the Solway Firth in the *Blood Raven,* and we'd used the *Ged* for the run up the Eden to Luel. Sygtrygg would stay back to deal with Frydys, and Snorri would stay back to deal with Sygtrygg, and Mairead would stay back to deal with Snorri. Thorfinn and Sinead would come with me; Goltrade would stay on the *Blood Raven* as a sort of maritime chaplain, and Skallagrim would come with us to lend his expertise and experience to the enterprise, whether he wanted to or not.

And there was no time like the present, they explained one afternoon on the barrowdown, while Sygtrygg and Thorfinn flew their hawks and everyone ate lunch and watched the kestrels hang still in the air, like a scream in a lake mist, before dropping on rodents or startled upland game birds flushed from their covert by the shadow of hawk wing. I lay in the long grass on the side of the barrow and watched the hawks against the Irish sky, and the Wicklow mountains were clear and blue in the distance across the bay. The hawks circled patiently on a thermal, all of Thorr's forest below them, as free as will, as impossibly real as Caitria. I closed my eyes.

And when I open them I see my clan gathered round the fire listening to stories. I hear the rhythm of drumming in the distance, I feel a cold fog. A little distance away, jugglers not unlike Æthelwulf's sons, except in their selection of props, are working the crowd.

This is a good time to be alive, and a good country to be alive in: Vineland the Good, the land of Leif the Lucky, one of the earliest Danish tourists to its rocky northeastern shore. It's possible to live the good life here, if you know how to do it. Money and a sense of detachment sure help, but all and all, unlike most places, Vineland the Good is exactly what it was advertised to be all those years ago.

These days I'm a man of leisure, rich enough to do what I want. I spend my summers in England, working the reenactment circuit. It's a nomadic life, but that's the kind of life I understand, moving from place to place, rubbing elbows with fire eaters and jugglers, craftsmen, travelers, academic dilettantes, middle-aged hippies, and weekend new age nudists: all the usual suspects. There are many more dangerous lives. I'm paid to tell stories about the old gods and heroes, to dress up in clothes I can wear like skin and sing verse to the accompaniment of Clannad on the Sony Discman. A good storyteller can make a life for himself on the reenactment circuit, join the tribe. I've at least learned how to work a crowd after all these years, and it's the kind of crowd I like: one with a good time on its mind and cold beer on board in the hot July afternoons.

> Let me show you a face—in disguise
> Uncover
> A color that's faded
> Swept aside by the tide.
> Scene after scene, later;
> There's a grey dust that's in our eyes

A misty cover;
That hides on the turning tide

Wooh . . .
The soul of the proud man drowns
Sad insinuation
Using words that are unwise
How they waver in your eyes
Wheels within wheels are turning
By now you know

Wooh . . .
The soul of the proud man drowns
For so long a proud man

As we face the fierce wind
And the turning tide.

And when winter comes I follow the Grateful Dead.
Look around: a Dead concert isn't much different than the
eighth century, especially a California show, and no matter
where the Dead play, the scene's a good place to meet
looking women. We exchange waves and nods, like old
souls hoping to recognize one another from past lives,
searching faces for a familiar smile. They're an acquired
taste, I admit, but worth what they put you through.

Once or twice a summer, Sinead and 'Finn meet their
hippie brother and we catch a few shows on the West Coast
tour. And always New Year, always the New Year shows.
Sometimes we like to remember, and there's no better
place than a Dead concert.

I've seen the band almost a thousand times, and every time
I think I see Caitria, but I can never quite get to her through
the women twirling on the fringes of the crowd, or across the
arena seething in the red and blue lights that spill from the
stage, or out in the parking lot marketplace where they sell
crystals and incense, sturdy peasant cloth and diaphanous
dresses of sheer fabric, rare and exotic culinary delights, for-
getfulness, *ofermod,* and luck. Even if you make your own
wyrd, it's true you always need luck, because there's always
a few wyrmtoothed arrows still outstanding.

DISCOVER THE MYRIAD WONDERS IN MARY GENTLE'S FANTASTICAL WORLD

from ROC

SISTERS IN FANTASY

EDITED BY

SUSAN SHWARTZ &
MARTIN H. GREENBERG

This collection gathers together fifteen all-original and thought-provoking stories by some of the most highly regarded women writing fiction today. From curses confronted and paths not followed to women gifted with magic as ancient as the earth itself, these powerful tales provide insight into sacrifices made and obstacles overcome by those with courage enough to welcome the consequences of their own actions.

from ROC

*Prices slightly higher in Canada.   (452925—$4.99)